Dear Reader,

And now for something completely different. . . .

We have some really wonderful stories in this volume of
Select Editions—intriguing tales full of twists and turns to
surprise you on every page, with endings that will leave you
breathless. And if that's not enough, we have *The Curious
Incident of the Dog in the Night-Time* by British author
Mark Haddon. I don't want to give away too much about this
extraordinary story except to say it is a truly unique, illustrated
family drama, with a little mystery thrown in. What makes it
unusual is the voice of the 15-year-old narrator, Christopher.
The humor and poignancy of his storytelling have been striking
a chord with readers worldwide, and we're very pleased to
share with you this special reading experience.

The Curious Incident is the kind of book
that immediately prompts readers to want to
learn more about the author and how he came
up with his story. With that in mind, we've
put together a special 8-page AFTER*WORDS*
section following the book, beginning on
page 569. There you'll find an interview with
Mark Haddon, as well as many other interesting tidbits about
him and his story.

Happy reading!

Very truly yours,

Laura E. Kelly

ACKNOWLEDGMENTS

Page 121: Lifetouch Inc. Page 285: Robert Doyle/OSD Photo.
Page 443: Suzanne M. Sheridan. Page 569: © Clare McNamee.
Pages 569–576: Interview © 2003 Powells.com. Page 570: RF/Corbis.
Page 571: The Reader's Digest Association, Inc./GID.
Page 572: © Corbis Sygma. Page 575: AP/Wide World Photos.

The original editions of the books in this volume are published and copyrighted as follows:

LETTER FROM HOME, published at $22.95 by Berkley Prime Crime, The Berkley Publishing Group, a division of Penguin Group (USA) Inc.; $34.50 in Canada
© 2003 by Carolyn G. Hart

PS, I LOVE YOU, published at $21.95 by Hyperion; published in Canada by HarperCollins Canada at $26.95
© 2004 by Cecelia Ahern
Lyrics to *With a Little Help from My Friends,* appearing on page 166, Copyright 1967 (Renewed) Sony/ATV Tunes LLC. All rights administered by Sony/ATV Music Publishing, 8 Music Square West, Nashville, TN 37203. All rights reserved. Used by permission.

THE PROMISE OF A LIE, published at $23.95 by Warner Books, a subsidiary of Time Warner Book Group, Inc.; $34.95 in Canada
© 2004 by Howard Roughan

THE CURIOUS INCIDENT OF THE DOG IN THE NIGHT-TIME, published at $22.95 by Doubleday, The Doubleday Broadway Publishing Group, a division of Random House, Inc.; published in Canada by Doubleday Canada at $29.95
© 2003 by Mark Haddon
Underground logo, fabric designs, and line diagrams are reproduced with the kind permission of Transport for London. Kuoni advertisement reproduced with the kind permission of Kuoni Travel Ltd. A-level maths question reproduced with the kind permission of Oxford Cambridge and RSA Examinations (OCR).

SELECT EDITIONS

SELECTED AND EDITED BY READER'S DIGEST

THE READER'S DIGEST ASSOCIATION, INC.
PLEASANTVILLE, NEW YORK • MONTREAL

SELECT EDITIONS

EDITORIAL

Global Editor-in-Chief: Laura E. Kelly

Managing Editors: Paula Marchese, Joseph P. McGrath

Senior Editors: Barbara K. Clark, Thomas S. Clemmons,
Mark Poirier, Amy M. Reilly

Editorial Administrator: Ann Marie Belluscio

EDITORIAL OPERATIONS

Director: James J. Menick

Art Director: Robin Arzt
Assistant Art Director: Gretchen Schuler

Senior Staff Copy Editors: Tatiana Ivanow, Marilyn J. Knowlton

Production Manager: Dianne Robinson
Production Associate: Lorraine Burton
Production Coordinator: Meg Ceccolini
Editorial Administrator: Christine Crisci

RIGHTS AND PERMISSIONS

Director: Lisa Garrett-Smith
Manager: Carol Weiss Staudter
Administrative Assistant: Arlene Pasciolla

INTERNATIONAL EDITIONS

Executive Editor: Gary Q. Arpin
Senior Editor: Bonnie Grande

CONTENTS

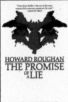

It was a summer of
secrets and mystery.
The summer when
everything changed.

Carolyn Hart

Letter from Home

OKLAHOMA
AUG-20'44

> "In *Letter from Home* the scene
> of the crime is bygone days in
> small-town Oklahoma. It took
> me back to my own boyhood
> and just such a summer...
> You'll enjoy it."
>   —Tony Hillerman

CHAPTER ONE

Dear Gretchen,
  You're rich and famous now. You've been all over the world,
seen things I'll never see, met people I'll never know. I saw you
once on TV going to a big night at the Kennedy Center. You had
on a white satin gown, and it looked like a diamond necklace
around your throat. That was a handsome man with you . . .

THE RUSTED IRON gate sagged from the stone pillar. A winter-brown
vine clung to the stones. Pale March sunlight filtered through the
bare branches of sycamores and oaks, throwing thin black shadows
as distinct as stylized brushwork in a Japanese painting. My cane
poked through a mound of tawny leaves, some wizened and wrinkled as old faces, some damp and soggy, smelling of must and rot
and decay. The rutted road looked much narrower than I remembered. When I'd last been in the cemetery, most of the headstones,
even those dating back to Indian Territory days, had stood straight.
Now many were tilted, and some had tumbled to the ground, half
hidden by leaves. Remnants of a late snow spangled shaded spots.

I walked slowly, stabbing my cane at the uneven ground. Nothing
looked familiar. Our graves were surely this way. . . . Oh, of course.
The weeping willow was gone. I'd always marked our family plot by

a huge willow, its dangling fronds shiny green in summer, bare and brown in winter. A stump leaned crookedly near the plot.

I paused to rest for a moment. The sharp wind rustled the bare branches of the sycamores and oaks. I shivered, grateful for the warmth of my cashmere coat and leather gloves. I plunged my left hand into a pocket of my coat. My gloved fingers closed around the letter. The name on the return address had not been familiar, but I had recognized the postmark. My first thought when I received the square cream envelope had been as instinctive as breathing: Why, it's a letter from home. Second came a quiver of utter surprise. Home? I'd not been back to the little town in northeastern Oklahoma since I was a girl. Home . . .

When I opened the envelope and lifted out three pages—the writing a dense, almost indecipherable scrawl—I almost threw the sheets away unread. The salutation stopped me: *Dear Gretchen.* No one had called me "Gretchen" for well over a half century. *Gretchen . . .* Across a span of time, I remembered a girl, dark-haired, blue-eyed, slim, and eager, who seemed quite separate and distinct from the old woman walking determinedly toward the graves.

I remembered that long-ago girl. . . .

GRETCHEN CLUTCHED THE folded sheaf of yellow copy paper and a thick dark-leaded pencil, sharp enough for writing but the point too blunt to break. That was just how Mr. Dennis did it when he covered the city council. Her first day at the *Gazette,* he'd waggled a thick handful of copy paper. "This is all you need, Gretchen. Take some paper and a couple of pencils, listen hard, make notes you can read, write your story fast."

It still seemed strange to walk toward Victory Café and not hurry inside. Victory Café—she was almost used to the name now. It used to be Pfizer Café, but after Pearl Harbor, when people began to talk about Nazis and Krauts as well as the Japs, Grandmother hired Elwyn Haskins to paint a new name in bright red and blue against a white background: VICTORY CAFÉ. There was a small American flag near the cash register, and the mirror behind the counter held pictures of men in the service. Anyone could bring a photo, and Grandmother would tape it up. Now people were beginning to believe in victory, especially since the invasion.

Gretchen stopped for the red light at Broadway and Main. She waited impatiently. The light was new, and lots of people honked their horns at it when they had to stop. There'd been a big fight in the city council about putting in a stoplight. Mayor Burkett got his way, insisting their town needed the light. After all, he'd pointed out, everything was different because of the war, and they had plenty of traffic—people stopping off from Highway 66 and soldiers coming over the Missouri line from Camp Crowder and local folks streaming into town to buy whatever shopkeepers had to offer. There wasn't much, but people had money from war work. Lots of townspeople, like Gretchen's mom, had gone to Tulsa to work in the Douglas plant. Mom was making good money, more than they'd ever seen—thirty-five dollars a week.

When the light changed, Gretchen hurried across the street. She wanted to run, but she held herself to a fast walk. She, Gretchen Grace Gilman, was on her way to the courthouse, the big red sandstone building that looked like a castle, with bays and turrets. The courthouse was her beat, and so was city hall on Cimarron Street. Of course, Mr. Dennis or Mr. Cooley covered the big stories, but there was plenty for Gretchen to write about. She'd been to both the courthouse and city hall first thing this morning, checked the sheriff's office for any overnight calls, asked the court clerk about lawsuits, dropped by the county records office to see about deeds registered, and scanned the police blotter at the police station. This was her last run to the courthouse and city hall for the day. She'd already turned in her stories for today's paper. Last deadline was one o'clock, but that was for late-breaking wire stories from the war front, especially the fighting in Normandy. Most of her stories were turned in by ten. The pressrun was at two.

She glanced across Main at the café. The windows needed a wash. Mrs. Perkins did a pretty good job, but she couldn't move as fast as Gretchen, and she didn't help Grandmother the way

Gretchen did when she worked there. That's how Gretchen had expected to spend the summer until the miracle happened: Mrs. Jacobs, the junior high English teacher, telling Mr. Dennis that Gretchen wanted to grow up to be a reporter and that she'd make a good hand while the *Gazette* was so short-staffed because of the war. Gretchen had put on her favorite dress—a yellow-and-white-checkered dirndl with starfish appliqués at the shoulder and near the hem and with white rickrack as an accent at the neck, waist, and skirt—and pulled on short white gloves and a yellow straw hat. She didn't have any good summer shoes, but she'd taken her white sandals and polished them and hoped Mr. Dennis wouldn't notice that the straps were frayed.

She'd never forget, never in a thousand million years, that May afternoon. School was almost out, and Mrs. Jacobs got her excused from last hour. It was only May, but it was hot, the temperature nudging toward ninety. Everybody said it was going to be a hot summer—the summer of 1944. But Gretchen didn't remember any summers when it hadn't been hot and dry.

When she'd got to the *Gazette* office, she'd stared at the door and been so scared, she'd almost turned and run away. Could she do it? She was editor of the *Wolf Cry,* the junior high newspaper. Mrs. Jacobs liked her stories, had given her bylines all this past year. One story, the one about Millard, Mrs. Jacobs had sent in to the interscholastic contest. When Gretchen won first prize, she'd felt funny, happy, and sad at the same time. But Millard would have been proud for her. Mrs. Jacobs had told Gretchen to cut out all her stories and take them to show Mr. Dennis. Mrs. Jacobs called them "clips."

Somehow, her hands sweaty, her stomach a hard tight knot, Gretchen opened the door and walked inside. Straight ahead was a square room with a half-dozen desks. A telephone shrilled. In one corner, the clacking Teletype spewed out paper in an endless stream, the very latest news from United Press. Only one desk was occupied. A stocky man, shiny bald except for a fringe of gray hair, typed so fast, it sounded like a machine gun. Smoke wreathed upward from a pipe cradled in a ceramic ashtray shaped like the state of Oklahoma. A door in the far wall banged open. A smell of hot metal rolled toward her. An old man with long sideburns and a big white mustache stuck out his head, shouting to be heard over a clattery metallic noise. "That newsprint ain't here yet, Walt. You better check again." The door slammed, cutting off the metal ping of the Linotypes, making the newsroom seem quiet in comparison. Gretchen walked slowly toward the occupied desk. "Mr. Dennis."

He continued to hunch over the big old typewriter, eyes squinting in concentration, fingers flying.

"Mr. Dennis."

His head jerked around. Deep lines grooved the editor's round face. His mouth turned down. Greenish-blue eyes glittered beneath bristly brows. He glowered. "What do you want, girl?"

Gretchen wanted to run away. But he'd told Mrs. Jacobs he had to have somebody quick. Gretchen thrust out her hand with the folder holding her clips. Her hand shook. "Mrs. Jacobs said for me to bring my clips. I'm Gretchen Gilman."

He grabbed his pipe, took a deep puff. His thick eyebrows were tufted like an owl's. He snapped, "I told her I wanted a boy. She said nobody was good enough. So here *you* are." The emphasis on the pronoun was sour. "How old are you, girl?"

Gretchen stood as tall as her five feet three inches would stretch. "I'm almost fourteen." Well, she'd be fourteen in September. That was almost, wasn't it?

"Fourteen." He heaved a sigh. "Damn this war." He puffed on the pipe, pinned her with his glittering eyes. "Can you write, girl?"

"Yes." Her answer came out clear and definite.

The editor studied her a moment longer, reached out for her clips, riffled through them, stopped to read one. He took so long, Gretchen knew he was reading it twice. When he looked up, his dark impatient glance swept her up and down. "Don't believe in women in a newsroom. Except for soc." He pronounced it "sock," his voice a rasp, reflecting a newsman's disdain for the fluff of the society page. "But there's a war on." He tapped the sheet. It was the story about Millard. "I guess you know that. Okay, girl. We'll give it a try." He handed back the clips. "You can start now. Take the plain yellow desk at the back. The metal desk belongs to Willie Hurst, sports. The desk that looks like a tornado hit it belongs to Ralph Cooley. He used to work for INS."

Gretchen's eyes widened. INS! Mrs. Jacobs had told her all about the three wire services: International News Service, Associated Press, and United Press. Nobody ever called them by those long names. They were INS, AP, and UP. To be a reporter for one of them was as magical to Gretchen as owning a flying carpet.

Mr. Dennis puffed out his cheeks in exasperation. "Used to." His tone was dry and a little sad. "But I got to use him. There's nobody else left. Joe Bob Terrell got called up. He left last week." The editor jerked his head. "The desk with the rose in a vase is Jewell Taylor's. Soc. Get on the phone, call the police station, ask if there's anything new on the blotter. You can come in every afternoon after school, and we'll see how you do. If you work out, you'll be full-time when school's out. Five bucks a week."

As Gretchen moved past, her heart thudding, the editor glanced at her hat. "School clothes will do from now on."

And here she was, a reporter for the *Gazette,* out on her beat. Gretchen took the courthouse steps two at a time. It seemed a long time ago that she'd first walked into the *Gazette* office. Now it was a familiar place. She still tensed whenever Mr. Dennis called her name, but he didn't glower at her anymore. Yesterday, when she'd written a story on Rose Drew's plans to go to San Diego to see her husband, a navy petty officer, before his ship left port, Gretchen almost hadn't turned it in. She'd laid the story next to her type-writer and poked in another sheet of copy paper and started the kind of story she knew Mr. Dennis expected: *Mrs. Wilford Drew will take the train to California next Tuesday in hopes of bidding her husband farewell before his ship leaves for the Pacific theater. Mrs. Drew has worked at Osgood Beauty Salon for eight years. She . . .*

Gretchen yanked out the sheet, threw it away. She picked up her first effort, pasted the three pages together, and placed them in the incoming copy tray on Mr. Dennis's desk. She went back to her desk and began typing up the list of civic-club meetings, shoulders tensed, waiting for Mr. Dennis to clear his throat, the grumbling roar that usually preceded a spate of impatient instruction.

He cleared his throat. "Girl."

She sat still and tight. Did he sound mad? There was a funny different tone in his voice. Was he going to fire her?

"Girl." A bark now. "What's your full name?"

She twisted in her chair. "Gretchen Grace Gilman, sir."

"Okay." He bent back to his work.

When the first copies of the paper came out of the pressroom, he tossed one toward her, then clapped his panama on his head and strode out of the office, heading for Victory Café. She unfolded the paper, and there on page 1, just below the fold, was her story:

Rose Drew's Journey

By G. G. Gilman

Staff Writer

"I got to go. In my heart, I know I got to go."

Rose Drew twisted a handkerchief as she spoke. She looked
at the photograph of her husband, Wilford, and . . .

G. G. Gilman . . . Gretchen clutched the newspaper. She burst out of the *Gazette* office and darted across the street, not caring that the light was red and a battered pickup honked at her. She pulled open the screen door of the café and ran to the kitchen, skidding past Mr. Dennis, who was settled at the counter with Dr. Jamison and Mayor Burkett. As she pushed through the swinging door, she shouted, "Grandmother, Grandmother, look!"

Her grandmother, yellow coronet braids a little disheveled, plump face red with exertion, wiped floury hands on her big white apron. She took the newspaper, peered nearsightedly as Gretchen pointed. *"Wunderbar, mein Schatz, wunderbar."* She spread the newspaper on the wooden counter near the refrigerator. "We shall cut it out, put it up for everyone to see. *Wunderbar.*"

And now here she was at the county courthouse, which crowned the slight rise in the town square, green lawn falling away in every direction. The American flag and the Oklahoma flag snapped on their poles. Dark green wooden benches were placed every so often along the sidewalks that led to the entrances on all four sides. A gazebo nestled beneath two huge cottonwoods near the corner of Cimarron and Broadway. The main steps of the courthouse, wide and shallow, faced Main Street.

Gretchen pulled the big bronze door handle. The door opened into a wide corridor. The floor was a speckled marble, greenish with dots of gold. The still air in the courthouse smelled like people, even when there was nobody in the hallways. Gretchen was reaching for the knob of the county clerk's office when a siren wailed outside. She swung around, ran to the end of the hall, and pushed up a creaky window. A black-and-white patrol car, its red light whirling, the siren rising and falling, pulled out of the parking lot next to city hall and swung onto Cimarron Street, going west. The tires squealed as it turned right onto Crawford. She lost sight of the car behind a row of elms. The city had two patrol cars: Sergeant Holliman in Car 1, Sergeant Petty in Car 2. Everybody was still shocked about Sergeant Petty. Nobody had ever heard of a woman policeman. But Chief Fraser jutted out his chin and demanded to know what he was supposed to do with every able-bodied man in the county in the service. As far as he was concerned, if women could weld bombers, they could patrol city streets.

Gretchen used the Cimarron Street exit. Despite the heat, she broke into a run. A single-story brick building housed the police station, fire station, and mayor's office.

The door to the police station was closed. Gretchen burst inside, swept the long room with a glance. There were several desks behind a wooden counter—a little like the *Gazette* newsroom, but the only sound was a muted radio, and the wooden desks were neat and orderly. The door to the chief's office was open. The office was dark.

Mrs. Morrison, her plump, placid face beaming, pushed back from her desk. "Hello, Gretchen. Here to check the records? I'll get the book for you."

"I heard the siren." Gretchen reached the counter and set her sheaf of copy paper on it, pencil poised. "Is there a wreck?"

Mrs. Morrison carried the ledger to the counter. "No. Just a call out on Archer Street. But you won't want that. The *Gazette* doesn't carry domestic-disturbance calls."

Archer Street? That was her street. A half-dozen small square frame houses straggled along the gravel road. Gretchen knew everyone in each house.

Gretchen bent to look at the list of citations: four of them—two speeding, one driving under the influence, a larceny. Her eyes brightened at the last one. Mr. Dennis would be interested to know somebody had stolen a scarecrow from the Hollis farm. Now, that could make a good story. Why would anybody steal a scarecrow? As she printed, she frowned. "I don't see anything about Archer Street."

"That call just came in, but like I said, Walt don't carry that kind of news. Families with troubles, well, no sense in making things worse."

Gretchen finished her notes on arrests. She turned her folded sheet over, looked at Mrs. Morrison. "Even so, I better get the information. Mr. Dennis says, 'Ask and you shall receive.' "

Mrs. Morrison's sweet, high laughter pealed. "Don't that sound like Walt! That man has no shame. Well, we got a call from Mrs. Crane that there was shouting and screaming next door at the Tatum house. Well, no telling what's wrong, but everybody knows Clyde's back for a furlough before his unit ships out, and everybody sure knows Faye's not been sitting home nights since he's been gone. It may be that Clyde's heard tell of her doings. And I can't think she's set a good example for that girl of theirs." Mrs. Morrison's thin penciled eyebrows rose. "The war's hard on everybody, but a woman has to learn how to be alone."

The Tatum house was three doors from Grandmother Pfizer's house. Gretchen had grown up running in and out of the Tatum house. Barb was just enough older that she treated Gretchen with casual disregard, sometimes welcoming Gretchen's wide-eyed admiration, other times brushing her off. Last year was Barb's first in high school. All the classes, from kindergarten through twelfth grade, were in the same big redbrick building, but there was a divide wide as the Arkansas River between junior and senior high. Barb ran around with the older girls now. Gretchen remembered when Barb was skinny and could skip rope a hundred times without stopping. She wasn't skinny now, and everyone noticed her when she came into a room. Gretchen felt a pang of envy. Barb's hair was a rich reddish-brown, and it curved in a perfect pageboy. Barb wasn't really beautiful, but she was interesting-looking, with deep-set eyes, a regal face with high cheekbones, a way of throwing out her hands as if she were inviting the world to be her friend.

Gretchen wrote down, *Tatum house. Screams. Yells.* She glanced at the wall clock—twelve minutes to five—guessed at the time she'd heard the siren: *Car 2 dispatched 4:40 p.m.* "Who was screaming?"

Mrs. Morrison settled behind her desk. "Oh, likely Faye was tellin' Clyde off. You know, he ought never to have married her. Some women are just damn fools about men, and they don't get no better with age. I swear, Faye's got a tongue that could strip bark off a gum tree. Well, Sergeant Petty will settle things down. And Clyde will be on his way soon enough."

Out in the heat, Gretchen shaded her eyes from the sun. She'd have to hurry to finish up at the courthouse before it closed. She walked fast, felt her cotton blouse sticking to her back. The main hallway was empty. At the court clerk's office, she noted that Mr. Edward Petree, 103 Cherry Street, had filed suit against his next-door neighbor, Mr. Coy Hendricks, 105 Cherry Street, for dumping out an old barrel of oil that had leaked into Mr. Petree's yard, ruining his vegetable garden. The county commissioner's office was already closed, and she'd have to wait until tomorrow. In the basement, the door to the sheriff's office was shut and locked.

She reached the *Gazette* office a few minutes after five. Nobody was there. Mr. Dennis was probably in the pressroom. She made some quick notes about tomorrow's stories, but she needed to get over to the café and get to work. Grandmother had protested at first, saying Gretchen worked all day at the *Gazette* and that was enough, but Gretchen knew how tired Grandmother got. Gretchen started off the day at the café and ended the day there. She and Grandmother were at the café by five to get ready to open at six. Gretchen didn't go to the *Gazette* until eight, so there was plenty of time to slap bacon into the huge skillets and flip eggs on the grill. Truckers coming through on Highway 66 would stop for the best breakfast on the road: bacon and eggs when they had them; hash browns, pancakes, and grits all the time. They made their own bread and rolls and corn bread. Gretchen did most of the cleanup after she got off from the *Gazette*. Grandmother would close up and go home by five. There was lots to do. Mrs. Perkins might be finished up with the dishes, but Gretchen scrubbed the tables and mopped the floor and saw to the trash. If everything went well, maybe she'd get home by six. Grandmother would have rested for a while and then fixed supper—macaroni and cheese and watermelon, Gretchen's favorite.

When Gretchen finished burning the trash in the incinerator at the edge of the lot behind the café, the sun was a hot red ball in the west. She looked down Archer Street. The graveled street curved up and down, following the gentle contours of the hilly countryside. The windows in all the boxy frame houses were up, the front doors open, welcoming any hint of breeze. But the houses were hot, all of them, even with fans. Grandmother said people got mad easier when it was hot—mad in the summer, blue in the winter.

Gretchen gave the ashes a final poke and swung up onto her bike. She rode slowly because it was hot, but she didn't care that sweat beaded her face, slipped down her back. The refrain sang in her mind: *G. G. Gilman*. She was almost past the Tatum house when she braked to a sudden stop.

The cover hung askew from the silver mailbox on its post next to the end of the rutted drive. Dandelions poked fluffy heads from grass that needed mowing and had gone to seed. The wooden steps to the porch were rickety, and one plank had a broken edge. The house had a frowsy air—some asphalt shingles missing, the white paint weathered and peeling.

Gretchen swung off her bike, leaned it on the kickstand. The house looked as it always had, no different at all. Mrs. Morrison was probably right. Mr. Dennis wouldn't put anything in the paper about the call to the police this afternoon. But it wouldn't hurt to knock on the door, see if Barb was home. Gretchen walked briskly to the porch. She looked through the screen door into the dim living room. Magazines spilled across the slipcovered sofa. A filled ashtray sat near a half-dozen nail-polish bottles and wadded tissues. There was an oval braided rug and two easy chairs, both slipcovered in shiny yellow chintz. Despite the disorder, the room glowed with color and life from the unframed paintings hanging on the walls.

Gretchen knocked. The rattle disappeared into the silence quick as a frog slipping into a pond.

A quick clatter of steps sounded. Faye Tatum hurried across the living room. Faye always moved fast. She stopped midway when she saw Gretchen. Her narrow face looked hard as marble. Her blond hair fell forward, a golden strand loose across one cheek. Her green eyes smoldered like a banked fire. She wore an apron over a cotton top and shorts. The apron wasn't tied, and the strings dangled on either side. There was something about the way the apron fell and the bareness of her legs that shocked Gretchen. Most women Mrs. Tatum's age wouldn't wear shorts around the house, only if they were going to a picnic on a hot summer day. But she was an artist, and everybody knew artists were different.

"Hello, Gretchen," Mrs. Tatum said. "Barb's not here." She sounded mad. And disappointed.

Gretchen began to back away. "Please tell her I came by."

Mrs. Tatum turned without answering.

Gretchen hurried toward her bike. The rest of the way home, she wondered about Mrs. Tatum. Had she shouted at her husband this afternoon? Or screamed? She was still mad when Gretchen came. But a scream was different from a shout.

Gretchen glanced at the Crane house. Like Grandmother said, everything was always neat as a pin at the Crane house. The lawn was freshly trimmed, though it had to be a losing battle against the blown puffs of dandelions from the ragged yard next door. Begonias flourished in the flower beds. Mrs. Crane would be proud to open her front door to company at any time of day or night. There would never be magazines strewn about or unemptied ashtrays.

Gretchen parked her bike behind her grandmother's house and hurried up the wooden steps into the kitchen.

Grandmother turned from the stove with a big smile. "So here you are. Just in time for supper so fine. We have salmon croquettes and fresh peas and Jell-O." Grandmother's German accent was still strong, her *w*'s often sounding like *v*'s.

Gretchen washed her hands at the sink. They sat across from each other at the white wooden table. Two more chairs were pushed against the wall on either side of the door to the living room. They pulled one to the table when her mother came on the bus from Tulsa. Her brother Jimmy's chair had been against the wall since he went overseas. His letters didn't come so often now, and when they did, he didn't write much, just how he wished he could be home and, when he came home, the first thing he wanted to do was have one of Grandmother's big hamburgers. And he asked after Mike Thompson. They hadn't written him that Mike had been killed in the fighting in Italy just three months before Millard's ship went down. There were two stars in the window of Thompson's Drugs. Mr. Thompson hardly ever came over to the café for lunch anymore, and Mrs. Thompson's clothes sagged against her wraith-thin body.

Grandmother passed the bowl of peas. "I put your story by the cash register. Mrs. Perkins said everybody thought it was good. She said Mrs. Jacobs had some company with her, and when they paid the check, Mrs. Jacobs pointed at the story and told everyone you were one of the best students she'd ever had and you were going to be famous someday."

Gretchen's spoon stopped midway to her mouth. "Mrs. Jacobs said that?"

Grandmother nodded. "*Ja.* When Mrs. Perkins told me, I wished I'd been there to hear. But we call your mother tonight."

Calling long distance was always exciting. They didn't make long-distance calls very often. When they did or when her mother called them, they talked loud and fast against a buzzing, scratchy background. The phone company asked everyone to keep their calls to five minutes because so many people needed to make calls.

Gretchen scarcely tasted the rest of her supper, though she loved salmon croquettes. She told Grandmother about her day, finishing with her last rounds. "When I got to the courthouse, there was a siren, so I went over to the police station. Sergeant Petty was on her way to the Tatum house. Mrs. Crane had called and said there were shouts and screams. Mrs. Morrison said that Barb's dad was home and getting ready to go overseas and that maybe he and Barb's mom got mad about something." Gretchen didn't want to tell Grandmother about Mrs. Tatum's being out at night, since that was the kind of thing that would make Grandmother say that Gretchen shouldn't go see Barb. "I stopped by on my way home. Mrs. Tatum looked like she was mad about something. So I guess she and Mr. Tatum had a big fight and Mrs. Crane called the police."

Grandmother put down her fork. "You won't put that in the paper?"

"I don't think so, but I have to tell Mr. Dennis."

Grandmother pushed the platter with croquettes closer to Gretchen. "I know. You have your job. You must do what Mr. Dennis says. But you see, I remember Clyde when he was a little boy. He was such a friend to your mama."

Gretchen's eyes widened. "I didn't know that, Grandmother."

"Oh, they played together all through school. Clyde was a nice boy, though he didn't like to share your mama. They'd fight about that sometimes, and she'd say she wanted to be friends with everybody, not just Clyde. They were best friends until she got in the pep club. She was so busy then. Everybody was her friend."

Grandmother pushed back her chair, went to the drainboard. She cut two generous slices of watermelon, set a serving at each place.

Gretchen carefully poked out the big shiny black seeds, cut her watermelon into dripping chunks.

Grandmother settled back in her chair. "I always thought perhaps someday . . . But your mama fell in love with your daddy in high school. She didn't see so much of Clyde then."

Gretchen had only a dim memory of her father—thick dark hair and bright blue eyes and a smiling face. She remembered laughter and being swung high in the air and nursery rhymes read in the glow of a flickering fire. And she remembered the gray, dark days after the accident and the fresh grave in the cemetery. Every time Mama came home from Tulsa, they went to the cemetery.

"Anyway"—Grandmother spoke with finality—"it would never have worked out for your mama and Clyde. I'm glad it didn't, because your mama loved your daddy. And once Clyde met Faye, he seemed happy as could be. She came to town when she was in high school. They got married soon after your mama and daddy. But sometimes I wonder if Clyde is jealous of Faye's painting. A man doesn't want to be second best in his home." Grandmother finished her watermelon. "Now it comes to the police being called. That's a bad way to send a man off to war. But Faye Tatum . . ." She gave a little head shake and sighed. "Well, we'd best be doing the dishes."

Gretchen popped up. She was suddenly tired to the bone, but she made her smile bright. "I'll do them, Grandmother. You go relax, listen to the radio." The six-thirty news would be on soon with Edward V. Kaltenborn. If Gretchen hurried, she'd hear most of it. And then they'd call Mother.

GRANDMOTHER BENT CLOSE to Gretchen, trying to hear. She always had Gretchen do the talking.

Gretchen frowned as she tried to catch the words on the other end: ". . . not home . . . take a message?"

The voice was unfamiliar, but her mother shared rooms with other war workers, and people seemed to come and go. "This is

Gretchen, Lorraine Gilman's daughter. Please tell her we called." So her mother would not know for a while about G. G. Gilman. "Tell her we are fine."

A spurt of cheery laughter. "Will do. She's fine, too. Out on a date with a navy man. Lucky gal."

GRETCHEN TOSSED RESTLESSLY on the bed. The small bedroom was hot. The electric fan's whir was cheerful, but the air didn't seem cooler at all. Disjointed words and indistinct images moved in the corridors of her sleep-drenched mind: *Lucky gal . . .* Mrs. Tatum's eyes . . . the shrill of the siren . . . G. G. Gilman . . . the smell of hot lead from the Linotypes . . . her fingers punching ever faster on the shiny keys of the tall Remington typewriter . . .

The rattle of the window screen overrode the clacking keys in Gretchen's dream.

"Gretchen, wake up!" The shrill cry rose into a nightmarish wail. "Oh, help me, Gretchen, help me!"

CHAPTER TWO

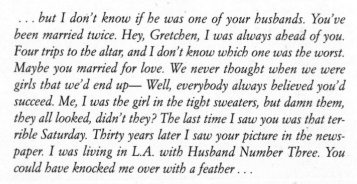

. . . but I don't know if he was one of your husbands. You've been married twice. Hey, Gretchen, I was always ahead of you. Four trips to the altar, and I don't know which one was the worst. Maybe you married for love. We never thought when we were girls that we'd end up— Well, everybody always believed you'd succeed. Me, I was the girl in the tight sweaters, but damn them, they all looked, didn't they? The last time I saw you was that terrible Saturday. Thirty years later I saw your picture in the newspaper. I was living in L.A. with Husband Number Three. You could have knocked me over with a feather . . .

A LINE OF BRICKS, some broken, edged the plot. There were seven graves. The oldest was that of Grandpa Pfizer. I didn't recognize my father's grave at first glance. The angel that had knelt on the granite stone was headless now. I'd always reached out to stroke the angel's wings. How many years had it been since anyone brought flowers for him?

When I'd entered the cemetery, I'd looked for the family plot, though I'd not come here today to visit these graves. But I had time enough to see them all. There had been no headstone on my grandmother's grave when I left town. I took a step, leaned against my cane, and bent down to touch the graven letters:

CHARLOTTE KLEIN PFIZER
Beloved wife of Karl Gerhard Pfizer
October 23, 1876–June 26, 1944

Oh, Grandmother, I loved you so. . . .

GRETCHEN SCRAMBLED OUT of bed, reached the window. Barb Tatum, her face chalk-white in the milky radiance of the moon, pounded on the window screen. "Gretchen, come quick. Mama's in trouble. Oh, Gretchen, help me." Barb's pink cotton nightgown had thin white straps over her shoulders and ended above her knees.

"Barb, what's wrong?" Gretchen yanked the hook free, pushed against the screen.

Barb's chest heaved as she struggled to breathe. "I ran. I ran all the way. Oh, my foot." She sank to the ground, clutched at her leg.

Gretchen darted to the wall by the bedroom door, flipped the light switch. She ran back to the window, looked out at Barb, pinioned in a square of brightness. Barb's head was bent. Her lustrous sorrel hair masked her face, tumbled over her bare shoulders. She held tight to her ankle. Blood spurted from a gash on the bottom of her right foot. "I must have run across some broken glass."

"Don't move. I'll get Grandmother."

"No!" Barb's voice was stricken. "We have to hurry. Mama needs help. Oh, Gretchen, I have to get back. I shouldn't have run away. Bring me something to bandage my foot."

Gretchen had always wished she looked like Barb, even though some of the girls didn't think Barb was really pretty. Her features were chiseled. Her nose was thin, her chin pointed, but her lips curved into a funny half smile whenever the boys were near—the kind of smile that promised a kiss when nobody was around to see. Her blue eyes glowed as if she saw things other people didn't see. Now those eyes were glazed and staring.

"You're hurt. I'll get Grandmother."

"No!" Barb's cry was desperate. "I don't want anybody to know. If you won't help me, I'll go back by myself." Barb was crying, swiping at her eyes, struggling to get up.

"Wait, I'm coming." Gretchen pulled on a T-shirt and shorts, slipped barefoot into her loafers. Her glance swept the room; then she reached for the pillow, shook the case free, rolled it into a long strip two inches wide. She carried it in one hand as she pushed the screen out, swung over the sill, and dropped softly to the ground. She hurried to Barb, knelt, and peered at her foot. "You've got dirt in it. We need to wash it up. I can get some water, but we need to call Dr. Jamison."

"We can't take the time." Barb yanked the strip of cloth out of Gretchen's hand. She slung the rolled pillowcase under her foot, crossed the ends over her instep, tied them tight. "Help me up."

They stood close together. Barb's fingers gouged Gretchen's arm. "Come on. I heard Mama scream." She pulled on Gretchen's arm, leaned against her for support, and limped across the lawn.

Gretchen knew it was very late. Archer Street lay quiet as a ghost town. All the houses were dark. All of them.

"Barb, what happened? Why did your mom scream?" Were Faye and Clyde Tatum fighting again?

"I heard somebody knock. Mama spoke, and her voice was real loud, and then the front door slammed against the wall. That's when Mama screamed." Tears streamed down Barb's face.

When they reached the front porch of the Tatum house, bright moonlight showed the front door open to darkness within.

"Mama? Mama?" Barb's voice was shrill in the silence.

Gretchen pointed at the dark doorway. "Were the lights off when you left?"

"When I got out of my window, I ran toward the front of the house. Light was coming around the shades in the living room. Then the light went out. I was scared. I turned and ran, and all of a sudden, I was at your house. I came to your window. Like we used to do a long time ago." Barb stepped toward the screen door. "Mama?"

No answer.

Barb reached out, yanked open the screen. She stepped into the dark living room, her hand brushing to her right. When the light came on, she clamped her hand over her mouth, but the sound of her scream pulsed against the dreadful silence in the room.

After one look, Gretchen grabbed Barb's arm, pulled her outside to the porch and down the steps. "Your dad— Where's your dad?" Gretchen turned away from the house, wishing she could run and scream and cry. She couldn't rid her mind of that terrible glimpse of Faye Tatum slumped on her back near the sofa, eyes wide and staring, tongue protruding from blanched lips, throat mottled with purplish bruises.

Barb wavered unsteadily. "Mama."

"We have to find your dad." Even as she spoke, Gretchen realized Mr. Tatum wasn't there. If he were in the house, he'd have heard Barb's scream and their high frightened voices. Where was he? Why hadn't he hurried to help Mrs. Tatum? "Who was in the living room with your mom?"

Barb whirled away. She ran a few steps, dropped. "My foot." She buried her face in her hands, her shoulders shaking.

Gretchen hesitated, looking toward the house, light now spilling out onto the porch. They had to get help. But she wasn't going back inside the Tatum house.

DR. JAMISON KNELT in front of the sofa. His graying hair was uncombed, and his shaggy beard tousled. He wound a final strip of tape around Barb's right foot, then pushed himself stiffly to his feet, giving a little groan, his tired eyes kind and sad.

Grandmother bustled out of the kitchen. She wore a blue cotton housedress and her everyday sturdy white shoes. Only her hair, hanging to her shoulders, indicated the oddness of the hour and the moment. "Here, Doctor, I have made coffee for you."

He took a cup. "Thank you, Lotte. I need this. I told the chief I'd come back." He sighed. "Will you see to Barb?"

Grandmother nodded. "Oh, yes. She can stay here."

Barb pushed to the edge of the couch, the sheet that Grandmother had brought her slipping to her waist. "But Daddy will wonder where I am."

Her face heavy, her mouth drooping, Grandmother looked at Dr. Jamison. Neither said a word.

"Daddy didn't come home for supper." Barb looked puzzled and frightened. "I don't know where he is."

A heavy knock thudded at the door.

Grandmother bustled across the room. "Come in, please to come in."

Chief Fraser stepped inside, ducking his head beneath the lintel. He pulled off his cowboy hat. Wiry gray hair was cut short and tight to his big head. His face bulged all over: massive forehead, distended cheeks, rounded chin. Tonight a stubble of beard emphasized the dewlaps beneath deep-set brown eyes. "Lotte, Doc, girls." He jerked his head toward the door. "If you can get down there, Doc, take care of things? We got what we need."

Dr. Jamison nodded. "All right, Buck." He placed the coffee cup on the table, picked up his satchel. As he passed the police chief, he muttered, "Clyde anywhere around?"

"Nope." The chief's bushy eyebrows bunched in a tight frown.

The door banged behind Dr. Jamison.

Barb stared at Chief Fraser. "You have to find my daddy. He doesn't know. Oh, poor Daddy." She pulled up the sheet.

Grandmother's voice was low. "Some coffee, Chief?"

"If it's not too much trouble, Lotte, that'd be real good." The heels of Chief Fraser's dusty black cowboy boots thudded as he walked slowly across the room. He settled into the brown imitation-leather morris chair. He dropped his hat on the floor. "Miss Barb, I reckon you know how sorry I am about your mama."

Barb pressed her hands to her face.

The chief cleared his throat. "Miss Barb, if I thought it would be easier, I'd talk to you another time. But it isn't going to be easier." His deep voice was low and quiet. "You got to climb a hard mountain, and nothing I can do will help. Except maybe I can ease some pain by finding out who did this thing."

Barb's hands fell. "Who . . ." She shivered. "I don't know who came. I heard Mama's voice, and the door banged, and I ran away."

The chief pulled a little notebook from the pocket of his tan shirt, flipped it open. "Let's go back a little bit, Miss Barb. I want to know what your mama and daddy did today."

Barb was suddenly still. "My daddy—he wasn't home tonight."

"We'll get to that." His tone was patient. "Now be a good girl and tell me about this morning. You got up . . ."

Barb wrapped her arms around a big red brocade throw pillow, propped her chin against the fringed edge. "We always get up at six-thirty. Mama's been working at the five-and-dime. She had to be there at eight. She'd come home for lunch at eleven, be back by quarter to twelve. She'd get home a little after four."

"Is that what happened today?"

Barb twined her fingers in the fringe of the pillow. "I guess so. I didn't get home till after five."

"So your mama wasn't taking any time off even though your daddy was home on furlough?"

"Mama had to go to work." Barb's tone was earnest. "We needed the money. Ever since Daddy was drafted, we haven't had enough money. That's why she got the job at Jessop's. She used to be at Millie's Gifts. She taught art classes in that little room at the back. But when Daddy was drafted, she got a job at Jessop's."

"Was your mama pretty sharp with your daddy about money?"

Barb stared at him, her eyes wide and frightened.

The chief never took his eyes off of Barb. "What did they talk about at breakfast?"

Barb relaxed against the arm of the sofa. "Mama got up late, and Daddy was still asleep. She had to hurry to get to work on time."

The chief slowly nodded. "What time did your daddy get up?"

"I don't know." Barb's fingers plucked at the golden tassels. "I left, too. I've been working at Mr. Durwood's office this summer. I just barely got there in time. I didn't see Mama again until supper."

"How about your daddy?" The chief's voice was as smooth as a cottonmouth gliding through dark summer water.

Barb clasped her hands tightly together. "He didn't come home for supper." She spoke so softly, it was hard to hear.

The chair creaked as the chief leaned forward. "Since he's been back, did he usually come home for supper?"

Barb stared at the floor. "Yes."

The chief squinted at her. "But you were home for supper."

"Yes." She closed her eyes. Tears edged from beneath her dark eyelashes.

The chief frowned. "What happened at supper?"

"When I got home, Mama was in the kitchen." Barb's words came haltingly. "Mama was banging the pots and pans. I asked her what was wrong, and she slammed down a plate, and it broke. She threw the pieces in the trash and said she didn't care. Then she took the pork chops—she'd got them special, used up all our stamps to have a good dinner for Daddy—threw them back in the icebox, and started to cry."

"How come she was so mad?"

"I guess it was because of the Blue Light." Barb's voice was low, almost a whisper. "Last night, Mama and Daddy went to the Blue Light. While they were there, somebody said how Mama was the best dancer in town and everybody loved to dance with her. Daddy didn't know she'd been going to the Blue Light while he was gone. They came home and had a fight. It woke me up. Daddy said she shouldn't have been going there by herself. It wasn't nice. Mama said there was nothing wrong with the Blue Light. People could go there and have fun. Mama can— Mama could dance better than anybody, and she loved to dance. That's all it was. She told Daddy she didn't think much of him that he'd want her to sit around and never go anywhere. And she slammed off to their room. Daddy made a bed on the couch. He didn't get up before we left. But Mama wasn't mad this morning."

"She wasn't?" The chief rubbed his nose. "What did she say?"

"She didn't say much. But she wrote Daddy a note, left it at his breakfast place. She told me it would all work out and we'd have a nice supper for him." Barb's face creased. "But when I got home for supper, she was mad again. I don't know why."

"Hmm." The chief glanced toward the cuckoo clock mounted over the mantel. "You say he wasn't there when you got home?"

"It was just Mama and me." Barb's voice was definite.

"Then you and your mama had supper?" The chief hooked his thumbs behind his suspenders and gently tugged.

Barb didn't answer.

"Miss Barb?"

Barb didn't look at the chief. "You had to know Mama to understand—whenever she got mad, she talked real fast and moved real fast. She ran into her room and put on a pretty dress: her green rayon with the white-flower print. She was carrying her compact when she came through the kitchen, putting on her powder, trying to make her face look like she hadn't been crying. But she was talking out loud to herself, and she ran out the door." Barb took a ragged breath. "And she was mad because Daddy had the car. She'd got used to having it all to herself. But he must have taken it."

"So your mama didn't have the car. Where do you suppose she went?" The chief loosened his suspenders.

Tears welled in Barb's eyes. "She had on her dancing shoes. I worried because it's a long way to the Blue Light. Almost a mile, but I guess she walked."

"Or maybe somebody gave her a ride. Well, we'll find out." The chief folded his arms over his chest. "And you, Miss Barb?"

"I cleaned up the kitchen. Then I went over to Amelia Brady's. She's a friend of mine. I didn't want to stay home by myself." She looked down at her hands. "I chipped the polish on my nails. Anyway, I went over to Amelia's, and we did our nails and played records until real late. When I got home, nobody was there. It must have been almost midnight. I went to my room and went to bed."

"Did you see your mama when she got home?"

"No." Barb slumped against the armrest.

A car door slammed outside. Steps pounded across the yard. The screen door rattled. "Chief, you in there?" The door opened, and Ralph Cooley, his faded brown hat perched on the back of his head, peered inside. His skinny face was flushed, his blue suit wrinkled. "There you are. H'lo, Gretchen, Mrs. Pfizer."

Gretchen had never seen Ralph Cooley when he didn't look like he'd slept in his clothes. He always reeked of whiskey and cigarettes.

The reporter stepped inside. "Mike Mackey called"—the funeral-home director always let the *Gazette* know about accidents—"so I came right over. The doc says somebody strangled Faye Tatum and her daughter ran up here for help." Cooley's bleary eyes settled on Barb. "Doc said the girl cut her foot. Okay, Chief, what's—"

Chief Fraser held up one hand. "I don't have time for you, Ralph."

The reporter peered around the room. "Where's Clyde Tatum?"

Chief Fraser heaved to his feet. "Git."

Cooley backed toward the door, his gait just a little unsteady. His slurred words were a taunt. "I saw Faye Tatum tonight at the Blue Light. Me and a lot of men." The door swung out. "Maybe I should talk to the county attorney."

Barb reached out a shaking hand. "You saw Mama?"

"Wait out front, Ralph." The chief spat out the words. "I'll be out in a minute."

Cooley tipped his hat, then banged outside.

The chief clumped back to the chair. "All right, Miss Barb. You been working in the county attorney's office this summer?"

Barb nodded.

"Thought I'd seen you there. Don't know how much you've learned about the law yet, but Mr. Durwood's the man who'll prosecute the case when we find out who killed your mama." He took a deep breath. "Now, Miss Barb, you're telling me you never saw your mama all day until you came home for supper, and you didn't talk to her after she got back from the Blue Light. How about your daddy? What time did he get home?"

Barb sat straight up. "He didn't come home. He never came home. He didn't come home for supper. And he wasn't home when I got back from Amelia's tonight."

Chief Fraser leaned forward. "How would you know? You went to bed."

Barb's eyes were stricken. "I wasn't asleep. I heard Mama come in. She slammed doors and paced back and forth. I heard her go in her room and run out again. There wasn't any other sound. If Daddy was there, he would have said something." Her voice was definite. "There was a knock at the front door. I heard Mama go answer, and she cried out something like 'You've got a nerve.' Somebody came in. There was a voice, but I couldn't hear the words. It was like somebody wanted Mama to be quiet. You know how people make a shushing noise? Then Mama yelled." Barb's face flattened in sick memory. "She was calling for help, and I ran away."

"Right thing to do, Miss Barb." The chief pushed to his feet. "Well, I guess that pretty much covers everything." He reached down a long arm to grab his hat.

Barb stood. "Chief, will you find Daddy? It's going to be awful when he finds out what's happened to Mama."

Gretchen got up, too. She realized she was more tired than she'd ever been. Her head ached; her body felt heavy. Through the screen, the night was turning gray. The sun would be up soon, and she and Grandmother would go to the café. Then she'd go to the *Gazette*. Mr. Dennis would want to know all about her and Barb's finding Mrs. Tatum. But Mr. Cooley would write the story. And she'd bet he'd tell all about seeing Barb's mom at the Blue Light.

Chief Fraser moved slowly, his bootheels thumping. He stopped at the front door. "One more thing, Miss Barb." He spoke quietly enough, but there was an edge to his deep voice. "How come the door to your room is locked?"

Barb's eyes widened, and her mouth hung slack.

The silence in the room pulsed. Gretchen frowned. Most people never even locked up their houses at night. Why would Barb lock the door to her bedroom? Why didn't Barb answer?

It was Grandmother who spoke. "Why, Chief Fraser," she said, her voice holding almost a tsk-tsk tone, "a girl all alone in her house late at night. That was it, wasn't it, Barb? You locked your door because your mama and papa weren't home."

"Yes," Barb said. "I didn't like being by myself. I just turned the lock and went to bed."

The chief frowned. "When you got up, was it because you heard your mama come home?"

"No. I heard Mama come in, and I knew she was still upset, and so I lay there, real still." Tears brimmed from her eyes. "She knocked on my door, but I pretended I was asleep. That's when somebody knocked on the front door. Everything happened real fast—somebody trying to shush her and Mama's cry. I knew something bad was happening, and all I could think of was getting away."

"And that's all you know, Miss Barb?" His voice was weary.

"That's all." Her voice wavered.

The chief clapped his hat on his head. "All right, girl. If you think of anything else, you call and I'll come."

Grandmother moved past him, pulled the door open.

The big man nodded. "Thank you, Lotte," he said, but his eyes still watched Barb, and his heavy face was dour.

Gretchen could see Barb's hands were clasped so tight, the knuckles blanched.

THE HOUSE WAS hot and still. The shades were drawn, but the summer sun peeked around the edges. Gretchen struggled awake. She stared at the alarm clock and felt a shock as she realized the time. She scrambled out of bed and hurried into the living room.

"Barb?" Even as she called, Gretchen knew the house was empty. They'd put Barb in Jimmy's room, but Barb was gone, and so was Grandmother.

The cuckoo clock chirped: ten o'clock. She was late.

Gretchen dressed fast, in a cool summer dress with a white piqué top and a red-and-white-checkered gingham skirt. She slipped barefoot into her white sandals. The phone rang as she was pouring a glass of orange juice. "Hello." She was breathless.

"Mein Schatz—"

"Grandmother"—Gretchen's voice was sharp—"you shouldn't have let me sleep. I'm late."

"That is why I have called. Do not worry, Gretchen. I spoke with Mr. Dennis, and he understood that you had no sleep. I told him you would be there at eleven, and he was pleased. Now, you must eat a good breakfast. There is a muffin and fresh strawberries. Oh, the pot is bubbling. I must go now."

Gretchen drank the juice, quickly ate the apple muffin. She gave her hair three quick swipes. She could be at the *Gazette* office in less than five minutes. But first . . .

THE DRAPES WERE drawn at the Tatum house. Gretchen opened the screen, knocked on the front door. The house lay quiet as death. But Barb should be here. She wouldn't have gone to work.

Gretchen stepped back. The screen door sighed shut. She hurried down the steps, hesitated, then walked around the side of the house. A recently painted white picket fence marked the boundary of the Crane yard.

The door to the Tatums' screened-in back porch wasn't latched. Gretchen listened hard, then slipped inside. "Barb?" The sweet scent of wisteria mingled with the sharper smells of paint and turpentine. Slowly Gretchen walked toward an easel and looked at the half-done painting. A woman in a white dress rested languidly on a white wicker sofa. The only color was the red rose in one trailing hand and the red cushion bunched behind her head. The woman's face was only partially glimpsed behind an open book held in the other hand.

The kitchen door squeaked open. Barb stood in the doorway. "Mama was a good painter." Barb stared at the unfinished painting with red-rimmed eyes. "She was happy when she painted."

Gretchen took two steps to stand just in front of Barb. "Why did you go off without telling me? Why didn't you answer the door?" She knew she sounded angry. She was. She hated the thought of Barb alone in the house.

Barb slumped against the wall. "I came home. I had to. I want to be here for Daddy." She took a deep breath. "But he hasn't come. I don't know what to do."

Gretchen picked her way carefully because this might be the wrong thing to do. "Maybe you ought to go on to the courthouse. When there's any word, they'll know."

Any word . . . Gretchen knew the police were looking for Mr. Tatum to tell him about Mrs. Tatum's murder. And, she thought coldly, to ask him where he was last night and whether he'd come in the front door and quarreled with his wife. "You said somebody knocked on the door. Your dad wouldn't have knocked."

"No. It wasn't Daddy." Barb's voice was dull but determined. "Daddy wouldn't knock. He'd just come in." Her eyes brightened. "That proves it wasn't Daddy." She gave a sigh of relief. "I told the chief, but I'm going to tell Mr. Durwood. He can make the chief understand."

Gretchen was almost all the way to the *Gazette* office before she wondered, What if no one believed Barb?

CHAPTER THREE

. . . when I saw your picture on the page with the editorials. The headline said "Around the World . . . by G. G. Gilman." You were in Rome, and it was something about happy Italian memories. That's nice, to have happy Italian memories. I wish I did. I had some good times—when I didn't remember home. That was always the trouble . . .

"GRETCHEN, *MEIN SCHATZ.*" I heard Grandmother's voice in my memory. It was as if she were here and speaking to me. In my heart, I felt like a girl again. Gretchen—that's how Grandmother knew me. I'd been G. G. Gilman in newsrooms around the world for most of my life. The nickname, derived from my initials, sounded like Gigi. I like to believe I carried it off with flair. No one patronized me. Or, to be honest, no one ever tried it twice. I hadn't been so tough in the beginning. The toughening started that sultry summer when Barb Tatum ran through the night to bang on my window screen. . . .

"PRETTY UGLY, HUH, kid?" Mr. Dennis's rounded face sagged into creases like an old bloodhound's. He leaned back in his swivel chair, arms folded. "You feel like telling me?" His tone was quiet.

Gretchen stood by his desk. She didn't answer.

Jewell Taylor, her bluish-white hair in a French twist, stopped typing. The feather on her wispy hat trembled. "Walt, don't make the child talk about it. Let Ralph handle it."

The editor puffed on his pipe. "Okay, Gretchen, I've got a couple of stories for you. The First Baptist Church has a new pastor. And there'll be a Red Cross bus to take volunteers to Tulsa Saturday to donate blood for the wounded overseas. But first, clear the wire." He jerked his head toward the clacking Teletype, paper oozing from the top, sloping down, and mounding on the floor.

Mrs. Taylor brushed back a loose tendril of her snowy hair. "Have I got room for that mug of the garden-club president?"

Dennis glanced toward the page layouts spread across his desk. "Nope. Too much jump from the Tatum story."

"All right." Mrs. Taylor was always good-humored. In her world, if a story didn't run one day, it would the next. As far as she was concerned, weddings and funerals and club meetings were the heart and soul of the *Gazette.* As she earnestly said, "What matters are people's names. That's what they look for in the paper."

But Gretchen knew that everyone would read about Faye Tatum

in this afternoon's *Gazette*. And, as Mr. Dennis had observed, Gretchen had been there. She took a step toward the editor. "Mr. Dennis, maybe if I wrote it all down . . . About last night."

He said quietly, "I'm not asking you to do that."

She rubbed tired eyes. "I know. I want to." If she put the fear and horror into words, the words would be separate and distinct from her, leaching the harsh images out of her mind and onto paper.

"Sure. Then see about the wire."

Gretchen slowly walked to her desk, sat down. For a while, she stared at the yellow copy paper. She started, stopped, started again. It took almost an hour. Finally she had three double-spaced pages. She pasted the sheets together, laid them in the copy tray. Mr. Dennis nodded his head in acknowledgment. Gretchen felt drained, but there was a sense of release.

The *Gazette* front door banged. Ralph Cooley strolled in, hat tilted to the back of his head, cigarette in his mouth, hand clutching a fistful of copy paper. He flapped the sheets. "Read all about it. 'Cops Hunt Killer. Dogs Called In.' "

Mr. Dennis's chair squeaked as he faced the door, leaned back. His face had a sour look Gretchen recognized. "What's kept you, Ralph? You went over there at nine."

Gretchen checked the clock: not quite noon. She grabbed her pica pole, the thin metal ruler with type sizes marked on the left and inches on the right, and hurried to the Teletype. Using her pica pole, she ripped the stories free, sorted them by origin. Each story had to be spiked. There were four spikes, one each for local, state, national, and international. The spikes were long, sharp nails that had been pounded through metal jar lids; then hot lead was poured in. When the lead cooled, the nails stood upright to serve as spikes for copy.

Cooley grinned as he slouched into his chair, tossed some crumpled notes by the typewriter. "Patience, Walt. There are currents. Tricky currents. Lots of door banging. The stalwart chief and the ambitious prosecuting attorney are toe-to-toe, ready to fight. Lurking on the sidelines, ready to jump in the ring, is the sheriff. This is going to be one hell of a battle, and I'm just the man to ferret out the real story."

"Yeah," Mr. Dennis said, his face still sour. He picked up a pencil, grabbed a sheet of paper. "What's the chief got, Ralph?"

Cooley rolled a sheet into the Remington. "The chief is going to feel a lot of heat if he doesn't find the husband pronto. The county attorney's been on the phone already, and he's pushing the chief hard. No trace yet of the husband. The sheriff's got some men out with dogs. Anyway, I've got a hell of a lead."

Cooley typed and talked at the same time. " 'Well-known artist Faye Tatum was strangled in her home Tuesday night after dancing the evening away at a local nightclub, according to Police Chief Harold "Buck" Fraser. Chief Fraser said police are seeking the victim's soldier husband, Sergeant Clyde Tatum, for questioning.' "

Cooley talked, typed, talked, typed, his words coming almost as fast as the staccato bursts of his typewriter keys. "Tatum's car is parked at the Blue Light. Has the keys in it." Cooley yanked out a sheet of copy paper, rolled another into the typewriter. "And hold on to your hat, Walt—I had a ringside seat last night. When I got to the Blue Light, Tatum was drinking at the far end of the bar. I didn't know who he was then, but I knew he was trouble. He was surly as hell, and everybody gave him a wide berth. Faye showed up about six-thirty, looking like a million dollars, with her hair in a pompadour and a fancy dress and . . ."

Gretchen frowned. She remembered the print. The green shirtwaist dress wasn't fancy. It was nice.

". . . she and Tatum had a shouting match. Somebody at the barbershop told Tatum that his wife was having gentlemen friends over at the house since he'd been gone." Cooley leaned back in his chair. "Faye screamed that it was a lie. She told Tatum he had a nasty mind and, as far as she was concerned, he couldn't get out of town soon enough and she was going to have a good time, no matter what. That's when Lou Hopper came around the bar, and before you could snap your fingers, she had Tatum out the door. You know her. She runs the Blue Light like a drill sergeant."

Gretchen knew all about the Blue Light. It was the biggest beer joint in the county, with a live band every night. She'd never been inside, but Millard had played in the band, sneaking out of his room at night and not telling his folks. That's how he got crossways with them and ran off to join the navy. Millard had liked Mrs. Hopper. Gretchen had spoken to her after Millard left, asked her to let Millard know he could come home, his parents weren't mad anymore. It wasn't too long after that that Millard wrote, sending a picture of himself in his white navy uniform.

"Lou doesn't want any trouble out there." Mr. Dennis made some notes. "Okay, Lou shoos him out. What time was that?"

"Maybe seven. Anyway, everything settled down. Everybody was jitterbugging, having a hell of a time." The Remington keys rattled. "Including Faye Tatum. She danced every dance. But with everybody. You know what I mean—no particular guy." He took a drag from his cigarette, frowned at the words on the sheet. "She put on quite a show. Jitterbug. Tango. Fox-trot. Good gams."

Gretchen had a snapshot-quick memory of the body sprawled in the untidy living room, legs agape. "She lived up the street from me." Gretchen was surprised she'd spoken. Mr. Cooley gave her a funny look, almost a sneer. Gretchen ripped off more wire copy. "She was exciting to be around. All the kids liked her." She stopped at a story about the fighting in Italy. Any news about the 45th Division was important. The 45th came from Oklahoma.

Cooley gave a husky rasp of laughter. "Just a dandy American mom—when she wasn't being a barfly."

Gretchen spiked the story. She whirled toward the reporter, her face burning. "Mrs. Tatum wasn't like that. Barb said her mom just loved to dance. That's all. Barb said her mom told her dad all she wanted to do was dance."

"Oh, sure. And there are leprechauns in my desk drawer." Cooley's mouth curved in a mocking grin. "Anyway, I can tell you that Faye was higher than a kite last night. Then she got belligerent, asking if anybody knew who'd said those things about her. That's when Lou talked to her. Faye quieted down. The last time I saw her, she was in the hallway leaning against the wall, holding on to the receiver at the pay phone. The chief wants to know who she talked to. He says that could be the key to the whole thing. The county attorney isn't impressed. Durwood says it looks pretty clear that the Tatums were having trouble. There was a disturbing-the-peace call from the next-door neighbor late in the afternoon."

"Faye didn't get killed yesterday afternoon." Mr. Dennis's voice was mild. "Gretchen, check the morgue for mug shots of Chief Fraser, Sheriff Moore, and Donny Durwood, the county attorney."

Gretchen walked to the big wooden filing cabinets in the corner, near the Teletype. She pulled out the drawer marked D-E-F.

Cooley yanked the last sheet from his typewriter. "She sure as hell croaked last night, and that happened after she and Tatum had their dustup at the Blue Light." Cooley scribbled a slug on the sheets, pushed back from his desk, and rolled his chair the two feet to the editor's desk.

Gretchen picked two photographs out of the files in D-E-F, found the sheriff's file in M-N-O. Chief Fraser looked like an old bulldog, but not as tired as he had last night. Sheriff Paul Moore's long face reminded her of a sheriff in the westerns, maybe because his eyes had a flat, cold stare and he wore a string tie. Donald Durwood, the county attorney, gazed straight at the camera, stalwart as an Eagle Scout—short blond hair, regular features, firm chin.

Mr. Dennis reached out for Cooley's copy. "Did Faye leave the Blue Light by herself?"

Gretchen placed the photos on his desk.

"She went out the door alone. Who knows?" Cooley rubbed his nose, gave a big yawn. "Anyway, she went home and got herself strangled. If you ask me, she was asking for it."

"Nobody asked you." Gretchen's voice was wobbly, but she glared at him, her gaze furious. "She was nice."

Cooley laughed. "She was an easy—"

The editor rattled the sheets. "That's enough, Ralph. Gretchen knew the woman. Let it go."

Cooley rolled his chair back to his desk, his glance at Gretchen sardonic. "The facts speak for themselves, kid."

Gretchen took a step toward Cooley. "Did you put anything in the story about Mrs. Tatum—about what kind of person she was?"

Cooley raised an eyebrow. His hands were poised above the keys. "What did her kid say? That she loved to dance?"

She loved to dance. But that wasn't everything. If that was all he'd written . . . "She was an artist."

Cooley yawned. "I'm going to get some lunch. Then I'll nose around the courthouse. Maybe they've got a line on her boyfriend." He shook out a cigarette. "Though I don't suppose that matters now."

The Teletype began to rattle. Gretchen ignored the paper coming out. She spoke loud and fast so she could get it all out. "Mr. Cooley, you could talk to some people who knew her. Some of the people who took art from her. Or somebody at the five-and-dime. They'd tell you what she was really like." About the way her laughter sounded light and free. Or the way she would rush out into the yard on a summer night and catch hands with Barb and the other girls playing in the yard and sing "Mairzy Doats."

Cooley gave her a hard stare. "Who, me? I'm no sob sister, kid. That kind of story belongs to Jewell. Or maybe you'd like to do it. Make everybody get their hankies out."

When the front door slammed behind him, Gretchen slowly turned toward Mr. Dennis. "He's going to make her sound cheap. Like she should have died."

Mr. Dennis folded his hands behind his head, frowned at her. "There's nothing in his story but the facts."

"The facts—" Gretchen stopped. She didn't know how to make him understand. Then she looked into bleak green eyes and knew that he understood everything.

Dennis nodded slowly. "That's right, kid. You're getting there faster than most. Depends upon which facts, doesn't it?" He poked at Cooley's copy. "Every fact in here is true. Ralph may have a smart mouth, but he gets it right. But you don't think the Blue Light and alcohol and people mad at each other tell the whole story about Faye Tatum. I'll tell you what—you go get a story about Faye. Only one thing you have to promise me."

"Yes, sir?" She stared into his mournful, skeptical, somber eyes.

"You got to promise that your facts will be true, too." The chair squeaked as he turned back to his desk.

GRETCHEN WALKED FAST despite the heat. She was in a hurry. Everybody in town would be talking about Faye Tatum and the Blue Light and her quarrel with Clyde. But Gretchen was determined that there would be something more to remember about Barb's mother. The place to start was with Barb.

At the courthouse, Gretchen went straight to the third floor. She opened the frosted glass door of the county attorney's office, stepped into a small anteroom. The door to Durwood's office to the left was closed. Wooden filing cabinets ranged against the opposite wall. The anteroom held three desks, the largest a brown walnut. On the big desk were a typewriter, a telephone, in- and out-boxes, a brown leather desk pad, and neat stacks of correspondence. Mrs. Holcomb, a buxom woman with shiny brown hair bunched in sausage-thick curls, held a flyswatter high above her head, poised to strike.

As the door clicked shut, she whispered, "Wait, Gretchen. Hush. Oh"—a sigh of frustration—"it's moved. If you hadn't come in just now . . . I hate wasps. What a morning." Abruptly she lurched forward, swung. The wasp tumbled to the shiny wooden floor. "There." She pushed back a tendril of loose hair. "Come in, my dear. What can I do for you? Mr. Durwood isn't here. If you're here about Mrs. Tatum's murder . . . Oh"—her voice dropped—"it's so awful. Poor little Barb. But Mr. Durwood did the right thing, hard as it was." She dropped into her chair. "The look on her face when she came out of his office just broke my heart. She walked past me like I wasn't even here. She went over to her desk and grabbed her purse from the drawer. I understand she's staying at your house. Will you tell her I wish I could help?"

"What happened in Mr. Durwood's office?"

"He had to let her go." Mrs. Holcomb's tone was mournful. "That's what he told me when he came out. He said that there can't be any appearance of favoritism before the law and if Barb worked at his office, why, people might think he wasn't going to do his job and make sure the police arrest Mr. Tatum."

"What if Mr. Tatum is innocent?" Gretchen raised her voice. "Barb heard someone knock on the front door. Her dad wouldn't knock."

Mrs. Holcomb shrugged. "Oh, my dear, there's all kinds of reasons he might knock. Maybe Faye locked the door. You know, they had a big fight at the Blue Light. Everybody heard her yelling at him. And there she is, dead not much later. Of course the police think Clyde's the one. Mr. Durwood says Barb didn't understand how her daddy's the main suspect. He hated having to tell her. She was real upset."

GRETCHEN OPENED THE screen door, stepped into a tumult of noise—people talking as they ate, the clatter of dishes, a rumble of laughter from a booth at the back. Mrs. Perkins gave her a harried look. "Gretchen, can you take some orders? We're swamped."

Gretchen hadn't had lunch yet, and it was past one o'clock. Mr. Dennis wouldn't mind if she took a few minutes to help out. She reached under the counter, found an apron, slipped it on.

In one of her trips to the kitchen, Gretchen fixed herself a bowl of the special—stewed okra and tomatoes with corn bread—and called hello to her grandmother. Grandmother smiled, but she was too busy to talk, moving swiftly from stove to counter.

At half past one, the county attorney and the sheriff came in. Chief Fraser wasn't with them. Maybe that was to be expected, considering how Ralph Cooley had said the prosecutor and the chief weren't getting along. Durwood was talking fast and gesturing energetically to Sheriff Moore. As the men crossed the floor, they stopped at almost every table. Durwood's curly blond hair was damp with sweat. His white dress shirt clung to him. As he reached out to shake hands or clap friends on the back, heavy gold cuff links glistened. The county attorney looked tense and worried, the sheriff grim. Gretchen had often seen them here at the café. Durwood always had a friendly word for everybody. Sometimes his wife, Sheila, met him here for lunch, and that was exciting, because she was a Winslow. Every town has its aristocracy. The Winslows lived on Hickory Hill. Everyone stood a little straighter when Sheila Durwood came by. Grandmother said Mr. Durwood and his wife were one of the town's finest young couples. There was talk of his running for the state senate.

"Hidy, Donny, Sheriff." Mayor Burkett came to his feet. "What's the latest on the murder? Are you making progress?" His plump face creased in concern. Mayor Burkett always wore a white suit and a straw boater in the summertime.

Gretchen edged nearer. She held the order pad.

Durwood's cheeks puffed in exasperation. "Some of us are." His tone was sour. "I can't get a straight answer out of the chief. Looks to me like he's wasting a lot of time out at the Blue Light. But Paul and I"—the county attorney jerked his head toward the sheriff—"are doing everything we can. The sheriff's got two search teams with dogs out. Nobody's seen Tatum since he left the Blue Light. His car's still in the parking lot, so we think he's on foot."

The mayor rocked back on his heels. His frown deepened. "Don't like the sound of it—a dangerous fugitive at large."

The sheriff shifted the lump of chewing tobacco in one cheek. "We're checking the bus and train stations in Tulsa. We'll find him if he's still around here. But he may have thumbed a ride on 66."

"One thing seems mighty clear. An innocent man would have come home, no doubt about it." The mayor's bulbous eyes challenged the county attorney and the sheriff. "I've called a special meeting of the city council for Friday night if we don't have this thing cleared up by then. The council expects to hear from both of you."

"You can count on us." Durwood met the mayor's gaze. "We'll be at the meeting. And we'll have plenty to report."

The sheriff cleared his throat. "I expect it will be over by Friday night." He jerked his head toward the booths. "Come on, Donny."

Gretchen followed them.

Durwood and the sheriff slid into a booth, and Gretchen took their orders. When she brought their lunches, she looked at the county attorney. His face was somber.

"Mr. Durwood"—Gretchen's fingers curled around the edges of the serving tray—"do you know where Barb is?"

"Barb?" He looked at Gretchen sharply.

The sheriff turned cold, inquiring eyes on Gretchen.

"Barb Tatum. I went to your office looking for her this morning. Barb said she was going to tell you about hearing a knock on the front door last night." Gretchen balanced her tray on one hip.

"Barb Tatum?" The sheriff raised a bushy eyebrow. "I hadn't heard about this."

Durwood fingered one of his cuff links, his face drawn in a tired frown. "The knock on the door? That's what she told me. But what else could she say? Poor kid. She's trying to protect her dad. But the minute she told me, I knew I had to let her go." Though he sounded hard and determined, his face was sad. "Here she was, trying to give evidence in a case I'll be handling. Obviously, we couldn't have her in the office. It looks like Clyde Tatum's going to be arrested for the murder of his wife and I'll prosecute. She was crying when she left."

Gretchen hesitated, then said quickly, "Last night, Barb came to my house for help. She told me then that she'd heard a knock on the door. And later, Barb told the chief her mother answered the door and said, 'You've got a nerve,' and then there was a struggle, and Barb ran away."

" 'You've got a nerve,' " the sheriff repeated. "Hmm. Could be somebody Faye didn't know well. Or didn't expect to see. On the other hand, after the fight she and Clyde had, maybe that's exactly what she'd say to him."

Durwood stared up at Gretchen. "So you were with Barb? Did you see anybody near the house?"

Mrs. Perkins clattered from behind the counter. "Gretchen, can you come help? We need you."

Gretchen glanced at the clock. Almost two. She needed to check in with Mr. Dennis. She would stay late this evening at the *Gazette* to make up for the time here at the café. So if Grandmother needed help for a few more minutes, that was okay.

Behind her, she heard the sheriff's gruff voice saying, "I suspect she died pretty quick. Tatum's a big, strong man. I'd guess he was long gone when the girls got to the house. He probably blundered out of the house and into the woods. That's where we'll find him, huddled in a thicket somewhere. Won't surprise me if he's dead."

Gretchen stopped at the kitchen door, turned her head to listen.

"Dead?" The county attorney sounded startled.

"Remorse," the sheriff said. "Clyde's no killer. I've known him since he was a boy. A woman can drive a man a long way down a dark path. I reckon right now, there's no one sadder than Clyde. Except his little girl."

CHAPTER FOUR

. . . remembering. You were nice to me, Gretchen. You tried to make me feel better about Mama. That first day after she died, the whole world caved in on me. I went to the county attorney's office to tell him about the knock on the door. He didn't believe me. He told me it looked like he was going to have to try and send my daddy to jail. He told me the police were looking for Daddy. But he didn't tell me why. I didn't find out until the chief came to your house that evening. Donny Durwood only said he was sorry and I couldn't work for him anymore. It was like nothing was real, not him or the streets or the cars or the people. . . .

A CARDINAL FLASHED through the air, red as a dancing flame. He and I and a chittering squirrel were the only living creatures in the cemetery, but familiar figures moved in my memory. Grandmother smiled at me, blue eyes shining. Mr. Dennis bent over yellow copy paper, then looked up with his sardonic, hopeful face. Donald Durwood sighed, and I heard his sad murmur: "Poor kid." Chief Fraser stood on the platform of the gazebo on the town square, defying them all. I stood amid the graves, surrounded by ghosts. . . .

MR. DENNIS WRINKLED his nose, plopped down the coffee mug. "Cold." By the time the pressrun ended, he always looked wilted. "Just like the trail for Clyde Tatum." He pointed at the front page of the *Gazette*. Faye Tatum's murder was the lead story. A three-column spread detailed the search under way for Clyde Tatum. Both stories had Ralph Cooley's byline. My story about Barb's coming to my window and our grisly discovery was just below the fold. It read, *By G. G. Gilman*. The Allied attack on Cherbourg rated a thirty-six-point two-column head at the upper left.

Gretchen felt wilted, too. She stood by Mr. Dennis's desk and wished for a big glass of iced tea. "They haven't found Mr. Tatum? Sheriff Moore thinks he may be dead."

Mr. Dennis leaned forward, face intent. "Let's say Clyde didn't kill Faye. Since he hasn't shown up, he most likely heard about her murder. He may be hiding out because he's scared. Or it could be that he doesn't know yet. He may have gotten out of town last night because he's mad at her. He may show up down at Sill, ready to ship out. There's a lot of stuff we don't know." Dennis's gaze dropped to the front page. "Damn. Broken font in the Cherbourg story." He picked up a red pencil, circled the head. The H in HARBOR was chipped.

"Mr. Dennis, I haven't found Barb anywhere." Gretchen felt the sheets of copy paper in the pocket of her skirt, the sheets that were still blank. "She can tell me about her mom's friends."

The editor frowned.

Gretchen looked at him anxiously. "Is it too late now for me to do the story?"

Mr. Dennis picked up his story log. "Try for Friday. That gives you tomorrow to find people. And Gretchen, that was good work, to talk to the sheriff and the county attorney." Dennis raised a bristly eyebrow. "So the mayor's going to demand answers at a specially called city council meeting. Durwood's been aching to tangle with the chief. If they don't find Tatum before then, the chief's going to have trouble. I'll tell you what, Gretchen. You can come to the council meeting with me Friday night and do a color story." He glanced at her, then continued smoothly. "I'll cover the meeting, while you take a look around, pick up the attitudes, describe the way people look and act."

A color story . . .

Gretchen brushed back a limp curl. "Why is Mr. Durwood against Chief Fraser?"

The editor's green eyes glinted. "Smart girl. That's the right question. The chief thinks Durwood's reckless and too quick to interfere with the police. Durwood thinks the chief is too cautious, wants too much evidence before he'll make an arrest. So"—Dennis pushed up from his chair—"you might get to see a little drama Friday night. But for now, you get on home."

THE SUN WAS a brilliant red in the west. At the café, Gretchen had hurried to get the floors mopped and the tables and booths set for tomorrow. Now Archer Street shimmered, and the three blocks home seemed endless. Tired, she was so tired. She needed to talk to Barb so she could find people who had known Faye Tatum.

A horn honked twice, and the chief's big green Packard nosed toward the shoulder. Gretchen stepped up to the open window.

The chief's smooth-crowned cowboy hat almost touched the interior roof. He looked somber, but his deep voice was gentle. "I'm on my way to your house, Miss Gretchen. Can I give you a ride?"

"Yes, sir." She pulled the door open and gingerly slid onto the leather seat, then pulled the door shut. The big seat was hot, but she sank back against the softness. As the big car rumbled down the street, Gretchen frowned. "Why are you coming to my house?" She sat bolt upright. "Is Grandmother all right?"

"Your grandma's fine. I'm coming to see Miss Barb."

"I've been looking for Barb all day."

"So've I." He turned into the graveled drive at Gretchen's house. "Seems she's been in the woods near her house and she came straggling out a little while ago. Sergeant Petty's been keeping an eye on the house. I guess Barb was waiting for her papa to come home."

Gretchen hurried ahead to open the front door. "Grandmother? I'm home. Chief Fraser's with me."

Her grandmother hurried out of the kitchen, a pot holder in one hand. "Chief Fraser, I was just getting supper ready. Will you stay and eat? We have tuna fish sandwiches and tomato soup tonight."

He stood in the doorway, holding his big hat. His eyes scanned the living room. The radio was on, and a smooth voice announced the news: "V-1 rockets struck in the heart of London today, and Londoners once again raced for cover, just as they had during the Blitz. . . ."

"No, ma'am, but thank you. Is Miss Barb handy?"

"That poor child." The older woman's dumpling face creased in concern. "So pale and tired, and nobody to help her. The only family is Faye's sister, Darla Murray. She's down in San Antonio with her husband. She can't come until Friday. She told me to call Reverend Byars." She gave a little headshake. "I talked to Reverend Byars, and he'll see to the funeral. They're thinking it will be Friday afternoon. He said Barb can come and live with them. They've got a houseful of kids and that big old rambling house. He's coming over tonight to see her. I told Barb to rest for a while in Jimmy's room—"

The hall door opened. "Have you found my daddy?" Barb's voice was tense and anxious.

"Not yet." The chief dropped his cowboy hat on a table. "I need to speak with you, Miss Barb."

She stared at him, her eyes forlorn, then slowly walked to the channel-back chair next to the sofa. Grandmother bustled to the radio and turned it off.

Gretchen and her grandmother sat on the brown mohair sofa. Gnarled hands clasped behind his back, the chief walked heavily across the room to look down at Barb, his protuberant cheeks red, his thick lips folded tight. Abruptly he cleared his throat and swung one hand toward her, pointing. "Who was the man coming in the night to see your mama?"

Barb sat frozen, her face stricken. "Man?"

The chief rocked back on his heels. "You didn't tell me that's why your mama and papa had a fight."

Barb came to her feet. "That's not why! Daddy was mad because she was going to the Blue Light. That's all that it was. I swear it. And Mama left him a nice note before she went to work."

The chief's face furrowed with disbelief. "Miss Barb, I got plenty of witnesses at the barbershop yesterday afternoon who heard your daddy explode. Seems he was lathered up getting a shave, and Ed Newton came in and made a crack about Faye Tatum's mystery boyfriend, and Clyde came out of his chair like a stung bronco. Ed told Clyde it was all over town that some man was visiting his house at night and Clyde should ask Faye what's what. Clyde stormed out of the barbershop, half his face still lathered. Now, Miss Barb, who was coming to see your mama?"

Barb sank blindly into the chair.

Grandmother drew her breath in sharply. "Chief Fraser, she is just a child. Why do you have to ask her things like this?"

"Lotte, I got to ask." His voice was harsh. "I've got to know who that man is. He may be in danger." His face looked older than time and full of sorrow. He swung back toward Barb. "I didn't want to believe your daddy killed your mama, but I've got to deal with what's happened. Clyde knew about the man, and Clyde's run away. If he's innocent, he's got to come home and tell us where he was last night. If he's guilty, well, the man your mama was seeing has to be warned. So you've got to tell me, Miss Barb, who he is."

Tears spilled down Barb's face. "It isn't true." She swallowed jerkily. "I tell you, it isn't true. Nobody came to see Mama. Mama wouldn't do that. It's a lie." She dissolved into hiccuping cries.

Grandmother rose. She was heavy, but she flew across the room, knelt by the chair to pull Barb onto her shoulder. She twisted to look up at the chief. "Of course this child doesn't know. No woman would let her daughter see that kind of thing."

The chief sighed. "I guess a woman letting a man steal into her husband's bed would keep it quiet. But I'm going to keep looking." He swung around. In two steps, he was at the door and scooping up his big hat. He gave Barb one last look, shook his head, and slammed out.

"TRY TO EAT a little soup, my dear." Grandmother spoke as if to someone who had been very ill for a long time.

Barb touched the spoon, left it lying on the table. "I can't. I keep thinking about Daddy."

Gretchen picked up half a tuna fish sandwich. "Look, Barb, you told the chief it wasn't true. They'll find out what happened."

Barb spoke almost in a whisper. "It wasn't true. But if Daddy thought it was . . ."

"We can't change what's happened," Grandmother said. "None of us made this happen. So you must trust in God."

Barb slowly began to eat. She finished half the bowl, ate part of a sandwich, then pushed back the plate.

"That is such a good girl. Now I will see to the dishes, and you and Gretchen listen to the radio." Grandmother started to rise from the table, then hesitated, one hand pressed against her chest.

"Grandmother!" Gretchen stood so quickly, her chair tumbled to the floor. She reached the older woman, who was now breathing quickly. "Are you sick? I'll call Dr. Jamison."

Grandmother sank back into her chair. "No, no. I am fine. Just a little catch in my chest. It will go away."

"You're tired, Grandmother." Gretchen took a tight grip on her grandmother's arm. "You lie down. Barb and I will do the dishes."

Grandmother slowly stood. "Yes, I will rest for a while. Thank you, Gretchen."

Gretchen helped her grandmother walk down the hall to the bedroom at the back. She settled her in the big green rocker. "I'll bring you some tea, Grandmother."

The old woman sagged against the cushions of the rocker, closed her eyes. "No, *mein Schatz*. I will just be quiet for a few minutes."

By the time Gretchen reached the kitchen, Barb had cleared the table and stacked the dishes. Gretchen got the dishpan out from beneath the sink, put on a kettle of water to boil. She washed, then scalded the dishes with boiling water. Barb dried.

The front doorbell rang.

Gretchen hurried into the living room. Barb waited in the kitchen doorway. She stared toward the front door, her face rigid.

The doorbell jangled again. The Reverend Byars peered through the screen. "Miss Gretchen, I've come to see Miss Barb. I've come to offer her our house as her new home."

Gretchen ran to the door. "Grandmother's resting. Please come in." She stood aside for him to enter. The fiery evening sun bathed the dusty yard in a brilliant orange light. Cicadas rasped, their summer song so loud, it masked the squeak of the screen-door hinges.

"Thank you, Miss Gretchen. We won't disturb your grandmother. I've come to offer sanctuary to Miss Barb." He looked at the stone-still figure. The preacher's voice was as thick and slow and sweet as molasses. Each word hung in the air like a dancer in a spotlight, eager for applause. Blond hair swooped in a high pompadour above an unctuous face. He lifted plump hands, palms up. "Let us pray." His head sank, and his voice soared. "Dear Lord, we gather here in Thy name always reverencing Thee and knowing that Thou does hear Thy children's call. Be with us now as we grieve for a lost soul and pray that Your child Faye shall be lifted out of sorrow and sin."

Gretchen felt buffeted by the sonorous flow of words. Was he saying that Barb's mother was bad?

The deep, rich voice rolled on. "I tried to counsel our sister Faye, and alas, she didn't heed my voice or that of her Savior. She went her own way, and we see the fruits of that decision. But with Your help, Good Lord, we shall surround her dear child, Barbara, with Your loving care and safeguard her from the temptations of the world and the devil. Amen." He lifted his head, his face wreathed in a forgiving smile. "Miss Barb, I've come to take you home."

Barb took a step back. "My daddy will come. I know he will. I'm going to stay at a friend's house tonight. I've talked to Amelia Brady, and I'm going there right now."

"Miss Barb"—his deep voice swooped low—"we cannot shut our eyes to facts. There's no question that last night's brutal act sprang from disorder between a man and wife, disorder that—"

"It wasn't Daddy." Her voice shook. "I tell you, it wasn't Daddy. I would have known." But her eyes were full of fear. "It was someone else."

The Reverend Byars frowned as the old grandfather clock chimed the hour. "Miss Barb, you will be happier to stay with your friend tonight, but we stand ready to welcome you. At any time." He moved briskly toward the door, impervious to Barb's pain. The last red rays of the evening sun flooded around him, glistened on his hair, turned his skin pink as a pig's. "Give my best wishes to your grandmother, Miss Gretchen. Good night, young ladies."

Barb didn't move until his car backfired its way into the street. Her eyes glittered with tears of rage. "Mama laughed at him. She said he was a silly little man who spent his life trying to scare everybody into heaven, saying nobody should drink or dance and that women in shorts were asking for trouble and deserved what they got. Mama said his problem was, he wanted every woman he saw. Mama told me that she'd heard about women he'd touched, and nobody could say anything, because who would believe it about the preacher. Now he's saying Mama was a bad woman. And there isn't anything I can do."

Gretchen reached out. "Yes, there is, Barb. There is."

"BARB DIDN'T GO with Reverend Byars?" Grandmother looked worriedly at Gretchen.

"She won't ever go there. She's gone to spend the night with Amelia. Reverend Byars prayed for Mrs. Tatum, but he made her sound bad."

"Oh, I see." Grandmother's face looked old and worn and infinitely sad. "Poor Barb. To have to listen to such as that. We will tell her she can stay with us as long as she wants." Grandmother lay heavy and still against the plumped cushions of the rocking chair. "You're a good girl, Gretchen." Her voice was just above a whisper. "You have had such a long day, a hard day. And to have seen what you have seen . . ."

Gretchen's hands clenched for an instant; then she willed away the image of Faye Tatum sprawled in death.

"Oh, dear child, I would have spared you if I could. Don't remember the way Faye died. Remember the way she lived. Faye is in heaven now, splashing paints on canvas, brighter paints on a bigger canvas than she ever had here on earth." Grandmother nodded solemnly. "The Bible tells us, 'God shall wipe away all tears from their eyes; and there shall be no more death, neither sorrow, nor crying; neither shall there be any more pain.' "

"Grandmother"—Gretchen's voice trembled—"I wish Barb was here. Reverend Byars talked about God, but it didn't help. And you help." Gretchen rushed to the rocking chair. She knelt, buried her face against warmth. She cried. With tears came release. Or was it Grandmother's faith? Gretchen felt her grandmother's hand gently stroking her hair. And heard the faint peal of the telephone in the kitchen.

Gretchen jumped to her feet. The ring was louder in the hall. She skidded into the kitchen, lifted the receiver. "Hello."

The operator's voice was thin against the background noises. "A collect call from Lorraine Gilman. Will you accept charges?"

Gretchen felt a surge of happiness. "Yes, oh, yes."

"Gretchen, honey, I just saw the paper. I was late getting home from my shift. I can't believe—"

Gretchen clung to the telephone. "Mother, oh, Mother. Can you come home? It's been so long. You haven't been home since May." Gretchen pictured her mother that last visit, her shiny blond hair in a new French twist, her blue eyes sparkling as she watched Gretchen's delight in the sack of new books she'd brought all the way from Oliver's Bookstore in Tulsa.

"Baby, I am coming home. On Saturday. I've got the day off. I've been planning—" She broke off. "But first, tell me what happened. About Faye. The paper says she was strangled and they're looking for Clyde. But there was a story written by you—G. G. Gilman." She spoke the name almost in awe. "I couldn't believe it. When I read it, I knew it was you. All about Barb running to get you and the two of you finding Faye. It made me feel like I'd been there. How did your story . . ."

Grandmother walked slowly into the kitchen. Gretchen pointed at the phone and smiled. "Mother," she whispered.

". . . get in our paper?"

"Mr. Dennis must have sent it out over the wire. He's supposed to give the wire service any story he thinks they might use."

"I've been half crazy ever since I read it. Is Mother all right?"

"Grandmother's fine." Even as Gretchen spoke, she knew that wasn't true.

"So the police really think Clyde killed Faye. I can't believe he hurt Faye. And Faye . . . Well, she might thumb her nose at bluestockings, but she wasn't a tramp. She wouldn't . . ." Her voice trailed off. "But who can say now, with the world the way it is?"

"Mother, the story in the *Gazette* makes her sound cheap. But Mr. Dennis said I could write a story about what she really was like—how she loved art and what a great mom she was to Barb and how she laughed a lot." Could she do it, could she, could she?

"Listen, honey, I've got to get off the phone. People are waiting. But I'll be home Saturday morning. Gretchen"—a pause and then a rush of words—"I'm bringing a friend. I know you'll like him a lot. See you, sweetie." The line went dead.

Slowly Gretchen hung up the receiver.

"Gretchen, what is wrong?" Grandmother gripped her arm. "Is something wrong with your mother?"

"No. She's coming home Saturday." *I know you'll like him a lot.*

Grandmother's eyes lighted. "But that is good."

"She's bringing someone with her." Gretchen tried hard to keep her voice even. "Mother said we will like him a lot."

CHAPTER FIVE

. . . Worst of all was knowing Daddy thought Mama made love with somebody else. When the chief said somebody told Daddy about a man going into our house late at night, I felt sick. You thought I stayed at Amelia's house that night, but I hid in the woods. . . .

COULD HAVE, WOULD have, should have. If you live long enough, there will be sadness and hopeless longing. If only I had . . . But what could I have done? Grandmother did her best. I did my best. I understand now that Grandmother had great courage. I see her as she was then, a woman of late middle age, her heart already weakening, daring to reach out. Oh, yes, she displayed enormous courage, because she was a woman intimidated by authority, anxious to fill out paperwork correctly, trying always to please. In the timeless silence of the cemetery, I remembered her . . .

GRETCHEN LAY RIGID as a board. Night pressed against the window, dark as a highwayman's cloak. Why did Mother have to bring someone home with her? It wouldn't be the same. Hadn't everything changed enough, with her mother gone to Tulsa and Millard dead and Grandmother painting VICTORY CAFÉ on the plate glass? Gretchen felt the hot prick of tears. Millard, so sweet and funny and nice to her, her best friend in all the whole world.

It was too hot for covers, so hot that the bed felt damp beneath her. She barely heard the click of the door. She lay still and looked through half-opened eyes at the open door and the shaft of light spilling in from the hallway. Grandmother stood just outside Gretchen's room, head bent as if listening. She held a wicker basket in one hand. Slowly she shut the door. The room was dark again.

Gretchen slipped out of bed. As she eased the door open, she heard the unmistakable click of the front-door lock. That was almost as startling as Grandmother's slipping quietly out into the night. They never locked the doors to the house. Why would they? And where was Grandmother going?

Gretchen ran down the hall and looked outside. Grandmother walked down the front walk, using a flashlight to find her way.

Gretchen raced back to her room, pulled on a blouse and pedal pushers. She stepped barefoot into her loafers, not taking the time for anklets. She moved swiftly to her window, unlatched the screen, dropped to the ground. The moon was hidden behind thick clouds, and shadows bunched dark as crow feathers.

When she reached the front yard, she saw Grandmother at the end of the street, slowly walking away from town. Gretchen slipped from shadow to shadow. Grandmother turned right at Maguire Road. There were occasional farmhouses set back from the road. Wearily Grandmother trudged forward.

They walked for another ten minutes and came over a rise. Grandmother stopped to look around; then she turned off the road, taking a path that plunged into a thicket of shrubbery.

Gretchen lost sight of Grandmother. She ran lightly to the path. She wished she had a light, but she took slow, careful steps, and gradually her eyes adjusted to the velvet-thick gloom. Suddenly there was a flicker of light. Gretchen edged behind a tree trunk. Only a few feet ahead, Grandmother played the light of her flashlight across the weathered wood of a ramshackle cabin.

The door creaked open. A big man in a crumpled khaki uniform was outlined in a dim glow of light. "Mrs. Pfizer"—his voice was eager, uncertain—"I wasn't sure you'd come after what they've been saying on the radio. They said the police are looking for me."

Grandmother placed a hand against her chest. "I know what they have said." She spoke quietly. "And I have remembered the little boy who was so good a friend to my Lorraine. I receive the call from the young woman who would not say who she was, but she said you needed for me to come, that you were innocent. And I listen to my heart, and it tells me you did not do this awful thing. So

I have come, and I have brought you food." She held up the basket.

He came down the steps, took the basket. "Are you all right, Mrs. Pfizer?" He gripped her arm, helped her up the steps.

"I will be fine." The words were labored. "I have walked fast, and I am not used to coming so long a way."

They stepped inside. Gretchen crept up the steps. She eased along the porch, her fingers touching the wooden boards. Suddenly she felt emptiness, then wool. A blanket! There was a blanket spread across a window. Cautiously Gretchen pulled the covering away from the frame, peered inside.

Most of the tiny room was jammed with discarded furniture. Two chairs sat on either side of a scarred table. A kerosene lantern atop a dingy iron range cast a fitful orange glow. Barb's father hunched over the basket, pulling out a drumstick and a wedge of corn bread. He looked dirty, tired, disreputable. Mother once said he looked like Tyrone Power. Not tonight. He looked beaten and drained, his hollow eyes wild and glazed.

Grandmother folded her hands. "Clyde, you must come home. This will not help you. And Barb needs her father."

He put down the drumstick, half eaten. "They're hunting for me. They think I hurt Faye." His lips began to tremble. "I wouldn't do that. I was mad at her because it broke my heart to think about her and another man. But if I'd gone home last night, she would be all right. And now she's dead. If I'd gone home . . ." He stared at Grandmother with tear-filled eyes.

Grandmother walked heavily around the table, sank into the chair. "The young woman who called me—if she can tell the police that you were with her . . ."

Clyde shook his head. "I can't tell the police about her. See, her husband's overseas, and his folks would be wild if they even knew she'd been at the Blue Light. But there wasn't anything to this. We were friends a long time ago, like me and Lorraine. She felt sorry for me when I got tossed out of the Blue Light. She came out after me. I was pretty drunk." He touched his head, winced. "We took a drive out to Hunter Lake. And she said Faye danced with everybody, that there wasn't a special guy, same as with her. She said she'd never seen Faye leave with anybody or anybody go out after her. Anyway, I fell asleep in the car, and she drove home. She brought out a blanket to me, and that's all I knew until this morning. She came running out and shook me awake and said that somebody had killed Faye and the police were looking for me. She said I had to get away from her place. I knew I couldn't go home. If the police arrested me, nobody would be looking for the man who killed Faye. I thought of this place, and I told her how to tell you to find me."

"If you were to tell the police what you have told me, then they would know to look for someone else."

"Tell them I got drunk and fell asleep in somebody's car? Do you think they'd believe me?" His tone was bitter.

Slowly Grandmother rose. "Clyde, I pray you will be careful. I am afraid you are in great danger."

"I'll be careful. I just need to talk to some people."

Grandmother turned toward the door.

He called after her. "I'll always be grateful that you came. And I promise I'll come home when I find out who hurt Faye."

Gretchen hurried to the steps and slipped into the darkness.

THE SOUND OF the shot exploded in Gretchen's mind. She knew it was the crack of a gun. One shot, and then shouts.

Gretchen rolled out of bed, ran to her window. She pushed out the screen. Up the street, a flashlight swept across the Tatum yard. "Kenny? Rosa?" Chief Fraser's deep voice boomed as he ran heavily toward the house.

Once again, Gretchen dressed quickly. She was almost to the window when her door opened and the light came on.

Grandmother's hair was tousled; her eyes, wide with fear. "Gretchen, what is happening? Where are you going?"

Gretchen poked her head out the window. She held up a hand for quiet as she listened to barking dogs and a woman's cry—

"Kenny, Kenny, answer me." Lights flared on in the houses on either side of the Tatum place. Mr. Kaufman stood on his front porch yelling, "What's going on out there?"

Gretchen was impatient. "I heard Chief Fraser. I think they're looking for Sergeant Holliman. I've got to find out what's going on. Grandmother, please call Mr. Dennis. Tell him something's happened at the Tatum house."

"At this hour?"

Gretchen's alarm clock showed the time—three-forty.

Gretchen swung her leg over the sill. "He won't mind." She dropped to the ground. She wished she had a pencil and paper. She heard Grandmother's protest, but she kept on going. The Crane house had lights on at the back, but the front door was closed. The Tatum house was still dark.

Another shout. "Chief, I've found Kenny. He's hurt."

Gretchen caught up with Chief Fraser as he strode along the side of the Tatum house. "Chief, has someone been shot?"

The chief flapped a long arm at her. "Get back, girl. I don't know what's happened."

Mr. Kaufman slammed his backyard gate. "What's going on?"

"Call an ambulance, Larry." The chief's voice was brusque. "I've got a man hurt—Sergeant Holliman."

Kaufman ran back toward his house.

The chief disappeared behind the Tatum house. Gretchen hurried to the end of the wall. A flashlight lay on the first tread of the back steps. The light flooded over Sergeant Petty, who was kneeling by a still figure. Sergeant Holliman lay on one side, an arm outstretched. A revolver was within inches of his fingers.

Sergeant Petty held a gun in her right hand. Her eyes scanned the night. "I don't find any blood. There's some swelling on the side of his head. He's unconscious, but he's breathing steady." She pulled a handkerchief from a back pocket, gripped the barrel of Holliman's gun, lifted it to her nose. "Kenny didn't shoot this gun. Chief, I didn't see a thing, but I thought I heard something funny. I called out real low for Kenny. All of a sudden, there was a kind of banging and scrambling and a thunk, like somebody got hit, and the shot. I didn't see anybody." She gestured at the thick tangle of undergrowth. "If anybody got in there, we won't find them now."

"Nope. Not now." The chief's voice was dour and angry.

"Gretchen!" Grandmother came around the side of the house. "Oh, there you are. I called Mr. Dennis, and then I got dressed." She stopped, pressed her hand against her chest.

"It's all right, Grandmother. I'll come home in a little while. Mr. Dennis might need me. Please."

A car screeched around the corner onto Archer Street, jolted to a stop. Mr. Dennis slammed out of a black Ford and ran across the lawn. "What's going on, Chief?"

"Sergeant Holliman's hurt."

A siren rose and fell. The ambulance came along the side of the house. The driver and his assistant moved quickly. They carefully eased Sergeant Holliman onto a stretcher, lodged him in the ambulance, and roared off to the hospital.

The chief swung his flashlight toward the porch, revealing an open kitchen door. "Looks like somebody got into the house. Holliman heard something, came up this way, and somebody knocked him down."

"The gunshot?" Sergeant Petty held Holliman's gun by the barrel.

The chief lifted his big shoulders, let them fall. "When Kenny comes to, maybe we'll find out. Come on, Rosa, let's take a look inside." He turned his flashlight on Mr. Dennis. "Police investigation. Nobody else can come in." The beam moved, lighted Gretchen, danced around her, touched on Grandmother. "Where's Miss Barb? She can help us check out the house, see if anything's missing."

Gretchen stepped forward. "She's at Amelia Brady's. Do you want me to call and ask her to come?"

He shook his head. "I'll talk to her in the morning. If anything's gone, we can't do anything about it now." He glanced at Mr. Dennis. "I'll talk to you in the morning, Walt. Ten o'clock."

"Aren't you going to call the sheriff? Get some deputies out here to look through the woods?" Mr. Dennis waved his hand at the dark mass of trees.

The chief scowled. "Don't need any help." He turned, stumped up the steps

Grandmother took Gretchen's arm. "Let's go home now."

"Thank you for calling me, Mrs. Pfizer," Mr. Dennis said.

"I would not have done so, but Gretchen insisted."

The editor nodded at Gretchen. "Good job. And Gretchen, here's what I want you to do in the morning. . . ."

AFTER HELPING GRANDMOTHER get started at the Victory Café, Gretchen rode her bike to the *Gazette* office, but didn't stop when she saw that the windows were still dark. She'd thought Mr. Dennis might have come in early, but he would likely be there by seven. She turned onto Archer Street. She would use the phone at home to call the Brady house. Mr. Dennis was counting on her finding Barb this morning before the chief saw her.

As she passed the Tatum house, she didn't see any trace of police. Did the chief still have someone watching the house?

Gretchen turned into her driveway. A slim figure rose from the swing on the front porch. Barb wore a striped cotton blouse and blue shorts. Her russet hair looked mussed and wilted.

"Barb"—Gretchen dropped the bike beside the steps, hurried onto the porch—"I'm so glad you're here. Listen, somebody broke into your house last night, and Chief Fraser wants you to go through the house with him and see if anything's missing."

Barb frowned. "Broke into our house? Why? Who did it?"

"Nobody knows. Come on, let's call the chief." Gretchen opened the front door.

Barb lifted a canvas bag and stepped inside. "I brought my stuff. I thought maybe I could stay here during the day. Amelia's mother—" She broke off, pressing her lips together.

Gretchen grabbed the bag. "Why don't you spend the night, too? You can stay with us as long as you want to."

"That's okay. I'll go back to Amelia's tonight. But last night, Mrs.

Brady talked and talked, and she's just like Reverend Byars." Barb pressed her hand against her mouth. "Oh, Gretchen, you know how Mama was. You're going to write that story about her, aren't you?"

"Yes." Gretchen looked away. She knew she could make Barb feel better. She could tell Barb that her father was safe, that he was hiding in the Purdy cabin. She could tell Barb that he had said he was innocent. But if the police ever found out that Grandmother had gone to the cabin, that she knew where a wanted man was hiding, she would be in terrible trouble.

THE OLD GREEN Packard rumbled into the Tatum drive. Gretchen and Barb stood near the front steps. It was already hot. Today would be a scorcher. Chief Fraser walked slowly.

"Morning, Miss Barb, Miss Gretchen. Appreciate your help." He held a tagged key in his right hand. "You know about last night, Miss Barb?" He looked at her with somber eyes.

"Gretchen said somebody broke in." Barb glanced toward the closed front door. "Do you know who it was?"

"No. But maybe we'll figure something out when we look around inside." The chief moved past them. He banged back the screen, unlocked the front door, held it open.

Barb gripped Gretchen's arm, her fingernails sharp as little knives. They stepped into the living room. Chief Fraser clicked on the light. Barb leaned against Gretchen and turned her face away from the center of the room, where they'd found her mother's body. The house was hot and still, with all the windows shut. There was a faint smell of paint and turpentine and old tobacco smoke.

"Miss Barb," Chief Fraser said briskly, "please look around the room. Do you see anything missing, anything out of place?"

Barb stepped away from Gretchen. She folded her arms tight across her front. "Nothing's changed." She took a deep breath.

The chief led the way to the narrow hall. "This first room . . ."

"Mama and Daddy's room." Barb walked slowly inside. Chief Fraser was close behind. The bed was unmade. Faye's clothing lay on chairs, hung from the bedpost, poked from open drawers.

"Were her things usually strewn around?" Chief Fraser frowned at the disarray.

Barb fingered the lace edge to the collar of a blouse. "Mama was always in a hurry. She wanted to be with people—me or Daddy or friends—and talk and laugh. Or she wanted to paint. She'd straighten everything up every so often and she'd be real proud of how tidy it was, and then the next minute, she'd toss something down and not give it a thought."

"So I guess there's no way to tell if anybody looked for something." He rubbed his face.

Barb pointed across the room. "Look! There's Daddy's duffel bag. And there on the dresser is his hairbrush and comb. So it wasn't Daddy who came. He'd take his things, wouldn't he?"

The chief frowned. "You'd think so, if it was him. But tell me this: Where's your daddy's gun? Where does he keep it?"

Barb turned to the closet. The door stood open. She reached up on the shelf. "He keeps it up—" She swept her hand back and forth. "Why, it's gone. Daddy's gun is gone!"

CHAPTER SIX

. . . I got a cot out of the shed and set it up back in the woods. I thought Daddy might come home, but I couldn't make myself stay in the house. I didn't think I'd fall asleep, but I did. A shot woke me up. I saw a man in dark clothes running on the path to Creek Road. I couldn't tell who it was. I sneaked up and heard everything the police said. That's why I came to your house in the morning. When the chief came and we went to my house, I couldn't believe it when I looked in the closet and Daddy's gun was gone. . . .

. . . AND FELT FOR a shining incalculable instant that Grandmother was beside me, her faith and goodness a bastion and a beacon. The feeling passed, and I was alone in the chill world of the dead, surrounded by souls, jostled by memories. The last time Mother had come home, we didn't bring flowers for Daddy. I'd resented it then. How hard-hearted I'd been. I'd not realized that Mother was still young that summer day in 1944. In her late thirties, impulsive, open to emotion, ready for laughter and love and happy days. I would never forget the yearning look . . .

THE TELETYPE CLATTERED. Gretchen worked fast, sorting the stories, the continuing siege at Cherbourg, Red troops at Vyborg, V-1 rocket attacks in London. It was already hot in the newsroom. Ralph Cooley, his hat tipped to the back of his head, a cigarette dangling from the side of his mouth, sat hunched at his typewriter. Mr. Dennis stood behind him, round face puckered in a frown beneath a green eyeshade, pipe clenched in his teeth, arms folded.

"The chief won't say Tatum's armed and dangerous, but"— Cooley's shoulders rose and fell—"anybody can figure it out. Holliman heard a noise from inside the house and went to the back porch to take a look. Somebody busted out the kitchen door and whammed him on the head. Holliman said he heard a shot and smelled gunpowder. The chief thinks whoever it was cracked Holliman on the head with a gun and the gun went off. With what she got this morning"—Cooley jerked his head toward Gretchen— "it seems pretty clear. We got a gun going off, and Tatum's gun is missing from his house. One plus one . . ."

Mr. Dennis took his pipe, held a match to the tobacco, drew hard. "The chief says an unidentified prowler broke into the house and a gun appears to be missing."

Cooley looked up at the editor. "So . . ." It was a challenge. "What's the chief thinking? Some stranger broke in and went straight to the place Clyde kept his gun? Face it, Walt, your Boy Scout is looking for trouble. If I were the guy who was fooling with Faye, I'd get out of town. Anyway, I've got a quote from the sheriff." Cooley cleared his throat. " 'Sheriff Paul Moore Thursday advised county residents that fugitive from justice Sergeant Clyde

Tatum, wanted for questioning in the murder of his wife, is believed to be armed and dangerous.' And that's my lead."

JESSOP'S FIVE-AND-DIME was four doors down from Victory Café. Shelving filled the middle of the store, and glass-topped counters ran along the walls. Gretchen hurried down the central aisle to the jewelry counter at the back. Lucille Winters wiped a cloth on the glass above the watch display. She looked up at Gretchen's quick steps on the wooden floor. Lucille's dark hair swept up in a high pompadour above a broad, open face, the cheeks bright with rouge. "Oh, Gretchen," she cried. "You were with Barb when she found her mama. I've felt so bad ever since I heard. How is Barb?"

Gretchen came close to the case. "Sad. Scared. Worried about her dad. Furious over what they're saying about her mom. That's why I came to see you. I want to write a story about what Mrs. Tatum was really like."

Lucille put down the cloth. "None of it's true—about Faye and another man. I know it's not. Faye was crazy about Clyde. I'll speak up for Faye and look everybody in the eye. I tell you, she loved Clyde and nobody else. Here's what she told me, and everybody who wants to think she was a bad woman can just put this in their pipe and smoke it. . . ."

Gretchen wrote as fast as she could.

JIM DAN PULLIAM rolled the tire toward the jacked-up car. He moved with muscular grace. Smears of oil streaked his hands and lower arms. He squatted and bounced the tire on the axle. As he slapped on the lug nuts with easy familiarity, he used the back of his hand to wipe sweat from his face. "Barb said her mother thought I was the best?" He darted a shy look at Gretchen.

Grasshoppers buzzed in the waist-high weeds behind the rutted, oil-stained patch of ground. Gretchen was intensely aware of Jim Dan—the smoky blue of his eyes, the thick tangle of chestnut hair that fell across his forehead, the way his jeans clung to his body. She dropped her eyes to the fan of copy paper. "Yes." Her answer seemed to come from a far distance. "Barb said her mother was sure you'd be an artist. A wonderful artist." She pushed away the sensations that had taken her by such surprise.

Right now, she needed to find out about Faye Tatum. She held fast to that thought, listened to Jim Dan's tentative, gentle voice.

"She never laughed at anybody." He picked up a wrench. "I mean, it was funny—she laughed a lot, but when she looked at your work, she was serious as she could be. Funny thing is, I was in a lot of trouble at school, but she didn't care about that. She . . ."

Gretchen nodded, her pencil flying.

MRS. PERKINS SLAPPED tuna fish salad on thick white bread. Her brown eyes gleamed. "Do you know what I heard the sheriff say? I couldn't help hearing. He was telling Mr. Durwood about the autopsy report they did on poor Faye." She shivered. "The sheriff said they found skin and blood underneath her fingernails."

"Skin and blood . . ." Gretchen repeated. "I don't understand."

"Oh, don't you see?" Mrs. Perkins slipped behind Gretchen, clamped her fingers on Gretchen's throat.

Startled, Gretchen lifted her hands, reached back, fastened on Mrs. Perkins's bony arms.

Mrs. Perkins loosed her grip. Her arms fell. She stood so close, her breath was warm on Gretchen's face. "Faye tried to get the hands off her neck. The sheriff said she fought real hard. She had long nails. He said Faye must have marked him up pretty good."

BETTY STEELE BUSTLED onto the screened-in porch, placed the tray on the wooden table next to the swing. "It's sweetened tea, Gretchen. With fresh mint." Soft curls framed a sweet, eager face with mild blue eyes and pink cheeks.

"Thank you, Mrs. Steele." Gretchen accepted the big glass. The sweet cold drink poured energy into her body. "Barb said you took a lot of her mom's classes at the gift shop." She put down the glass, picked up her pencil and the fan of yellow copy paper.

Tears glistened in Mrs. Steele's eyes. "Faye was the most alive person I ever knew. She loved painting and teaching people how to do it. I never knew anybody who loved painting as much as she did."

GRETCHEN RESTED HER bike against the back steps of the Blue Light. The kitchen door was open. A radio played Glenn Miller. A half-dozen cars were parked in front. Gretchen wasn't sure why she'd come. She'd talked to Mrs. Hopper last fall, when she'd tried to get word to Millard that his folks weren't mad at him anymore. Gretchen remembered a big woman in a purple dress, with a dead-white face and bushy red hair and tired eyes.

Gretchen knocked on the screen door. A skinny little woman stamped to the door. "Go away, kid. We don't need whatever—"

Gretchen lifted her voice. "I need to see Mrs. Hopper."

The woman snapped a dishtowel at flies buzzing over the dishes on an uneven counter. "You selling something?"

"No. Please, tell Mrs. Hopper that I'm here for Faye Tatum." Gretchen's tongue felt thick—she was so thirsty.

"The one that got herself killed? Lou don't know nothing about that. I can tell you, she don't want to talk about it."

"Please, go ask her if she liked Faye. If she did, she'll want to talk to me."

The sharp-featured woman shrugged. As her shoes clumped on the wooden floor, Gretchen jumped off the steps and hurried to the water faucet on the side of the foundation. She crouched, turned the handle, let warm water slip through her fingers until it cooled, then pooled water into her hands and drank thirstily.

The screen door banged. Lou Hopper stood on the top step, her hands splayed on her hips. Mercurochrome-red hair flared in thick curls to the sides of her head. Thin black eyebrows, shiny as tar, arched in half moons above dark eyes cold as a winter pond.

Gretchen scrambled to her feet. "Mrs. Hopper, I'm Gretchen Gilman and—"

"I remember you." The rough voice was brusque. "Millard's friend." Mrs. Hopper pressed her lips together in a tight line.

Gretchen looked up, and their eyes met. For an instant, Millard was there with them, his round face bright with happiness.

"Damn war." Mrs. Hopper cleared her throat. "Josie said you asked if I liked Faye Tatum. Why?"

"People are saying a lot of bad things about Mrs. Tatum. Mostly because she came here to dance. I want to write a story for the *Gazette* telling people what she was really like. You can help me."

Bright red lips twisted. "Gilman . . . G. G. Gilman." She gave a hoot of laughter. "So people'll think you're a man." She lifted her big shoulders in a shrug. "Why not? Give 'em hell, kid. I'm all for you. But I don't talk to cops, and I don't talk to reporters."

"If you liked Faye, why won't you say so?"

"I run a beer joint, kid. Who cares what I say? People come here to laugh and dance and forget the war. I don't talk about 'em."

"All I want to know is what you thought about Faye Tatum. Everybody says she was a tramp, because she came to the Blue Light. If you say that isn't so—"

"Do you think anybody in town will care what I say?" Her voice was sharp. "Poor Faye. She wasn't looking for trouble." Mrs. Hopper came down the steps, her face bleak. "All right, I'll talk to you about Faye. Nobody else. And I don't give a damn what the bluenoses think. Because you know something—they're wrong. . . ."

GRETCHEN RODE HER bike slowly. She was almost past the Crane house when she realized the front door was open. Gretchen slowed, stopped. Mrs. Crane had been the nearest neighbor to the Tatums. She had called the police Tuesday afternoon; she clearly kept an eye on the house next door.

A ruffled white curtain moved at a front window.

Gretchen swung off her bike and started up the walk. She had enough now for a good story, but it wouldn't be complete if she didn't talk to Mrs. Crane.

She lifted her hand to knock, but quick footsteps sounded. Mrs. Crane looked through the mesh of the screen door. Permed gray hair in tight curls bristled from her narrow head. Skin sagged from sharp bones. Her mouth drooped as if she'd just said something sad. The brightness of pansy-blue eyes was almost startling in the seamed face. She held up the evening paper and pointed at Ralph Cooley's headline: ARMED AND DANGEROUS. "Gretchen, do you know about this?" She yanked open the door. "I'm so upset. Come in and let me get you some iced tea. You sit down, and I'll be right back."

Gretchen stepped inside. The living room was almost a twin in size to that in the Tatum house, but here everything was fresh and clean, washed and polished.

Gretchen sat on the blue chintz sofa in a pool of summer heat. Mrs. Crane talked as she bustled about the kitchen. "I've felt so bad about Faye, but I never thought anything like that would happen. When I called the police, I was frightened for Clyde because Faye was out of control. I've never heard anyone scream like that in all my life." She pattered into the living room, placed a tray on the coffee table. "I brought you some watermelon, too."

"Thank you." Gretchen lifted the glass, welcomed the sweet, bitingly cold tea. The watermelon was sweet, too, and crunchy.

"Anyway, my husband, William, always said to me, 'Least said, soonest mended.' And, oh, if I hadn't told my sister-in-law Penelope Newton about seeing that man late at night, maybe none of this would have happened. I should have known that Penelope always tells Ed everything, and Ed was at the barbershop telling everybody there about a man coming to see Faye." The words buzzed like flies swirling over a picnic. "I was scared to death Tuesday afternoon when I heard those screams and shouts. I was in the kitchen, and I heard the back door slam and Clyde yell, and pretty soon, Faye's voice was shrill and loud, and she said he was awful and that it was all a lie and what kind of man was he to believe that kind of garbage about his wife. Clyde yelled that she was a"—pause—"a bad woman, and a minute later, she shouted she was going to get the gun and shoot him dead and show him what happened to liars. That's when I ran to the phone and called the police. Anyway, Clyde was gone before the police car got here. I'll never forget how Faye sounded, screaming that she was going to shoot him dead."

Gretchen felt confused. Faye Tatum threatened Clyde? "Are you sure it was Mrs. Tatum who—"

"I know what I heard. Just like I know what I saw late at night at that house." She sat up very straight, and her cheeks flamed. "No one can call me a liar. That's what I told Faye when she called—" She gave a tiny gasp, and her eyes widened.

"Mrs. Tatum called you? From the Blue Light?" Gretchen's voice was eager. "The chief wants to know who she called that night."

"Oh, Gretchen, it was awful." Mrs. Crane's voice trembled. "She'd been drinking, and she was all upset. Ed Newton had told her what I'd said to Penelope." Tears trickled down the worn cheeks. "Oh, how I wish I hadn't done that. I made up my mind I wouldn't ever tell anybody about what I'd seen, not ever again. But when she asked me why I lied about her, I told her it wouldn't do any good to pretend with me, because I saw what I saw, and I told her chapter and verse. She got real quiet. I guess she knew it wasn't any use calling me a liar. But none of that matters now. She made mistakes. I don't know anybody in this lifetime who hasn't."

Gretchen frowned. "Chief Fraser said it could be real important to know who she talked to." But if it was just Mrs. Crane, it didn't make any difference at all.

Mrs. Crane folded her plump arms across the starched front of her blue housedress. "Least said, soonest mended. Don't you go and tell anybody what I said. You hear, now?"

"You need to tell the chief. He's trying everything to find out who was coming to see Mrs. Tatum and—"

"Oh, no." Mrs. Crane held up her hands in protest. "No. I won't talk to him. It won't do Chief Fraser a bit of good to come see me. I know there was a man. I saw him plenty of times, but who it was is God's business, not mine. I don't recall now who it was. And I've said all I ever intend to say." She folded her lips tight as a closed coin purse.

Gretchen knew Mrs. Crane had recognized that stealthy visitor, but she'd made up her mind never to tell.

THE SMELL OF apple pie scented the house. Gretchen smiled as she hurried toward the kitchen. "Grandmother?"

Grandmother turned, her face lighting with love. "*Mein Schatz,* everything is ready for your mama to come home on Saturday. For dinner, we will have fried chicken and mashed potatoes and gravy and peas and"—she pointed at the pie cooling on the drainboard—"your mama's favorite."

And Gretchen's favorite. But the prospect of pie and seeing her mother couldn't erase the hard lump in her stomach. Mama's friend. Why did she have to bring someone home with her?

Grandmother's smile slipped away. "Gretchen, what is wrong?"

Gretchen felt the burn of tears prompted by fatigue and worry and uncertainty. And jealousy. Instead of answering, she tossed the *Gazette* on the table and forced a smile.

Grandmother walked to the stove, lifted the lid. "Hmm, do you smell the bratwurst, Gretchen? Supper is almost ready."

Gretchen hurried to her room and changed into a white cotton blouse and seersucker shorts. When she came back, she set the table, thinking, as she always did, how bare the table looked with only two plates.

"*Mein Gott.*" Grandmother's voice was low and strained.

Gretchen jerked around. Grandmother was bent over the counter, looking at the front page of the *Gazette.* Gretchen moved to stand close. She touched her grandmother's rigid arm.

Grandmother walked slowly to her chair, slumped into it.

"Grandmother . . ." Gretchen didn't know what to say. She couldn't let Grandmother know that she'd followed her to the cabin.

"Our supper . . ." Grandmother's face crinkled with worry.

GRETCHEN FELT HOT and uncomfortable lying in bed wearing her blouse and shorts. But she knew Grandmother would go to the cabin tonight to ask Clyde Tatum about the gun. She fought to remain awake. She felt the night press against her, closing her mind, pushing her down, down into darkness.

Gretchen woke. Grandmother—where was she? Fear swept her.

Gretchen pushed out of her bed, not bothering to be quiet. The house had that unmistakable feel of emptiness. She slipped on her loafers. She knelt, reached under her bed, and pulled out Jimmy's .22 pistol, which she'd hidden there earlier. She went to the window, dropped to the ground, and ran through the night, the pistol in her hand. The bright moonlight coated the trees and road with cream.

How could she have fallen asleep? What if he had the gun? God, please don't let him hurt Grandmother.

At the clearing, she hesitated. No light shone from the front window of the cabin. But there had been a blanket tacked there. Gretchen eased up the steps, crept across the floor, reached out, felt the roughness of wool and heard the low murmur of voices. Grandmother's voice! Gretchen cautiously pulled the edge of the blanket away from the frame. Clyde Tatum and Grandmother stood by the front door, so near that Gretchen saw the thick black bristles on Tatum's unshaven face. Gretchen's fingers tightened on the butt of Jimmy's gun. Her eyes swept the counter and the stove and the rickety wooden table, two pans, the remnants of a meal, the lantern, Grandmother's picnic basket, a copy of the *Gazette*. No gun. No gun anywhere.

". . . when I find out who killed her . . ." His voice grated.

"Oh, Clyde." Grandmother touched his grimy cheek. "I beg of you. Give this up. Come with me. We shall tell the police—"

"Tell the police! They'll throw me in jail." He took a deep breath. "I was out last night. I tried to catch Ed Newton, but there was always somebody around. I'm going to talk to him—just him and me—and he's going to tell me where he heard this stuff about Faye. I can talk to whoever it was. Maybe some guy had been bothering her and she told him to get lost and he came after her. And if he hurt Faye—"

"Then it will be time to go to the police." Grandmother clasped her hands together. "Chief Fraser is a good man. He will listen."

Clyde rubbed at his face. "As soon as I find out, I'll tell him. Now you better get home. I didn't want you to come here again."

"I had to come. That gun—who could have taken it, Clyde?"

He rubbed his cheek, frowned. "I don't know."

Grandmother shook her head. "The police and the men hunting for you will have guns. Clyde, we should go now and tell them it wasn't you." Grandmother clasped his strong, tanned arm.

"Not yet. I got to talk to Ed Newton." He gave her a quick, gentle hug. "You go home now. It will be all right."

Grandmother turned toward the door.

Gretchen ran to the edge of the porch, jumped. She reached the fringe of the woods and plunged into darkness.

CHAPTER SEVEN

. . . That's when I started drinking at night. I took a bottle of bourbon from the house and hid it in the woods. I started drinking so I could forget. But I never, ever could. Whiskey and men, starting that summer . . .

. . . IN MOTHER'S EYES and the way she'd hugged me, held me so tight. I smiled and felt warm despite the cold eddy of the March wind rustling the bare limbs of the cottonwoods, swirling leaves across the graves. We shared so much laughter, Mother and I, and she was always so proud of me. Through my life, I wore that pride like a shield, deflecting envy, uncharitableness, indifference, hatred. Her grave wasn't in this cemetery, but she was here with me now. Perhaps it is only the old who know that the unseen is as real as the seen. I knew that. I knew, too, that nothing could alter the past, but it was important to know truth. I was still seeking truth. . . .

"IT'S GOING TO be a hell of a dog and pony show." Ralph Cooley snickered. "Everybody's mad: the mayor, the chief, the sheriff, the county attorney, the bluenoses who think anybody who'd go inside the Blue Light's tainted by hell."

Gretchen rolled in a fresh sheet of copy paper, tried to ignore

Cooley's chatter as he typed, smoked, relished the coming city council meeting. In her wastebasket, wadded-up sheets puffed like cheerleaders' pom-poms. She tried another beginning: *Five friends remembered Faye Tatum. . . .*

She ripped out the sheet, squeezed it, added another crumpled ball. Mrs. Hopper couldn't be called a friend. There had been no warmth in her rough voice. Her observations were unemotional, brusque, her tone remote.

The minute hand on the old wall clock made a distinct click when it reached the hour. She heard it now and looked up, her face taut. She'd been working all morning, and she didn't have anything. "Mr. Dennis, I don't have the story on Mrs. Tatum."

Mr. Dennis gave her a casual smile. "You'll do fine. Keep it simple. Tell it the way it happened."

Keep it simple. . . . Gretchen lifted her hands, began to type, a word, another, more, then faster and faster:

WHO WAS FAYE TATUM?

Five people described her for the *Gazette.* Each knew her in a different way. Lucille Winters worked with Faye at Jessop's Five-and-Dime. Jim Dan Pulliam is an aspiring artist whom Faye encouraged. Betty Steele took classes from Faye. Lou Hopper owns the Blue Light, where Faye loved to dance. Martha Crane lived next door to Faye.

Faye Tatum still loves and laughs and paints and dances in the memories of those who knew her. . . .

When she finished writing, Gretchen read over the copy, corrected typos, put her name and a slug—*Memories*—in the upper-left-hand corner. She marked the page numbers in the upper right. She pasted the sheets together. The story ran twenty-eight inches, the longest she'd ever written. Was it stupid? Would Mr. Dennis wonder why he'd ever hired her?

The floor creaked. A shadow fell across her desk. "Let me see, Gretchen." Mr. Dennis reached down, took the copy.

When he was done, he nodded and turned away, carrying the

pages. He walked back toward his desk, then said over his shoulder, "Yeah, Gretchen, I'm sending it out on the wire. With your byline."

She sat very still. . . . *On the wire*—her story would go out on the wire.

GRETCHEN SLIPPED ON her dull blue wool crepe dress. It was her best winter dress, and the pleated skirt felt heavy as a blanket. She'd be hot as blazes, but none of her summer church clothes were dark. Why did people wear dark clothes to a funeral? To show they were unhappy? Gretchen tucked the question in her mind.

Grandmother was waiting in the living room, wearing her best navy silk dress and a blue straw hat. Her white-blond hair was freshly braided in a coronet. She held a blue pottery bowl covered with waxed paper. "I have made a fruit salad. Barb and her aunt are at the house, so I thought we'd take it there." Her round face creased. "I don't know if people will come to the house after the funeral."

Gretchen reached out for the bowl. Murder changed everything. Murder had turned Faye Tatum into a bad person. At least that seemed to be how the Reverend Byars saw Faye. How many people in town felt the same way?

Two unfamiliar cars were parked in the rutted drive of the Tatum house. A mud-streaked green coupe was nosed in close to a pile of logs. Behind it, a shiny black sedan gleamed with fresh wax. Gretchen held the bowl in one hand, braced Grandmother's elbow with the other. Grandmother moved slowly, as if each step took effort. Her gait was leaden, like an old, old woman's.

The Tatums' rusted gate still hung from its hinge. The front door was open. Gretchen moved ahead of Grandmother, lifted one hand. Before she could knock, the screen door swung out.

Barb, her face white as a clown's greasepaint, held the screen. She, too, wore a dark dress. She didn't say a word. Red-rimmed eyes, glazed with misery, stared emptily.

Gretchen stepped inside even though she wanted to turn and run, flee from this square room with its awful freight of memory.

Grandmother climbed the steps, breathing heavily. She came inside, folded Barb in her arms, held her tight.

Footsteps clipped on the hardwood floor. "Come in. I'm Darla Murray, Faye's sister." Darla Murray's voice was sharp. Her face was a heavier version of Faye's. She, too, might have been beautiful, but her green eyes were hard and cold.

Grandmother patted Barb once more. "Mrs. Murray, we are neighbors to Faye and Clyde. This is my granddaughter, Gretchen. She has brought the salad."

Mrs. Murray waved a thick hand, the nails a bright red. "Oh, you can put it in the kitchen. I don't know whether we'll need anything. Some people brought dishes, but I've got to get on the road as soon as the burial's done." She glared at Barb. "And you have to get your things ready to go to the preacher's house."

Barb's stricken face turned toward Gretchen. "I'll take the salad." She reached out, grabbed the bowl, limped toward the kitchen. Gretchen followed. Barb went to the doorway to the back porch, slumped against the doorframe, facing the easel with the unfinished painting.

"Barb," Gretchen called softly.

Barb turned and looked at Gretchen dully, her face heavy with sadness and despair. "Daddy didn't come home. They're going to bury Mama, and he isn't here. Aunt Darla said what could Mama expect? No man would put up—" She buried her face in her hands. "Oh, God, I wish I was dead. That's what Daddy thought. That's what he thought and—"

A crisp handclap sounded from the doorway.

Barb's head jerked up. Her eyes blazed.

"Time to go." Barb's aunt adjusted her hat, dropped down a short veil. "Come on, girl."

Barb started across the kitchen, then whirled back to the porch.

Mrs. Murray clapped her hands on her broad hips. "What do you think—"

Barb came through the door, clutching a paintbrush. She held it tight to her body.

"You can't take that—"

"I'm going to take it. I am." She moved across the floor, stopped by Gretchen. "You and your grandmother will sit with us, won't you? And come in the car? There's room. There's only me and Aunt Darla. Please, Gretchen, say you'll come."

THEY SAT, THE four of them—Barb's aunt and Barb and Grandmother and Gretchen—in the family room that overlooked the pews. In the chapel, only a handful of mourners sat in wooden pews. Of those, only two were young: Jim Dan Pulliam and a soldier. Gretchen was puzzled. Where were Barb's friends? She'd always had plenty of friends. But murder changed everything.

The Reverend Byars waved a manicured hand and shouted, "Our sister, if her heart is repentant, will find forgiveness and peace. And someday, brothers and sisters, we, too . . ." Gretchen was intensely aware of Grandmother's soft sobs, a handkerchief pressed to her face, and of the rigidity of Mrs. Murray, her bulky body still as stone, though tears slipped down her hard face, and, most of all, of Barb, who trembled like a brown leaf swept by a November wind.

". . . know that hell awaits us if we pursue the path of damnation." The Reverend Byars's voice still hung in the air when the organist began to hammer out "The Old Rugged Cross."

The door to the family room opened, and the funeral-home director stepped inside. "Mrs. Murray, Barb, if you wish to go by the casket now . . ."

Barb grabbed Gretchen's arm, clung so tight, it hurt. Mrs. Murray stood, started forward.

Grandmother held out her hands. "Come, girls." She made a soft sighing sound. "I will be with you both. And please to remember that our lovely Faye is not here. She is in heaven with Jesus. 'And God shall wipe away all tears from their eyes; there shall be no more death, neither sorrow, nor crying; neither shall there be any more pain.' " She took Barb's hand.

Barb clutched Grandmother's arm as they walked slowly through the door into the chapel. It wasn't until they stopped beside the casket with its single spray of white flowers that Gretchen saw the paintbrush in Barb's hand. She reached out, pressed the brush against the wood, held it there for an instant. "Mama . . ."

COTTONWOOD LEAVES RUSTLED. Splotches of shade from an oak splashed across the graves. Dirt clods mounded beside the new gravesite. The dank smell of disturbed earth mingled with the summer scent of new-mown grass. The rasp of cicadas rose and fell.

The small circle of listeners was held captive by the red-faced minister. Mrs. Crane, Lucille Winters, and Mrs. Steele were sweltering in the heat. Barb's aunt glanced furtively at her wristwatch. Jim Dan Pulliam and the young soldier stood a little separate. The sun burnished Jim Dan's hair. He wasn't like the others. Not to Gretchen. Was it because he was young? Or because she found him attractive, wished she knew him better? The soldier was young, too, but there was nothing remarkable about him. He hunched his stocky shoulders, his cap tight in his hand, and watched Barb, his eyes squinting against the sunlight, his lips folded tight. Donny Durwood's face glistened with sweat. He mopped his cheek with a crumpled handkerchief. Sheriff Moore stood unmoving beside the county attorney. His dark-skinned drooping face was unreadable, but his eyes darted from person to person, probed the thick grove of trees. Of the officials, only Chief Fraser stared at the casket poised above the grave. Deep lines scored the chief's heavy face. He looked exhausted. And sad. Ralph Cooley's wrinkled hat was tilted down onto his face. He scrawled rapidly on a handful of copy paper. Mr. Dennis's suit coat hung open. He fingered his heavy watch chain impatiently.

Not even the shrill bursts of the cicadas could overcome the impassioned rhetoric of the Reverend Byars. "This poor sinner must now regret the path that led to her destruction. Had she fulfilled her solemn promises made before God and man, she would be here today, a wife and mother. But she chose to flout the laws of God—"

"No, no, no!" Barb's deep cry exploded.

The Reverend Byars's thick lips hung apart, like the flaccid mouth of a gaffed fish. For an instant, no one moved or spoke.

Wild-eyed, trembling, Barb backed away from the grave. "Mama didn't. I tell you, it's a lie. I won't stand here and listen. I won't."

"Barb, shut your mouth." Darla Murray's face twisted in fury. "Don't disgrace us even more. Faye's done that already."

Barb hunched her thin shoulders, clenched her hands tight. Suddenly she whirled and ran toward the woods.

"Barb, come back." Darla Murray's shout was sharp and ugly.

The young soldier bolted after Barb, caught her at the edge of the woods. He pointed to the road, where a half-dozen cars were parked.

"The wrath of God follows those who defy him!" the Reverend Byars shouted. "There is a place in hell for those who will not hear. Let us bow our heads in prayer. Dear Lord, forgive those who . . ."

The sound of a car motor drowned out the words.

THE FUNERAL-HOME car pulled onto the rough Tatum drive.

As Gretchen reached for the door handle, Darla Murray snapped, "The car can take you home." She stared at the house. "No sign of Barb." She sniffed. "Well, if the girl won't behave, there's nothing I can do. The preacher said he'd take her in. Not that I wouldn't have her if I could. But I can't. Ted and I are squeezed in a tiny apartment near the base, and I don't have any room at all." She clambered awkwardly out of the backseat.

Grandmother leaned forward. "Barb can stay with us."

Mrs. Murray lifted her shoulders in a shrug. "She has to stay somewhere. And the preacher may not take her now." She closed the door. "Tell her I'll write."

The black car backed out, turned, took them to their house.

Gretchen fixed supper. She made tuna fish salad on thick white crusty bread, poured fresh iced tea.

They sat at the white kitchen table. Gretchen was ravenous. Grandmother sipped her tea and ate slowly, her face weary.

"I don't blame Barb for running away," Gretchen said. "I would have, too. Reverend Byars was saying awful things. I talked to

Lucille Winters for my story. She said it couldn't be true about Mrs. Tatum—that she was seeing another man."

Grandmother's face lightened. "And that is in your story?"

"Yes. It's in tonight's paper." How could she have forgotten to tell Grandmother? "I'll go get it." She dashed outside, found the paper next to the steps, opened it, and there was her story across the bottom of the page, a thirty-six-point head:

FRIENDS REMEMBER FAYE TATUM,
WIFE, ARTIST, FRIEND, TEACHER

Grandmother held the page close to her eyes. When she put the paper down, her face glowed. "Oh, Gretchen, this whole long day I have struggled to remember Faye the way she was. You have made her live again. God will bless you." She picked up the *Gazette,* touched the story with her fingertips. After supper, she took the newspaper with her to her old cane rocker and sat beside the radio listening to the news with Edward Kaltenborn.

Gretchen was almost finished with the dishes when the phone rang. She hurried, wiping her hands on a tea towel. "Hello."

"Gretchen, hi. Listen, I had to call you."

Gretchen frowned. "Wilma?" It sounded like Wilma, but her voice was stiff, like she was talking to the principal. Wilma Fuller was the most popular girl in their class. The third floor of the Fullers' huge old Victorian house had once been a ballroom. Sometimes as many as fifteen girls spread out their sleeping bags there on a Friday night after the movies. They'd stay up most of the night and drink Cokes and talk about boys and practice different hairdos.

"Yeah. Anyway, I've got to rush. There's not going to be a slumber party tonight. I just wanted you to know so you wouldn't come over." She spoke fast. "Sorry, Gretchen, I have to go. See you."

Gretchen slowly replaced the receiver.

The radio switched off. "Gretchen?"

Gretchen walked to the living room. She made her voice brisk. "It's okay, Grandmother." But that wasn't true. "It was Wilma Fuller."

Grandmother relaxed against the cushions. "Oh, yes. It's Friday night." She tried to smile. "And you will go to Thompson's and—"

Gretchen interrupted before she would have to tell Grandmother what Wilma said. "Not tonight. Mr. Dennis wants me to come to the city council meeting. The mayor wants to know why they haven't arrested Mr. Tatum."

"Oh." Grandmother sighed. "I wish . . ." She didn't finish.

Gretchen stopped beside the rocker. "Will you go to bed early? I'll lock up when I get back from the meeting."

Grandmother's face was drained. "Yes, I will. But tomorrow we will celebrate to have your mother home."

Gretchen bent down, kissed Grandmother's cheek. She moved fast, finishing her last check of the kitchen, hurrying to her room to change, grabbing a pencil and copy paper. She stopped at the telephone, picked up the receiver. She gave the operator Tonya Harris's number.

"Hello?" Tonya's voice was high and sweet.

"Tonya, this is Gretchen. About the slumber party—"

A gasp. "Oh. Didn't Wilma call you?"

"Yes. But I just wanted to know. There is a slumber party, isn't there?"

"Oh, Gretchen, I'm sorry. Reverend Byars is mad about that story on Mrs. Tatum. He told everybody it was just like consorting with the devil, to write things that make her sound like she was a good person. Wilma's dad—he's a deacon—said she couldn't have you over again. Oh, Gretchen, I'm sorry." Tonya hung up.

THE LOT BEHIND the courthouse was full. People milled around outside city hall. Gretchen, trying to squeeze past a clot of men near the shallow front steps, caught bits of their conversations: ". . . can't get in . . . packed . . . sheriff said no progress . . ."

"Make way!" The deep shout parted the crowd jammed on the walk in front of city hall. Mayor Burkett bustled importantly down the steps, followed by Sheriff Moore and County Attorney Durwood. Behind them, Chief Fraser and Sergeant Holliman carried a rectangular oak table. Chief Fraser's face bulged in a grim frown. A lumpy white bandage swathed the left side of Sergeant Holliman's head. His uniform cap was perched on the back of his head.

Mayor Burkett gestured toward the city square. "There will be plenty of room on the square. We'll set up in the gazebo."

Those who had come early and squeezed inside city hall came streaming out. A knot of men fanned out to make way for Sheila Durwood, slim and elegant in a white shantung dress with turquoise sleeves. There was always space for her—she was a Winslow. Gretchen spotted Mr. Dennis and Ralph Cooley and hurried to join them. They wormed their way right up to the steps of the gazebo. The crowd pressed close. Gretchen made notes as the four council members took their places.

Gretchen knew all the council members: Mr. Thompson, the druggist; Mr. Evans, the town's richest lawyer; Mr. Wilkins, who owned Wilkins Plumbing; and Mr. Randall, Best Department Store.

Mr. Dennis bent down, whispered, "Keep your ears open for comments from the crowd, Gretchen."

Ralph Cooley rubbed his nose. "Durwood's brought out the heavy artillery."

Gretchen looked up at him. "Artillery?"

"The little woman." Cooley's voice was derisive. "Everybody says she runs him pretty good. Wants to be the governor's wife, and he damn sure better make the grade."

The police chief and his sergeant stood to the left of the council members. Sheriff Moore and County Attorney Durwood were on the other side. The mayor bustled importantly to the front of the gazebo. Gretchen thought about the man in the dirty khaki uniform hiding in the cabin. These people wanted him run down and caught.

Mayor Burkett boomed, "Fellow citizens, welcome. As your mayor, I am determined that public concerns shall always be promptly addressed. My fellow council members share that commitment. The safety of our families—"

A shout came from the back of the crowd. "How come you ain't caught Tatum yet?"

Gretchen turned, stood on tiptoe. A rangy farmer's leathery face twisted in a scowl.

A skinny man in a seersucker suit waved a copy of the *Gazette*. "The paper says he's got a gun. I don't want to leave my wife and kids alone. But she's ready for him. I got the shotgun waiting."

Voices rose. The crowd moved toward the gazebo. Mayor Burkett cried, "Wait a minute here. We're here to—"

Chief Fraser strode forward. He glared at the crowd, stern as a bulldog, all bulging eyes and cheeks and blunt chin. "If Clyde Tatum's out there, we're going to find him. Nobody's seen him since he left the Blue Light Tuesday night just after seven o'clock. Faye Tatum left at midnight. Clyde's car is still in the Blue Light parking lot. We got dogs out there Wednesday morning. They ran around the lot, to and from the door, and then they sat on their butts. Now, what does that tell us?" Nobody spoke. "Clyde left in a car. We don't know who took him. We don't know where he went. We've checked the buses and the trains, got word out on the Teletype." Chief Fraser turned his hands palms up. "Not a trace. Nobody saw him near Archer Street. Nobody saw him with Faye. And Faye didn't have a car to come and get him. Yet all of you"—he swept that big hand toward the crowd, swung to look at the mayor and county attorney and each council member—"are positive that Clyde strangled Faye."

The county attorney glanced at his wife. Her head tilted in an almost imperceptible nod. Durwood took a step forward.

The chief spat out the words. "There's no evidence."

"Wait a minute, wait a minute." Durwood's voice flowed out cool and certain as a river. He suddenly seemed in his element, his smile deprecating, patient. "Let's look at the facts. Faye Tatum and her husband quarreled Tuesday afternoon. They quarreled again at the Blue Light. Faye was strangled in her living room just after midnight. The police were on the scene within minutes." Durwood walked to the edge of the steps, looked out at the crowd. "Did the police find Clyde Tatum there? No. Did Clyde Tatum return to his home that night? No." Each question and answer was louder. "An innocent man would rush to the police, demand they find his wife's killer. Instead, Tatum goes to earth, like a fox. But Wednesday night, he goes to his house, and even though there are officers there, he gets inside, gets his gun. And he gets away." Durwood swung toward the chief. "Where's Clyde Tatum?"

The crowd roared. "Where is he? Where is he?"

"That's what we all want to know." Mayor Burkett waggled a plump finger at Chief Fraser. "How come you let him slip through your fingers Wednesday night?"

Chief Fraser said sharply, "The man who broke in wasn't seen—"

"Broke in?" The county attorney flung his arms wide. "There was no evidence of a break-in when Sheriff Moore and I examined the house on Thursday. Maybe you found something we didn't."

Chief Fraser walked slowly across the planks, stood face-to-face with the county attorney. "We don't know how the intruder got in. The house was locked up but—"

"So it looks like he had a key. Right?"

"Maybe. But you know what, Donny?" The chief's voice was hard. "Clyde Tatum left his keys, including the key to the front door, in his car." Fraser reached in his pocket, pulled out a metal key ring with a half-dozen keys dangling from it. "Clyde Tatum didn't have a key to his house."

Durwood frowned. "He could have had another key."

"Sure he could. So could somebody else. But you want to talk about facts." The chief glared at Durwood. "The fact is, we don't know who got in the house or how he did it."

A chair scraped. Councilman Evans cleared his throat. "Chief Fraser, what is the status of the investigation?"

"The search for Clyde Tatum continues. We are seeking leads to Faye Tatum's actions the night she died. We know she used the pay phone at the Blue Light. Who did she talk to? Did somebody follow her home from the Blue Light? We know she was surprised by the person who killed her. Her daughter overheard Faye say, 'You've got a nerve coming here.' "

Sheriff Moore ambled forward. "For my money, Clyde Tatum

killed his wife, and there's only two possible reasons he's not in jail:
Tatum's dead, or somebody's hiding him. Because we've hunted."
He jerked his big head toward Chief Fraser. "The chief and his
men, me and my men. We've looked. So if Clyde's not dead, he's
still hiding, and the only way he can hide is with help. When we find
him, we're going to find out who helped him. Make no mistake—
whoever helped Clyde is going to rot in jail. That's a promise."

CHAPTER EIGHT

*. . . You remember Buddy Wilson? He was so kind to me the day
they buried Mama. I almost told Buddy when I finally figured out
what happened to Mama. But I don't think even Buddy would
have believed me. I was scared, so scared. I had to get away. We
ran away to Tulsa and got married by a justice of the peace. I was
sixteen. Nobody looked too hard at how old you were in those
days, not when the guy had on a uniform. I went out to the Coast
with him. He shipped out in September. . . .*

. . . ABOUT THAT SUMMER. All these years, I'd refused to remember
that Saturday. But age is a merciless companion. There is something
within us when we are old that accepts reality. We look back, gazing
in wonder at occasional moments in the sun but seeing the darkness
and shadows, the unintended consequences of our struggles. . . .

CIMARRON STREET BLAZED with light and movement. People
greeted neighbors as they walked toward their cars. Some people
stood talking in clumps. Mr. Dennis nodded toward Gretchen. "I'll
give you a ride home. I'm parked in the alley behind the *Gazette*."

"Thank you." Her voice could scarcely be heard over the angry,
scared rumble of the crowd.

The farther they walked from the town square, the quieter it was.
When they drove away, Gretchen remembered the sheriff's bleak

voice: . . . *rot in jail . . . rot in jail . . .* If the sheriff found out about Grandmother, would he put her in jail?

"Gretchen?"

She jerked toward him. "Yes?"

"Are you all right?" Mr Dennis's face furrowed in concern as he braked in front of her house.

"Yes, sir." But she wasn't. She could scarcely keep from flinging open the door and running to the Purdy cabin. She had to hurry.

"You're tired. You worked all day. And there was the funeral." He pulled his pipe from his pocket. "Don't come in tomorrow. Enjoy your mom's visit. I'll do the story on the crowd."

As she opened the door, Gretchen held tight to her sheaf of copy paper. She had good notes: the Reverend Byars with a petition calling for the padlocking of the Blue Light; Mrs. Gordon saying somebody broke into her barn and took fishing tackle; the Whittle sisters on Colson Road demanding police protection . . .

Gretchen shut the car door, leaned in the open window. "I'm okay. I'll come in early. I'll get the story done before Mother and— Before she comes." Before Mother and the man arrived. Maybe she didn't even care if she got home before Mother arrived.

The porch light was on. She stepped inside, closed the door, carefully placed her notes on the stand below the mirror. She tiptoed down the hall, trying to be quiet, but the wooden floor creaked. Grandmother's bedside light flashed on.

Gretchen stopped at her bedroom door. "I'm home."

"The meeting . . ." Grandmother's voice was dull and very faint.

Gretchen hurried across the floor. "I'll tell you about it tomorrow. Nothing really happened." *(. . . rot in jail . . . rot in jail . . . rot in jail . . .)* "But people are frightened." Gretchen patted a heavily veined hand, reached up, clicked off the lamp. "Good night."

Once in her room, Gretchen changed into shorts and a top and loafers, grabbed a flashlight and Jimmy's gun from its hiding place in her top dresser drawer, quietly eased open the screen of her window, and dropped softly to the ground.

Heavy clouds obscured the moon. The night was hot and still.

Faraway lightning crackled. Gretchen reached the faint path that angled into the woods. Tucking Jimmy's .22 under one arm, she cupped her hand over the flashlight lens, using just enough light to find her way. She crept through the night, burdened by fear. She was shaking when she reached the overgrown clearing and the dark cabin. She flicked off the flashlight and stared, seeking even the barest hint of light from the gloom-shrouded shanty.

Nothing. No light. No sense of life or occupancy, simply darkness and an overwhelming sense of danger. The steps creaked as she climbed. She froze, head bent forward. Behind her, grasses rustled.

Gretchen whirled. The circle of woods was darker than the overgrown clearing. She had a feeling of a watchful presence, malevolent, hurtful, malignant. She snapped on the flashlight, swung it back and forth, the beam sliding across the trees and wild grasses and tangled ferns. Nothing moved.

She yanked the flash toward the cabin. The spear of light swept past the closed door and illuminated the open window, the sash raised halfway. The door remained shut. She walked across the porch. She held the flashlight in her left hand, the .22 in her right.

"Mr. Tatum? It's Gretchen Gilman." Her words fell into silence. Awkwardly, gripping the flashlight in her thumb and forefinger, she curved the rest of her hand around the door handle, turned it. She pushed, and the door swung in. She stepped slowly into the cabin, the tongue of light flicking in every direction.

Thunder rumbled in the distance. She was half glad Clyde Tatum was gone, half sorry. She'd intended to tell him what the sheriff said and beg him to protect Grandmother.

Lightning flashed, pouring blue light across the jumbled mass of junk. Gretchen turned her light to the worn wooden tabletop. She moved the beam slowly and stopped. There's where the picnic basket—Grandmother's picnic basket with her name, "Pfizer," burned in black letters into the wooden handle—had sat. Now there was only the tabletop with scraps of brown paper on it.

She came closer. The paper was torn from crumpled old grocery sacks. A big, thick leaded pencil lay near the pieces of paper. There were names printed, five or six, on one piece. Gretchen scarcely glanced at the scraps. She had to find the picnic basket.

Sweat beaded her face. She bent low, looked up and down and around, behind boxes, beneath tables. She was on her hands and knees when she found the basket, wedged beneath a rickety table. Gretchen grabbed the wooden handles, tugged it free. She felt relief so overwhelming, she was almost dizzy. She dropped the gun inside and closed the lid. Would he notice that the basket was gone? It didn't matter. Nothing mattered but protecting Grandmother. She hurried through the door, pulled it shut behind her.

She was at the steps, the light from the flash dancing across the grass-choked clearing, when fear washed over her again. She held tight to the basket, looked out at the dark mass of trees. There was someone near. There was danger—evil—close to her.

Panic swept her. She flicked off the flashlight and jumped from the porch. When she reached the woods, she slipped onto the path, trusting to her night vision, quiet as a fox. She eased open the picnic basket, dropped the flashlight inside. She yanked out the gun, held it tightly in her hand.

One stealthy step, another and another, she crept on and on, fear searing her soul. Once beyond the woods, she clung to the dark edge of the road. As she reached Archer Street, the rain began. At the house, she darted toward the back steps and set the basket down. She took out the flashlight. Grandmother would find the basket in the morning. She would believe Clyde Tatum had left it. Whatever happened, there was nothing to link Grandmother to the cabin.

AS GRETCHEN SETTLED at her desk, the early morning sun spilling through the front windows and the hard feel of the typewriter keys combined to reassure her. She would not think of those moments in the woods. She unfolded her notes from the city council meeting and began to write.

She was almost finished when Mr. Dennis arrived. His eyes were doleful, but he tried to sound jolly. "Hey, Gretchen—long john?" He held up a white cardboard box from Lyon's Bakery.

"Yes, sir. Thank you."

He brought the long john on a cracked yellow saucer. Gretchen took a bite, but the still-warm cake and delectable brown sugar icing had no taste.

In a moment, she typed –30– at the bottom of the page, pasted the sheets together, handed him the story.

He stood beside her. Mr. Dennis scanned copy faster than anyone she'd ever known. He nodded, said, "Good," and turned away, carrying her story.

Gretchen hesitated, then moved determinedly to his desk. "Mr. Dennis, I wondered what it meant last night when the sheriff said somebody must have been helping Mr. Tatum."

Mr. Dennis's light green eyes seemed to look all the way into her mind and heart. She shouldn't have asked. She scarcely breathed.

"Sheriff Moore's nobody's fool. Clyde's been missing since Tuesday night. Now it's Saturday. Where's Clyde been staying? How has he got food? Oh, it's pretty clear Clyde's had help." His bristly gray eyebrows bunched. "Listen, girl, if you know anybody—like Barb, maybe—who knows where Clyde is, tell them to warn him. People have got their guns out. Clyde better turn himself in pronto."

Gretchen backed away, shaking her head. "Barb doesn't know where her dad is. I just wanted to be able to tell her what happened last night, and I didn't understand what the sheriff meant."

The editor's lips turned down in a sour grin. "Just what he said, girl—somebody's going to rot in jail, right along with Clyde."

THE TATUM HOUSE had a look of abandonment. The windows were closed, the shades drawn.

Gretchen walked up the rutted drive. A battered coupe, missing the right front fender, was parked behind a honeysuckle shrub. The screen door of the back porch banged open. Barb stood on the top step. Her long auburn hair shone in the summer sun, the kind of hair that should have framed beauty, not an old-young face with misery-filled eyes. When Gretchen was a few feet away, Barb plucked at a strap of her halter. "Have they found my dad?"

Gretchen shook her head. "No."

Barb let go a little breath. "Daddy—"

Gretchen burst out, talking fast. "They had a meeting of the town council about your dad. Everybody's pretty upset."

Barb's dark, despairing eyes demanded more.

"People are talking about getting out their guns. The sheriff said somebody's going to jail for helping your dad hide out. And Mr. Dennis is afraid that somebody's going to shoot your dad."

"Why should they shoot Daddy? He wouldn't hurt anyone. He'd never hurt—" Barb broke off, as if hearing her own words. "Oh, Daddy. Oh, God, he loved Mama. He loved her."

And he killed her. Barb didn't say it, but the realization was there in her pain and sorrow. Barb stumbled blindly down the steps.

The back door banged open. "Barb, honey, don't cry." The young soldier jumped to the ground, took her in his arms. Barb clung to him, sobbing. He had a kind face, freckled and open, and his big hand was gentle as he stroked her long reddish-brown hair.

Gretchen backed away, then walked slowly to her front yard. The door was open. Grandmother would be in the kitchen, making sure everything was ready for lunch. She'd tell Grandmother what Mr. Dennis said and then admit she'd followed Grandmother to the cabin. They could go to the cabin together and persuade Mr. Tatum to come back with them. That would keep him safe. They could bring him home and call Chief Fraser.

She hurried up the steps. She stepped into the hall and smelled the sweet musky scent of roses. On the letter stand, Grandmother's best cut-glass bowl overflowed with roses from the backyard. The living room was neat as a pin, and the dining-room table was already set with china and crystal and silver.

Peace washed over Gretchen. "Grandmother?"

"Gretchen." It was Grandmother's voice, the cadence sweetly familiar but the sound so slight, it might have been a dream.

Gretchen plunged toward the kitchen.

Grandmother sat slumped in a wooden chair, her face pale. Her blue eyes were huge and staring.

"Grandmother!" Gretchen picked up limp hands that were cold and clammy to the touch.

"*Ach,* I will be fine. Please to get me some coffee."

"Dr. Jamison." Gretchen's heart thudded. "I'll call him." She let loose her grip, whirled toward the phone.

"No. I will be fine." Grandmother placed one hand on the kitchen table, pushed herself straighter in the chair. "I have worked too fast. But I want everything perfect for my Lorraine. Now, you must help me. I will sit here, but please bring me some coffee."

The percolator was on the back burner on low. Gretchen poured the pungent black brew into a thick white china cup, added two teaspoons of sugar and a quarter inch of cream.

Grandmother managed a smile as she took the cup. "Your mama will be here soon, and I want you to ask her to go to the lake." She paused, drew in a breath as though it was hard to find air for her words. "It is so hot today. I shall urge her to go, too. I shall say that I want her—and her friend—to have a real holiday. I will tell her that I have worked too hard this week and I wish to stay here and rest, and then when you come back from your swim, we shall have our special dinner."

"Grandmother," Gretchen begged, "please let me call Dr. Jamison. He will come—"

A car turned into their drive.

"They are here." Grandmother waved her hands at Gretchen. "Go see. Hurry. I shall come."

Gretchen ran to the front door. The dark blue Buick was dusty, but sunlight reflected off its shiny chrome grille. Gretchen shielded her eyes. The passenger door swung out. Wiry blond curls poked from beneath a saucer of a hat with a bright pink feather.

"Mother! Mother!" Gretchen jumped down the steps, ran. Her mother ran, too, despite her high heels and tight skirt. They came together, and Gretchen felt the loving pressure of her mother's arms.

"Oh, baby, it's so good to see you." Lorraine stood back, holding Gretchen at arm's length. "You're so grown up, G. G. Gilman."

She laughed. "Come on, G.G., I want you to meet Sam. I hope—"

He was standing beside them. Gretchen didn't want to look at him. His shadow fell between them. She stared at the elongated streak.

"Hi, Gretchen. Lorraine's told me a lot about you." He had an easy voice, warm and friendly. "You read faster than Clark Kent changes into Superman and you write better than Lois Lane."

Gretchen slowly turned. He was a big man, taller than her daddy had been. Beneath his white cap, his blunt face was burned coppery red. He had deep grooves in his cheeks, like he laughed a lot. His uniform was crisp, all white with dark shoulder boards.

She stared at him, unsmiling.

Abruptly his face looked older, heavier.

"Lorraine." Grandmother stood on the top step, her round face smiling, her best dress a vivid blue. But she was so pale.

"Mother." Lorraine whirled, and in an instant, she was up the steps, her arms around Grandmother. "Mother, here's Sam. Sam Hoyt. He's a petty officer, and he's going back to California next week. I met him last week at Crystal City. I went on Friday night with a bunch of the gals from the plant. I was riding the Ferris wheel, and he was in the car behind ours. We got stopped at the top, and Jenny rocked it, and I was so scared. When we got down to the ground, Sam called out that I had a nice scream. I thought he wanted to know where to get ice cream, and the first thing you know, we were all on our way to Hawk's." She paused, breathless.

"Mrs. Pfizer," he said with laughter in his deep voice, "I didn't used to eat ice cream, but now it's my favorite food."

"We have homemade ice cream for today. And apple pie so fine." Grandmother beamed. "Come in now, out of the hot sun."

They walked into the living room. Lorraine took Sam by the hand. "I want you to see this picture of Jimmy." Sam stood close as they looked at the photographs on the mantel.

Sam Hoyt's dark eyes met Gretchen's.

Gretchen looked away.

Grandmother sat in her easy chair. "We have so much pride now,

Mr. Hoyt. Our brave Jimmy. And Gretchen works so hard. She helps me at the café every day, and then she goes to the newspaper office, and her stories are in the paper every night. Lorraine, will you and Mr. Hoyt take Gretchen to the lake? It will be so much fun for all of you. I will find a suit of Jimmy's for Mr. Hoyt to wear."

Lorraine clapped her hands. "Oh, Sam, that does sound like fun. I haven't been swimming in forever. And then we'll have Mother's wonderful food." She looked hesitantly at her mother. "We have to leave right after lunch. Sam promised his folks we'd come by this afternoon. They live in Tahlequah."

"You're leaving that soon?" Gretchen stared at her mother.

Lorraine reached out her hands.

Gretchen backed away. "I better get my suit."

IT WAS ALMOST the way it had been before the war—a summer day at the lake with her mom and Jimmy. The feel of the water was the same, and the shouts of the big boys as they jumped from a tower into deep water, and the high squeals of the little kids as they made sand castles and played toss. Teenage girls stretched out on towels and blankets. The jukebox blared *Besame Mucho.* The smell of hot dogs and popcorn mingled with the scents of honeysuckle and suntan lotion and car exhaust and water. Hunter Lake was just as it had always been. It was Gretchen who was different.

Gretchen's gaze darted across the water. There they were— Mother and Sam, swimming side by side on their way out to the wooden float. It was a long way out. Not many people swam out to the float—the older boys sometimes, but usually only if a pretty girl had gone there first. Gretchen dived, swam fast. She didn't pause until she reached the square wooden raft bobbing in the water. She came up beside it, held on to the warm wood. She looked around, seeing no one. Mother and Sam must have dived down and come up underneath the float in the gauzy brownish-green two-foot space between the platform and the water. Gretchen took a deep breath, curled down. She kicked and rose in the water, a hand outstretched to grip the rough edge of one of the barrels supporting the platform. Her head came out of the water. She blinked the water from her eyes. Her mouth opened, but no sound came. In the wavering moss-green light, Lorraine and Sam embraced, their bodies melded into a single form, her hand, the fingernails a glossy red, tight against his neck, drawing down his face to her uplifted lips.

The water closed over Gretchen's head as she dived down, down and away.

CHAPTER NINE

. . . Maybe Buddy and I could have made a go of it if he hadn't been killed in the war. But I couldn't stay off the bottle. Buddy's folks came out to California. I was living in Long Beach. Funny, I never knew you were there at the same time. They came out and found me drunk and Rod dirty and hungry. Rodney James Wilson, Jr.—I named him after Buddy. I loved Rod, yet every time I looked at him, it all came back to me, that summer. But he was just a baby, and none of it was his fault. That's the problem. Everything was my fault. . . .

WAS IT JEALOUSY that caused me to run away from the lake that day? Of course. I didn't want to lose Mother. I didn't want to share her. I never had a chance later to ask her if she knew why I left the lake. There was so much I never told her, never told anyone. Perhaps it is only now that I understand what that summer cost me. . . .

GRETCHEN STOPPED RUNNING. She gasped for breath. Her heart pounded. Tears mixed with sweat, stinging her flushed face. Mother had only met him a week ago. How could she kiss him like that?

She moved forward, her swimsuit uncomfortable beneath her blouse and shorts. She'd grabbed her clothes from the backseat of the car, pulled them on, slipped her feet into her sandals, used a borrowed pencil to scrawl a note that she placed on the front seat:

Gone home. Gretchen. All she thought about was escape. But every step on the road took her nearer to the Purdy cabin.

She hesitated. She didn't want to go into the woods. But some-one had to warn Clyde Tatum. Gretchen forced herself forward.

Abruptly she plunged into the murky half-light, moving fast before she could change her mind. She brushed against wild hydrangeas. Bracken ferns clutched at her. She plunged into the overgrown clearing. The cabin almost seemed a part of the woods. The rotten steps sagged. The dirt-grimed windowpanes were as blank as dead eyes. "Mr. Tatum!" Her voice wavered, high and shrill. "Mr. Tatum, it's Gretchen Gilman, Barb's friend."

Despite the sounds of summer and the rustle of the woods, silence flowed over her, thick and quiet as fog rising from a pond. She reached down, rubbed one ankle. She was eaten up by chiggers. "Mr. Tatum—" She broke off. He wasn't here.

She took a deep breath. She would have to leave a note warning that people were looking for him and they had guns. The door was open. She was in a hurry now, eager to leave a message and be gone.

She reached the doorway, stopped.

"Oh . . ." The voice, scarcely audible, was hers, a faint moan of sound. "Oh . . . oh . . ." She backed away. She carried with her an indelible memory of the dim, crowded, junk-filled cabin and the body of Clyde Tatum slumped over the table.

She jerked about, clattered down the steps, thrashed through the grass, flailed into the woods, tearing through creepers and vines. She stumbled over a log, fell, scrambled to get up, and knew she was lost. Trembling, she stared around the forest. She needed to retrace her steps, find the path to the road. She had to get help somewhere. She felt sick with horror. Barb's dad was dead, dead, dead. . . .

"You are surrounded." The deep, heavy voice boomed through the woods. "Come out with your hands up. We are armed."

Gretchen ducked behind a white ash, pressed against the thick trunk. The shouted commands continued. Cautiously she slipped back the way she'd come and peered into the clearing.

Sheriff Moore stood at the bottom of the cabin steps, a bullhorn in one hand, his big black service pistol in the other. The gun in his hand moved back and forth slowly, gently, like the head of a swaying cobra. Fanned in a semicircle behind him were Chief Fraser, Sergeant Holliman, Sergeant Petty, and Donald Durwood.

"Maybe the note's a hoax," Durwood said. "This place doesn't look like anybody's been here in years."

"Quiet." The sheriff took a slow step forward. "Come out of there, Tatum. Or I'm coming in to get you."

"Wait a minute." Chief Fraser gripped Moore's elbow. "Give me a chance. Let me go up there."

The chief started forward. The sheriff lifted his hand. The gun, big and black, pointed at the door. And at the chief's back.

"Clyde, Chief Fraser here." The steps creaked as the chief climbed. "Listen, it's time to come out." He reached the doorway. "Clyde . . ." The chief's big shoulders slumped. "Oh, God."

The sheriff shouted, "Careful, now, careful!" The county attorney's face creased in a tight frown. Sergeant Holliman ran toward the porch. Sergeant Petty lowered her gun, her eyes fearful.

Chief Fraser looked at them. "It's over. Put your guns up. Clyde's blown his head to hell and gone." He kneaded his cheek with his fist. "I thought he was innocent. I was wrong."

Donald Durwood stretched out his hands. The lion-head cuff links in his starched white shirt glistened in the sunlight. "If we'd found the note earlier, we might have got here in time."

Chief Fraser walked heavily across the porch. "It wouldn't have made any difference. Clyde's been dead for hours. The blood's all dried. If we'd found the note last night, maybe we would have got here in time. Whoever stuck it under the wiper of the cruiser must have put it there after the rain. Somebody knew Clyde was here." He nodded his head toward the sheriff. "It's just like Paul said last night. I expect that person was at the town square and went home and thought about it and decided to turn him in. But Clyde was already dead by then."

Sheriff Moore thumped up the steps. "Think he's been hiding out here ever since he killed Faye?"

The chief massaged the side of his face. "Probably. I don't guess it matters now. Clyde killed Faye, and he couldn't live with it. Let's wrap it up."

Gretchen eased toward the path. She hurried up the trail. When she reached the road, she stopped and stared. So many cars—the chief's old Packard, a police cruiser, a black Ford, a black Cadillac. If she'd come along here, walking home from the lake, a few minutes ago, she would have seen the cars and recognized the Packard and the police car, and she would have gone down the path to see what was happening. She plunged back into the woods. She was halfway to the clearing when she came face-to-face with Sergeant Petty.

The police officer jolted to a stop. "Mercy, girl, what are you doing here?"

"I saw the cars in the road, and I wondered why. I came to see." She tried to look past the sergeant.

"This is no place for you." The sergeant's voice was sharp.

Gretchen stood her ground. "Have you found Mr. Tatum?" She tried to peer down the path. "Isn't the Purdy cabin around here?"

Rosa Petty's face hardened. "Police business, Gretchen. This is off-limits for now. Move along now."

Gretchen didn't budge. "I'm here for the *Gazette*."

Twigs snapped. Chief Fraser loomed up behind Sergeant Petty. "Go on, Sergeant. I'll deal with this."

The sergeant brushed past. Gretchen forced herself to look straight at the chief, hoping he wouldn't see her guilt and fear. If she'd told someone sooner, Clyde Tatum might be in jail—and alive. "I was walking home from the lake—"

He didn't care. "You know where Barb Tatum is?"

"I'm not sure." It wouldn't do for anyone to know that Barb was with the soldier. "I can find her. Is it about her dad?"

The chief's face creased. He took a deep breath. "Clyde's dead. Shot himself. See if you can find Barb. Take her to your house. I'll come there"—he glanced at his watch—"about two o'clock."

"What do I tell her?"

"Tell her the truth." His voice trembled with anger and hurt. "I never believed Clyde killed Faye, but he did. Tell her that sometimes people we love do bad things. Tell her he was a good man at heart and he loved her and she should remember him that way." His defiant voice cracked. "Tell her that her daddy's dead and he's past suffering now. And he's sorry."

"Sorry?" How did the chief know?

"He wrote a note. I'll bring it with me when I come." The big man turned away, walked heavily up the trail toward the cabin.

THE SCREEN DOOR slammed open. Lorraine's eyes flashed as she stood on the top step. "Gretchen, where have you been? We couldn't find you anywhere. And then we ran to the car and found that note. I don't know when I've been so upset."

Gretchen pressed her hand against her lips. She wanted to cry or shout. She wanted to run away, but she had to find Barb. She had to tell Barb.

Her mother's face changed. She plunged down the steps, took Gretchen in her arms. "Gretchen, what's wrong? What happened?"

Gretchen clung to her mother. "They found Clyde Tatum. He killed himself."

"Gretchen!" Grandmother's voice was high and faint from the doorway. "What is it that you say?" She leaned against the doorframe, her plump face ashen, one hand pressed against her chest.

Gretchen hurried to her grandmother. "It's over." Chief Fraser's words gave her strength. "Grandmother, no one can do anything now for Mr. Tatum. The chief said he's past suffering now."

"Clyde . . ." Grandmother's face crumpled.

"Come inside, Mother." Lorraine's voice quivered. She jerked her head toward Sam. Together they helped Grandmother, who sagged against them.

Gretchen stopped just inside the door. "Mother, I've got to find Barb. I promised Chief Fraser." She looked at the grandfather clock: almost noon. They should be sitting at the table with crisp fried chicken and mashed potatoes and green peas and gravy. Almost noon. The *Gazette* went to press early on Saturday afternoons for the Sunday paper. The *Gazette*... "Excuse me." She turned toward the kitchen. "I have to call Mr. Dennis."

Gretchen grabbed the receiver. She gave the operator the *Gazette* number. She looked away from her mother's questioning face.

Mr. Dennis answered on the first ring. "City desk."

"Mr. Dennis, this is Gretchen. They've found Clyde Tatum dead at the old Purdy cabin. He shot himself."

Her mother said sharply, "Who's Gretchen talking to?"

Grandmother's voice was faint. "Her editor at the newspaper."

"The newspaper." Lorraine sounded strange.

"Oh, but she must." Grandmother's defense was swift. "It is her job, you see. Mr. Dennis has to know. For tomorrow's paper."

On the phone line, there was a perceptible pause. Mr. Dennis cleared his throat. "When?"

"They think sometime last night. I was on my way home from the lake, and I saw the cars on the road. I went to see."

"The Purdy cabin. How'd they find him?"

"Somebody left a note on one of the police cars saying he was there. Sergeant Petty didn't find it until this morning. The chief said he died last night."

"Clyde's gun?" Mr. Dennis barked.

"I don't know." She hadn't seen a gun.

"Ralph'll get all that. Good work, kid." Mr. Dennis's voice was crisp. "Gretchen, you okay?"

"Yes." Another lie.

There was a pause. "I'm sorry, girl. Try not to think about it."

"Yes, sir." She hung up the receiver and wished she could stay where she was, safe in Grandmother's kitchen. The house smelled like Sunday dinner, familiar and comforting as church bells.

A gentle hand touched her arm. "Gretchen."

She looked at her mother. Their eyes met, held, Lorraine's uncertain, worried, sad. "Baby . . ."

Gretchen wanted to fling herself into her mother's arms and cry.

Footsteps sounded. Sam came up behind Lorraine, slipped his arm around her shoulders. "Nobody expects something like this to happen to neighbors." His voice was reassuring.

"More than neighbors." Tears rolled down Lorraine's cheeks. "I grew up playing with Clyde. He spent a lot of time at our house."

Sam spoke softly. "We need to get your mom to lie down. And I can call my folks, tell them we can't come this afternoon."

Lorraine straightened, used her hands to wipe her cheeks. "No. We're going to your folks'." There was a determination in her voice that Gretchen didn't understand.

Lorraine held out her hands toward Gretchen. "You'll take care of Mother, won't you?" She reached up, touched Gretchen's cheek. "Oh, baby, I know it's hard. But everything's hard now. I'm afraid every time someone knocks on the door that Jimmy's dead. People come to work, and you know what's happened—their eyes are red, and they walk like they don't care where they're going or if they ever get there. And now Faye and Clyde and poor little Barb. And here you are in the middle of something you don't even understand, and there's nobody here to help you. Gretchen, if I could make it better, I would. But please, will you understand if I don't stay?"

"Sure." Gretchen ducked her head, squeezed past them. "I have to find Barb. I promised the chief."

GRETCHEN WENT STRAIGHT to the back door of the Tatum house. She knocked on the screen door. "Barb! Barb!"

The soldier came to the kitchen doorway. "Barb doesn't want to see anybody."

Gretchen pulled open the screen. "I have to talk to her. I've got bad news."

"Bad news . . ." He stood, head bent for an instant, then walked stolidly into the house.

Gretchen stepped onto the porch. Faye's painting—the one she'd been working on—was close enough to touch. The canvas was spotted. The rain had blown through the porch. A tarp lay in a crumpled heap near her foot. No one had bothered to cover the painting before the storm. On impulse, Gretchen bent, grabbed the tarp, draped it over the painting.

"What difference does it make now?" Barb's voice was dull.

Gretchen whirled toward the kitchen.

Barb walked heavily onto the porch. "It's Daddy, isn't it?"

"I'm sorry." Gretchen wanted to help Barb, but nobody could. "Your dad's dead."

Barb didn't move.

Gretchen spoke fast. "He shot himself last night. At the Purdy cabin. They found him a little while ago. I promised Chief Fraser I'd come and get you."

"Get me?" Brooding eyes focused on Gretchen.

Gretchen felt as if Barb were as distant as a faint star in the night sky. "I told the chief I'd bring you to my house. He's coming at two o'clock. Your dad left a note."

THE DOOR BANGED as Gretchen came inside. The hot living room was empty and dim; the shades, drawn. A fan was whirring in one corner. Gretchen looked into the dining room. The lace table-cloth was draped in a diamond shape. Two place settings remained.

Steps sounded in the kitchen. Sam Hoyt, holding a dish towel in one hand and a filled china plate in the other, walked toward the table. "We saved your lunch, Gretchen." He was once again in his crisp white uniform, a yellow apron tied around his middle.

She stood in the archway. "Where's Mother?"

"She's with your grandmother." He placed the plate on the table. "Did you find the girl?"

"Yes." Gretchen almost turned to go down the hall to Grand-mother's room, but what good would it do? Mother was getting ready to leave, going away with this stranger. Gretchen slipped into the chair. Fried chicken and mashed potatoes and cream gravy and peas—her favorite dinner. She began to eat, ignored Sam.

He looked toward the front door. "I thought you were bringing her here. I've got another plate ready. Is she all right?"

"No." Her tone was scornful. Barb all right? What kind of fool was he? "She didn't want to come now. She'll be here at two, when the police chief comes."

Sam returned to the kitchen, came back with a tall glass of tea. "Would you like sugar?"

"No, thank you." The food had no taste, but she ate, one mouthful after another.

He cleared his throat. "Gretchen . . ."

She didn't answer, but she watched him out of the corner of her eye. He looked tired and sad.

"Gretchen, the war has changed everything. It used to be we had time to get to know people. But now, first thing you know, people are here or there, and we can't count on tomorrow coming."

Gretchen put down her fork, twisted to face him.

"I just want you to know that I think your mother is . . . Well, I don't have to tell you how special your mother is."

"Sam?" High heels clattered on the wooden floor. Lorraine burst into the dining room. "Oh, baby, did Sam take care of you? I knew he would." She looked around. "Is Barb here?"

Sam took off the apron. "She's coming in a little while."

"Oh." Lorraine sighed. "I wish we could stay." She took a deep breath. "But we can't."

Gretchen pushed back her plate.

Lorraine came close. Her hands touched stiff shoulders. "I love you, baby."

Gretchen managed a whisper. "Love you, too."

Lorraine lifted one hand. Her fingers smoothed a dark curl at the side of Gretchen's face. Gretchen looked up.

Lorraine's smile was tremulous. "You're going to do all right, honey. Today. Tomorrow. Whatever happens, you can handle it. Even something as awful as Faye and Clyde."

Gretchen pushed away the memory of Clyde Tatum slumped over the table.

"You know, I've been thinking and thinking." Lorraine clasped her hands together. "Clyde loved Faye. I know that. I don't think he ever in a million years meant to hurt her. He cared too much, and he was angry and hurt. That's why he ran away. He couldn't live with what he'd done."

Gretchen wanted to say that he had told Grandmother, sworn to her, that he didn't kill Faye. Gretchen heard him. But she couldn't tell her mother. Or anyone. And neither could Grandmother.

Lorraine bent down, pressed her cheek against the top of Gretchen's head. And then she moved away.

GRETCHEN PUT THE cup with hot tea on the bedside table. Grandmother lay unmoving in the big double bed. She slept, one hand tucked beneath her chin. Her face, moist with perspiration, looked old and heavy, pale and worn.

Gretchen wandered into the living room, pausing to straighten a crocheted arm cover on the sofa. Despite the fan, the room was heavy with heat. And so quiet. It didn't seem real that her mother had been there for a while—her mother and Sam Hoyt.

The grandfather clock chimed twice. A car turned into the drive. Gretchen went to the front door as Chief Fraser's old green Packard rocked to a stop. He opened the door, got out, then ducked his head to reach inside for his hat and a manila envelope. As he walked across the yard, dust scuffing beneath his cowboy boots, he craned his neck. "Miss Barb here?"

Gretchen held open the door. "She's coming."

In the living room, he settled in the biggest chair, planted his boots on the floor, placed his hat and the envelope on a side table, next to the lamp.

"Would you like some iced tea, Chief?" Gretchen spoke softly.

"Sure would." Chief Fraser looked around. "Nobody here?"

"Grandmother's resting. She doesn't feel very well. And Mother had to leave." But she didn't have to go.

The screen door opened. Barb stood just inside the door. "My dad . . ." Her face was the dull white of a soft winter snow.

The chief pushed up from the chair, moved heavily across the room. He stood, looking down at Barb. "Barb, your daddy shot himself sometime last night. At the Purdy cabin. Looks like he'd been staying there since the night your mama died. We traced the gun. It's his. One bullet gone. His fingerprints on the stock. He left a note." He walked to the end table, picked up the manila envelope.

"A note to me?" Barb's voice was dry and stiff.

Chief Fraser lifted his big head. "This here's evidence, I guess. The county attorney told me I didn't ought to take it with me. But I told him we didn't have a murder investigation any longer. All we got is heartbreak, a man who couldn't bear it when his wife cheated on him—"

"Mama never did!" Barb's cry was high and shrill.

The chief held up a callused hand. "Hear me out, Miss Barb. It don't help now to say it was any way other than what happened. Your mama was lonely. Lots of people are lonely now, their menfolk gone. People do the best they can. Your mama did her best, but I want you to understand that your daddy did his best, too. In my heart, I know nobody grieved for your mama more than Clyde. That's why he wrote this note." The chief rattled the envelope. He slowly pulled out an irregular piece of heavy brown paper.

Gretchen recognized the paper, torn from a grocery sack just like the pieces she'd seen on the table in the cabin. Gretchen wished she'd taken the time to look at those pieces of paper. Probably they contained the list of people Clyde hoped could tell him the name of the man who came in the darkness to his house to see Faye. But the chief would no longer search for that visitor. Faye's late-night visitor was safe.

Barb slowly walked toward the chief, took the scrap of paper from him. She looked down. "Oh, God . . ." Her head jerked up; she stared wildly from the chief to Gretchen and began to shake, her entire body rippling like a flag in a high wind. "Oh, Daddy . . . Daddy." She gasped for breath, then ran blindly across the room, yanking the door open, plunging out into the hot afternoon.

The chief took a step toward the door, then stopped. "Guess

she's got to face it her own way, but she had a right to see that note. I don't care what anybody says. There's no case to build, no matter how much Donny Durwood complains. It's all finished and done with—Durwood be damned. Barb can keep that scrap of paper. It's all she's got left from her daddy, hard as it is, little as it is."

Gretchen hurried to the door, looked out. The graveled street lay quiet and empty. Barb must have run all the way home.

It wasn't until the green Packard had pulled into the street that Gretchen realized she'd never asked Chief Fraser what the note said.

IT WAS ALMOST time for the pressrun. Soon the Sunday papers would be stacked, ready to deliver in the morning.

Gretchen pushed through the door to the newsroom. Ralph Cooley leaned back in his chair, crossed feet up on his desk. Mr. Dennis, pencil gripped in his fingers, hunched over yellow copy paper. His pipe smoldered in a big brass ashtray.

The reporter slouched to his feet. "Look who's here! Maybe Gretchen knows." He ambled toward her.

Gretchen didn't answer Ralph. She turned away from him, walked toward Mr. Dennis's desk.

The editor tapped the sheets of yellow copy paper. "We got the story, Gretchen, thanks to you."

Ralph sauntered after her, stood on the opposite side of the editor's desk. "Not all the story. According to Durwood, the chief took the prime piece of evidence with him. What I want to know is this: Where's the note Clyde Tatum wrote? I want to see it. How do we know he wrote it?"

"He wrote it." Gretchen laced her fingers together. "The chief gave it to Barb." Gretchen swallowed. "Barb cried."

Ralph rocked back on his heels. "Oh. She recognized his hand-writing. I guess that wraps it up. The show's over."

"I told you to drop it, Ralph." Mr. Dennis's voice was sharp. "Chief Fraser's no fool. And the sheriff told us what Clyde's note said."

Gretchen looked at the editor. "What did the note say?"

Mr. Dennis picked up his pipe, poked at the embers. "Not a lot, Gretchen. Enough." His face wrinkled, and he said carefully, repeating what he'd heard, " 'I didn't mean to kill Faye. Tell Barbie I love her—' "

Tell Barbie I love her—

Gretchen felt the sting of tears. No wonder Barb cried and ran away.

THE SWEET REFRAIN of "Do, Lord" hung in the evening sky like the settling cry of birds. Youthful voices rose in the dusk, competing with the twilight rasp of the cicadas. They sat on folding chairs on a grassy lawn beside the church, holding hands, the circle unbroken. The girls all wore pretty summer dresses. Gretchen had taken her accustomed place in the circle, but she felt as if she were invisible. The girls spoke past her or over her or around her. Gretchen had always been a part of this group, and now, though she still sat among them, she was not.

As the last refrain sounded, the youth director said, "Let's close with a prayer." Everyone stood, still holding hands. The director, Mr. Haskell, prayed for servicemen around the world, fighting to keep them free and—"Please hold in your hearts a special prayer for Barbara Tatum and her parents, Faye and Clyde . . ."

Wilma's hand jerked in Gretchen's. All around the circle, there was movement.

". . . and help all of us to support Barbara in her hour of need. Thank you, God, for hearing our prayer. Amen." Mr. Haskell wiped his perspiring face. "Good night, everyone, good night."

Gretchen hung behind, watched her friends leave. They were on their way to the town square. Tonight a barbershop quartet was going to perform at the gazebo.

Gretchen felt hot and cold as she walked home. It was still close to a hundred, even though it was dark now. But deep inside, she was cold. She didn't have any friends now. Not since she'd written the story about Faye Tatum. Would people forget as time went on?

Maybe. If she stopped working at the *Gazette,* told them she'd only written the story because Mr. Dennis had asked her to, they might be her friends again.

"I'd rather die." Gretchen said it aloud. She wouldn't quit. She would write the best stories she could write, no matter what. Deeper than the sense of loss and loneliness was pride. Her story was good. Mr. Dennis had sent it out on the wire. In other cities, places she would never be, people she would never know had read that story, and for a moment, Faye Tatum lived and breathed and moved in other minds because of Gretchen.

She reached Archer Street and stopped to stare at the Tatum house. Gretchen knew it was empty. Not a glimmer of light shone. In the silver of the moonlight, the house looked shrunken, drawn in upon itself, like a body with the soul departed.

Gretchen walked slowly toward the steps of her own house. She paused just inside the door, heard Grandmother's voice. ". . . oh, so happy I am for you. If only Gretchen were here . . ."

Gretchen ran across the living room.

Grandmother stood by the telephone. Her lips curved in a happy smile. "Lorraine, Lorraine, here she is. Our Gretchen has come home just in time to speak with you." And she held out the receiver.

Gretchen scarcely took in the words, her mother's voice almost lost in the roar of sounds behind her—voices and whistles and the rumble of train wheels. ". . . don't have much time . . . off the train at Albuquerque . . . on our way to California . . . Sam and I . . . his leave was up. . . . Oh, Gretchen, we got married last night."

Gretchen gripped the receiver with all her strength, holding on. "Married?" Her lips felt stiff.

"Oh, baby, I love him so. And I love you. I'll call when we get there. Baby, I've got to go."

THE FEATHER—MAYBE from a peacock, it was so long and blue— on Mrs. Taylor's hat swooped perilously near Mr. Dennis's pipe.

"What's the problem, Jewell?" Mr. Dennis's gaze was wary.

The diminutive society editor perched on the edge of Mr. Dennis's desk. "During the coffee hour at church yesterday, I talked until I was blue in the face. I insisted loudly that the *Gazette* does not condone unfaithfulness on the part of wives . . ."

Gretchen rose from her desk, walked slowly toward Mr. Dennis and Mrs. Taylor.

". . . that the *Gazette* upholds the sanctity of the family, that the *Gazette*—"

Mr. Dennis held up his hand. "I got it, Jewell. Did anybody listen to you?"

The society editor slowly shook her head. She reached out, took Gretchen's hand. "Gretchen, it was a wonderful story. I told them that, too." She pushed up from the desk. "Back to the trenches."

Mr. Dennis looked up at Gretchen. "You getting a lot of flak?"

She had to tell him the truth. "Some."

He was silent for a moment. "Are you sorry you wrote about Faye?" There was no inflection in his voice.

"No." Her story—out on the wire.

He squinted at her and slowly smiled. "You'll be all right."

Gretchen went back to her hard chair, smoothed her fingers across the typewriter keys. She lifted her hands and began to write about an injured soldier who wanted to be a veterinarian. She was almost finished when Mrs. Taylor slapped down her phone, flung out her hands, and exclaimed, "Marry in haste! Repent at leisure!"

Gretchen frowned. Marry in haste—that's what her mother had done. She'd run away to California with a man she'd only known for a week.

Mrs. Taylor picked up her notebook and pushed back her chair. "Walt, I don't know how to handle this. Jane Wilson's a fine woman, and I'll tell you she was crying so hard, I could barely understand her, but she wants the wedding story to be in the paper. But what will people think? Barb's parents dead, and the awful way they died, and then her running off and marrying Rodney Wilson. Do you think I should just write it the way I would any wedding story?"

Gretchen pulled the last sheet of paper from her typewriter, wrote *–30–*. So Barb had married her soldier. Gretchen put her story in the incoming copy tray.

Mr. Dennis's telephone shrilled. He reached out, scooped up the receiver. *"Gazette."*

"And who won't marry a soldier these days?" Mrs. Taylor's feather quivered as she typed fast. "On their way to California . . ."

Gretchen was turning away, when she saw the editor wince. He looked at her, and there was all the sadness in the world in his eyes. "Heart attack? She's gone?"

Gretchen felt frozen. Her mouth curved into a soundless "O." She wanted to cry or run, twist and turn, cover her ears, somehow escape the words that she knew were coming.

Mr. Dennis pushed up from his chair. He reached out, took her arm. "Gretchen, your grandmother . . ."

HER DARK DRESS was hot. The straw hat chafed her forehead. Her hands clenched, and the gloves felt tight against her fingers. Beside her, her cousin Hilda sobbed. Cousin Ernst stood with his gray head bowed, heavy face solemn, hat clasped in his hands.

"Unto God's gracious mercy and protection we commit you. The Lord bless you and keep you. The Lord make His face to shine upon you and be gracious unto you. The Lord lift up His countenance upon you and give you peace, both now and evermore. Amen."

As the mourners walked slowly toward the cars that lined the gravel road, Gretchen twisted for one last look at the casket with its blanket of white flowers, and the gaping gravesite. Grandmother . . .

The cars filled Archer Street and their drive and the lawn. Gretchen and Cousin Hilda and Cousin Ernst stood by the dining-room table greeting Grandmother's friends. Gretchen shook hands and endured embraces, and all the while, she braced herself for what she knew would come.

There were only a few members of Grandmother's Sunday school class still working in the kitchen, when Cousin Hilda brushed back a dank gray curl that had slipped loose from her tight bun. "Have you packed, Gretchen?"

Gretchen straightened the lace cloth on the walnut end table by Grandmother's chair. "I can't come out to the farm yet, Cousin Hilda. I have to stay here until Mother calls."

Cousin Hilda pressed her fingers against her temples. "Oh. Oh, yes. Don't you have any idea where they are? Or how to get in touch with them?" Her lips thinned into a harsh line. "I'll have to say, your mother certainly has acted irresponsibly, going off into the blue."

"His leave was up." Gretchen glared at Cousin Hilda. "That's why they got married now. It's the war. She's gone to California with him. Sam's stationed there. She'll call soon. I know she will. Anyway, I've got to stay here. She doesn't know about Grandmother. I have to stay." And she wasn't going to go and live on the farm with Cousin Hilda and her taciturn husband, Ernst. Not now. Not ever.

Cousin Hilda patted her handkerchief against her face. "Lorraine has to know. But I don't feel good about leaving you alone."

"I'll be all right." Abruptly Gretchen reached out, gripped thin, muscular arms. "Thank you, Cousin Hilda."

The older woman's face crumpled. She stifled a sob with her handkerchief, whirled, walked toward the door.

GRETCHEN SAGGED AGAINST the cushions of the sofa. Tired, so tired . . .

The past few days, she'd worked all day at the *Gazette,* gone to Victory Café early and late. Cousin Hilda had taken over the kitchen.

Gretchen fished an ice cube from her tea glass, crunched. She picked out another cube, wiped it on her face. She was so hot. Maybe she'd sleep outside tonight, set up a cot.

The phone rang.

Gretchen's head jerked up. She bolted across the living room to the kitchen, grabbed the receiver. "Hello."

The operator's voice was thin. "I have a collect call from—"

"I accept. Mother? Oh, Mother, Grandmother—" She choked with sobs.

"Gretchen, oh, God, honey, tell me." Her mother's voice faded in and out.

". . . and the funeral was yesterday, and Cousin Hilda wants me to come to the farm—"

"Oh, no. You'll come here. To me and Sam." Lorraine's voice was firm. "We're bunking with some of Sam's friends. Everybody's looking for a place to live. But it doesn't matter, baby. We'll manage if we have to sleep on the beach."

THE THUNDEROUS CLATTER of steel on steel, a hiss of steam, an acrid smell of burning fuel, and the train roared into the station.

Gretchen lifted her cosmetic case. Her heart thudded. She started toward the steps to the car. People jostled her—women with children, soldiers, sailors. California, California . . . She was almost to the steps. A porter with grizzled hair helped the elderly woman in front of Gretchen. "All aboard. All aboard."

"Gretchen, Gretchen!" The brusque bark sounded to her left.

Gretchen slipped to one side, passengers streaming past, everyone in a hurry. She looked up at Mr. Dennis. He thrust an envelope toward her. ". . . almost didn't make it . . . just found out." He paused, panting. ". . . old friend on the *Long Beach Press-Telegram,* 604 Pine Avenue . . . take this to him."

She grabbed the envelope and was caught up in the flow of travelers. She looked back and caught one last glimpse of Mr. Dennis, hat tilted to the back of his head. He looked envious, sad, admiring. She stepped into the car. Clutching the envelope, she found a seat.

As the train pulled out of the station, Gretchen propped her feet on her overnight case. The iron wheels clacked beneath her.

On the envelope, Mr. Dennis had scrawled, in thick black pencil, *Harry.* The envelope wasn't sealed. She tipped out folded sheets. On three pages were the clips of her story on Faye Tatum. The cover letter read:

Harry—read this. Hire her. Walt

CHAPTER TEN

. . . Do you know how many times I wanted to tell the truth? I never could. You see, there was Rod. You probably don't know about him. No reason you should. I'm so proud. He's a great artist. Everybody in the Southwest knows him. He has a mural in the Gilcrease Museum, and the Getty out in California commissioned him to do an acrylic painting, and it's famous. Rod called it Left Behind, *and it's a railroad track on the prairie. Buddy's folks raised Rod. They hardly ever let me see him. I felt so bad about everything, I never fought them. They're both gone now. I couldn't have said anything while they were alive. Or while Rod was alive. . . .*

I TURNED AWAY from Grandmother's grave. A faraway peal of church bells marked the noon hour. I'd driven about the town when I arrived that morning. So much was the same and so little. The *Gazette* offices were gone. The Victory Café was an insurance agency. I'd been shocked at how small the courthouse seemed. Long ago, I'd thought the building huge, and I remembered running up the steps that hot June day, filled with excitement and energy. I was a reporter. . . .

The letter—I reached into my pocket, touched the envelope—the letter from home had brought so many memories: bright, dark, happy, sad, sharp, blurred. I had not been able to resist the plea in the final paragraph:

> *I can tell the truth now. Will you come, Gretchen?*
> *Barb*

I pulled down the rim of my glove, looked at my watch—almost time. I walked across the leaves, my cane poking the winter-hard ground.

Old oaks and elms and cottonwoods stood like sentinels among the graves. My goal was over the hill—a family plot I'd never visited. I'd received clear directions when we spoke on the phone.

I saw her when I reached the top of the hill. There was a hollow here, a little valley of graves, nestled between two low hills. She waited for me near the new grave, the one heaped with flowers.

When we faced each other, the mound of flowers between us, we were silent for a moment. Her face held remnants of beauty despite the puffy pouches beneath her blue eyes, the crinkled skin that told of illness as well as age, the sagging mouth that revealed more clearly than words the loss of hope and joy. Her cloth coat, a rough tweed, was black speckled with gray. The hem dangled loose in front. Her black shoes were fashionable but cheap.

Would I have recognized Barb Tatum? No. Not the Barb who had enthralled our little world, face vibrant, eyes eager.

Barb clasped her hands together. She had no gloves. Her hands were arthritic, the joints red and swollen. "You look good, Gretchen. Distinguished."

I recognized the lilt of southern California in her words.

I glanced down at the topmost funeral spray, jonquils, their bright yellow blossoms already faded. "I'm sorry, Barb."

"We have to stop meeting like this." Her tone was brittle. "Always standing beside a new grave." Her worn face crumpled. She stifled a sob behind a bunched, reddened hand.

I came around the end of the grave, pulling a Kleenex from my purse.

She took it, swiped at her eyes. "I know Rod's all right. He'd been so sick, Gretchen. Leukemia. He suffered so bad. He doesn't hurt now. I'm the one who hurts. Not Rod." She looked at me hopefully. "You being a reporter, I'll bet you checked him out after I wrote. He really is famous."

"Yes." Barb's son was famous indeed.

Barb leaned down, broke off a jonquil bloom. "Rod asked me once about Mama and Daddy. I got up and left the room. I didn't want him to see my face. Later, there was a painting, a woman in black kneeling before two graves. He never asked again." Barb brushed loose a yellow petal. It floated lazily down to the leaf-strewn ground, a splash of color against the winter-dried leaves. "I expect Rod knows now. I expect Mama and Daddy were there to greet him, along with Buddy and his folks." Her glance at me was sharp. "Do you think I'm silly?"

My voice was gentle. "Faith is never silly, Barb."

"Anyway, I know Rod's all right." She leaned forward, gently placed the flower on the tumbled mass of sprays. "Rod understands. My priest says everybody who dies has to forgive everyone who's hurt them." Her eyes glistened. "A lot of people had to forgive me, Gretchen. But that's not why I wrote you. See, the whole world thinks Daddy killed Mama, and I got to tell the truth before I die. I'm the only one who knows. Oh, Gretchen, can I ever make you see?"

I clenched my hand on the knob of my cane. How could Barb or anyone else change the fact that Clyde Tatum killed his wife and shot himself?

She reached up, those painful fingers tugging at a thick flannel muffler as if it were hard to breathe. "You got to remember how awful it was, finding Mama dead, hearing that she and Daddy quarreled. I couldn't believe Daddy would hurt Mama like that, but finally, like everybody, I thought Daddy was guilty. He was a jealous man, and he loved Mama. Maybe he loved her too much. When he heard that a man was coming to our house late at night, what else could he believe but that Mama was having an affair? That was the first awful blow, knowing that Daddy believed Mama was unfaithful. I couldn't sleep for grief. But the second was worse, when Chief Fraser gave me that note that Daddy wrote."

The note—Mr. Dennis had told us what Clyde wrote. I didn't remember the words now. It had been too many years.

"Then I knew." The eyes that moved to mine held an agony of pain. "That's why I married Buddy. I had to get out of town—I was so scared. I wanted to tell Chief Fraser, but I knew he'd never believe me. I couldn't prove a thing."

"Prove what?"

"Who killed Mama. And Daddy." She pulled her purse from under one arm, opened the clasp. She reached inside, carefully pulled out a plastic folder. She handed it to me.

I held it loosely in my gloved hands. The piece of paper—a scrap from a brown grocery sack—looked old and limp. I strained to read the faded scrawl:

I didn't mean to hurt Fay. Please tell Barbie I love her—

That was all. Two sentences, one unfinished, no signature.

I felt an icy prickle down my back. Chief Fraser saw this note; he took it from beneath the slumped body of Clyde Tatum. "Oh, God, Barb . . ." I breathed the words.

"You see. Oh, Gretchen, you see!" Triumph lifted her voice, and she almost sounded young.

I willed my hands not to shake. It was as clear as though Clyde Tatum stood there beside us, ever young, his grieving face stubbly with beard, his uniform crumpled and dirty, his smooth muscular arms outstretched. *Fay* . . . Clyde would never have misspelled his wife's name, dropped the *e*. And *Barbie?* His pet name for his daughter was Sugarbee, sometimes Sugar. Not Barbie. Never Barbie.

I smoothed a gloved finger over the plastic protecting the faded letters. "He wrote it."

She folded her arms tight across the bulky front of her old tweed coat. "He was telling us."

Clyde had written those jerky letters because someone stood with a gun at his head. In his last, desperate seconds, trapped by the man who'd killed his wife, Clyde tried to tell those who would find his body that he wrote under duress, the gun stolen from his house held inches from his temple. Chief Fraser read right over the spelling of Faye's name. How many people in this world cannot spell, never notice when words are right or wrong? So many. So very many.

Barb shuddered. "He died thinking Mama made love with him.

That's the worst part. That's what I can't forget. Or forgive. Daddy never knew it was me."

Her eyes met mine. It was as though I looked into her soul, weighted with the shackles of shame. "Yes. There was a man coming to our house. But he came for me, Gretchen, for me. I thought I was so sexy, that it was all so exciting, that he was so handsome. I never thought what could happen. Now it all seems stupid. Everybody screws around." Her voice was hard, bitter. "And Mama died and Daddy died because I was sleeping with Donny Durwood. What a waste."

I shook my head. "It would matter even now, Barb—a grown man sleeping with an underage girl. Especially a married man."

"Donny . . . I never saw him again. I wish I could stop hating him." Her tone was metallic, unyielding. "I doubt he meant to hurt Mama. She was yelling, and he got scared. You know, I never thought of him. Not that night. Because Mama had pounded on my door. I locked it when she yelled for me to come out, that she knew what I'd been doing, and . . ."

Across the years, I remembered Mrs. Crane saying how she'd told Faye chapter and verse when she called from the Blue Light.

". . . she was going to find out everything that had happened from me and that there was going to be hell to pay. I guess she called Donny from the Blue Light . . ."

Two calls that terrible night, not one.

". . . and he came over to try and talk her out of telling anyone. And when she yelled at him, he must have tried to make her be quiet. And he killed her. But Daddy— Oh, God, he killed Daddy in cold blood."

"I saw him that Saturday." I understood now. Donny Durwood had been clever. Clever and desperate, guilty of murder, but seeing a way to safety. Everyone thought Clyde Tatum was guilty. If Clyde committed suicide, leaving a note behind, Durwood was safe. The woman who had helped Clyde reach the cabin had become frightened. Perhaps she decided Clyde was guilty, especially after the gun was stolen from the Tatum house. Did she go that sultry night to the town square, hear Donny Durwood's confident accusation? Whatever her motive, she tucked a note beneath the wiper of Donny Durwood's car. It was Durwood who slipped through the darkness of the woods, his scratched arms hidden beneath long sleeves, and awaited Clyde's return from another fruitless effort to find Faye's killer. After he killed Clyde, Durwood placed the note on the police cruiser. I remembered the sense of danger and evil in the darkness that hot summer night.

I spoke slowly. "That morning when they found your dad, Durwood looked sick." Sick and shaken, distraught, burdened forever. "Barb, there are killers and killers." I'd covered trials, seen murderers who were stupid or angry or scared or vicious. "Durwood had to care about justice. He would never have become a prosecuting attorney, not even for attention or political gain or power, unless he cared about right and wrong." What would it do to such a man to become as bad as the criminals he prosecuted?

"Donny drove his car into a tree a few years later." Barb's voice was cool. "Drunk." She lifted her chin. "I was glad. It made it better somehow that he was dead. That's when I could look at Rod and not see Donny."

"Rod?"

Barb's lips trembled. "I told you I was bad, didn't I? That everything was my fault? I had to get married. I was pregnant." Tears slid down her cheeks unchecked. "But maybe that was the only good I ever did—having Rod. Letting Buddy's parents take him. They loved him, you know. Loved everything he did, everything he said. He was Buddy's boy, and then when he became an artist, it was like they were farmyard chickens and there was a peacock among them. That's why I never could say anything. I couldn't do that to Rod. Or to Buddy's folks. But they're gone now. Whatever I say now can't hurt them. I guess I'm looking for peace, Gretchen. And I thought of you." Barb brushed back a tangle of dyed red hair. "I was afraid you wouldn't come. You didn't have to."

"No. I didn't have to come." There isn't much a woman my age has to do. It's easy to say no. But when the letter arrived, I'd just returned from a family holiday in Hawaii. We'd stayed on Kauai, splashed in the surf, played tennis, picnicked, run with the children across golden sand. My children and grandchildren came as my guests. I thrust my gloved hand into my coat pocket, felt the letter, and looked down at the spray of jonquils, their fading yellow blossoms a harbinger of the spring yet to come. It was simply a holiday, but a holiday made possible by my working years. I never forgot how my career began. I still have the yellowed clips of the story I wrote about Faye Tatum, the story that I carried with me to California and to the future.

". . . you're a writer. You could tell what really happened. That Mama was faithful to Daddy and that he never killed her, he never did."

Yes. I was a writer. I could tell the story of Faye and Clyde Tatum, and of their daughter, Barb, and the little girl down the street. . . .

–30–

CAROLYN HART

Carolyn Hart is the author of two successful mystery series (Henrie O and Death on Demand), as well as stand-alone books for both adults and children. When she started writing in the 1980s, the mystery field was "the province of dead English ladies and hard-boiled American private eyes." She was able to make her mark, she says on her website, www.carolynhart.com, when she decided, "I am not going to give any thought to the market." It is writing her books her own way that has made her a best-selling author.

While *Letter from Home* has a nostalgic, almost melancholy tinge, one thing that permeates many of Hart's mystery novels is a sense of fun. "Murder is never funny," she says, "but people are very funny." Her sense of humor is clear when one learns about her pet felines—the "charming and huge" Cat-A-Thomas and the imperious Sophie, "who bites"—

or that she is a "maybe-next-year" Chicago Cubs fan.

Hart was born in Oklahoma City. Her first fiction about her home state was a short story that, interestingly enough, tells of a young girl named Gretchen during World War II. Hart met her husband-to-be, Phil, on a student trip to Europe during her junior year of college. They had a great journey then, she says, and they are *still* having a great journey.

"I am not going to give any thought to the market."

Sometimes, you have to look at life

in a whole new way.

One

$\mathcal{H}$OLLY held the blue cotton sweater to her face, and the familiar smell immediately struck her, an overwhelming grief knotting her stomach and pulling at her heart. Pins and needles ran up the back of her neck, and a lump in her throat threatened to choke her. Panic took over. Apart from the low hum of the fridge and the occasional moaning of the pipes, the house was quiet. She was alone. Bile rose to her throat, and she ran to the bathroom, where she collapsed to her knees before the toilet.

Gerry was gone, and he would never be back. That was the reality. She would never again run her fingers through his hair, never share a secret joke across the table at a dinner party, never cry to him when she got home from a hard day at work and needed a hug. She would never share a bed with him again, never be woken up by his sneezes each morning, never laugh with him until her stomach ached, never fight with him about whose turn it was to get up and turn the bedroom light off. All that was left was a bundle of memories and an image of his face that became more and more vague each day.

Their plan had been very simple: to stay together for the rest of their lives. A plan that anyone within their circle would agree was accomplishable. They were best friends, lovers, and soul mates destined to be together, everyone thought. But as it happened, one day destiny greedily changed its mind.

The end had come all too soon. After complaining of a migraine for a few days, Gerry had agreed to Holly's suggestion that he see his doctor. This was done one Wednesday on a lunch break from work. The doctor thought it was due to stress and agreed that at the very worst, he might need glasses. Gerry had been upset about the idea he might need glasses. He needn't have worried, since as it turned out, it wasn't his eyes that were the problem. It was the tumor growing inside his brain.

Holly shakily steadied herself to her feet. He had been thirty years old. By no means had he been the healthiest man on the earth, but he'd been healthy enough. When he was very sick, he would bravely joke about how he shouldn't have lived life so safely. Should have taken drugs, should have drunk more, should have traveled more, should have jumped out of airplanes. Growing older became something he wanted desperately to accomplish rather than merely a dreaded inevitability. How presumptuous they both had been never to consider growing old as an achievement.

Holly drifted from room to room while she sobbed her fat, salty tears. Her eyes were red and sore. None of the rooms provided her with any solace. Gerry would not be happy with this, she thought. She dried her eyes and tried to shake some sense into herself.

JUST as she had every night for the past few weeks, Holly fell into a fitful sleep in the early hours of the morning. Each day, she found herself sprawled uncomfortably across some piece of furniture; today it was the couch. Once again, it was the phone call from a concerned friend or family member that woke her up. They probably thought all she did was sleep. Where were their phone calls when she listlessly roamed the house like a zombie searching the rooms for . . . for what? What was she expecting to find?

"Hello," she answered, her voice hoarse from all the tears.

"Oh, sorry, love. Did I wake you?" Every morning, Holly's mother called to see if she had survived the night alone.

"No. I was just dozing. It's okay."

"Your dad and Declan have gone out, and I was thinking of you, pet." Why did that sympathetic voice always send tears to Holly's eyes? Her mother shouldn't have to be worried. Everything should be normal. Gerry should be here, rolling his eyes up to heaven and trying to make Holly laugh while her mother yapped on. So many times, she would have to hand the phone to Gerry, as her fit of giggles would take over. Then he would chat away, ignoring Holly as she jumped around the bed, pulling her silliest faces just to get him back. It seldom worked.

"It's a lovely day, Holly. It would do you the world of good to go out for a walk. Get some fresh air."

"Um, I suppose."

"Maybe I'll call around later, and we can have a chat."

"No thanks, Mum. I'm okay."

"Well, all right, then. Give me a ring if you change your mind. I'm free all day."

"Okay. Thanks, though."

"Right, then. Take care, love. Oh, I almost forgot. That envelope is still here for you—the one I told you about. You might want to collect it. It's been here for weeks."

"It's probably just another card."

"No, I don't think it is, love. It's addressed to you, and above your name it says, 'The List.' I'm not sure what that means. It's worth just taking a—"

Holly dropped the phone.

"GERRY, turn off the light!" Holly giggled as she watched her husband undress before her. He danced around the room performing a striptease, slowly unbuttoning his white cotton shirt. He raised his left eyebrow toward Holly and allowed the shirt to slide from his shoulders, caught it in his hand, and swung it over his head.

Holly giggled again.

"Turn off the light? And miss all this?" he grinned cheekily while flexing his muscles. He wasn't vain but had much to be vain about, thought Holly. His body was perfectly toned. He wasn't a tall man, but he was tall enough to make Holly feel safe when he stood protectively beside her five-foot-five body. Most of all, she loved that when she hugged him, her head would rest neatly below his chin.

He lowered his boxers, caught them on the tips of his toes, and flung them at Holly, where they landed on her head.

"Well, at least it's darker under here anyway," she laughed.

Gerry dived into bed, snuggled up beside her, and tucked his freezing-cold feet underneath her legs.

"Aaaagh! Gerry, your feet are like ice cubes." Holly knew he had no intention of budging an inch. "Gerry!"

"Holly," he mimicked.

"Didn't you forget something? The light?"

"Ah, the light," he said sleepily, and pretended to snore loudly.

"Gerry!"

"I had to get out and do it last night, as I remember."

"Yeah, but you were right beside the switch a second ago!"

"Yes . . . just a second ago," he repeated sleepily.

Holly sighed. She hated having to get out of bed when she was nice and snug, step onto the cold wooden floor, then fumble around in the darkness on the way back. She tutted.

"I can't do it all the time, you know, Hol. Someday I might not be here, and then what will you do?"

"Get my new husband to do it," Holly huffed, trying her best to kick his cold feet away from hers.

"Ha!"

"Or just remember to do it myself before I get into bed."

"Fat chance, my dear. I'll have to leave a message on the light switch before I go, just so you'll remember."

"How thoughtful of you, but I would rather you just leave me your money."

"And a note on the central heating. And on the milk carton."

"Ha-ha. You're very funny, Gerry. Hey, why don't you just leave me a list in your will of things to do if you think I'll be so incompetent without you?"

"Not a bad idea," he laughed.

"Fine, then, I'll turn off the bloody light." Holly grudgingly got out of bed and switched it off. She held out her arms in the darkness and slowly began to find her way back.

"Hello? Holly, did you get lost? Is there anybody out there, there, there, there?" Gerry shouted out to the black room.

"Yes, I'm hhhhowwwwwwcch!" she yelped as she stubbed her toe against the bedpost.

Gerry snorted and sniggered underneath the duvet. "Number two on my list: Watch out for bedpost."

"Oh, shut up, Gerry, and stop being so morbid," Holly snapped back, cradling her poor foot in her hand.

"Want me to kiss it better?" he asked.

"No. It's okay," Holly replied. "If I could just put them here so I can warm—"

"Aaaaah! Bloody hell, they're freezing!"

"Hee-hee-hee," she laughed.

So that was how the joke about the list had come about. It was a silly and simple idea that was soon shared with their closest friends, Sharon and John McCarthy. It was John who had approached Holly in the school corridor when they were just fourteen and muttered the famous words, "Me mate wants to know if you'll go out with him." After days of emergency meetings with her friends, Holly eventually agreed. "Aah, go on, Holly," Sharon had urged. "At least he doesn't have spots all over his face, like John."

How Holly envied Sharon right now. Sharon and John had married the same year as Holly and Gerry. Holly was the baby of the bunch at twenty-three; the rest were twenty-four. Some said she was too young and lectured her about how she should be traveling the world and enjoying herself. Instead, Gerry and Holly traveled the world together, because when they weren't, well, *together,* Holly felt like she was missing a vital organ from her body.

Her wedding day was far from being the best day of her life. She had dreamed of a fairy-tale wedding, like most girls, with a princess dress and beautiful weather, in a romantic location surrounded by all who were near and dear to her. The reality was quite different.

She woke up in her family home to screams of "I can't find my tie!" (her father), or "My hair looks shite!" (her mother), and the best one of all: "I look like a bloody whale! There's no way I'm goin' to this bleedin' weddin' looking like this. Holly can find another bridesmaid. Oi! Jack, give me back that hair dryer. I'm not finished!" That statement was made by her younger sister, Ciara, who on a regular basis threw tantrums and refused to leave the house, claiming she had nothing to wear, regardless of her bursting wardrobe. She was currently living somewhere in Australia. Holly's family spent the rest of the morning trying to convince Ciara how she was the most beautiful woman in the world. All the while, Holly silently dressed herself, feeling like shite. Ciara eventually agreed to leave the house when Holly's typically calm dad screamed at the top of his voice, to everyone's amazement, "Ciara, this is Holly's bloody day, not yours! I don't wanna hear another peep out of you."

So when Holly walked downstairs, everyone oohed and aahed, while Ciara, appearing like a child who had just been spanked, looked at her tearily and said, "You look beautiful, Holly." All seven of them squashed into the limo—Holly, her parents, her three brothers, and Ciara—and sat in terrified silence all the way to the church.

The day seemed to be a blur to her now. She had barely had time to speak to Gerry, as they were both being pulled in opposite directions to meet Great-aunt Betty from the back arse of nowhere, and Grand-uncle Toby from America, who had never been mentioned before but was suddenly an important member of the family.

By the end of the night, Holly's cheeks were sore from smiling for photographs, and her feet were killing her from running around all day in very silly little shoes not designed for walking. But as soon as Holly stepped into the honeymoon suite with Gerry, her worries of the day faded and the point of it all became clear.

Tears once again rolled down Holly's face, and she realized she had been daydreaming again. She sat on the couch with the phone still off the hook beside her. Time seemed to pass her by these days without her knowing what hour or what day it was. She couldn't remember the last time she had eaten. Had it been yesterday?

She shuffled into the kitchen wearing Gerry's dressing gown and her pink DISCO DIVA slippers, which Gerry had bought her the previous Christmas. She was his Disco Diva, he used to say. Always the first on the dance floor, always the last out of the club. Huh, where was that girl now? She opened the fridge and stared in at the empty shelves. Just vegetables and yogurt, long past its sell-by date. She shook the milk carton. Empty. Third on his list . . .

CHRISTMAS two years ago, Holly had gone shopping with Sharon for a dress for the annual ball they attended at the Burlington Hotel. Shopping with Sharon was always a dangerous outing, and Holly spent a disgraceful amount of money on the most beautiful white dress she had ever seen.

"Sharon, this will burn a huge hole in my pocket," Holly guiltily said, running her fingers over the soft material.

"Aah, don't worry. Gerry can stitch it up for you," Sharon replied, followed by her infamous cackle. "Buy the damn thing, Holly. It's the season of giving and all that."

"You are so evil, Sharon. I'm never shopping with you again. This is, like, half my month's wages."

"Holly, would you rather eat or look fab?" Was it even worth thinking about?

The dress was cut low, which showed off Holly's chest perfectly, and it was split to the thigh, displaying her slim legs. Gerry hadn't been able to take his eyes off her. It wasn't because she looked so beautiful, however. He just couldn't understand how on earth that little slip of material had cost so much. Once at the ball, Ms. Disco Diva overindulged in alcoholic beverages and succeeded in destroying her dress by spilling red wine down her front. While Holly tried but failed to hold back her tears, the men at the table drunkenly informed their partners that number fifty-four on the list prevented you from drinking red wine while wearing an expensive white dress. Later, when Gerry knocked his pint over onto Holly's lap, she announced seriously, "Rule fitty-fife: *Neffer effer* buy a 'spensive white dress." A toast was made to Holly and to her profound addition to the list.

Was it possible that Gerry had kept his word and written a list for her before he died? She had spent every day with him up until his death, and he had never mentioned it, nor had she noticed any signs of him writing one. No, Holly, pull yourself together, and don't be stupid. She so desperately wanted him back that she was imagining all kinds of crazy things. He wouldn't have. Would he?

HOLLY was walking through an entire field of tiger lilies. The wind was blowing gently, causing the silky petals to tickle the tips of her fingers as she pushed through the long green strands. The ground felt soft beneath her bare feet, and all around her, birds whistled as they went about their business. The sun was so bright, she had to shield her eyes, and with each brush of wind, the sweet scent of the lilies filled her nostrils. She felt so happy, so free.

Suddenly the sky darkened, and her sun disappeared behind a gray cloud. The wind picked up, and the air chilled. The petals of her tiger lilies were racing through the air wildly, blurring her vision. Sharp-pebbled stones scraped her feet, and she felt afraid. In the distance, a gray stone was visible. She wanted to run back to her pretty flowers, but she needed to find out what was ahead.

Bang! Bang! Bang! She raced over the sharp stones, collapsed to her knees in front of the gray slab, and let out a scream of pain as she realized it was Gerry's grave. *Bang! Bang! Bang!* He was trying to get out! She could hear him!

Holly jumped from her sleep to a loud banging on the door. "Holly, please let me in!" *Bang! Bang!* Confused and half awake, she made her way to the door to find a frantic-looking Sharon.

"Holly, I've been banging on the door for ages!"

Holly looked around outside, still not fully alert. It was bright and slightly chilly, must be morning.

"Well, aren't you going to let me in?"

"Yeah, Sharon, sorry. I was just dozing on the couch."

"You look terrible, Hol." Sharon studied her face before giving her a big hug.

"Wow, thanks." Holly rolled her eyes and turned to shut the door. Sharon was never one to beat around the bush, but that's why Holly loved her so much, for her honesty. That's also why Holly hadn't been around to see Sharon for the past month. She didn't want to hear the truth. She didn't want to hear that she had to get on with her life. She just wanted . . . Oh, she didn't know what she wanted. She was happy being miserable. It somehow felt right.

"It's so stuffy in here. When's the last time you opened a window?" Sharon marched around the house, opening windows and picking up empty cups and plates. She brought them into the kitchen, where she then proceeded to tidy up.

"You don't have to do it," Holly protested weakly. "I'll do it."

"When? Next year? I don't want you slumming it while the rest of us pretend not to notice. Why don't you go upstairs and shower, and we'll have a cup of tea when you come down."

A shower. When was the last time she had even washed? Sharon was right; she must look disgusting with her greasy hair and dirty robe. Gerry's robe. But that was something she never intended to wash. She wanted it exactly as Gerry had left it.

"Okay, but there's no milk. I haven't got around to . . ." Holly felt embarrassed by her lack of care for the house and for herself.

"Ta-da!" Sharon sang, holding up a bag Holly hadn't noticed her carry in. "Don't worry, I took care of that."

"Thanks, Sharon." A lump formed in Holly's throat.

"Hold it! There will be no tears today! Just fun and laughter and general happiness, my dear friend. Now shower, quick!"

HOLLY felt almost human when she came back downstairs. She was dressed in a blue tracksuit and had allowed her long blond hair to fall down on her shoulders. She gasped as she looked around the house. She couldn't have been half an hour, but Sharon had tidied, polished, and vacuumed. She followed the noise she could hear to the kitchen, where Sharon was scrubbing the counters.

"Sharon, you absolute angel! I can't believe you did all this. And in such a short space of time."

"Ha! I was beginning to think you'd fallen down the plughole. You would and all, the size of you." She looked Holly up and down. "Okay, I just bought some vegetables and fruit, and there's cheese and yogurts, pasta and tinned foods. And there are microwave dinners in the freezer. That should do you for a while, but by the looks of you, it'll last you the year. How much weight have you lost?"

Holly looked down at her body; her tracksuit, with the waist tie pulled to its tightest, still drooped to her hips. She hadn't noticed the weight loss at all. She was brought back to reality by Sharon's voice again. "There's a few biscuits to go with your tea. Jammy Dodgers, your favorite."

That did it. The Jammy Dodgers were the icing on the cake. Holly felt the tears start to run down her face. "Oh, Sharon," she wailed, "thank you so much. You've been so good to me, and I've been such a horrible friend." She sat at the table and grabbed Sharon's hand. "I don't know what I'd do without you." This is what Holly had been dreading, breaking down in front of people, but she didn't feel embarrassed. Sharon sat opposite her, patiently holding her hand as if it were normal.

"I'm your best friend, Hol. If I don't help you, then who will?" Sharon gave her an encouraging smile.

"Suppose I should be helping myself."

"Pah!" Sharon waved her hand dismissively. "Whenever you're ready. Grieving is all part of helping yourself anyway."

She always said the right things.

"Thanks for coming round, Sharon." Holly gratefully hugged her friend, who had taken off work to be with her. They spent the rest of the day laughing and joking about old times, then crying, followed by some more laughing, then more crying again. It had been good being around the living again instead of moping around with the ghosts of her past. Tomorrow was a new day, and she intended to begin it by collecting that envelope.

Two

$\mathcal{H}$OLLY started her Friday morning well by getting up early. However, although she had gone to bed full of optimism, she was struck afresh by the harsh reality of how difficult every moment would be. Once again, she awoke to a silent house, but there was one small breakthrough. For the first time, she had woken up without the aid of a telephone call.

She showered and dressed in her favorite blue jeans, trainers, and a T-shirt. She made a face at her reflection in the mirror. She had black circles under her eyes, and her lips were chapped and chewed on, and her hair was a disaster. First thing to do was to go down to her local hairdresser's and pray they could squeeze her in.

"Jaysus, Holly!" her hairdresser, Leo, exclaimed when he saw her. "Look at the state of ya! People make way! Make way! I have a woman in a critical condition!" He winked at her and proceeded to push people from his path, pulling out the chair for her.

"Thanks, Leo. I feel really attractive now," Holly muttered.

"Well, don't, 'cos you're in bits. Sandra, mix me up the usual. Colin, get the foil. Tania, get my little bag of tricks from upstairs— Oh, and tell Paul not to bother getting his lunch; he's doing my twelve-o'clock." Leo ordered everyone around, his hands flailing wildly as though he were about to perform emergency surgery.

"Oh, sorry, Leo. I didn't mean to mess up your day."

"I wouldn't do it for anyone else but you, love. So how have you been?" He rested his skinny behind on the counter facing Holly. Leo must have been fifty, yet his skin was so flawless and his hair, of course, so perfect that he didn't look a day over thirty-five. He was enough to make a woman feel like crap.

"Terrible."

"Yeah, you look it. Ah, well, at least by the time you walk out of here, you'll have one thing sorted. I do hair, not hearts."

Holly smiled gratefully at his odd little way of showing he understood. "Thanks, Leo," she said. He went to work on her hair, putting on his funny little concentrating face. Holly giggled.

"You laugh now, Holly, but wait till I accidentally give you a stripy head of color. We'll see who's laughing then."

"How's Jamie?" Holly asked, keen to change the subject before she embarrassed herself.

"He dumped me," Leo said, pushing aggressively with his foot on the chair's pump, causing her to jerk wildly in her chair.

"Oh, Leo, I'm sorry. You two were great together."

He stopped pumping and paused. "Yeah, well, we're not so gree-aat together now, missy. I think he's seeing someone else. Right. I'm going to put two shades of blond in—a golden color and the blond you had before. Otherwise it'll go that brassy color that's reserved for prostitutes only."

"Oh, Leo, I'm sorry. If he has any sense at all, he'll realize what he's missing."

"He mustn't have any sense; we split up two months ago. I've had enough of men. I'm just going to turn straight."

"Leo, now that's the most stupid thing I've ever heard."

HOLLY bounced out of the salon with delight. Without Gerry's presence beside her, a few men looked her way, something that made her feel uncomfortable, so she ran to the safety of her car and prepared herself for her parents' house. So far, today was going well. It had been a good move to visit Leo. Even in his heartbreak, he worked hard to make her laugh. Holly took note of it.

She pulled up to the curb outside her parents' house in Portmarnock and took a deep breath. To her mother's surprise, Holly had called her first thing to arrange a time to meet up. It was three-thirty now, and Holly sat outside in the car with butterflies in her tummy. Apart from the visits her parents had paid her over the past two months, Holly had barely spent any time with her family. She didn't want all the attention; she didn't want the intrusive questions about how she was feeling and what she was going to do next. However, it was time to put that fear aside. They were her family.

Her parents' house was directly across the road from Portmarnock Beach. She parked the car and stared across the road to the sea. She had lived here from the day she was born till the day she moved out to live with Gerry. She had loved waking up to the sound of the sea lapping against the rocks and the excited call of the seagulls. Sharon had lived around the corner, and on the hottest days of the year, the girls would venture across the road and keep an eye out for the best-looking boys. Holly and Sharon were the complete opposite of each other—Sharon with her brown hair, fair skin, and huge chest; Holly with her blond hair, sallow skin, and small chest. Sharon would be shouting to the boys and calling them over, Holly fixing her eyes on her favorite and not moving them till he noticed. Holly and Sharon hadn't changed all that much since.

She didn't intend to stay long, just to have a little chat and collect the envelope that she had decided could possibly be from Gerry. She rang the doorbell and placed a smile on her face.

"Hi, love! Come in," said her mother with the welcoming, loving face that Holly just wanted to kiss every time she saw her.

"Hi, Mum." Holly stepped into the house. "You on your own?"

"Yes. Your father's out with Declan, buying paint for his room."

"Don't tell me you're still paying for everything for him."

"Your father might be, but I'm not. He's working now, so he has a bit of pocket money. Although we don't see a penny of it," she chuckled, and brought Holly to the kitchen and put the kettle on.

Declan was Holly's youngest brother and the baby of the family, a twenty-two-year-old child studying film production at college. He constantly had a video camera in his hand.

"What job has he got now?"

Her mother rolled her eyes to heaven. "He's joined some band. The Orgasmic Fish, I think they call themselves. If he goes on one more time about how famous they're going to be, I'll go mad."

"Ah, poor Deco. Don't worry, he'll eventually find something."

"I know. He'll find his way."

They brought their mugs into the sitting room and settled down in front of the television. "You look good, love. I love the hair. Any luck with a job yet?"

"No, not yet, Mum. I haven't even started looking. I don't quite know what I want to do."

Her mother nodded. "Take your time and think about what you like, or you'll end up rushing into a job you hate, like the last time."

The last job Holly had had was working as a secretary for an unforgiving slimeball in a solicitor's office. She'd been forced to leave when the little creep failed to understand that she needed time off to be with her dying husband. Now she had go looking for a new one. For a new job, that is. At the moment, it seemed unimaginable to go to work in the morning.

Holly and her mother relaxed, falling in and out of conversation until Holly finally built up the courage to ask for the envelope.

"Oh, of course, love. I completely forgot about it. I hope it's nothing important."

"I'll find out soon enough."

They said their good-byes after a while, and Holly couldn't get out of the house quickly enough.

Perching herself on the grass overlooking the sand and sea, Holly ran her hands over the thick brown envelope. The address had been typed onto a sticker, so she couldn't even guess the origin. Above the address were two words, thick and bold—THE LIST.

Her trembling fingers gently tore at the package. She turned it upside down and shook the contents out. Out fell ten tiny envelopes, the kind you find on a bouquet of flowers, each with a different month written on it. Her heart missed a few beats as she saw a loose page underneath the pile. It was from Gerry.

With tears in her eyes, she read the familiar handwriting knowing that the person who had sat down to write to her would never be able to do so again. She ran her fingers over his words knowing that the last person to have touched the page was him:

My darling Holly,

I don't know where you are or when exactly you are reading this. I just hope it finds you safe and healthy. You whispered not long ago that you couldn't go on alone. You can.

You are strong and brave, and you can get through this. We shared some beautiful times together, and you made my life. But I am just a chapter in your life. Remember our wonderful memories, but please don't be afraid to make more.

Thank you for doing me the honor of being my wife. For everything, I am eternally grateful.

Whenever you need me, I'm with you.

Love forever,
Gerry

PS, I promised a list, so here it is. The following envelopes must be opened exactly when labeled and must be obeyed. I'm looking out for you, so I will know.

Holly broke down, sadness sweeping over her, yet she felt relief that Gerry would somehow be with her for another little while. She leafed through the small white envelopes. It was April now. She had missed March, and so she delicately picked out that envelope and opened it. Inside was a small card with Gerry's handwriting on it:

Save yourself the bruises and buy yourself a bedside lamp!
PS, I love you . . .

Her tears turned to laughter. Gerry was back!

Holly read his letter over and over in an attempt to summon him to life again. Eventually, when she could no longer see the words through her tears, she looked out to the sea.

She closed her eyes and breathed in and out along with the gentle sighing of the waves. She thought about how she used to lie by Gerry's side during his final days and listen to his breathing. She had been terrified to leave him just in case that was the time he chose to leave her. When she returned to his bedside, she would sit in terrified silence and watch his chest.

But he always managed to hang on. He had baffled the doctors with his determination to live; Gerry kept his good humor right up until the end. He was so weak, but they would giggle together late into the night, and other nights they would hold each other and cry. Holly remained strong for him. Looking back, she knew that she needed him more than he needed her.

On the second of February, at four in the morning, Holly held Gerry's hand tightly as he took his last breath. She didn't want him to be afraid, and she didn't want him to feel that she was afraid, because at that moment, she wasn't. She had felt relief that his pain was gone and that she had been there with him. She felt relieved to love him and to be loved by him, and relief that the last thing he saw was her smiling face, assuring him it was okay to let go.

The days after were a blur. She occupied herself making funeral arrangements. She was thankful that his suffering was over. It didn't occur to her to feel the bitterness she felt now. That feeling didn't arrive until she went to collect her husband's death certificate.

As she sat in the crowded health clinic waiting for her number to be called, she wondered why on earth Gerry's number had been called so early in his life. She sat sandwiched between a young couple and an elderly couple, and it all just seemed unfair. Squashed between the shoulders of her past and her lost future, she felt suffocated. She shouldn't have had to be there. It just wasn't fair.

After presenting the official proof of death to bank managers and insurance companies, Holly returned home to her nest and locked herself away from the world. That was two months ago, and she hadn't left the house until today. And what a welcome she had been given, she thought, smiling down at the envelopes. Gerry was back.

"Wow," was all Sharon and John could say as the three of them sat around Holly's kitchen table in silence, staring at the contents of the package.

"But how did he manage to . . ."

"But why didn't we notice him . . ."

"When do you think . . . He was on his own sometimes. . . ."

Holly and Sharon sat looking at each other while John tried to figure out how his terminally ill friend had managed to carry out this idea all alone.

"Wow," he eventually repeated after coming to the conclusion that Gerry had done just that.

"Are you okay, Holly?" Sharon asked. "I mean, how do you feel about all this? It must be . . . weird."

"I feel fine. Actually, I think it's the best thing that could have happened right now. It's funny, though, how amazed we are, considering how much we all went on about this list."

"I think Gerry was the only one who took it really seriously," Sharon said.

There was a silence. "Well, let's study this more closely," John said. "There's how many envelopes?"

Holly sorted through the pile. "There's March, which is the lamp one, April, May, June, July, August, September, October, November, and December. A message for every month left in the year."

"Hold on!" John's blue eyes twinkled. "It's April now."

"Oh, I forgot about that! Oh, no. Should I open it now?"

"Go on," encouraged Sharon.

Holly picked up the envelope and pulled out the little card.

A Disco Diva must always look her best. Go shopping for an outfit, as you'll need it for next month!
PS, I love you . . .

"Ooooh," John and Sharon sang with excitement. "He's getting cryptic!"

HOLLY lay on her bed like a demented woman, switching the lamp on and off with a smile on her face. She and Sharon had gone shopping in Bed Knobs and Broomsticks in Malahide and had eventually agreed on the beautifully carved wooden stand and cream shade, which matched the cream and wooden furnishings of the master bedroom. And although Gerry hadn't physically been there, Holly felt that they had made the purchase together.

She had drawn the curtains of her bedroom in order to test her new merchandise. How easily this could have ended their nightly arguments, but perhaps neither of them wanted to end them. It had become a routine, something familiar that made them feel closer. How she would gladly get out of her cozy bed for him now, gladly walk on the cold floor. But that time was gone.

The sound of Gloria Gaynor's "I Will Survive" snapped her back to the present. Her mobile phone was ringing. "Hello?"

"G'day, mate. I'm hooooome!" shrieked a familiar voice.

"Ciara! I didn't know you were coming home!"

"Neither did I, actually," said Holly's little sister. "But I ran out of money and decided to surprise you all."

"Wow, I bet Mum and Dad were surprised, all right."

"Well, Mum's organizing dinner tonight to celebrate. The whole family."

"Did I mention that I'm going to the dentist to have all my teeth pulled out? Sorry, I can't make it."

"I said the same thing to Mum, but we haven't all been together for ages. When's the last time you've seen Richard and Meredith?"

"Richard was in flying form at the funeral. Had things to say, like, 'Did you consider donating his brain to medical science?' "

"Oh, gosh, Holly, the funeral. I'm sorry I couldn't make it."

"Ciara, don't be silly. It was far too expensive, flying from Australia. So when you say the whole family, you mean . . ."

"Yes. Richard and Meredith are bringing our little niece and nephew. And Jack and Abbey are coming. Declan will be there in body if not in mind, and Mum, Dad, me, and you."

Holly groaned. As much as she moaned about her family, she had a great relationship with her brother Jack, who was a schoolteacher. He was only two years older than she, so they had always been close growing up, always getting up to mischief (usually aimed at their eldest brother, Richard). Jack was similar to Holly in personality, and she considered him the most normal of her siblings. It also helped that she got along with his girlfriend, Abbey, and when Gerry was alive, the four of them often met up for dinner.

Ciara was a whole different kettle of fish. Jack and Holly were convinced she was from the planet Ciara, population one. Ciara had the look of her father: long legs and dark hair. She also had various tattoos and piercings as a result of her world travels. A tattoo for every country, her dad used to joke. A tattoo for every man, Holly and Jack were convinced.

Of course this carry-on was frowned upon by the eldest of the family, Richard, born with the illness of being an eternal old man. His life revolved around rules, regulations, and obedience. When he was younger, Holly could never remember him going out to social-ize. She and Jack thought it was a wonder he met his equally joy-less wife, Meredith. Probably at an anti-happiness convention.

It's not as though Holly had the worst family in the world; it's just that they were a strange mix. These huge clashes of personalities usu-ally led to arguments at the most inappropriate times. They could get along, but that was with everyone really being on their best behavior.

Holly and Jack often met up for lunch or for drinks. Holly en-joyed Jack's company and considered him to be not only a brother but a real friend. Lately they hadn't seen much of each other. Jack understood Holly well and knew when she needed her space.

The only time Holly caught up on her younger brother Declan's life was when she called the house looking for her parents and he would answer. Declan wasn't a great conversationalist. He was a twenty-two-year-old "boy" who didn't quite yet feel comfortable in the company of adults.

Ciara, her twenty-four-year-old little sister, had been away for the entire year, and Holly had missed her. They were never the kind of sisters to swap clothes and giggle about boys, their tastes differed so much. But as the only two girls in a family of brothers, they formed a bond. Ciara was closer to Declan—both of them dream-ers. Jack and Holly had always been inseparable as children, and friends as adults. That left Richard. Holly dreaded his insensitive questioning of her life. But tonight was to be a welcome-home dinner for Ciara, and at least Jack would be there.

So was Holly looking forward to tonight? Absolutely not.

THAT EVENING, HOLLY reluctantly knocked on the door to her family home and immediately heard the pounding of tiny feet.

"Mummy, Daddy, it's Aunty Holly! It's Aunty Holly!"

It was Nephew Timothy, Nephew Timothy.

His happiness was suddenly crushed by a stern voice. "Timothy! What did I tell you about running in the house! Go stand in the corner and think about what I said. Do I make myself clear?"

"Yes, Mummy."

"Ah, come on, Meredith. Will he hurt himself on the carpet?"

Holly laughed to herself; Ciara was definitely home.

The door swung open, and there stood Meredith, looking even more sour-faced than usual. "Holly," she nodded.

"Meredith," Holly imitated.

Once in the living room, Holly looked around for Jack, but he was nowhere to be seen. Richard stood in front of the fireplace with his hands in his pockets, giving a lecture to their father, Frank, who sat uncomfortably in his favorite armchair. Holly blew her poor father a kiss, not wanting to be brought into their conversation. He smiled and pretended to catch her kiss.

Declan was slumped on the couch, wearing his ripped jeans and SOUTH PARK T-shirt, puffing on a cigarette while Meredith warned him of the dangers of smoking. Ciara was hiding behind the couch throwing popcorn at Timothy, who stood facing the wall in the corner. Abbey was pinned to the floor by five-year-old Emily.

"Hi, Ciara." Holly gave her sister a big hug. "Nice hair."

"You like it?"

"Yeah. Pink is really your color."

Ciara looked satisfied. "That's what I tried to tell them," she said, squinting at Richard and Meredith. "So how's my big sis?"

"Oh, you know"—Holly smiled weakly—"I'm hanging in there." She wandered into the kitchen, where she found Jack at the table with his feet up, munching on some food.

He smiled and stood up from his chair. "I see you got roped into coming to this thing as well." He held out his arms to offer her one of his big bear hugs. "How are you?" he said quietly into her ear.

"I'm okay." Holly kissed him on the cheek before turning to her mother. "Darling Mother, I am here to offer my services."

"Oh, aren't I just the luckiest woman in the world, having such caring children," Elizabeth said sarcastically. "I hope you two won't be getting up to any mischief tonight. I would like this to be an argument-free zone for a change."

"Mother, I am shocked the thought even crossed your mind." Jack winked across to Holly.

"All right," Elizabeth said, not believing a word of it. "Well, there's nothing to be done here. Dinner will be ready in a minute."

A few moments later, everyone made their way to the dining room, oohing and aahing as Elizabeth brought out the food. Holly had always loved her mother's cooking. "Hey, poor little Timmy must be starving out there!" Ciara exclaimed to Richard. "He must have done his time by now."

Ciara loved to wind Richard up. After all, she had to make up for lost time. She had been away for a year.

"Ciara, it's important that Timothy know when he has done something wrong," explained Richard.

"Yeah, but couldn't you just tell him?"

The rest of the family tried hard not to laugh.

"Stop it, Ciara," Elizabeth snapped.

"Or you'll have to stand in the corner," Jack added sternly.

The table erupted with laughter, bar Meredith and Richard.

"So, Ciara, tell us about your adventures," Frank moved on.

Ciara's eyes lit up. "I had the most amazing time, Dad. I'd definitely recommend Australia to anyone."

"Awful long flight, though," Richard said.

"Did you get any more tattoos?" Holly asked.

"Yeah, look." With that, Ciara stood up and pulled down her trousers, revealing a butterfly on her behind.

Mum, Dad, Richard, and Meredith protested in outrage, while the others sat in convulsions of laughter. This carried on for a long time. Finally, when Ciara had apologized and Meredith had removed her hands from Emily's eyes, the table settled down.

"They are revolting things," Richard said in disgust.

"I think butterflies are pretty, Daddy," said Emily.

"Emily, I'm talking about tattoos. They can give you all sorts of diseases." Emily's smile faded.

"Richard dear, do you think that Timmy might want to come in now for some food—" Elizabeth asked politely.

"It's Timothy," Meredith interrupted.

"Yes, Mother, I think that would be okay."

Timothy walked into the room with his head down and took his place silently. Holly's heart leaped out to him. How cruel to treat a child like that. Her sympathetic thoughts diminished immediately as she felt his little foot kick her shin underneath the table.

"Holly, what are you doing for your birthday?" Abbey asked.

"That's right," shouted Ciara. "You're gonna be thirty!"

"I'm not doing anything big," Holly warned everyone. "I don't want any party or anything."

"Oh, you have to," said Ciara.

"She doesn't have to if she doesn't want to," Frank said.

"Thank you, Dad. I'm just going to have a girly night out clubbing or something. Nothing mad, nothing wild."

"Yes, I agree with you, Holly," said Richard. "Those birthday celebrations are always a bit embarrassing. Grown adults acting like children, drinking too much. You're quite right."

"Well, I actually enjoy those parties, Richard," Holly shot back. "I just don't feel in the mood, that's all."

There was silence until Ciara piped up. "A girly night it is, then."

"Can I tag along with the camera?" asked Declan.

"For what?"

"Just for some footage of clubs and stuff for college."

"Well, if it'll help . . . But as long as you know, I won't be going to all the trendy places that you like."

"No, I don't mind where you go. . . . Ow!" he shouted, and stared menacingly at Timothy. Timmy stuck out his tongue, and the conversation continued on.

Eventually it grew late, and everyone began to leave one by one.

Holly stepped into the chilly air and walked to her car alone. Her mum and dad stood at the door waving her off, but she still felt lonely. Usually she left dinner parties with Gerry, and if not with him, then she was returning home *to* him. But not tonight or the next night or the night after that.

Three

STANDING in front of the full-length mirror, Holly inspected herself. She had carried out Gerry's orders and had purchased a new outfit. What for, she didn't know, but several times every day, she had to drag herself away from opening the envelope for May. There were only two days left until she could, and the anticipation left her no room to think of anything else.

She had settled on an all-black outfit to suit her current mood. Black fitted trousers slimmed her legs and were tailored to sit over her black boots. A black corset that made her look like she had a bigger chest finished the outfit off perfectly. Leo had done a wonderful job on her hair, tying it up and allowing strands to fall in loose waves around her shoulders.

She didn't feel thirty. But then again, what was being thirty supposed to feel like? When she was younger, she thought a woman of that age would be so wise and knowledgeable, so settled in her life, with a husband and children and a career. She had none of those things. There was nothing about being thirty worth celebrating.

The doorbell rang, and Holly could hear the excited chatter and giggles of the girls outside. She tried to perk herself up, took a deep breath, and plastered a smile on her face.

"Happy birthday!" Sharon, Abbey, Ciara, and her good friend Denise—whom she hadn't seen in ages—all yelled in unison.

Holly stared back at their happy faces and was immediately cheered up by their enthusiasm. She ushered them into the living room and waved hello to the camera being held by Declan.

"No, Holly. You're supposed to ignore him!" hissed Denise, and she dragged Holly by the arm onto the couch, where they all surrounded her and started thrusting presents in her face.

"Open mine first!" squealed Ciara.

"I think we should pop open the bubbly first and *then* open the pressies," said Abbey.

"Ciara, I promise to open yours first," Holly said.

Abbey raced into the kitchen and returned with a tray full of champagne flutes. "Anyone for champers, sweetie darlings? Holly, you can do the honors." Abbey handed her the bottle.

Everyone ran for cover and ducked as Holly began removing the cork. "Hey, I'm not that bad, everyone!"

The girls cheered and crawled out of their hiding places as they heard the pop. "Okay, now open my present!" Ciara screamed.

"Ciara!" they all shouted.

"After the toast," added Sharon. Everyone held up a glass.

"Okay. Here's to my bestest friend in the whole world, who has had such a difficult year, but throughout, she's been the bravest and the strongest person I've ever met. She's an inspiration to us all. Here's to her finding happiness for the next thirty years. To Holly!"

"To Holly," they all chorused. The girls' eyes were sparkling with tears as they took a sip of their drink except, of course, for Ciara, who had knocked back her glass of champagne.

"Okay," said Ciara. "First you have to wear this tiara because you are our princess for the night, and second here's my present!"

The girls helped Holly put on the sparkling tiara that went perfectly with her black glittery corset. She carefully removed the tape from the parcel and looked inside the box. "What is it?"

"Read it!" Ciara said excitedly.

Holly read out loud from the box: "It's a 'battery-operated' . . . Ciara, you naughty girl!" The girls laughed hysterically.

Declan looked like he was about to throw up.

Holly gave her sister a hug.

"Okay, me next," Abbey said, putting her parcel on Holly's lap.

Holly opened Abbey's present. "Oh, Abbey, it's beautiful!" She held up the sterling silver–covered photo album.

"For your new memories," Abbey said softly.

"It's perfect," Holly said, wrapping her arms around Abbey and squeezing her. "Thank you."

"Mine is less sentimental." Denise handed her an envelope.

"Oh, brilliant!" Holly exclaimed as she opened it. "A weekend of pampering in Haven's health-and-beauty clinic! Oh, Denise, thank you!" Holly winked at Sharon. "Okay, last but not least."

It was a large silver frame with a photograph of Sharon, Denise, and Holly at the Christmas Ball two years ago.

"I'm wearing my 'spensive white dress!" That had been the last ball she and Gerry had been to. "This will take pride of place," she announced, placing it beside her wedding photo on the mantel.

"Okay, girls," yelled Ciara. "Let's get some serious drinking done!"

Two bottles of champagne and several bottles of red wine later, the girls stumbled out of the house and piled into a taxi. Holly insisted on sitting in the passenger seat and having a heart-to-heart with John, the driver, who probably wanted to kill her by the time they reached town.

"Bye, John!" they all shouted to their new best friend before falling out onto the curb in Dublin city. They had decided to chance their luck in Dublin's most stylish club, Boudoir.

The club was reserved for the rich and famous only, and it was a well-known fact that if you weren't rich and famous, you had to have a member's card to be granted access. Denise walked up to the door, coolly waving her video-store membership card in the bouncers' faces. Believe it or not, they stopped her.

The only famous faces they saw overtaking them to get into the club as they fought with the bouncers to get in were a few newsreaders from the national TV station, whom Denise smiled at, and she hilariously kept repeating, "Good evening," very seriously to their faces. Unfortunately, after that, Holly remembered no more.

HOLLY AWOKE WITH HER head pounding. Her mouth was as dry as Gandhi's sandal. She leaned up on one elbow and tried to open her eyes, which were somehow glued together. The room was bright, very bright, and it seemed to be spinning. Holly caught sight of herself in the mirror ahead and startled herself. Had she been in an accident last night? She collapsed flat on her back again. Suddenly the house alarm began wailing. Oh, take whatever you want, she thought. Just bring me a glass of water. After a while, she realized it wasn't the alarm but the phone ringing beside her bed.

"Hello?" she croaked.

"Good, I'm not the only one," said a desperately ill voice.

"Who are you?" croaked Holly again.

"My name is Sharon, I think. The man beside me in bed seems to think I know him." Holly heard John laughing loudly.

"Sharon, what happened last night? Please enlighten me."

"Alcohol happened last night—lots and lots of alcohol."

"Any other information?"

"Nope," Sharon said drowsily.

"Know what time it is?"

"Two o'clock. It's afternoon, Holly."

"Oh. How did that happen?"

"Gravity or something. I was out that day in school."

"I think I'll go back to sleep. Maybe when I wake up, the ground will have stopped moving."

"Good idea. Oh, and Holly, welcome to the thirties club."

Holly groaned, "Night."

Seconds later, she was asleep. She awoke at various stages to answer the phone, conversations that seemed part of her dreams.

Eventually, at nine o'clock that night, she decided to treat herself to Chinese takeaway. She sat snuggled up on the couch in her pajamas, watching TV while stuffing her face. After the trauma of being without Gerry for her birthday the previous day, Holly was surprised to notice that she felt very content with herself. It was the first time since Gerry had died that she was at ease with her own company. There was a slight chance she could make it without him.

Later that night, Jack called. "Hey, sis, what are you doing?"

"Watching TV, having Chinese," she said.

"Well, you sound in good form. Unlike my poor girlfriend."

"I'm never going out with you again, Holly," she heard Abbey scream in the background.

"She says she can't remember anything."

"Neither can I. Maybe it happens as soon as you hit thirty."

"Or maybe it's just an evil plan you all hatched, so you wouldn't have to tell us what you got up to." He laughed. "Anyway, I was ringing to ask if you're going to Declan's gig tomorrow night."

"Where is it?"

"Hogan's pub."

"No way. There is no way I'm ever setting foot in a pub again, especially to listen to some loud rock band."

"Well, don't drink, then. Please come, Holly. We hardly got a chance to talk at dinner."

"Well, we're hardly going to have a heart-to-heart with the Orgasmic Fish banging out their tunes," she said sarcastically.

"They're actually called Black Strawberries now, which has a nice sweet ring to it, I think," he laughed.

Holly groaned, "Oh, please don't make me go, Jack."

"You're going. Declan will be chuffed when I tell him. The family never usually goes to these things."

WHEN Holly arrived at Hogan's pub the next evening, the place was jammed. Situated in the center of town, Hogan's was a popular three-story club. The second floor was a trendy nightclub where the young, beautiful people went. The first floor was a traditional Irish pub for the older crowd. The basement was dark and dingy and was where bands usually played.

Holly was finding it difficult to breathe in the stuffy, smoky basement. The tiny bar in the corner was surrounded by a huge crowd of young students in scruffy jeans. She waved at Declan to let him know she was there, but decided not to make her way over, as he was surrounded by a crowd of girls. She wouldn't want to cramp his style. Holly had missed out on the whole student scene, having decided not to go to college and instead working as a secretary. Gerry had studied marketing at Dublin City University, but he never socialized much with his college friends.

Finally Declan made his way over.

"Well, hello, Mr. Popular. I feel privileged you chose to speak to me," Holly said.

Declan rubbed his hands together. "This band business is great! Looks like I'll be getting a bit of action tonight," he said cheekily.

"As your sister, it's always a pleasure to be informed of that," Holly replied sarcastically. She found it impossible to maintain a conversation with Declan, as he refused eye contact with her and instead scoured the crowds.

"Okay, Declan, just go flirt with these beauties. Why be stuck here with your old sister."

"Oh, no. It's not that," he said. "We were told there might be a record company guy coming to see us tonight."

"Oh, cool!" Holly's eyes widened with excitement. She looked around and tried to spot someone who looked like a record company guy. Her eyes fell upon a man who seemed older than the rest of the crowd, more her own age. He wore a black leather jacket, black slacks, and a black T-shirt and stood staring at the stage. Yes, he was definitely a record company guy, as he had stubble all around his jaw.

"Over there, Deco!" Holly pointed at the man. Declan's smile faded. "No, it's just Danny," he yelled, and then wolf-whistled to grab the man's attention.

Danny twirled around and made his way over. "Hey, man," Declan said, shaking his hand.

"Hi, Declan. How are you set?" The man looked stressed.

"Yeah, okay," Declan nodded.

"Sound check go okay?"

"There were a few problems, but we sorted them out."

"Good." Daniel turned to greet Holly. "Sorry for ignoring you there. I'm Daniel."

"Nice to meet you. I'm Holly—"

"Oh, sorry," Declan interrupted. "Holly, this is the owner; Daniel, this is my sister."

"Hey, Deco, we're on," yelled a blue-haired boy.

"See you two later," and Declan ran off.

"Good luck!" yelled Holly. "So you're a Hogan," she said, turning to face Daniel.

"Well, no. Actually, I'm a Connelly," Daniel smiled. "I just took over the place a few weeks ago."

"Oh." Holly was surprised. "I didn't know they sold the place. So are you going to change it to Connelly's, then?"

"Can't afford all the lettering on the front. It's a bit long."

Holly laughed. "Well, everyone knows the name Hogan's; it would probably be stupid to change it."

Daniel agreed. "That was the main reason, actually."

Suddenly Jack appeared at the entrance, and Holly waved him over. "I'm so sorry I'm late," he said, giving her a hug.

"He's about to go on. Jack, this is Daniel, the owner."

"Nice to meet you," Daniel said, shaking his hand.

"Are they any good?" Jack asked him, nodding at the stage.

"To tell you the truth, I've never even heard them play."

"That was brave of you," laughed Jack.

"I hope not too brave," Daniel said as the boys took to the stage.

The crowd cheered, and Declan took on his moody persona as he lifted his guitar strap over his shoulder. The music started, and after that, there was no chance of carrying on any kind of conversation. The crowd began to jump up and down, and once too often, Holly's foot was stomped on. Daniel battled through the crowd and climbed behind the bar. He returned minutes later with drinks and a stool for Holly. The music wasn't Holly's type of thing, and it was so loud, it was difficult for her to tell if the Black Strawberries were actually any good. The name said it all, though, really.

After four songs, Holly had had enough, and she gave Jack a kiss good-bye. "Nice meeting you, Daniel!" she screamed, and made her way back to civilization. Her ears continued to ring all the way home in the car. It was ten o'clock by the time she got there. Only two more hours till May. And that meant another envelope.

HOLLY sat at her kitchen table nervously drumming her fingers on the wood. Staying awake for two more hours had proved more difficult than she thought; she was obviously still tired from overindulging at her party. It was eleven-thirty p.m. She had the envelope on the table in front of her, and she could almost see it sticking its tongue out and singing, *"Na-na na-na-na."*

Each time Holly opened an envelope, she felt a connection with Gerry. She felt as though he were sitting right beside her and laughing at her reactions. She felt as though they were playing a game together, even though they were in two different worlds.

The small hand of the clock eventually struck midnight. Once again, she treasured every moment of the process. She carefully tore open the seal, slid the card out, and opened it.

> Go on, Disco Diva! Face your fear of karaoke at Club Diva this month, and you never know, you might be rewarded.
> PS, I love you . . .

She felt Gerry watching her, and the corners of her lips lifted into a smile, and she began to laugh. She kept repeating, "No way!" whenever she caught her breath. Finally she calmed down. "Gerry, you bastard! There is no way I am going through with this!"

Gerry laughed louder.

"This is not funny! You know how I feel about this, and I refuse to do it. No way. Not doing it. I hate karaoke!"

"You have to do it, you know," laughed Gerry. "Do it for me."

The sound of the phone caused Holly to jump in her seat. It was Sharon. "Okay, it's five past twelve. What did it say?"

"What makes you think I opened it?"

"Ha!" Sharon snorted. "Twenty years of friendship qualifies me as being an expert on you. Now come on, tell me."

"I'm not doing what he wants me to do," Holly stated bluntly.

"Why? What is it?" John said from their downstairs phone.

"Gerry wants me to sing karaoke at Club Diva. I don't even know where that is."

The other two burst out laughing so loud, Holly had to remove the phone from her ear. "Phone me back when the two of you shut up," she said angrily, hanging up.

A few minutes later, they called back.

"Okay." Sharon had an overly serious "let's get down to business" tone in her voice. "I'm fine now. Don't look at me, John," she said away from the phone. "Holly, I'm sorry, but I just kept thinking about the last time you—"

"Yeah, yeah, yeah," Holly interrupted. "You don't need to bring it up. It was the most embarrassing day of my life."

"Oh, Holly, you can't let a stupid thing like that put you off. It was only a little fall . . ."

"Yes, thank you! I remember it just fine! Anyway, I can't even sing, Sharon. I think I established that fact the last time."

Sharon was very quiet.

"Sharon, are you still there?"

There was no answer.

"Sharon, are you laughing?" Holly gave out.

She heard a little squeak, and the line went dead.

"HAPPY birthday, Holly! Or should I say, Happy belated birthday?" Richard laughed nervously. Holly's mouth dropped open in shock at the sight of her older brother standing on her doorstep. This was a rare occurrence; in fact, it may have been a first. "I brought you a potted mini phalaenopsis orchid," he said, handing her a potted plant. "Shipped fresh and ready to bloom."

Holly fingered the tiny pink buds. "Gosh, Richard. Orchids are my favorite!"

"Well, you have a nice big garden here anyway, nice and"—he cleared his throat—"green. Bit overgrown, though."

"Would you like to come in, or are you just passing through?" *Please say no, please say no.* Despite the thoughtful gift, Holly was in no mood for Richard's company.

"Well, yes, I'll come in for a little while." He wiped his feet for a good two minutes at the door. He reminded Holly of her old math teacher at school, dressed in a brown cardigan, with brown trousers that stopped just at the top of his neat brown loafers.

Richard never seemed comfortable in his own skin. He looked as if he were being choked to death by his tie, and his smile never seemed to reach his eyes. He was the drill sergeant of his own body, punishing himself every time he lapsed into human mode. And the sad thing was that he thought he was the better for it. Holly led him into the living room and placed the ceramic pot on the TV.

"No, no, Holly," he said, wagging a finger. "It needs to be in a cool, draft-free location, away from sunlight and heat vents."

"Oh, of course." Holly searched around the room in panic.

"That little table in the center—it should be safe there."

Holly placed the pot on the table. "Can I get you a tea or coffee?" she asked, expecting him to say no.

"Yes, great," he said, clapping his hands together. "Tea would be splendid. Just milk, no sugar."

Holly returned with two mugs of tea and placed them down on the coffee table. She hoped the steam rising from the mugs wouldn't murder the poor plant.

"You just need to water it regularly and feed it during the months of spring." He was still talking about the plant. Holly nodded, knowing full well she would not do either of those things.

"I didn't know you had green fingers, Richard. Do you do much work in your garden?"

"Oh, yes. I love to work in the garden," he said, smiling.

Holly felt as though a stranger were sitting beside her. She realized she knew very little about Richard and he equally knew little about her. But that was the way Richard had always liked to keep things. He never shared exciting news with the family or told them how his day went. He was just full of facts, facts, and more facts.

"So," she announced, far too loudly for the echoing room, "anything strange or startling?" *Like, why are you here?*

"No, no, nothing strange. Everything is ticking over as normal."

He took a sip of tea, then a while later added, "I just thought I would pop in and say hello while I was in the area."

Holly forced a smile. "How are Emily and Timmy?"

His eyes lit up. "They're good, Holly. Worrying, though."

"What do you mean?"

"Oh, there isn't one thing in particular. Children are a worry, in general." He looked her in the eye. "But I suppose you're glad you'll never have to worry about this children nonsense."

There was a silence. Holly sat frozen on her chair; she couldn't believe he had the audacity to say that to her.

"So have you found a job yet?" he continued on.

"No," she spat out.

"What are you doing for money? Have you signed on the dole?"

"No, Richard," she said. "I get *widow's* allowance."

"Ah, that's a great, handy thing, isn't it?"

"Devastatingly depressing is more like it."

The atmosphere was tense. Suddenly he slapped his leg with his hand. "I better get back to work," he announced, standing up. "Anyway, nice to see you, and thank you for the tea."

"You're welcome, and thank you for the orchid," Holly said through gritted teeth. He marched down the path to his car.

Holly fumed as she watched him drive off. That man made her blood boil. He hadn't a clue about anything.

HOLLY woke up the next morning still fully dressed and lying on her bed. She could feel herself slipping into her old habits again. All her positive thoughts of the past few weeks were melting away. It was so bloody tiring trying to be happy all the time, and she just didn't have the energy. Who cared if the house was a mess? Who cared if she didn't wash for a week? Who bloody cared? Her phone vibrated beside her, signaling a message. It was from Sharon.

CLUB DIVA PHONE NO. 36700700
THINK BOUT IT. KARAOKE WUD B FUN.
DO IT 4 GERRY?

Gerry's bloody dead, she felt like texting back. But ever since she had begun opening the envelopes, he didn't feel dead to her. It was as though he were just away on holiday. Well, the very least she could do was ring the club and suss out the situation.

She dialed the number, and a man answered. She couldn't think of anything to say, so she quickly hung up. Oh, come on, Holly, she told herself. It's really not that difficult.

Holly pressed REDIAL. The same voice answered, "Club Diva."

"Hi. I was wondering if you do karaoke nights there?"

"Yes, we do. They are on a Tuesday night."

"Okay, em, well, I was wondering if, em . . ." Holly took a deep breath. "My friend might be interested in singing."

"What's your friend's name?"

Holly froze. "Em, her name is Holly Kennedy."

"Well, it's actually a karaoke competition on Tuesday nights. Every week, two people out of ten are chosen till the six people sing in the final. But unfortunately, the names have all been entered in advance. Your friend could try again at Christmas."

"Oh, okay."

"By the way, the name Holly Kennedy rings a bell. Would that be Declan Kennedy's sister?"

"Eh, yeah. Do you know her?" said a shocked Holly.

"I met her here the other night with her brother."

Was Declan going around introducing girls as his sister? The sick and twisted little . . . No, that couldn't be right.

"Declan played a gig in Club Diva?"

"No, no. He played with his band in the basement."

"Is Club Diva in Hogan's?"

"On the top floor. Maybe I should advertise a bit more!"

"Is that Daniel?" Holly blurted out, and then kicked herself.

"Eh, yeah. Do I know you?"

"Em, no! Holly just mentioned you in conversation, that's all." Then she realized how that sounded. "Very briefly. She said you gave her a stool." Holly began hitting her head softly on the wall.

Daniel laughed. "Oh, okay. Well, tell her if she wants to sing at

Christmas, I can put her name down now. You wouldn't believe the amount of people that want to sign up."

"Really," Holly said weakly. She felt like a fool.

"Oh, by the way, who am I speaking to?"

Holly paced her bedroom floor. "Em, you're speaking to Sharon."

"Okay, Sharon. Well, I have your number on caller ID, so I'll call you if anyone backs out."

"Okay, thanks a lot."

He hung up.

Holly leaped into bed, throwing the duvet over her head as she felt her face going purple with embarrassment. Ignoring the ringing phone, she hid under the covers, cursing herself for being such a bimbo. Eventually she crawled out of bed and hit the button on her answering machine.

"Hi, Sharon. I must have just missed you. It's Daniel here, from Club Diva." He paused. "I was just looking through the list, and it seems somebody entered Holly's name a few months back, unless it's another Holly Kennedy. Anyway, call me back so we can sort it out. Thanks."

Holly sat shocked on the edge of her bed.

Four

SHARON and Holly met up with Denise on her lunch break in Bewley's Café, overlooking Grafton Street. They often met up there to watch the world go by. Sharon always said it was the best window-shopping she could ever do, as she had a bird's-eye view of all her favorite stores.

"I can't believe Gerry organized all this!" gasped Denise when she heard the news. She flicked her long brown hair behind her shoulders, and her bright blue eyes sparkled enthusiastically.

"It'll be a bit of fun, won't it?" Sharon said excitedly.

"Oh, God." Holly had butterflies in her stomach just over the thought of it. "I still really, really don't want to do it, but I feel I have to finish off what Gerry started."

"That's the spirit, Hol," said Denise. "What are you planning on singing?"

"I have no idea. That's why I called this emergency meeting."

"Okay, well, what CD are you listening to at the moment?" Denise asked.

"Westlife?" she looked at them hopefully.

"Then sing a Westlife song," Sharon encouraged. "That way, at least you'll know all the words."

Sharon and Denise began to laugh uncontrollably. "You might not get the tune right," Sharon forced out between hacking laughs.

"But at least you'll know the words!" Denise managed to finish for her before the two of them doubled over at the table.

First Holly was angry, but looking at the both of them crouched over, holding their stomachs in hysterics, she had to giggle. They were right: Holly was completely tone-deaf and hadn't a note in her head. Finding a song she could actually sing was going to prove impossible. Finally Denise looked at her watch and moaned about having to get back to work.

The three girls left Bewley's and walked toward the clothes store where Denise was manager. Grafton Street was busy, as usual. At every stretch of the road, there was a busker fighting for attention from the crowds, and Denise and Sharon embarrassingly did a quick Irish dance as they passed a man playing the fiddle. He winked at them, and they threw some money into his tweed cap.

"Right, you ladies of leisure, I better head back to work," Denise said, pushing the door to her shop open. As soon as her staff saw her, they scarpered from gossiping at the counter and immediately began to fix the clothes rails. Holly and Sharon tried not to laugh. They said their good-byes and went to collect their cars.

It was four o'clock by the time Holly got out of town and started home. Evil Sharon had convinced her to go shopping, which resulted in her splashing out on a ridiculous top she was far too old to wear. She really needed to watch her spending from now on; her funds were running low, and just the thought of looking for a job was depressing. She phoned her mum and checked if it was all right for her to call around.

"Of course you can, love"—Elizabeth lowered her voice—"as long as you know that Richard is here." What was with all the little visits?

Holly contemplated heading straight home, but he was her brother. As annoying as he was, she couldn't avoid him forever.

She arrived to a loud and crowded house, and it felt like old times again. Her mum was setting an extra place at the table just as she walked in. "Oh, Mum, I hope you didn't go to too much trouble."

"No trouble at all, dear. It just means that poor Declan will have to go without food for the day, that's all," she said, teasing her son, who was taking his seat. He made a face at her.

"So, Mr. Hard Worker, why aren't you in college?" Holly said.

"I've been in college all morning," Declan replied, "and I'm going back in at eight o'clock, actually."

"That's very late," said her father, pouring gravy on his plate.

"Yeah, but it was the only time to book the editing suite."

"Is there only one editing suite, Declan?" piped up Richard.

"Yeah." Ever the conversationalist.

"Don't they have the funds for another editing suite?"

"No. It's only a small college, Richard."

"I suppose the bigger universities would be better equipped. They're better all-round."

And there was the dig they were all waiting for.

"No, I wouldn't say that. The facilities are top of the range. And the lecturers work in the industry. It's not just textbook stuff."

Good for you, Declan, Holly thought.

"What's your project on, Declan?" Frank asked.

"It's too messy to go into, but basically, it's on club life in Dublin."

"Ooh, will we be in it?" Ciara asked excitedly.

"I might show the back of your head or something," he joked.

"Well, I can't wait to see it," Holly said encouragingly.

"Thanks." Declan put his fork down and started laughing. "Hey, what's this I hear about you singing in a karaoke competition?"

"What?" Ciara's eyes nearly popped out of her head.

Holly pretended not to know what he was talking about.

"Ah, come on. Danny told me." Declan turned to the rest of the table. "Danny owns the place I did the gig the other night, and he told me Holly entered a karaoke competition in the club upstairs."

Everyone oohed and aahed about how great it was. Holly refused to give in. "Declan, Daniel's just playing games with you. Everyone knows I can't sing!" She laughed as if the thought were ridiculous.

Declan persisted. "I saw your name on the list! Don't lie!"

She might as well tell them. "It's a complicated story, but basically, Gerry entered my name in months ago because he really wanted me to do it, and I feel I have to go through with it."

Her family stared at her.

"Well, I think that's a wonderful idea," her dad announced.

"Yes," added her mum, "and we'll all be there to support you."

"No, Mum. You really don't have to. It's no big deal."

"There's no way my sister is singing in a competition without me being there," declared Ciara.

"Hear, hear," said Richard. "We'll all go. I've never been to a karaoke. It should be fun. When is it on?" He took out his diary.

"Eh, Saturday," Holly said. Richard began writing it down.

"It is not," Declan burst out. "It's next Tuesday, you liar!"

"Damn!" cursed Richard, much to everyone's surprise. "Has anyone got any Tipp-Ex?"

HOLLY could not stop going to the toilet. She had gotten practically no sleep, and she looked just the way she felt. There were huge bags under her eyes, and her lips were bitten. The big day had arrived—her worst nightmare, singing in public.

Her friends and family had been as supportive as ever, sending her good-luck cards. Sharon and John had even sent her a bouquet of flowers, which she placed on the draft-free, heat-vent-free coffee table beside her half-dead orchid.

Holly dressed in the outfit Gerry had told her to buy in April and cursed him all throughout. She left her hair down so it could cover her face as much as possible, and piled on the waterproof mascara, since she could foresee the night ending in tears.

John and Sharon collected her in the taxi, and she refused to talk to them, cursing everyone for forcing her to do this. She couldn't sit still. She kept opening and closing her bag to keep herself occupied.

"Relax, Holly," Sharon said. "Everything will be fine."

"Bug off," she snapped.

They finally reached Hogan's, and much to her horror, the club was absolutely jammed. Her family had saved a table beside the toilet, as requested.

Richard was sitting awkwardly on a stool, looking out of place in a suit. "So tell me about these rules, Father. What will Holly have to do?" Frank explained, and her nerves began to build even more.

"Gosh, that's terrific," Richard said, staring around in awe. Holly didn't think he'd ever been in a nightclub before.

The sight of the stage terrified Holly; it was much bigger than she had expected. Jack was sitting with his arm around Abbey's shoulders; they both gave her a supportive smile. Holly scowled at them.

"Hi, Holly," Daniel said, approaching her with a clipboard. "First up is Margaret, then Keith, and then you're up, okay?"

"So I'm third."

"Yeah, after—"

"That's all I need to know," Holly snapped rudely. She wished that everyone would leave her alone, but Daniel was still talking.

"Look, Holly, I'm really sorry to disturb you again, but could you tell me which of your friends is Sharon?"

"Over there." Holly pointed to Sharon. "Hold on, why?"

"I just wanted to meet her in person. We spoke on the phone." He headed over to Sharon, and Holly leaped from her stool.

"Sharon, hi. I'm Daniel. We spoke on the phone."

"On the phone? What's your name again?"

"Em, it's Daniel."

Holly gestured wildly to her behind Daniel's back. He cleared his throat nervously. "Yes. You called the club?"

"No, sweetie. You've got the wrong girl," Sharon said.

Daniel appeared confused. Holly nodded her head frantically.

"Oh . . ." Sharon said. "Oh, Daniel! God, I am so sorry. My brain cells seem to be going a bit dead. Must be too much of this," she laughed, picking up her drink.

Relief washed over Daniel's face. "Okay then, well, it's nice to finally meet you in person," he said, and walked away.

"What was that all about?" Sharon asked Holly as soon as he was out of earshot.

"I'll explain it to you later," said Holly as their karaoke host for the evening was just stepping up onstage.

"Good evening, ladies and gentlemen," he announced in his DJ voice. "We have an exciting night ahead of us. First up, we have Margaret from Tallaght to sing the theme to *Titanic*, 'My Heart Will Go On,' by Celine Dion. Please put your hands together for Margaret!" The crowd went wild. Holly's heart raced.

When Margaret began to sing, the room became so quiet, you could almost hear a pin drop. Holly watched everyone's faces. They were all staring at Margaret in amazement, including Holly's family, the traitors. Margaret's eyes were closed, and she sang with such passion, it seemed she had lived every line of the song.

"Wasn't that incredible?" the DJ announced. The crowd cheered again. "Next up, we have Keith—last year's winner—and he's singing 'America,' by Neil Diamond. Give it up for Keith!"

Holly didn't need to hear any more and rushed into the toilet.

She paced up and down, trying to calm herself. Her knees were knocking; her stomach was twisted in knots. She looked at herself in the mirror and tried to take big deep breaths. The crowd applauded outside, and Holly froze. She was next.

"Wasn't Keith terrific, ladies and gentlemen?"

Lots of cheers again.

"Well, it doesn't get any better than that! Next we have a newcomer. Her name is Holly. . . ."

Holly ran to the cubicle and locked herself in. There was no way in this world they were getting her out of there.

"Holly Kennedy, are you here?" the karaoke host's voice boomed. The applause died down as everyone looked around in search of Holly. Well, they would be a long time looking, she thought. She closed her eyes and prayed for this moment to pass.

Outside, the club sounded quiet. A sense of calm engulfed her as she realized they were moving on to the next singer. Her shoulders relaxed. The panic was over, but she decided to wait until the song began before she made a run for it.

Outside the cubicle, Holly heard the toilet door open and slam.

"Holly?" It was Sharon. "I know you're there, so just listen, okay?"

Holly sniffed back the tears that were beginning to well.

"I know that this is an absolute nightmare for you, but you need to relax, okay?" Sharon paused.

"What?" the DJ's voice said into the microphone. "Ladies and gentlemen, it appears that our singer is currently in the toilets." The entire room erupted in laughter.

"Sharon!" Holly's voice trembled in fear.

"Holly, you don't have to do this. Nobody is forcing you . . ."

"Ladies and gentlemen, let's let Holly know that she's up next," yelled the DJ. Everybody began to chant her name.

"But if you don't do this, I know you'll never forgive yourself. Gerry wanted you to do this for a reason."

"HOLLY! HOLLY! HOLLY!"

"Oh, Sharon," Holly repeated again, panicking. Suddenly the walls of the cubicle felt like they were closing in on her; beads of sweat formed on her forehead. She burst through the door, her eyes red and puffy, black lines of mascara streaming down her face.

"I can't sing, Sharon," Holly whispered.

"I know that! Screw them! You're never gonna see their ugly mugs ever again. Who cares what they think? I don't. Do you?"

Holly thought about it for a minute. "No," she whispered.

"What? I didn't hear you. Do you care what they think?"

"No," she said, a little stronger.

"Louder!" Sharon shook her by the shoulders.

"No!" she yelled.

"Louder!"

"NOOOOOOOOO! I DON'T CARE WHAT THEY THINK!" Holly screamed. The two of them began to giggle.

"Just let this be another silly Holly day so we can laugh about it a few months from now," Sharon pleaded.

Holly washed away her smudged mascara lines, took a deep breath, and charged toward the door like a woman on a mission. She opened the door to her adoring fans, who were all chanting her name. She took an extremely theatrical bow and headed to the stage to the sound of claps and laughter.

Holly had everybody's attention now whether she liked it or not. She stood with her arms folded and stared at the audience. The music started, and her whole table held their thumbs up. It was corny but strangely comforting. Holding the microphone tightly, with an extremely shaky and timid voice, she sang, *"What would you do if I sang out of tune? Would you stand up and walk out on me?"*

Denise and Sharon howled with laughter at the wonderful choice of song and gave her a big cheer. Holly struggled on, singing dreadfully, looking like she was about to burst into tears. Just when she felt she was about to hear boos, her family and friends joined in with the chorus. *"Ooh, I'll get by with a little help from my friends; yes, I'll get by with a little help from my friends."*

The crowd laughed, and the atmosphere warmed a little more. Holly prepared herself for the high note coming up and yelled at the top of her lungs, *"Do you neeeed anybody?"* A few people helped her out to sing, *"I need somebody to love."*

"Do you neeeed anybody?" she repeated, and held the microphone out to the crowd, and they all sang. She felt less nervous now and battled her way through the rest of the song. The people down the back continued on chatting; the bar staff carried on serving drinks. When she had finally finished singing, a few polite tables up front and her own table were the only people to acknowledge her. The DJ took the microphone and managed to say between

laughs, "Please give it up for the incredibly brave Holly Kennedy!"

Her family and friends cheered. Denise and Sharon approached her with cheeks wet from tears of laughter.

"I'm so proud of you," Sharon said, throwing her arms around Holly's neck. "It was awful!"

"Thanks for helping me, Sharon." Holly hugged her friend.

Abbey cheered. Jack shouted, "Terrible! Absolutely terrible!" Holly's mother smiled, and Holly's father could barely look her in the eye, he was laughing so much.

Declan waved at her from across the room and gave her the thumbs-down. Holly hid at the table and sipped on her water while she listened to everyone congratulating her on being so desperately bad. She couldn't remember the last time she had felt so proud.

John shuffled over and leaned against the wall beside her. He said, "Gerry's probably here, you know," and looked at her with watery eyes.

Poor John. He missed his best friend too. She gave him an encouraging smile. He was right. Holly could feel Gerry's presence. She could feel him wrapping his arms around her and giving her one of the hugs she missed so much.

After an hour, the singers had finally finished, and Daniel and the DJ headed off to tot up the voting slips. The DJ played a pathetic CD of a drumroll as Daniel took to the stage in his black leather jacket and was greeted by wolf whistles and screams from the girls. Richard looked excited and crossed his fingers at Holly.

"Okay, so the two people that will be going through to the final are"—Daniel paused for dramatic effect—"Keith and Samantha!"

Holly jumped up and danced around in a huddle with Denise and Sharon. Richard looked on, confused, and the rest of Holly's family congratulated her on her victorious loss.

Holly sat back down and sipped her drink thoughtfully. Sharon and John seemed engrossed in a heated discussion; Abbey and Jack were like love-struck teenagers, as usual; Ciara was snuggling up to Daniel; and Denise was . . . Where was Denise?

Holly looked around the club and spotted her sitting on the

stage, striking a very provocative pose for the karaoke host. Holly's parents had gone home, which left . . . Richard. Richard sat looking like a lost puppy, taking a sip from his drink every few seconds.

Holly moved over and sat opposite him. "Enjoying yourself?"

He looked up. "Yes, thank you, I'm having fun, Holly."

"I'm surprised you came, actually. I didn't think this would be your scene."

"Oh, you know, you have to support the family."

"So where's Meredith tonight?"

"Emily and Timothy," he said, as if that explained it all.

"You working tomorrow?"

"Yes," he said suddenly, knocking back his drink, "so I best be off. You were a great sport tonight, Holly." He looked around awkwardly at his family, debating whether to interrupt them and say good-bye, but eventually he went off through the thick crowd.

Holly was alone again. As much as she wanted to grab her bag and run home, she knew she should sit this one out. There would be plenty of times when she would be the only singleton in the company of couples, and she needed to adapt. Just sit it out, she told herself.

Holly smiled as she watched her sister nattering away to Daniel. Ciara was nothing like her; she was so carefree. Ciara had never managed to hold down a job or a boyfriend; her brain was always somewhere else, lost in the dream of visiting another far-off country. Holly turned her attention to Jack, still lost in a world with Abbey. She wished she could be more like him, the cool teacher all the teenagers respected. Holly sighed and drained her drink.

Daniel looked over. "Holly, can I get you another drink?"

"No thanks, Daniel. I'm heading home soon anyway."

"Ah, Hol," protested Ciara. "It's so early! You're staying. Get her a vodka and Coke," she ordered Daniel, "and I'll have the same."

"Ciara!" Holly exclaimed, embarrassed at her sister's rudeness.

"No, it's okay. I asked," Daniel said, and headed off to the bar.

"Ciara, that was so rude," Holly gave out to her sister.

"What? It's not like he has to pay for it. He owns the bloody place," she said defensively. "Where's Richard?"

"Gone home."

"No! He's supposed to be driving me home!" Ciara threw everyone's coats into a pile while she rooted around for her bag.

"Ciara, you'll never catch him. He's gone far too long."

"No, I will. He's parked ages away. I'll get him while he's passing." She found her bag and legged it out the door, yelling, "Bye, Holly. Well done!"

Daniel returned with the drinks and sat down opposite Holly. "Where's Ciara gone?" he asked.

"Oh, she's really sorry, but she had to chase my brother for a lift." Holly started laughing. "You must think we're the rudest family in the world. Ciara's a bit of a motormouth; she doesn't mean what she says half the time."

"Hey, it's fine. Just means there's more drink for you." He stared past her shoulder with amusement. "Well, it looks like your friend is having a good night."

Holly swirled around and saw Denise and the DJ wrapped around each other. Her provocative poses had obviously worked.

"Oh, no. Not the horrible DJ who forced me to come out of the toilet," Holly groaned.

"That's my friend Tom O'Connor from Dublin FM. The karaoke went out live on the radio tonight," he said seriously.

"What?"

Daniel's face broke into a smile. "Only joking. Just wanted to see the look on your face."

"Don't do that to me," Holly said, putting her hand on her heart. "Having the people in here hear me was bad enough, never mind the entire city as well."

"If you don't mind me asking, if you hate it so much, why did you enter?" Daniel asked.

"Oh, my hilarious husband thought it would be funny to enter his tone-deaf wife into a singing competition."

Daniel laughed. "You weren't *that* bad! Is your husband here?" he asked, looking around.

Holly smiled. "Yeah, he's definitely here . . . somewhere."

Five

HOLLY secured her bedsheet onto the washing line with a peg and thought about how she had bumbled around for the remainder of May trying to get her life into some sort of order. Days went by when she felt confident that her life would be okay, and then the feeling would disappear, and she would feel her sadness setting in once more. She found herself immobile for hours in the sitting room, reliving every memory that she and Gerry had shared, every argument they had had, wishing she could take them back. She tortured herself for when she held grudges instead of forgiving him or when she went straight to sleep some nights instead of making love to him. The bad times had all been such a waste of time.

Then there were days when she would walk around in a daydream with nothing but a smile on her face, catching herself giggling when a joke of theirs would suddenly pop into her head. That was her routine. She would fall into days of depression, then finally build up the strength to snap out of it until the tiniest thing would trigger her tears again. It was a tiring process.

She read Gerry's original letter over and over, trying to read between the lines and guess the hidden message. The fact was that she would never really know exactly what he meant, because she would never speak to him ever again. It was this thought that she had the most difficulty trying to come to terms with, and it was killing her.

Now May had gone and June had arrived, bringing bright, long evenings and beautiful mornings. It seemed as though the whole of Ireland had come out of hibernation. It was time to get up early with the songbirds, time to stop hiding in the dark.

June brought another letter from Gerry.

Holly had sat out in the sun, reveling in the new brightness of life, and read the fourth letter. Gerry had listed the items in the house that belonged to him and explained what he wanted Holly to do with each of his possessions. At the bottom, it read:

> PS, I love you, Holly, and I know you love me. You don't need my belongings to remember me by. You don't need to keep them as proof that I existed or still exist in your mind. You don't need to wear my sweater to feel me around you. I'm always wrapping my arms around you.

Holly almost wished he would ask her to do karaoke again. She would have jumped from an airplane, run a thousand miles—anything except empty his wardrobes and rid herself of his presence. But he was right, and she knew it. The physical Gerry was gone.

It was an emotionally draining experience. It took her days to complete. She relived a million memories with every garment and piece of paper. Every time an item left her fingers, it was like saying good-bye to a part of Gerry all over again. It was so very difficult.

Despite her wishes to do this alone, Jack had called round and she had appreciated it. He was there for her when she cried, and he was there when she finally clapped her hands together, ridding her skin of the dust that remained.

So many objects, so many memories: Gerry's wedding tuxedo, his suits, shirts, and ties that he would moan about having to wear to work. The fashions of the years gone by—'80s shiny suits and shell tracksuits bundled away. A snorkel from their first time scuba diving, a shell that he picked from the ocean floor ten years ago, his collection of beer mats from every pub in every country they had visited. Valentine's Day cards from Holly. His golf clubs for John; books for Sharon; memories, tears, and laughter for Holly.

His entire life bundled into twenty refuse sacks.

His and her memories bundled away into Holly's mind.

Each item unearthed dust, tears, laughter, and memories. She bagged the items, cleared the dust, wiped her eyes, and filed away the memories.

HOLLY'S MOBILE BEGAN TO ring, and she ran to the kitchen to answer the phone. "Hello?"

"I'm gonna make you a star!" Declan's voice screeched hysterically, and he broke into uncontrollable laughter.

Holly searched her brain to figure out what he could be talking about. "Declan, are you drunk?"

"Maybe jus a li'l bit, but that's completely irrevelant."

"Declan, it's ten o'clock in the morning!" Holly laughed. "Have you been to bed yet?"

"Nope. I'm on the train home now. I'm in Galway. The 'wards were on last night."

"Oh, sorry for my ignorance, but what awards were you at?"

"The student media 'wards, and I won!" he yelled, and Holly heard what sounded like the entire carriage celebrating with him. She was delighted for him.

"And the prize is that it's gonna be aired on Channel Four next week!" There were more cheers this time, and Holly could barely make out what he was saying. "You're gonna be famous, sis!" was the last thing she heard before the line went dead.

She rang her family to share the good news but learned that they had all received a similar phone call. Ciara chattered on like an excited schoolgirl about how they were going to be on TV and said that Daniel had offered Club Diva so they could watch next Wednesday on the big wall screen. Holly was excited for her brother and rang Sharon and Denise to let them know the news.

"Oh, this is brill news, Holly!" Sharon whispered excitedly.

"Why are you whispering?" Holly whispered back.

"Oh, old wrinkly face here decided it would be a great idea to ban us from accepting personal calls," moaned Sharon, referring to her boss. "She says we spend more time chatting on the phone to friends than doing business." Suddenly Sharon spoke up and became businesslike. "May I take your details please?"

Holly laughed. "Is she there?"

"Yes, absolutely," Sharon continued.

"Okay, well, I won't keep you very long, then. The details are that we're all meeting up in Hogan's on Wednesday night to watch it."

"That's great." Sharon pretended to take her details.

"Brilliant. We'll have fun. Sharon, what will I wear?"

"Hmm . . . brand-new or secondhand?"

"No, I can't afford anything new, so probably something old."

"Okay . . . red."

"The red top I wore to your birthday?"

"Yes, exactly. What's your current state of employment?"

"To be honest, I haven't even started looking yet." Holly chewed the inside of her mouth and frowned.

"And date of birth?"

"Ha-ha, shut up," Holly laughed.

"I'm sorry. We only give motor insurance to ages twenty-four and older. You're too young, I'm afraid."

"I wish. Okay, I'll speak to you later."

"Thank you for calling."

HOLLY sat at the kitchen table wondering what she should wear next week. She wanted to look sexy and gorgeous for a change. Maybe Denise had something in the shop. She picked up the phone and called her at work.

"Hello. Casuals," answered a very polite Denise.

"Hello, Casuals. Holly here. I know I'm not supposed to call you at work, but Declan's documentary won some student-award thingy, and it's gonna be aired on Wednesday night."

"Oh, that's so cool, Holly! Are we gonna be in it?"

"Yeah, I think so. We're all meeting up at Hogan's to watch it. You up for that?"

"Of course! I can bring my new boyfriend, Tom?" she giggled.

"The karaoke guy?" Holly asked in shock.

"Yeah, of course! Oh, Holly, I'm so in love!" she giggled again.

"In love? But you only met him a few weeks ago!"

"I don't care. It only takes a minute, as the saying goes."

"Wow, Denise, I don't know what to say. It's great news!"

"Try not to sound too enthusiastic," Denise said sarcastically.

"Anyway, I can't wait for you to meet him. You'll really like him."

"Denise, are you forgetting that I met him already?" Holly said.

"Yeah, I know, but I'd rather you meet him when you're not acting like a demented woman hiding in toilets."

Holly rolled her eyes. "Look forward to it, then."

HOLLY arrived at Hogan's and made her way upstairs to Club Diva. It was only seven-thirty, so the club wasn't officially open yet. She was the first to arrive and settled herself at a table right in front of the big screen.

A smashing glass made her jump, and she looked up to see Daniel behind the bar, a dustpan and brush in his hand. "Oh, hiya, Holly." He looked at her in surprise. "I didn't realize anyone had come in."

"It's just me. I came early." She walked over to greet him.

"You're really early," he said, looking at his watch. "The others probably won't be here for another hour or so."

Holly looked confused. "But doesn't the show start at eight?"

"I was told nine, but I could be wrong." Daniel reached for that day's paper. "Yep, nine o'clock, Channel Four."

"Oh, no. I'm sorry. I'll wander around town for a bit."

"Don't be silly. You can keep me company," he said, smiling. "So now, what can I get you?" His smile was infectious.

"Well, this is great. I'll have a sparkling water, please."

He reached behind him to the fridge to retrieve the bottled water. Holly realized what it was that made him look so different; he wasn't wearing his trademark black. He was wearing faded blue jeans and a light blue shirt that made his blue eyes twinkle. The sleeves of his shirt were rolled up to just below his elbows. Holly could see his muscles through the light fabric. She quickly averted her eyes as he slid the glass toward her.

"Can I get you anything?" she asked him.

"No thanks. I'll take care of this one."

"Please. You've bought me plenty of drinks. It's my turn."

"Okay, I'll have a Budweiser. Thanks." He leaned against the bar and continued to stare at her.

"What? Do you want me to get it?" Holly laughed, jumping off her stool. "I always wanted to work behind a bar when I was a kid," she said, grabbing a pint glass and pulling down on the tap.

"Well, there's a spare job if you're looking for one," Daniel said.

"No thanks. I think I do a better job on the other side of the bar," she laughed, filling the pint glass. She took out her purse and handed him money. "Keep the change," she smiled.

"Thanks." He turned to the cash register. "Has your husband deserted you again tonight?" he teased.

Holly wondered how to answer him. "Daniel, I don't mean to make you uncomfortable, but my husband passed away."

Daniel blushed slightly. "Oh, Holly, I'm sorry. I didn't know."

"It's okay. I know you didn't." She smiled to show him it was all right. "Gerry died in February."

"But I thought you told me he was here the other night."

"Oh, yeah." Holly looked down at her feet with embarrassment. "Well, he wasn't here," she said, looking around the club, "but he was here." She put her hand on her heart.

"Ah, I see. Well then, you were even braver the other night than I thought," he said gently. Holly was surprised by how at ease he seemed. She felt relaxed in his presence, as if she could talk openly without fear of crying. She briefly explained the story of the list.

"So that's why I ran off after Declan's gig that time."

"It wasn't because they were so terrible, by any chance?" Daniel joked. "Ah, yes, that's right. That was the thirtieth of April."

"Now you're getting the gist," she laughed.

"I have arrived!" announced Denise as she swanned into the club, dolled up to the nines in the dress she had worn to the ball last year. Tom strolled in behind her, refusing to take his eyes off her.

"You're dressed up," Holly remarked. In the end, she had decided to just wear a pair of jeans, black boots, and a very simple black top. She hadn't been in the mood to get all dressed up.

"It's not every day I get to go to my own premiere, is it?"

Tom and Daniel greeted each other with hugs. "Baby, this is my best friend, Daniel," Tom said, introducing Denise to Daniel.

Daniel and Holly raised their eyebrows at each other and smiled, both registering the use of the word "baby."

"Hi, Tom." Holly shook his hand after Denise had introduced her, and he kissed her on the cheek. "I'm sorry about the last time I met you. I wasn't feeling very sane that night."

"Oh, that's no problem," Tom smiled. "If you hadn't entered, then I wouldn't have met Denise, so I'm glad you did."

After a while, Holly discovered she was enjoying herself; she wasn't just pretending to laugh. She was genuinely happy. The thought of that made her even happier, as did the knowledge that Denise had finally found someone she really loved.

Minutes later, the rest of the Kennedy family arrived, along with Sharon and John. Holly ran down to greet them.

"Okay, everyone!" Declan stood on a stool. "Because Ciara couldn't decide what to wear tonight, we're all late and my documentary is about to start any minute. So if you can all sit down."

"Oh, Declan," Holly's mother admonished him.

Holly laughed and settled down to watch the documentary. As soon as the announcer introduced it, everybody cheered.

The words "Girls and the City" appeared over a beautiful nighttime shot of Dublin, followed by a shot of Sharon, Denise, Abbey, and Ciara all squashed in the back of a taxi. Sharon was speaking. "Hello! I'm Sharon, and this is Abbey, Denise, and Ciara."

Each of the girls posed for her close-up as she was introduced.

"And we're heading to our best friend Holly's house because it's her birthday today. "Tonight it's gonna be just us girls and NO men."

The scene changed to the girls surprising Holly with shouts of "Happy birthday" at her door.

"We are gonna do lots of drinking."

Now Holly was popping open the champagne; then the girls were knocking back shots, and eventually it showed Holly with the crooked tiara on her head, drinking out of a champagne bottle with a straw.

"We are gonna go clubbing."

There was then a shot of the girls in Boudoir, doing some very embarrassing moves on the dance floor.

Sharon was shown next, speaking sincerely. "But nothing too mad. We're gonna be good girls tonight!"

The next scene showed the girls protesting wildly as they were escorted out of the club by three bouncers.

HOLLY stared in shock over at Sharon, who was equally surprised. The men laughed their hearts out and slapped Declan on the back. Holly, Sharon, Denise, Abbey, and even Ciara slithered down in their seats with humiliation. What on earth had Declan done?

Holly held her breath. What exactly had the girls all conveniently forgotten? The truth terrified her.

Once again, a new title took over the screen—"Journey to the City"—and showed the girls in the seven-seater taxi. Holly had actually thought she was quite sober at that stage. "Oh, John," she moaned drunkenly to the taxi driver from the passenger seat, "I'm thirty today. Can you believe it?"

John glanced over at her and laughed, "Sure, you're only a young one still, Holly." The camera zoomed in on Holly's face, and she cringed at the sight of herself. She looked so sad.

"But what am I gonna do, John?" she whinged. "I have no job, no husband, no children, and I'm thirty! Did I tell you that?"

"Ah, Holly, worry about all that shite tomorrow, love."

The camera stayed with Holly as she leaned her head against the window, lost in thought for the rest of the journey. Holly couldn't get over how lonely she looked. She didn't like it. She looked around the room in embarrassment and turned back in time to see herself screaming to the girls on O'Connell Street.

"Okay, girls. We are going to Boudoir, and no one is going to stop us, especially any silly bouncers who think they own the place," and she marched off in what she thought at the time was a straight line. All the girls cheered and followed after her.

The scene immediately jumped to the two bouncers outside Boudoir, shaking their heads. "Not tonight, girls, sorry."

"But," Denise said calmly, "do you not know who we are?"

"No." They both stared over their heads, ignoring them.

"Huh!" Denise put her hands on her hips. "But this is the very, very famous, em, Princess Holly from the royal family of . . . Finland." On camera, Holly frowned at Denise.

Her family howled with laughter. "You couldn't write a script better than this," Declan laughed.

"Oh, she's royalty, is she?" the bouncer with a mustache smirked. "Finland got a royal family, Paul?"

"Don't think so, boss."

Holly gave them both a royal wave. "You see?" Denise said. "You'll be very embarrassed if you don't let her in."

"Supposing we let her in, then; you'll have to stay outside." Mustache Man motioned for the people behind them to pass.

"Oh, no, no," Denise laughed. "I'm her lady-in-waiting."

"One must have a drink," Holly said. "One is dreadfully thirsty."

Paul and Mustache Man snorted and tried to keep a straight face. "No, honestly, girls, you need to be a member."

"But I am a member of the royal family!" Holly said.

Denise pleaded. "The princess and I will be no trouble at all."

Mustache Man raised his eyes to the sky. "All right, then. Go on in," he said, stepping aside.

"God bless you," Holly said as she passed.

"She's out of her mind," laughed Mustache Man, regaining his composure as Ciara's entourage approached.

"Is it okay if my film crew follow me in?" Ciara said confidently in a brilliant Australian accent.

"Hold on while I check." Paul turned his back and spoke into his walkie-talkie. "Yeah, that's no problem. Go ahead."

"That's that Australian singer, isn't it?" Mustache Man said.

"Yeah. Good song, that."

"Tell the boys inside to keep an eye on the princess and her lady. We don't want them bothering that singer with the pink hair."

As Holly watched the image of the inside of Boudoir on the screen, she remembered being disappointed by the club. There had always been a mystery as to what Boudoir looked like. The girls had read in a magazine that there was a water feature that Madonna had apparently jumped into one night. Holly had imagined a huge waterfall cascading down the wall of the club, while all the glamorous people sat around it and occasionally dipped their glasses into it to fill them with more champagne. But instead of her champagne waterfall, what Holly got was an oversized fishbowl in the center of the circular bar. The room wasn't as big as she thought it would be, and on the far side was a huge gold curtain. At the top of the room was a massive king-size bed on a tilted platform. On top of the gold silk sheets were two skinny models dressed in gold body paint and gold thongs. It was all a bit too tacky.

"Look at the size of those thongs!" gasped Denise. "I have a plaster on my baby finger bigger than those."

Beside her in Club Diva, Tom began to nibble on Denise's baby finger. Holly returned her gaze to the screen.

"Good evening and welcome to the twelve-o'clock news. I'm Sharon McCarthy." Sharon stood in front of the camera with a bottle in her hand serving as a microphone. Declan had angled the camera so he could get Ireland's famous newsreaders in the shot.

"Today, on the thirtieth birthday of Princess Holly of Finland, her royal self and her lady-in-waiting succeeded in being granted access to the famous celebrity hangout Boudoir. Also present is Australian rock chick Ciara and her film crew and—" Sharon held her finger to her ear as though she were receiving more information. "News just in . . . and it appears that Ireland's favorite newsreader, Tony Walsh, was seen smiling just moments ago. Here I have a witness to the fact. Welcome, Denise." Denise posed seductively at the camera. "Denise, can you tell us what happened?"

"Well, I was just over there beside his table, minding my own business, when Mr. Walsh took a sip of his drink and smiled."

"Denise, this is fascinating news. Are you sure it was a smile?"

"Well, it could have been trapped wind causing him to make a face, but others around me also thought it was a smile."

"So there were others who witnessed this?"

"Yes. Princess Holly here saw the whole thing."

The camera panned across to Holly, where she stood drinking from a champagne bottle with a straw. "So, Holly, can you tell us— was it wind or a smile?"

Holly looked confused, then rolled her eyes. "Oh, wind, sorry. I think it's this champagne that's doing it to me."

Club Diva erupted in laughter. Holly hid her face in shame.

"Okay then," Sharon said, "so you heard it here first. The night when Ireland's grimmest presenter was seen smiling. Back to you at the studio." Sharon's smile faded as she looked up and saw Tony Walsh standing beside her. She gulped and said, "Good evening," and the camera was switched off. Everyone in Club Diva was laughing at this stage. The whole thing was just so ridiculous.

The scene changed, and the words "Operation Gold Curtain" came up. Denise screamed, "Oh, my God, Declan, you bastard!" and rushed off to the toilet to hide. Declan chuckled.

"Okay, girls," Denise was announcing on-screen. "It is now time for Operation Gold Curtain. Time to infiltrate the VIP bar!"

"You mean, this isn't it?" Sharon said sarcastically, looking around Boudoir.

"No! That's where the real celebs go!" Denise said excitedly, pointing at the gold curtain, which was blocked by possibly the biggest and tallest man on the planet. "Girls, Abbey and Ciara are in there. Why aren't we?"

Once Sharon and Holly had heard that Abbey and Ciara were in the room, they sat up and listened attentively to Denise.

"Okay, girlies, here's what we're gonna do," said Denise.

Holly turned away from the screen and nudged Sharon. Holly couldn't remember doing any of these things. Sharon turned to face her and shrugged. Nope, she wasn't there that night either.

The camera followed the girls as they approached the gold curtain and loitered around like idiots. Sharon finally built up the courage to tap the giant on the shoulder, causing him to turn around. Denise got down on her hands and knees and stuck her head through the curtain to the VIP bar. Holly kicked her in the bum to hurry her along.

"I see them," Denise hissed loudly. "They're speaking to that Hollywood actor guy!" She took her head back out and looked at Holly. Unfortunately, the giant bouncer turned his head just in time.

"No, no, no!" Denise said. "This is Princess Holly of Finland. I am bowing to her. Join me!"

Sharon quickly got on her knees, and the two of them began to worship Holly's feet. Holly looked around awkwardly as everyone in the club began to stare, and she once again gave the royal wave.

"Oh, Holly!" her mother said, trying to catch her breath after laughing so hard.

The big burly bouncer spoke into his walkie-talkie. "Boys, got a situation with the princess and the lady."

Denise looked at both girls in panic and mouthed, "Hide!" The girls jumped to their feet and fled. The camera searched through the crowds but couldn't find them.

From her seat in Club Diva, Holly groaned loudly as it finally clicked with her what was about to happen.

Paul and Mustache Man rushed upstairs to the gold curtain. "What's going on?" Mustache Man asked.

"Those girls tried to crawl through to the other side," the big man said. You could tell his previous job involved killing people if they tried to crawl to the other side.

"Where are they?" Mustache Man asked.

The big man looked away. "They're hiding, boss."

Mustache Man rolled his eyes. "Well, start looking for them."

The camera secretly followed the three bouncers as they patrolled the club, looking under tables and behind curtains. There was a bit of commotion at the top of the club, and the bouncers headed toward the noise to sort it out. The two dancers in gold body paint had stopped dancing and were staring with horrified expressions. The camera panned across to the king-size bed. Underneath the gold sheets, there appeared to be three pigs fighting under a blanket. Sharon, Denise, and Holly rolled around screaming at one another, trying to make themselves as flat as possible so they wouldn't be noticed. A crowd gathered, and soon the music was shut down. The three big lumps suddenly stopped squirming and froze.

The bouncers pulled the covers off the bed. Three very startled-looking girls, appearing like deer caught in headlights, stared back at them.

"One just had to get forty winks before one left," Holly said with her royal accent, and the other girls burst out laughing.

Everyone at Club Diva howled with laughter.

The scene changed to "The Long Journey Home," and the girls were in the taxi. Abbey sat like a dog, with her head hanging out the window by order of the taxi driver: "You're not throwing up in my cab." Her face was purple. Sharon and Denise had fallen asleep.

The camera turned to Holly, sitting in the passenger seat. This time, she wasn't talking the ear off the driver; she rested her head on the seat back and stared straight into the night. Holly knew what she was thinking as she watched herself. Time to go home to that empty house alone again.

"Happy birthday, Holly," Abbey's tiny little voice trembled.

Holly turned around to smile at her and came face-to-face with the camera. "Are you still filming with that thing? Turn it off!" and she knocked the camera out of Declan's hand. The end.

As Daniel went to turn the lights up in the club, Holly slipped quickly away through the nearest door. She needed to collect her thoughts before everyone started talking. She found herself in a tiny storeroom, surrounded by empty kegs. She sat down on a keg and thought about what she had just seen. She felt confused and angry at Declan. He had told her that he was making a documentary about club life, but he had literally made a show of her and her friends.

Yet the last thing she wanted to do right now was to scream at Declan in front of everyone. If it had been anyone else but her on the TV, Holly would have thought it very deserving of the award. But it *was* her. She didn't mind so much the bits of her and her friends being so silly; it was more the sneaky shots of her unhappiness that bothered her.

Salty tears trickled down her face. She had seen on television how she truly felt—lost and alone. She cried for Gerry; she cried for herself with heaving sobs. She didn't want her family seeing the loneliness she tried so hard to hide. She just wanted Gerry back.

She heard the door open behind her and felt big, strong arms wrapping themselves around her frail body. She cried as though months of built-up anguish were all tumbling out at once.

"Didn't she like it?" she heard Declan ask worriedly.

"Just leave her be," her mum said softly, and the door was closed again. Daniel stroked her hair and rocked her softly.

After crying what felt like all the tears in the world, she stopped and let go of Daniel. "Sorry," she sniffed.

"There's no need to be sorry," Daniel said gently.

She sat in silence while trying to compose herself.

"If you're upset about the documentary, there's no need."

"Yeah, right," she said sarcastically, wiping her tears.

"No, really. You all looked like you were having a great time. Nobody but you noticed whatever's upsetting you."

Holly felt mildly better. "Are you sure?"

"I'm sure. Now, you really have to stop hiding in all the rooms in my club. I might take it personally," he said, and smiled.

"Are the girls okay?" There was loud laughter from outside.

"They're fine," he said. "Ciara's delighted everyone will think she's a star, Denise has finally come out of the toilet, and Sharon just can't stop laughing—although Jack's giving Abbey a hard time about throwing up on the way home."

Holly giggled. "Thanks, Daniel."

"You ready to go face your public?" he asked.

"Think so." Holly stepped outside to everyone sitting around the table sharing jokes and stories. Holly joined the table and sat beside her mum. Elizabeth gave her daughter a kiss on the cheek.

"So is it okay?" Declan asked Holly, afraid he had upset his sister.

Holly threw him a look. "Only if you're nice to me for the next few months."

Declan made a face. He was stuck, and he knew it. "Yeah, whatever," he said.

Six

*H*OLLY was standing over the sink with her sleeves rolled up, scrubbing the pots, when she heard the familiar voice.

"Hi, honey."

She looked up and saw him standing at the open patio doors. "Hello, you," she smiled.

"Miss me?"

"Of course."

"Have you found that new husband yet?"

"Of course I have. He's upstairs asleep," she laughed, drying her hands.

Gerry tutted. "Shall I suffocate him for sleeping in our bed?"

"Ah, give him another hour or so. He needs his rest."

He looked happy, she thought, still as beautiful as she remembered. He stared at her with his big brown puppy eyes.

"Are you coming in?" she asked.

"No. I just popped by to see how you are. Everything okay?" He leaned against the door ledge, hands in his pockets.

"So, so," she said. "Could be better."

"I hear you're a TV star now," he grinned.

"A very reluctant one," she laughed. "I miss you, Gerry."

"I haven't gone far," he said softly.

"You leaving me again?"

"For the time being."

She smiled. "See you soon."

Holly woke up with a smile on her face and felt like she'd slept for days. "Good morning, Gerry," she said happily. The phone rang beside her. "Hello?"

"Oh, my God, Holly. Just take a look at the weekend papers," Sharon said in a panic.

HOLLY IMMEDIATELY THREW on a tracksuit, drove to her nearest newsagent, and began to leaf through the pages. The man behind the counter coughed loudly, and Holly looked up at him. "This is not a library, young lady. You'll have to buy that," he said.

"I know," she said, irritated. Honestly, how was anyone supposed to know which paper to buy if they didn't know which paper had what they were looking for? She picked up every single newspaper and slammed them down on the counter, smiling sweetly at him.

The man started to scan them into the register one by one.

She stared longingly at the chocolate display in front of her and grabbed two king-size bars from the pile. One by one, the rest of the chocolate began to slide onto the floor. She bent down with a red face to pick them up. The shop was silent, apart from a few coughs from the queue forming behind her. Then she remembered she needed milk, so she rushed to retrieve a pint from the fridge.

She made her way back to the top of the queue and added the milk. The newsagent stopped scanning. "Mark," he yelled.

A spotty young teenager appeared from the aisles, a pricing gun in his hand. "Yeah?" he said grumpily.

"Open the other till, will ya, son?" He glared at her.

Holly made a face at him.

Mark dragged his body over to the second till, and the queue rushed over. Holly grabbed a few packets of crisps from below the counter and added them to her purchases.

"Anything else?" the newsagent asked sarcastically.

"No, thank you. That will be all." She paid her money and fumbled with her purse, trying to put the change back in.

"Next." The newsagent nodded to the customer behind her.

"Excuse me," Holly said. "Could I have a bag, please?"

"That'll be twenty cents."

Holly found her money again, slammed the coin on the counter, and began to fill the bag with her items.

"Next," he said. Holly began stuffing the bag full in panic.

"I'll wait till the lady is ready," the customer said politely.

Holly smiled at him appreciatively, and as she turned to leave the shop, Mark, the boy behind the counter, startled her by yelling, "Hey, I know you! You're the girl from the telly!"

Holly swirled around, and the bag handle broke from the weight of all the newspapers. Everything went rolling in all directions.

The friendly customer got down on his knees to help her while the rest of the shop watched in amusement.

"It is you, isn't it?" the boy laughed.

Holly smiled up weakly at him from the floor.

"I knew it!" He clapped his hands together. "You're cool!"

Holly's face went red. "Em, could I have another bag, please?"

"Yeah, that'll be—"

"There you go." The friendly customer placed a twenty-cent coin on the counter. The newsagent looked perplexed and continued serving the customers.

"I'm Rob," the man said, helping her put all her chocolate back into the bag, and held his hand out.

"I'm Holly," she said, a little embarrassed by his over-friendliness as she took his hand. "And I'm a chocoholic."

He laughed.

"Thanks for the help," she said gratefully, getting to her feet.

"No problem." He held the door open for her. He was good-looking, she thought, a few years older than her, and had the oddest-colored eyes, a kind of gray-green color.

He cleared his throat.

She blushed, suddenly realizing she had been staring at him like a fool. She walked out to her car and placed the bulging bag in the backseat. Rob followed her over. Her heart did a little flip.

"Hi again," he said. "Em, I was wondering if you would like to go for a drink?" Then he laughed, glancing at his watch. "Actually, it's a bit too early for that. How about a coffee?"

He was a very confident man, and he rested coolly against the car, his hands in the pockets of his jeans, acting as though asking a stranger out for coffee was the most natural thing in the world. Was this what people did these days?

"Em . . . " Holly thought about it. What harm could it do to go for a coffee with a man who had been so polite to her? The fact that he was absolutely gorgeous also helped. But regardless, he seemed like a nice, decent man to talk to.

She was just about to say yes when he glanced down at her hand and his smile faded. "Oh, sorry. I didn't realize . . . I have to rush off anyway." He smiled quickly at her and took off down the road.

Holly stared after him, confused. Had she said something wrong? She looked down at her hand and saw her wedding ring sparkle back at her. She sighed loudly and rubbed her face tiredly.

Holly wasn't in the mood to go home. She was sick of staring at the walls all day. Across the road, her local café, the Greasy Spoon, was setting up tables outside. Her stomach grumbled. She took her newspapers from the car and wandered across the road.

A plump lady was cleaning the tables. "Want to sit here, love?"

"Yes. I'll have the Irish breakfast."

"No problem, love." She waddled into the café.

Holly flicked through the pages of the tabloids and came to a small article in the review section that caught her eye.

"GIRLS AND THE CITY" A HIT IN THE RATINGS

For any of you who missed the outrageously funny "Girls and the City" last Wednesday, do not despair. It will be back soon. The hilarious fly-on-the-wall TV documentary, directed by Irishman Declan Kennedy, follows five Dublin girls out for a night on the town. They lift the lid on the mysterious world of celebrity life in trendy club Boudoir and provide us with thirty minutes of stomach-aching laughter.

Ratings revealed 4 million people tuned in, in the U.K. The show is to be repeated Sunday at 11:00 p.m. on Channel 4. This is must-see TV, so don't miss it!

Holly tried to keep her cool. This was obviously great news for Declan but disastrous for her. Having that documentary aired once was bad enough.

She flicked through the rest of the papers and saw what it was Sharon was ranting about. Every single tabloid had an article about the documentary, and one had even printed a photograph of Denise, Sharon, and Holly from a few years ago. How they got their hands on it, she did not know. And she wasn't too happy with the use of the words "mad girls," "drunken girls," and how they were "well up for it." What did that even mean?

Holly's food finally arrived, and she stared at it in shock— sausages, bacon, eggs, hash browns, baked beans, fried potatoes, tomatoes, and toast. Holly looked around her with embarrassment, hoping no one would think she was a complete pig. She hadn't had much of an appetite lately, and she finally felt ready to eat.

Holly stayed in the Greasy Spoon much longer than she expected, and by the time she reached her parents' house in Portmarnock, it was almost two o'clock. She rang the doorbell for the fourth time, and still no one answered. She pressed her face against the living-room window to see if there was any sign of life and heard the screaming match.

"CIARA, GET THE DAMN DOOR!"

"NO, I SAID! I . . . AM . . . BUSY!"

"WELL, SO AM I!"

Holly rang the doorbell again, just to add fuel to the fire.

"DECLAN!" Ouch, that was a bloodcurdling scream.

"GET IT YOURSELF, YOU LAZY COW!"

Holly took out her mobile phone and rang Declan's mobile.

"Yeah?"

"Declan, open the door now, or I'll kick it in," Holly growled.

"Oh, sorry. I thought Ciara had answered it," he lied.

He opened the door in his boxer shorts, and Holly stormed in.

"Mum and Dad are out," he said lazily.

Holly headed upstairs and knocked on Ciara's door.

"Don't come in," yelled Ciara from inside.

Holly opened the door anyway.

"I told you not to come in!" wailed Ciara, sitting on the floor with a photo album on her lap and tears streaming down her face.

"Oh, Ciara, what's wrong?" Holly said. She couldn't remember the last time she'd seen her sister cry.

"Nothing's wrong," Ciara said, snapping the album shut and sliding it under her bed. She wiped her face roughly.

Holly crossed the room to join her sister on the floor. She wasn't sure how to deal with Ciara like this. "If there's something upsetting you, you know you can talk to me about it, don't you?"

Ciara nodded her head and burst into tears again. Holly wrapped her arms around her sister, stroking her silky pink hair.

"Do you want to tell me what's wrong?" she asked.

Ciara gurgled some sort of reply and slid the photo album back out. She opened it with trembling hands and flicked a few pages.

"Him," she said sadly, pointing to a photograph of her and some guy Holly didn't know. Holly barely recognized her sister. The photograph was taken on a boat overlooking the Sydney Opera House. Ciara was sitting happily on the man's knee with her arms around his neck. She had blond hair, and her features looked much softer.

"Is that your boyfriend?" Holly asked carefully.

"Was," Ciara sniffed, and a tear landed on the page.

"Is that why you came home?"

Ciara gasped for breath. "We had a fight."

"Did he . . . He didn't hurt you or anything, did he?"

"No," Ciara spluttered. "It was just over something really stupid, and I said I was leaving, and he said he was glad. . . ." She started sobbing again. Holly held her in her arms and waited. "He didn't even come to the airport to say good-bye to me."

Holly rubbed Ciara's back. "Has he called you since?"

"No, and I've been home for two months, Holly," she wailed.

"Then maybe he's not the right kind of person for you."

"But I love Mathew, Holly, and it was only a stupid fight. I booked the flight because I was angry. I didn't think he would let me go. . . ." She stared for a long time at the photograph.

Ciara's bedroom windows were open, and Holly listened to the familiar sound of the waves from the beach. Holly and Ciara had shared this room while they were growing up, and a weird sense of comfort embraced her as she listened to the familiar noises.

Ciara began to calm down beside her. "Sorry, Hol. This is minor compared to what happened to you. I feel stupid crying about it."

"Losing someone you love is always hard, no matter if they're alive or . . ." Holly couldn't finish the sentence.

"It's just that you've been so brave, Holly. And here I am crying over a stupid boyfriend I only went out with for a few months."

"Me? Brave?" Holly laughed. "I wish."

"Yes, you are," Ciara insisted. "Everyone says so. If I were you, I'd be lying in a ditch somewhere."

"Don't go giving me ideas, Ciara." Holly smiled at her.

"You're okay, though, aren't you?" Ciara said worriedly.

Holly slid her wedding ring up and down her finger. She thought about that question for a while.

"I'm lots of things, Ciara. I'm lonely, I'm tired, I'm sad, I'm happy, I'm lucky, I'm unlucky—I'm a million things every day, but I suppose okay is one of them."

"And you're brave," Ciara assured her. "And in control."

"No. You were always the brave one. As for being in control, I don't know what I'm doing from one day to the next."

Ciara's forehead creased. "I am far from being brave, Holly."

"Yes, you are. All those things that you do, like jumping out of airplanes and snowboarding off cliffs—"

"Oh, no, that's not brave; that's foolish. Anybody can bungee jump off a bridge. You could do it if you had to."

"Yes, and if your husband died, you would cope if you had to. There's nothing brave about it. There's no choice involved."

Ciara and Holly stared at each other, aware of the other's battle.

Ciara was the first to speak. "I guess you and I are more alike than we thought." She smiled at her big sister, and Holly hugged her tightly. "Well, who would have thought?"

IT WAS eight o'clock when Holly finally drove up her driveway, and it was still bright. She had spent hours chatting with Ciara about her adventures in Australia. Ciara had changed her mind at least twenty times about whether or not she should call Mathew in Australia. By the time Holly left, Ciara was adamant she would never speak to him again, which probably meant she had called him by now.

Holly walked up the path to the front door and stared at the garden curiously. Was it her imagination, or did it look a little tidier?

It had always been Gerry's job to do the garden. He wasn't necessarily a keen gardener; it was just that Holly was an incredibly unkeen gardener, so somebody had to do the dirty work. Their small patch of grass surrounded by a few shrubs and flowers now looked like an overgrown field. When Gerry died, the garden had died along with him.

This thought reminded Holly of the orchid. She rushed inside and poured water over the thirsty-looking plant. Then she threw a chicken curry into the microwave and thought back over her day, deciding it had been good, apart from one isolated incident.

She looked down at her wedding ring. When that man had walked away, Holly had felt so awful. He had given her that look as if she were about to initiate an affair. She felt guilty for even considering his invitation for coffee.

Gerry had died when they were both still very much in love, and she couldn't just fall out of love because he wasn't around anymore. She still felt married, and going for a coffee would have seemed like she was betraying her husband. Gerry was gone almost five months now, but her heart and soul still belonged with him.

When the microwave beeped, her dinner was ready. She took the dish out and threw it straight into the bin. She had lost her appetite.

Later that night, Denise rang her in a tizzy. "Switch Dublin FM on quick!" Holly raced to the radio and flicked the switch. "I'm Tom O'Connor, and you're listening to Dublin FM. If you've just joined us, we're talking about bouncers. In light of the amount of persuasion it took the 'Girls and the City' girls to blag their way into the club Boudoir, we wanna know your thoughts on bouncers. Do you like them? Are they too strict? The number to call is . . ."

Holly picked the phone back up. "Well?" Denise said.

"What the hell have we started, Denise?"

"I know," she giggled. "Did you see the papers today?"

"Yeah. It's all a bit silly, really."

They listened to the radio. Some guy was giving out about bouncers, and Tom was trying to calm him down.

"Oh, listen to my baby," Denise said. "Doesn't he sound sexy?"

"Em, yeah. I take it you two are still together?"

"Of course." Denise sounded insulted. "Why wouldn't we be?"

"Well, it's been a while now, Denise, that's all. And you always said you couldn't be with a man for over a week!"

"Yes, well, Tom is different, Holly," Denise said breathily. "It's like he's my soul mate. He's so thoughtful, always surprising me with little gifts. He makes me laugh all the time, and I haven't gotten sick of him, like all the other guys. Plus he's good-looking."

Holly stifled a yawn. Denise tended to say this after first going out with all her new boyfriends and then would quickly change her mind. Then again, perhaps Denise meant what she said this time. After all, they had been together for several weeks now.

"I'm very happy for you," Holly said genuinely.

THE next day, Holly dragged herself out of bed to go for a stroll in the park. She needed to start doing some exercise, and she also needed to start thinking about job-hunting. Everywhere she went, she tried to picture herself working in that environment. She had ruled out clothes stores, restaurants, hotels, and pubs, and she certainly didn't want another office job, which left . . . nothing.

She sat down on a park bench opposite the playground and listened to the children's screams of delight. She thought about the stinging remark Richard had made about never having to bother with that children nonsense. She wished so much she could have a little Gerry running around the playground. She and Gerry had just started talking about having children a few months before he was diagnosed. They used to lie in bed for hours trying to decide names and imagine what it would be like to be parents.

Well, think of the devil, Holly thought, seeing Richard leaving the playground with Emily and Timmy. He looked so relaxed as he chased the children around the park. They looked like they were having fun—not a very familiar sight. She zipped up her extra layer of thick skin in preparation for their conversation.

"Hello, Holly!" Richard, spotting her, walked across the grass.

"Hello," Holly said, greeting the kids as they ran over to her and gave her a big hug. It made a nice change. "You're far from home," she said to Richard. "What brings you all the way here?"

"I brought the children to see Grandma and Granddad, didn't I?" he said, ruffling Timmy's head.

"And we had McDonald's," Timmy said excitedly.

"Oh, yummy!" Holly said. "Isn't your daddy the best?"

Richard looked pleased.

"Junk food?" Holly questioned her brother.

"Ah." He waved his hand dismissively and sat down beside her. "Everything in moderation, isn't that right, Emily?"

Five-year-old Emily nodded her head as though she had completely understood her father.

"One McDonald's meal isn't going to kill them," Holly agreed.

Timmy grabbed at his throat and pretended to choke. His face went red as he made gagging noises, and he collapsed on the grass and lay very still. Richard and Holly laughed.

"Oh, dear," Richard joked. "Looks like we were wrong, Holly. The McDonald's did kill Timmy."

Holly looked at her brother in shock for calling his son Timmy. Richard got up and threw him over his shoulder. "Well, we better go bury him now." Timmy giggled as he dangled upside down.

"Oh, he's alive!" Richard laughed.

"No, I'm not," giggled Timmy.

"Okay, we best be off," laughed Richard. "Bye, Holly."

"Bye, Holly," the children cheered, and Richard walked off with Timmy slung over his shoulder as little Emily skipped and danced beside her father, gripping his hand.

Seven

BARBARA finished serving her customers, and as soon as they left the building, she ran into the staff room and lit up a cigarette. Swords Travel had been busy all day. Melissa, her workmate, had called in sick, so she was stuck by herself. As soon as November came, with those depressing dark nights and sheets of rain, everyone came running in the door, booking holidays to hot, sunny countries.

With her boss finally out to run errands, Barbara had been really looking forward to her cigarette break. Of course, just her luck, the bell over the door sounded just then. She silently cursed, puffing on the cigarette and reapplying her lipstick. She left the staff room expecting to see the customer sitting behind the counter, but instead, the old man was still slowly making his way.

"Excuse me?" the weak voice called.

"Hello, sir. How can I help you?" she said, surprised at how young the man actually was. His body was hunched, and the walking stick in his hand seemed to be the only thing preventing him from collapsing. His skin was pasty, but he had big brown eyes that seemed to smile at her. She couldn't help but smile back.

"I was hoping to book a holiday," he said, "but I was wondering if you could help me choose a place."

Usually Barbara would have silently screamed at the customer for making her do this impossible task. Most of her customers were so fussy, she could be sitting there for hours. But she surprised herself.

"No problem, sir. My name is Barbara. Why don't you take a seat, and we'll search through the brochures." She pointed to a chair and looked away so she didn't have to watch him struggle. "Now," she said, "any country in particular you would like to go to?"

"Em, Spain. Lanzarote, I think. A summer holiday."

They looked through the brochures until the man found a place he liked. Barbara was happy he took her advice into account.

"Okay, any month in particular?" she said.

"August?" he asked.

"August is a good month. Would you like a sea view?"

He stared into space with a smile. "A sea view, please."

"Good choice. Can I take your name and address, please?"

"Oh, this isn't actually for me." Those brown eyes looked sad. "It's a surprise for my wife and her friends."

"Well, that's very thoughtful of you, sir." She finished taking his details, and he settled the bill.

"Do you mind if I leave the arrangements with you? I'd be afraid of leaving papers around. I won't be telling her till July, so could it be kept quiet till then?"

"That's no problem at all, sir."

"Thank you for your help, Barbara," he said.

"It's been a pleasure, Mr. . . . Clarke?"

"It's Gerry," he smiled.

"It's been a pleasure, Gerry. Your wife will have a wonderful time. My friend went there, and she loved it."

"Well, I better head home. I'm not even supposed to be out of bed." He smiled again and slowly walked to the waiting taxi.

IT WAS the first of July, and Barbara sat grumpily behind the counter of the travel agency. It was the hottest day of the year; all her customers kept strolling in wearing little shorts and skimpy tops. Barbara squirmed in her chair in her incredibly itchy uniform. She banged on the fan as it suddenly stalled.

"Leave it," Melissa moaned. "That'll only make it worse."

"As if that could be possible," Barbara grumbled.

"What is it with you today?" Melissa laughed.

"Oh, nothing much. It's just the hottest day of the year, and we're stuck in this crappy job in this stuffy room."

"Why don't you go outside to get some air, and I'll deal with this customer." Melissa nodded to the woman making her way in.

"Thanks, Mel," said Barbara, grabbing her cigarettes.

"Hello. Can I help you?" Melissa smiled at the woman.

"Yes. I was wondering if Barbara still works here."

Barbara froze just as she was reaching the door. She groaned and headed back to her seat. "Yes, I'm Barbara."

"Oh, good! I was afraid you might not work here anymore."

"Can I help you?" Barbara asked.

"Oh, God, I really hope you can," the lady said a bit hysterically, and rooted through her bag. "I received this today from my husband, and I was wondering if you could explain it to me."

Barbara frowned at the crumpled piece of paper on the counter. A page had been torn out of a holiday brochure, and written on it were the words "Swords Travel Agents. Attn: Barbara." "Can't you ask your husband for more information?" Barbara said.

"No. He's not here anymore," the lady replied sadly.

"Okay. Maybe your name will come up on the computer."

"It's Holly Kennedy." Her voice shook.

"Holly Kennedy, Holly Kennedy." Melissa repeated her name after listening in on their conversation. "Oh, hold on. I was about to call you this week! That's weird. I was under strict instructions not to ring you until July for some reason—"

"Oh!" Barbara interrupted. "You're Gerry's wife?"

"Yes!" Holly threw her hands to her face. "He was here?"

"Yes, he was." Barbara smiled and tapped away on the computer. "Let me explain. Gerry arranged a holiday for you and a Sharon McCarthy and a Denise Hennessey to go to Lanzarote for a week, arriving on the twenty-eighth of July, to return home on the third of August. He was adamant that he find the perfect place for you."

"When did he come in?" Tears poured from Holly's eyes.

"The booking was made on the twenty-eighth of November."

"November?" Holly gasped. "Was he on his own?"

"Yes, but there was a taxi waiting for him the whole time." Barbara told her as much as she could remember.

"Oh, thank you, Barbara. Thank you so much." Holly reached over the counter and gave her a big hug.

"No problem at all." Barbara hugged her back. "Let us know

how you get on," she smiled. "Here's your details." She handed Holly a thick envelope and watched her walk out. Barbara sighed, thinking the crappy job might not be so crappy after all.

HOLLY eventually arrived at her house and waved to Sharon and Denise, who were sitting on her garden wall bathing in the sun. They jumped up and rushed over to greet her.

"You both got here quick," she said, trying to inject energy into her voice. She felt completely and utterly drained.

"Sharon left work as soon as you called, and she collected me from town," Denise explained, studying Holly's face.

"Oh, you didn't have to do that," Holly said lifelessly as she put the key in the door.

"Hey, have you been working in your garden?" Sharon asked, looking around and trying to lighten the atmosphere.

"No. It's either my neighbor or a little leprechaun lives down the end of my garden," Holly said as the door opened. "Why don't you two make yourselves comfortable in the living room, and I'll follow you in a minute." She headed into the toilet to splash cold water on her face. She needed to snap out of this daze, to take control of her body and be as excited as Gerry had intended.

When she felt a little more alive, she joined the girls in the living room. She pulled the footrest to the couch and sat opposite them.

"Okay. I'm not going to drag this one out. I opened the envelope for July today, and this is what it said." She handed them the small card that had been attached to the brochure:

> Have a good Holly day!
> PS, I love you . . .

"Is that it?" Denise wrinkled up her nose, unimpressed.

"Well, Holly, I think it's a lovely note," Sharon lied. "It's so thoughtful, and it's . . . a lovely play on words."

Holly had to giggle. "No, you fool!" she said, hitting Sharon with a cushion. "This was inside." Holly handed them the crumpled page that was torn from the brochure.

She watched with amusement as the girls tried to figure out Gerry's writing. "Oh, my God!" Denise gasped.

"What?" Sharon demanded. "Did Gerry buy you a holiday?"

"Girls," Holly said with a smile beginning to spread across her face, "he bought *us* a holiday!"

The girls opened a bottle of wine.

"Oh, this is incredible," Denise said after the news had sunk in. "Gerry's such a sweetie."

Holly nodded, feeling proud of her husband, who had once again managed to surprise them all.

"So you went down to this Barbara person?" Sharon asked.

"Yes, and she was the sweetest girl," Holly smiled. "She sat with me for ages, telling me about their conversation."

"That was nice," Denise said. "When was it, by the way?"

"He went in at the end of November."

"November?" Sharon looked thoughtful. "That was after the second operation."

Holly nodded. "The girl told me he was pretty weak."

"Isn't it funny that none of us had any idea at all?" Sharon said.

They all nodded silently.

"Well, it looks like we're all off to Lanzarote," Denise cheered, and she held her glass up. "To Gerry!"

"To Gerry!" Holly and Sharon joined in.

After Denise and Sharon had headed off home, Holly wandered around her garden, wondering about the leprechaun who had been tidying it up. As she walked back in her door, the phone rang. She ran to answer it. "Hello?" she panted.

"What were you doing, running a marathon?"

"No. I was chasing leprechauns."

"Oh, cool."

The oddest thing was that Ciara didn't even question her.

"It's my birthday in two weeks."

Holly had completely forgotten. "Yeah, I know, Ciara."

"Well, Mum and Dad want us all to invite friends to a barbe-cue. So will you tell Sharon and John, Denise and her DJ bloke, and that Daniel guy too?" She laughed hysterically. "He's yummy!"

"Ciara, I hardly know the guy. Ask Declan to ask him."

"No, because I want you to subtly tell him that I love him and want to have his babies."

Holly groaned.

"Stop it," Ciara gave out. "He's my birthday treat!"

"Okay, I'll call the others and . . ."

Ciara had already hung up.

Holly decided to get the most awkward phone call out of the way first, and she dialed the number to Hogan's.

"Hi, Daniel? It's Holly Kennedy."

"Who?"

Holly dived onto her bed in embarrassment. "It's Holly Kennedy? Declan's sister?"

"Oh, Holly, hiya. Hold on while I go somewhere quieter."

Holly was stuck listening to "Greensleeves," and she danced around her bedroom and started singing along.

"Sorry, Holly," Daniel laughed. "You like 'Greensleeves'?"

"Em, no, not really." Her face went scarlet. "I was just ringing to invite you to a barbecue."

"Oh, great. Yeah, I would love to go."

"It's Ciara's birthday on Friday week—you know, my sister, Ciara. Well, she wanted me to invite you and to subtly tell you that she wants to marry you and have your babies."

Daniel started laughing. "Yes, that was very subtle, all right."

"Em, well, Denise and Tom are coming, and Declan, so you'll know plenty of people."

"Are you going?"

"Of course!" She was just about to hang up when a thought popped into her head, "Oh, one more thing. Is that position behind the bar still available?"

THANK God it was a beautiful day, Holly thought as she walked around to the back of her parents' house. It had rained all week, and Ciara was in hysterics about her barbecue. Luckily for everyone's sake, the weather had returned to its former splendor.

Holly followed the sounds of laughter and was glad to see that the garden was full with family and friends. Denise had already arrived with Tom and Daniel, and they had all flaked out on the grass. Sharon had arrived without John, and she was sitting chatting to Holly's mum, no doubt discussing Holly's progress in life.

Ciara was standing in the middle of the garden, screaming at everyone and loving being the center of attention. She was dressed in a pink bikini top, to match her pink hair, and blue denim cutoffs.

Holly approached with her present, which was immediately grabbed and ripped open. "Oh, Holly, I love it! I'm gonna wear it now, actually," Ciara said, ripping out her current belly-button ring and piercing the butterfly with its pink wings through her skin.

"Ugh"—Holly shuddered—"I could've gone without seeing that."

There was a beautiful smell of barbecued food in the air, and Holly's mouth began to water. She went to join Denise, Tom, and Daniel on the grass.

"Hi, Daniel." She greeted him with a kiss on the cheek.

"Hi, Holly. Long time no see." He handed her a beer. It was weird seeing him out of his wintry clothes; he was dressed in a navy vest and navy combat shorts and a pair of trainers. She watched his biceps as he took a slug of his beer. She had had no idea he was that fit.

"You're very brown," she commented, trying to think of an excuse for being caught staring at his biceps.

"And so are you," he said, purposely staring at her legs.

Holly laughed and tucked them up underneath her. "A result of unemployment. What's your excuse?"

"I was in Miami for a while last month."

"Ooh, lucky you. Did you enjoy it?"

"Had a great time," he nodded. "Have you ever been?"

She shook her head. "But at least us girls are heading off to Spain next week. Can't wait." She rubbed her hands together excitedly.

"Yes, I heard that. I'd say that was a nice surprise for you." He gave her a smile, his eyes crinkling at the corners.

They chatted together for a while about his holiday. "I hope you didn't go to Miami with another woman, or poor Ciara will be devastated," she joked, and then kicked herself for being so nosy.

"No," he said seriously. "We broke up a few months ago."

"Oh, I'm sorry to hear that. Were you together long?"

"Seven years." He looked away, and Holly could tell he didn't feel comfortable talking about it, so she quickly changed the subject.

"By the way, Daniel, I wanted to thank you for looking out for me after the documentary. Most men run when they see a girl cry."

"No problem at all, Holly. I don't like to see you upset."

"You're a good friend," Holly said, thinking aloud. "Maybe I can get to know as much about you as you know about me," she laughed. "I think you know my whole life story."

"Yeah, I'd like that," Daniel agreed.

"Did you give Ciara that birthday present?" Holly asked.

"No," he laughed. "She's been kind of . . . busy."

Holly spotted her sister flirting with one of Declan's friends. So much for wanting Daniel's babies. "I'll call her over, will I?"

"Go on," Daniel said.

"Ciara," Holly called, "got another pressie for you!"

"Ooh!" Ciara screamed with delight. "What is it?" She collapsed on the grass beside them.

Holly nodded over at Daniel. "It's from him."

"Would you like a job working behind the bar at Club Diva?"

Ciara's hands flew to her mouth. "Oh, Daniel, that would be brill!" she squealed, and threw her arms around him.

Any excuse, Holly thought. "Okay, okay, that's enough, Ciara. You don't want to kill your new boss."

Suddenly the garden became very quiet, and Holly's parents appeared with a large birthday cake, singing "Happy Birthday." Someone followed behind them with a huge bouquet of flowers. Her parents placed the cake on a table, and the stranger removed the bouquet from his face.

"Mathew!" Ciara gasped. Her face went white.

"I'm sorry for being such a fool, Ciara." Mathew's Australian accent echoed around the garden. He looked like he was acting out a scene from an Australian soap, but then drama always seemed to work for Ciara. "I love you! Please take me back!" he announced. Everyone turned to Ciara to see what she would say.

Ciara's lower lip started to tremble. She ran over to Mathew and jumped onto him, throwing her arms around his neck.

Holly was overcome with emotion, and tears welled in her eyes. Declan grabbed his camera and began filming.

Daniel wrapped his arm around Holly's shoulders. "I'm sorry, Daniel." She wiped her eyes. "I think you've just been dumped."

"Not to worry," he laughed. "I shouldn't mix business with pleasure anyway." He seemed relieved.

Holly continued to watch as Mathew spun Ciara around in his arms.

"Oh, get a room!" Declan yelled, and everyone laughed.

HOLLY smiled at the jazz band as she passed and looked around the bar for Denise, Tom, and Daniel. They had arranged to meet up in the girls' favorite bar, Juicy, known for its extensive cocktail menu and relaxing music. Holly spotted Denise snuggling up to Tom on a large black leather couch in a conservatory area that overlooked the river Liffey. Daniel sat opposite Denise and Tom, sucking fiercely on a strawberry daiquiri, eyes surveying the room.

"Sorry I'm late," Holly apologized, approaching her friends.

"You're not forgiven," Daniel said quietly into her ear as he gave her a welcoming hug and kiss.

Denise looked up at Holly and smiled, Tom waved slightly, and they returned their attention to each other.

"I don't know why they bother inviting other people out. They just sit there staring into each other's eyes, ignoring everyone else. They don't even talk to each other! And then they make you feel like you've interrupted them if you strike up a conversation," Daniel said, taking another sip from his glass. He made a face at the sweet taste. "And I really need a beer."

Holly laughed. "Well, I've come to rescue you." She picked up the menu and surveyed the choice of drinks. She chose one with the lowest alcohol content and settled down in the cozy chair. "So, Mr. Connelly, you know everything about me. Tonight I am on a mission to find out about you, so be prepared for my interrogation."

Daniel smiled. "Okay, I'm ready."

Holly thought about her first question. "Where are you from?"

"Born and reared in Dublin." He took a sip of the red cocktail and winced again. "And if any of the people I grew up with saw me drinking this stuff and listening to jazz, I'd be in trouble."

Holly giggled.

"After I finished school, I joined the army," he continued.

Holly was impressed. "Why did you decide to do that?"

He didn't even think about it. "Because I hadn't a clue what I wanted to do with my life, and the money was good."

"So much for saving innocent lives," Holly laughed.

"I only stayed with the army for a few years. My parents had moved down to Galway to run a pub, and the idea of that appealed to me. So I moved down to Galway to work there, and eventually my parents retired, I took over the pub, decided a few years ago that I wanted to own one of my own, worked really hard, saved my money, took out the biggest mortgage ever, and moved back to Dublin and bought Hogan's. And here I am talking to you."

Holly smiled. "Well, that's a wonderful life story, Daniel."

"Nothing special, but a life all the same." He returned her smile.

"So where does the ex come into all this?" Holly asked.

"She's right in between running the pub in Galway and leaving to come to Dublin."

"Ah, I see," Holly nodded, understanding. She drained her glass and picked up the menu again. "I think I'll have Sex on the Beach."

"When? On your holidays?" Daniel teased.

Holly thumped him playfully on the arm. Not in a million years.

Eight

"We're *all going on our summer Holly days!*" the girls sang in the car all the way to the airport. John had offered to drive them, but he was fast regretting it. They were acting like they had never left the country before. Holly felt like she was back at school and off on a school tour. Her bag was packed with packets of sweets and magazines, and they couldn't stop singing cheesy songs. Their flight wasn't until nine p.m., so they wouldn't arrive at their accommodations until the early hours of the morning.

They reached the airport and piled out of the car. John lifted their suitcases out of the boot, they gave him a hug, and they dragged their luggage across the departure lounge to the long check-in queue. After thirty minutes of queuing, they finally checked in and headed over to the boarding gate.

Four hours later, the plane landed at Lanzarote Airport. The girls made their way to the luggage reclaim and stood for almost an hour waiting for their bags while the majority of the crowd went out to their coaches. Finally they headed off to meet their holiday rep.

"Kennedy, McCarthy, and Hennessey?" the young woman dressed in a red uniform said in a thick London accent.

The girls nodded.

"Hi. I'm Victoria, and I'll show you to the coach." She led the girls outside.

It was two o'clock in the morning, and yet a warm breeze greeted them. Holly smiled to the girls, who felt it too; now they were really on holiday. They stepped onto the coach.

Forty-five minutes later, they reached Costa Palma Palace. There was a long driveway, and tall palm trees lined the center of the drive. A large fountain was lit up with blue lights outside the main entrance. The girls were booked into an apartment that contained one bedroom with twin beds, a small kitchen and living area with a sofa bed, a bathroom, and a balcony. Holly stepped onto the balcony and looked out to the sea. Although it was too dark to see anything, she could hear the water gently lapping up against the sand. She closed her eyes and listened.

"Cigarette, cigarette, must have cigarette." Denise joined her, ripping the cigarette packet open and inhaling deeply. "Ah, that's much better. I no longer have the desire to kill people."

Holly laughed; she was looking forward to spending time with her friends.

"Hol, do you mind if I sleep on the sofa bed so I can smoke?"

"Only if you keep the door open, Denise," Sharon yelled from inside. "I'm not waking up in the morning to the stink of smoke."

"Thanks," Denise said happily.

At nine o'clock that morning, Sharon woke Holly up. "I'll be down on the beach if you want me," she said. Holly sleepily mumbled some response. At ten o'clock, Denise jumped on her in bed, and they decided to get up and join Sharon at the beach.

The sand was hot, and they had to keep moving so as not to burn the soles of their feet. They spotted Sharon sitting under the shade of an umbrella reading her book.

"Oh, this is so beautiful, isn't it?" Denise looked around.

Sharon looked up from her book and smiled. "Heaven."

Holly looked around to see if Gerry had come to the same heaven. Nope, no sign of him. All around her were couples—couples massaging sun cream onto each other, couples walking hand in hand along the beach. Holly didn't have time to be depressed, as Denise had stepped out of her sundress and was hopping around on the hot sand in nothing but a skimpy leopard-skin thong.

"Will one of you put sun cream on me?"

Sharon put her book down. "I'll do it."

Denise sat at the end of Sharon's sun bed. "You know what, Sharon? You'll get an awful tan line if you keep that sarong on."

Sharon looked down at herself. "What tan? I never get a tan. I've nice Irish skin, Denise. Didn't you know that the color blue was the new brown?"

Holly and Denise laughed. As much as Sharon tried to tan over the years, she just ended up getting sunburned. She had finally given up and accepted the fact that her skin was meant to be blue.

"Besides, I look like such a blob these days, I wouldn't want to scare everyone off."

Holly looked at Sharon, annoyed at her for calling herself a blob. She'd put a little weight on but was by no means fat.

The girls relaxed by the beach for the rest of the day, occasionally dipping themselves into the sea to cool down. They ate lunch at the beach bar. Holly gradually felt all the tension working its way out of her muscles, and for a few hours, she felt free.

That night, they enjoyed dinner in one of the many restaurants that lined the busy street not far from the complex.

"I can't believe it's ten o'clock and we're heading back to the apartment already," Denise said while staring longingly at the huge choice of bars around them.

People overflowed from the outdoor bars and onto the streets; music vibrated from every building. Holly could almost feel the ground pulsing beneath her. Neon lights flashed, and tanned young bodies hung out in big groups around outdoor tables.

Looking at the average age of the clientele, Holly felt old. "Well, we can go to a bar if you want," she said uncertainly.

Denise scanned the bars in order to choose one.

"All right, beautiful." A very attractive man stopped and flashed his pearly whites at Denise. "Are you coming in here with me?"

Denise stared at the young man for a while, lost in thought. Sharon and Holly smirked at each other, knowing that Denise wouldn't be going to bed early after all.

Finally Denise snapped out of her trance. "No thanks. I have a boyfriend, and I love him!" she announced. "Come on, girls," she said to Holly and Sharon, and walked off toward the hotel.

The two girls remained on the street, mouths open in shock.

They couldn't believe it. They had to run to catch up with her.

"What are you two gawking at?" Denise smiled.

"You," Sharon said, still shocked. "Who are you, and what have you done with my man-eating friend?"

"Okay." Denise held her hands up in the air and grinned. "Maybe being single isn't all it's cracked up to be."

Holly lowered her eyes and kicked a stone along the path as they made their way back to their resort. It sure wasn't.

"Well, good for you, Denise," Sharon said happily, wrapping her arm around Denise's waist and giving her a little squeeze.

A silence fell between them as the music faded away slowly, leaving only a beat of the bass in the distance.

"That street made me feel so old," Sharon said suddenly.

"Me too!" Denise's eyes widened. "Since when did people start going out so young?"

Sharon began to laugh. "Denise, *we* are getting older."

"Well, it's not like we're *old* old. I mean, we could stay out all night if we wanted to. We just . . . are tired. We've had a long day. Oh, God, I do sound old," Denise rambled on.

Sharon watched Holly with concern. "Holly, are you okay? You haven't said a word."

"Yeah, I was just thinking," Holly said quietly.

"Thinking about what?" Sharon asked softly.

Holly looked at the girls. "I was thinking about Gerry."

"Let's go down to the beach," Denise suggested, and they slipped off their shoes and let their feet sink into the cool sand.

The sky was clear, and a million stars twinkled as if someone had thrown glitter up into a massive black net. The full moon rested over the horizon. The girls sat in its path, the water gently lapping before them. Holly filled her lungs with fresh air.

"That's why he brought you here, you know," Sharon said, watching her friend relaxing.

Holly closed her eyes and smiled.

"You don't talk about him much, Holly," Denise said.

Holly slowly opened her eyes. "I know."

Denise drew circles in the sand. "Why not?"

Holly thought for a while. "I don't know whether to be sad or happy when I talk about him. It's like if I'm happy, certain people judge and expect me to be crying my eyes out. When I'm upset, it makes people feel uncomfortable." She stared out to the sparkling sea. "I can't tease about him in conversation like I used to, because it feels wrong. I can't talk about things he told me in confidence, because they're *his* secrets."

The three girls sat cross-legged on the soft sand.

"John and I talk about Gerry all the time." Sharon looked at Holly with glittering eyes. "We talk about the times he made us laugh, which was a lot. We even talk about the times we fought. Things we loved about him and things he did that annoyed us."

Holly raised her eyebrows.

Sharon continued. "Because to us, that's just how Gerry was. He wasn't all nice. We remember *all* of him."

There was a long silence.

Denise was first to speak. "I wish my Tom had known Gerry."

Holly looked at her in surprise. A tear ran down Holly's cheek.

"Gerry was my friend too," Denise said. "I tell Tom things about him just so he knows that one of the nicest men on this earth was my friend. I can't believe that someone I now love so much doesn't know a friend I loved for ten years."

Holly reached out to hug her friend. "Well then, we'll just have to keep telling Tom about him, won't we, Denise?"

THEY didn't bother meeting up with their holiday rep the next morning, as they had no intention of going on any tours. Instead, they spent the day at the beach.

"You ever hear from Gerry's parents, Holly?" Sharon asked as she and Holly lounged on their inflatable rafts in the sea.

"Yeah. They send me postcards every few weeks."

"So they're still on that cruise? Do you miss them?"

"To be honest, I don't think they feel we have any connection anymore. Their son's gone, and they have no grandchildren."

"That's bull, Holly. You're their daughter-in-law."

"Oh, I don't know," Holly sighed.

"They're a bit backward, aren't they?"

"Yeah, *very*. They hated me and Gerry 'living in sin,' as they said. Couldn't wait for us to get married. And then they couldn't understand why I wouldn't change my name."

"Yeah, I remember that," Sharon said.

"Hello, girls." Denise floated out to meet them.

"Hey, where have you been?" Holly asked.

"Oh, chatting to some bloke from Miami. Nice guy."

"Miami? That's where Daniel went on holiday," Holly said.

"Hmm," Sharon replied, "nice guy, Daniel, isn't he?"

"Really nice," Holly agreed. "Very easy to talk to."

"Tom was telling me he's been through the wars recently," Denise said, turning to lie on her back.

Sharon's ears pricked up. "Why's that?"

"Oh, he was engaged to some chick, and it turns out she was sleeping with someone else. That's why he moved to Dublin and bought the pub, to get away from her."

"I know. It's awful, isn't it?" Holly said sadly.

"Where did he live before?" Sharon asked.

"Galway. He used to run a pub there," Holly explained.

"Oh," Sharon said. "He doesn't have a Galway accent."

"Well, he grew up in Dublin and joined the army; then he left and moved to Galway, where his family owns a pub; then he met Laura; they were together for seven years, were engaged to be married, but she cheated on him, so they broke up, and he moved back to Dublin and bought Hogan's." Holly caught her breath.

"Don't know much about him, do you?" Denise teased.

"Well, if you and Tom had paid the slightest bit more attention to us the other night in the pub, then maybe I wouldn't know so much about him," Holly replied playfully.

Denise sighed loudly. "I really miss Tom," she said sadly.

"Did you tell the guy from Miami that?" Sharon laughed.

"No. I was just chatting to him," Denise said defensively. "To be honest, nobody else interests me. It's really weird. I don't even *notice* other men."

Sharon smiled at her. "I think they call it love, Denise."

They lay in silence for a while, all lost in their own thoughts, allowing the gentle motion of the waves to soothe them.

"Bloody hell!" Denise yelled. "Look how far out we are!"

Holly sat up immediately. They were out so far from shore, everybody on the beach looked like ants.

"Oh, God!" panicked Sharon.

"Start swimming, quick!" Denise yelled, and they all started splashing. After a few minutes of tirelessly going at it, they gave up. To their horror, they were even farther out. It was no use—the tide was moving out too quickly, and the waves were just too strong.

"Help!" Denise screamed at the top of her lungs, and waved her arms around wildly.

"I don't think they can hear us," Holly said.

"Oh, could we be any more stupid?" Sharon ranted.

"Forget about that, Sharon," Denise snapped. "We're here now, so let's all scream together."

They all sat up on their rafts. "Okay, one, two, three . . . HELP!" They all waved their arms frantically.

Eventually they stopped screaming and stared in silence at the dots on the beach. Holly tried to hold back her tears. "We might as well save our energy," she said.

The three of them huddled together on their rafts and cried. There was nothing more they could do, Holly thought, beginning to panic even more. It was starting to get chilly, and the sea was looking dark and ugly. What a stupid situation to get themselves into. Through all her fear and worry, Holly managed to surprise herself by feeling completely humiliated. She wasn't sure whether to laugh or cry.

"At least one good thing came out of this," she said.

"There's a good thing?" Sharon said, wiping her eyes.

"Well, the three of us always talked about going to Africa," she giggled. "And by the looks of things, we're halfway there."

The girls looked out to sea to their future destination. "It's a cheaper mode of transport too," Sharon joined in.

Denise stared at them as if they were mad, and just one look at her lying in the middle of the ocean naked with only a leopard-skin thong was enough to set the girls off laughing.

"What?" Denise looked at them, wide-eyed.

"I'd say we're in deep, deep trouble here," Sharon giggled.

"Yeah," Holly agreed. "We're in way over our heads."

They lay there laughing and crying for a few minutes more till the sound of a speedboat caused Denise to start waving frantically again. Holly and Sharon laughed even harder at the sight of Denise's chest bouncing up and down as she waved.

"It's just like a regular night out with the girls," Sharon giggled, watching Denise being dragged to the boat by a muscular lifeguard.

"I think they're in shock," one lifeguard said to the other as they dragged the remaining hysterical girls onto the boat.

"Quick, save the rafts!" Holly blurted out through her laughter.

"Raft overboard!" Sharon screamed.

The lifeguards looked at each other worriedly as they wrapped warm blankets around the girls and sped back to shore.

A large crowd appeared to be gathering. The girls looked at one another and laughed even harder. As they were lifted off the boat, there was a huge applause. "They clap now, but where were they when we needed them?" Sharon grumbled.

"Traitors," Holly giggled. They all cracked up laughing again and were ushered away to be looked at by a doctor.

That night, the girls realized the seriousness of what had happened, and their moods drastically changed. They sat in silence throughout dinner, thinking about how lucky they were to be rescued and kicking themselves for being careless. Holly had reacted unusually out there in the water. After the initial panic of thinking she was going to die, she became giddy as she realized that if she did die, she would be with Gerry. It bothered her to think that she didn't care whether she lived or died. She needed to change her perspective on life.

THE NEXT MORNING, HOLLY woke to the sound of Sharon throwing up in the toilet. She followed her in and gently held back her hair.

"You okay?" Holly asked worriedly after she had stopped.

"Yeah. It's just those bloody dreams I had all night. I dreamed I was on a boat and on a raft. I think it was just seasickness."

"I had those dreams too. It was scary yesterday, wasn't it?"

Sharon smiled weakly. "I'm never going on a raft again."

Denise arrived at the bathroom door a moment later, already dressed in her bikini. She and Sharon decided to head to the pool, while Holly went down to the beach alone, carrying the small beach bag that contained her all-important letter from Gerry.

Holly couldn't believe that she had fallen asleep before midnight the previous night. She had planned to get up quietly without waking the girls, sneak out to the balcony, and read the next letter. How she fell asleep in all her excitement was beyond her.

At the beach, she positioned herself away from the shouts of children playing and stereos blaring. She found a quiet corner and made herself comfortable on her beach towel. The waves crashed and fell. It was morning, and already the sun was hot.

She carefully pulled the letter out of her bag and ran her fingers along the word "August." She gently tore open the seal.

> Hi, Holly,
>
> I hope you're having a wonderful holiday. You're looking beautiful in that bikini! I hope I picked the right place. It's the place you and I almost went for our honeymoon, remember? I'm glad you got to see it in the end.
>
> Apparently, if you stand at the very end of the beach near the rocks and look around to the left, you'll see a lighthouse. I'm told that's where the dolphins gather. I know you love dolphins. Tell them I said hi.
>
> PS, I love you, Holly . . .

With shaking hands, Holly put the card back into the envelope and secured it safely in her bag. She felt as if Gerry were here with her as she stood up and rolled up the beach towel. She quicky ran to the end of the beach, which suddenly stopped because of a cliff. She put her trainers on and began to climb the rocks.

And there it was, exactly where Gerry had described it: The lighthouse sat high on the cliff, bright white, as though it were some sort of torch to heaven. Holly carefully climbed over the rocks and made her way around the little cove. She was on her own now. It was completely private. And then she heard the noises. The squeaks of dolphins playing near the shore, away from all the tourists on the beaches. Holly collapsed on the sand to listen to them talk.

Gerry sat beside her.

He may even have held her hand.

HOLLY felt happy enough to head back to Dublin, relaxed, de-stressed, and brown. Just what the doctor ordered. That didn't stop her from groaning when the plane landed in heavy rain.

"It looks like the garden leprechaun didn't do any work while you were away," Denise said when John reached Holly's home.

Holly gave her friends a big hug and a kiss and made her way into her quiet, empty house. There was a horrible musty smell in-side, and she moved to the patio doors to let the fresh air circulate.

She froze as she turned the key in the door and stared outside. Her entire back garden had been re-landscaped. The grass was cut. The weeds were gone. The garden furniture had been polished. A fresh coat of paint gleamed from her garden walls. Flowers had been planted, and underneath the great oak sat a wooden bench. Holly looked around in shock. Who on earth was doing all this?

Nine

$\mathcal{I}$N THE days following her return from Lanzarote, Holly kept a low profile. It wasn't something she, Denise, and Sharon had talked about, but after living in each other's ears for a week, Holly was sure they all agreed, it was healthy to spend some time apart. Ciara was impossible to get hold of, as she was either working at Daniel's club or spending time with Mathew. Jack was spending his last few precious weeks of summer freedom down in Cork, and Declan was . . . Well, who knew where Declan was.

She wasn't exactly bored with her life, but it just seemed so . . . pointless. She'd had the holiday to look forward to, but now again, she felt she had no real reason to get out of bed in the morning. And compared to last week in Lanzarote, Dublin was wet and ugly.

Some days, she never even got out of bed; she just watched television and waited for next month's envelope from Gerry, wondering what journey he would take her on next. When he was alive, she'd lived for him, and now that he was gone, she lived for his messages.

Something that she did feel she should do was to catch the garden leprechaun. After interrogating her neighbors, she still knew nothing more of her mystery gardener. Eventually she had herself convinced that a gardener was working on the wrong garden, so she checked the post every day for a bill that she was going to refuse to pay. But no bill arrived—of that variety anyway. Plenty of others arrived: electricity bills, phone bills, insurance bills. Everything that came through her door was a bloody bill, and she hadn't a clue how she was going to continue paying them all. But she had become numb to all those irrelevant problems in life.

One morning, Denise called her. "Hiya. How are you?" she asked.

"Oh, full of the joys of life," Holly said sarcastically.

"Me too!" Denise giggled in response.

"Really? What's got you so happy?"

"Oh, nothing much, just life in general," she giggled again.

Of course, just life. Wonderful, beautiful life.

"So what's happening?"

"I'm calling to invite you out for dinner tomorrow night. We're all meeting at Chang's at eight."

"Who's we?"

"Sharon and John and some of Tom's friends. We haven't been out together for ages, so it'll be fun!"

Holly rolled her eyes. "Okay then, see you tomorrow." She hung up feeling angry. Had it slipped Denise's mind that Holly was still a grieving widow? She stormed upstairs and opened her wardrobe. Now what piece of old and disgusting clothing would she wear tomorrow night, and how on earth was she going to afford an expensive meal? She could barely afford to keep her car on the road. She grabbed all her clothes from her wardrobe and flung them across the room, screaming her head off until she finally felt sane again.

HOLLY arrived at the restaurant at eight-twenty, as she had spent hours trying on different outfits. Eventually she settled with the one she had been instructed to wear by Gerry for the karaoke, just so she could feel closer to him.

As she was walking toward the table in the restaurant, her heart sank—Couples "R" Us.

She paused halfway there and quickly sidestepped, hiding behind a wall. She wasn't sure she could go through with this. She looked around to find the easiest escape route—the fire escape beside the kitchen door. The moment she stepped out into the cool fresh air, she felt free again. She walked across the car park, trying to formulate an excuse to tell Denise.

"Hi, Holly."

She froze and slowly turned around. Daniel was leaning against his car smoking a cigarette.

"Hiya, Daniel. I didn't know you smoked."

"Only when I'm stressed."

"You're stressed?" They greeted each other with a hug.

"I was figuring out whether to join the Happy Couples."

Holly smiled. "You too?"

He laughed. "I won't tell them I saw you if that's what you want."

"So you're going in?"

"Have to face the music sometime," he said grimly.

Holly thought about what he'd said. "I suppose you're right."

"You don't have to go in if you don't want to. I don't want to be the cause of you having a miserable night."

"On the contrary, it would be nice to have another loner in my company. There are so very few in existence."

Daniel laughed again and held out his arm. "Shall we?"

Holly linked his arm. "By the way," she said, "I have to leave early to catch the last bus." She hadn't had money to fill the car for days.

"Well then, we have the perfect excuse. I'll say I'm driving you home and you have to be home by . . ."

"Half-eleven?" At twelve, she planned on opening the September envelope.

"Perfect time." He smiled, and they walked into the restaurant.

"Here they are!" Denise announced as they approached the table.

Holly sat beside Daniel. "Sorry we're late."

"Holly, this is Catherine and Thomas, Peter and Sue, Joanne and Paul, Tracey and Bryan—John and Sharon you know—Geoffrey and Samantha, and last but not least, this is Des and Simon."

Holly smiled and nodded at all of them.

"Hi. We're Daniel and Holly," Daniel said smartly.

"We had to order already," Denise explained. "But we ordered loads of dishes so we can all share them."

Holly and Daniel nodded.

Everyone fell into conversation, and Daniel turned to Holly. "Did you enjoy your holiday?"

"Oh, I had a fabulous time," she answered. "We took it easy and relaxed. Didn't do anything wild and weird."

"Just what you needed," he smiled. "I heard about your near-death experience."

Holly rolled her eyes. "I bet Denise gave you the exaggerated version."

"Not really. She just told me about how you were surrounded by sharks and had to be airlifted by a helicopter."

"She didn't!"

"No, not really," he laughed.

"Okay, everyone," Denise called. "You're probably wondering why Tom and I invited you all here tonight. Well, we have an announcement to make." She looked at everyone and smiled.

Holly's eyes widened.

"Myself and Tom are getting married!" Denise squealed.

Holly's hands flew up to her mouth. She did *not* see that one coming. "Oh, Denise!" she gasped, and walked around the table to hug them. "That's wonderful news! Congratulations!"

She looked at Daniel's face; it had gone white.

They popped open a bottle of champagne, and everyone raised their glasses for a toast. "Hold on! Hold on!" Denise stopped them. "Sharon, did you not get a glass?"

Everyone looked at Sharon, who was holding a glass of orange juice in her hand.

"None for me, thanks," she said.

"Why not?" Denise huffed, upset that her friend wouldn't celebrate with her.

Sharon looked at John. "Well, I didn't want to say anything, because it's Denise and Tom's special night. . . ."

Everyone urged her to speak.

"Well, I'm pregnant! John and I are going to have a baby!"

Holly froze in shock. She did *not* see that one coming either. Tears filled her eyes as she went to congratulate Sharon and John. Then she sat down and took deep breaths. This was all too much.

"So let's make a toast to Tom and Denise's engagement and Sharon and John's baby!"

Everyone clinked glasses, and Holly ate dinner in silence, not really tasting anything. After dinner, she and Daniel made their excuses to leave, and nobody really tried to persuade them to stay. Holly left her last thirty euro toward the bill.

They drove in the car in silence. Holly wanted to feel happy for her friends, but she couldn't shake off the feeling of being left behind. Everyone else's lives were moving on except hers.

Daniel pulled up outside her house. "Do you want to come in for a tea or coffee or anything?" She was sure he would say no and was shocked when he accepted her offer. She really liked Daniel, but right now, she just wanted to be alone.

"That was some night, wasn't it?" Daniel said, sipping his coffee.

She shook her head. "Daniel, I have known those girls all my life, and I did *not* see any of that coming. Sharon wasn't drinking when we were away, and she did throw up a few mornings, but she said it was seasickness." Holly's brain went into overdrive as things started to add up.

"Seasickness?" Daniel asked, confused.

"After our near-death experience," she explained.

"Oh, right." This time neither of them laughed.

"It's funny," he said, settling down into the couch. Oh, no, Holly thought. He's never going to leave the house now. "The lads always said that myself and Laura would be the first to get married. I just didn't think Laura would be getting married before me."

"She's getting married?" Holly asked.

"He used to be a friend of mine too," he laughed bitterly.

"Obviously, he's not anymore."

"Nope."

They sat in silence for another while, and Holly watched the clock. It was ten past twelve. She really needed to get him out of the house so she could open the envelope.

He read her mind. "So how're the messages from above going?"

Holly sat forward. "Well, I've another one to open tonight, actually. So . . ." She looked at him.

"Oh, right," he said, jumping up. "I better leave you at it."

Holly bit her lip. "Thanks a million for the lift, Daniel."

"No problem at all." They gave each other a quick hug.

"See you soon," she said, feeling like a bitch, but her guilt faded as soon as she closed the door. "Right, Gerry," she said. "What have you got in store for me this month?"

She held the envelope tightly and glanced up at the kitchen clock. It was twelve-fifteen. Usually Sharon and Denise would have called her by now. It seemed news of an engagement and a pregnancy beat the news of a message from Gerry. Holly scorned herself for being so bitter. She wanted to be back in the restaurant right now, celebrating with her friends, like the old Holly would have done. But she couldn't bring herself even to smile for them.

She was jealous of their good fortune. She was angry with them for moving on. Even in the company of friends, she felt alone; in a room of a thousand people, she would feel alone. But mostly, when she roamed the rooms of her quiet house, she felt so alone.

She couldn't remember the last time she'd felt truly happy. She missed going to bed at night with absolutely nothing on her mind. She missed the feeling of being loved, of knowing Gerry was watching her as she watched television or ate her dinner. She missed sensing his eyes on her as she entered a room. She missed his touches, his hugs, his words of advice, his words of love.

She hated counting down the days till she could read another one of his messages, because they were all she had left of him, and after this one, there would be only three more. And she hated to think of what her life might be like when there would be no more Gerry. Memories were fine, but you couldn't hold them.

She slowly opened her seventh envelope:

> Shoot for the moon, and if you miss, you'll be among the stars. Promise me you will find a job you love this time!
>
> PS, I love you . . .

Holly reread the letter, trying to discover how it made her feel. She had been dreading going back to work for such a long time now, had believed that she wasn't ready. But now she knew she had no choice. If Gerry said it was to be, it would be. Holly's face broke into a smile. "I promise, Gerry," she said happily. She studied his writing for a long time, and when she was satisfied she had analyzed every word, she rushed over to the kitchen drawer, took out a notepad and pen, and began to write her own list of possible jobs:

1. FBI Agent—Am not American. Do not want to live in America. Have no police experience.
2. Lawyer—Hated school. Hated studying.
3. Doctor—Ugghh.
4. Nurse—Unflattering uniforms.
5. Waitress—Would eat all the food.

6. Beautician—Bite my nails, and wax as rarely as possible. Do not want to see areas of other people's bodies.

7. Secretary—NEVER AGAIN.

8. Actress—Could not possibly outdo my wonderful performance in the critically acclaimed "Girls and the City."

9. Hotshot businesswoman in control of life—Hmm . . . Must do research tomorrow.

Holly finally collapsed onto her bed and dreamed of being a hotshot advertising woman making a huge presentation on the top floor of a skyscraper overlooking Grafton Street. Well, he did say aim for the moon.

She woke up early the next morning, excited from her dreams of success, and walked to her local library to look up jobs on the Internet. The librarian directed her to the row of computers on the far side of the room. "It's five euro for every twenty minutes online."

Holly handed over her last ten euro. It was all she had managed to take out of her ATM that morning before the machine beeped INSUFFICIENT FUNDS. She couldn't believe that was all she had left.

"No, no," the librarian said, handing back her money. "You can pay when you finish."

Holly reached the computers and realized that there were none free. She stood drumming her fingers on her handbag and looking around. Her eyes nearly popped out of her head as she spotted Richard tapping away. She tiptoed over and touched him on the shoulder. He jumped with fright and swirled around in his chair.

"Hiya," she whispered.

"Oh, hello, Holly. What are you doing here?" he said uneasily, as though she had caught him doing something naughty.

"I'm just waiting for a computer," she explained. "I'm finally looking for a job," she said proudly.

"Oh, right." He shut down his screen. "You can use this one."

"Oh, no. You don't have to rush for me," she said quickly.

"Not at all. I was just doing some research for work."

"All the way over here?" she said, surprised. "Don't they have computers in Blackrock?" She wasn't quite sure what Richard did for a living, and it would seem rude to ask him after he'd worked there more than ten years. She knew it involved wearing a white coat, wandering around a lab, and dropping colorful substances into test tubes.

"My work brings me everywhere," Richard joked awkwardly. He said a quick good-bye and made his way over to pay at the desk.

Holly sat down at the computer and quickly became engrossed in her job-hunting.

Forty minutes later, she made her way to the desk. The librarian tapped away on the computer. "That's fifteen euro, please."

Holly gulped, "I thought you said five for twenty minutes."

"Yes, that's right," she smiled at her.

"But I was only online for forty minutes."

"Actually, you were on for forty-four minutes, which cuts into the extra twenty minutes."

Holly lowered her voice. "This is embarrassing, but I only have the ten on me now. Can I come back with the rest later today?"

The librarian shook her head. "I'm sorry, but we can't allow that. You need to pay the entire amount."

"But I don't have the entire amount," Holly protested.

The lady stared back blankly.

"Fine," Holly huffed, taking out her mobile.

"Sorry, but you can't use that in here." She pointed to the NO MOBILE PHONES sign on the counter.

Holly looked at her and counted to five in her head. "So we have a little problem here, don't we? Can I go outside to use the phone?"

"As long as you stand in front of the entrance." The lady shuffled papers and pretended to go back to work.

Holly stood outside the door and thought about whom to call. She didn't want Denise and Sharon to know about her failures, now that they were both so blissfully happy. She couldn't call Ciara, because she was on a day shift at Hogan's pub. Jack was back teaching, Declan was at college, and Richard wasn't even an option.

Tears rolled down her face as she scrolled down through the list of names in her phone book. The majority hadn't even called her since Gerry had died. She turned her back on the librarian so the woman wouldn't see that she was upset. How embarrassing to actually have to call somebody to ask for five euro. It was even more humiliating that she had absolutely nobody to call. She dialed the first number that came into her head.

"Hi. This is Gerry. Please leave a message after the beep, and I'll get back to you as soon as I can."

"Gerry," Holly said, crying, "I need you."

AN HOUR later, Holly was snuggled up on the couch with her mum in Portmarnock. She felt like a teenager again. Her mum had picked her up at the library, dealt with the librarian, and brought her home for tea.

"I rang you last night. Were you out?" her mum said.

Holly took a sip of tea. Oh, the wonders of the magical tea. The answer to all of life's little problems. You have a gossip, and you make a cup of tea; you get fired from your job, and you have a cup of tea; your husband tells you he has a brain tumor, and you have a cup of tea. . . .

"Yeah. I went out to dinner with the girls and about a hundred other people I didn't know." Holly rubbed her eyes tiredly.

"How are the girls?" Elizabeth said fondly. She had always gotten along well with Holly's friends, unlike Ciara's friends, who terrified her.

Holly took another sip of her tea. "Sharon's pregnant, and Denise got engaged," she said, staring off into space.

"Oh," Elizabeth squeaked, not sure how to react in front of her obviously distressed daughter. "How do you feel about that?" she asked softly, brushing a hair away from Holly's face.

Holly stared down at her hands and tried to compose herself. She wasn't successful, and her shoulders began to tremble.

"Oh, Holly," Elizabeth said sadly, moving closer to her daughter. "It's perfectly normal to feel like this."

Holly couldn't manage to get any words out of her mouth.

The front door banged. "We're hoooome!" Ciara announced.

"Great," Holly sniffed, resting her head on her mum's chest.

"Where is everyone?" Ciara shouted, banging doors closed around the house.

"Just a minute, love," Elizabeth called out, angry that her moment with Holly was ruined.

"I have news!" Ciara's voice got louder as she got nearer to the living room. Mathew burst open the door, carrying her in his arms. "Me and Mathew are moving back to Australia!" she yelled happily into the room. She froze as she saw her upset sister in her mum's arms. She quickly jumped down from Mathew's arms, led him out of the room, and closed the door silently behind them.

"Now Ciara's going, too, Mum." Holly cried even harder, and Elizabeth wept softly for her daughter.

HOLLY stayed up late that night talking to her mum about everything that had been bubbling up inside her for the past few months. And although her mother offered many words of kind reassurance, Holly still felt as trapped as before. She stayed in the guest bedroom that night and woke up to a madhouse the following morning. Holly smiled at the familiarity of the sound of her brother and sister running around the house, screaming about how they were late for college and late for work. The world went on, simple as that, and there was no bubble big enough to protect her.

At lunchtime, Holly's dad dropped her home and squeezed a check for five thousand euro into her hand.

"Dad, I can't accept this," Holly said, overcome with emotion.

"Take it," he said gently. "Let us help you, love."

"I'll pay back every cent," she said, hugging him tightly.

She stood at the door and waved her father off down the road. She looked at the check in her hand, and immediately a weight was lifted from her shoulders. She could think of twenty things to do with this check, and for once, buying clothes wasn't one of them.

She sat in the spare room in front of her computer and began to type up a C.V. It took her two hours to finally print out something half decent. She laughed, hoping she would manage to fool her future employers into thinking she was a capable worker. She dressed smartly and drove down to the recruitment office in the car she had finally managed to fill with petrol. There was to be no more time wasting. If Gerry said to find a job, she was going to find a job.

A COUPLE of days later, Holly sat out on her new garden furniture in her back garden, sipping on a glass of red wine. She looked around at the neat landscaped lines and decided that whoever was working on her garden had to be a professional. She breathed in the sweet scent of the flowers. It was eight o'clock, and already it was beginning to get dark. The bright evenings were gone, and everybody was once again preparing for winter hibernation.

She thought about the message she had received on her answering machine that day. It had been from the recruitment agency. The woman on the phone said that there had been a great response to her résumé, and already Holly had an interview lined up for a job selling advertising space for a magazine that circulated throughout Dublin. It was something she had absolutely no experience in. But Gerry had told her to shoot for the moon. . . .

Holly also thought about the phone call she had just received from Denise. Denise didn't seem to be at all bothered by the fact that Holly hadn't talked to her since they'd gone out for dinner. Denise had been full of talk about her wedding in January. All Holly had to do was make a few noises to let her know she was still listening, although she wasn't.

Sharon hadn't called since the day after she had announced her pregnancy. Holly knew she would have to call Sharon soon, but she just couldn't bring herself to do it. She was still trying to get her head around the fact that Sharon and John were managing to achieve everything that everyone had assumed Holly and Gerry would do first. Sharon had always said she hated kids, Holly thought angrily. Holly would call Sharon when she was good and ready.

It began to get chilly, and Holly took her glass of wine inside. All she could do was wait for her job interview and pray for success.

She went into the sitting room, turned on her and Gerry's favorite CD of love songs, snuggled up on the couch with her wine, closed her eyes, and pictured them dancing around the room together.

THE following day, she was awoken by the sound of a car in her driveway. She got out of bed and peeped through the curtains and jumped back as she saw Richard step out of his car. She wasn't in the mood for one of his visits. She paced her bedroom floor, feeling guilty as she ignored the doorbell ringing.

She breathed a sigh of relief as she heard his car door bang shut. She stepped into the shower and twenty minutes later came downstairs. A scraping noise from outside made her prick her ears up. There it was again. A scraping noise and a rustling . . . Holly's eyes widened as she realized that her leprechaun was outside.

She crept into the living room and got down on her knees. Peering above the windowsill, she gasped as she saw Richard's car still sitting in the driveway. What was even more surprising was the sight of Richard on his hands and knees planting new flowers. She crawled away from the window and sat on the carpet in shock.

A few minutes later, she peeked out from behind the curtain again and saw Richard packing up his gardening equipment. As soon as he drove down the road, she ran outside and hopped into her car. She was going to chase her leprechaun.

She managed to stay three cars behind him, just like they did in the movies, and she slowed down as she saw him pulling over. He parked his car and went into the newsagent, returned with a newspaper, and crossed the road to the Greasy Spoon.

She backed into a free space, crossed the road, and looked inside the café. Richard was sitting with his back to her, hunched over his paper and drinking a cup of tea. She marched over happily with a smile on her face. "Richard, do you ever go to work?" she joked loudly, causing him to jump. She was about to say more but stopped herself as he looked up with tears in his eyes.

She pulled out a chair and sat down beside him. "Richard, what's wrong?" She awkwardly patted his arm.

Tears continued to roll down his face. "I'm sorry for crying," he said, embarrassed. He wiped his eyes with a tissue.

"Hey, it's my new hobby these days, so don't knock it."

He smiled sadly. "Everything just seems to be falling apart."

"Like what?" she asked, concerned at her brother's transformation into somebody she didn't know at all. She had seen so many sides to him over the past few months, he had her slightly baffled.

Richard gulped back his tea. He looked doubtful.

"Richard, I've recently learned that talking about things helps," Holly said gently. "I won't laugh; I won't say anything if you don't want me to. I won't tell a soul what you tell me," she assured him.

He looked away and spoke quietly. "I lost my job."

Holly remained silent and waited for him to say more. After a while, Richard looked up to face her.

"Richard, I know you loved your job, but you can find another one. Hey, I lose my jobs all the time—"

"I lost my job in April, Holly." He spoke angrily. "It is now September. There's nothing for me, not in my line of work."

"Oh." Holly didn't know quite what to say. "But Meredith is working, so you still have a regular income. Just take the time you need to find the right job—"

"Meredith left me last month." This time, his voice was weaker.

Holly's hands flew to her mouth. "The kids?"

"They're living with her," he said, and his voice cracked.

"Oh, Richard, I'm so sorry," she said, fidgeting with her hands. Should she hug him or leave him alone?

"I'm sorry too," he said miserably.

"It wasn't your fault, so don't tell yourself it was."

"Wasn't it?" he said, his voice beginning to break. "She told me I was a pathetic man who couldn't even look after his own family."

"Oh, never mind that silly bitch. You are an excellent father and a loyal husband," she said, and realized she meant every word of it. "Timmy and Emily love you because you're fantastic with them, so don't mind what that demented woman says." She wrapped her arms around him and hugged him while he cried.

Richard's tears finally subsided, and he pulled away from her.

"Where are you staying?" she asked.

"In a B and B down the road," he said, pouring another cup of tea. Your wife leaves you, and you have a cup of tea. . . .

"You can't stay there. Why didn't you tell any of us? What about Mum and Dad?" she asked.

Richard shook his head. "No. I wouldn't want to dump myself on them. I'm a grown man now."

"Oh, don't be silly. There is nothing wrong with returning to the house you grew up in now and again. It's good for the soul."

He looked uncertain. "I don't think that's such a good idea."

"Ciara's heading back to Australia in a few weeks."

His face relaxed a little.

Holly smiled. "So what do you think?"

Richard smiled, and it quickly faded. "I couldn't ask Mother and Father, Holly. I wouldn't know what to say."

"I'll go with you, and I'll talk to them for you. Honestly, Richard, they'll be delighted. You're their son, and they love you. We all do," she added, placing her hand over his.

"Okay," he finally agreed, and she linked her arm in his as they headed out to their cars.

"Oh, by the way, Richard. Thank you for my garden." Holly smiled at him, then leaned over and kissed him on the cheek.

"You know?" he asked, surprised.

She nodded. "You have a huge talent."

Her brother's face relaxed into a shy smile.

Ten

$\mathcal{T}$WO days later, Holly looked at herself in the toilet mirror of the office building where her interview was taking place. She had lost so much weight since she had last worn her old suits that she had had to purchase a new one. It was black with light pink lines going through, and she matched it with a light pink top underneath. She felt like a hotshot advertising businesswoman in control of her life, and all she needed to do now was to sound like one.

She took a seat in the waiting area and looked around the office. The colors were warm and cozy, and the light poured in from the large Georgian windows. Holly could sit there all day thinking. Her heart didn't even jump as her name was called.

"Shoot for the moon," she whispered to herself.

She knocked on the door, and a deep voice told her to enter. "Hello," she said more confidently than she felt. She walked across the room and held out her hand to the man who had stood up from his chair. He greeted her with a smile and a warm handshake. He looked to be in his late fifties, with a big physique and silver hair.

"Holly Kennedy, isn't it?" he said, taking his seat and glancing down at her C.V. She sat opposite him.

"That's right," she said, resting her sweaty hands on her lap.

He put his glasses on the end of his nose and flicked through her C.V. in silence. Holly glanced around his desk, and her eyes fell upon a silver photo frame with three pretty girls close to her age all smiling at the camera. When she looked up, she realized he had put the C.V. down and was watching her. She smiled and tried to appear more businesslike.

"Before we start talking about you, I'll explain who I am and what the job entails. I'm Chris Feeney, founder and editor of the magazine. As you know, the running of any media organization is hugely reliant on the advertising we receive. Unfortunately, our last man had to leave us in a hurry, so I'm looking for somebody who could begin work almost immediately."

Holly nodded. "That would be no problem at all—in fact, I'm eager to begin work as soon as possible."

"I see you've been out of the workforce for over a year now, am I correct?" Chris stared at her over the rim of his glasses.

"Yes, that's right. Unfortunately, my husband was ill, and I had to take time off work to be with him."

"I see. Well, I hope he's fully recovered now."

Holly wasn't sure—did he want to hear about her personal life? Then she realized he was waiting for an answer.

"Well, no, actually, Mr. Feeney. Unfortunately, he passed away in February. He had a brain tumor."

"I'm very sorry," Chris said. "It must be hard for you being so young and all. . . ." He looked down at his desk. "My wife lost her life to breast cancer just last year."

"I'm sorry to hear that," Holly said sadly.

"They say it gets easier," he smiled.

"So they say," Holly said grimly. "Apparently, gallons of tea does the trick."

He started to laugh, a big guffaw of a laugh. "I've been told that one too, and my daughters inform me that fresh air is also a healer."

Holly laughed. "Ah, yes, the magic fresh air; it does wonders for the heart. Are they your daughters?" She looked at the photograph.

"Indeed they are," he said. "My three little doctors who try to keep me alive," he laughed. "Unfortunately, the garden no longer looks like that," he said, referring to the photograph.

"Wow. Is that your garden?" Holly said, wide-eyed.

"That was Maureen's specialty. You can't get me out of the office long enough to sort through that mess."

"Oh, don't talk to me about gardens," Holly said, rolling her eyes. "I'm not exactly Ms. Green Fingers myself."

They looked at each other and smiled.

"Anyway, getting back to the interview," Mr. Feeney said. "Have you experience working with the media at all?"

"Yes, I have, actually." She returned to business mode. "I worked in an estate agents, and I was responsible for advertising new properties, so I was on the other end of what this job requires."

"But you have never actually worked on a magazine?"

Holly racked her brains. "I was responsible for printing up a weekly newsletter for a company I worked for . . ." She rambled on and on, as she went through every job she'd ever worked at. Eventually she grew bored at the sound of her own voice. She was under-qualified for this job and she knew it, but she also knew that she could do it if he would give her the chance.

Mr. Feeney took off his glasses. "I see. Well, Holly, you have a great deal of experience in the workplace, but I notice you haven't stayed in any job for longer than nine months."

"I was searching for the right job for me," Holly said, her confidence now totally shattered.

"So how do I know you won't desert me?" He smiled.

"Because this is the right job," she said seriously. "Mr. Feeney, I'm a very hard worker. When I love something, I give it one hundred percent. What I don't know, I am more than willing to learn. If you put your trust in me, I won't let you down." She stopped herself just short of getting down on her knees and begging for the damn job. Her face blushed as she realized what she had just done.

"Well then, I think that's a good note to finish on," Mr. Feeney said, smiling at her. He stood up and held his hand out. "Thank you for taking the time to come down here. We'll be in touch."

HOLLY decided to drop in on Ciara at work, where she could have a bite to eat. She rounded the corner and entered Hogan's pub. It was packed with smartly dressed people on their lunch breaks. Holly found a small table in the corner.

"Excuse me," she called out loudly, and clicked her fingers in the air. "Can I get some service here please?"

The people around her threw her looks for being so rude to the staff. Ciara swirled around with a scowl. "I was about to smack the head off you," she laughed, approaching the table.

"I hope you don't speak to all your customers like that," Holly teased.

"Not all of them. You having lunch here today?"

Holly nodded. "Mum told me you were working lunches. I thought you were working in the club upstairs?"

"That man has got me working all the hours under the sun. He's treating me like a slave," Ciara moaned.

Daniel walked up. "Did I hear someone mention my name?"

Ciara's face froze. "No, no. I was just talking about Mathew. He has me up all hours of the night. I'm, like, his sex slave." She wandered over to the bar to get a notepad and pen.

"Sorry I asked," Daniel said, staring at Ciara, bewildered. "Mind if I join you?" he asked Holly.

Holly pulled out a stool for him. "Okay, what's good to eat here?" she asked, looking through the menu.

Ciara mouthed, "Nothing," behind Daniel's back.

"The toasted special is my favorite," Daniel suggested.

Holly nodded her head. "Okay."

Ciara stuck her fingers in her mouth and pretended to gag as she walked away.

"You're looking very smart today," Daniel said to Holly.

"Yes, well, I was just at a job interview." Holly winced at the thought of it. "Let's just say I won't expect a call anytime soon."

"Oh, well, not to worry," Daniel said, smiling. "Still have that job upstairs if you're interested."

"I thought you gave that job to Ciara."

"Holly, you know your sister; we had a bit of a situation. Some guy at the bar said something she didn't quite like, so she served him his pint over his head."

"Oh, no!" Holly gasped. "I'm surprised you didn't fire her."

"Couldn't do that to a Kennedy family member, could I?"

Ciara arrived with Holly's food, frowned at her sister, and turned on her heel.

"Have you spoken to Denise or Sharon lately?" asked Daniel.

"Just Denise," she said, looking away. "You?"

"Tom has my head done in with all this talk of weddings. Wants me to be his best man."

"How do you feel about it?"

"Ah . . ." Daniel sighed. "Happy for him in a selfish kind of way."

"Know how you feel. You haven't spoken to your ex lately or anything?"

"Who, Laura? Never want to see the woman again."

"Is she a friend of Tom's?"

"Not as friendly as they used to be, thank God."

"So she won't be invited to the wedding, then?"

Daniel's eyes widened. "You know, I never thought of that."
There was a silence. "I'm meeting up with Tom and Denise tomorrow night to discuss the wedding plans, if you feel like coming out."

Holly rolled her eyes. "Gee, thanks, well, that just sounds like the
best fun ever, Daniel."

Daniel started laughing. "I know. That's why I don't want to go
on my own. Call me later if you want to go anyway."

Holly nodded.

HOLLY'S heart began to pound as she drove down her street and
spotted Sharon's car outside her house. It had been a long time
since Holly had spoken to her. She should have been to visit
Sharon, and she knew it. She pulled up, got out, and walked toward
Sharon's car and was surprised to see John stepping out. There was
no Sharon to be seen.

"Hi, Holly," John said grimly, banging the car door.

"John, where's Sharon?" she asked.

"I just came from the hospital."

Holly's hands flew to her face. "Oh, my God! Is she okay?"

John looked confused. "Yeah. She's just having a checkup. I'm
going back to collect her after I leave here."

"Oh," Holly said, feeling stupid.

"You know, if you're that concerned, you should call her." John's
icy-blue eyes stared straight into hers.

Holly bit her lip, feeling guilty. "Yeah, I know. Why don't you
come inside, and I'll make us a cup of tea."

She flicked the switch on the kettle and busied herself while John
made himself comfortable at the table.

"Sharon doesn't know that I'm here, so I would appreciate it if
you didn't say anything."

"Oh." Holly felt even more disappointed. Sharon hadn't sent
him. She didn't even want to see her.

"She misses you, you know."

Holly carried the mugs over to the table. "I miss her too."

"It's been a while now, Holly. The two of you used to speak to each other every day." John took the mug from her hand.

"Things used to be very different, John," Holly said angrily.

"Look, we all know what you've been through."

"I know you all know what I've been through, John, but you don't seem to understand I'm still going through it! I can't move on with my life like you're all doing and pretend nothing's happened."

"Do you think that that's what we're doing?"

"Well, let's look at the evidence, shall we?" she said sarcastically. "Sharon's having a baby. Denise is getting married—"

"Holly, that's called living. You seem to have forgotten how to do that. I miss Gerry too. He was my best mate. I lived right next door to him all my life. We went to school together; we played on the same football team. I was his best man at his wedding, and he was at mine! Whenever I had a problem, I went to Gerry; whenever I wanted to have a bit of fun, I went to Gerry. I told him some things that I would never have told Sharon, and he told me things he wouldn't have told you. Just because I wasn't married to him doesn't mean that I don't feel like you do."

Holly sat stunned. John took a deep breath before he spoke again.

"Yes, it's difficult. Yes, it's the worst thing that has ever happened to me in my life. But I can't stop going to the pub because there's two blokes on the stools Gerry and I used to sit on. I can't stop going to football matches because we used to go all the time."

Tears welled in Holly's eyes, and John continued talking.

"Sharon knows you're hurting, but you have to understand that this is a hugely important time in her life, too, and she needs her best friend to help her through it."

Holly sobbed hot tears. "I'm trying, John."

"I know you are." He grabbed her hands. "But Sharon needs you. Avoiding the situation isn't going to help anyone."

"But I went for a job interview today," she sobbed childishly.

John smiled. "That's great news, Holly. And how did it go?"

"Shite," she sniffed, and John started laughing. He allowed a silence to fall between them before he spoke again.

"She's almost five months pregnant, you know."

"What?" Holly looked up in surprise. "She didn't tell me!"

"She was afraid to. She thought you might get mad at her."

"Well, that was stupid of her to think that," Holly said, wiping her eyes aggressively. She looked away. "I meant to call her, I really did. I picked up the phone every day, but I just couldn't do it. Oh, I'm sorry, John. I'm truly happy for the both of you."

"Thank you, but it's not me that needs to hear this."

"But I've been so awful! She'll never forgive me now!"

"Oh, don't be stupid, Holly. It's Sharon we're talking about here. She'll have it all forgotten about by tomorrow."

Holly raised her eyebrows at him hopefully.

"Well, maybe not tomorrow. Next year, perhaps . . . and you'll owe her big time." His icy eyes warmed and twinkled at her.

"Stop it!" Holly giggled. "Can I go with you to see her?"

BUTTERFLIES fluttered around in Holly's stomach as they pulled up outside the hospital. Sharon stood alone, waiting outside to be collected. She looked so cute, Holly had to smile at the sight of her friend. She couldn't believe Sharon was almost five months pregnant. As Holly looked at her dressed in a polo neck and jeans, she could see the swelling of a tiny bump. And it suited her. Holly stepped out of the car, and Sharon's face froze.

Oh, no. Sharon was going to scream at her. She was going to tell her she hated her and that she was a crappy friend and that . . .

Sharon's face broke into a smile, and she held her arms out. "Come here to me, you fool," she said softly.

Holly ran into her arms. There, with her best friend hugging her tight, she felt the tears begin again. "Oh, Sharon, I'm so sorry. I'm a horrible person. I'm so so so so so so so sorry to—"

"Oh, shut up, you whiner, and hug me." Sharon cried, too, and they squeezed each other for a long time as John looked on. Linking arms, they walked to the car.

The three of them headed back to Holly's house. She and Sharon weren't quite ready to leave each other again after just making up. They had so much to talk about. Sitting around her kitchen table, they made up for lost time.

"Sharon, Holly went for a job interview today," John said when he managed to get a word in edgewise.

"Ooh, really? I didn't know you were job-hunting already."

"Gerry's new mission for me," Holly smiled.

"Oh, was that what it was this month? So how did it go?"

Holly grimaced and held her head in her hands. "It was awful, Sharon. I made a total fool of myself."

"Really?" Sharon giggled. "What was the job?"

"Selling advertising space for that magazine *X*."

"Ooh, that's cool. I read that at work all the time."

"What kind of magazine is it?" asked John.

"It has fashion, sports, culture, food, reviews . . ."

"And adverts," Holly joked.

"What was so wrong with the interview? You can't have been that bad." Sharon reached for the pot of tea.

"I think it's bad when the interviewer asks if you have any experience and you tell him you once printed up a newsletter." Holly banged her head playfully off the kitchen table.

Sharon burst out laughing. "I hope you weren't referring to that crappy little leaflet you printed up on the computer."

John and Sharon howled with laughter.

"Ah, well, it was advertising the company," Holly giggled.

"Remember, you made us all go out and post them around people's houses! It took us days to do!"

"Hey, I remember that," John laughed. "You sent me and Gerry out to post hundreds of them one night. Well, we shoved them in the skip at the back of Bob's pub and went in for a few pints."

Holly's mouth dropped open. "You sly little bastards! Because of you two, the company went bust and I lost my job!"

"Oh, I'd say it went bust the minute people took a look at those leaflets, Holly," John teased.

"Shut up, you," Holly laughed. "Hey, what else did you and Gerry get up to that I don't know about?"

John's eyes danced. "Ah, a true friend never reveals secrets."

But something had been unlocked. And after Holly and Sharon threatened to beat some stories out of him, Holly learned more about her husband that night than she ever knew. For the first time since Gerry had died, the three of them laughed and laughed all night, and Holly learned how to be able to talk about her husband. It used to be that the four of them gathered together—Holly, Gerry, Sharon, and John. This time, three gathered to remember the one they lost. Soon they would be four again, with the arrival of Sharon and John's baby.

Life went on.

THAT Sunday, Richard visited Holly with the kids. She had told him he was welcome to bring them by whenever it was his day with them. They played outside in the garden while Richard and Holly finished off their dinner and watched them through the patio doors.

"They seem really happy, Richard," Holly said.

"Yes, they do, don't they?" He smiled as he watched them chasing each other around. "I want things to be as normal for them as possible. They don't quite understand what's going on."

"What have you told them?"

"Oh, that Mummy and Daddy don't love each other anymore and that I moved away so that we can be happier."

"And they're okay with that?"

"Timothy is okay, but Emily is worried that we might stop loving her and that she will have to move away." His eyes were sad.

Poor Emily, Holly thought, watching her dancing around. She couldn't believe that she was having this conversation with Richard. He seemed like a totally different person these days. But then again, they now had something in common. They both understood what it was like to feel lonely and unsure of themselves.

"How's everything going at Mum and Dad's house?"

Richard swallowed a forkful of potato and nodded. "Good. They're being extremely generous."

"Ciara bothering you at all?"

"Ciara is . . . Ciara," he smiled. "We don't see eye to eye on a lot of things."

"Well, I wouldn't worry about that," Holly said, trying to stab a piece of pork with her fork. "The majority of the world wouldn't see eye to eye with her either." Her fork finally made contact with the pork, and she sent it through the air to the kitchen counter.

"And they say pigs don't fly," Richard remarked as Holly crossed the room to retrieve the piece of meat.

Holly giggled, "Hey, Richard, you made a funny!"

He looked pleased. "I have my moments, too, I suppose. Although I'm sure you think I don't have many of them."

Holly sat back down in her seat slowly, trying to decide how to phrase what she was going to say. "We're all different, Richard: Ciara is eccentric, Declan is a dreamer, Jack is a joker, I'm . . . Well, I don't know what I am. But you were always very controlled. It's not necessarily a bad thing."

"You're very thoughtful," Richard said after a long silence.

"Pardon?" Holly asked, feeling confused.

"I've always thought you were very thoughtful."

"When?" Holly asked incredulously.

"Well, I wouldn't be sitting here eating dinner, with the kids running around having fun outside, if you weren't thoughtful now, but I was referring to when we were children."

"Jack and I were always so awful to you," she said softly.

"You weren't *always* awful, Holly." He gave her an amused smile. "Anyway, that's what brothers and sisters are for, to make each other's lives as difficult as possible. It forms a great basis for life, toughens you up. Anyway, I was the bossy older brother."

"So how does that make me thoughtful?" Holly asked.

"You idolized Jack. You used to follow him around and do exactly what he told you to do." He started laughing. "I used to hear him telling you to say things to me, and you would run into my room terrified and blurt them out and run away again."

Holly looked at her plate, feeling embarrassed.

"But you always came back," Richard continued. "You would creep into my room and watch me working at my desk. I knew that was your way of saying sorry." He smiled. "None of our siblings had a conscience in that house. Not even me. You were the only one."

THE next day, Holly jumped around the house ecstatically as she replayed the message on the answering machine for the third time.

"Hi, Holly," came the gruff voice. "This is Chris Feeney here from magazine X. I'm just calling to say that I was very impressed with your interview. Em . . ." He stalled a bit. "Well, no doubt you'll be delighted to know that I've decided to welcome you as a new member of the team. I would love you to start as soon as possible, so call and we'll discuss it."

Holly rolled around her bed in terrified delight and pressed the button again. She had aimed for the moon, and she'd landed!

Eleven

HOLLY stared up at the tall Georgian building, and her body tingled with excitement. It was her first day of work, and she felt good times were ahead of her in this building. It was situated in the center of town, and the busy offices of magazine X were on the second floor above a small café. She had gotten very little sleep the night before due to nerves and excitement; however, she didn't feel the same dread that she usually felt before starting a new job. Her family and friends had been ecstatic, and before she left the house that morning, she had received a beautiful bouquet of flowers from her parents.

But although she had felt excited when she sat down to eat her breakfast, she had also felt sad. Sad that Gerry wasn't there to share her new start. They had performed a little ritual every time Holly started a new job. Gerry would wake Holly up with breakfast in bed, and then he would pack her bag with ham-and-cheese sandwiches, an apple, and a bar of chocolate. Mind you, they only did that on her first day; every other day, they would tumble out of bed—late, as usual—race each other to the shower, and then grab a quick cup of coffee. They would kiss good-bye and go their separate ways, then start all over again the next day. All those tedious routines day after day when their time was so precious . . .

This morning, she awoke to an empty house in an empty bed to no breakfast. She had allowed herself to imagine that when she woke up, Gerry would miraculously be there to greet her, but with death, there were no exceptions. Gone meant gone.

Now, poised at the entrance, Holly checked herself to see that she looked presentable and made her way up the wooden staircase. She entered the waiting-room area, and the secretary she recognized from the interview came from around the desk to meet her.

"Hi, Holly," she said happily, shaking her hand. "Welcome to our humble abode." She looked to be about the same age as Holly and had long blond hair. "I'm Alice, by the way. He's waiting for you."

"I'm not late, am I?" Holly asked, glancing at her watch.

"No, not at all." Alice led her down to Mr. Feeney's office. "Don't mind Chris and all the other lot; they're all workaholics. I think Chris actually lives in his office. The man isn't normal," she said, tapping on his door lightly and leading her in.

"Who's not normal?" Mr. Feeney asked, standing from his chair.

"You." Alice smiled and closed the door behind her.

"See how my staff treat me?" Mr. Feeney's handshake was once again warm and welcoming, and Holly felt immediately at ease.

"Thank you for hiring me, Mr. Feeney," she said genuinely.

"You can call me Chris, and there's no need to thank me. Follow me, and I'll show you around the place." He started leading her down the hall. The walls were covered by framed covers of every X magazine that had been published for the last twenty years.

"In here is our office of little ants." He pushed open the door, and Holly looked into the huge office. There were about ten desks in all, with people sitting in front of their computers and talking on the phone. They looked up and waved politely. Holly smiled at them. "These are the wonderful journalists who help pay my bills," Chris explained. "That's John Paul, the fashion editor; Mary, our food woman; and Brian, Steven, Gordon, Aishling, and Tracey. Everyone, this is Holly." They smiled and waved again.

Chris led her to the room next door. "This is where all our computer nerds hide. That's Dermot and Wayne, and they're in charge of layout and design, so you'll be keeping them informed about what advertisements are going where. Lads, this is Holly."

"Hi, Holly." They both stood up and shook her hand and then continued working on their computers.

"I have them well trained," Chris chuckled, and headed back down the way they had come. Holly glanced at the walls, feeling excited. This was like nothing she had ever experienced before.

"In here is your office," he said.

Holly couldn't stop herself from smiling. She had never had her own office before. The small room was just big enough to fit a desk and filing cabinet. There was a computer on the desk with piles of folders. Opposite the desk was a bookcase crammed with stacks of old magazines. The huge Georgian window practically covered one entire wall, and the room had a bright and airy feel to it.

She placed her new briefcase on the desk. "It's perfect," she said.

"RIGHT, Ciara, are you sure you've got your passport?" Holly's mum asked for the third time since leaving the house.

"Yes, Mum," Ciara groaned. "I told you, it's right here."

"Show me." Elizabeth twisted around in the passenger seat.

"No! You should just take my word for it. I'm not a baby."

Declan snorted, and Ciara elbowed him. "Shut up, you."

"Ciara, just show Mum the passport so you can put her mind at rest," Holly said tiredly.

"Fine," she huffed, lifting her bag to her lap. "It's in here, Mum. No, actually, it's in here. . . . No, maybe I put it . . . Oh, crap!"

"Bloody hell, Ciara," Holly's dad growled, slamming on the brakes and turning the car around.

"What?" she said defensively. "I put it in here, Dad. Someone must have taken it out," she grumbled, emptying her bag in the car.

"Ciara," Holly groaned as a pair of knickers went flying over her face.

Holly sat squashed in the backseat with Declan and Ciara. Richard was driving Mathew and Jack, and they were probably at the airport already. This was their second time returning to the house, as Ciara had forgotten her lucky nose ring.

An hour after setting off, they reached the airport in what should have been only a twenty-minute drive.

"Pet, keep in touch with us a lot more this time, won't you?" Elizabeth cried as she hugged her daughter.

"Of course I will, Mum. Don't cry, or you'll get me started too."

A lump formed in Holly's throat, and she fought back the tears. Ciara had been good company over the last few months and had always succeeded in cheering Holly up.

Holly stood on the tips of her toes to hug the enormous Mathew. "Take care of my sister."

"Don't worry. She's in good hands," he smiled.

"Look after her now, won't you?" Frank smacked him on the back. Mathew was intelligent enough to know it was more of a warning than a question.

"Bye, Richard," Ciara said. "Stay away from that Meredith bitch. You're far too good for her." She gave him a big hug and Declan too. "You can come over anytime you like, Dec—maybe make a movie or something about me. And Jack, look after my big sis," she said, squeezing Holly tightly. "I'm gonna miss you," she said sadly.

"Me too." Holly's voice shook.

"Okay, I'm going now before all you depressing people make me cry," she said, trying to sound happy.

Holly stood in silence with her family and watched as Ciara and Mathew walked hand in hand out the door. Even Declan had a tear in his eye but pretended he was about to sneeze.

"Just look at the lights, Declan." Jack threw his arm around his baby brother. "They say that helps you sneeze."

Declan stared up at the lights and avoided watching his favorite sister walking away. Frank held his wife close as she waved at her daughter while tears rolled down her cheeks.

They all laughed as the alarm went off when Ciara walked through the security scanner and was ordered to empty her pockets, followed by a frisk.

"Every bloody time," Jack laughed. "It's a wonder they agreed to let her into the country at all."

HOLLY drummed her fingers on her desk and stared out the window. She was absolutely flying through her work this week. She didn't know it was possible to actually enjoy work. She happily sat through lunch breaks and even stayed late. But it was only her third week, after all; give her time. The office had a lighthearted banter, and she loved feeling like she was part of the team. She still had her miserable days, but the excitement of her job was spurring her on.

She glanced back down at her work again; a freelancer had written an article on how he traveled around Ireland trying to find the cheapest pint, and it was very amusing. There was a huge gap at the bottom of the page, and it was up to Holly to fill it. She flicked through her book of contacts, and an idea came to her immediately. She picked up the phone and dialed.

"Hogan's."

"Daniel? Hiya, it's Holly."

"How are you doin', Holly?"

"I'm grand, thanks. You?"

"Couldn't be better. How's that snazzy job of yours?"

"Well, actually, that's why I'm calling. Do I remember hearing you say you needed to advertise Club Diva more?" Well, he had actually thought that he was saying it to Sharon, but she knew he wouldn't remember that minor detail.

"I do recall saying that, yes."

"Good. Well, how would you like to advertise it in magazine *X?*"

"Is that the name of the magazine you work on?"

"No. I just thought it would be an interesting question, that's all," she joked. "Of course it's where I work!"

"Oh, of course, I'd forgotten. That's the magazine that has offices just around the corner from me," he said sarcastically. "The one that causes you to walk by my front door every day, and yet you still don't call in. Why don't I see you at lunchtime?" he teased.

"Oh, everyone here eats their lunch at their desks," she explained. "So what do you think about the ad?"

"Yeah, sure, that's a good idea."

"Okay, well, I'll put it in the November issue. You'll be a millionaire after this goes to print."

"I better be," he laughed. "By the way, there's a launch party for some new drink next week. Can I put you down for an invite?"

"Yeah, that would be great. What new drink is it?"

"Blue Rock. Tastes like shite, but it's free all night."

"Wow, you're such a good advertisement for it," she laughed. "When is it on?" She took out her diary and made a note of it. "That's perfect. I can come straight after work."

"Well, make sure you bring your bikini. It has a beach theme."

"But it's winter, you nutter."

"Hey, it wasn't my idea. The slogan is 'Blue Rock, the hot new drink for winter.'"

"Ugghh, how tacky," she groaned. "Okay, thanks, Daniel. Have a think about what you want your ad to say."

"What time do you finish work?"

"Six."

"Why don't you come around here at six, and I'll take you somewhere to have a bite?"

"Will do." She hung up and sat quietly for a moment. Then she went next door to Chris's office, a thought occurring to her.

"What's up?" he said. "Take a seat."

"Well, you know Hogan's, around the corner?"

Chris nodded.

"I was just on to the owner to place an ad, and he was telling me that they're having a launch party for a new drink. It has a beach theme; all the staff will be in bikinis and that kind of thing."

"In the middle of winter?" He raised his eyebrows.

"It's apparently the hot new drink for winter."

He rolled his eyes. "Tacky."

"That's what I said. Anyway, I just thought it might be worth finding out about and covering."

"That's a great idea, Holly. I'll get one of the lads onto it."

Holly smiled. "By the way, did you get that garden sorted yet?"

Chris frowned. "I've had about ten people come down to look at it. They tell me it'll cost six grand."

"Wow, six grand! That's a lot of money."

"Well, it's a big garden, and a lot of work needs to be done."

"My brother will do it for five," she blurted out.

"Five?" His eyes nearly popped out of his head. "That's the lowest I've heard yet. Is he good?"

"Remember I told you my garden was a jungle?"

He nodded.

"Well, it's a jungle no longer. He did a great job on it, but he works alone, so it takes him longer."

"For that price, I don't care. Have you his business card?"

"Eh, yeah. Hold on and I'll get it." She stole some impressive-looking card stock from Alice's desk, typed up Richard's name and mobile number in fancy writing, and printed it out.

"That's great," Chris said. "I think I'll give him a call now."

"No, no," Holly said quickly. "He's up to his eyeballs today. You'll get him easier tomorrow."

"Right so. Thanks, Holly."

HOLLY couldn't concentrate during the last hour of work; she kept watching the clock, willing the time to go more slowly. Why didn't it go this fast when she was waiting to open her messages from Gerry? She opened her bag to check that Gerry's eighth message was still tucked safely in the inside pocket. As it was the last day of the month, she had brought the October envelope with her to work. She wasn't sure why, but she couldn't face leaving it on the kitchen table. She was only hours away from being that much closer to him again, and while she willed the clock to move faster so she could read it, she was also dreading her dinner with Daniel.

At six o'clock on the button, she heard Alice switch off her computer and clatter down the stairs. She prayed Chris would dump another load on her desk just so she would have to stay late. She and Daniel had been out together millions of times, so why was she worrying now? But there was something in his voice that worried her, and something happened to her stomach when his voice came on the phone that made her feel uneasy about meeting up with him.

She slowly shut down her computer and packed her briefcase. Everything she did was in slow motion, as though that would prevent her from having dinner with Daniel. She hit herself over the head. It was a *business* dinner. Finally she headed outside.

Her heart beat wildly as she spotted Daniel walking down the road to meet her. The cool autumn months had arrived, so he was back wearing his black leather jacket with blue jeans. His black hair was messy, and stubble lined his chin. He had that just-out-of-bed look. Holly's stomach lurched again, and she looked away.

"I'm so sorry, Daniel," she apologized. "I got tied up," she lied.

"Don't worry about it." He smiled at her. "So where would you like to go?"

"How about in there?" Holly said, looking at the small café on the ground floor of her office building. She wanted to go to the least intimate and most casual place possible.

Daniel scrunched up his nose. "I'm a bit hungrier than that, if you don't mind. I haven't eaten all day."

They walked along together, and eventually he settled on an Italian restaurant. Inside, it was quiet, with just a few candlelit tables occupied by couples. When Daniel stood up to take his jacket off, Holly quickly blew out the candle on their table.

"They make you sick, don't they?" Daniel laughed, following Holly's gaze to a couple who were kissing across the table.

"Actually, no," Holly thought aloud. "They make me sad."

Daniel hadn't heard her, as he was busy reading through the menu. "What are you having?"

"A Caesar salad."

"You women and your Caesar salads," Daniel teased.

Holly tried to control the conversation, steering it into safe territory, and they spent the evening talking about the launch party and the ad. She wasn't in the mood for discussing their private feelings and thoughts tonight; she wasn't even quite sure what exactly they were right then. She left the restaurant feeling a little panicked about why she had been so uncomfortable with a man that she was certain only wanted to be her friend.

She stepped outside the restaurant for a breath of fresh air while Daniel kindly paid the bill. He was extremely generous; there was no denying that. It just didn't feel quite right to be eating in an intimate restaurant with anyone other than Gerry.

She froze and tried to hide her face as she spotted a couple walking toward her. "Holly, is that you?" she heard a familiar voice.

"Hello there!" She tried to sound surprised.

"How are you?" The woman gave her a feeble hug. "What are you doing standing out here in the cold?"

"Oh, you know . . . I was just having a bite to eat," Holly smiled, pointing at the restaurant.

"Well, good for you." The man patted her on the back. "It's good to get out and do things on your own."

She glanced at the door. "Yes, it's nice to do that—"

"There you are!" Daniel laughed, stepping outside. "I thought you had run off on me." He wrapped his arm around her shoulders.

Holly smiled at him weakly and turned to face the couple.

"Oh, sorry. I didn't see you there." Daniel smiled at the couple. The couple stared back at him stonily.

"Daniel, this is Judith and Charles Clarke—Gerry's parents."

HOLLY pressed down on her car horn and cursed at the driver in front of her. She was fuming. She was mad at herself for being caught in a bad situation when really there was nothing to it. She had a headache, and the stupid traffic all the way home was driving her insane. Poor Daniel, she thought sadly. Gerry's parents had been so rude to him. Oh, why did they have to see her the one time she was happy? They could have come round to the house any day of the week to see her living the life of the perfect grieving widow. Well, screw them, she thought angrily.

She stopped at every traffic light she met, and all she wanted to do was to go throw a tantrum in the privacy of her own home. She picked up her mobile, but she couldn't reach Sharon or Denise.

She decided Ciara would cheer her up, but just as she pulled up outside her parents' house, she remembered Ciara wasn't there, and her eyes filled with tears. Once again, she had nobody.

She rang the doorbell, and Declan answered.

"What's wrong with you?"

"Nothing," she said, feeling sorry for herself. "Where's Mum?"

"In the kitchen with Dad talking to Richard. I'd leave them alone."

"Oh, okay." She felt lost. "What are you up to?"

"I'm just watching what I filmed today. It's for a documentary on homelessness. Do you wanna watch it?"

"Yeah." She smiled gratefully and settled on the couch. A few minutes into the video, and Holly was in tears, but for once, they weren't for herself. Declan had done a heartrending interview with a remarkable man who was living on the streets of Dublin. She realized there were people far worse off than she, and the fact that Gerry's parents had bumped into her and Daniel seemed such a stupid thing to worry about.

"Oh, Declan, that was excellent," she said, drying her eyes when it had finished. "Are you happy with it?"

"It's hard to be happy about the fact that what he has to say is so bad that it's making a great documentary," Declan shrugged. "Anyway, I'm going to bed. I'm absolutely knackered." He kissed her on the top of her head as he passed, which touched Holly. Her baby brother was growing up.

She glanced at the clock on the mantelpiece and noticed it was almost twelve. She reached for her bag and took out the October envelope and tore the seal open. When she slid the card out, a dried sunflower fell onto her lap, along with a pouch of seeds. His message read:

A sunflower for my sunflower. To brighten the dark October days you hate so much. Plant some more, and be safe in the knowledge a warm and bright summer awaits.

PS, I love you . . .

PPS, Could you please pass this card on to John?

Holly lifted the second card that had fallen onto her lap.

To John,

Happy 32nd birthday. You're getting old, my friend, but I hope you have many, many more birthdays. Enjoy life and take care of my wife and Sharon. You're the man now!

Lots of love,

Your friend Gerry

PS, Told you I'd keep my promise.

Holly reread every word Gerry had written. She stood up from the couch and felt a new bounce in her step. She couldn't wipe the grin off her face. She tapped lightly on the kitchen door.

"Come in," Elizabeth called.

Holly stepped in and looked around at her parents and Richard sitting at the table with cups of tea in their hands.

"Oh, hello, love," her mum said, getting up to give her a hug and a kiss. "I didn't hear you come in."

"I was just watching Declan's documentary," Holly beamed.

"It's great, isn't it?" Frank stood up to hug her.

Holly nodded and joined them at the table. "Have you found a job yet?" she asked Richard.

He shook his head sadly, as though he were going to cry.

"Well, I did."

He looked at her, disgusted that she could say such a thing. "Well, I know *you* did."

"No, Richard. I mean, I got *you* a job."

"You what?"

"You heard me. My boss will be calling you tomorrow."

His face fell. "Oh, Holly, that's very nice of you indeed, but

I have no interest in advertising. My interest is in science."

"And gardening."

"Yes, I like gardening." He looked confused.

"That's why my boss will be calling you—to ask you to work on his garden. I said you'd do it for five thousand. I hope that's okay."

He was completely speechless, so Holly kept on talking.

"And here's your business cards." She handed him the pile.

Richard read the cards in silence. Then suddenly he started laughing and jumped out of his chair, pulling Holly with him, and danced her around the kitchen while her parents looked on and cheered.

Twelve

"OKAY, this is the last one, I promise, girls!" Denise called as her bra was sent flying over the changing-room door.

Sharon and Holly groaned and collapsed onto their chairs again. "You said that an hour ago," Sharon complained, kicking off her shoes and massaging her swollen ankles.

"Yeah, but I mean it this time. I have a really good feeling about this dress," Denise said, full of excitement.

"You said that an hour ago too," Holly grumbled.

They had been dragged to every wedding-gown boutique in the city, and Sharon and Holly were exhausted. Whatever excitement they had felt for Denise had been drained from their systems. And if Holly heard Denise's irritating squeals one more time . . .

"Ooh, I love it!" Denise shrieked.

"Okay, here's the plan," Sharon whispered to Holly. "If she walks out of there looking like a meringue sitting on a bicycle pump, we are going to tell her she looks beautiful."

Holly giggled. "Oh, Sharon, we can't do that!"

"Ooh, wait till you see!" Denise shrieked again.

"On second thought . . ." Holly looked at Sharon miserably.

"Ta-da!" Denise stepped out of the dressing room, and Holly's eyes widened. She looked at Sharon uncertainly and tried not to laugh at the look on her face.

"Do you like it?" Denise squealed again, and Holly winced.

"Yes," Sharon said unenthusiastically.

"Do you think Tom will be happy when he looks down the aisle and sees me walking toward him?"

"Yes," Sharon repeated.

"Do you think it's worth the money?"

"Yes."

"Oh, but does it make my bum look enormous?"

"Yes."

Holly looked at Sharon, startled, realizing she wasn't even listening to the questions anymore.

Denise carried on, obviously not even listening to the answers. "So will I get it—"

"No!" Holly interrupted before Sharon said yes again.

"No?" Denise asked. "Is it because it makes me look fat?"

"No."

"Do you not think Tom will like it?"

"No."

"Do you think it's worth the money, though?"

"No."

"Oh." She turned to face Sharon. "Do you agree with Holly?"

"Yes."

"Okay then, I trust you two," Denise said sadly. "To be honest, I wasn't really that keen on it myself."

Sharon put her shoes back on. "Okay, Denise, let's go get something to eat before I drop dead."

The three of them trudged into Bewley's Café and managed to grab their usual spot by the window overlooking Grafton Street.

"I hate shopping on Saturdays," Holly moaned, watching as people bumped and crushed one another on the busy street below.

"Gone are the days of shopping midweek, now you're no longer a lady of leisure," Sharon teased, picking up her club sandwich.

"I know, and I'm so tired, but I feel like I've earned the tiredness this time," Holly said happily.

"Tell us about the episode with Gerry's parents," said Sharon.

Holly rolled her eyes. "They were just so rude to Daniel."

"Too right. They can't tell you who to see and who not to see," Sharon gave out.

"Sharon, I'm not seeing him." Holly tried to get the record straight. "We were just having a business dinner."

"Ooh, a *business* dinner!" Sharon and Denise giggled.

"Well, it was that, and it was also nice to have a bit of company." Holly smiled. "When everyone else is busy, it's nice to have someone else to chat to. Especially male company."

"Yeah, I understand," Sharon nodded. "It's good for you to get out and meet new people anyway."

Denise giggled. "Well, Holly, I'm glad you get along with him, because you're going to have to dance with him at the wedding."

"Why?" Holly looked at Denise, confused.

"Because it's tradition for the best man to dance with the maid of honor." Her eyes sparkled.

Holly gasped, "You want me to be your maid of honor?"

Denise nodded, full of excitement. "Don't worry. I already asked Sharon, and she doesn't mind."

"I would love to!" Holly said happily. "But Sharon, are you sure you don't mind?"

"I'm happy just being a blown-up bridesmaid. I'll need to borrow Denise's marquee to wear as a dress."

"I hope you don't go into labor at the wedding," Denise said.

"Don't worry, Denise. I won't be due till the end of January. Oh, by the way, I forgot to show you the photograph of the baby!" Sharon pulled a small photograph from her bag.

"Where is it?" Denise moved the scan closer.

"There." Sharon pointed out the area.

"Whoa, that's one big boy!" Denise exclaimed.

Sharon rolled her eyes. "Denise, that's a leg, you fool. We still don't know the sex yet."

"Oh," Denise blushed. "Well, congratulations, Sharon. It looks like you're having a little alien."

"Stop it, Denise," Holly laughed. "I think it's beautiful."

"Good." Sharon looked at Denise, and Denise nodded. "Because I wanted to ask you something. John and I would love it if you would be our baby's godmother."

Holly gasped with shock, and tears filled her eyes.

"Hey, you didn't cry when I asked you to be maid of honor," Denise huffed.

"Oh, Sharon, I would be honored!" Holly gave her friend a hug.

HOLLY pushed through the crowds in Hogan's pub and made her way upstairs to Club Diva. She gasped as she approached the door. A group of young muscular males dressed in swimwear were banging out Hawaiian drumbeats. Female models in skimpy bikinis greeted guests by wrapping multicolored leis around their necks. Holly could barely recognize the club; it had been transformed.

The bar staff were dressed in their bikinis and swimwear, and they lined the entrance with trays of blue drinks in their hands. Holly lifted a drink from the tray and took a sip, trying not to make a face from its overly sweet taste. The floors were scattered with sand, each table was sheltered by a huge bamboo umbrella, the barstools were all big kettledrums, and there was a wonderful barbecue smell in the air. Holly darted to the nearest table, helped herself to a kebab, and found herself facing Daniel.

"Em, hello. The place looks great," she said.

"Yeah, it worked well, all right." He looked pleased. Daniel wore faded blue jeans and a blue Hawaiian shirt with big pink and yellow flowers. He still hadn't shaved, and Holly wondered how painful it would be to kiss him with that sharp stubble. Not for her to kiss him, of course. Somebody else . . .

"Daniel," she said, "I'm really sorry about the other night."

"I only felt uncomfortable for you, Holly. They shouldn't be able to tell you who to see and who not to see." He smiled and placed his hands on her shoulders as though he were going to say something more, but someone called him from the bar, and he rushed over to sort the problem out.

"But I am *not* seeing you," Holly muttered to herself. Daniel had called her almost every day since that episode, and she realized she looked forward to his calls. There was that niggling thing at the back of her mind again. Holly saw Denise and wandered over to join her on the sun bed, where she was sipping the blue concoction.

"So what do you think of the hot new drink for winter?" Holly indicated the bottle.

Denise rolled her eyes. "Tacky. I've only had a few, and my head is spinning already."

Holly enjoyed herself that evening, laughing and chatting with Denise and Tom. She barely got to speak to Daniel, as he was too busy running around being the manager. She watched as he gave orders to his staff, and they immediately got to work. It was obvious his staff had great respect for him. He got things done. Every time she spotted him heading over to her group, somebody stopped him for an interview or just for a chat. Most of the time, to Holly's annoyance, he was stopped by young girls in bikinis.

DENISE banged the till closed with her hip and handed the receipt over the counter to the customer. "Thanks," she smiled, but her smile quickly faded as soon as the customer turned away from the counter. She sighed loudly, staring at the long queue in front of the cash register, grumpily grabbed the item of clothing from the next customer, de-tagged it, scanned it, and wrapped it.

"Excuse me, are you Denise Hennessey?" she heard a deep, sexy voice ask. She looked up to see a police officer before her and tried to think if she had done anything illegal in the past few days. When she was satisfied she was crime-free, she smiled. "Yes, I am."

"I'm Officer Ryan, and I was wondering if you would accompany me to the station, please."

It was more of a statement than a question, and Denise's mouth dropped open. He was no longer the sexy officer; he was the evil "lock her up in a tiny cell with a luminous orange jumpsuit and no hot water or makeup type" officer. Denise gulped, "What for?"

"Everything will be explained to you down at the station." He walked around the counter, and Denise looked at the long line of customers helplessly. Everybody just stared back at her.

"Check his ID, love," one of the customers shouted.

Her voice shook as she demanded to see his ID, which was a completely useless operation, as she had never seen a police ID before, nor did she know what a real one would look like. Her hand trembled as she studied it closely, but she didn't read a thing.

"I refuse to go until you tell me what this is about," she said.

"Ms. Hennessey, if you just work with me here, then there will be no need to use these." He took out a pair of handcuffs.

"But I didn't do anything!" she protested, starting to panic.

"We can discuss that down at the station." He began to get irate.

Denise crossed her arms across her chest. "I said I will not go with you until you tell me what this is about."

"Okay then," he shrugged. "If you insist." He opened his mouth to speak, and she yelled as she felt the cold silver handcuffs being slapped around her wrists. She was in so much shock, she couldn't speak as he led her out of the shop.

"Good luck, love," the customer shouted again.

Images of sharing a cell with a psycho murderer jumped into Denise's mind. Maybe she would find a little bird with a broken wing and nurse it and teach it to fly to pass the years inside.

Her face reddened as they stepped out onto Grafton Street, and the crowds immediately scattered. Denise kept her eyes down, hoping nobody she knew would spot her. Her heart beat wildly as she was led toward a beat-up-looking minibus, the well-known color blue of the police, with blackened-out windows. Denise sat in the front row of seats behind the driver, and although she could sense people behind her, she sat rigidly in her seat, too terrified to turn around and meet her future fellow inmates.

"Where are we going?" she asked as they drove past the police station. Officer Ryan ignored her.

"Hey, I thought you were taking me to the station!"

No answer.

"I haven't done anything wrong!"

Still no answer.

"Dammit, I'm innocent, I tell you!"

Denise started kicking the chair to get his attention. Her blood started to boil, when the officer pushed a cassette into the player. Denise's eyes widened at the choice of song.

Officer Ryan stood up, a big grin on his face. "Denise, you have been very naughty." He made his way in front of her. She gulped as he started to gyrate his hips to the song "Hot Stuff."

She was about to give him a great big kick between his legs when she heard whooping and laughing. She twisted herself around and spotted her sisters, Holly, Sharon, and about five other friends. She finally figured out what was really happening when her sisters placed a veil on her head, screaming, "Happy hen party!"

"Oh, you bitches!" Denise spat at them.

The girls continued to hold their stomachs with laughter.

"You are so lucky I didn't kick you in the balls!" Denise screamed at the gyrating garda.

"Denise, this is Paul," her sister Fiona giggled, "and he's your stripper for the day."

Denise narrowed her eyes. "I almost had a heart attack, I hope you know! What will my customers think? And my staff!"

Sharon giggled. "They were all just playing along."

"When I go back to work, I'm going to fire the lot of them."

"Don't worry," her sister said. "We told your staff to inform the customers after you left the shop."

Denise rolled her eyes. "Well, knowing them, they deliberately won't, and I will be fired."

"Denise, stop worrying!" Fiona said. "Your boss thought it was funny. Now relax and enjoy the weekend."

"Weekend? Where are we going for the weekend?" Denise looked around at her friends, startled.

"We're going to Galway. And that's all you need to know," Sharon said mysteriously.

THE ROOM WAS STILL SPINNING. Having closed her eyes, Holly was now unable to sleep. It was five o'clock in the morning, which meant that she had been drinking for almost twelve hours. Her stomach became queasy, and she sat up on the bed.

She turned to face Denise so that they could talk, but the sound of her friend's snores ended all thought of communication. Holly sighed. She wished she hadn't drunk so much, but with all the talk of husbands, she dreaded to think what the next two days would be like. Denise's friends were twice as bad as Denise. They were loud and hyper and acted exactly the way girls should on a hen weekend, but Holly didn't have the energy to keep up with them.

It felt like only yesterday that Holly had had her own hen party, but in fact, it was more than seven years ago. Back then, she had been so excited and the future looked so bright. She was to marry the man of her dreams and live and grow with him for the rest of their lives. Now life had become a nightmare for her.

Yes, she had managed to drag herself out of bed every morning. Yes, she had succeeded in finding a new job. But these were just formalities, something else to check off on the "things that normal people do" list. Nothing she had done so far had managed to fill that hole in her heart.

Holly pretended to have a coughing fit just so the girls would wake up. She needed to talk; she needed to cry; she needed to vent all her frustrations and disappointments. But what more advice could they give her? She repeated the same old worries over and over. Sometimes her friends would succeed in getting through to her, and she would feel positive and confident, only to find herself thrown back into despair days later.

After a while, Holly tired of staring at the four walls, threw on a tracksuit, and made her way back downstairs to the hotel bar.

CHARLIE groaned with frustration as the table down the back of the bar began to roar with laughter again. He wiped down the bar counter and glanced at his watch. Five-thirty, and he was still here working. He had thought he was lucky when the girls from the hen party had gone to bed earlier than expected, and he was about to go home when this arrogant crowd arrived from a nightclub in Galway city. They weren't even residents of the hotel, but he had to serve them because the group included the daughter of the owner. She and her arrogant boyfriend, and he couldn't stand them.

"Don't tell me you're back for more!" he laughed as one of the women from the hen party walked in. She bumped into the wall as she tried to make her way to the high stool.

"I just came down for a glass of water," she hiccuped.

"There you go." Charlie placed a glass of water on a beer mat.

She squinted at his nametag. "Thanks, Charlie."

"Did you girls have fun tonight?"

Holly sighed, "I suppose."

"Are you okay?" Charlie watched her. He had a horrible feeling she was going to cry, but he was used to it at this stage. A lot of people became emotional when they drank.

"I miss my husband," she whispered, her shoulders trembling.

"How long are you here for?" he asked.

"The weekend," she told him.

Charlie laughed. "Have you never gone a weekend without seeing him?"

Holly frowned. "Only once. And that was at my own hen party, seven years ago." A tear spilled down the woman's face.

"Don't worry," Charlie said gently. "Your husband's probably miserable without you."

"Oh, God, I hope not." Holly's eyes widened.

"Well then, see?" he said. "I'm sure he hopes you're not miserable without him either. You're supposed to be enjoying your life."

"You're right," Holly said, perking up. "He wouldn't want me to be unhappy."

"That's the spirit." Charlie smiled, then jumped as he saw his boss's daughter coming over with one of those looks on her face.

"Hey, Charlie," she yelled. "Maybe if you stopped chatting and did a bit of work, me and my friends wouldn't be so thirsty."

Holly's mouth dropped open. That woman had a nerve. And

her perfume was so strong, it made Holly start to cough lightly.

"I'm sorry, do you have a problem?" The woman's head darted toward Holly, and she looked her up and down.

"Yes, actually," Holly slurred, taking a sip of her water. "Your perfume is disgusting, and it's making me want to throw up."

Charlie dropped to his knees behind the counter to pretend to look for a lemon to slice and started laughing.

"What's the delay here?" a deep voice inquired. Charlie shot to his feet at the sound of her boyfriend. He was even worse. "Why don't you sit down, honey, and I'll bring the drinks over," he said.

"Fine. At least *someone* is polite around here," she snapped, and stormed back to her table. Holly watched her hips go boom-boom-boom as they went from side to side.

"How are you?" the man beside Holly asked, staring at her chest.

"I'm fine," Holly replied shortly, staring straight ahead.

"I'm Stevie," he said, holding out his hand to her.

"I'm Holly," she mumbled, and took his hand lightly.

"Holly, that's a lovely name." He held her hand much too long. "Can I buy you a drink, Holly?" he asked smoothly.

"No thanks. I have one here." She sipped on her water again.

"Okay. I'm just going to bring these drinks down, and I'll be back to buy the lovely Holly a drink." He smiled at her creepily as he walked away. Charlie rolled his eyes as soon as the man turned his back.

"Who the hell is that eejit?" Holly asked, looking bewildered, and Charlie laughed, delighted that she hadn't fallen for him.

Charlie lowered his voice. "That's Stevie, boyfriend of Laura, that blond bitch. Her dad owns this hotel, which means I can't exactly tell her where to go, although I would love to."

Holly stared at the beautiful woman, thinking nasty thoughts. "Anyway, good night, Charlie."

"You off to bed?"

She nodded. "It's about time. It's after six." She tapped on her watch. "I hope you get home soon."

"I wouldn't bet on it," he replied, and watched her leave the bar.

Stevie followed after her, and Charlie, thinking this was suspicious, made his way closer to the door, just to make sure she was okay. The blonde, noticing her boyfriend's sudden departure, left her table at the same time. They both stared down the corridor in the direction Holly and Stevie had headed.

The blonde gasped, and her hand flew to her mouth.

"Hey!" Charlie called out angrily as he witnessed a distressed Holly pushing a drunken Stevie away from her. Holly wiped her mouth, disgusted with his attempts to kiss her. She backed away from him. "I think you have the wrong idea here, Stevie. Go back to the bar to your girlfriend."

Stevie wobbled slightly and slowly turned to face Laura.

"Stevie!" she shrieked. "How could you?" She ran from the hotel in tears, closely followed by a protesting Stevie.

THE next day, Holly and Sharon went for a long walk on the beach just outside Galway city. Although it was October, the air had warmth in it, and Holly didn't need her coat. She stood in a long-sleeved top and listened to the water gently lapping.

"Are you okay?" Sharon wrapped her arm around her friend.

Holly sighed. "Every time someone asks me that question, Sharon, I say, 'I'm fine, thank you,' but to be honest, I'm not. Do people *really* want to know how you feel?" Holly smiled. "The next time someone asks, I'm going to say, 'Well, actually, I'm not very well at all, thank you. I'm feeling a bit depressed and lonely.' Then I'll say how it pisses me off when everyone says time is a healer. Nothing is healing at all, and every morning I wake up in my empty bed, it feels like salt is being rubbed into those unhealing wounds. And then I'll say how much I miss my husband and how I feel like I'm just waiting for my world to end so that I can join him." Holly took a deep breath. "What do you think?"

"Ooh!" Sharon jumped.

Holly frowned. "I say all that, and all you can say is, 'Ooh'?"

Sharon placed her hand over her bump and laughed. "No, you silly. The baby kicked! Feel it!"

Holly placed her hand over Sharon's swollen belly and felt the tiny little kick. Both their eyes filled with tears.

"Oh, Sharon, if only my life were filled with perfect little moments like this, I would never moan again."

"But Holly, nobody's life is filled with perfect little moments."

"Ooh!" They both shrieked again.

"This little boy is going to be a footballer, like his daddy!"

"Boy?" Holly gasped. "You're having a boy?"

Sharon nodded happily, and her eyes glistened. "Holly, meet baby Gerry. Gerry, meet your godmother, Holly."

HOLLY smiled as she flicked through the pages of the November magazine she had worked on. It would be out in the shops tomorrow, the first of November, and she felt so excited. Her first magazine would be on the shelves, and she could also open Gerry's November letter. Tomorrow would be a good day.

Although she had only sold the ad space, she felt great pride in being a member of a team that produced something so professional-looking. And she felt she had really proved herself. She had taken her job by the reins and guided it through to success.

Time to get working on the December edition. But first she had to call Denise.

"Hello? Disgusting, stuffy, and ridiculously expensive clothes shop. Pissed-off manager speaking, how can I help you?"

"Denise," Holly gasped, "you can't answer the phone like that!"

Denise giggled, "I have caller ID, so I knew it was you."

"Hmm." Holly was suspicious; she didn't think Denise had caller ID on her work phone. "I got a message you called earlier."

"Oh, yeah. I was just ringing you to confirm you were going to the ball. Tom is going to buy a table this year."

"What ball?"

"The Christmas ball we go to every year, you dope."

"Oh, yeah. The Christmas ball. Sorry, but I can't make it this year."

"But you don't know what date it's on yet," Denise protested. "It's on the thirtieth of November this year. You can make it!"

"Look, Denise, I'm sorry," Holly said. "But Gerry and I went together for the past ten years. I would find it a bit difficult."

"Oh, sorry. I didn't think," said Denise. "Don't go if you don't feel comfortable. We'll all understand."

Holly hung up, promising to call later to give her a decision. It was only a stupid ball, and she didn't have to go if she didn't want to. However, it was a stupid ball that was hugely representative of Holly and Gerry's time together. It was a night they had both enjoyed, a night they would share with their friends. If she went without him, she would be destroying that tradition, replacing happy memories with an entirely different one. She didn't want to do that.

She wanted to hang on to every shred of memory of the two of them together. It was scaring her that she was forgetting his face. She still rang his mobile phone, paying the mobile company every month just to hear his voice on his answering machine. His smell had faded from the house, his clothes long gone. She clung to every little bit of him that she could. She didn't want to let go, because he was all she had. But she didn't really have him, so she felt lost.

Later, after leaving the office, Holly poked her head into Hogan's. She was feeling much more at ease with Daniel. Since that dinner where she had felt so uncomfortable in his company, she had realized that she was being ridiculous. Before, the only close friendship she had ever had with a man was with Gerry, and that was a romantic relationship. The idea of becoming so close to Daniel seemed strange and unusual. Holly had since convinced herself that there didn't need to be a romantic link for her to share a friendship with an unattached man. Even if he was good-looking.

Holly smiled as he walked over to greet her. "Are you going to that ball?" she asked, and scrunched up her nose.

He smiled and scrunched up his nose, and she laughed. "Well, it's going to be another case of Couples 'R' Us." He pulled out a high stool for her at the bar, and she sat down.

Holly giggled, "Well, we could just be rude and ignore them all."

"Then what would be the point in going?" Daniel sat beside her and rested his leather boot on the footrest of her chair. "You don't expect me to talk to you all night, do you? We've talked the ears off each other by now; maybe I'm bored of you."

"Fine, then!" Holly pretended to be insulted. "I was planning on ignoring you anyway."

"Phew!" Daniel wiped his brow. "I'm definitely going, then."

Holly became serious. "I think I really need to be there."

Daniel stopped laughing. "Well then, we shall go."

Holly smiled at him. "I think it would be good for you, too, Daniel," she said softly.

He turned away. "Holly, I'm fine," he said unconvincingly.

She kissed him good-bye on the forehead. "Daniel Connelly, stop trying to be all macho and strong. It doesn't wash with me."

Thirteen

$\mathcal{H}$OLLY was running late as she rushed around her bedroom trying to get dressed for the ball. She had spent the past two hours applying her makeup, crying and smudging it, and then reapplying it.

"Cinderella, your prince has arrived!" Sharon yelled upstairs.

Holly's heart raced. She had completely forgotten her reasons for going to the ball. Now she was faced with only the negatives.

Reasons not to go: She would spend all night crying, she would be stuck at a table of so-called friends who hadn't talked to her since Gerry had died, she looked like crap, and Gerry wouldn't be there.

Reason to go: She had an overwhelming feeling she needed to go.

She breathed slowly, trying to prevent a whole new batch of tears from appearing. "Holly, be strong. You can do this," she whispered to her reflection in the mirror. She repeated this over and over again until a creak at the door made her jump.

"Sorry," Sharon apologized, appearing from around the door. "Oh, Holly, you look fabulous!" she said excitedly.

"I look like crap," Holly grumbled.

"Stop saying that," Sharon said angrily. "I look like a blimp, and do you hear me complaining? Accept the fact that you're a babe!" She smiled at Holly in the mirror. "You'll be fine."

John shouted up the stairs. "Come on, girls! The taxi's waiting. We have to collect Tom and Denise."

Before Holly followed Sharon downstairs, she slid open the drawer of her dressing table and took out the November letter from Gerry she had opened weeks ago. She needed his words of encouragement. She slid the card from the envelope and read:

> Cinderella must go to the ball this month. And she will look glamorous and beautiful and have the time of her life, just like always. But no white dresses this year.
>
> PS, I love you . . .

Holly took a deep breath and followed Sharon downstairs.

"Wow," Daniel said, "you look fabulous, Holly."

"I look like crap," Holly grumbled, and Sharon shot her a look. "But thanks," she quickly added. Denise had helped her choose a black halter-neck dress, with a split to the thigh up the middle.

They all piled into the seven-seater taxi. For once, the traffic on the streets of Dublin cleared, and after picking up Tom and Denise, they made it to the hotel in record time.

They stepped up to the table just inside the function room. The woman sitting behind it smiled. "Hello, Sharon. Hello, John. Hi, Denise. Oh, gosh. Hello, Holly! It's so good of you to come, considering . . ." She flicked through the guestlist to tick off their names.

"Let's go to the bar," Denise said, linking her arm in Holly's.

As they walked across the room to the bar, a woman Holly hadn't spoken to for months approached her. "Holly, I was sorry to hear about Gerry. He was a lovely man."

"Thank you." Holly smiled and was dragged away again by Denise. They finally reached the bar.

"Hi there, Holly," a familiar voice behind her said.

"Oh, hello, Paul," she said, turning to face the businessman who sponsored the charity. He was tall and overweight, with a bright red face, probably due to the stress of running one of Ireland's most successful businesses. That and the fact that he drank too much.

"You're looking as lovely as always." He gave her a kiss on the cheek. "Can I get you a drink?"

"Oh, no thanks," she smiled.

"Ah, let me." He held his hand up to attract the barman's attention. "What'll you have?"

Holly gave in. "A white wine, then, please, if you insist."

"I might as well get a drink for that miserable husband of yours," he laughed, searching the room for Gerry. "What's he having?"

"He's not here," Holly said, feeling uncomfortable.

"Why not, the dryshite! What's he up to?" Paul asked loudly.

"Em, he passed away early in the year, Paul," Holly said gently, hoping not to embarrass him.

"Oh"—Paul reddened even more and stared down at the bar— "I'm very sorry to hear that." He looked away.

"Thank you," Holly said, counting the seconds in her head till he made an excuse to leave the conversation. He left after three seconds, saying he had to bring his wife her drink. Holly was left standing at the bar alone, as Denise had made her way back to the group with their drinks. She picked up her wine and headed over.

"I have arrived!" a loud voice announced at the door. Holly turned to see Jamie, the party animal. "I have again dressed in my penguin suit, and I am ready to partaaay!" He did a little dance, attracting stares from around the room. He made his way around their circle, greeting the men with a handshake and the women with a kiss on the cheek. When he got to Holly, he glanced to Daniel a couple of times, pecked her on the cheek, and rushed off. Holly angrily tried to swallow the lump in her throat. His wife, Helen, smiled timidly at Holly but didn't come over.

Holly was laughing at one of Sharon's stories when she felt a tapping on her shoulder. She turned to face a sad-looking Helen.

"Hi, Helen," she said happily.

"How *are* you?" Helen said quietly, touching Holly on the arm.

"I'm fine," Holly smiled. "You should listen to this story. It's very funny."

"I mean, how are you since Gerry . . ."

"Since Gerry died, do you mean?"

Helen appeared to wince. "Well, I didn't want to say."

"It's okay, Helen. I've accepted that's what happened."

"It's just that I haven't seen you for a very long time, so I was beginning to get worried."

Holly laughed. "Helen, I still live around the corner from you. If you were worried about me, I was never that difficult to find."

"Oh, yes, but I didn't want to intrude."

"Friends don't intrude, Helen," Holly said.

The bell was rung, signaling that it was time to take their places in the dining area, and the crowds began to swarm in. Holly made her way over to the table and took her seat.

"Are you okay?" Daniel asked quietly from beside her.

"Yes, I'm fine, thank you," she replied, taking a sip of wine.

"You don't have to give me that answer, Holly. It's me," he laughed.

Holly smiled and groaned. "People are being very nice by offering me their sympathies, but I feel like I'm back at his funeral again."

He nodded. "When Laura and I broke up, for months, everywhere I went, I was telling people we had broken up."

"Any word on Laura, by the way?" Holly asked. She enjoyed having bitching sessions about Laura, even though she had never met her. She loved to hear stories about her from Daniel, and then the two of them would spend the night talking about how much they hated her. It passed the time, and right now, Holly really needed something to talk about.

Daniel's eyes lit up. "Yes, actually, I do have a bit of gossip. A friend of mine named Charlie, who works as a barman in Laura's dad's hotel, told me her boyfriend tried to come on to some other woman and Laura caught him, so they split up." He laughed evilly.

Holly froze. "Daniel, what hotel does her father own?"

"The Galway Inn. It's brilliant, isn't it? I can tell you, if I ever met the woman who split them up, I would buy her the most expensive bottle of champagne I could find."

Holly smiled weakly, "Would you, now." Holly stared at Daniel curiously. She would have bet all her money against those two ever being together; she didn't seem his type. "Em, Daniel?"

He smiled at her, eyes still twinkling. "Yes, Holly."

"Well, I was wondering. Laura sounds like a bit of a bitch, to be honest." She studied his face to see if she had insulted him. "My question is, really, whatever did you see in her? You're so different— at least you sound like you're so different."

He broke into a sad smile. "Laura isn't really a bitch, Holly. Well, for leaving me for my best friend she is, but as a person, when we were together, never. Dramatic, yes. You see, I loved the drama of our relationship. I found it exciting; she enthralled me." His face became animated. "I loved waking up in the morning and wondering what kind of mood she would be in. I loved the passion of our fights, and I loved how we would make love after them. She would make a song and dance about most things, but I suppose that's what I found attractive about her. I used to tell myself that as long as she kept making a song and dance about our relationship, I knew she cared. She didn't treat me badly, Holly. She was just—"

"Dramatic," Holly said, finally understanding. He nodded.

She watched his face as he got lost in another memory. She supposed it was possible for anybody to love anybody.

"You miss her," she said gently.

Daniel snapped out of his daydream and stared deeply into Holly's eyes. A shiver went down her spine. "Wrong again, Holly Kennedy." He nodded his head and frowned, as though she had said the most bizarre thing ever. "Completely and utterly wrong." He picked up his knife and fork and began to eat his salmon starter.

After dinner and a few bottles of wine, Daniel took Holly by the hand and led her to the dance floor. As soon as they reached it, the song ended and Eric Clapton's "Wonderful Tonight" began. Holly gulped. She had only ever danced with Gerry to this song.

Daniel placed his hand lightly on her waist and gently took her hand, and they began to circle around. Holly was stiff. Dancing with another man felt wrong. A tingle went down her spine, and she shuddered. Daniel must have thought she was cold, and he pulled her closer to keep her warm. She was led around the floor in a trance until the song ended.

She had been doing so well. Even with everyone asking her about Gerry, she had remained calm. But the dance had shaken her. Perhaps it was time to go home while the going was good.

She made her way back to the table to say good-bye to everyone. "You're not leaving me here on my own," Daniel laughed. "We can share a cab."

Holly was slightly irritated when Daniel hopped out of the taxi and followed her to her house, as she was looking forward to opening the last envelope from Gerry. It was a quarter to twelve. She even called another taxi to arrive at her house in half an hour, just to let him know he couldn't stay too long.

"Ah, so this is the famous envelope," Daniel said, picking the tiny envelope up from the kitchen table.

Holly's eyes widened; she felt protective over that envelope, and she wasn't happy with Daniel touching it.

"December," he said, reading the outside and running his fingers along the lettering. Eventually he placed it back on the table, and she breathed a sigh of relief.

"How many more envelopes are left?" Daniel asked, taking his overcoat off and walking over to join her at the counter.

"That's the last one." Holly's voice was husky.

"So what are you going to do after that?"

"What do you mean?" she asked, feeling confused.

"Well, as far as I can see, that list is like your bible, your ten commandments. What the list says goes, as far as your life is concerned. So what will you do when there aren't any more?"

"I'll just live my life," she replied, turning her back and filling the kettle with water.

"Will you be able to do that?" He walked closer to her. "You'll have to make your own decisions then," he said softly.

Holly rubbed her face tiredly. "Daniel, what's this about?"

He swallowed hard and adjusted his stance, trying to make himself comfortable. "I'm asking you this because I'm going to say something to you now, and you are going to have to make your own decision." He looked her in the eye, and her heart beat wildly. "There will be no list; you'll have to follow your own heart."

Holly backed away a little. A feeling of dread pulled at her heart. "Daniel, I don't think that this is the right time to talk about . . ."

"This is a perfect time," he said. "You know what I'm going to say to you, Holly, and I *know* you know how I feel about you."

Holly's mouth dropped open, and she glanced at the clock.

It was twelve o'clock.

GERRY touched Holly's nose and smiled to himself as she wrinkled up her nose in her sleep. He loved watching her sleep; she looked like a princess, so beautiful and peaceful.

He tickled her nose again and smiled as her eyes slowly opened. "Good morning, sleepyhead."

"Good morning, beautiful." She cuddled closer to him and rested her head on his chest. "How are you feeling today?"

"Like I could run the London marathon," he joked.

"Now, that's what I call a quick recovery." She lifted her head and kissed him on the lips. "What do you want for breakfast?"

"You," he said, biting her nose.

"Not on the menu today, unfortunately. How about a fry?"

"No," he frowned. "That's too heavy for me," and his heart melted as he saw Holly's face fall. He tried to perk himself up. "But I would love a big, huge bowl of vanilla ice cream!"

"Ice cream!" she laughed. "For breakfast?"

"Yes," he grinned. "I always wanted that for breakfast when I was a kid, but my darling mother wouldn't allow me to have it."

"Then ice cream you shall have," Holly said happily, hopping out of bed. "Okay, I'll be back in a minute." He heard her racing down the stairs and clattering around in the kitchen.

Lately he had noticed her racing around every time she left his side. It was as though she were afraid to leave him for too long, and he knew what that meant. He had finished his radiation therapy, and it had failed. Now all he could do was lie around, as he felt too weak to get up most of the time. He was afraid of where he was going, afraid of what was happening to him, and afraid for Holly. He wanted to stay with her and carry out every promise they had ever made to each other, but he knew he was fighting a losing battle.

He and Holly had become even closer over the past few months, which was something he knew was a bad idea for Holly's sake, but he couldn't bear to distance himself from her. He was enjoying the chats till the early hours of the morning and giggling just like when they were teenagers. But that was on their good days.

They had their bad days too.

He wouldn't think about that now. And his new little project was keeping him busy. As he mapped out his plan to remain even when he was gone, he was also fulfilling a promise. At least there was one he could follow through on.

He heard Holly thudding up the stairs; his plan was working.

"Babe, there's no more ice cream left," she said sadly. "Is there anything else you would prefer?"

"Nope." He shook his head. "Just the ice cream, please."

"But I have to go to the shop to get it," she complained.

"Don't worry, hun. I'll be fine for a few minutes." He lifted his mobile off the bedside table and placed it on his chest.

"Okay"—Holly bit her lip—"I'll only be down the road."

She gave him a kiss and raced down the stairs.

As soon as Gerry knew he was safe, he pulled back the covers. He sat on the edge of the mattress, waiting for the dizziness to pass; then he made his way to the wardrobe. He took out an old shoebox from the top shelf. He took out the empty envelope and wrote "December" on the front. Today was the first of December, and he moved himself forward one year, knowing he wouldn't be around. He imagined Holly to be a karaoke genius, relaxed from her holiday in Spain, and, hopefully, happy in a new job she loved.

He imagined her on this very day in one year's time, and he thought hard about what to write. Tears filled his eyes as he placed the full stop beside the sentence. He kissed the page, wrapped it in the envelope, and hid it back in the shoebox. He made his way back to his phone, ringing on the bed.

"Hello?" he said, trying to control his voice. He smiled when he heard the sweetest voice on the other end. "I love you, too, Holly."

"No, Daniel, this isn't right," Holly said, upset, and pulled her hand away from his grip.

"But why isn't it right?" he pleaded.

"It's too soon," she said, feeling so confused.

"Too soon because that's what people have been telling you or because that's what your heart's telling you?"

"Oh, Daniel, I don't know!" she said, pacing the floor. "Please stop asking so many questions!" Her head spun. This felt so wrong. "I can't, Daniel. I'm married! I love Gerry!" she said in a panic.

"Gerry?" he asked, his eyes widening as he went over to the table and grabbed the envelope. "This is Gerry! This is what I'm competing with. It's a piece of paper, Holly. It's a list you have allowed to run your life for the past year. Right now, you have to think for yourself. Gerry's gone," he said gently, "and I'm here. I'm not saying I could ever take his place, but at least give us a chance."

She took the envelope from his hand and hugged it. "Gerry's not gone," she sobbed. "He's here every time I open these."

There was a silence as Daniel watched her crying. "It's a piece of paper," he said softly.

"Gerry is not a piece of paper," she said angrily. "He was a human being that I loved. He is a million happy memories."

"So what am I?" Daniel asked quietly.

"You," she took a deep breath, "are a kind, caring, and incredibly thoughtful friend who I respect and appreciate—"

"But I'm not Gerry," he interrupted her.

"I don't want you to be Gerry. I want you to be Daniel."

"How do you feel about me?" His voice shook slightly.

She stared at the ground. "I feel strongly about you, Daniel, but I need time. . . ." She paused. "Lots of time."

"Then I'll wait." He smiled sadly and put his arms around her. The doorbell rang. "That's your taxi." Holly's voice shook.

"I'll call you tomorrow." He kissed her on the top of her head, and he made his way to the front door. Holly continued to stand in the middle of the kitchen holding the envelope, going over the scene that had just occurred. She stood there for quite some time.

Still in shock, she eventually made her way up the stairs. She wrapped herself in Gerry's robe and climbed into bed like a child, tucked herself under the covers, and flicked on the bedside lamp. She stared at the envelope, thinking about what Daniel had said.

She took the phone off the hook. She needed to savor this special and final moment, to say good-bye to Gerry's contact with her.

She slowly tore open the envelope, trying not to rip the paper.

Don't be afraid to fall in love again. Open your heart and follow where it leads you. Remember, shoot for the moon.

PS, I will always love you . . .

"Oh, Gerry," she sobbed, and her shoulders shook as her body heaved from the pain of her tears.

She got very little sleep that night, and the times she did nod off, her dreams were obscure images of Daniel's and Gerry's faces and bodies mingled together. She awoke in a sweat at six a.m. and decided to get up and go for a walk to clear her jumbled thoughts. Her heart felt heavy as she walked along the path of her local park.

How on earth had she found herself in this situation? She wasn't looking to become entangled in some ridiculous love triangle. The third person wasn't even around. And anyway, if she were in love with Daniel, wouldn't she be the first person to realize it? If she didn't love him, then she should come right out and say it. But she was thinking about it.

And why was Gerry urging her to find a new love? What had he been thinking when he wrote that message? Had it been so easy for him to resign himself to the fact that she would meet someone else?

After hours of tormenting herself, she headed home. "Okay, Gerry," she announced as she stepped inside. "I've been for a walk, and I've thought deeply about what you said, and I've come to the conclusion that you lost your mind when you wrote that message."

She had three weeks left at work until she could take her Christmas holidays, which meant she would have to avoid Daniel for fifteen working days. That seemed possible. She hoped that by the time of Denise's wedding, she would have made a decision. But first, she had to get through her first Christmas alone.

"OKAY, where do you want me to put it?" Richard panted, dragging the Christmas tree into her living room. A trail of pine needles led all the way out the living-room door, down the hall, and out to her car. Holly sighed. She would have to vacuum the house again.

"Holly!" Richard repeated, and she jumped from her thoughts.

"You look like a talking tree, Richard," she giggled. All she could see were his brown shoes sticking out, resembling a skinny stump.

"Holly," he grunted, losing his balance slightly under the weight.

"Oh, sorry," she said quickly. "Over by the window."

He made his way over. "There now," he said, wiping his hands and stepping back to look at his work.

Holly frowned. "It looks a little bit bare, don't you think?"

"Well, you will have to decorate it, of course."

"Richard, I was referring to the fact that it only has about five branches left. It's got bald patches," she moaned.

"I told you to buy a tree earlier, Holly. Not leave it until Christmas Eve. I sold the best ones weeks ago."

Holly frowned. She really didn't want a Christmas tree this year. Richard had insisted, though, and Holly felt that she had to help him out with his new Christmas tree–selling venture, in addition to his flourishing landscaping business. But the tree was awful, and no amount of tinsel could hide that.

She couldn't believe it was Christmas Eve already. She'd worked overtime to get the January issue of the magazine ready. She had ignored all of Daniel's calls and had ordered Alice to tell him she was in a meeting if he ever called the office. He called the office nearly every day. She didn't intend to be rude, but she needed time. Richard's stare snapped her back to reality. "Sorry, what?"

"I said, would you like me to help you decorate it?"

Holly's heart fell. That was her and Gerry's job, nobody else's. Every year without fail, they would put the Christmas CD on, open a bottle of wine, and decorate the tree.

"I'm sure you've better things to be doing."

"Well, actually, I would quite like to do it," he said. "Usually myself, Meredith, and the children do it together."

"Oh." Holly hadn't even thought about Richard's Christmas as being difficult. "Okay then, why not?" she smiled.

Richard beamed, and he looked like such a child.

"But the thing is, I'm not too sure where the decorations are. Gerry stored them in the attic somewhere."

"No problem," he smiled encouragingly. "That used to be my job too." He bounded up the attic stairs.

Holly opened a bottle of red wine and pressed PLAY on the CD player; Bing Crosby's "White Christmas" played softly in the background. Richard returned with a black sack slung over his shoulder and a dusty Santa hat on. "Ho-ho-ho!"

Holly giggled and handed him his glass of wine.

"No, no"—he waved his hand—"I'm driving."

"You can have one glass, Richard," she said, feeling disappointed.

"No, no," he repeated. "I don't drink and drive."

Holly threw her eyes up to heaven and knocked back his glass of wine. By the time Richard left, she had finished the bottle. Then she noticed the red light flashing on the answering machine. Hoping it wasn't from who she thought it was, she hit the PLAY button.

"Hi, Sharon. It's Daniel Connelly here. Sorry to bother you, but I had your phone number from when you called the club months ago. I was hoping you could pass on a message for me. Denise has been so busy, I couldn't rely on her to remember." He laughed. "Anyway, I was wondering if you could just tell Holly that I'm going down to my family in Galway for Christmas. I haven't been able to get through to her on her mobile, and I don't have her home number, so if you could just tell her that I'll have my mobile with me if she wants to reach me." He paused. "Anyway, I'll see you all at the wedding next week. Okay, thanks. Bye."

The second message was from Denise saying Daniel was looking for her; the third message was from Declan, also telling her Daniel was looking for her; and the fourth message was from Daniel again.

"Hi, Holly. It's Daniel here. Declan gave me your number. I can't believe you never gave me your home number, yet I've a sneaking suspicion I've had it all along. . . ." There was a silence as he exhaled. "Anyway, I really need to talk to you, Holly. I think it should be before we see each other at the wedding. Please, please take my calls." Another deep exhalation. "Okay, well, that's all. Bye."

Holly pressed PLAY again, lost in thought.

She sat in the living room staring at the tree. She cried. Cried for her Gerry and for her baldy Christmas tree.

Fourteen

"HAPPY Christmas, love!" Frank opened the door to a shivering Holly standing on the doorstep.

"Happy Christmas, Dad." She smiled and gave him a bear hug. The smell of pine mixed with wine and Christmas dinner cooking in the kitchen filled her nostrils, and she was hit with a pang of loneliness. Christmas was Gerry. It was their special time together, when they would hide from the stresses of work and just relax and entertain their friends and family and enjoy their time alone. She missed him so much, it gave her a sick feeling in her stomach.

She had visited the graveyard that morning to wish him a happy Christmas. It was the first time she had been there since the funeral. Gerry had wanted to be cremated, which meant that she had to stand in front of a wall that had his name engraved on it. She told him about her year and what her plans were for the day; she told him Sharon and John were expecting a baby boy and they were calling him Gerry. She told him that she was to be the baby's godmother and that she was to be maid of honor at Denise's wedding. She explained what Tom was like, because Gerry had never met him, and she talked about her new job. She wanted to get some deep spiritual feeling that Gerry was there with her, but she really just felt like she was talking to a drab gray wall.

All in all, it hadn't been a good morning.

"Oh, happy Christmas, dear!" Elizabeth announced, walking out of the kitchen with open arms. Holly started to cry. Elizabeth's face was flushed from the heat of the kitchen, and the warmth of her body warmed Holly's heart.

"I'm sorry"—Holly wiped her face—"I didn't want to do that."

"Hush," Elizabeth said, hugging her even tighter.

Holly had called around to visit her mother the previous week in a panic and explained what had happened between her and Daniel.

"So how do you feel about him?" Elizabeth had asked.

"I like him, Mum. I really do. But I don't know if I'll *ever* feel ready for another relationship. He's not Gerry, but I'm not expecting him to be. I don't know if I'll ever love the same way again. I find it hard to believe that will happen, but it's a nice thought to have that maybe someday I could."

"Well, you don't know if you can if you don't try," Elizabeth said encouragingly. "It's important not to rush into things, Holly. I know you know that, but all I want is for you to be happy. You deserve it. Whether it's with Daniel, the man on the moon, or without anybody—I just want you happy."

As comforting as her mother had been to her that day, Holly was no closer to making her decision.

The rest of Holly's family joined them in the living room. They gathered around the tree and exchanged gifts, and Holly allowed the tears to flow all throughout. She hadn't the energy to hide them or to care. But the tears were a strange mixture of happiness and sadness. A peculiar sensation of feeling alone yet loved.

Eventually they sat down for their meal, and Holly's mouth watered. Everyone oohed and aahed at the food before them.

"I got an e-mail from Ciara today," Declan announced. "She sent this picture." He passed around the photograph he had printed.

Holly smiled at the sight of her sister lying on the beach, eating barbecued Christmas dinner with Mathew. Her hair was blond and her skin was tanned, and they both looked so happy. After traveling around the world searching, Ciara had finally found contentment.

"They're saying it might snow today," Holly announced.

"No, it won't snow," Richard said. "It's too cold for that."

Holly frowned. "Richard, how could it be too cold to snow?"

He wiped his fingers on the napkin that was tucked into his black woolly jumper with a Christmas tree emblazoned across the front. "It needs to get milder before it can snow."

Holly giggled. "Richard, it's about minus a million in the Antarctic, and it snows there. That's hardly mild."

"That's the way it works," he said matter-of-factly.

"Whatever you say." Holly rolled her eyes.

"He's right, actually," Jack added after a while, and everyone stopped chewing to stare at him. That was not a phrase they often heard. Jack went on to explain how snow worked, and Richard helped him out on the scientific parts. They both smiled at each other and seemed satisfied they were Mr. Know-it-alls. Abbey raised her eyebrows at Holly, and they shared their secret look of shock.

"You want some vegetables with your gravy, Dad?" Declan asked, seriously offering him a bowl of broccoli.

Everyone looked at Frank's plate and laughed.

"Ha-ha," Frank said, taking the bowl from his son. "Anyway, we live too close to the sea to get any."

"To get what? Gravy?" Holly teased, and they laughed again.

"Snow, silly," he said, grabbing her nose like he used to when she was a child.

"Well, I bet you all a million quid that it snows today," Declan said, eagerly glancing around.

"Oh, well, you better start saving, Declan, because if your brainiac brothers say it ain't so, it ain't so!" Holly joked.

"Better pay up, then, boys." Declan nodded toward the window.

"Oh, my God!" Holly exclaimed. "It's snowing!"

Everyone deserted the dinner table and threw on their coats to run outside like excited children. Elizabeth wrapped her arms around her daughter's shoulders. "Well, it looks like Denise will have a white Christmas for her wedding," she smiled.

Holly's heart beat wildly at the thought of Denise's wedding. In just a few days, she would have to confront Daniel. As though her mother had been reading her mind, she asked Holly quietly, "Have you thought about what to say to Daniel yet?"

Holly glanced up at the snowflakes glistening down from the black star-filled sky in the moonlight. The moment felt so magical; right there and then, she made her final decision.

"Yes, I have." She smiled and took a deep breath.

"Good"—Elizabeth kissed her on the cheek—"and remember, God leads you to it and takes you through it."

"He'd better. I'm going to need Him a lot over the next while."

"SHARON, don't carry that case. It's too heavy!" John yelled at his wife, and Sharon dropped the bag angrily.

"John, I am not an invalid. I am pregnant!"

"I know that, but the doctor said not to lift heavy things!" He walked to her side of the car and grabbed the bag.

"Well, screw the doctor. He's never been bloody pregnant," Sharon yelled, watching John storm off.

Holly banged down the boot of the car loudly. She had had enough of John and Sharon's tantrums all the way to Wicklow. Now all she wanted was to relax in the hotel.

She grabbed her bag and glanced up at the hotel. It was more like a castle. As the venue for their New Year's Eve wedding, Tom and Denise couldn't have picked a more beautiful place. The building was covered in ivy climbing up its aging walls, and a huge water fountain adorned the front courtyard. Acres of lush green gardens crept out around all sides. Denise didn't get her white Christmas wedding after all; the snow had melted minutes after it had arrived.

Holly dragged her bag behind her over the cobblestones and was suddenly sent flying as someone tripped over her luggage.

"Sorry," she heard a singsong voice say, and she looked back angrily to see who had almost caused her to break her neck. She watched the tall blonde as her hips went boom-boom toward the hotel. Holly frowned. She knew that walk from somewhere.

Laura.

Oh, no, she thought, panicking. Tom and Denise had invited Laura after all! She had to find Daniel quickly so that she could warn him. And then if the moment was right, she would finish off that chat with him. She rushed toward the reception area.

It was crowded with angry people and luggage. Denise's voice was instantly recognizable above all the noise.

"Look, I don't care if you've made a mistake! Fix it!" Denise held her hand up in a very startled receptionist's face. "I don't want to hear any more excuses. Just get ten more rooms for my guests!"

Holly gulped. Denise looked possessed. Holly queued in line behind the other guests, and twenty minutes later, she reached the top.

"Could you tell me what room Daniel Connelly is in, please?"

The receptionist shook his head. "I'm sorry, we can't give out guests' room numbers."

"Look, I'm a friend of his," Holly explained, and smiled sweetly.

The man smiled politely. "I'm sorry, it's against policy—"

"Listen," she yelled, and even Denise shut up screaming beside her, "it's very important you tell me!"

"Holly"—Denise placed her hand on her arm—"what's wrong?"

"I need to know what room Daniel's in!" Holly yelled.

Denise looked startled. "It's room three forty-two."

"Thank you!" Holly ran off in the direction of the elevators.

She rushed down the corridor, dragging her bag behind her and checking the door numbers. When she reached his room, she knocked furiously on the door. She took a deep breath as the door was pulled open.

She stopped breathing. It was Laura.

"Honey, who is it?" she heard Daniel's voice call. He walked out of the bathroom with only a tiny towel wrapped around his body.

"You!" Laura screeched.

Holly glanced from Laura to Daniel and back to Laura again. She gathered from their seminakedness that Daniel had already known Laura was coming to the wedding. Daniel's face was a picture of shock. Laura's face was stormy. Holly's mouth had dropped open. Nobody spoke for a while.

"What are *you* doing here?" Laura finally hissed.

Holly's mouth opened and closed like a goldfish's.

Daniel's forehead wrinkled in confusion as he stared from one girl to the other. "Do you two . . ." He stopped as if the question were totally ridiculous. "Do you two know each other?"

"Ha!" Laura's face twisted in contempt. "I caught this little bitch kissing my boyfriend," Laura yelled, and then stopped herself.

"Your *boyfriend?*" Daniel yelled.

"Sorry . . . ex-boyfriend," Laura mumbled, staring at the floor.

A small smile crept across Holly's face. "Yeah. Stevie, wasn't it? A good friend of Daniel's, if I remember correctly."

Daniel's face reddened as he looked at them both, seeming completely lost. Laura stared back at Daniel, angrily wondering how this woman knew her boyfriend—her current boyfriend, that was.

"Daniel's a good friend of mine," Holly explained.

"So have you come to steal him too?" Laura said bitterly.

"Oh, please. Like you're one to talk."

"You kissed Stevie?" Daniel said. He looked angry.

"No, I did not kiss Stevie." Holly rolled her eyes.

"You did too!" Laura yelled childishly.

"Oh, would you ever shut up?" Holly looked at Laura and laughed. "I take it you're back with Daniel. What does it matter anyway?" She then turned to Daniel. "No, I did not kiss Stevie. We were down in Galway for Denise's hen weekend, and Stevie was drunk and tried to kiss me."

"Oh, you're such a liar," Laura said. "I saw what happened."

"And so did Charlie," Holly told Daniel. "So ask him if you don't believe me, but if you don't believe me, I really don't care. I came to have that chat with you, but you're obviously busy." She glanced down at his skimpy towel. "So I'll see you both later, at the wedding." And with that, she turned on her heel and marched down the corridor to the elevator, dragging her suitcase behind her.

She pressed the button and breathed a sigh of relief. She didn't even feel angry with Daniel. In fact, in a childish way, she was glad he had done something to stop them from having their little chat. So she had been dumped and not the other way around. But Daniel couldn't have been that much in love with her if he was able to go back to Laura so quickly. Ah, well, at least she didn't hurt his feelings.

But she did think he was a complete fool for taking Laura back.

DENISE looked at Holly excitedly at the head table of the hotel's function room as someone rapped a spoon against their glass and the speeches began. Holly fumbled nervously with her hands in her lap, going over and over her speech in her head and not even listening to what the other speakers were saying.

She should have written it down, because now she couldn't remember the start of it. Her heart beat wildly as Daniel sat down and everyone applauded. She was next, and there was to be no running into the toilets this time. Sharon grabbed her trembling hand, and Holly smiled back at her shakily. Denise's father announced that Holly was going to speak, and the room turned to face her. She stood up and spotted John sitting at a table with his and Gerry's friends. John gave her the thumbs-up, and Holly's speech went out the window as a new one formed in her head.

"Please forgive me if I get a little emotional while I speak, but I am just so happy for Denise today. She is my best friend. . . ." She paused and glanced down at Sharon. "Well, one of them."

The room laughed.

"And I am so delighted that she has found love with a wonderful man like Tom. Finding someone you love is a wonderful feeling. But finding a true soul mate is an even better feeling. A soul mate understands you like no other, loves you like no other, will be there for you forever, no matter what. I know a thing or two about that, and I know that Denise has found a soul mate in Tom." A lump formed in Holly's throat, and she took a moment to compose herself. "I am honored to have been asked to share this beautiful day with Denise and Tom, and here's to them having many more beautiful days like this together."

Everyone cheered and reached for their glasses.

"However!" Holly raised her voice over the crowd and held her hand up. The noise died down, and once again, all eyes were on her.

"However, some guests here today will be aware of the list that a marvelous man thought up." John's table cheered. "And one of those rules was to *never ever* wear a 'spensive white dress."

John's table went wild, and Denise broke down in hysterics remembering the fateful night when that rule was added to the list.

"So on behalf of Gerry," Holly said, "I will forgive you, Denise, for breaking that rule, only because you look so amazing. And I will ask you all to join me in a toast to Tom and Denise and her very, very 'spensive white dress. I should know, because I was dragged around every bridal shop in Ireland!"

The guests all held up their glasses. "To Tom and Denise and her very, very 'spensive white dress!"

Holly's face beamed. And then the party began.

TEARS formed in Holly's eyes as she watched Tom and Denise dancing together for the first time as husband and wife, and she remembered that feeling. That feeling of excitement, of hope, of pure happiness and pride, a feeling of not knowing what the future held but being so ready to face it all. And that thought made her happy. She wouldn't cry about it; she would embrace it. She had been given a wonderful gift: life. Sometimes it was cruelly taken away too soon, but it was what you did with it that counted.

"Could I have this dance?" She looked up to see Daniel smiling down on her.

"Sure." She smiled back and took his hand.

"May I say that you're looking very beautiful tonight?"

"You may," Holly smiled. Denise had chosen a beautiful lilac-colored dress for her with a corset top, and there was a large slit up the side. Her hair was pinned up, allowing some curls to tumble down around her shoulders. She felt beautiful. She felt like Princess Holly, and she giggled to herself at the thought.

"That was a lovely speech you made," he smiled. "I realize that what I said to you was selfish of me. You said you weren't ready, and I didn't listen," he apologized.

"That's okay, Daniel. I don't think I'll be ready for a long time. But thank you for getting over me so fast." She nodded over at Laura, who was sitting moodily on her own at the table.

Daniel bit his lip. "I know it must seem crazy fast to you, but when you didn't return any of my calls, even I got the hint you weren't ready for a relationship. And when I went home for the holidays and met up with Laura, that old flame just sparked again. You were right; I never got over her. Believe me, if I hadn't known with all my heart that you weren't in love with me, I never would have brought her to the wedding."

Holly smiled at Daniel. "Sorry for avoiding you all month. I was having a bit of 'me' time. But I still think you're a fool." She shook her head as she watched Laura scowl back at her.

Daniel sighed, "I know she and I have a lot to discuss over the next while, and we're really going to take things slowly, but like you said, for some people, love just lives on."

Holly threw her eyes up to heaven. "Oh, don't start quoting me on that one," she laughed. "Ah, well, as long as you're happy, I suppose. Although I don't see how you ever will be." She sighed dramatically, and Daniel laughed.

"I am happy, Holly. I guess I just can't live without the drama." He glanced at Laura, and his eyes softened. "I need someone who is passionate about me, and for better or for worse, Laura is passionate. What about you? Are you happy?" He studied Holly's face.

Holly thought about it. "Tonight I'm happy. I'll worry about tomorrow when tomorrow comes. But I'm getting there. . . ."

HOLLY flicked through the newspapers to see which one contained a photo of Denise and Tom on their wedding day. It wasn't every day that Ireland's top radio DJ and a girl from "Girls and the City" got married. That's what Denise liked to think anyway.

"Hey," the grumpy newsagent yelled at her, "this is not a library. You either buy it or put it down."

Holly sighed and began to gather every newspaper from the newsstand once again. She had to take two trips to the counter due to the weight of the papers. Once again, a queue had formed behind the till. Holly smiled and took her time. She made her way with the last of the papers and began to add chocolates to the pile.

"Oh, and can I have a bag, too, please?" She batted her eyelashes. The old man stared at her angrily. "Mark!" he yelled.

The spotty teenager appeared from the shopping aisles.

"Open the other till, son," the man ordered. Half the queue behind Holly moved over to the other side.

"Thank you." Holly made her way to the door. Just as she was about to pull it open, it was pushed from the other side, causing her purchases to spill out all over the floor.

"I'm so sorry," the man said, bending down to help her.

"Oh, it's okay," Holly replied politely.

"Ah, it's you! The chocoholic!"

Holly looked up, startled. It was the friendly customer with the green eyes who had helped her before.

Holly giggled. "We meet again."

"Holly, isn't it?" he asked, handing her the chocolate bars.

"That's right. Rob, isn't it?" she replied.

"You've a good memory," he laughed.

"As do you," she grinned, and got back onto her feet.

"Well, I'm sure I'll bump into you again soon." Rob smiled and made his way over to the queue.

Holly stared after him in a daze. Finally she walked over. "Rob, is there any chance you'd like to go for that coffee today? If you can't, that's fine. . . ." She bit her lip.

He glanced down nervously at the ring on her finger.

"Oh, don't worry about that." She held her hand out. "It only represents a lifetime of happy memories these days."

He nodded understandingly. "In that case, I would love to."

They crossed the road and headed over to the Greasy Spoon.

Holly smiled as she sat at the table waiting for him to bring back the drinks. He seemed nice. She gazed out the window and thought about what she had learned. She was a woman who had taken advice from a man she loved and tried her hardest to help heal herself. She now felt confidence within herself to reach for what she wanted.

She was a woman who made mistakes, who sometimes cried on a Monday morning or at night alone in bed. She was a woman who often became bored with her life and found it hard to get up in the morning. She was a woman who more often than not had a bad hair day, who wondered why she couldn't drag herself to the gym more often. She was a woman who sometimes just got things wrong.

On the other hand, she was a woman with a million happy memories, who knew what it was like to experience true love and who was ready to experience more life, more love, and make new memories. Whether it happened in ten months or ten years, Holly would obey Gerry's final message. Whatever lay ahead, she knew she would open her heart and follow where it led her.

In the meantime, she would just live.

Talk about the luck of the Irish! Cecelia Ahern, the 22-year-old daughter of Ireland's prime minister, is smart, talented, gorgeous, and even rich, thanks in part to the instant success of *PS, I Love You.*

Just how did this young writer become so fortunate? Hard work, determination, a belief in herself, and, yes, a dash of luck. While growing up in Dublin, Ahern had always noodled around with writing. When she finished college, the choice was either look for a job or write a book. Bravely she opted to give writing a go. A night owl by nature, she'd work from ten p.m. till six a.m., writing in longhand. Then she'd go to bed, wake up at three p.m., and edit and type what she'd written the night before.

"I hibernated," Ahern says. "Every time I went out or had to do something, I'd think I should be home, writing." This breakneck pace paid off, and the book was completed in only three months.

Ahern says her novel is not autobiographical. Although the book deals with grief and loss, Ahern has never experienced the death of a close loved one, apart from her grandparents. Likewise, the Kennedy family is nothing like her own. In real life, she has just one sister. And her parents are "calm and loving" but "very different" from the parents in her book.

"Every time I went out or had to do something, I'd think I should be home, writing."

Every perfect murder

starts with a perfect lie.

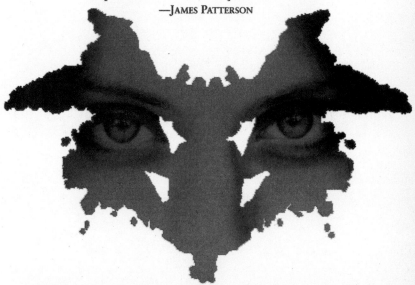

"A knockout thriller with one of the most
suspenseful courtroom sequences I've read."
—JAMES PATTERSON

HOWARD ROUGHAN
THE PROMISE
OF A LIE

A Novel by the Author of *THE UP AND COMER*

PART I

TO BE perfectly blunt and unprofessional, my lineup that day read like the maladjusted all-star team of Manhattan.

My nine-o'clock was a bulimic, twice-divorced executive who was having an affair with her married boss.

My ten-o'clock was a guilt-ridden kleptomaniac who could never keep what he stole. He was always revisiting stores to put things back.

Then came my eleven-o'clock—a sexually compulsive cellist.

A couple of hours for lunch and paperwork, then my two-o'clock: a soap-opera actor who could no longer distinguish between himself and the character he played.

Next up was my three-o'clock. Don't get me started on my three-o'clock.

Finally, there was my last patient of the day. My four-o'clock. The main reason I remember that day at all.

His name was Kevin Daniels. A struggling young writer who'd written seven screenplays and had yet to sell any of them. Kevin's frustration had manifested itself in a bitter hatred of the very people he wanted to impress. To Kevin, Hollywood was infested with, and I quote, "culturally retarded wayward whores destined to make feel-good-movie johns out of all of us."

But on this particular afternoon, an overcast Thursday in the middle of October, Kevin arrived at my office with an uncharacteristic smile. He professed to having significant news.

"I've had a moment of intense clarity, an epiphany," he said. He leaned forward and lowered his voice to a whisper. "I need to be in the belly of the beast. I'm moving to Hollywood."

I nodded, my face giving away nothing.

"I flew out there last weekend and rented a place in the Hollywood Hills. I'll be heading back there for good the day after tomorrow."

"You're not wasting any time, are you?"

"Not if I can help it."

"Have you told your parents?" I asked.

"They cosigned on the new apartment."

"I take it that means they approve?"

"I wouldn't go that far," said Kevin. "But what about you, David? Do you approve of my moving?"

I cautioned myself. Much about psychotherapy was predicated on the belief that an opinion should never do more harm than good. My job was not to ferret out right from wrong in any absolute sense. Only what was right or wrong for a particular patient.

"I'm not sure my thoughts have anything to do with approving or disapproving," I said. "The important thing is that no one has more control over your life than you do. While that won't guarantee success, it will guarantee you the right to make your own decisions."

He shrugged. "I can live with that."

After looking at each other in silence for a few seconds, we both realized that continuing to talk merely because we had time left in the hour would be silly. We shook hands, and I wished him luck.

And that's how it came to be. Why I remember that day so well. I'd told Kevin what I'd been telling him repeatedly over four years—that no one can have more control over your life than you do. *Pretty good advice,* I thought.

Too bad it was wrong. *Dead* wrong.

I know this because Kevin's leaving created an opening in my schedule . . . and the person who filled it was going to be all the proof I needed.

THE VERY NEXT NIGHT around eight o'clock.

I watched as Parker poked his index finger at the doorbell. As the three of us stood there, waiting, I took the opportunity to complain one more time.

"I can't believe I let you two talk me into coming," I muttered.

"Nonsense," Parker replied. "You wouldn't be here unless you wanted to be."

"That's very shrink of you," I said.

"And that's a *nondenial* denial," said Parker.

I chuckled. "There's the lawyer I know and love."

Parker's wife, Stacy, gave him a nudge. "Will the lawyer I also know and love ring the doorbell again?" she said. "I don't think anyone heard us."

Parker rang the bell again. The door opened almost immediately.

"*Omigod!* Will you look who's here," she practically shrieked. Cassandra Nance, all ninety-eight pounds of her, stood before us. A little black dress draped her shoulders as if it were still on the hanger. The woman was thin. "Come in, come in," she said.

Air kisses, initial pleasantries, and the customary bottle-of-wine handoff. A rented man in a tuxedo took our coats. Cassandra led us into the party. By that point, I was resigned to the situation. This was the appearance to keep up appearances, and I was prepared to put in the good effort. But before that could happen, I needed to say hello to Mr. Bartender. After a brief conversation with the guy, I was handed my bourbon and water. Two quick sips, and I was ready.

I looked around. Seemingly every ethnicity, ideology, and sexual orientation was represented—all happily conversing with one another and all somehow connected to our hostess.

My connection was originally through Parker and Stacy, my escorts for the evening. Parker Mathis was my freshman-year roommate at Columbia. Over the course of four years, we became best of friends. That we'd each decided to remain in the city after graduation practically made us brothers. I had even forgiven Parker for growing up to be a criminal defense attorney.

But to the extent I could kid him for his lapse of judgment in choosing a career, I had to hand it to him for his success in choosing a bride. Stacy Mathis was smart, witty, attractive, and the founder of a women's crisis center in Harlem. The complete package topped off by a halo.

For the next couple of hours, I made the rounds, shaking hands and trading anecdotes, happy to discover that my group social skills, while a bit rusty, hadn't completely deserted me.

Then, en route to another bourbon and water, I felt a tug on my arm courtesy of Cassandra. She was standing with a few other people. "David, you absolutely have to hear this!" she announced.

"Hear what?" I asked, obliging her.

"Nathan's theory, that's what. It's positively Neanderthal."

I waited a moment as feet shuffled left and right to make room for me in the conversation. The Cocktail Two-step.

"Oh, c'mon, Cassandra, you can't pretend to tell me you disagree," said the man I presumed was Nathan. We hadn't met.

"Nathan Harris," he said to me. We shook hands.

"David Remler," I told him.

"Yes, I know. I read your book."

"Go on, Nathan," Cassandra said. "Tell David what you were saying. I'm curious what our resident psychologist will make of it."

Nathan was fortyish, thin, tan out of season, impeccably groomed. The word "dapper" came to mind. So did "pompous." "I have this theory," he began, "about the true difference between men and women. Very simply, I believe men are superior to women when it comes to all things tangible—things that we can actually touch. For example, men are far better than women when it comes to building things. I don't just mean in terms of physical construction. I'd include the planning and design as well. All the great architects have been men. Consider the arts, at least those with a tangible component. Holding a brush and palette, molding clay—all the great painters and sculptors have been men as well. Even when it comes to making money, men are better at it than women."

Nathan paused and took a sip of his drink. "Ah, but women," he said, wagging his index finger in the air. "When it comes to the intangible—the things you can't touch—women have us men beat by a mile. When it comes to feelings and emotions, women rule and men are powerless. And don't think women don't know this. They know it all too well and take full advantage, often luring men into a serene sense of being in control, only to suddenly turn the tables."

"So," said Cassandra, turning to me with a frown, "what do you think of Nathan's theory?"

"I think it's very interesting," I answered, knowing full well that that alone wasn't going to get me off the hook.

"You'll have to do better than that, David," she said, shaking her head. "You have to tell us what you really think."

What I really thought at that moment was that I should've taken a different route to the bar.

"Well, let's see," I began. "You seem to be saying, Nathan, that while men are the hands of our collective culture, women represent the heart. Numerous exceptions notwithstanding, that's a pretty tenable idea. However, the notion that women use this difference as a way of tricking and deceiving—I don't really buy that. To me, that paints a rather unflattering, not to mention inaccurate, picture of what I've always considered the more compassionate sex. Wouldn't you agree, Cassandra?"

She looked ready to kiss me. "I couldn't agree more."

"Sold!" I announced. I shook the empty glass in my hand. "Now if you'll all excuse me, I seem to need a refill."

Not so fast, David.

"Interesting," Nathan Harris said, scratching his temple. "Let me ask you something, though, David. Can you honestly say that you've never been taken advantage of emotionally by a woman?"

"I don't think so," I answered. "Of course, the night is young."

Everyone found that amusing except Nathan. "I'm afraid I don't really buy *that*," he said, throwing my words back at me. "Somewhere along the line, surely you've been the victim of a woman."

"Nathan dear, don't you think we're getting a bit personal?" Cassandra had come to my rescue. The party's hostess was informing one of her guests that he was perhaps in bad form.

"I'm not asking him to name names or reveal intimate details," said Nathan indignantly. "I'm simply asking him to be honest." He turned to me. "You can be honest with us, David, can't you?"

That about did it. Nathan was becoming more pompous by the minute. It was time to put him in his place. A thought was jelling, and I was about to say a few things I knew I'd later regret.

"Excuse me, do you mind if we borrow David for a moment?"

It was a welcoming and familiar voice. Parker, with Stacy by his side, had leaned in over my shoulder. I was being sprung. Parker already had ahold of my arm and was pulling me away.

"I'm afraid I've been summoned," I told the group. It happened so fast that Nathan could do nothing except stare helplessly.

A safe distance later, I thanked Parker and Stacy for their timely appearance.

"We figured as much," said Parker.

"Like I said, I don't know how I let you two talk me into coming to this thing."

"Oh, c'mon," said Stacy, "you're having a good time. Admit it."

"If I do admit it, can we leave?"

Soon thereafter, the three of us shared a cab home. We discussed (read: "gossiped about") the people we'd encountered that evening. No shame to be had. That's what cab rides home are for.

At Sixty-ninth and Third, the taxi pulled over to let me out. Once out on the sidewalk, the autumn night air crisp and biting, I watched as their cab sped off, fully aware of the inevitable: Now it was I who'd be discussed by Parker and Stacy. They'd continue to wonder, as they surely had since the day it happened, that in missing her, as I still did, would I also miss out on the rest of my life? At the time, I was kind of wondering that myself.

It had been nearly three years since my wife, Rebecca, died at the age of thirty-one. She was four months pregnant at the time.

Rebecca and I owned an apartment in Manhattan. In addition, we owned a cottage out in Connecticut. Our weekend retreat.

Often Rebecca would get a jump on the weekend with a Thursday night drive out to the cottage. As a freelance writer, she made her own hours. Hardly the case for me. As a psychologist, I may have made a good living, but I still only got paid by the hour. I'd work a full day on Friday and join Rebecca that evening at the cottage after taking the train up to Danbury.

Such was the case that second weekend in November. Or at least it was supposed to be until everything changed. On that Friday evening, instead of Rebecca's picking me up at the station, as she usually did, a policeman was there, waiting. His job was to take me to the county coroner's office.

Earlier that morning, a freezing rain had fallen. Rebecca had left the cottage during the worst of it to pick up groceries.

It was a head-on collision. An eighteen-year-old kid behind the wheel of his parents' Lexus. He hadn't been drinking or smoking pot. The kid was just a kid, driving too fast. He lost control of the car and spun into the oncoming lane. Right into Rebecca.

In time, I found I could deal with talking about her death. It was *thinking* about it that I couldn't handle. I could easily disengage from the concern and curiosity of others, but I couldn't escape my own thoughts . . . and the frequency with which they'd turn to Rebecca. And our baby.

It was too early to know if we were having a boy or a girl. Rebecca had every intention of finding out the sex as soon as she could, but in the meantime, we didn't discuss names. That was my suggestion. Waiting until we knew the sex meant fifty percent less arguing, I joked. Agreeing not to discuss names, however, didn't mean we weren't thinking about them. I know I was.

A few weeks after Rebecca died, I was looking through the closet for a pair of gloves. What I found, instead, was one of those baby-name books. I never knew Rebecca had purchased one, and given the hiding place, I guess that's how she wanted it.

I sat down on the floor in front of the closet and began flipping through the pages.

Then I came across it. Tucked in the page that ended the *S*'s and began the *T*'s was a piece of white paper. Rebecca had written a sentence near the top. It read, *Things we will teach our child . . .* Underneath, she'd jotted down the following:

> *To love.*
> *To laugh.*
> *To laugh some more.*
> *To listen and learn.*
> *To say please and thank you.*
> *To have opinions.*
> *To respect those of others.*
> *To be honest.*
> *To be a friend.*
> *To be yourself.*

How long I stayed there on the floor, I can't remember. I read what Rebecca had written over and over until I memorized it. I put the paper back in the book. The next day, I went to a bank and rented a safe-deposit box. I placed the book in it. I told myself that if I ever forgot any part of Rebecca's list, I'd come and remind myself. I've yet to go back.

THERE was a brief message waiting for me when I arrived at my office Monday morning. It was from Mila, or Mamka (Czech for "Mom"), as I was fond of calling her. I think she was fond of my calling her that as well. She'd never had any kids.

Mamka, a.k.a. Mila Benninghoff, was my secretary, bookkeeper, insurance-company liaison, and all-around godsend. At seventy, she made it look easy. Mila oversaw the scheduling of my appointments, my correspondence, my billing, and everything else in my day-to-day life. All from her apartment. Which was fine by her and exactly how I wanted it, for two reasons: One, the workload didn't mandate someone's sitting out in my reception area full-time. Two, it had been my experience that receptionists tended to make some people in therapy uncomfortable, and those people generally had enough to be uncomfortable about on their own.

So from her rent-controlled one-bedroom apartment near Gramercy Park, Mila would call me in between my appointments to pass along any messages—those she fielded herself and those forwarded by my answering service. Mila's message that afternoon regarded the opening in my schedule created by Kevin Daniels's departure for Hollywood. I'd told her about it, and she was going to get back to me after checking the waiting list.

"David, it turns out there is someone on the list," began Mila's message. "His name is Sam Kent, and he'll be your Thursday four-o'clock." I wrote it down in my calendar.

THAT afternoon, I was meeting Debra Walker Coyne, my esteemed literary agent, for lunch at the Four Seasons to discuss the outline for my second book.

The reason there was going to be a second book was due to the surprise success of my first, *The Human Pendulum*. It spent eleven weeks on the *Times* nonfiction bestseller list.

If I believed in such things, there'd be significant temptation to ascribe my book's success to cosmic reparations—meaning that were it not for Rebecca's death, I never would've written the thing. When she was alive, I had no desire to be an author. After she was dead, I still had no desire. What I had, however, was time. Lots of time. So I wrote a book.

Did I know what I was doing? Absolutely not. Had I even a smidgen of knowledge about publishing—what sold and what didn't—I would've nixed the idea. How many people, after all, could've been interested in David Remler's sardonic take on human behavior? Plenty, it turned out.

It happened like this. Months before my book was published, a rabbi from the Upper West Side was arrested for murder. According to the district attorney, the rabbi, who was married, was having a sexual relationship with a female member of his congregation. When the affair went sour and the woman threatened to expose him, he allegedly went to her apartment and strangled her.

At first, the evidence seemed overwhelming. The rabbi's fingerprints were at the scene, and a nosy neighbor had seen him leaving. On top of that, the woman was strangled with wire, the gauge of which matched that of a half-used spool found in the rabbi's home.

Finally, there was the diary. The woman had kept a detailed account of her relationship with the rabbi. Apparently, it was a creepy read. Particularly fascinating were the numerous references to the rabbi's threatening to harm the woman if she betrayed his trust. The last entry was dated the morning of the woman's death. It read, simply, *I think he's going to kill me today.*

The arrest of the rabbi and the ensuing trial were perfect fodder for every news outlet in the city. It was a whopping good story. It had murder, sex, religion. Then it had me.

All thanks to Ethan Greene. Ethan was an enterprising prosecutor with the Manhattan D.A.'s office. He was also on the spot. His superiors were convinced they had their man, rabbi or not, and in Ethan, they believed they had the prosecutor to nail him.

Despite all the evidence, though, the case turned out to be anything but a slam dunk. The rabbi claimed the woman was very unstable and had somehow decided the two of them were destined to be romantically involved. The rabbi said he'd tried to counsel the woman, while also being quite clear about the impossibility of his ever being more to her than a spiritual adviser. As for his being at the woman's apartment, he was merely making a house call, trying one last time to help. It was no use, though. On that day, said the rabbi, he left the woman's apartment believing she needed psychiatric care. He called a hospital to inquire about a program. Phone records indicated as much.

Was the rabbi telling the truth? Or lying to save himself?

No matter how the jury digested the rabbi's story, the defense would still have to address the question: Who killed the woman?

Simple. She killed herself.

It could've happened. Or so suggested a medical expert put on the stand by the rabbi's defense team. Suicide by self-garroting. Physically achievable, claimed the expert. The expert went on to cite two other cases in which the same type of suicide was thought to have occurred. Suddenly things were looking up for the rabbi.

That's when I got the call from Ethan Greene. Having read about the trial in the paper, I thought I knew what he wanted. A way to come back at the defense. Testimony from a psychologist saying that the woman's profile made her incapable of inventing a love affair, let alone ending her life. That had to be it, right?

Wrong. Ethan Greene's problem wasn't the woman, but the jury, he said. He had to convince them it was okay to convict a rabbi, to put away a "holy man."

"Fair enough, but why me?" I asked.

Ethan explained. He'd first heard of me over dinner with an old college friend, discussing the dilemma presented by the rabbi. Ethan's friend mentioned my book and how it might apply. Ethan purchased *The Human Pendulum* the following morning. He liked what he read. He loved one part in particular:

> I'm reminded of the woman who killed her children the same month she won a "Teacher of the Year" award. Then there's that nice family man who raised millions of dollars for charity, yet one day dragged a guy out of his car and kicked him to death—all because the guy had the temerity to honk at him after the light turned green.
>
> These are stories we hear from time to time and will continue to hear time and time again. They won't go away. Nonetheless, we persist in thinking of them as aberrations, anomalies in the spectrum of human behavior.
>
> Quickly we try to ascertain the mitigating factors: Medication the person was taking. A suppressed trauma from childhood. Postpartum depression, excessive stress, the playing of violent video games. Anything and everything. Just so long as we don't have to confront the disturbing reality: Good people can do

very bad things. Because to accept that notion means we're all capable of doing the unspeakable.

It means that we're all at risk on the Human Pendulum.

My initial response to Ethan's plea for help was a polite yet firm no. He persisted, though, pointing out that my testimony could be crucial in getting the jury to accept what they already knew—that the rabbi, like the rest of us, wasn't impervious to temptation. Still, I continued to say no, and Ethan continued to implore me. That's when the real point was made clear: He wasn't exactly *asking*.

"Dr. Remler, you will be testifying in my case. The only question is whether you'll be a friendly witness or a hostile one. I don't like subpoenas. They're a lot of paperwork, but if that's what it's going to take, so be it."

Two days later, I got called to the stand and nervously spoke to the unfortunate reality that there's no tenured status for do-gooders. Human behavior, I said, is like the fine print of a mutual fund prospectus: Past performance doesn't guarantee future results.

I never once looked at the rabbi. For the most part, I fixed my gaze on Ethan while intermittently acknowledging the jury. To my eyes, they seemed as if they really didn't care about Dr. Remler and his precious book. When I stepped down from the stand, Ethan gave me a shrug that I took to mean, *Well, it was worth a shot.*

Closing arguments came the next day. The verdict three days after that. The legal pundits on cable were pretty much all in agreement. Not guilty. I was prone to agree.

Of course, I of all people should've known better than to try to predict human behavior. "This just in," announced the radio host of the jazz station I listened to when eating lunch in my office. I sat at my desk with a tuna sandwich, waiting to hear if it would be one word or two. It was one: "guilty."

Ethan Greene had prevailed. Later that night, I watched on the news as he stood in front of the courthouse and spoke to reporters. Then the footage of Ethan switched to footage of some older Hispanic woman. She looked familiar. Yes, she'd been in the first row, third from the right. In this age of the postverdict interview, here was this woman, one of the jurors, telling the reporter what had really influenced her decision. "I guess what really made the difference for me was that psychologist witness. The one with the book."

Ditto, said the young man in a business suit standing next to her. He'd sat somewhere in the second row of the jury box. He claimed it was my testimony that helped him overcome what had been one of his main obstacles: believing a rabbi could ever do such a thing.

Ten seconds later, my phone was ringing. I picked it up to hear Parker. "Congratulations," he said. "You're about to become a best-selling author."

"What makes you say that?" I asked.

"Because you just demolished one of the oldest tenets of trial law: the character witness. Now every attorney and law prof in the land will have to read your book to see what all the fuss was about. You wait."

I didn't have to wait long. Within days, my editor called to say that a second printing of the book had been ordered. My agent, Debra Walker Coyne, was fielding calls from a horde of news programs, all wanting me to make an appearance. Ultimately, I agreed to do one show: *Charlie Rose.* By the time it aired, Parker's prediction had come true—I was a *New York Times* best-selling author.

AT FOUR on the nose, I double-checked my calendar for the correct name of my new patient—Mr. Sam Kent, according to Mila. I got up from my desk and opened the door to the reception area. What I saw wasn't quite what I expected. I hesitated.

"Is something wrong?" she asked.

Sitting on the couch against the wall was a woman, a black shoulder bag by her side. She was wearing a long raincoat with a high collar, and a gray Yankees baseball cap, the rim barely clearing her eyes. A soft blue.

"I'm sorry," I answered. "You're not—"

"I am. Sam Kent. Short for Samantha." We shook hands.

"My secretary told me you were *Mr.* Sam Kent," I said. "The Sam name notwithstanding, I assume you spoke with her."

"E-mailed, actually. When I first called a few months back, I got your service. I gave them my e-mail address because I was moving and my phone number would be changing. Your secretary and I ultimately traded e-mails."

"Well, that explains it," I said. "Come on in." I motioned with my arm, and Sam Kent stepped into my office. She removed her raincoat. She had on blue jeans and a red sweatshirt.

"Where should I sit?" she asked. They always did.

"Sofa or chair, whichever you prefer."

She preferred the chair, a wingback opposite mine. We both sat. I looked at my new patient. She was now visibly upset.

"I'm sorry," she said, wiping away a tear. "I promised myself I wouldn't do it, but I still did. Right off the bat, no less."

"You mean cry?"

"No," she said. "Lie. You asked me whether I had talked to your secretary. I told you I didn't give a phone number, because I was moving." She wiped away another tear. "I was never moving."

I got up, grabbed a box of tissues off my desk, and walked it over to her. She took one and dabbed her eyes.

"Okay," I said, returning to my chair. "I take it there was some reason you didn't want to give out your phone number."

"It's the same reason that I'm here," she said. "My husband."

Usually, a first session is nothing more than an extended introduction. The immediate concern is getting to know each other. Occasionally a patient delves right into things. Whatever it is he or she is carrying around has grown beyond heavy. It's time to unload. This was one such occasion.

"Your husband—what is it about him that brings you here?"

She reached for another tissue. Wiped her eyes. Proceeded to look into mine. "I'm here because I want to kill him," she said.

I didn't flinch. "When you say you want to kill him, are you speaking literally or figuratively?" I asked.

"Both," she said. "Though it's the *literally* that has me worried."

"That you might actually do it?"

"That and how I could be so crazy even to think such a thing."

"Let's put your murdering ways on the back burner for a moment. I'm still a little confused about how your husband has anything to do with not giving out your phone number."

"That's easy," she said. "Say your office calls and he picks up or he hears a message. I couldn't have that. He can't find out I'm seeing a therapist, because he'd know I'd be talking about him."

"He wouldn't like that, huh?"

"You have no idea."

She was right. I had no idea. That would have to change. While there was no rush, I chose to seize the opportunity she was giving me. "What does your husband do for a living?"

"He's a venture capitalist. He has a firm downtown."

"Wall Street?"

"That's where the money is, he likes to say."

"Does he work a lot?" I asked.

"All the time."

"Is the firm successful?"

"Very," she said. The subtext being *very* very.

"What about children? Do you have any?"

"A little boy," she said, her expression warming. "He's two."

"How is your husband with him?"

The warm expression faded. "Like I said, he works all the time."

"And how many years have you been married?"

"Five."

"Do you love him?"

"I told you I wanted to kill him. I don't love him."

"Why haven't you left him?"

"Because if I did, he'd be the one killing me."

Here we go again, I thought. "Literally?" I asked.

"Figuratively," she answered. "He told me that if I tried to divorce him, he'd make sure I'd never get custody of our son."

"How would he accomplish that?"

"Do we have to talk about it now?"

"Not if you don't want to," I said. "As for my next question, you can chalk it up to professional obligation. Has he ever hit you?"

She shook her head. "No. He's too smart for that. But he belittles my every move, questions my every motive. He's turned my family against me, as well as my friends. He tells me I'm not as pretty as I once was. Or as thin."

"When he says and does these things, what do you do in return?"

"I wish I could say I gave it right back. I wish I was that strong. I'm not. It hurts too much. And he knows it. He feeds off of it."

With that, the timing seemed right. At some point during every first session, I asked the same question. "What do you want to gain by coming here?"

"The strength to stand up to him," she said. "Once and for all."

She reached for another tissue, and I decided to keep the remainder of the session as light as possible. We talked about her background. She'd been raised in Larchmont, north of Manhattan. Only child. Parents retired in Tempe, Arizona. She graduated from Brown. Dreamed of being a fashion designer. Ended up working as a buyer for Bergdorf's. Met her husband at a trunk show.

After fifty minutes, we agreed to meet once a week. Same day and time: Thursday, four o'clock. The subject turned to payment. She reiterated how important it was that her husband not know she was going to a therapist. "He sees all my checks and credit-card charges," she said. "Can I pay you in cash?"

I told her I didn't see why not.

She reached into her bag and removed a bank envelope. Three crisp one-hundred-dollar bills were taken out and handed to me.

"Wouldn't your husband notice the bank withdrawal?"

"A girl has to have her walking-around money, doesn't she?" Sam put her raincoat back on and adjusted her Yankees cap. It was one of those fashionable kinds, styled to look as if it were old, made from gray flannel.

"Are you a fan?" I asked.

"My uncle was a season ticket holder while I was growing up. He took my dad and me to a lot of games. Pretty good memories."

We shook hands.

"So I'll see you next week," she said.

Sam Kent. Samantha Kent. Mrs. Samantha Kent.

She left my office, and I sat behind my desk to jot down notes. I recorded the essentials. A physical description of her: early thirties, attractive, affluent without pretense. A few facts: places lived, jobs, anything that could've shaped who she was. Finally, in bullet-point fashion, I recounted the conversation about her husband.

I never once asked his name. If she'd offered it up, fine. My experience, however, was that it was harder for some patients to be forthcoming about their problems when discussing others by name. Her husband, therefore, would remain "the husband."

The mind works in mysterious ways. So must a psychologist.

"HELLO, David."

"Hi, Mamka," I said. *"Rád te˘vozím."*

Mila chuckled. "You just told me it was good to drive me."

"Damn. You have to admit I was close, though, wasn't I?"

"Yes. You're getting much better, David."

Mila had come to my office for her regular visit—every other Tuesday at five o'clock. The main purpose of our meeting was for me to sign checks she'd brought along. Utilities, the lease, and other things relating to the practice. Occasionally I also signed books. People would call and ask if they could send a copy of *The Human Pendulum* for me to autograph. Some wanted it for their library. Others, while never admitting it, wanted it for eBay.

"By the way," I said after signing the last of the checks, "my new patient, Mr. Sam Kent? He's not a he. He's a she. Sam is short for Samantha. Anyway, for reasons I can't go into—you know, patient privacy and all—she's going to be paying me in cash. So if you could deposit this with the rest of the checks," I said, handing her the three hundred dollars Sam had given me.

"Sure." She put the cash in a folder she used for the checks. "Oh, one other thing," she said. "Don't forget, you've got the Kesper Society cocktail party this Friday."

I frowned. "Can't you write me a note? You know, say I'm too sick to attend?"

She frowned back. "Now, what kind of Mamka would I be if I did something like that?"

"The best kind."

TWO days later, I welcomed Sam Kent back to my office. Her jeans and sweatshirt were replaced by a sharp-looking gray flannel suit. Her blond hair, which had last been tucked beneath a Yankees cap, was now straight down and long. A very polished look.

"I think you've exceeded the dress code," I said.

"Fancy lunch with a girlfriend," she explained, dropping into the wingback opposite mine. "I confided in her about coming to see you, and she knew who you were. She read some article on you."

"Is that right?"

"Yes, and she mentioned you lost your wife a few years back."

"That's true."

"I'm so sorry. I was wondering . . ." Her voice trailed off. "Well, did it help or hurt that you were a psychologist? What I mean is, given what you do for a living, I'd think you'd be almost too aware of your emotions to grieve, as one normally would."

A lot of patients did this. Assumed that because they were revealing their deepest, darkest, most intimate secrets, they were entitled to know everything about me. But Sam caught herself.

"What am I *doing?*" she gasped. "This is none of my business."

"It's okay," I said. Which it was. Also pretty refreshing.

"This is about me, and let's keep it that way," she said.

"Okay," I replied immediately. "You mentioned that if you tried to divorce your husband, he'd make sure you'd never get custody of your son. How would he do that?"

"I don't like to think about it," she said.

"Perhaps by telling me, you—"

"I tried to kill myself," she said, her voice remaining calm.

I expected tears. There weren't any. Her face was expressionless.

"When did this happen?" I asked.

"A few years ago."

"Before you were pregnant?"

"*God,* yes."

"What is it you did?"

"I swallowed thirty Halcions with a bottle of wine," she said.

"Yet here you are today," I said.

"My husband found me. He was supposed to be at dinner with a client. The client called him to cancel—an emergency at home. Ironic, huh? My husband came back to our place, and there I was. He saw the empty bottle of pills near the bed and asked how long it had been since I took them. I told him it had been long enough, which it hadn't, because I was still pretty lucid. My husband went to the medicine cabinet and grabbed a bottle of ipecac. He force-fed me a couple of ounces, and the next thing I knew, I was puking my guts out. Thirty pills had gone down. Twenty-eight came back up."

"What happened next?" I asked.

"I slept like a baby and woke up the next morning."

"You didn't go to the hospital?"

"No. I knew I was going to be all right. At least physically," she said. "That night, a hospital wasn't going to do anything for me mentally. I assured my husband I didn't need to go."

"He was okay with that?"

"I'm sure he felt relieved," she said. "Better to have a wife who committed suicide than a wife who's known to all his friends and associates as the one who'd *tried* to commit suicide."

"So you never told anyone about that night?" I asked.

"Not until this moment, no."

"And your husband?"

"Not a soul, *yet.* That's his leverage. It's also the answer to your original question," she said. "If I ever file for divorce, he swears he'll tell the court about my trying to kill myself. Which means, there goes my son. Courts don't award custody to suicidal mothers."

"It's not as cut-and-dry as you think," I said. "Determinations have to be made. In your case, a court might trust that you pose no risk to yourself."

"That's the problem. The word 'might.' There's too much at stake for me to put faith in a word like that."

"So instead, you live a compromised life with your husband."

"Because it means being with my son, yes."

"It's strange, though, Sam. The more I listen to you, the less I understand your husband's motivations. What's in it for him?"

"The ultimate freedom, that's what," she replied. "He does whatever he wants, whenever he wants, *who*ever he wants."

"You're saying he's had affairs?"

She nodded.

"Have you confronted him about it?"

"He'd just deny it and accuse me of being paranoid."

I had no follow-up to that. I simply sat there, looking at Sam Kent, seeing a woman who needed out of her marriage, and fast. That's why she'd come to me. To give her the strength to walk away, she'd said. The question was how I was going to accomplish that.

"What are you thinking?" she asked, breaking the silence.

"I'm thinking you deserve better," I said.

IT'S good to have at least one friend who's a lawyer. I'd shared that observation with Parker as a segue into asking him for what I wanted—free legal advice.

I dialed his office the next morning, a Friday, between my ten- and eleven-o'clock sessions. His secretary put me through.

"Can I pick your brain?" I asked. "It's about a patient."

"Whoa. It must be serious. You've never once told me anything about any of your patients. Not that I ever asked."

"Well, consider this your lucky day," I said. "It's a woman who wants to divorce her husband. They have a two-year-old son. Before the kid was born and before the woman was pregnant, she tried to commit suicide. An entire bottle of sleeping pills. Her husband found her and got her to vomit everything up. She ended up being fine. Physically, at least. Now here's the tricky part—not only did they not go to the hospital after it happened, they never sought any professional counseling."

"Why not?" he asked.

"Neither wanted to deal with the aftermath," I told him. "Now the husband is threatening to spill the beans to keep her from the kid if she tries to divorce him. So if she goes through with it and files, what chance does she have at custody? How much of a role will her attempted suicide play?"

"First off, this is family law, and I'm not," Parker said. "Then again, far be it from me not to think I know everything. So here we go. Will the suicide play a role? Yes. How much? It depends. A custody case, as it should be, is geared toward the well-being of the child. Anything that even hints at jeopardizing that well-being is fair game. Do you think your patient is still a threat to herself?"

"Personally, I don't," I answered. "Professionally, though, I couldn't say for sure. We've only had two sessions. On the plus side, the suicide attempt was three years ago."

"A point in her favor," he said. "Does the husband have money?"

"Yeah. Why?"

"Quality of representation. A good lawyer won't be banking on some doctor saying she's unfit to be a mother. He'll assume she gets the medical thumbs-up going in, and make it his mission to redefine the battlefield."

"Which would be what?"

"The rest of her behavior," he said. "Specifically, those things that either show or promote questionable judgment on her part. Does she drink, is she taking any antidepressants, has she ever been arrested? Nothing goes unscrutinized. Everything gets magnified. One speeding ticket, okay. Two speeding tickets, and she's got a death wish."

"Assume that my patient is otherwise a model citizen," I said.

"Then she's got a fighting chance. Given that she's got good lawyers, they'll be digging up dirt on the husband. Even if he's a

Boy Scout, they'll be nailing him for his lack of judgment when his wife tried to check out. It was his responsibility to get her to a hospital. That he didn't take her goes beyond stupid." Parker paused. "You know, if you want, I can put you in touch with a guy who handles nothing but custody cases."

"I might take you up on that later," I said. "One last thing, though. Absent all the facts, give me her odds . . . ballpark."

"Sixty percent," he said. "Sixty-five if she's pretty."

What if she's very pretty? I wanted to ask, but thought better of it. Instead, I remarked, "Those aren't such bad odds. Thanks."

I hung up the phone and thought of Sam Kent. Her voice telling me her story, the details of a life in retreat. She didn't have a marriage; she had an arrangement. I could hear the catching of her breath as she cried in my office. It was the sound of suffocation.

I wanted to help her, restore her confidence, and there was nothing wrong with that. I wanted to help all my patients. That was my job. But this was different, and I knew it.

The wall was beginning to be chipped away—the separation between patient and doctor.

Put down the chisel, David, I told myself. Let the wall stand.

THE Kesper Society was started by Arnold Kesper, as in the satellite-hoarding conglomerate Kesper Communications and as in more money than God. The man was somewhat eccentric—a personality trait not uncommon among billionaires—and he rarely missed an opportunity to reinforce the image.

Fittingly, Kesper managed to be eccentric even with his charitable giving. In effect, he held competitions. Under the guise of better acquainting himself with all of the world's problems, he, along with his wife, would throw huge, lavish cocktail parties twice a year and invite representatives from various causes. He'd mingle with them, listen to what they had to say, and then, after presumably giving it some thought, decide how much to bestow on each cause.

The good news was that being invited to one of these parties was to know you were getting some funding. The bad news was that the exact amount was a function of the impact you made in those pressure-filled few hours. Word had it that the more you kissed up to Kesper, the more zeros were added on to your donation check.

Bennett Larson, Crescent House's top financial lobbyist, called two days prior to let me know he was going to be out of town for the event. I wasn't happy to hear it. Bennett Larson was an all-smiling, joke-telling, natural schmoozer—the Money Whore, as he freely admitted. Anything for a good cause, though.

Which was precisely what Crescent House was—a free psychotherapy and analysis clinic for the poor and uninsured that I'd recently been named a board member of after having volunteered there for more than two years. With only one location, in Queens, Crescent House had set its eyes on expanding to the other boroughs and to other cities. There were plenty of therapists willing to donate their time. But securing the bricks and mortar, not to mention the real estate on which to break ground, required a much higher level of generosity. The Arnold Kesper variety.

So that Friday evening, sans Larson, I, along with some of the others filling out the Crescent House board, descended on the Great Hall at the Metropolitan Museum of Art, the site of the latest Kesper Society cocktail party. That Crescent House had been invited at all remained no small achievement.

An hour and a half into the cocktail party, we were finally getting our audience with "the man." One of Kesper's minions, a petite and humorless-looking woman clutching a clipboard, had us all gather in a designated area before bringing over Kesper. "Mr. Kesper, may I present the representatives from Crescent House," said the woman. Then, in a hushed tone, she introduced each of us to her boss by name. We might as well have been at the Vatican.

Given that, maybe the question he threw at me wasn't from so far out of left field. Up until that point, the conversation had been relatively innocuous. Kesper asked about what we did at Crescent House, and we answered the best we could. He expressed his admiration for our efforts and genuinely seemed to understand our objectives. Then Kesper looked directly at me.

"Tell me, Dr. Remler, did you think he was guilty?" he asked.

"I'm sorry?" I said.

"The rabbi in that trial," said Kesper. "Did you think he was guilty? Because I'm not so sure. I tend to think he was innocent. Though from what I understand, your testimony sure did him in."

I was slightly taken aback. My involvement with that trial was the last thing I expected to be discussing with Arnold Kesper.

"I think it was certainly possible the rabbi was guilty," I told Kesper. "Though it was hardly a clear-cut case."

The billionaire shook his head. "That's far too diplomatic of an answer," he said. "I'd have to believe that, deep down, you have a very strong opinion one way or the other. Am I wrong?"

"You're not wrong," I said. "I just think it might be better if that strong opinion remained that way. Meaning deep down."

Kesper pursed his lips. "Dr. Remler," he said, "I'd be dismayed if your reticence is on account of not wanting to appear disagreeable with me. Maybe you'd like some assurance that speaking your mind will have no bearing on my intentions for Crescent House."

"I don't think that's really necessary," I said.

"Oh, of course you do. I'd be lying if I didn't admit your not indulging me about that rabbi—not revealing your innermost thoughts on his guilt or innocence—would indeed adversely impact my feelings toward Crescent House. I agree it might not be fair. Nonetheless, it's honest. So I'm afraid that puts us at an impasse."

All eyes settled on me, waiting for a response. I cleared my throat. "Guilty as sin," I crowed.

"What's that?" said Kesper, who no doubt heard me perfectly.

"I said I believe the rabbi was guilty. Guilty as sin."

"That's what I thought you said." He stuck his hands in his pockets and hunched his shoulders forward. "It's amazing what we'll do for money, isn't it?"

I said nothing. So Kesper continued, his voice now relentlessly cheerful. "At least in your case, it was for a good cause." His hands reappeared from his pockets, and he clapped two times loudly. "Thank you, Dr. Remler. Thank you, Crescent House. Thank you very, very much." He backed up a few steps before walking away.

And that was Arnold Kesper.

I stuck around just long enough to polish off three bourbon and waters in ten minutes. Those, combined with the three I had prior to meeting Kesper, meant I was extremely good to go.

Out the front of the Met and into the brisk night air. I stood there under a streetlamp for a moment, breathing it in. That's when I heard the voice over my shoulder. "Fancy meeting you here."

I TURNED around and saw a figure coming down the steps. A long black dress and a red shawl draped over her shoulders. A purse held in her hand. A familiar person in an unfamiliar setting. Then I realized I was looking at Sam Kent.

She walked up to me. "For a moment, I thought you didn't recognize me."

"For a moment, I didn't," I told her. "I think this is what you call 'out of context.' "

"I know. Isn't this funny? The two of us being at the same function. Though I'm surprised I didn't see you inside."

"Me, too," I said. "So what cause were you shilling for?"

"My husband's firm handles the charitable trust for the Kesper Society," she said. "According to philanthropic etiquette, that makes me a member."

"Where's your husband?" I asked somewhat warily.

"Singapore," she said with a strained smile. "He always manages to be away for these things, which leaves it up to me to represent the both of us. Any other event, and I'd take a pass. But for all of Arnold Kesper's eccentric, ego-driven ways, he really has helped a lot of people. Nice suit, by the way."

I instinctively looked down at myself. "Thank you."

Good form would've had me returning the compliment, telling Sam she looked nice herself. Which she did. But she was a patient. At that moment, I was trying hard to remember that.

Sam looked at her watch. "So where are you off to now?"

"I guess home," I said.

"That's what I hate about these parties—they ply you with booze and give you just enough finger food to make you hungry." She glanced around. "Hey, you know what? I should buy you dinner."

"And why's that?" I asked.

"Because you've been helping me. I feel I owe you," she said.

"Not with my rates, you don't."

She was determined. "Wait, don't tell me," she said. "You're thinking that wouldn't reflect too well upon you—the two of us being seen together. Socializing with your patients must be a no-no."

"It is frowned on by those who care about that kind of thing."

"Does that mean you don't?"

"No. I do. I'm simply not as fanatical about it," I said. "But as far as going to a restaurant is concerned, I'm afraid appearances do come into play."

"There you have it. That's our solution. Instead of buying you dinner, I'll cook it for you."

"Sam, I'm not sure that—"

"It's pretty funny when you think about it. To avoid the suggestion of impropriety, we're forced to do something far more suggestive." She put a hand on her hip. "So what will it be, David? Your place or mine? Wait a minute. I just realized we can't go to my place. Celeste, our nanny, is there watching my son tonight. She's quite a blabbermouth. Her seeing you would *really* not be a good thing. So it looks like it's your place." She stood and stared at me.

At last, it was the moment to make a graceful exit. Instead, I said nothing. I was too busy noticing the things I shouldn't have. The sheen of her hair. The snugness of her dress. The fact that I was seriously considering her offer.

I was a man who knew better. But I was also a man who hadn't felt anything for another woman in quite some time. That man had also drunk six bourbon and waters on an empty stomach.

"There's really nothing in my refrigerator," I said.

She smiled. "Don't worry. I'll make do."

Sam went to the curb and began hailing a cab. Had it taken a few minutes for one to come along, I probably would've gotten cold feet. Nixed the whole idea. But a cab rolled up within seconds. I did my best not to read too much into that. *Fate* was such a big word.

DOORMEN in New York City can be counted on for two things: The first is, saying what is pleasant and expected; the second is, simultaneously thinking otherwise. "Good evening, Dr. Remler," was all the one on duty said as Sam and I walked into my building. But to read his mind? *Hey, maybe that poor guy isn't gay after all.*

Sam and I had the elevator to ourselves. "I kind of miss having them," she said. "Doormen, that is."

"Your building doesn't have them?"

"No. We live in a town house," she said. "When I was single, though, I lived in a doorman building. Made me feel safer."

"I'd say the same, but anytime I happen to come home really late, the guy here has usually nodded off."

"How long have you lived here?" she asked.

"About three years."

She nodded slightly while appearing to put one and one together. It made three. As in how many years it had been since my wife died.

Once in my apartment, I took off my coat, and Sam handed me her shawl. I hung them both up. While I went to turn on some lights, she disappeared on a self-guided tour. I stayed in the living room, stacking newspapers and scooping up empty beer bottles.

Sam called out from my library. "I pictured more paneling."

"I hope you're not disappointed."

"Quite the opposite," came back her voice. "I told myself that if I spotted a pipe rack, I'd leave immediately."

She walked out of the library and headed down the hallway to the bedrooms. First the guest's, then mine.

She reappeared. "I like your place," she said. "No pretensions."

She eyed a picture on an end table. She picked it up. "Are these your parents?"

"Yes."

"They're adorable." Sam stared at the photo a little more.

"You told me your folks live in Arizona. Tempe, right?"

"Yes." The way she replied made me think she wanted to add something. Or maybe had left something out. I looked at her as she stared some more at the picture frame in her hands.

"Is everything all right?" I asked.

"I'm sorry. I get this way sometimes when I look at other people's parents. My parents out in Tempe are actually my adoptive parents. I didn't mention it at the time, because—"

"That's okay; you don't have to explain," I said.

"Apparently, my real father died in some factory accident before I was born. As for my birth mother, all I know is her address and that she's really poor, which was why she had to give me up."

"You've never wanted to make contact with her?"

"When I was younger, I was far too angry about the whole thing. As I got older, I thought it was too complicated, and as you well know, that's the last thing my life needs."

"I can see why you'd think that, but taking care of one unresolved issue can often do wonders for working out another."

"It's been so long, though. I can't help thinking I'd only be meeting a stranger and not my real mother."

"Perhaps at first. In time, that would change."

This was turning into a session, and that was wrong. I was about to change the subject, when she saw fit to change it on her own. She put the picture down. Next to it happened to be the phone.

"Do you mind if I call home?" she asked. "I want to let Celeste know where I am."

"Sure. No problem."

Sam picked up the phone and dialed. I went into the kitchen to get rid of the beer bottles. I could hear her telling the nanny that she'd dropped by a friend's apartment and wouldn't be home for a bit. Sam called out to me, "David, what's your number here?"

I walked to the entrance of the kitchen and told her. She repeated the number back to Celeste.

"I always feel I've got to give her two ways to reach me," said Sam after hanging up. "She's got my cell-phone number, but I don't trust those things. Half the time, you can never get through to someone."

"I know what you mean."

She glanced over my shoulder. "So is that the kitchen?"

"Ready and waiting," I said.

"Good. Then let the magic begin."

I followed her into the least-used room in my apartment and watched as she took a few seconds to size it up. "You weren't kidding," she said after opening the refrigerator and taking a look.

"I know. I told you it's a barren wasteland."

Sam turned on her heels and eyed the cabinets. "Pasta," she said.

I opened a cabinet by the stove. On the top shelf, behind some microwave popcorn and a couple of cans of soup, sat a box of linguine.

She took the box from my hands, went back to the fridge, and grabbed a few things: eggs, butter, a jar of capers. She opened the freezer and started poking around.

I heard an "Aha!" She held up a package of chopped sirloin. "Now I need a big bowl and half your spice rack."

I got her the bowl and opened a lazy-Susan cabinet littered with various seasonings. "Do you want an apron?" I asked.

"Probably a good idea," she said.

I dug one up and gave it to her. "So what are we making here?"

"It doesn't really have a name."

"Interesting. The no-name linguine. I like the sound of that."

Sam tilted her head. "Me, too," she said. "It implies no responsibility on the part of the chef."

Smiling, I leaned on the counter and watched as she got busy. Meat in the microwave to defrost. Egg whites, spices, and some capers in the bowl. "You actually know what you're doing," I said.

"It's all a façade," she replied.

"Can I help in some way?"

She thought about it for a moment. "You can open up some wine. You do have a spare bottle lying around, I hope?"

"I think so," I said. Truth be told, I knew so. Wine happened to be the holiday gift of choice for many of my patients. Over the years, I'd been given more bottles than I knew what to do with.

I brought back a cabernet, uncorked it, and filled two glasses. "To the no-name linguine," I said, toasting.

Sam raised her glass. "And to better days ahead," she added.

It was a natural opening.

"Listen, Sam, normally I'd be discussing this with you in my office, but given the circumstances, it makes sense to bring it up now. I spoke to a friend about your situation. He's a lawyer and—"

Her face flushed with concern. "You didn't mention my name, did you?" she asked, her voice nearly panicked.

"No, no. There's nothing I told my friend that could betray your privacy. I wanted to get professional advice about your husband using your suicide attempt against you to get custody of your son."

"What'd your friend say?"

"Well, while he's a very good attorney, he doesn't practice family law. So this isn't definitive by any means. His take was that you stood a decent chance of winning if you went to court."

"Based on what?"

"A few things: the amount of time that's passed since the attempt, your not being a mother when it happened, and the most important factor—that you *are* a mother now. A good one, at that."

She seemed somewhat dazed. "The prospect of having to be judged, of having everything dragged out in a courtroom . . . I don't know if I can handle that."

"I think you can. What you *can't* handle is your life as it is now."

We were interrupted by three loud beeps: the microwave over the stove. The meat had defrosted, and I walked over to take it out. One hand pulled the door of the microwave open, while the other— I grabbed my left hand, writhing in pain.

"What happened?" she said. Then she quickly realized that the burner was on. "Oh, my God, I forgot to put the pot on it."

I looked down at the inside of my throbbing hand. I'd been branded by a GE Profile range.

"I'm so sorry," she said. "I am so, so sorry."

"It's okay," I told her. "I'll be all right."

"Wait," she said. "You're supposed to put butter on a burn."

She went to the refrigerator and found a tub of Country Crock. She scooped some out and began rubbing it into my hand.

"You know, technically, I don't think that's butter," I said.

Sam picked up the tub and spun it around slowly. "Whatever this is, it's got one-third fewer calories than margarine."

"Great. We certainly wouldn't want my hand to get fat."

She laughed out loud. What I was going for. A little levity.

I was feeling better, and it appeared she was as well. That's when we both noticed: We were standing six inches apart. Facing each other. Our hands touching and our eyes locked. Staring.

She was beautiful skin. She was full lips. I wanted to kiss her. Maybe I would have forsaken my professional responsibilities and done exactly what I shouldn't. But at that moment, I looked down and noticed the embroidered words on Sam's apron: KISS THE CHEF! It was the same apron I'd originally given Rebecca.

I backed away. Sam let go of my hand.

"Are you okay?" she asked. "You look like you've seen a ghost."

I had.

IT COULD'VE been awkward after that. It wasn't. Instead, Sam finished cooking. We ate, talked, drank the wine, and acted as if nothing had happened. Which it hadn't.

After heaping praise on Sam's no-name linguine and insisting I'd take care of the cleanup, I watched as she tried to suppress a yawn.

"I think it's past my bedtime," she announced. "Would you do me a favor and see me into a cab downstairs?"

"I'll go one better," I said. "I'll see you all the way home."

"Don't be silly. You don't need to do that."

"But I do. In the name of gentlemen everywhere."

She cocked her head. "Okay. But I live on the Upper West Side."

"Oh, *now* you tell me!"

She laughed and grabbed her purse. I fetched my coat, as well as her shawl. Out the door, down the elevator, up to the street corner, and into a cab.

"Fifty-six West Eighty-first, off Central Park West," Sam told the driver. I added that we'd be making a round-trip. We were off.

We talked about current movies. She'd seen a lot; I'd hardly seen any. Then I asked, "When does your husband get back?"

She turned to me. "To think it was almost a perfect evening."

"I'm sorry."

"I'm kidding," she said. "He gets back tomorrow night."

We stopped at a light. I looked out the window at some sign for a yoga studio.

"I really do hate him, David," she said as the light flashed green and we turned.

"Which is why you've got to seriously consider what we talked about. You can win. You can get out . . . with your son."

"You make it sound so easy."

"It won't be. I know that. But I can help you through it."

The cab came to a stop. Fifty-six West Eighty-first Street. "Home sweet home," she said sarcastically.

I looked out the window at her town house. Brick with columns. Tall windows. Flower boxes. Right over the entrance was a gigantic stone eagle with its wings spread.

"Yeah, I know, the bird is huge," she said. "Let's just say I'm not the one who picked it out."

She turned back to me. And there it was. Close together, face-to-face. Temptation all over again. Though it was easier this time to turn it down. I had practice.

"So I'll see you Thursday, right?" I said.

"Yes, Thursday," she said, reaching for the door handle.

I reached for mine. "Wait, let me walk you to your door."

"No. It's okay." She smiled and put her hand on top of mine. "Thanks, David. Thanks for everything."

I watched as she stepped out of the cab and walked up the entrance to her town house. She reached into her purse, found her keys, and waved. The cabbie sped off, but not before I got one last look at her. Sam Kent. Beautiful. Vulnerable.

My patient.

TWO NIGHTS LATER, I WAS awakened by a phone call. It was around two-thirty a.m. My eyes half closed, I answered it. "Hello?"

I heard nothing on the other end.

"Hello?" I said again.

Finally a voice—Sam's. "I did it," she said faintly.

"What are you talking about? What did you do? Did you leave your husband?"

"No, David," she said. "I killed him."

I shot up in bed, jolted by what she'd just said. But there was something else. How she sounded. Drained. Listless.

"Sam, where are you?" I asked.

I could hear soft crying. "Home."

"Listen to me. Have you taken sleeping pills?"

No reply.

"Damn it, Sam. Answer me!" I yelled at the top of my lungs, wanting to know if she was trying to kill herself . . . again.

"It was the only way, David," she whispered. "The only way." Then I heard a thump. It was the phone hitting the ground.

PART II

PANTS, sweatshirt, socks, sneakers. I reached for my wallet on the bureau and instead knocked it onto the floor. I kneeled down to pick it up and smacked my head hard against an open drawer. I felt nothing. There was no time to feel pain.

Could she really have done it? Of course she could've done it.

Ready to go. No, wait—keys. I dashed out of the bedroom straight to the sofa table in the living room. A little ceramic bowl from Mexico. That's where I always kept them. The keys. Where were they? I checked the kitchen. They were sitting by an empty glass of what had been a double bourbon and water. My homespun version of Sominex. How fitting—sleeping pills.

She was dying with each passing second.

I yanked on an overcoat, slammed the apartment door behind me. Down the elevator and a sprint past the doorman, who—big surprise—was asleep behind his desk. Out on the street, I didn't so much hail a cab as jump in front of one.

"Eighty-fifth and Central Park West," I barked at the driver. No, wait. That wasn't the address. "Actually, make that Eighty—" I stopped. Eighty-what? I couldn't remember. "Just head to Central Park West in the Eighties as fast as you possibly can," I said. He flipped the meter, and we were off.

Up ahead, the light turned yellow. If the driver had hit the gas, we could've made it. Instead, he slowed to a stop before it went red. Clearly, some additional incentive was in order.

"I'll give you two bucks for every red light you don't stop for."

The driver scratched his beard. "Not worth the risk," he groused.

"Make it five bucks, then," I said.

That seemed to alter things a bit. "I'll see what I can do."

Two blocks later, he swerved into the bus lane to dodge a line of cars stopped at a light and made his first five bucks. His head whipped back and forth through the intersection to check for crossing traffic. Not to mention cops.

The police. I'd neglected to call them. That was a mistake. The fact was, I'd reacted as David Remler, the guy who'd been with Sam in his apartment two nights prior. Not the David Remler who'd seen her as a patient for the past two weeks.

I quickly checked my pockets. Sure enough, there was something else I'd neglected to do—bring my cell phone.

"You're bleeding," the driver said. I watched in his rearview mirror as he pointed. "There, on your forehead."

I reached up above my eyes and felt around. Dry, dry . . . then wet. Mushy and warm to the touch by my right temple. I brought my hand down and saw the blood. With my other hand, I checked my pockets for a tissue or napkin. There was nothing.

"Here," said the driver. I looked up to see him passing back a crumpled ball of paper towel. Unraveling it, I ignored what appeared to be mustard stains, and folded it into a square. I pressed the paper towel against the gash to try to stem the bleeding.

We were getting close. North on Central Park West in the Seventies. I peered out my window, waiting to see something that would jog my memory. A store. A building. A sign.

I saw it. Right before the corner of Eighty-first Street, an actual sign, tucked inside a second-story window. Big, with all caps: GO YOGA! I remembered seeing it that night riding back with Sam. We'd turned immediately after.

"Turn on Eighty-first!" I yelled at the driver.

Three seconds later, he did, screeching left on red. "What's the number?" the driver asked as we straightened out.

"I'll know it when I see it," I told him. Then, "There, on the left! That's it." Sam's town house. The statue of an eagle.

The driver hit the brakes and flipped the meter off. A total of $8.50, it read. "Plus nine red lights," he reminded me.

It was really only seven, but I wasn't about to argue. I was already halfway out of the cab, and I tossed sixty bucks over the partition. He sped off the moment my door closed.

Sam's town house was completely dark. I rushed up the steps and reached the double doors. I pounded on them with my fist. The prospect of getting Sam to let me in seemed altogether nonexistent.

I grabbed the doorknob and was about to— *What the . . .*

Around went my wrist. The spring latch snapped. No resistance. I couldn't believe it. Sam had wanted me to come save her. The front door had been left open on purpose. In I went.

The only light was filtering in from the street, creating a few shadows, nothing more. What I couldn't see I could feel—the hollow expanse of a large foyer and the underlying stillness of the rooms around it. I groped for a light switch, finding a round knob. A crystal chandelier lit up above me.

"Sam!" I yelled out. No answer.

I yelled her name again, louder. Nothing.

There were archways to other rooms on my left and right, a huge, curving mahogany staircase in front of me. I ventured to think, *Where would I be if I'd just killed my husband and tried to commit suicide?*

Upstairs, my gut told me. I ran, screaming Sam's name. I reached the second floor and hit another light switch. There was a wide hallway before me with two doors on each side, another door at the end. All were closed.

Anxiety, adrenaline, impatience, and, most of all, fear. Fearing the worst behind each door. First up, a guest room. It had that minimal, barely used look. That's all it had, however.

I darted across the hall and barged through door number two. It was a small study. I saw a couch, a chair, a lot of books, and a desk. But no Sam. No husband.

The next door over—another bedroom. Larger, though no more lived in. I yelled out Sam's name. There was sweat running down my forehead, and I went to wipe it. Instead, I was wiping blood. A wide red smear left on the back of my hand.

Across the hall again. I stormed in on a bathroom. A sink, a toilet, and a shower curtain, pulled taut from one end to the other. I froze. It was my own personal horror flick. The slow walk up to the curtain. The bracing for what lay in wait. The quick grab and pullback. Only to find an empty tub.

Four doors down, one to go.

It was the one facing me when I got to the top of the stairs. Presumably the master bedroom. I breathed in, exhaled, and reached for the knob, turning and pushing. But the door was locked.

"Sam!" I called out. I pounded with my fist. Nothing.

She had to be in there. Then another thought: They were *both* in there—Sam and her husband. A murder-suicide?

I took a few steps back and steeled myself. Time to find out.

Everything I had left I put into the heel of my right foot. Over and over, I kicked. The wood shuddered with each kick until the door finally ripped open, flying on its hinges and slamming against the wall. I stepped in. An immediate rush of cold air hit me as I stood amid shadows of billowing drapes. Every window was open.

The light from the hallway spilled in over my shoulder. I flipped a wall switch. Frantically I scanned past a dresser and a night table. Across an unmade bed, thick with covers. Too thick, I realized.

That's when I began to see. The shape of a head . . . possibly an arm . . . what looked to be a pair of legs. I approached the bed, gripped the corner of the duvet, and gave a swift yank.

Lying there, facedown on the bed, was a man. A very dead man. There was blood all over and all around him. He was wearing a pair of sweatpants and a T-shirt. The T-shirt was riddled with tears, each one being where a knife had entered his body. It didn't matter that there was no knife to be seen. It was that obvious.

"I killed him," Sam had said. "I killed my husband."

My mind grappled with images of what must've happened. The anger being unleashed by her. How it was incongruous with the woman I was getting to know. Therein lay a real regret—that I hadn't gotten to know her well enough. Or fast enough.

I stared at the back of Sam's husband, unable to see his face. That didn't seem right. For whatever reason, I felt as if I needed to see it. As if none of this was really happening until I did. I reached down under his right shoulder and began to lift. *So that's what they mean by deadweight.* Finally the body rolled over.

I had my pick of things to make me shudder. The blood that had gathered on his chest, thick and sticky. The fact that his eyes were open, fixed with fear and panic, and seemingly boring into mine. But the most unsettling was this: When I looked at the face of Sam's husband, I couldn't help thinking, *I somehow know him.*

I had this feeling that it wasn't the first time I was seeing this guy. Not in a picture, but in person. I couldn't remember when and where exactly. Only that it felt very real.

That thought immediately took a backseat. It had to. I'd found Sam's husband, but not Sam. There were more rooms to search.

I bolted out of the bedroom and down the stairs. I bounced from room to room, going everywhere.

The library off the foyer, over to the living room and the dining room. To the den, then into the kitchen and a walk-in pantry. I covered every inch of the place. I searched every room and opened every door. Yet no sign of Sam. I checked the basement.

Where is she?

Truth was, I hadn't a clue. The one thing I was sure of was that Sam wasn't in that town house. She could've gone anywhere. At that very moment, she could've been lying on a sidewalk or in an alley, drifting off to a permanent sleep. I had to call the police.

I climbed back up the stairs. In the kitchen, I saw a cordless phone on the counter. I took a step toward it. That's as far as I got, though.

"Freeze!"

I spun around to see two cops at the entrance of the kitchen. One was short, the other tall. Both had their guns drawn, and both barrels of those guns were pointed directly at my chest.

"Thank God," I said with a deep exhale.

"Put your hands up!" the short cop barked in response.

Up went my hands. "Officers, I—"

"Who are you?" the second cop, the tall one, asked me.

"My name is Dr. David Remler, and I'm a psychologist here in the city," I said. I started to reach for my wallet.

The two officers cocked their guns. "Keep your hands in the air!" was the gist of what they both shouted.

"Sorry! Sorry!" I raised my hand back up and swallowed hard. "I only wanted to show you some ID."

"Just tell us what you're doing here," said the first cop.

"I got a call . . . one of my patients . . . Sam Kent," I began. I was sounding like a telegram, but the more I stared at the guns, the more out of breath I became. "Actually, Sam is short for Samantha. Anyway, she told me she'd killed her husband and—"

First cop: "Wait a minute, *who* said this?"

"Her name is Samantha Kent. This is her home," I said.

"She told you she killed her husband?"

"Yes."

"Where is she?" asked the second cop.

"I don't know," I said. "I thought she was here. That's why I'm here. But I've searched absolutely everywhere, and I can't find her."

Second cop: "What about the—"

"He's upstairs," I said with a grimace. "I'm afraid she was telling the truth. It's pretty bloody."

I saw both cops look at the blood on my forehead.

"How'd you hurt yourself?" the first cop asked.

"Oh, this," I said. "This is from my hitting my head back at my apartment in the rush to get over here. It's not what you think."

"And what would that be?" intoned the first cop.

"Maybe that I had something to do with—"

The second cop jumped in. "What'd you say your name was?"

"David Remler," I answered. "Dr. David Remler."

He nodded. "Dr. Remler, show us that ID, slowly."

"Yes, sir," I told him. I pulled out my driver's license. My business card. My American Psychological Society card.

The second cop approached me, his gun still aimed at my chest. He looked everything over and gave a quick "he is who he says he is" head bob to his partner.

The thought of Sam quickly resurfaced. "There's something else," I said. "We've got to hurry. I'm convinced that wherever Samantha Kent is now, she's got a handful of sleeping pills in her."

"What makes you say that?" said the first cop.

"Number one, the way she sounded on the phone," I said. "Number two, I'm her psychologist."

"You're saying she's suicidal?" said the second cop.

"I'm just saying that I'm her psychologist," I replied.

First cop: "You sure she's not here in the house?"

"Almost positive," I said. "Can we check the neighborhood?"

"First," said the second cop, "show us where the husband is."

THE rhythm and routine of a murder in Manhattan.

Or at least what happens after the murder. When the victim is found. When the system kicks in. When a bunch of people show up who make their living off of other people dying.

But for a time, it was just me and the cops. At their request, I'd led them to Sam's husband. Up the stairs and down the hallway. I turned back to them at the entrance of the master bedroom. "It was locked," I said in response to their curious looks at the smashed-in door. "I had to kick it open."

We went in. The room felt even colder than it had before. Despite my coat, I let go with a few shivers. My escorts didn't seem to mind. They checked the bathroom and the walk-in closet. All clear. They hovered over the bed and took a good long look.

The first cop looked at me. "Is this how you found him?"

"He was under the covers," I answered. "I pulled them back."

"What about the body itself?" he said. "Did you touch him?"

"He was facedown. I rolled him over," I said.

Immediate frown. "Why?"

"I guess to see his face," I said.

"Why?" he asked again. "Did you know him?"

I still had the feeling I did, yet I couldn't figure out how. Saying "Maybe" seemed like a really bad idea, given the circumstances. It was the sort of word used by people who had something to hide. "No," I said, "I didn't know him." And like that, I was on record.

There was no follow-up question, nothing that suggested they didn't believe me. Instead, procedure took over. The second cop called in to his precinct, reported there'd been a homicide, and gave Sam's address. When he hung up, I started to press the issue about trying to find Sam.

"All right," said the second cop. "What does she look like?"

I described Sam Kent. Five foot six. Thin. Blond hair.

"Any idea what she might be wearing?"

"No."

The second cop called his precinct again and made what amounted to a "be on the lookout" request for anyone on patrol. He also asked that all the emergency rooms in the area be checked. He relayed the information about Sam, right through the part about the sleeping pills, in a dispassionate monotone that suggested a lunch order rather than a life-or-death situation. But I didn't care. It got done. That meant there was still hope.

"C'mon," I was told.

The cops had to see for themselves that there was nobody else in the town house. While the first one took me downstairs and kept a watch on me in the foyer, the second went room by room.

As I stood there with the cop, I heard the sound of gunshots out on the street. I spun on my heels toward the front door and was about to hit the deck. The cop didn't flinch.

"Firecrackers," he said calmly. "It's Hackers' Night."

It took me a moment to get my calendar and jargon in order. I realized that it was October 30, the night before Halloween. When I was growing up in suburbia, we called it Mischief Night. Apparently, the urban translation was a tougher-sounding Hackers' Night.

The silence settled back in. I was growing increasingly impatient. "Isn't there something I can do to help you?" I asked the cop.

"There's going to be plenty you can do," he replied. "In a few minutes, the detectives will get here, and you can give them your full cooperation."

"Of course," I said. Another question occurred to me. "There's one other thing," I said. "I was about to call nine one one when you guys showed up. How'd you know to come? Did a neighbor call?"

"An alarm," the cop said. "Silent. You must have tripped it."

"But the front door was open," I said.

"It wouldn't matter, so long as the system was on." He motioned with his head up to the ceiling. "Motion detectors," he said.

We were joined just then by the second cop. "Nothing," he said, referring to his search of the town house.

"Good," said the first cop. He glanced at his watch. As if on cue, the homicide detectives arrived—two of them. They were followed by a couple of EMTs and two additional detectives from the crime-scene unit. Soon thereafter, two guys from the morgue showed up.

After checking out the bedroom upstairs and huddling for a few minutes with the two cops, the homicide detectives approached me and introduced themselves.

"Dr. Remler, I'm Detective Joseph Trentino, and this is my partner, Detective Frank Lopez."

I looked at them. Trentino, fortyish, was average height, stocky, and square-jawed. He wore thick-rimmed glasses and was losing his hair. His partner, Frank Lopez, was slightly taller, thinner, and—thanks to his full head of hair—younger-looking.

The first question was simple, open-ended, and expected. "Why were you here?" asked Trentino.

I told them everything. How Sam was my patient. The phone call from her. Rushing to the town house and frantically searching. Everything right up until I was told to freeze.

The two detectives took a few notes. Then came their follow-ups. Trentino fired off the first few. "At what time did you say Ms. Kent called you?" he asked.

"It was around two-thirty."

"How do you know?"

"At some point in the cab ride over here, I looked at my watch for the first time. By then, it was a little before three," I said.

Trentino scribbled in his pad. "The front door was open?"

"Yes."

"The door to the master bedroom was locked, though?"

"Yes."

"You kicked it in?"

"Yes."

"Once inside, you saw the victim there on the bed, right?"

"Actually, no," I said. "I saw what looked like a body underneath the covers. As I told the officers, I pulled them back."

"And the guy was staring up at you?" said Detective Lopez.

I gave Lopez a wary look. There was a chance he didn't know. There was also a chance the detective was testing me.

"I rolled him over. He was originally facedown."

Lopez grimaced. "You rolled him over because . . ."

I shrugged. "I'm not sure, to be perfectly honest."

Trentino flipped back a page in his notes. "I see you told the officers you don't know the victim," he said, staring down at his pad.

The lesser of two evils. It was pretty much what I was choosing between. Stand by my earlier statement, even though it wasn't necessarily the case. Or explain as convincingly as I could that there was a chance I did know the guy. My head was swirling.

"No, I didn't know the guy," I said.

And like that, I was *really* on record.

More questions followed. Mostly about what Sam had said to me on the phone. From there, the focus shifted to my forehead. The gash. No sooner had I explained again about hitting my dresser drawer than Detective Trentino flagged down an EMT. "Let's see if we can't clean away the blood there on Dr. Remler," said Trentino.

The EMT obliged. With some damp cloth and a cotton swab on a stick, he wiped and dabbed away the blood. Once the wound was clear, two butterfly bandages were applied.

"Good to go," said the EMT when finished.

What a great idea, I was thinking. Being able to leave. Going home, going to bed. The adrenaline that had kicked in with Sam's phone call had run its course. In its place now was staggering fatigue. I looked at my watch—quarter to four.

"Guys, can I have a word with you for a second?"

Trentino and Lopez had just resumed their questioning when the first cop approached. He pulled the two detectives aside. I watched and waited as the cop filled them in on something. A minute later, I was told what it was.

"We've had a chance to confirm some facts," Trentino said. "For starters, as you claim, a Samantha Kent does indeed live here. Though it turns out Kent is her maiden name. Did you know that?"

"No, I didn't."

Trentino continued. "Her husband's name is Conrad Birch. Or should I say *was,* because that's him upstairs, all right."

Conrad Birch . . . Birch . . . Birch. I repeated the name over in my head, relieved it didn't immediately ring a bell.

"Finally," said Trentino, "it looks like you are who you say you are, Dr. Remler. Your practice checks out, and your home address checks out. So we've only got one other thing to ask you. Which is, you're not planning on leaving town anytime soon, are you?"

"No," I said. "I have no plans to leave town."

"Good," he said. "Then go home and get some sleep."

I stood there . . . not going. "What about Samantha?" I asked.

"We've got people looking for her," said Lopez.

"Just the same, I want to stick around for when you find her," I said. "Better yet, I'd like to help in the search."

"We appreciate that," said Trentino. "But the best thing you can do for everyone's sake is to go home, get some rest. When we find Ms. Kent, you'll be among the first to know."

"All right," I said. "Let me give you my home phone number."

"It's okay; we'll get it," Trentino told me.

"It's unlisted, though," I said.

"Not to us," he replied.

I said good night to the detectives. Good morning would've been more accurate. Walking out of Sam's town house, I could see the first hint of dawn illuminating the sky. A new day. Halloween, actually. But also a Monday. In about three hours, I was supposed to be sitting in my office, listening to someone talk about his fears and frustrations. *Oh, yeah?* I could say smugly, glaring back at my patient. *Let me tell you about* my *problem. . . .*

Back home at last, I checked the answering machine. Maybe Sam had tried to call me again. It wasn't blinking. I picked up the phone.

Mila once told me that the older she got, the less sleep she needed. "It's my body's way of telling me that there'll be time for that soon enough," she'd said. I thought of her words as I dialed.

It rang only once before she answered.

"Mila, it's David," I said.

I told her nothing of what had happened or where I'd been. What she heard was that I wasn't feeling well. My appointments would have to be canceled. Dr. Remler was taking a sick day.

She didn't pry. Still, she could read between the lines. It wasn't a head cold; it was something else. Something I couldn't explain.

"I hope you feel better," she said.

"Thank you, Mamka."

I hung up and poured myself a finger of bourbon. Then another after that. I knew it was the only way I'd ever get any sleep.

I thought about the detectives, Trentino and Lopez. The questions they asked and the questions they didn't. They'd concerned themselves strictly with the events of the evening. Not once had they asked about Sam or what her motive might have been. They only wanted to know what had led to Conrad Birch's getting killed. Again, I was left wondering, Where did I know him from?

Nowhere closer to an answer and having achieved the proper numbness from the bourbon, I was ready to sleep.

AGAIN, it was the phone that woke me. Ringing in my bedroom. Ringing in my head. I rolled over to the nightstand. A clumsy reach for the phone and a groggy hello.

"Dr. Remler?" the voice said. "This is Detective Trentino. We met—"

"Yes, last night."

"We were wondering if we could have a few more minutes of your time."

"Uh, sure," I answered. "Is there any news about Sam?"

"That's what we want to talk to you about," said Trentino.

"Why can't you tell me now?"

"We *can* tell you now, Dr. Remler. We're actually standing outside your apartment. We tried knocking and ringing the bell but—"

"I was asleep. I'm sorry." I looked at my watch: It was almost noon. "Give me a minute. I'll be right with you," I said.

I put on the same pants, sweatshirt, socks, and sneakers I'd had on the night before, then went to let the detectives in. "Sorry about that," I said as I opened the door.

"No problem," they both replied.

We stood there, in the entryway, for a moment. "So what is it? Did you find her?" I asked, bracing.

334 | *Howard Roughan*

"We found her, all right," said Lopez.

I exhaled. "She's alive?"

"Very much so."

"Where was she found?" I asked.

Trentino took it from there. "That's the thing. She found *us*. When she returned home this morning . . . from a trip to Boston."

My face probably said it all. Perplexed. "I don't understand."

"Neither do we," said Trentino. "However, she was definitely in Boston last night. All weekend, in fact."

"That doesn't make any sense," I said.

"No, it doesn't. Certainly not in relation to what you've told us. But here's where it really gets weird," said Trentino. *"Samantha Kent says she's never even met you before."*

I was standing in my apartment not more than three feet away from Detectives Trentino and Lopez. I could hear them perfectly. Yet the one word that kept coming out of my mouth was this: "What?"

What were they talking about? What did they mean Sam had been in Boston? What was this about her saying she'd never met me?

"We're talking about Samantha Kent, right?" I said. "Five foot six. Thin. Blond hair, past her shoulders?"

"Actually, the Samantha Kent whom we met, the one who lives at Fifty-six West Eighty-first Street, is a little taller," said Trentino.

"But she's blond and thin, right?"

"Yes, she is."

"Okay, so I was off a bit with her height."

"That depends," said Lopez. "The Samantha Kent we talked to—the Samantha Kent married to Conrad Birch—is five foot ten."

"That's impossible. There's no way she's that tall, and what is this stuff about Boston?"

"Samantha Kent was checked in at the Ritz-Carlton on Friday, Saturday, and Sunday night. She was there for some conference—"

"The Children's Aid Society," said Lopez.

Trentino nodded. "We've got people from the conference, as well as hotel employees, confirming they saw her there. Hey, do you think I could have a glass of water?"

As segues went, that one was pretty strange. "Huh?" I uttered.

"I'm sorry," said Trentino. "It's been a long night. I'm very thirsty. Would it be possible for me to get some water?"

My look at him was, *You've got to be kidding.* "I'll be right back," I said, heading for the kitchen. I pulled a glass from the cabinet and began filling it up at my cooler.

"Nice kitchen." From over my shoulder. Lopez's voice.

I turned to see that the two detectives had decided to keep me company. I handed Trentino his glass of water. "Detectives, in light of everything you've told me, I think I should see for myself this woman you're talking about," I said.

"You mean the real Samantha Kent?" asked Lopez.

I ignored the inference that I was either crazy or lying or both. "Don't you agree we should arrange a meeting?" I asked.

"Yes, that meeting should happen," said Trentino. "Though she's pretty shook up right now and not exactly taking visitors."

"Particularly someone she doesn't know," added Lopez. "Excuse me, *claims* she doesn't know."

"That's the point," I said. "To clear up all this confusion."

Trentino ran a hand through what little hair he had left. "Like I said, Dr. Remler, we'll arrange for you to see her."

"Good," I said.

"Hey, did you know you're missing a knife?"

I turned to Lopez, who'd asked the question, and followed his gaze to the thick wooden block by my stove. There were seven knives for eight slots in the block. In a flash, I realized what was going on. "What are you saying?" I asked.

Lopez walked over to the block and pulled out one of the knives. "I was asking whether you knew there was a knife missing from your set. That's all. Why, what are *you* saying?"

I eyed them both. Really seeing them for the first time. "Detective Lopez, you and I see a knife block with seven handles protruding out of it, plus an empty slot," I began. "But you don't know it was a set to begin with. So when you ask if I know I'm missing a knife, my question to you is, Do you really know that I am?"

"Dr. Remler, there's no need to be angry," said Trentino.

"You're right. The only need I've got is for you to quit with the innuendos. I've answered every one of your questions and offered to help in any way possible. If what I've told you isn't matching up with what you've learned, then let's figure out who's in error."

"I'm sorry if you've got the wrong impression," said Trentino. The tone was calmer, more affable. It was also very forced. "We appreciate your candor, and we're well aware you've cooperated fully with us. Rest assured, we'll get to the bottom of all this."

"Yes," said Lopez. "Soon enough."

The two detectives thanked me for my time and told me they'd be in touch. I showed them to the door. Before stepping out to the hallway, they each gave me a prolonged look.

"Happy Halloween," said Lopez.

Alone again in my apartment, I returned to the kitchen to make some coffee. There on the counter sat the glass of water Detective Trentino had asked for. It was as full as when I'd handed it to him. The man who'd claimed to be very thirsty hadn't taken a single sip.

I picked up the phone and immediately dialed.

HIS secretary put me through.

"Hey, what's up?" came Parker's voice.

"Plenty. I need to talk to you. Can I come by your office?"

"Yeah, no problem. You okay?" he asked.

"I'm not sure."

"Tell you what, meet me here at one o'clock, okay?"

"Okay."

I took a quick shower and threw on some clean clothes, then grabbed a cab. Parker was in his office, waiting for me.

"What happened?" he asked, looking up at my forehead and the two butterfly bandages holding it together.

"It's a long story," I said. There was so much to tell, and I hadn't really given any thought about how to tell it. I decided the best place to start was with the part Parker already knew. "Do you remember that patient I was telling you about the other day?"

"You mean the woman with the kid?"

My head immediately dropped. *The kid.* The detectives didn't say anything about him. Nor did I ask. Where was he in all this? Presumably okay, I figured. Though it seemed a lot of my presumptions were now being challenged.

I gathered my thoughts and settled into explaining what had happened as best I could. Parker, meanwhile, was doing his very best to wear two hats—that of a friend and that of a lawyer. Being the friend, he showed concern. Being the lawyer, he wanted to know the who, what, when, where, and why.

"Here's the thing," he said ultimately. "There are two sets of facts: what you know and what you've been told. The first set—what you know—includes only what you can prove. What you've been *told,* on the other hand—the second set—is what's making up most of your story. Especially the confusing parts." He flung out his hands. "So right away, you know what you have to stop doing."

I looked at him, unsure.

Parker leaned in. "You've got to stop treating *both* sets like they're the truth. Take the detectives, for instance. They think you're hiding something, and they want to find out what it is."

"But I'm not."

"Irrelevant. So that's the first thing. Being able to discern what's for real and what's merely bait."

"The stuff about Sam Kent's being out of town, her saying she doesn't know who I am—you're telling me it might not be true?"

"No. I'm telling you not to believe it simply because you're told it," said Parker. "Example: You said the detectives claimed Sam was at the Ritz-Carlton in Boston. She *may* have been there, but there's no way the detectives have gotten around to proving that yet. Until they do, they'll act as if they have. It turns up the heat on you."

"That's legal?"

"It's all relative. Somebody was murdered, which happens to be extremely far down on the list of things that are legal. I think the word for what the detectives have is 'leeway.' "

"So what am I supposed to do?"

"Exactly this. Talk to a lawyer," he said. "The visit the detectives made to your apartment—that charade about a glass of water to get into your kitchen—was all about one thing. What's more, it's the one thing I'm sure they didn't tell you."

"What's that?"

"They found the murder weapon."

"The knife?" I asked.

"Yep. Now they want to know if it could belong to you. What you've got to focus on is everything you know for sure, the stuff you can prove. Gather everything that establishes Samantha Kent as your patient. For starters, did she pay you by check or credit card?"

"She paid me in cash," I said, barely above a whisper.

"She did?"

"Yeah. She said she didn't want her husband to know she was seeing a therapist. She told me he saw all the canceled checks and credit-card bills."

"Did one of your other patients see her in your office?"

I thought about it. "No, I don't think so."

"Wait. She would have to go through Mila to get to you, right?"

"E-mail. She exchanged e-mails with Mila after first contacting my service. They never actually talked."

"David, how could—" Parker stopped. "Sorry," he said.

"It's all right," I assured him. "Let me explain."

I told him about my first session with Sam. Her going on about not giving Mila a phone number, because she was moving. Then Sam's fear of her husband. Her fear that she might kill him.

"How serious did you think she was?" he asked.

"Not enough to report her, if that's what you're asking."

"So what do we got?" said Parker. "You were treating a woman who claimed to be Sam Kent. She's not. You don't know who she really is, nor can you prove she even exists."

"My notes," I said. "What about my notes?"

"That's the problem. They're *your* notes. They prove nothing."

I thought of something else. "What about her phone call to me at home? Can't we trace the number?"

"Did she call you on your cell?"

"No. Landline."

He shook his head. "LUDs only cover outgoing calls."

"Lugs?"

"*LUDs,*" he said. "Local usage details, otherwise known as your phone records."

Then a click in my head, the spark of remembrance. "The party," I said. "The Kesper Society cocktail party. *She was there.*"

Bingo, said Parker's eyes. "You mean a roomful of people saw the two of you together?"

"Not exactly," I said, deflated. "She approached me outside on the sidewalk as I was leaving. She was dressed to the hilt and came down the steps of the museum as if she'd been inside."

"How'd she know you'd be there?" he asked.

"I have no idea."

"Come to think of it, she could've read it in the paper. The Kesper people put out a press release naming the different organizations invited—she could've seen Crescent House listed somewhere. But she had to give you a reason for her being there, right?"

"She told me her husband managed the charitable trust for the Kesper Society."

"She was alone, though?"

"Yes. She said her husband was traveling."

Parker shook his head slowly. "It's incredible when you think about it," he said, almost impressed. "I mean, what that implies. The planning, the maneuvering, the—"

"There's something else," I said.

I told him what happened after the Kesper party, her coming back to my apartment and making me dinner. How fitting—the no-name linguine prepared by the woman using someone else's name.

Parker listened intently to the details of that night, the sexual underpinning being quite obvious.

"Tell you didn't . . ." His voice trailed off.

"No, I didn't," I said. "She just cooked me dinner."

"Was she ever by herself in the kitchen?"

I thought about it. "At some point, I left to get a bottle of wine."

"I wonder where she put the knife," he said. "She had to get it out of your apartment somehow."

"You think—"

"More than think. You're missing a knife, all right. The same knife used to kill Conrad Birch." Parker leaned back in his chair. "Congratulations, David. You're being framed for murder."

ON THE bright side, I didn't have to rush back to work.

"Take tomorrow off, too," Parker told me. "You need to be available all day in case I set something up with the detectives."

"What for?"

"To air everything out. Otherwise you're a sitting duck. But there are a couple of things you've got to do first," Parker said. "Try to figure out how you know Conrad Birch, if at all. If this woman has done a number on you, the odds are, there's some connection to be made. If we know what it is, I'm confident about going to the detectives."

"And if I can't figure it out?"

"Then we press our luck and wait a bit. The one thing the detectives don't have is any inkling of a motive. My bet is, they'll be paying you another visit."

"Do I cooperate?"

"Not anymore," he said. "If they come to talk to you again, don't say a word. Call me, and we'll take it from there. In the meantime, I'm going to make a few calls. A couple of friends of mine in uniform might know something about the investigation."

"What else do I have to do?"

"Go over your session notes you took on the woman," he said. "Look for clues, a mistake, something she said that tips her hand. No matter how clever she's been, nobody's perfect. Buy one of those minirecorders in case she's foolish enough to call you again."

"Okay. What else?"

"I think that's it," he said. "On second thought, you should have your forehead checked out. You might need a stitch or two."

"The EMT thought the butterfly bandages would be enough."

"What EMT? You mean at the town house last night?"

"Yeah. The detectives had one of the medical guys look at it."

"And he cleaned it for you?"

"Yeah, why?"

Parker thought for a second. "It's nothing. Everything's going to be fine," he said. "Just hang in there, okay?"

"Do I have a choice?"

Parker shook his head and let out a laugh.

I STARTED to walk back uptown to my office. Every other block seemed to bring a new revelation. Another piece to the puzzle that was the fake Samantha Kent. My Mystery Patient.

The bit about her nanny. What was her name? Celine? Celeste? I was pretty sure it was Celeste. Celeste was the reason that dinner had to be cooked at my place. Then, back at my apartment, she was the one supposedly on the other end of the phone, taking down my number. My *unlisted* number. It would be needed two nights later, when I got the call.

The favor she asked me—escorting her from my apartment into a cab. She knew it was no favor at all. It was my obligation as a *gentleman*. She had worked out a very crafty way of telling me her address. All intended to make sure I'd remember when the time came. When I had to rush to her rescue.

Oh, how easy I'd made it for her. I joined her in the cab and went along for the ride. Even then she nearly gave my memory too much credit. I almost couldn't remember the address. But she knew I'd find it if I had to crisscross every block on the Upper West Side. And just to make sure, she went out of her way to prompt me about that huge eagle over the entrance.

My Mystery Patient. She must have killed Conrad Birch. She must have had a key to his town house. She must have known the real Samantha Kent would be out of town. But why did she want Conrad Birch dead, and why was I being set up to take the fall? I was becoming more convinced that I knew Conrad Birch somehow. It would mean she and I both knew him without knowing each other. Yet there still had to be a connection between the two of us. For some reason, she'd sought me out. Why?

I took a few more steps and stopped. I raised my hand and marched out into the street, looking for the first available cab. I had a feeling I knew where a few more answers were waiting, and it was exactly where I was heading. But the time for walking was over. I was now in a hurry.

IT WAS almost creepy. The darkness, the stillness of my office. I'd spent hours there alone so many times, and yet this time somehow felt different—as if I were trespassing on my own property.

I flipped on some lights and approached my credenza, pulling out a drawer. The file for Samantha Kent wasn't what I went to first. Instead, I went straight to the *B*'s. BAXTER . . . BERNSTEIN . . . BIBBY, until . . . there it was: BIRCH, CONRAD.

I'd known the guy from somewhere, all right. That somewhere being my office. I removed his file, took it over to my desk, sat down, and opened it. As soon as I did, I knew why my memory of him was so hazy. There was only a single page in his folder. It was from our first, and our last, session together.

Conrad Birch had been a foot dipper—those people who, for any number of reasons, decide not to continue with therapy after their initial exposure to it. Their interest is fleeting, as if they'd dipped their foot in the pool and decided they weren't up for the swim.

My eyes immediately went to the upper-right corner of the page. The date. It had been just over a year since Conrad Birch had sat in my office. I tried to picture him. His clothes or a certain idiosyncrasy. It was no use. Any remnant of that day had been buried.

I raced through my notes. It seemed Conrad Birch had come to me with a problem as common as it was complex. The guy was having an affair, and he was worried. He said he couldn't leave his wife and understood he had to end it with his mistress. However, he feared how she'd take the news. She had a temper. She had a mean streak. He wanted to know how he should handle it.

That was it. The gist of what I'd written . . . other than a single last bullet point: *discussed how best to break with mistress.*

Was there a connection? Was his mistress my Mystery Patient? A jilted lover seeking revenge? While that suggested a motive for murder, it left unclear why she'd want me to take the fall.

I went to my credenza and flipped through the *K*'s. My forefinger came to a stop on the newest name tab: KENT, SAMANTHA.

I returned to my desk and went over what I'd written. Three pages representing two sessions. I was looking for a mistake, a slipup. As Parker put it, something she'd said that tipped her hand.

The problem was, everything was about tipping her hand. She made me think she was in a disastrous marriage, wed to an emotionally manipulative man. "I'm here because I want to kill my husband," she'd confessed.

It wasn't possible to lay down your cards more than that. And all for one purpose—so when she called me telling me that she'd gone through with it, I'd *believe.* I'd jump, a puppet on a string.

I closed the file. Slammed it, actually. The more I read, the more I came to realize what a dupe I'd been. It could've happened to anyone, I tried to tell myself. But it had happened to *me,* and I felt disgusted. Worse than that, I felt helpless.

THE slender man with silver hair was putting on his Burberry coat. I saw him as I spun through the revolving doors. Then he saw me. "*Thank God* you're here, Dr. Remler," he called out.

I had left the office, the two files in hand, and cabbed it back to my apartment. There in the lobby was Robert Gordon, the building's owner. "I came down as soon as I was called. This has never happened before in any of my buildings, so I wasn't sure about all the legalities. I called my attorney to see if they could do such a thing without your being here."

"Mr. Gordon, I'm afraid I don't—"

"Turns out, a search warrant entitles them to free rein."

"A what?"

"A search warrant," he repeated. "It happened a little while ago. Two detectives arrived, along with a policeman, to search your apartment. They ordered the super, Javier, to open your door. Javier called my office immediately and— Dr. Remler, wait!"

I was already gone, heading straight for the elevators. As I hit the UP button, Mr. Gordon stationed himself next to me.

"When did you say this happened?" I asked.

"About an hour and a half ago," he said, catching his breath. "They were in your apartment up until ten minutes ago."

The elevator arrived. I stepped in and pressed the button for the twenty-second floor. As the doors started to close, Mr. Gordon said, "As you might imagine, Dr. Remler, the building will have to conduct its own inquiry regarding this situation."

At my floor, the elevator doors opened. For some reason, I expected to see a web of yellow tape down around my apartment. Probably because I'd seen so much of it the night before at the town house. Instead, when I reached my door, there wasn't anything to indicate I'd had company, welcome or not. Somehow that almost made it worse.

As I opened the door, I prepared for the worst: drawers turned upside down, clothes strewn everywhere, the obligatory ripped pillow, with feathers still floating in the air.

I stood in the doorway and looked. There were no feathers. In fact, the place looked pretty much as I'd left it. *Pretty much.* When I stepped in, the signs were there. Cushions were rearranged, wall hangings slightly askew. That was just the living room.

The room to check after that was a no-brainer. I walked into my kitchen and immediately saw what I expected. Which is to say, I didn't see it at all. I no longer possessed a knife set. They'd taken the entire block. *They.* Who was I kidding? I had little doubt Detective Lopez was the one gleefully wrapping the thing up in an evidence bag. Not that Trentino didn't also have his fun. That glass of water I'd given him—the one he never took a sip out of—was sitting in the same spot on the counter. Only now it was empty.

I was really starting to dislike these guys.

AFTER Mr. Gordon left, I poured myself a drink. After that, I picked up the phone and dialed. It was Stacy who answered.

"Hi, David," she said. "He's right here."

Parker got on the line. "Hey, buddy."

"The bastards came and searched my apartment."

"I know," he said. "I caught wind of it about twenty minutes ago. A friend of mine from downtown."

"They took the knives."

"Makes sense, considering that they found the murder weapon."

"Where'd they find it?"

"In the alley next to the town house. The knife was clean—no blood and no prints—but it was found directly beneath one of the windows of the master bedroom."

"So they can march into my apartment and take my knives?"

"Among other things."

"What do you mean?"

"I don't know yet, but they found something else implicating you besides the knives," he said. "What does it say on the property voucher?"

"The what?"

"It's a piece of paper they're required to leave behind. It lists what was removed."

"I haven't seen it," I said. "Where would it be?"

"It's supposed to be readily visible, but sometimes they like to have a little fun, like taping it to the toilet seat."

"Hilarious."

I checked in my bathrooms. I checked in my bedrooms. In the library, on the seat of the chair behind my desk, was the property voucher. Holding it in place was clearly an example of "having a little fun": a book-cum-paperweight taken from my shelf—Dostoyevsky's *Crime and Punishment*.

I read Parker what was on the voucher. Indeed, there were two things listed, except the second item—after the knives—wasn't what you'd call specific: *Misc. Paper.*

"What's that supposed to mean?" I asked.

"They don't want us to know yet. Take a look on your desk there. Do you notice anything missing?"

I thumbed through a few stacks of papers. "Offhand, I don't."

"We'll find out. Did you learn anything at your office?"

"I did. I checked my files. Conrad Birch had come to me for a single session a little over a year ago. He was having an affair and wanted to end it. Birch was worried about how his mistress would take the news. He described her as having a mean streak."

"You think—"

"It's possible," I said, "that my Mystery Patient was his mistress."

"That would explain a lot, wouldn't it?"

"Yes, except why it is I had to be involved."

"Right," said Parker. "And that was your only involvement with Birch? One session?"

"That was it."

"Okay, now just tell me he didn't pay for the session in cash."

"Wouldn't that be something?" I said with a half laugh. "But I'm sure it was by check or credit card. I'll have Mila look into it."

"Not that we're rushing to prove any connection," he said. "I mean, the good news is, we know how you know him. The bad news is, you told the police you didn't."

"Couldn't we simply explain the circumstances?"

"We could, though I've got to think about that. They can't sub-poena your patient files, so it's a question of how they'd find out."

"I don't want to lie, Parker."

"You also don't want to go to jail."

I took a deep breath. "This is really happening, isn't it?"

"I'm afraid so."

"When does it begin to get better?"

He didn't say anything. There was an ominous silence.

"Parker, what is it you're not telling me?"

"It's like this," he said. "But before you freak, trust me. It's not as bad as it sounds. . . . Tomorrow, you're going to be arrested for the murder of Conrad Birch."

I started to freak. He let me go for a bit, as if I were a blue marlin that had just been hooked. Only when I started to ramble on about prison did my best friend decide it was time to reel me in.

"All right, this is what I've been able to negotiate so far," he said. "I spoke to the D.A.'s office, and the cops are in line with this. They're not going to come and get you. We're going to go to them. That way, there'll be no flashbulbs going off. Turns out, Conrad Birch was a pretty big deal on Wall Street."

In a flash, the first session I had with Samantha Kent came back to me. Make that the fake Samantha Kent. She'd claimed her husband was a venture capitalist downtown. I'd even asked her if that meant Wall Street. I remembered because of the way she'd answered. It was a phrase she claimed her husband had often used. *That's where the money is.*

Like that, her duplicity became all the more staggering. I explained this to Parker, and we agreed: The idea of my Mystery Patient being Conrad Birch's mistress was gaining momentum.

"Back to my impending incarceration," I said.

Parker continued. "We're going to make this as civil as possible. I've promised the D.A.'s office your cooperation, and they've promised a meeting. The arrest is going to happen, but the meeting gets us an up-close look at what they think they've got on you. It also means you'll be processed faster."

"Is that supposed to cheer me up?"

"Yes, because you'll get a same-day arraignment and won't have to spend a night in lockup. You'll thank me later."

"They've agreed to all this?"

"It wasn't easy. Now let's talk about posting bail. How much are you worth? Stocks, bonds, savings. Try roughing out a number."

I started doing the math. Royalties from *The Human Pendulum* had proved a windfall. "Three and a half million," I told him.

"How much of that is liquid?"

"Close to two."

"Good," he said. "Push comes to shove, I can always secure a bond for you if necessary."

"Thanks."

"Hey, that's what friends are for."

"I always knew you'd be my friend. Who would've thought you'd also be my lawyer?"

"I'm not going to be your lawyer."

"What are you talking about?" I asked. "Is it a conflict thing?"

"No, it's not that," he said. "I'm a really good criminal defense attorney. But part of what makes me so good is that I know when a prospective client needs something different from what I can offer. Or, in certain situations, something better."

"I think you're selling yourself short, Parker."

"Not in this case. This one's going to be high-profile. Which means you need someone with an equally high profile leading your charge, someone who's more used to playing in that arena."

"Are you sure?"

"Never more so," he said. "I've already made the arrangements. Meet me in the lobby of the Chrysler Building tomorrow morning at nine."

"You're going to introduce me to the guy who's better?"

"No," said Parker. "I'm going to introduce you to the guy who's the best."

BEFORE going to bed that night, I called Mila to tell her I'd be out another day. At least. I also confirmed what she'd already suspected: It had nothing to do with my being sick.

I apologized for being less than honest and further apologized for not being able to give her the whole story. I did reveal that the problem related to my newest patient, Samantha Kent. Or, as I told Mila, a woman posing as Samantha Kent.

On the heels of that, I asked Mila if she could dig up the billing paperwork on Birch.

"Is there a connection?" she asked while going through her files.

"Quite possibly," I said, leaving it at that. She didn't press me.

"Here it is," she said. "He paid by check. June of last year. Do you want me to get it over to you?" she asked.

"No. Hold on to it for now. I'll let you know when I need it."

"No problem. Anything else?"

There was one more thing. I asked her about those initial e-mails sent by my Mystery Patient. "Any chance you still have them in your computer?"

Mila's silence was answer enough. She'd deleted them.

I wasn't surprised. Given the lengths gone to by my Mystery Patient to live up to her moniker, I doubted she would've left a trail.

"Sorry, David," said Mila.

"Don't worry about it." I hung up the phone and stared blankly at the wall. It was my word against the world.

That night, I got a good, solid twelve minutes of sleep.

At a little past nine the next morning, I met Parker in the lobby of the Chrysler Building, Forty-second and Lex.

As we rode the elevator up to the forty-fifth floor, Parker gave me a little background about the man we were on our way to see.

"His name is Victor Glass."

He was the managing partner of Edwards, Vode, Isadore & Locke. It was one of the oldest firms in the city, as revered as it was feared. "The founders were ruthless," explained Parker. "Dog kickers, candy from a baby—you get the idea. And just in case you don't, consider the firm's acronym."

He waited as I strung together the first letters of the founders' names: Edwards, Vode, Isadore & Locke. I smiled, amused.

"Of course, that was a long time ago," he said. "They're all dead now. In-house counsel for Hell, Incorporated, if I had to guess."

Which brought him back to Victor Glass.

Parker described him as a tough-talking, charismatic guy's guy who could go from turning the screws to turning on the charm and back again in a heartbeat. Throw in the fact that he possessed a brilliant legal mind, and you had a criminal defense attorney who'd managed to win more than eighty percent of his cases.

We got off the elevator and entered the spacious, ultramodern reception area of Edwards, Vode, Isadore & Locke. Not what I expected, given the firm's long history. The space was a melding of curves and harsh angles, set off by minimalist furniture, sleek lighting, and bizarre artwork.

"They've redecorated," said Parker, looking around.

We approached a sharply dressed receptionist, who pressed a button and announced our arrival into a tiny wraparound headset. Her voice was elegant and practiced. "Mr. Glass will be with you in just a couple of minutes."

We had a seat on what was a park bench made out of leather. Parker reached into his briefcase. "Here," he said, handing me a glossy folder. "Victor's press kit."

I took the folder and stared at Parker with a raised eyebrow. "The man has a press kit?"

"Yep."

I opened the folder and began thumbing through tear sheets and reprinted articles. Victor Glass had been featured in everything from the *Harvard Law Review* to *Playboy.* As I looked at his photo, I realized I'd seen him before. Probably on TV.

I kept thumbing through the kit. A lot had been written about Victor Glass. Then I came across something written *by* Victor Glass. It was a piece in the *New York Times* entitled DUMB JUSTICE. The argument was simple. Lawyers have educational requirements. Judges have educational requirements. Why not juries?

It was a fascinating read. Especially the last two paragraphs:

Ten of the twelve jurors in the O. J. Simpson trial hadn't graduated from college. Should this prevent them from enjoying any of the freedoms in our society? Of course not. Should this prevent them from determining the freedoms of another human being? You better believe it.

Circumstances preventing one from going to college are relevant in a job interview—but not the justice system. Too much is at stake. The fact is, education level bears directly on one's ability to reason, including the weighing of testimony and evidence. And what job could possibly hold more responsibility than being a juror?

"Just so you know, we fired the decorator," he said.

I looked up to see Victor Glass standing in the reception area. His suit jacket was off, his shirtsleeves rolled back to the elbows. He hadn't sent his secretary, choosing instead to greet us himself. It was a nice touch.

"Aw, it's not so bad," Parker said, getting up.

"Yeah, if you're Ray Charles," said Victor.

The receptionist tried to contain a laugh as Victor walked over and gave Parker a hearty handshake. Each expressed how good it was to see the other. I stood up, and Parker made the introduction. "Victor, this is David Remler."

"It certainly is," he said. "I understand this isn't one of your better weeks."

"And it's only Tuesday," I said.

Victor flashed a smile. His teeth were whiter than white. Suddenly I understood the notion of someone having movie-star good looks. Trim, fit, his hair combed back, he was the guy you'd normally see playing the part of a lawyer in a movie. Only Victor was the real thing and, if Parker was right, one of the best there was.

And he couldn't have been more than forty.

"Why don't we head back to my office," he said. "We'll talk about what luck we might have with the rest of the week."

We followed Victor down a long corridor. When we got to his office, in the corner of the building, we found that he had two gatekeepers: one a blonde, the other a brunette.

"Hold my calls, Ashley, will you?" he said to the blonde. The brunette got up and followed us into Victor's office.

"You guys want coffee?" Victor asked.

We declined. Secretary No. 2 turned with a polite smile and left.

"All right, then," said Victor. He motioned us over to a seating area that included four oversize club chairs. I sat in one and looked around. Along the near wall was a colossal bookcase. In the corner, in front of a huge panoramic view of the East River, was Victor's massive desk. No wonder the guy seemed larger than life.

We were all seated.

Parker had already given Victor the big picture. Nonetheless, Victor wanted to hear it all from me. Start to finish. Beginning with the very first time a woman came into my office and introduced herself as Samantha Kent.

I spoke as clearly and calmly as I could.

Along the way, Victor cut in with a few questions. On the surface, he was filling in the gaps—things I either hadn't been clear about or had simply neglected to mention. Below the surface, he was putting my story to the test—asking me about the details. He didn't seem so concerned with my answers as with the way I gave them. Meaning, was I remembering or fabricating?

"And that brings us to our being here this morning," I said.

Victor took a moment to review the notes he'd made. Then he stared right into my eyes. "So did you kill Conrad Birch?"

"I just told you I didn't," I said with a note of defiance.

"No," said Victor. "What you told me was everything that supports the *argument* you didn't."

The distinction was a little lost on me.

"That's all right," he said. "Your body language says it all. You didn't kill Conrad Birch."

"It's nice to have my lawyer believe me," I said facetiously.

"Yeah, except I'm not going to be your lawyer," said Victor.

I looked at Parker, who looked as confused as I did.

I threw my hands up. "Doesn't anyone want to represent me?"

"What I mean is, I won't be lead counsel," Victor said. "That is, if we do indeed go to trial."

"Why not?" I asked.

"Because I'm a guy, that's why." He was about to explain, when Parker jumped in. He'd caught on fast.

"Because you'll be standing trial for killing a guy, and in your defense, you'll be blaming it on a woman," said Parker.

"A woman who we, as yet, can't prove exists," Victor said. "The prosecutor will stack the jury with chicks and make sure they all have a clear view of the grieving widow sitting in the front row. So the last thing you need is some slick guy like me standing up to argue for the entire trial. I'll be there. I won't be silent. But what you really need defending you is a pair of boobs."

"And a great pair at that," came a voice.

We all turned to look. She was leaning against the door, dressed in a white blouse and a black skirt that came right above her knees. She was wearing a confident smile. My lead counsel had arrived.

"SPEAK of the devil," said Victor as she walked into the room. The three of us got up.

"No, Victor. *You're* the devil," she said. She reached Parker first and put out her hand. "I'm Terry Garrett."

"Parker Mathis," he said. They shook.

She turned to me. But instead of extending a hand, she simply looked me over. "Oh, good. You're attractive," she said. "Maybe we'll want a jury stacked with chicks, after all."

Parker shot Victor a look. *A jury stacked with chicks?* It was the same phrasing Victor had used.

"Am I mistaken, or do the walls have ears?" said Parker.

Victor shrugged. "Sorry. It's just that men in trouble talk more self-consciously when a woman is in the room. Given the specifics of David's predicament, I wanted to make sure we didn't have any filtering up front. I also didn't want to make you have the same conversation twice." Victor pointed at the speakerphone device on a nearby end table. "This way, Terry's up to speed."

"Big Brother lives," said Parker as the four of us sat down.

"Terry is the latest addition to our family," Victor continued. "She came to us from Weiss, Stone, and Wilcox out in L.A."

"Excellent firm," said Parker.

"Yeah, well, Weiss still isn't talking to me," said Victor.

Terry smiled. "Victor would prefer to think he stole me away. Truth is, I was always an East Coast girl at heart."

"Second in her class at Harvard Law," said Victor.

"Yes, and all my mother wanted to know was who was first," said Terry.

"I think we had the same mother," said Parker.

Terry laughed. Parker laughed. Victor cracked a follow-up joke. I gazed at all three with a face that said, *I hate to break up all the fun, but I'm about to be arrested today!* They all picked up on the look, and we quickly got back to business. Actually, the "we" didn't really include me. I'd given them the ball, and they were running with it, brainstorming angles and discussing possibilities. For example, were there any security cameras in my building that might have recorded my comings and goings and with whom? If so, were the tapes saved and for how long?

I threw out another idea—finding the cabdriver who took me to the town house that night. Surely he'd remember a guy who paid him an extra five bucks for every red light he ignored.

"I'm afraid it fails as an alibi," said Terry.

What ruled it out was the fact that every window in Conrad Birch's bedroom had been left open. The cold temperature that night had chilled his body to the point of preservation, effectively extending the time-of-death estimate by a few hours. That would've given me ample time to kill Birch, go home, and come back again via the cab under the pretense of helping my patient.

Eventually, my legal troika moved beyond the facts of the case to strategizing how the rest of the day should play out. First up would be our meeting with the detectives and the D.A.'s office. After that, I'd be processed and there'd be the arraignment.

As Terry, Victor, and Parker debated tactics, I sat there, listening. Pondering it all, I wouldn't describe my feelings as comfortable.

"Are you okay, David?" Terry asked after a bit.

"As a matter of fact, no," I answered. "I've been sitting here for over an hour, waiting to hear one thing: why a woman would want to pose as Conrad Birch's wife and frame me for his murder."

"Why?" said Victor. "David, this might sound strange, but that question isn't relevant. Making a jury believe it was possible in the first place—that's what we have to worry about."

"Just the same, I'd still like to know."

"I don't blame you," said Terry. "But that's the problem with irrational behavior: Everyone always approaches it looking for a rational explanation." She gave me a slight smile. "I think I got that from a book called *The Human Pendulum*. Ever hear of it?"

"Rings a bell," I told her.

"Which leads me to a question I'm pretty sure I already know the answer to," she said. "In everything you and this Mystery Patient talked about, I bet she never mentioned your book, right?"

"No. I'm fairly certain we never discussed it," I said.

"It's just a hunch, but I'll bet you a million dollars she's read *The Human Pendulum* front to back. If not a few times over."

Victor nodded and then peeked at his watch. "It's time," he said.

"You're right," said Parker. He turned to me. "Are you ready?"

"As ready as I'll ever be," I answered.

We all stood up.

"Okay, then," said Victor, walking over and putting a hand on my shoulder. "Let's go get you arrested."

Part III

I THINK it was David Byrne and his group, Talking Heads, who summed it up best with a simple lyric: *How did I get here?*

The here was New York Supreme Court, specifically a chair at the defendant's table. To my right was Terry Garrett; to my left, Victor Glass. It was a lawyer sandwich, and I was the meat.

But first that question: How did I get here?

It had been seven months since that initial meeting in Victor Glass's office. Seven months since I'd been introduced to Terry Garrett. From that point on, it had been a crash course in the American legal system.

Lesson 1: Beware of free medical attention.

From the spacious confines of Victor's office that first day, we traveled to a cramped interrogation room at the Twentieth Precinct.

By the numbers, the teams were evenly matched. On one side of the table were Detectives Trentino and Lopez. They were joined by an assistant district attorney by the name of Glenn Hemmerson. He was a thin man, roughly forty, with dark eyes, big ears, and a haircut that suggested either he or his barber had served in the military.

On the other side of the table was my team: Parker, Terry, and Victor. Three fifty, three fifty, and five hundred an hour, respectively. Parker was reducing some of the sting by giving me the best-friend discount—one hundred percent off. Still, he had placed me in very capable hands.

Terry was razor-sharp and possessed an unflinching poise. She also, for lack of a better phrase, knew how to "work it." While the two detectives could care less that she was very attractive, Hemmerson, the A.D.A., couldn't get past it. So whenever Terry talked, her eyes—long lashes and all—always fixed on Hemmerson. He was too busy loving it to question it.

Then there was Victor.

Never had I seen a guy who could control a room like him. He was arrogant, bellicose, and unreasonable. A real loose cannon. . How much of it was an act, I didn't know. What I did know was that he was able to keep the other side on their collective heels and therefore dictate the meeting's flow.

But as much as I derived pleasure from watching Detectives Trentino and Lopez perform with a little less swagger, there was no denying the evidence they'd gathered. It was worse than I thought.

I was at the scene of the crime for a reason I couldn't prove. Strike one. The murder weapon had belonged to me. Strike two.

Then came this development: motive. And where did it come from? The library in my apartment. The *Misc. Paper* of the property voucher finally defined.

It was a typewritten letter—hand-signed—that Conrad Birch had apparently sent me a month earlier. As Hemmerson placed a photocopy of the letter on the table in front of me, I replayed that evening with my Mystery Patient. Her self-guided tour of my apartment. The playful quips shouted out from my library—how if she spotted a pipe rack, she'd be making a quick exit. Buying her the time she needed to plant the letter. To deliver strike three.

I leaned over and read it. Victor, Terry, and Parker gathered behind me and did the same. Two short paragraphs. Conrad Birch was writing to let me know he didn't appreciate the way I'd threatened him. He couldn't wire me the money because of a banking error. There was nothing sinister going on, he stressed. He'd soon clear everything up. Until then, he asked that I remain patient.

"Can you tell us what this letter is all about, Dr. Remler?" asked Hemmerson.

"No, he can't," said Victor quickly before I could respond. "Not until we get a handwriting analysis on the signature."

Hemmerson smirked. "Fair enough," he said. "But perhaps it's time to give Dr. Remler a second chance at a question he's already answered." He turned to me. "Did you know Conrad Birch?"

I immediately looked to Victor, who didn't bat an eyelash.

"Mr. Birch had been a patient of Dr. Remler's," Victor said. "Albeit for only one session."

"Excuse me?" said Hemmerson, his tone incredulous.

"You heard me," replied Victor. He reached into a folder and pulled out the copy of Birch's check, courtesy of Mila.

Hemmerson glanced at it. "Why did your client lie?"

"Not revealing the identity of a patient is Dr. Remler's professional prerogative."

"Barring unmitigating circumstances, yes. But the guy was dead. Murdered, I might add."

"That doesn't change a thing."

Hemmerson rolled his eyes. "Then what about Dr. Remler's Mystery Patient? Why didn't he extend her the same privilege?"

Victor came right back. "It was a life-or-death situation."

"You mean, the life or death of someone he can't prove exists."

"How quickly we forget who actually has the burden of proof."

Again, Hemmerson smirked. "It's hardly a burden."

The subject was dropped, if only for the time being, which pretty much underscored the reality of that meeting. The certain inevitability of everything that would follow.

"One last thing," said Hemmerson. "Would you care to discuss how and why your client's blood was found on the victim?"

Parker wasted no time. "First off, you know that Dr. Remler admitted to incidental, after-the-fact contact with Mr. Birch," he stated coolly. "And as for how you even have a sample of Dr. Remler's blood, well, we'll discuss that when we get to the issue of illegally obtained evidence."

"Am I supposed to understand what you're talking about?" asked Hemmerson.

"Why don't you ask your detectives?" Parker answered. "When they had an EM technician clean a cut on Dr. Remler's forehead, I'm sure they asked permission to retain his blood for analysis."

I remembered Parker's original hesitation when I told him about the EMT. He knew what had gone down between the detectives and the technician. He knew that without even being there.

The A.D.A. glanced at Trentino and Lopez, who weren't about to admit to anything. "It's perfectly good evidence," Hemmerson said.

Parker shook his head. "Perfectly inadmissible is more like it."

Terry interceded. "Gentlemen, why don't we move on," she said while locking eyes with Hemmerson. His hard edge immediately softened, and he enthusiastically agreed. He was absolutely smitten.

Lesson 2: Don't slouch.

Fingerprints. A mug shot. The requisite paperwork. After all the posturing in the meeting, the outcome was what was expected. I was read my rights and officially arrested. Murder in the second degree. By the time I was transported to central booking down on Centre Street, the clock on the wall said half past one.

At a little before two, I was in a holding area, waiting for my arraignment. I looked up in the corner to see a security camera staring back. It reminded me of yet another dead end in trying to prove my Mystery Patient existed: After checking with the management office for my building, Terry had learned that none of the security cameras were the kind that recorded.

At four-thirty, I was led out of the holding area by a gray-haired, potbellied officer into the courtroom. I saw Parker first. He was seated on the aisle on the other side of the room. Next to Parker sat Terry. She gave me a quick smile and reassuring nod. Then came a signal I didn't understand at first. Terry placed the back of her hand underneath her chin while slowly pushing back her shoulders.

Huh?

She pushed her shoulders back a little more, and I got it: *Sit up straight, David.* That's what she was telling me. I was getting my first bit of coaching on being a defendant. Look good. Look sharp. In other words, good posture mattered. To judges and juries alike.

But at the arraignment, it was just a judge. A relatively young one, at that. Blond hair, square jaw, and horn-rimmed glasses. He talked fast and always with his hands.

A few minutes later, I was the next contestant. It was my gang of three and me again, but before our feet even came to a stop before the judge, he began firing away. "Do you waive a—"

"Yes, we waive a reading, Your Honor," fired back Victor.

Right off the bat, there were a few exchanges between the judge and the A.D.A., Hemmerson. He was all business and barely glanced in my direction when summarizing the people's case against me.

The only disarray arrived with the request from Hemmerson that I be remanded. That term I knew. Victor immediately began singing my praises as a model citizen. He implored the judge to set bail and at a reasonable amount. Hemmerson countered by pointing out the severity of the crime I was charged with. The public interest *required* that I remain incarcerated.

Victor was about to respond, when Parker jumped in. "Your Honor," he said, "Dr. Remler is a psychologist with numerous patients who depend on his counseling day in and day out. As you know, he's guilty of nothing at this moment, so I would ask that you weigh the adverse effects of removing Dr. Remler from the lives—"

The judge interrupted. "You don't think, Counselor, that the patients will flee their doctor once they learn of his predicament?"

Parker smiled. "With all due respect, sir, I imagine it will be quite the opposite."

"Why's that?"

"Simple," he replied. "Misery loves company."

Call it a minor miracle. The judge leaned back in his chair and chuckled. He grabbed his gavel and lifted it up. "Bail is set at a million dollars," he announced. *Bang.* The gavel came down.

Lesson 3: A grand jury will indict a ham sandwich.

By the time I got home from my arraignment after posting bail, there was a throng of reporters and camera crews camped outside the lobby. I could only imagine the look on the face of my dear old landlord, Mr. Robert Gordon, when he heard about that.

At least he wouldn't have to watch it on the news. As soon as my cab turned the corner and was met by a fleet of news vans, I had the driver pull around to the service entrance. I ducked in unscathed.

When I got to my apartment, I had messages from the *Times,* the *Wall Street Journal,* the *News,* and *Newsday.* CNN, CNBC, and all the local network affiliates had also tried to contact me. "The best thing to do is let your machine pick up everything for a few days. After that, no one will bother you again until the trial," Parker said.

Until, not *if* there's a trial. I discovered that there were now three—not two—absolute certainties in the world: death, taxes, and a grand-jury indictment of David Remler.

The hearing was scheduled for three weeks after my arraignment. It was my assumption I'd testify. I assumed wrong. Victor explained that no matter how eloquent and persuasive I thought I could be, at the end of the day I'd be a liability to myself.

I asked why.

"Memory," said Victor. "Right now, you may or may not be able to recall what's happened in the past month with one hundred percent accuracy. Six months from now, something will be blurry, if not lost completely. And that's all they need. Say one thing before the grand jury and another at the trial, and—*pow!*—the prosecutor's got you on an inconsistency. After that, you're Pinocchio."

I looked at Victor while mulling over his words.

"Besides," he added, "a grand jury will indict a ham sandwich if presented with one."

And there it was. Lesson No. 3 delivered.

THE trial, fast-tracked because of its high-profile status, got under way at the beginning of May, but you wouldn't know it by looking at a thermometer. What had been an extremely cold and damp spring wasn't done yet, and summer seemed like a long way away.

Who are all these people? That was my first reaction upon walking into the courtroom. The aisles on either side were packed with spectators, who, almost in unison, turned to stare. If they'd been standing and smiling, I would've known what it felt like to be a bride.

Parker was already seated in the first row, directly behind the defendant's table. It was a location that very much represented his involvement in the case—always hovering in the background.

"Stacy wanted to be here, but she had some crisis up at the center," Parker said as he sidestepped out to the aisle to greet me.

"Imagine that," I replied. "A crisis at a women's crisis center."

He smiled. "Good. You're loose. It's important to be loose."

Parker nodded as Terry and Victor came over. They wanted to discuss a final detail regarding the opening statement. Parker had been involved with the crafting of it.

A few minutes later, a door opened to the right of the bench. The jury was about to be let in. Parker returned to his seat, and the rest of us headed to the defendant's table.

We sat down. Terry to my right. Victor to my left. Me in the middle. In the middle of it all.

And you may ask yourself, Well, how did I get here? That's how.

I SIGHED. "WE'RE NOT doing very well, are we?"

Terry looked up at me from the notes she'd been poring over on her desk. The two of us were back in her office. The trial was three days old. "David, we haven't stepped up to the plate yet," she said.

"But they sure have. I feel like we're getting hit really hard."

Terry's mouth curled up at the corners. "This Mystery Patient of yours gave the prosecution a whole lot to work with."

"Then why are you smiling?" I asked.

Her eyes narrowed. "Because it's our turn now."

That it was. The prosecution had rested. With their exhibits A through what felt like Z; their extensive serology reports; their handwriting expert, who verified Conrad Birch's signature on the letter planted in my library; and their detailed testimony from Detectives Trentino and Lopez, even I was wondering if maybe I did actually kill Conrad Birch. I could only imagine what the jury must have been thinking.

The jury.

When it came to what went on inside a courtroom, there was little Victor didn't have an opinion about. The one thing in which he took particular pride was juries.

"Do you play gin, David?" he asked.

"Not as much as I drink it."

"It's like this," he plowed on. "The jury pool is the hand you're dealt. Right away, you've got your keepers, the people you know you want for sure. Then the real strategy starts—knowing who you need and who you'll have to toss to get them. Of course, no matter how much skill you've got, you still need some luck to win."

Terry's approach to juries was more up my alley. "I look at it this way," she'd said on the eve of jury selection. "By and large, authors are viewed with a fair amount of reverence. One of our objectives, therefore, would be to select as many people as possible who've read *The Human Pendulum.* The prosecution would have the opposite objective. But the actual message of *The Human Pendulum* turns all that on its head. Your book maintains that we're all susceptible to evil, given the right circumstances. No one is immune."

I nodded. "Including the author."

"*Especially* the author," said Terry. "You can't be familiar with your book without considering the possibility that through the murder of Conrad Birch, you've managed to prove your point."

"So we shoot for a jury of nonreaders, those who aren't familiar with the book, right?"

"Right. We sacrifice reverence for ignorance."

She was right. Come jury selection, one of the first questions Hemmerson asked the candidates was whether they were familiar with *The Human Pendulum.* Those who were became his best friend. Meanwhile, those who weren't became Terry's best friend.

In the end, reality won. The people who made me a best-selling author were few and far between among the jury pool.

"Gin!" declared Victor.

Of the seven women and five men picked, none had ever read *The Human Pendulum.* Only two had ever heard of it.

Still, Hemmerson had a grand time with the book just the same. As he liked to remind the jury, I'd put my premise into practice. On the trial's second day, he stood directly in front of the judge's bench and loudly announced to the entire courtroom that he'd already contacted the Guinness World Records people. For with *The Human Pendulum,* I'd written the world's longest confession.

Quipped an on-air reporter that evening, sans rim shot, "You might say they're really throwing the book at Remler."

I WAS still in Terry's office, lamenting the efforts of Hemmerson and the prosecution, when Victor strolled in. "So does he or doesn't he?" was his first question.

He wasn't wondering if I dyed my hair. Does he or doesn't he *testify?* That's what Victor was asking.

The risk was that Hemmerson might trip me up, make me contradict myself. But if I held my own—or appeared sympathetic—the reward could be a veritable fountain of reasonable doubt.

"Tough call," said Terry. "Particularly because Hemmerson has been given a really long leash. I swear, it's like Lomax has never met a defense objection he couldn't overrule."

She was referring to Barton Lomax, the judge, an old and rigid man who didn't seem to sit on the bench as much as grow out of it. In his nearly thirty years of presiding over cases in Manhattan, he'd proved himself to be ornery, caustic, impatient, and wholly intolerant of anyone who dared challenge his authority.

Terry regarded me for a moment, still weighing the decision of whether I should testify. "Let's wait and see," she said. "We'll take a measure of things in a couple of days and decide then."

Victor didn't hesitate. "Okay, you're the boss."

She put her hand to her ear. "What's that?"

"Cute," said Victor. He turned to me. " 'You're the boss'—that's by far her favorite expression."

"Only when you say it, boss," she added.

He chuckled. "Okay, so what else?"

"Witness list," she said. "Let's go over it."

For the next twenty minutes, we discussed the array of people who I hoped would be saving my butt. None were solely character witnesses, since my maiden voyage into authorship had pretty much established character as being irrelevant.

Next up: damage assessment. It started first and foremost with Detectives Trentino and Lopez. Big hitters for the prosecution. Hemmerson had both detectives recount all their conversations with me. Trentino first, followed by Lopez. While it bordered on redundant, the echoing of their testimony furthered the notion that what both men were saying was fact and not merely opinion.

Hemmerson made sure to include a few damning tidbits that went beyond the facts. Example: "Tell me, Detective Lopez, did you notice anything strange about the defendant when you visited him at his apartment?"

"I did," began Lopez. "Dr. Remler appeared a little out of it. Both Detective Trentino and I could smell alcohol on his breath."

"Do you think he was intoxicated at the time?"

"I couldn't say for certain without administering a Breathalyzer. But Dr. Remler was inconsistent in his behavior, at times cooperative but at other times quite abusive."

Hemmerson acted shocked—*shocked!*—by this development. "Did you feel threatened?" he asked.

"That's a relative term for me, since I carry a firearm," said Lopez, his chest seemingly expanding. "Suffice it to say, I don't believe he was acting in a rational manner."

Terry hit back on her cross-examination. She trapped Lopez a bit with his implication I'd been drinking. She asked if he thought it was possible he smelled alcohol on my breath the night before at Conrad Birch's town house. She'd stressed the word "possible," and Lopez seized on it as if he'd been given a loophole from the truth.

"Possible?" he repeated. "Yes, I think it's possible."

"Then why didn't you administer a Breathalyzer or have Dr. Remler's blood drawn? Your mere suspicion in that situation would've satisfied any court's definition of just cause."

Lopez didn't have an answer for that. But the accusation had been made, the suggestion planted—the doctor was a drunk.

If there was a silver lining, though, it was that I realized I *was* drinking too much. Or for the wrong reasons. First came Rebecca's death, then this trial. I was relying on the bottle to dull the pain. The problem was that it threatened to dull everything.

So I decided I'd go on an alcohol-free diet for a while. Cold Wild Turkey. I shouldn't need four bourbons to close my eyes at night.

Now, three days later and sitting in Terry's office discussing the detectives, I'd yet to have a drink.

From that issue to another: Mila. The poor woman wanted to help me. But she'd been a helpless pawn in my being framed and, as a result, was a key witness for the prosecution.

Said Hemmerson in court, "Ms. Benninghoff, you never actually saw this woman whom Dr. Remler was calling Sam Kent, right?"

"I'm sure she—"

"Just yes or no, please, Ms. Benninghoff."

"No, I never saw this woman," Mila said to Hemmerson. "But what I was trying to—"

"Thank you, Ms. Benninghoff. Did you ever see any payment from her other than the cash Dr. Remler gave you?"

"But you don't understa—"

"*Yes* or *no*, Ms. Benninghoff."

"No."

"Which means that she very well could've been a fabrication on the part of Dr. Remler, correct?"

"No."

"No? Why not, Ms. Benninghoff?"

"Because I don't believe David would ever do such a thing."

"Precisely," said Hemmerson. "You trusted him. And he knew you trusted him. Which made it all the more easy for him to accomplish his deception."

That's when Terry objected for probably the third time in three minutes. The latest was to point out that Hemmerson hadn't actually bothered to ask Mila a question in that last exchange. Judge Lomax was quick to respond—small miracle—"Sustained."

Said Lomax, with more than a hint of sarcasm, "Here's a yes or no for you, Mr. Hemmerson. Do you actually have another question for the witness?"

Hemmerson took the talking-down-to in stride. He'd made his point. "No, Your Honor. No further questions."

"Your witness, Ms. Garrett."

Terry stood up to cross-examine. "Ms. Benninghoff, the prosecution would have us believe that it was Dr. Remler who sent the initial e-mails to you under the guise of Sam Kent. But if Dr. Remler's objective was to create the appearance of a patient who he could later claim was Conrad Birch's mistress, why would he make you first believe his patient was a man?"

"I have no idea."

"Neither do I," said Terry before turning to the judge. "No further questions, Your Honor."

At the time, I didn't know what she was getting at. Now, back in her office, she was about to let on.

"They're painting you as a criminal mastermind, David. You not only fooled strangers, you fooled people who knew you very well. You were cunning, brilliant. You know what we have to do?"

"What's that?" I asked.

Terry grinned. "We've got to show them they're right. That you are, in fact, a criminal mastermind."

Confused, I looked at her, while Victor laughed out loud. "I like it," he said. "I like it a lot. It's the one thing the prosecution hasn't delivered on. If you're so clever, how come you were dumb enough to get caught so easily? Approach it like that, and the jury starts to wonder if maybe the real mastermind isn't on trial."

"Don't you see, David? If we can make them wonder, we can make them believe," said Terry, "that your Mystery Patient is very much for real and very much at large."

THE next night, I ate Chinese takeout in my kitchen. A couple of hours after downing my fortune cookie, I flipped on the late local news. The top story was about a murder in Queens. The second story was about a suicide in upstate New York.

I sat there, bewildered, as the anchorwoman spoke of the "rabbi murder trial that had riveted the city" the previous year. The screen switched to footage of the rabbi and, after that, the woman he'd been found guilty of killing. The anchorwoman's face returned. "Tonight," she said, "that rabbi is dead."

It was an apparent suicide. "Sources" reported that the rabbi had left behind a suicide note. In it, he confessed to his crime. He had, in fact, murdered the woman.

In a most ironic twist, he'd killed himself in the very same fashion that his defense lawyers had tried to pin on his victim—suicide by self-garroting. The rabbi was off to make peace with God.

I continued to watch the news up through the sports and the weather. Then I turned off the television and went to bed. I didn't know exactly how to feel.

So, in the end, I felt nothing.

MONDAY morning, a little before nine. In a matter of minutes, the first witness for the defense—*my* defense—was going to be called. I stood between Victor and Terry as Judge Lomax was announced. Then, out of the corner of my eye, I saw her.

Sam Kent. Samantha Kent. Mrs. Samantha Kent. The real one.

For the first time, I was seeing her in person. There'd been a couple of pictures in the papers, and I'd gained a sense of what she looked like. Yet as much as our lives had suddenly intersected, I didn't really know much about her.

What little I did know came from the brief stories accompanying those newspaper pictures. That and what was relayed to me by Terry based on statements Samantha Kent made to the police. One thing was clear: My Mystery Patient had done her homework. Posing as Samantha Kent, she appropriated far more than a name.

Being an only child. Growing up in Larchmont, New York. Attending Brown. Even the former job as a buyer for Bergdorf's.

How she knew all this could've stemmed more from pillow talk than research. Over the course of their affair, Conrad Birch could've told her things about his wife. Either way, my Mystery Patient had really gotten into her role.

One thing she didn't appropriate was the family business. It didn't play into the sympathy card. Samantha Kent was the only child of Archibald Kent, founder of Kent Oceanic. They made most of the world's cargo ships and a lot of money in the process. At age seventy-seven and a widower, "Archie" Kent supposedly had a net worth of four billion dollars. That made Samantha one serious heiress.

But it was what my Mystery Patient flat out made up that proved most pivotal. Two things in particular.

One was the nanny, Celeste. Samantha Kent and Conrad Birch

never had a nanny. Because, two, *there was no kid*. The two-year-old boy at the center of everything—the pending custody battle and, ultimately, the desire to kill Birch—was a complete fabrication.

Which meant that along with the pictures I'd already seen of the real Samantha Kent, I was able to add one more: a portrait of a woman in a state of disbelief. Especially when it came to my alibi.

She'd said she didn't know her husband had ever seen a psychologist. Considering what Conrad Birch told me in that one session we had together—that he was cheating on his wife—I was inclined to believe her. So what *did* Samantha Kent know?

She knew that she came home from a trip to learn her husband had been brutally murdered. She knew that the knife used to stab him was a knife I once owned. She knew that a letter signed by her husband had been found in my apartment and that it strongly suggested I had a motive.

I was now staring at her. The real Samantha Kent was more blond than she appeared in any picture I'd seen. Her hair was now different, too. It fell straight to her shoulders, parted on one side and angling across her forehead. She was also thinner in person, with pronounced cheekbones. She was forty, forty-five at the outside. In total, she was attractive, although in a way that suggested she had once been far more so.

Then she turned my way, staring right at me. And if the weight of her gaze was any indication, she didn't like what she saw.

"YOU may call your first witness, Ms. Garrett."

Terry stood from her chair and adjusted her suit jacket with a slight tug. "Thank you, Your Honor," she said. "The defense calls Dr. Hans Lenbakker." And so began Operation Brilliant Idiot.

A succession of witnesses called in strategic order. One to show my uncompromising genius in plotting a complex murder. The next to show how utterly stupid I was in trying to pull it off. Brilliant and idiot. Repeated enough times to make the jury get the point. I was neither smart enough nor dumb enough to commit this crime.

Dr. Hans Lenbakker was sworn in and took a seat in the witness-box. While his gray beard was neatly trimmed, he had just enough Einstein rumple about him to suggest formidable intelligence.

Terry had the doctor give a brief history of his educational background and professional credentials. His specific area of expertise was the dating of paintings, along with paper- and parchment-based writings. By the time he got to his current stint as director of the Smithsonian's Artifact Authentication Board, I could tell the jury was suitably impressed.

Terry strode back to the defense table, opened a folder, and removed a page of loose-leaf notepaper sheathed in clear plastic. She approached Dr. Lenbakker with it. "I'm showing you what's been marked defense exhibit A," she said to him. "Do you recognize it?"

"Yes. I've examined it."

With that, Terry began reciting aloud my notes on Conrad Birch. Our one session together. The admission that he was having an affair. The feeling that he couldn't leave his wife. The fear of having to break it off with his mistress. "Fear," Terry repeated. She listed my bullet points that said the mistress had a temper, a mean streak, then looked up at the jury. "Dr. Remler then writes that Conrad Birch had, and I quote, 'overwhelming concern for how mistress will react.' "

She handed the plastic-covered page to Dr. Lenbakker. "As you know, Doctor, these are notes that my client has offered as being a record of his one and only session with Conrad Birch," she said. "Based on your examination of the document, and in your expert opinion, when were they written? Last month? Last year?"

"Much longer than a year, closer to two years. The breakdown of the ink particles alone would heavily support that. The oxygenation would all but guarantee it."

"So, Dr. Lenbakker, if Dr. Remler had intended to fake the fact that he once treated Conrad Birch in order to construct an alibi, what you're saying is that he was brilliantly planning to kill Mr. Birch for nearly *two* years?"

"Objection!" shouted Hemmerson. "First off, the murder itself was over seven months ago. More important, Dr. Lenbakker has been called to verify ink, not the intentions of the defendant."

"Sustained," said Judge Lomax.

"I'm sorry," she said. "I have no further questions, Your Honor."

"Your witness," said Lomax with a nod toward Hemmerson.

The assistant D.A. stood up. "We have no questions."

"Very well, then. Ms. Garrett, your next witness."

Terry had barely made it back to her seat. "Your Honor, in the time since the cross-examination of Detectives Trentino and Lopez, the defense has realized additional questions for them pertinent to our case. Given their presence in the courtroom today, I'd like to call them back to the stand."

Hemmerson began to make an objection, but Lomax squashed it with a raised palm. "I'll allow it," he said.

Terry had told me it was common for detectives to attend the trials of their cases beyond the days they were testifying. A vested interest sort of thing. Nonetheless, neither she nor Victor was about to bank on it. So they let drop to a reporter the day before that they had a surprise witness lined up. Predictably, that reporter later asked the detectives if they knew who it was.

"The defense calls Detective Joseph Trentino," announced Terry.

Surprise.

After making it to the stand and swearing to tell the whole truth, Trentino sat down and Terry did a little recapping. "Detective Trentino, you've got a psychologist at the scene of a crime who explains he's looking for a patient of his. He tells you his patient has confessed to killing her husband. Only it turns out, the husband is not her husband—he's someone else's husband. What's more, the patient has been pretending to be that husband's real wife. Sounds pretty confusing, doesn't it? Almost hard to believe."

"Yes."

"I mean, if I were trying to make up an alibi, I certainly wouldn't choose one as far-fetched as that. Would you?"

Hemmerson objected on the grounds that it called for speculation. Terry countered that the detective had heard many alibis in the line of duty and that he was uniquely qualified to comment on the viability of the one put forward by her client. Lomax instructed Trentino to answer the question.

Said the detective, "As alibis go, it didn't seem very plausible. No, it wouldn't have been my choice."

"In other words, if Dr. Remler were fabricating his alibi, he'd been pretty stupid about it, right?"

"Those are your words, not mine."

Terry nodded. "What if I said Dr. Remler could've been smarter about making up an alibi, if that was indeed what he was doing? Could those be *our* words, Detective Trentino?"

"Sure, okay. Yes, he could've been smarter."

"Good. Thank you," she said. She paced a bit without saying anything. "Now, let's go back to that fateful night in the Birch home when the police first found Dr. Remler. He was coming up from the basement, correct?"

"That's what the two officers on the scene reported."

"Do you know what Dr. Remler was doing in the basement?"

"He told us he was searching for his patient."

"And you believed it—what Dr. Remler was telling you?"

"At first."

"And do you still believe that?"

"I don't know," he snapped.

Terry, incredulous: "You don't know if you believe him?"

"That's right. I don't know."

"Maybe this will help," she said, turning to the jury. "Dr. Remler's fingerprints were found in practically every room in that town house, including the basement. That would be consistent with someone who was looking for someone else, wouldn't it?"

Hemmerson objected. "I fail to see the point of this line of questioning." The toss of a life preserver to his flailing witness.

Judge Lomax squinted at Terry. "Ms. Garrett, could you either get to your point or move on, please?"

"Your Honor, my point is simple. The prosecution would have us believe that my client plotted and carried out a complex murder. But if that were the case, it would've been pretty stupid of him to leave his fingerprints all over the place. Unless, of course, my client is telling the truth, which is what I'm trying to prove—that Dr. Remler truly was looking for his patient that night and that she truly did kill Conrad Birch."

"Hell, you can't even prove she exists."

Terry froze for a moment. Trentino, the seasoned detective, had let his emotions overtake his brain. He'd blurted out something without thinking, and while it may have been true, it also played right into Terry's hands.

"You're right, Detective. And why can't we prove she exists? Because that's exactly what she wants. It's how she intends to get away with this murder. She's manipulating you, just like she did Dr. Remler. But you're helping her get away with it!"

"Detective Trentino is not on trial here!" Hemmerson shouted.

Lomax promptly scolded Terry for her tactics. He also reminded Trentino that he was on the stand to answer questions and not to inject commentary. In other words, *If you had kept your trap shut, buddy, maybe she wouldn't have given you such an earful.*

Said the judge, "Do you have any further questions for the detective, Ms. Garrett?"

"No, I don't," she said.

Lomax asked Hemmerson if he wanted to requestion Trentino. He didn't. He was in damage-control mode, the best move being to get his detective off the stand as fast as possible.

"You can step down," said Lomax.

Trentino did, but not without casting a cold stare at his least favorite woman in the room. Terry returned the stare and then some. Victor turned to me, beaming. "That's my girl," he whispered.

I nodded with a quick smile of my own. The proud boss was reflecting on the prowess of his recent addition to the firm and his decision to make her lead counsel on the case.

I had another thought. What if there was more to it than that? *That's my girl.* My mind raced with the idea that Victor and Terry were an item. He was a good-looking guy; she was a good-looking woman. They worked together and knew each other to be smart and talented. It was more than conceivable. And I didn't like it.

The reason should've been because of the possible complications. I was on trial for murder and could ill afford a lovers' spat jeopardizing my defense. Yet that was the last thing I was thinking about. Truth was, I simply didn't want Terry to be seeing someone. Not Victor. Not anyone. A crush had crept up on me.

I told myself I was crazy. It hadn't been that long since I'd taken an interest in a woman, and she ended up framing me for murder. Now I was having thoughts about my attorney. Was I that starved for attention?

Terry continued with her strategic list of witnesses. There was the coroner, who testified that Conrad Birch was definitely asleep before he was stabbed. This meant less of a struggle for the killer, if any at all. Very smart of me.

Then there was the policeman who had found my knife—the murder weapon—in the alley directly below Birch's bedroom. I obviously must have thrown it out the window. Very stupid of me.

Back and forth. Back and forth. Terry proceeded with her witnesses, sowing the seeds of doubt with a deft and efficient hand. My Mystery Patient seemed to be coming to life in that courtroom.

Operation Brilliant Idiot was rolling right along. Brilliantly. But then the wheels fell off.

IT WAS their one and only rebuttal witness.

The defense had rested, my case made. And without my having to assume the risk of testifying. The time was a little before three on a Wednesday. Hemmerson stood up and, looking at Judge Lomax, announced, "Your Honor, the prosecution calls Gabrielle Dennis."

I could hear Victor and Terry utter in unison, *"Who?"*

We all turned and saw a bombshell of a young woman get up

from her seat in the back of the courtroom. She looked to be in her mid-twenties, with auburn hair and a top-heavy figure that left little doubt as to where she stood on the issue of breast implants.

The young woman walked past our table and up to the witness stand. As she was sworn in, Victor said, "Get ready to pounce."

Terry nodded and began to jot down a note. Victor opened his briefcase and took out his BlackBerry. He began to quickly type.

Hemmerson approached the young woman. "Could you please state your name for the court?"

She leaned in to the microphone. "My name is Gabrielle Dennis."

"You're here today, Ms. Dennis, because you knew the victim, Conrad Birch, correct?"

"Yes, that's right."

"And in what capacity did you know Mr. Birch?"

She didn't hesitate for a moment. "I was his mistress."

The courtroom launched into a collective murmur with a few scattered gasps. Lomax asked for order, and everyone began to quiet down. That's when Terry pounced. "Your Honor, we've had no advance notice of this witness, and given her claim, the timing of her appearance is dubious at best."

Hemmerson jumped right in. "Your Honor, the timing is not only genuine, it's logical. Ms. Dennis only became known to the D.A.'s office yesterday evening. She heard news reports of the defense's claim and believed it was her duty to come forward."

"Is the prosecution claiming that they themselves haven't had time to vet this witness?" Terry asked incredulously.

"Justice is a twenty-four-hour-a-day operation," said Hemmerson with a smirk. "We've had ample time."

"But not enough time to inform the defense. How convenient."

Hemmerson threw a nasty look at Terry before addressing the judge again. "Your Honor, if you let me proceed, you'll discover this is a legitimate witness. Ms. Dennis has information that I believe will alter the course of this trial."

Lomax raised his hand and declared that the questioning of the witness could continue. All eyes returned to Ms. Gabrielle Dennis.

"When did you first become involved with Conrad Birch?" Hemmerson asked.

"About two and a half years ago."

"How did you meet?"

"We worked out at the same gym, Max Fitness." she said. "We were on treadmills next to each other one day. I was having a problem with setting a program, and he offered to help."

"In terms of a sexual relationship, did he initiate the affair?"

"We were two consenting adults, but I'd say that's accurate."

"Did you know he was married?"

"Yes, I knew he was married. He told me he was."

Right then, I realized Samantha Kent was sitting through all this. It was bad enough for me. Her level of discomfort had to have been something else entirely. I stole a quick glance to confirm she was indeed sitting in the same seat she'd been in for the past week.

She wasn't in that seat or any other. I was relieved. She certainly didn't need to hear the testimony of Gabrielle Dennis.

Hemmerson continued the questioning of his surprise star witness. "How long did the affair last, Ms. Dennis?"

"About nine months."

"Now, Ms. Dennis, you became aware of the defendant's claim that Conrad Birch had been a patient of his and told him of having an affair, correct?"

"Yes."

"According to the defendant's handwritten notes, this affair took place roughly two years ago, which would seem to coincide with the time in which you were involved with Conrad Birch, right?"

"Yes."

"Furthermore, you've heard in news reports that the defense is suggesting this mistress was Dr. Remler's Mystery Patient, correct?"

"Yes, that's right."

"So I have to ask you, then," he said with a bit of dramatic pause, "have you ever been a patient of Dr. David Remler's?"

She looked directly at me. "No, I have not," she said.

"Have you ever even met him before?"

"No, I have not."

"Which is why you came forward, isn't it?"

"Yes. I didn't think it was fair."

"Ms. Dennis, you've displayed real courage in coming forward," said Hemmerson. "I have no further questions."

Judge Lomax: "Your witness, Ms. Garrett."

Instead of getting up, Terry asked her first question from her seat. "Ms. Dennis, where did you and Conrad Birch usually do it?"

"Objection!" shouted Hemmerson. "She's trying to demean the witness!"

"I'll rephrase the question," said Terry. She stood and walked in front of the defense table. "Ms. Dennis, where did you and Mr. Birch conduct the affair?"

She answered, not very loudly, though, "Mainly in hotels."

"Could you name one of them for us?"

With barely a beat in between, she did. "The Wall Street Inn."

"Did you ever pay for a room there?"

"No. Conrad did that."

"Did you ever see him pay by credit card?"

"I never saw him pay at all," she said. "We just—"

Terry interrupted. "You didn't want to be seen together in public. So it's not like anyone ever saw you together, right?"

"We were discreet, yes."

I glanced at Victor, who was reading something on his Black-Berry. Terry looked at her watch. She was quite deliberate about it. "Ms. Dennis, would you consider yourself to have a temper?"

"I can get mad about things, if that's what you mean."

"No. What I'm asking is that if someone described you as having a mean streak, do you think it would be an accurate assessment?"

She mulled the question over. "No, I don't think it would be."

Terry nodded. "Would it surprise you, then, that Conrad Birch told my client he thought that's exactly what his mistress had?"

"No, actually, it wouldn't."

"Why's that?"

"Conrad had a tendency to exaggerate. Sometimes even lie. He was having an affair, after all."

"I see," said Terry, now looking at the jury. "So someone having an illicit affair is more likely not to tell the truth. That's interesting, because you were also having an illicit affair."

"But—"

"At least that's what you're claiming today." Terry had talked right over her. "Tell me, Ms. Dennis, what do you do for a living?"

"I'm an actress."

Terry paused. The answer was an unexpected windfall. The implication of someone playing a part. "Are you currently working?"

"No, I'm not."

"When's the last time you did work?"

"Well, I'm also a waitress."

"I see. But in terms of the acting, when's the last time you got paid to do that?"

"Maybe six months ago. It was for a commercial."

Hemmerson objected. "Are we in court or on the Bravo channel?"

Lomax agreed. "Keep it moving, Ms. Garrett. It's getting late."

Terry's face lit up. It was as if Lomax had said the magic words. "I agree, Your Honor, it is getting late. Given that, combined with the surprise nature of the witness, I'd like to request that we adjourn until tomorrow morning."

Lomax looked at his watch. The clock on the wall was behind him. It was ten of five. Close enough for a full day, he apparently thought. "Court is in recess until tomorrow morning at nine."

Gabrielle Dennis stepped down as the rest of the people in the courtroom gathered their things and stood. Terry walked over to Victor and me.

"Did he e-mail you back yet?" she asked Victor with a nod toward his BlackBerry.

"Yeah. He's starting on it right away."

I looked at the two of them. "Starting on what? Who's 'he'?"

"You'll see," said Victor.

His name was Anthony Magnetti, but Victor called him "The Magnet." The reason was simple, he explained. The guy could pull almost any information about anyone right off his computer. Or anyone else's computer.

"There are hackers, and then there's The Magnet," said Victor to me. He seemed unaware he was talking about the guy the way a kid talked about a superhero.

The man who showed up at Victor's office after we returned from court was not about to inspire a Saturday morning cartoon. Anthony Magnetti, a.k.a. The Magnet, was around five and a half feet tall and easily three hundred pounds. The guy was somewhere between geek and hip. His thick black glasses were countered by a black leather biker jacket. A ponytail hung down his back.

"The Magnet has arrived!" exclaimed Victor, getting up from behind his desk. The two hugged like old friends. Victor's secretary—the brunette—hovered until her boss could inquire about a drink.

"Coffee, please. Light and sweet," said The Magnet.

The Magnet. I hadn't persuaded myself to call him that when Victor made the introduction. "David, meet The Magnet."

"Anthony Magnetti," he said, sticking his hand out.

"Hi, Anthony," I said, shaking it. "David Remler."

Victor returned to his desk. "Let me just buzz Terry."

Terry had been in her office, checking her mail. While we waited for her, we settled into Victor's big club chairs and engaged in small talk. Victor expressed his frustration with the Knicks, while The Magnet reported that he was a few days away from cracking the Pentagon's new internal-file encryption code. Victor's brunette secretary returned with The Magnet's coffee.

Then Terry arrived. "Hey, Anthony," she said. "Three cases since I've been here, and three dates with you. People are going to talk."

"Good," he said. "I'll be able to tell you what they say—a buddy of mine is teaching me wiretapping."

I had to know the guy for only a minute to know he was serious.

Terry warmly shook hands with The Magnet and sat down in the fourth, and final, club chair. Let the briefing begin.

From the moment Victor first e-mailed him, The Magnet had been busy digging up everything he could find on Gabrielle Dennis, the woman claiming to be Conrad Birch's mistress.

"Okay," said Terry. "The possibilities are as follows. One, she's the real deal and is telling the truth. Two, she's a plant—"

"Or, should we say, *im*plant," cracked Victor.

The Magnet put his coffee down and flipped a page on his notepad. "Gabrielle Dennis's breast-enlargement surgery was performed in Manhattan four years ago by Dr. Rueben Stolzmier at a cost of six thousand four hundred and eighty-seven dollars."

The office fell silent for a moment.

Then, like a ringmaster, Victor shouted with a wide grin, "The Magnet, ladies and gentlemen!"

I couldn't help asking the question. Maybe it was just wide-eyed curiosity. "Anthony, how could you find that out?"

He looked at me. "Trust me, you don't want to know."

Terry continued. "As for the third, and final, possibility, it's this: Gabrielle Dennis is trying to jump-start her career." She turned to The Magnet. "Anthony, what's the deal with the gym?"

He flipped back to the first page of his notes. "She and Birch were both members during that time," he said. "The gym uses a MagSeven card-swipe system to ID people and chart usage patterns. The data pools centrally with all its other branches behind a weak virtual network perimeter, so tracking their visits was easy."

"Stop showing off, Anthony," said Terry with a smile.

The Magnet smiled back and cut to the chase. "As I was saying, Gabrielle Dennis was much more of a regular than Conrad Birch."

"And in terms of overlapping?" asked Terry.

"Only eighteen times from the first date you gave me."

"Okay, so Gabrielle Dennis and Conrad Birch could've met as she claimed they did," said Victor.

"Or that's just the way she knew about him," said Terry. "What about the Wall Street Inn, Anthony? Or any other hotels?"

"Birch had four credit cards, plus a corporate card from his firm," he answered. "None showed any Manhattan hotel."

"He would've paid cash. Credit cards are an infidelity trail," said Victor. "Not that I'm the voice of experience on that."

"Of course not," said Terry.

Damn. There it was again. That nagging feeling Victor and Terry were involved. Had he just winked at her when he said that?

"What about the girl's finances?" asked Terry.

"What finances?" said The Magnet with a smirk. "Gabrielle Dennis gives new meaning to 'struggling actress.' She has one checking account with Chase, with three overdraws in the past three years. No lump-sum payments or steady increase in deposits during the time she claims she was with Birch."

Victor stood up and walked over to his windows. "So what I'm hearing is nothing that's out-and-out suspicious on the one hand, versus on the other hand—"

Terry jumped in. "Nothing in her testimony today that she couldn't have picked up from television or the newspapers."

The Magnet reached for his coffee. "Have you checked the autopsy report on Birch to see if he had any moles or beauty marks you could call her on?"

"I thought about that," said Terry. "I checked, and he didn't."

"What else, Mag?" Victor asked.

"I got into most every drugstore chain. She had a prescription for Xanax a year back, with three refills, but who hasn't, right?" He scoured his notes some more. "There is one other thing," he said. "It does make you wonder about her real motivation."

"What is it?" asked Terry, sitting up in her chair.

"Her phone records," said The Magnet. "Two days ago Gabrielle Dennis placed three calls to EpicOne Media. EpicOne Media publishes the *National Tabloid.*"

"The notion that she's trying to sell her story hurts her credibility," said Terry. "But it doesn't prove the story wrong."

The Magnet shrugged. "I didn't think it was your smoking gun."

"Though it's not bad, as far as ammo goes," said Victor. He looked at his watch and then up at Terry. She nodded.

"On that note, why don't we let you go, Anthony," she said.

The Magnet pushed off the arms of his club chair with a slight grunt and stood. As we shook hands, I thanked him for his efforts. Victor gave him another hug, and Terry volunteered to walk him out of the office. "Back in minute," she said.

As they left, Victor headed for his bar. "Want a drink?"

"No. I'm all set," I lied. Few things sounded better than a drink at that moment. Fortunately, one of those things was the sound of my mental Magic Marker crossing off another day on my "how long it's been since I've had a drink" calendar. Ten days and counting.

Terry returned. She sat back down, kicked off her heels, and put her feet up on the glass table. Victor finished pouring what, of course, had to be my poison of choice—bourbon—and joined us.

"So what are we thinking?" asked Terry.

"Fifty-fifty, Gabrielle Dennis is telling the truth," said Victor. "Though if she's lying, I'd put my money on you making her crack."

"That's a big 'if,' " she said.

There was a rap on the door. Victor's secretaries were standing there. "All right if we head out, Victor?" asked the blonde.

Victor nodded. "Yes," he told them. "Have a good night."

They wished us the same before turning on their heels to leave.

When they were out of earshot, Terry kidded, "Do you *really* need two secretaries, Victor, or is it just a male-power-trip thing?"

"Oh, it's definitely a male-power-trip thing," he said, grinning. "Sometimes one woman just isn't enough." He started to laugh.

"Of course!" exclaimed Terry.

Victor and I both looked at her. *What?*

"I just figured out what we have to do tomorrow," she said.

Terry stood up from her chair, rubbed her temples, and began to explain. When she was finished, Victor had only one thing to say. "What are you two doing here when you should be rehearsing?"

THE next morning, Terry rose to her feet in the courtroom and informed Judge Lomax that she had no further questions for Gabrielle Dennis. "Instead, Your Honor, I'd like to call Dr. David Remler to the stand."

Does he or doesn't he?

"I do," I told the clerk with my right hand raised. The whole truth and nothing but.

Lomax motioned for me to be seated. Terry approached and, despite her game face, managed to give me a reassuring nod. "You begged me to put you on the stand, didn't you, Dr. Remler?"

I smiled like I was supposed to. "I don't know about begged," I replied. "It was more like 'strongly urged.' "

The quip brought a smattering of laughter from the courtroom.

"Either way," said Terry, "I had no intention of having you testify. Up until yesterday, I felt we'd done a pretty good job of proving your innocence. But then we heard from a young woman named Gabrielle Dennis." She paused. "Had you ever seen her before, Dr. Remler?"

"No, I hadn't," I said.

"There's no way she's the woman who became your patient—the one claiming to be Samantha Kent—is there?"

"No. It's not the same woman."

"So, seeing Gabrielle Dennis testify yesterday that she was involved with Conrad Birch during the time he told you he was having an affair, well, that must have come as quite a shock," she said. "If Gabrielle Dennis was not the patient who framed you, then who are we supposed to believe? You or her?"

Terry sounded as if she was turning on her own client.

It made my response sound that much better. "Actually, I think the logical choice is to believe both of us."

Terry cocked her head. "How do you figure that?"

"I think the prosecution has done me a favor. With Gabrielle Dennis, they proved I was telling the truth about Conrad Birch—that he was, in fact, an adulterer."

"Yes," said Terry. "But they're trying to suggest that because his mistress wasn't your Mystery Patient, you've been lying."

I looked at Terry. "Really, the only thing the prosecution has proved is that *one* of his mistresses wasn't my patient," I said calmly.

"What are you suggesting, Dr. Remler? That once you're not a one-woman man, who's to say you're a one-*mistress* man?"

"Exactly," I said. "As a psychologist, I've seen examples of both men and women who've had more than one extramarital affair at the same time. But what's also key is that, at least with the patients I've treated, there's an utter reluctance to admit it."

"Why do you think that is?"

"I see it as a societal boundary. While we frown on those who have affairs, we have come to accept it as commonplace. But two affairs simultaneously? The stigma is double."

"But Conrad Birch told you about his affair. Are you saying such a stigma would prevent him from telling you about another affair?"

"Yes, though in the case of Conrad Birch, we have to remember the purpose of our meeting in the first place. He was concerned about ending a relationship with a woman who had a mean streak. Guilt never really came into play."

"But again, the prosecution has claimed you've fabricated this whole story right down to your patient notes written nearly two years ago. What do you make of that?"

"It would mean I not only had tremendous patience in plotting a murder but was also the recipient of tremendous luck: I somehow guessed that Conrad Birch was having an affair."

Terry walked toward the jury box. "In other words," she said, "you're not only a psychologist but a member of the Psychic Friends Network."

There was a smattering of laughter from the courtroom.

Terry looked at Judge Lomax. "I have no further questions."

Before she could even get back to her seat, Hemmerson had stood and fired his first shot. "Dr. Remler, tell me, the knife used to fatally stab Conrad Birch over fifty times—was it your knife?"

"Yes."

"Yes, it was your knife," Hemmerson repeated. "And the letter that clearly stated how your relationship with Conrad Birch was more than doctor and patient, and signed by Conrad Birch—a signature that no one in this room disputes—where was it found?"

"The letter was found in my apartment."

"You don't deny you were at the scene of the crime, correct?"

"Correct."

"That your alibi is that you were coming to the aid of a patient, a woman you cannot prove exists, correct?"

I tried to keep my composure. "Yes, that's right."

Hemmerson did his own walk toward the jury. "Now, if I understand you correctly, you'd like us to believe that Conrad Birch was the Don Juan of Manhattan, that he had a whole harem of women."

"That's not what I said."

"You're right. You suggested he was having more than one affair at the same time. That's a convenient argument, don't you think? The fact is, you can't prove Conrad Birch was involved with more than one woman any more than you can prove your Mystery Patient exists. Do you disagree?"

"No, I don't. I've simply explained what happened the night Conrad Birch died—my version of the events that took place."

"You certainly have, Dr. Remler. And it's quite an *unbelievable* version." He turned to Lomax. "Nothing further, Your Honor."

QUESTION: When is a tie the same as a win?

Answer: When your attorney says it is.

Terry and I were sharing a cab, heading back uptown. She was returning to her office, and I was going home.

As the buildings passed my window in a blur, I couldn't figure how Terry managed to sound so upbeat in the wake of my testifying. Sure, I came across decent enough when she was asking the questions. But any sense of relief disappeared with Hemmerson and his cross-examination. I thought the guy had me for lunch.

"Not so," said Terry. "Hemmerson rubbed your nose in the evidence, but there was nothing new. The jury's already heard it all. More important, Hemmerson didn't really go after you on the multiple-mistress angle. He danced around the thing, but didn't touch the psychology of it. He knew it wasn't his turf. That means we've got a jury contemplating the very real and *reasonable* possibility that Conrad Birch had more than one affair going on."

"So Hemmerson *didn't* have me for lunch?"

"Light snack, maybe," she said. "That's why I called it a tie. And let's face it, a tie is as good as a win."

I looked at Terry. "I was with you up until 'let's face it,' " I said.

"It's all about expectations, David. When jurors watch a prosecutor go after a defendant, they're looking for the knockout. You're either innocent or guilty, and in either case, the verdict has to be unanimous. By holding your own with Hemmerson, it's as if he's the one who failed. The onus was on him to score the knockout."

I stared ahead silently. We'd had a full thirty blocks of conversation about the trial, and I realized there were another thirty blocks before Terry would get out. I decided to change the subject. "Is this what you always wanted to do? Practice law?"

"I knew I wanted to be an attorney since I was twelve."

"Sounds like you remember the exact moment."

"I do. It's when I saw Paul Newman in *The Verdict.*"

I started to laugh. "That's so weird. I wanted to be a psychologist ever since I saw Judd Hirsch in *Ordinary People.*"

"Wow," said Terry. "Two impressionable young people letting Hollywood dictate their entire future."

"What's pretty amazing is that we both followed through on it."

"You have, perhaps. I've still got a ways to go."

"What do you mean?"

"The plan was that I was going to represent the poor," she said.

"What happened to your plan?"

"Nothing. It's still there, just revised. As much as I want to do 'low-income law,' I realize I don't want to live like the people I'm representing. So the revised plan has me doing 'high-income law' for about ten years. That should pay the bills for happily ever after."

"I'm impressed."

"Don't be. I haven't done it yet."

"You will."

Terry gave me an appreciative look. Eyes that said thank you in a very real way. In that moment, we weren't lawyer and client. It was a little awkward. Because we both knew that lawyer and client was exactly what we were.

The cab pulled up in front of the Chrysler Building.

"It's time to be brilliant," Terry said. She was referring to the crafting of her closing argument.

"How much of it have you written?" I asked.

"About two thirds."

"That's good. You're almost done."

"Yes, except the one third remaining is the part that's supposed to make twelve people say 'not guilty.' "

I tapped my index finger on my temple. "Tell me, please, that you have it all right up here."

"Piece of cake." She winked and offered to give me some money for the cab. I declined.

"You need to save up for when you don't make three hundred and fifty bucks an hour," I said.

I WENT home, later climbing into bed that night without having a drink. Eleven days and counting. At seven forty-five the next morning, my phone rang.

"Hello?"

"David, it's Terry." Her voice was anxious.

"Is something wrong?"

"I'm not sure," she said. "I got a call five minutes ago from Judge Lomax. He wants all counsel to meet in his chambers at nine-thirty. And he specifically asked that you be there as well."

"What do you think the reason is?"

"I don't have a clue. I called Victor to let him know, and he has no idea either. The only thing Lomax would say was that 'something highly unusual has happened.' "

PART IV

JUDGE'S chambers. Nine-thirty on the dot. All were assembled.

I'd met Terry and Victor out in the hallway first. Victor, who clearly possessed an extensive grooming regimen to begin with, nonetheless looked to have applied an extra spit and polish.

As for Terry, she struck me as having also spent a few extra minutes in front of the mirror. Her hair, normally worn down, was tucked back neat behind a black barrette, the sheen of which matched her perfectly tailored blazer and skirt.

So what was my excuse?

"You missed a button," Terry said to me right away.

I looked down, and sure enough, the shirt beneath my tie was bunched up around my stomach. I made the correction.

"There we go," she said. "Much better."

I nodded. Then I immediately threw back my shoulders and straightened my posture. She smiled.

"So what's our best guess?" I asked.

"Can't imagine what it would be," said Terry.

Victor glanced at his watch. "It's time to find out."

The two of them turned and began walking. I fell in line behind them. We continued to the end of the corridor. Lomax's door was open, and the three of us stepped inside. Lomax wasn't there, but already seated and waiting were Hemmerson and the two other prosecutors who'd been assisting him—a young man and woman.

"Hello, Glenn," said Victor.

"Morning, Victor. Morning, Terry."

Hemmerson turned to me with a slight nod. I took a seat on the couch to the side of Lomax's desk.

Judge Lomax entered his office. In one hand was a coffee mug, in the other an ominous red folder. He took a seat behind his cluttered desk and began making room for the folder. "Are we all here?" he asked, head down and shuffling some papers.

"Yes," said Hemmerson.

"Yes," said Terry.

Lomax looked up. His eyes were searching, and immediately it became obvious whom they were searching for—the defendant. When they found me, I tried to gauge his expression, but the old man was wearing one serious poker face.

He hit a button on his phone and leaned in to the speaker. "Eunice, could you come in here, please?"

A slender gray-haired woman entered the office with a stenograph machine. She took a seat behind Lomax without acknowledging anyone. No eye contact whatsoever.

Said Lomax, "I want there to be a transcript of this meeting due to the unorthodox nature of what's about to occur and the impact it will have on this case."

Eunice typed away, her fingers a near blur.

"For the record, the defendant, Dr. David Remler, is present in addition to his counsel. Also present is the prosecution team." Lomax turned to me. "Dr. Remler, what I'd like you to do right now is describe for us the woman you claim was your patient."

I exchanged a glance with Terry, who gave me a nod. "She was around five foot six. Thin. Blond hair, past her shoulders if worn down," I said.

That's when Lomax opened the red folder. Barely. He slid his hand in and pulled something out—a color Polaroid. He held it up to me. "Dr. Remler, is this the woman you described?"

I leaned forward and studied the photograph. It was of a woman standing on a city street corner in broad daylight. She was thin, medium height, with blond hair about shoulder length. Everything matched the description of my Mystery Patient except for one thing: It wasn't her.

"No," I said, "that's not the woman."

"Are you sure?" asked Lomax. "Take a good look."

I already had. "Yes, I'm sure that's not her."

I could tell Victor and Terry didn't know how to react to my answer, though disappointment made the most sense. Had the woman in the photograph been my Mystery Patient, the defense of Dr. Remler would've taken a considerable turn for the better.

Hemmerson smiled. The prosecution had dodged a bullet.

But wait. There would be another shot.

Lomax returned the photograph to his red folder and took out a second one. This one wasn't a Polaroid. This photograph was square, maybe five by five. He held it up to me, as he'd done the first time. I stared in disbelief.

Eureka. There she was. My Mystery Patient. Thin, medium height, and blond hair about shoulder length. Except this time it was definitely her. The fake Samantha Kent. Although the shot was taken at night, there was plenty of light around her. She was wearing a long black dress and a red shawl draped over her shoulders.

"Dr. Remler?" Lomax said. "Dr. Remler?"

I needed to say something, if only for Eunice and her stenograph machine. The transcript had to make official what everyone had already gathered. "That's her. That's definitely her," I said.

The shock of seeing the photo quickly gave way to the realization of where it had been taken. She was standing under a streetlamp before the steps leading up to the Metropolitan Museum of Art, venue for the Kesper Society cocktail party. Which meant . . .

"What is it, Dr. Remler?" asked Lomax. He was staring at me. He obviously had picked up on my expression—a look of putting one and one together in my mind. Turned out, he knew exactly what I was thinking.

My Mystery Patient wasn't standing alone. Lomax revealed that the photograph in his hand was only half a photograph. The other half had been folded back. With a flip forward, the picture became complete. My Mystery Patient and me. Standing side by side.

Hemmerson was no longer smiling. Cut to Victor and Terry. Their disappointment was now the look of marvelous opportunity.

"Your Honor, I demand an explanation!" barked Hemmerson.

"First of all, calm down, Counselor," Lomax said. "Second, listen to what I'm about to tell you without interrupting me." He swung his eyes over to Victor and Terry. "That goes for all of you."

So began the explanation. "When I returned here to my chambers yesterday after court was adjourned, there was a FedEx envelope waiting for me. Judges don't normally open anything they're not expecting. However, the sender was listed as NYU Law School, where I'm a guest lecturer, so I opened the envelope. Inside was a photograph and a typewritten note." Lomax went to his folder again and pulled out a piece of paper. "There was only one sentence, and it read as follows," he said. *"Dr. Remler is telling the truth."*

He continued. "Naturally, the contents of this envelope gave me considerable pause, first and foremost because of where the envelope came from. Or at least where I thought it came from. I went about contacting several people I know at NYU Law School, none of whom had any knowledge of the envelope.

"That's when I called FedEx. According to the tracking number, the envelope was mailed from one of their midtown locations. Paid for in cash. Beyond that, there was nothing they could tell me."

"Excuse me, Your Honor."

Lomax threw Hemmerson a cold stare. "What did I tell you about interrupting?"

Hemmerson apologized, and Lomax went on. "Putting aside the anonymity of the sender, the primary issue for me, as it relates to the trial, is the consequence of my having seen this picture. Which is what I'm sure Mr. Hemmerson wanted to interrupt me about. I showed two photographs to Dr. Remler. Yet I stated there was only one in the envelope sent to me.

"The reason for this is simple. The law requires that I assume Dr. Remler is innocent. I also have to assume he had nothing to do with sending me this photograph. But if that's the case, what I can't rely on as proof is Dr. Remler's word." Lomax picked up the first picture he had shown me—the Polaroid. "Which is why there's another photograph. In other words, I needed a control group."

The guy had been testing me.

"Yesterday, not long after receiving the envelope, I had Eunice here go out on the street with an instant camera we keep in the office. I asked her to find and take a picture of a woman who fit Dr. Remler's description of his alleged patient. This way, I could know that Dr. Remler, a man whose freedom lies in the balance, wasn't simply being an opportunist." Lomax stopped and examined the shot briefly. "I think Eunice did a very nice job, by the way."

I glanced at Eunice as she recorded Lomax's compliment. She gave the slightest of smiles.

"You've now seen how I've utilized that photograph, as well as the one sent to me. You've also seen how Dr. Remler responded. For some of you, my actions might challenge your sense of a judge's prerogative. While I'll give both sides an opportunity to register their opinion, please keep one thing in mind: From a legal standpoint, I've already done my homework on this."

The judge leaned back in his chair and put his hands behind his head. It was the body-language equivalent of *Bring it on.*

Hemmerson brought it first. "How do we know the defendant himself or someone representing him didn't mail you the picture?"

Terry gave me a quick stare to make sure I kept my mouth shut. While my instinct was to defend myself, we had the best possible person to defend us—the judge.

Said Lomax, "While it's conceivable Dr. Remler and/or his counsel sent me the picture, it begs the question as to why they waited until now. Because if you look closely, you'll see it wasn't taken recently. In fact, it was taken many months ago. Right around the time of Dr. Remler's arrest."

"Is there some kind of date printed on it?" asked Hemmerson.

Lomax shook his head coyly.

"Then how could you know that?"

"Because I happen to be a fan of Mark Rothko," he said. Lomax pointed with his forefinger. "You see that swath of red in the background? That's the banner for what was the Rothko exhibit. I know because I went to it—*last October.*"

And like that, Mark Rothko became my favorite artist of all time.

A stymied Hemmerson cut his losses on that angle and moved to another. "Your Honor, be that as it may, your leeway as a judge also permits you to ignore the contents of the envelope."

"It does indeed," replied Lomax, putting the picture down. "The problem with that, however, is twofold. First, someone out there knows I received the picture. If I choose to disregard it, it doesn't mean everyone else will. Who's to say the press won't get the same anonymous envelope in the mail? Then what?"

Hemmerson was dumbfounded. "How on earth could you let the threat of media exposure dictate your actions?"

Lomax shook his head. "It's not the press that has me concerned. I said the problem with ignoring the envelope was twofold. It's the second fold that has me concerned." He picked up the picture again. "If this woman was indeed Dr. Remler's patient, it means she's still at large. Hell, even if she wasn't his patient, she's still out there. Only by finding her will we know for sure. Whether she's a material witness, suspect, or innocent bystander, we need her to be found. Ignoring her doesn't make her go away."

So much for dumbfounded. Now Hemmerson looked panicked. "Are you suggesting what I think you're suggesting?"

"Yes. I'm suspending the trial. A further police investigation is needed. They might want to start by showing this photograph to Samantha Kent. The real one. Maybe she'll recognize the woman."

"And if it turns out this whole thing was a hoax or a desperate attempt to prevent a guilty verdict, what then?" Hemmerson asked.

"Then we start again," said Lomax.

"But don't you see? That's a win-win for the defense."

"That's odd," interjected Terry, clearly unable to resist at that point. "I thought this was about justice, not who wins or loses."

Victor cleared his throat. "Your Honor, I don't know what your intention is regarding the dismissal of the jury, but I'd like you to wait at least a day."

"What for?"

"So Samantha Kent can see the photo before the media gets wind of the suspended trial," said Victor. "I'd hate to think this woman would know something was up before we got a positive ID on her."

It was a good point, and the judge knew it. "I see," he said. "Does the prosecution have a problem with that?"

Hemmerson rubbed his temples. "With all due respect, on my list of problems relating to this case, that one pales in comparison."

"I'll take that as a no," said Lomax. He proceeded to act out a cough. "I'm feeling a bit under the weather." He turned to Eunice. "Would you please instruct the bailiff that today's session will be canceled due to illness?"

Again, Eunice gave the ever so slightest of smiles.

Lomax glanced at Victor, who nodded. "I appreciate it, Your Honor." He cracked a smile. "I do hope you're feeling better soon."

IT WASN'T quite a celebration that night, though it shared many of the same telltale signs—smiles, jokes, laughs, drinks, and more drinks. There was even a toast.

"To the Phantom Photographer!" said Victor, raising his glass.

We all readily drank to that. Mine happened to be of the Diet Coke variety.

Victor, Terry, and I had been joined by Parker and Stacy. We were camped out in the swank Bar and Books on Hudson Street.

In listening to Victor, I couldn't help saying the words over in my head. The Phantom Photographer. I speculated on who took the picture. And why? I had no doubt that sending the picture to Lomax was an attempt to help me, but it seemed highly unlikely that that was the purpose of taking the picture. What was the original motive for tailing me like that? Or was it even me who was being tailed?

Naturally, I wasn't alone in pondering these questions. "How did our man Hemmerson react?" asked Parker.

"Not very well," said Terry.

"Parker, you should've seen the way Terry and Hemmerson got into it toward the end," said Victor. "It was beautiful." He put his arm around Terry and picked up his glass. "To Terry Garrett and her excellent work in *People* versus *Dr. David Remler.*"

"Hear, hear!" we all said. As we clinked glasses, I couldn't help watching Victor's hand give Terry's shoulder a squeeze. Was it sexual? Just friendly? Sexual disguised as just friendly?

I was staring at Terry's shoulder—post-squeeze—when I felt something. It was her eyes. She was looking at me looking at her shoulder. I looked up, and our eyes met. She smiled briefly, and I looked away like a nervous schoolboy.

We continued to talk, tell stories, and laugh for a while longer. Stacy got Victor to pledge money to her women's crisis center on behalf of his firm. In addition, Terry offered to throw in some pro bono work. After joking that he and Stacy should leave before anyone changed their mind, Parker looked at his watch. "Seriously, though, it is getting late."

He and Stacy stood, and we said our good-byes.

Then there were three. Victor, Terry, and I continued to have a good time. Certainly, there was nothing outwardly awkward about the situation, but I'd be lying if I said there wasn't a part of me that was determined not to leave the two of them alone.

As it turned out, it was Victor who left Terry and me alone. He'd spotted someone he knew toward the front of the bar. In his words, an "old chum from law school."

"Be right back," he told us. Then there were two.

A few seconds of silence passed.

"We're not, by the way," Terry said.

"Excuse me?"

"Victor and me. We're not an item."

I looked at her blankly. At least that was the look I was going for.

"Oh, *puleeeze,*" she said.

So much for the façade. "Okay, maybe I was wondering a bit," I admitted.

"I thought you wanted to know. Turns out, I was right. Though now that I think about it, if Terry Garrett were to marry Victor Glass, I wouldn't have to get new monogrammed towels."

"Do you actually have monogrammed towels?"

"No."

"You also don't strike me as the type who would take another man's name."

"Ah, that's where you're wrong."

"Really?"

"If only for the children. A mommy and daddy should have the same last name."

"So you want kids?"

"I do," she said. "I already have a name picked out. It's going to be the same whether it's a boy or a girl. Did you ever read *To Kill a Mockingbird*?"

"Sure," I said.

"I want to name my first child Atticus."

"You better pray for a boy."

"What about Atty?" she said. "That could be a girl's name."

"Not if you ever want her to like you."

She laughed. "Do you mind if I ask you a personal question?"

"Go ahead."

She crinkled her mouth. "Did you and your wife want children?"

As soon as she finished the question, she regretted it. All because of my expression. There was no way I could hide my discomfort. It was as if I could feel the sudden pallor in my face.

"I should've known better," she said. "I'm sorry."

"Don't be," I told her. I took a breath. "It's just that when my wife died, she was four months pregnant."

Terry grabbed her forehead. "Oh, God. David, I didn't—"

"Really, it's okay. How could you know?" I was about to say something to try to lighten the mood, when I happened to look down at my hand. To think I didn't even feel it.

Her hand was on top of mine.

She'd obviously been caught up in the moment, and as soon as I saw it, she saw it, too.

"Sorry," she said, slowly lifting her hand. "That was stupid of me. I mean, it wasn't intentional, but it was stupid all the same."

"What if I said it wasn't?"

She blinked slowly. "Then I'd remind you that you're my client. It's like you and one of your patients. It's not ever supposed to happen."

I immediately slouched. "It almost did happen with me."

"Your Mystery Patient? That was different," she said. "For all intents and purposes, you were seduced. She took advantage of you emotionally."

Terry's last sentence launched a flashback. That guy at Cassandra's party. His theory—the difference between men and women. His question: *Can you honestly say that you've never been taken advantage of emotionally by a woman?* I guess I no longer could.

"Still," I said to Terry, "I feel like some pathetic guy who falls for any woman who gives him the time of day."

She rolled her eyes. "Wow, that makes me feel really special."

"You know what I mean. Besides, you're the one telling me you're not interested."

A coy smile. "I never said that. I was merely pointing out the circumstances."

"You mean, attorney and client."

"Exactly," she said.

"You're right," I said. "It would be wrong. But maybe the only thing wrong is the timing."

"Maybe. But I can't think about that—or, more specifically, you—in that way and represent you at the same time."

"That settles it," I said. "You're fired." I laughed before she could think I was serious. "How about this? We'll make a deal. When this thing is over and, hopefully, I'm not heading off to jail, you and I have dinner."

"I think we have a deal," she said.

I extended my hand. "Then we'll shake on it."

Terry glanced over at the bar and put her hand in mine. When I squeezed, she pulled me forward.

"What are you doing?"

"Taking a chance," she said.

We were face-to-face, inches apart. Terry leaned in and put her lips onto mine. We kissed.

I was stunned that she'd just done that. But I couldn't have been more happy about it. "You realize your boss is twenty feet away?"

"Keenly aware of it," she said.

We both looked over at Victor, who had his back turned to us. His "old college chum" turned out to be a fetching young blonde.

Terry shrugged. "Well, there go my monogrammed towels."

LIMBO. There was no better way to describe the feeling. As nice as it was not having to go to court, I couldn't help thinking how much harder it would be if I eventually did have to go back. Priority number one: not getting my hopes up too high.

Resuming some semblance of a life in the meantime—that was priority number two. The key to doing that was going back to work. Take my mind off my problems by focusing on the problems of others. Fact was, I'd left all my patients in limbo.

Which was why a good number of them had decided to leave me. Though there were certain things New Yorkers could abstain from for a while, a weekly mental-health fix didn't seem to be one of them. So when the doctor was away, some of the patients did stray.

On the flip side, my remaining patients expressed a stronger faith in me than ever before, and I actually picked up a few new ones. Despite returning to the Swiss-cheese schedule of appointments that had marked the early days of my practice, I was heartened that there weren't more holes than there were.

On Thursday, at four o'clock, I looked up to see Mila poking her head into my office. Right on time. Instead of meeting every other Tuesday at five, as we usually had, she'd asked if we could turn it into a weekly meeting for a while because, with my being out of the office, the bills and other business-related issues had piled up.

"No problem," I'd told Mila. "When do you want to do it?"

"How about Thursdays at four?"

"Sounds good."

Mila obviously thought that filling the hour my Mystery Patient had occupied was in my best interest. I wasn't about to say no.

I waved her in. *"Rád te vidím,"* I said.

She nodded with approval. "It's good to see you, too," she said.

Ever since her testimony at the trial, Mila had felt terrible. She so much wanted to help me, and the mere thought that she couldn't drove her crazy. After I assured her a dozen times that she'd done nothing wrong, her guilt began to subside. When she heard the news of my trial's suspension, there was no stopping her tears of joy.

"What's going to happen now?" she asked, taking a seat.

"First the police are showing the picture to Samantha Kent to see if she recognizes the woman. Obviously, we hope she does."

"What if she doesn't?"

"The police release the picture to the press. It's printed in every local newspaper and gets shown on every newscast. Odds are, somebody out there will recognize her. Of course, finding out who she is—that's one thing. Catching her might be another," I said.

I looked at my watch. I realized that most of the day had passed without hearing from Terry. She had told me she'd call once the police had visited Samantha Kent. Instead of having her come in to the station, they were going to show the picture to her at her new apartment. It was no surprise she'd moved to a new address, given what had happened at the old one.

In the meantime, there were indeed some checks to sign with Mila. Rent, electricity, and the like didn't have much sympathy for my limbo status. At about a quarter to five, Mila left my office. As I started to pack up for the day, the phone rang.

It was Terry. "Things took a little longer than planned."

"But Samantha Kent was shown the picture, right?"

"Yes. She saw it. She didn't recognize the woman."

"Damn," I said. "So how come it took all day?"

"Trentino and Lopez decided they wanted to show it to some of the neighbors from the town house, as well as some of Birch's coworkers. Unfortunately, no one recognized your Mystery Patient."

"What now?"

"You're going to see the picture of her on your eleven-o'clock news tonight. I wouldn't be surprised if it's the lead story. Starting tomorrow, the phone tips should start pouring in."

"You really think so?"

"You'll see. The public loves a manhunt. Kidnappers, snipers, you name it. The fact that, in this case, it's a woman—and a good-looking woman at that—only makes it sexier."

We ended the call by agreeing to speak the following morning. The last thing Terry explained was the wording the police were providing for the news media. My Mystery Patient was not to be labeled a "possible suspect." Rather, "The authorities believe she might have valuable information regarding the death of Conrad Birch." Yeah, like maybe why she killed him.

That night, sitting on the couch in my apartment, I tuned in to the late local news. There was a full-screen picture of my Mystery Patient with the phone number to call.

I undressed for bed, embracing the possibility that this was the beginning of the end. A happy ending. That's when I got the call.

"DID you miss me, David?" I stood there, stunned. It was my Mystery Patient. Late at night and calling me again. Only this time she sounded a lot more awake. "Because I certainly missed you."

I wanted to scream and curse, unleash my rage. She'd played me for a fool, and I'd played right along. Which was why I remained calm. Because I was being given a golden opportunity—to learn something about the fake Samantha Kent. And to get it on tape.

The minirecorder that Parker had suggested I buy was right there in the drawer of my bedside table. I grabbed the recorder and lifted it to the top of the phone by my ear. With a slow press of my thumb, we were rolling.

"I take it you watched the news tonight," I said.

"Oh, c'mon!" she scoffed. "You're not going to scream at me?"

"It's tempting."

"But let me guess—the shrink in you says not to, right?"

"Something like that."

A sigh. "I've got to tell you, if I'd known I was being photographed, I would've smiled more."

"I doubt you're smiling now, though."

"David, you're either smarter than I gave you credit for or the recipient of some incredibly dumb luck."

"Call it what you want. The fact remains, you're going to have a hard time shopping at your local supermarket tomorrow."

"I know. What a shame," she said, laughing.

"In a way, I find it kind of ironic," I said. "Being framed only to be saved by a picture."

She snickered. "Is that what you think you are? *Saved?*"

"Let's put it this way: I'd rather be me right now than you."

"I wouldn't be so sure, David. Life is full of surprises. People never know as much as they think they do."

"Starting with your real name. You could fix that right now."

"What, and spoil the mystery?"

"At least tell me this. Why me? Why set me up?"

"That's easy. Murder 101. The best way to cover your tracks is to lead everyone to somebody else. And who more *deserving* than the psychologist who turned Conrad against me?"

"What are you talking about?"

"You know exactly what I'm talking about." She lowered her voice, making it deep. *"My therapist thinks this affair is destructive. My therapist thinks I really should end this and try to fix my marriage."*

This was an avalanche of revelation—my Mystery Patient was indeed the mistress. Or at least one of two mistresses, if a certain buxom woman was telling the truth at the trial.

It seemed that Conrad Birch had done what so many before him had done—pawned off the guilt of a difficult life decision by blaming the therapist. It was so common in my profession that we had a name for it: the Shrink Rap.

My Mystery Patient continued. "Tell me, David, what's it like to have so much power over people's lives?"

"I should ask the same of you."

"No. What I've done is simply give you a taste of your own slick medicine. I saw how you work firsthand, remember?"

"What? That I tried to help you?"

"You were playing God, and a self-serving one, at that," she shot back. "Do you move in on all your vulnerable female patients?"

"That wasn't part of your plan? To make me attracted to you?"

She snickered. "Yes, it was part of the plan, but it worked because of something else I knew—that you're either too arrogant or too ignorant to consider the consequences of what you do for a living. The sacred advice you dispense as you sit in your cocoon of an office. That's why you had no problem telling Conrad what you did."

"I didn't turn him against you," I insisted. "He used me. He was trying to take the easy way out. I never told him those things."

She snickered again. "You actually expect me to believe you."

"You'd rather believe the guy who left you and went back to his wife? Think about it," I said. "Can you honestly tell me he never misled you up until that point?"

"He lied to me plenty of times. That's why I killed him."

I glanced at the recorder in my hand, the tape spinning.

"He lied to you. Perhaps even more than you knew," I said. "You followed the trial, didn't you? Another woman came forward claiming she was the mistress, did you know that?"

Silence.

"I said did you know that? Because if she was telling the truth, it means he was lying to you that much more."

"Even more of a reason to kill him, then."

"Yet you'd still take his word over mine?"

"It looks that way, doesn't it?"

"But what about—" I stopped. I realized I was trying to make a rational argument to someone who embodied the irrational. What was the point? I had what I needed. She'd admitted to everything.

It was as if she'd read my mind. "Did you get all of it?" she asked.

"All of what?"

"You've got a lousy poker voice, David. You were recording the conversation, weren't you?"

"No," I lied. "I wish I were, though."

She laughed. "Even if you're lying, you're still telling the truth."

"What's that supposed to mean?" I asked.

"It's like I told you—life is full of surprises. Want one more?" She paused. "I'm not done yet. First I took care of Conrad. Now it's time for that bitch of a wife he ran back to. Tonight she dies." *Click.*

SO MUCH for remaining calm.

The last time I was on the phone with this woman, she told me she'd killed Conrad Birch. She may have lied about being married to him, but she sure was telling the truth about the killing part. Now she was telling me Samantha Kent was next.

The threat was real. It was as real as she was. Something the tape would prove once and for all. I pressed REWIND and waited a few anxious seconds. I pressed PLAY and listened. What I heard was a sharp, piercing whistle amid static.

In a fumbling panic, I rewound the tape farther. I got the same sound, nothing of our conversation. I checked the batteries. Fidgeted with the volume. Ejected the tape and put it back in. I was running out of remedies.

Even if you're lying, you're still telling the truth. It didn't make any sense when she said it. Now it made all the sense in the world. I told her I hadn't been recording the conversation. I thought I was lying. I wasn't. The truth was, I hadn't recorded anything.

"Nine one one emergency," the operator said.

As soon as I made the call, I wondered, What was I going to say? That a woman's life had been threatened by another woman, only I didn't really know who the second woman was, let alone the address of the first?

I hung up and ran to my kitchen, where I had Terry's home number written down on a pad. I looked at the clock on the stove: It was past midnight.

After four or five rings, Terry answered. She'd been sleeping and was barely awake when I started to tell her what had happened. She was wide-awake by the time I finished.

"Stay there by the phone, and I'll call you back." She hung up.

Terry was off and running. Still, I felt little relief. Someone's life was in jeopardy, and there was only so much I could do. What if it was too late? What if Samantha Kent was already dead?

I returned to my bedroom with Terry's number and sat on the bed. Five minutes passed. I leaned back against my headboard. Twenty minutes passed. I looked at the phone and willed it to ring. A half hour had gone by without hearing back from her.

Finally the phone rang. I answered in a heartbeat.

"David, it's Terry."

"Where are you?"

"Samantha Kent's apartment building," she said. "I need you to get over here."

"Where is it?"

"Ten-thirty Park Avenue, on the corner of Eighty-fifth."

"Terry, what happened?"

"I'll explain later. Just get over here fast, and bring the tape recorder." She hung up before I could say another word.

AT LEAST two blocks before reaching Samantha Kent's apartment building, I saw the red-and-blue dance of flashing lights and assumed the worst. The lights belonged to two police cars. As I got out of the cab, Terry and I saw each other almost simultaneously. She was inside the lobby, visible through the large glass double doors of the entrance. Before I could go in, she came out and took me by the arm, pulling me to the side.

"Good news and bad news," she said. "The good news is, nothing happened. No one tried to kill Samantha Kent tonight."

I did a quick exhale. "What's the bad news?"

"The same thing. No one tried to kill Samantha Kent tonight, and you've got two detectives inside thinking you cried wolf."

"Trentino and Lopez think I fabricated this? How could they believe I made up that phone call?"

"The same way they believe you killed Conrad Birch," she said. "Did you bring the tape?"

"Yeah." I reached into my pocket and pulled out the recorder. "Like I said, she must have done something—used a device, maybe—because all you hear is a high-pitched whistle."

I pressed PLAY so Terry could listen to it. I watched her grimace at the shrill sound. "She did something, all right."

"Maybe the police will have an idea what it was."

She shook her head. "This tape is strictly between us, for now. It's the only copy. You never hand cops the only copy of anything. Tomorrow we'll get The Magnet on it. If he can't figure out what happened, he'll know someone who can."

I started to put the recorder back in my pocket.

"On second thought, why don't you let me hold that," she said.

I handed it over. In doing so, I had my first chance to focus on Terry rather than what she was saying. I'd woken her up from a deep sleep, and here she was looking as attractive as ever. But it was the wrong time for me to be anything but her client.

"Why couldn't you fill me in on the phone?" I asked.

"When I called you, Trentino and Lopez were within earshot. I didn't want them to hear anything."

"How'd you get in touch with those two in the first place?"

"I didn't. Victor did."

"You called Victor?"

"Didn't have to. He was lying right next to me."

I froze. Terry laughed. I shook my head, slightly embarrassed.

"Oh, you should've seen your face," she said. "*Yes,* I called Victor right after I hung up with you. I wanted him to be the one to call the police. He's a better alarmist when need be. In fact, he's upstairs in Samantha Kent's penthouse trying to get her to consent to police protection."

"Do you think she needs it?"

"Probably not. Given our killer's star turn on the eleven-o'clock news, she's probably en route to a faraway place. That said, better safe than sorry."

"I agree."

"Yeah, except Kent has refused the protection."

I was about to ask why, but I knew why. *I* was why. "She thinks I killed her husband."

"Yeah. The Mystery Patient idea was never really a big hit with her," said Terry facetiously.

"Still, can't the police do it anyway?"

"Not without consent. But they'd rather keep an eye on you."

"Let 'em."

She smiled and looked at her watch.

"Are we waiting for something?" I asked.

"Yes—the real reason why you're here. You have to give a statement. Tell them what happened, minus the part about you recording the conversation."

"What if they ask if I did?"

"If they do, tell them yes. They'll ask if you have the tape with you, and you can tell them no." Terry patted her pocket where she put the recorder. "This way, you won't be lying. At that point, I'll step in and tell them we'll have to make a copy before we can hand it over."

Just then Victor poked his head out from the entrance. "There you guys are," he said. He looked at Terry. "You holding the recorder?"

"Yep."

"We'll get to the bottom of that tomorrow," he said. "I'm thinking The Magnet could probably help us."

"I'm thinking the same thing," said Terry. "Any luck with Samantha Kent's agreeing to the police protection?"

"That's a big no-go," said Victor. "Though the woman wanted to press charges for harassment, David."

"That's ridiculous."

"No kidding," he said. "Our detective friends were considering it. And if we're out here any longer, they'll think we're plotting something." He turned back toward the entrance. "C'mon."

Terry and I followed Victor inside the lobby, where Trentino and Lopez were waiting. They looked *extremely* unhappy.

"Let's make this quick," said Trentino with a pronounced scowl.

"If you'd like to make it really quick, Detective, we can skip it altogether," Victor said with a sarcastic grin.

Lopez glared at me. "You mean, like pretend the phone call never happened?"

"Oh, that's good," said Terry back to him. "Because you wouldn't want to reveal your bias in the investigation, would you?"

I stood there, watching the sparks fly. That's when a cooler head prevailed.

"Excuse me, would one of you happen to have any aspirin?"

We all turned to the voice. It belonged to the distinguished-looking doorman. Slender, gray-haired, and easily in his sixties, he was sitting behind a desk along the wall. In a polite yet pointed manner, he was very cleverly asking us to shut up and get on with it.

So I began telling Trentino and Lopez what happened. The phone call and what was said—her wanting to kill Samantha Kent, as well as why she set me up. Her whole Murder 101 speech.

As the detectives listened, with Trentino taking notes, there was no snickering. Not a single expression of disbelief. When Lopez asked me whether or not I'd been drinking prior to getting the call, I answered that I hadn't been, and that was the end of it. We were courteous. We were respectful. We spoke in hushed tones.

Then all hell broke loose. It started with the doors of the elevator opening, though that's not what everyone heard first. Rather, it was the yelling, her yelling. *"You son of a bitch!"*

Samantha Kent was coming at me, finger pointed, screaming, calling me a murderer.

She was wearing a long robe, only socks on her feet. She yelled, *"I swear to God I'll kill you!"*

Trentino and Lopez cut her off before she could reach me. The screaming became louder. *"Police protection? Ha! The only protection I need is from you!"*

I was shocked. We all were. The poised, stoic Samantha Kent from the courtroom had succumbed to raw emotion. The night's events had triggered her breaking point.

Trentino and Lopez began forcing her back toward the elevator. As the doors closed, she disappeared with them, and within seconds, so did the commotion. A hushed quiet resumed. I exchanged weary glances with Terry and Victor. Then I peeked over at the doorman, who'd watched and heard it all. There was little doubt in my mind that we were both thinking the same thing: We could've all used some aspirin.

I WALKED home. Terry and Victor each offered to share a cab with me, but I declined. I needed the air. I needed some space. It was nearing three in the morning, and the streets of Manhattan certainly offered more of both than usual.

I tried to focus on what I really needed—some answers. More than ever, my Mystery Patient had left me wondering, Why did she call? Why did she tell me what she did? Why did she say she was going to murder Samantha Kent that night and not do it?

It occurred to me that the phone call may have been nothing more than a reminder of how much control my Mystery Patient still had over me. Even in her absence, I remained her pawn.

The mere thought of that word brought me back to my days at Columbia and one of my psych professors—Dr. Alvin Wexler.

An avid chess player, Dr. Wexler held the game up as a metaphor for practically everything. Our hopes, our dreams, our fears, could be better understood through a better understanding of chess.

As I walked those last few blocks to my apartment, I found myself recalling something Dr. Wexler had told me. I'd received a B minus on a case-study analysis I thought I'd nailed. I approached Dr. Wexler, wanting to know why I hadn't received a higher grade.

"That's easy," he said. "You only saw what was in front of you."

When I asked what he meant, he asked me if I played chess.

"A little," I lied.

"Then you can appreciate its paradox, how it's a game of infinite possibilities defined by a finite set of movements. Ultimately, chess is played in your head and not on the board in front of you," he said. "If you only play what you see, you'll never win. To excel in chess—and in anything else for, that matter—you have to imagine. You have to see beyond what's in front of you."

He eyed me closely. "In other words, Mr. Remler, your paper

proved only that you'd read the case. But those who scored higher proved that they'd read *into* the case. They saw beyond the facts."

I pushed through my building's revolving door and into the lobby. Walking by the doorman, who was fast asleep at his desk, I stepped onto the elevator and hit the button for my floor. The entire way up, I continued to hear Dr. Wexler, his words resonating, the meaning sinking in. All along, I'd been staring blankly at the chessboard. It was time to start using my head.

A LITTLE over fourteen hours. That's how long it took. From the moment I stepped off the elevator to the moment I made that fateful determination.

The first three were spent copping barely enough sleep to get me through the day at the office—six sessions I didn't dare cancel. It wasn't until after my four-o'clock had left that I managed any answers. One big answer, really. I was being set up again.

My Mystery Patient had every intention of killing Samantha Kent. She'd merely lied about when. She also had every intention of making me the prime suspect. *Again*. The night before was all about laying the groundwork.

She calls. I cry wolf. Everybody comes. The wolf's not there. Everybody goes home.

Those were the facts. That was the chessboard—there for everyone to see. Except now I was onto her game. I saw the move to come. It was the one in which Samantha Kent turns up dead . . . and everybody comes looking for me.

No, I told myself. I wasn't going to let it happen.

I DIALED from my office. The phone rang half a dozen times before someone picked up. "Ten-thirty Park Avenue," said the man.

"Yes, hi. This is Fiorillo Florist over on Madison," I said. "We've got a delivery for one of your residents. Her name's Kent, Samantha Kent. Could you tell me if she's at home right now?"

The question threw the guy off-balance for a second. He cleared his throat. "This is the doorman. Whatever you've got for her, drop it off, and I'll make sure she gets it."

"My customer insisted that this be hand-delivered."

"We don't give out information on our residents."

"Sure, I understand," I said. "Here's the thing, though. This customer plopped down three hundred bucks on the bouquet, and he doesn't want it sitting around. So I tell you what—if she's home right now, I'll send someone over, and you can take it from there."

A heavy sigh. "Yeah, she's here," he said.

It was all I needed to know.

The next call was to Hertz. Early evening on a Friday meant limited availability. Fifteen minutes and a ridiculous day rate later, I was behind the wheel of a beat-up white Hyundai Accent.

My destination was Ten-thirty Park Avenue. Home to Samantha Kent and her penthouse apartment. Where I knew she was.

The rest was simple. Find a parking space across the street from her building that offered a good view of the entrance. Then sit, watch, and wait.

Actually, there's never been anything simple about finding a parking space in Manhattan. The one I got took forty minutes of being double-parked with my hazards on. The car leaving happened to be the one I was blocking.

It was a tight squeeze. I was practically kissing bumpers front and back. With the engine off, I made a quick call from my cell to the doorman. Chances were slim that Samantha Kent had left while I was in transit, but I had to make sure she was still there. She was.

My weekend plans were settled. If Samantha Kent was heading out, I was following her. If she wasn't, I was staying put. Either way, I'd still need to eat, but I was in the take-out capital of the world. If a restaurant could deliver to the front door of an apartment, they could certainly deliver to the front door of a parked car.

After eight hours in the Hyundai, though, that aching no-sleep joint pain had settled in, as had the boredom. Worst of all, I was beginning to question what I was doing.

Still, I kept my eyes trained on that apartment building.

Dawn. With it came a calculated risk. A nap. Two hours to try to offset the effects of the previous twelve. The word "refreshed" didn't really come to mind when I awoke. However, I was in good enough shape to carry on.

At nine-thirty, a cab pulled up. Cabs were tricky. It was difficult to see who was getting out of them. I craned my neck to get a glimpse of the new arrival. It was a man. I watched as he—

Out of the corner of my eye. Walking toward the entrance. Big black sunglasses. Large shoulder bag. A long raincoat with a high collar. She was looking straight ahead. Inconspicuous. Incognito.

No one would've recognized her. Including me. Were it not for one thing: the Yankees cap, gray flannel. The same cap she had on in my office that first day.

My hand swung toward the Hyundai's door, blindly reaching for the handle. I barreled out of the car, my eyes fixed on her as she was turning into the building's entrance. She was all that I saw. Until it was too late.

I heard the screeching skid of tires, and the rest was a blur. The front of the van, the impact, the pavement. When I opened my eyes, I was flat on my back, looking up at an overcast sky. Then came the pain, in a continuous loop from my knees to my hips. A couple of people came rushing over, no doubt asking me if I was okay. But I couldn't hear them. Another person joined the circle hovering over me—a young man. He was the driver of the van.

My muddled gaze traveled down from his face to something he was wearing. It was a smock, white with orange and green lettering across the chest. The smock said MAXINE'S BOUQUET. Irony of ironies—I'd been hit by a florist.

I saw the person standing next to him. The doorman from Samantha Kent's building had come out to see what had happened. Like the others, he was staring down, waiting for me to move.

412 | *Howard Roughan*

The sight of him sucked the fog out of my head in an instant. The woman in the gray flannel Yankees cap, my Mystery Patient—she was on her way to Samantha Kent's apartment.

I jolted up and climbed to my feet. The pain was excruciating, yet I was off just the same, pushing past people and straight into the entrance of Ten-thirty Park Avenue.

"Hey!" I heard behind me. While everyone probably wanted to know where I was going, there was one man who *needed* to know: the doorman. Between a sprint and a hurried walk was my limping jog—right through his lobby.

I reached the two elevators and smacked the UP button. One of the doors opened immediately. Before stepping on, I took a quick glance over my shoulder. The doorman was heading right for me.

I pressed PH, and the door began to close. In the last second, I caught a glimpse of the doorman arriving too late. His face was very pissed off.

Up went the elevator. A moment to catch my breath—and to realize how much pain I was in. Yet I was lucky. Had the van driver been any slower on his brakes, I would've been dead, for sure.

But was I too late? Would Samantha Kent survive as well?

The elevator door opened. I got off and listened. There were two apartments: at three o'clock and nine o'clock. Hearing nothing, I started left, when over my shoulder I heard a crash. I turned and rushed to the opposite door. A twist of the knob, and I was in.

I heard a scream, raw and guttural. There was grunting and what sounded like gasping for air. It was coming from down the hallway in front of me. As fast as I could, I ran past a kitchen and a dining room. The noise—the struggle—getting louder as I got closer. Until it was right in front of me.

What I saw first was the knife, the long, steel blade raised in the air and angled straight down. It was trembling. *They* were trembling. Standing toe-to-toe, Samantha Kent fending off the downward thrust of my Mystery Patient. Their arms were extended, locked at the elbows, but of the two of them, only Samantha Kent's legs were buckling. She was fighting a losing battle.

Do something, David. Head down, teeth gnashing, I charged across the room and tackled high. Her Yankees cap went flying. So did the rest of her. As we tumbled and headed toward the ground, I tried to spot the knife. Had it dropped? I couldn't see it.

I also couldn't see the wall. I careened into it. The impact was hard. On the heels of being tattooed by that delivery van, the feeling was agony.

The knife was on the floor a yard away. But so was my Mystery Patient. She rolled left, then right, woozy from our collision.

Get the knife, David. I pushed off the wall and onto my knees. I was dizzy. The room was spinning. Wait! There were *two* knives in front of me. Two of everything—double vision. Two knives: one real, the other not. How fitting. Unfortunately, it was the fake Samantha Kent who knew which one was real.

Her body stretched, and her hand reached. I couldn't stop her. She started to get up. Like a punch-drunk fighter, I did the same. I was back to seeing one of everything again. My Mystery Patient was standing before me with the knife gripped in her hand.

She lunged, but it wasn't a lunge. It was a bullet ripping through her. In the back and out the front. Fired from a gun held tightly in the hands of Samantha Kent. The one and only.

The body of the woman I'd once known as my patient went rigid. Then it went limp. She fell to the ground as the blood seeped from her stomach. It was soaked up like a sponge by a beige carpet, and for the first time, I noticed where I was. Where we all were. It was the living room.

Though not for my Mystery Patient. She was dead.

As soon as Samantha Kent pulled the trigger and quite possibly saved my life, she collapsed to the floor. I thought maybe she'd been stabbed while defending herself, but as I rushed to her side, there was no blood to be seen. My best guess was that she'd fainted.

"Freeze!"

Man, did that ever sound familiar. Slowly I turned to face two cops with their guns drawn, and slowly I put my hands up.

Right behind the two cops were two paramedics. They all thought they were responding to an accident, a guy hit by a delivery van. They didn't expect to arrive on the scene and learn from a ticked-off doorman that said guy had decided to make a mad hobble up to the penthouse. Of course, that was nothing compared to their hearing the gunshot while stepping off the elevator.

So there I was. One dead woman, one unconscious woman, and me. *I can explain everything, Officers. . . .*

Luckily, I didn't have to. As one paramedic confirmed the death of my Mystery Patient, the other waved some smelling salts under Samantha Kent's nose. She came to. She was shaky, groggy, and a little dizzy, for sure. But she was also something else. Thankful.

Samantha Kent rose slowly to her feet. As tears began to trickle down her cheeks, she walked over to me. I lowered my arms, while the cops lowered their guns. The woman who earlier had screamed that she wanted to kill me wanted to hug me now.

"Thank you," she said softly.

I hugged her back. "Thank *you.*"

She squeezed a little tighter, and I nearly fainted from the pain. The paramedics made it clear there was a hospital and an X-ray machine in my immediate future. Even more immediate was the cops' need to figure out what had happened.

We went into a den, away from the image of death sprawled on the carpet. That's where Samantha Kent did her best to explain. Beginning with the phone call she'd received the day before.

It was from a woman claiming to work in the human resources department of Conrad Birch's firm. The woman said she needed a spousal signature on some documents so the final dividends from Birch's 401(k) money could be paid out. She offered to come by Samantha Kent's apartment the next morning, since she herself lived not too far away. A time was set: nine-thirty, Saturday morning. Like that, my Mystery Patient was in.

"She looked so normal when I opened the door," said Samantha Kent. "I led her back to the living room and offered to make coffee. I never even made it to the kitchen."

Prompting her to turn around was what she described as a rustling noise. "It wasn't loud or anything, yet for some reason, it made me glance over my shoulder. Thank God I did."

What she saw was the woman pulling a large knife out of her bag. "The next thing I knew, she was charging right at me." Samantha Kent shuddered, as if reliving the moment. "The rest was a blur."

She described the way she tried to fight off the woman. "I wasn't as strong as she was. I didn't know how much longer I could hold her off. And then . . ." She couldn't finish the sentence.

I finished it for her. "That's when I showed up, I guess."

The cops turned to me. Up until that point, they hadn't made the connection. "You're that psychologist," said one of the cops. I watched the other cop as he looked at Samantha Kent. He didn't say anything, though I could tell what he was thinking: *And you're that murdered guy's wife.* Putting it together, both turned in the direction of the living room, where the paramedics were assisting the guys from the morgue. Almost in unison, they asked, "Is she . . ."

I nodded. "Yes," I said. She was my Mystery Patient.

I began to explain how it happened that I was there. Hearing myself talk, I realized how unbelievable it must have sounded. When I finished, the looks were priceless. They knew I had to be telling the truth. Who on earth could ever make something like that up?

One of the cops cracked a joke to that effect, and in the first real moment of levity, everyone allowed for a brief chuckle. Laughing hurt like hell, and there was no way to hide it.

"You should really go to the hospital," Samantha Kent said.

The cops agreed, saying they could fill in any blanks on their report later. They called to the paramedics, who came to the den.

"We'd like you to go as well, Ms. Kent," said one of them.

She'd have nothing to do with it. "I'm okay," she said. "What I'd really like is to answer any further questions you might have, Officers. Then I'm going to pack a suitcase, check into a hotel, and call my Realtor. Would any of you gentlemen like to buy an apartment?"

Just then a stretcher was brought in for me. I climbed aboard and let the paramedics strap me in. Immediately we were off.

An hour later, X-rays at Lenox Hill Hospital showed three broken ribs. "A hat trick," claimed the doctor who examined me. "Avoid comedy clubs, shiatsu massages, and all middleweight-title fights."

"There's nothing you can do?"

"Nothing the body doesn't do better and faster by itself."

"What about the pain?"

"That I can do something about. Wait here, and a nurse will get you a Percodan prescription."

"Here" was a curtained-off area of the emergency room. I realized I should probably get in touch with a few people and fill them in. That's when I also realized I left my cell phone back in the Hyundai.

The need for a phone was instantly abated by a familiar voice outside the curtain. "Paging Dr. Remler . . . Dr. Remler."

"C'mon in, Parker."

And Stacy right behind him. They maneuvered around the curtain and immediately shook their heads upon seeing me.

"What the hell were you thinking?" asked Parker.

Stacy kissed me on the forehead. "My hero!" she gushed.

I filled them in on what had happened. They could hardly believe it. Then I asked how they'd heard.

"Terry called me," said Parker. "She should be here any minute."

"How'd she know?"

"A reporter buddy of Victor's was monitoring the police band, looking for tomorrow's story. He called Victor, who's in Connecticut playing golf. Victor got in touch with Terry."

As if on cue, she poked her head around the curtain. "Thank God!" she said. She was clearly more than my lawyer at that moment, and I watched as Parker and Stacy pretended not to notice.

I told the story again to Terry. Parker and Stacy hardly minded. Even after hearing it a second time, they still couldn't get over it.

"So after all this, who was she?" asked Stacy.

I'd been wheeled out of Samantha Kent's apartment before the determination could be made. "You'd think she'd have some identification on her," I said. "Maybe not."

"We'll know soon," said Terry. "I'll make some calls in a bit."

So for a bit more time, my Mystery Patient would remain a mystery. The difference now was that I was certain she had no further moves to make. It was a terrific feeling that I could sum up in one word: "checkmate."

There was just one problem, though. Something I didn't know. *There was more than one game being played.*

PART V

13

HER name was Haley Morgan. Age thirty-two. Only child of Adam and Shirley Morgan. Both deceased. Lived by herself in a studio apartment in Chelsea.

She did a few small acting jobs and some modeling, mainly catalogue stuff. In lean times, which was most of the time, she worked as an office temp. That was the hook. A little over two years before, she'd been assigned for a few months to a Wall Street investment firm. The same firm where Conrad Birch worked.

End of story. At least as far as the papers and local news broadcasts were concerned. In the twenty-four hours after my leaving the hospital—and in between a steady diet of Percodan and sleep—I took it all in.

"But there's more, isn't there?"

I looked across the table and watched Terry react to my question with a knowing smile. Two days after the fact, and we were having our agreed-to "when this whole thing is over" dinner.

"Yes, there's more. The press haven't gotten ahold of her rap sheet yet. Two priors—one for cocaine possession, the other for theft of a doctor's prescription pad," she said. "Sad thing is, Haley Morgan was a smart girl. Graduated from Vassar."

"Did you get all this extra stuff from The Magnet?" I asked.

"No. From her actual police file. As you might imagine, those guys are pretty tail-between-the-legs on this one. The more they feed us, the less we'll rub their noses in it publicly. Hemmerson left a message on my voice mail at work. He did his best to sound gracious, even said he wanted to buy me a drink."

"What a guy. Any chance you'll hear from Trentino and Lopez?"

"The same chance you will," she said. "Somewhere between slim and none. That reminds me, though. Victor mentioned he was going to call you. Did you hear from him?"

"Yes. A congratulatory call. He told me what I did took guts, and I told him that 'stupidity' was probably a better word. As Victor put it, all that mattered was the result."

"He's very Machiavellian that way," she said. "Though he does have his Miss Manners side as well. He wrote Samantha Kent a note on behalf of the firm. A nice touch."

"I agree. What did the note say?"

"I don't know. She almost didn't get it. Victor had it messengered, only to find out she's not living in her apartment anymore. A doorman revealed she'd checked into the Drake."

"She did say something about going to a hotel. Can't blame her."

Terry filled me in on her recent chat with The Magnet. She'd asked him how Haley Morgan had been able to prevent me from recording our telephone conversation.

Explained Terry, "It's called a sprayer. It's this device that emits a high-frequency pitch preventing the magnetic recording of any fiber-optic transmission. They're available on the Internet."

"What isn't? Nonetheless, it strikes me as odd that Haley Morgan would know about a device like this, let alone have one," I said.

"There's something else," Terry said. "Apparently, Anthony did a little checking into Haley. About a year ago, she had an abortion."

I nodded with slow understanding. It might explain why Haley hated Conrad Birch so much. Also why she chose to make a child the centerpiece of her deception.

Our plates were cleared; the table, brushed free of crumbs. A touch of symbolism, perhaps, since it was about then that Terry and I realized this was supposed to be a date, not a debriefing session.

The conversation moved from the past to the future.

Usually, couples got the background down about each other—hometowns, hobbies, number of siblings—before any emotional connection was struck. With Terry and me, it was the opposite. The trenchlike experience of the trial, the time vested in a shared effort, had allowed our feelings to take shape and then bond. Straggling behind were the basic facts.

One of them, my widower status, Terry tackled head-on. She had no problem discussing my emotional connection to someone else, and what could've been a minefield in our relationship turned out to be the most meaningful exchange we'd had so far.

Watching her listen to me and then follow up with the right questions, I knew she understood that this was a part of who I was. I knew I was finally ready to move on with my life.

I held Terry's hand as we walked a few blocks after leaving the restaurant. I didn't let go during the cab ride back to my apartment. We kissed in the elevator. We kissed outside my door.

We stood facing each other in my bedroom. "I haven't done this for a few years," I said.

"Would you like me to draw a diagram or something?"

"No. The mechanics I remember. It's the nuances I might be a little rusty on."

"Sounds like you're about to give a piano recital."

I looked into her eyes, not wanting to blink. The more I stared at her, the more comfortable I felt. There was no pain. No broken ribs. No reminders of a life I'd been afraid to let go of.

She gently pressed her body against mine, whispering in my ear, "I think this is going to be good."

THE word had gotten out, and out of the woodwork they came—the people from my not-too-distant past who'd kept their distance.

There were the former patients who wanted to return. There were the tenants in my building who no longer had to look away when walking by me.

Then there was my esteemed literary agent, Debra Walker Coyne.

To be fair, she'd had no aversion to talking to me during the whole ordeal. She'd phoned to discuss business—foreign licensing of my book, that sort of thing—and never failed to ask how I was doing and express her support. Nonetheless, I couldn't help harboring a cynical suspicion that she had it all worked out in her head. Guilty or innocent, I was a good book in the making.

Cut to the Grill Room at the Four Seasons. Her usual table.

"So how's my favorite best-selling and now truly famous author doing?" said Debra, standing up to give me a kiss on the cheek. "I knew there was no way you could've stabbed someone fifty times over. Your writing style is far too succinct. That's why your next book has got to be about this whole experience."

"I'm not sure this is something I really want to capitalize on," I said as I sat down and unfolded my napkin.

As if to change the subject while making sure to stay right on it, she asked me about some of the players involved—the detectives, my lawyers, the grieving widow. Most notably, she was curious about Haley Morgan, my Mystery Patient.

I told her what I knew, which wasn't much.

Debra frowned. "Did you at least find out if the police discovered anything where she lived?"

"Like what?"

"If you want to know the truth about a woman, all you have to do is rummage through her closets."

"I don't think that's an option."

"Maybe, maybe not. But you really should inquire with the police. I'll bet you they've gone through her apartment."

The thought had never occurred to me, and my blank expression said as much. Debra continued. "This woman nearly ruined your life, David. Just from a professional standpoint, aren't you the least bit curious about her?"

We ordered and ate, and all along, Debra kept up the full-court press on my writing about the ordeal. As she paid the hefty bill, I figured the least I could do was promise her I'd think about it.

After saying good-bye, I began walking uptown along Park

Avenue. *Just from a professional standpoint, aren't you the least bit curious about her?*

The more I walked, the more Debra's words echoed in my head. She'd asked a good question. I'd asked the same question myself. Repeatedly. Only to suppress the answer every time.

But no longer. As much as I wanted to leave Haley Morgan behind and get on with my life, I now realized I couldn't. She may have been dead, but her impact was living on. And it didn't take a rocket scientist to figure out why.

Haley had singled me out and made me her victim. The incredible anger I felt because of that had blocked any other emotion I might have felt for her. With her gone, however, the anger was starting to dissipate. Regret was creeping in.

If only she'd been my patient for real. If only Haley Morgan had come to me as Haley Morgan. Maybe she couldn't have been helped. All I knew was, I'd never know for sure. Which was precisely what was consuming me. Because I wanted to know something more. Until I did, there'd be other words echoing in my head as well: *No one can have more control over your life than you do.*

I came to a corner and a DON'T WALK sign. As I stood there, waiting, I happened to glance over at some benches in front of an office building. Sitting on one were two older men staring at what was between them—a chessboard.

I took out my cell phone and dialed.

ETHAN Greene looked at me as if I had three heads. "Do you realize what you're asking me to do?" We were at a bar near Rockefeller Center. I'd barely touched my Diet Coke.

"Yes," I said. "A favor."

"No. You're asking me to break the law."

"It's a small fracture, at best."

"Since when did you become the legal expert?"

"Since you dragged me into court to help you win your case."

Ethan took a sip of his beer. "Assuming for a second I get you into her apartment, what is it you intend to do?"

"I just want to look around for something that can help me better understand what motivated this woman. I have a feeling there's more to know."

"What are you telling me? This is a hunch?"

"Not quite that random. I spent a lot of time with her," I said.

"Yes, as she was *pretending to be someone else.*"

"I realize that, but I have to believe parts of her, the real her, managed to slip through. I just want to know what those parts are."

"But what if you're wrong? What if there's nothing to know?"

"If that's what I find out, fine," I said. "It's the not knowing either way that's bothering me."

Ethan emptied his glass and set it down hard on the bar. "Okay," he said. "But you didn't get the key from me. You'll have it, but it won't touch my hands at any time."

I thanked him profusely and asked when I could be expecting it.

"Tomorrow, two days tops."

The next morning, a little after nine, there was a loud knock on my door. I opened it to see a bike messenger with dreadlocks. He asked me if I was Dr. Remler.

I told him I was.

He gave me a small manila envelope and was off.

THE cab dropped me off on Eighteenth Street between Ninth and Tenth avenues. I unlocked the glass door to Haley's brownstone and strolled in as if I lived there. Looking around the foyer, though, I was pretty glad I didn't. While far from a rathole, it had nondescript down to a tee. Everything seemed gray. The only color came from the Chinese take-out menus scattered by the mailboxes.

I headed up the stairs. Arriving on the third floor, I saw a web of yellow tape. The message was loud and clear: Keep out. Quickly I took out a pair of latex gloves from my pocket. It wasn't as if anyone had any reason to be taking fingerprints. Still, on they went.

I walked up to Haley's door, maneuvered around the yellow tape, and slid the key into the lock. With one twist, I entered her apartment. It was a small studio.

I stood in the middle of the room and did a three-sixty. A bed, a bookcase, a chest of drawers, a sofa, a kitchenette. Scattered clothes, magazines, and books. All novels—beach reads, mainly.

I checked Haley's closet. Suitcases and shoe boxes crammed the shelf above the crush of hanging clothes. A fan, a humidifier, and an overstuffed hamper took up the floor.

I stepped back and turned, facing the rest of the apartment.

The more trivial the items I saw, the more I realized where pay dirt might lie. A diary, for instance. A yearbook, even. But neither was anywhere to be found.

I began to think of my conversation with Ethan. *But what if you're wrong? What if there's nothing to know?*

Word for word, I remembered my answer: *If that's what I find out, fine. It's the not knowing either way that's bothering me.*

I sat down on Haley's sofa and wondered if I really meant it. Could I leave and be satisfied? Could I just walk away now and never look back? To my surprise, the answer was yes.

Maybe it was the same thing that had brought me there—all my years as a therapist. I'd learned the hard truth: There is only so much you can do to help someone . . . including yourself.

I stood up, took a breath, and headed for the door. I was simply going to walk away. But just for the hell of it, I took one look back.

The next thing I knew, I was on an airplane.

THE seat-belt sign lit up, and the captain announced our descent. The temperature in Atlanta, he said, was seventy-two degrees.

On the way to the airport, I'd made the call on my cell phone, posing as a telemarketer. I asked if her name was Evelyn Stark. She said it was. She also said she wasn't interested in whatever it was I was selling, and hung up.

I'd gotten what I needed—confirmation. The knowledge it was her, Evelyn Stark. *Haley's birth mother.*

Haley was indeed adopted, just like she'd told me. Only when she told me, she was posing as Samantha Kent.

It had become clear with a card. A Hallmark with flowers and the words *For My Daughter* on the front. The card was inside a yellow envelope, a corner of which was peeking out from beneath a jewelry box on Haley's chest of drawers. When I was looking from a few feet away, it was barely visible. When I was looking back from the doorway of her apartment, it was practically neon.

The message inside was brief:

> To my daughter Haley,
> It means so much that you've found me after all these years. Thank you for forgiving me. I won't tell anyone what you've told me.
>
> Love, Evelyn

Immediately, I'd flashed back to the conversation with Haley about her mother, how making contact could be a good thing. Again, real advice for a real situation in an otherwise complete lie.

But what amazed me was that it was such a paradox. The warmth of reconnecting with her birth mother amid the brutally cold murder of Conrad Birch. Not to mention my being framed for it.

Then there was the last line on the card: *I won't tell anyone what you've told me.* Had Haley really discussed what she'd done? It seemed so unlikely. All I knew for sure was, I'd be leaving Haley's apartment the same way I arrived—wanting to know more.

And pointing me in the right direction was the front of the envelope in the upper-left-hand corner, a return address sticker:

> Ms. Evelyn Stark
> 114 Traeger Mill Road
> Griffin, GA 30224

Three-plus hours and one Delta Shuttle later, I was renting a car at the Atlanta airport. The free map at the counter got me to Griffin. A gas-station attendant got me right to the house, a tiny ranch.

She opened the door.

"Ms. Stark, my name is Dr. David Remler."

It took only one look at her to know the woman standing before me in a worn, faded blue robe had the hardened gaze of someone who had nothing left to fear. This was the woman who'd put Haley Morgan up for adoption.

And now I was about to tell her Haley was dead.

"I'm here about your daughter," I said.

"My daughter?"

Her cold stare said it all—I knew something I wasn't supposed to know. "Yes, ma'am," I said. "I'm a psychologist."

"Haley never mentioned a psychologist. Is she your patient?"

Present tense. She had no idea Haley was dead.

"Ms. Stark, I'm afraid I have some horrible news for you."

The cold stare remained fixed on me as I told her. Finally she asked when it happened and where. "Last week in Manhattan," I said. She nodded and fell silent. I expressed how sorry I was, and she nodded again.

"I'm going to make some coffee," she announced. She only made it one step. She nearly collapsed to the ground. I caught her just in time, and she clung to me as if I were her capsized boat. The tears started, and she cried, the sound muffled against my shirt.

"Come, let's sit down," I said. I practically carried her to a couch in a wood-paneled room to my right.

After a few minutes, Evelyn Stark began to compose herself. I knew that meant she was going to want the details of her daughter's death. I'd have to edit, I told myself, but there was only so much I could leave out.

I decided to steer the conversation more to Haley's life, as opposed to her death. My motivation wasn't a hundred percent altruistic. I was looking for some answers of my own.

"So you obviously got to know Haley," I said.

"Only since last year."

She explained how she'd always wondered about her daughter. She wanted to find her, except she knew that if they were to meet, it would have to be Haley who initiated it. Lo and behold, she did.

"Last fall, she called me," said Evelyn. "A few weeks later, she came here for a visit. I haven't had many happy days, but that was one of them."

"Did Haley talk about being involved with a married man?"

"No."

"Did she seem angry about anything?"

"Not really."

With each shake of Evelyn's head, I became more disheartened. I'd felt so strongly about tracking down this woman and talking to her, so strongly that there was something to learn.

"Ms. Stark, what *did* you and your daughter talk about?"

"We talked about a lot of things, trying to make up for the lost time. It sounded like she was raised by a good family. She went to college, and she told me about the modeling she'd done. She was very pretty." Evelyn stopped. "Would you like to see the picture?"

"What picture's that?"

She explained that Haley had brought a camera down with her, and they'd taken some pictures using that "thingy" where you could press a button and then hurry into the picture. A week later, she said, Haley mailed her a copy of one of the shots.

Evelyn got off the couch and went to a cluttered bookcase. She pulled down a small box from the top shelf. "I keep it in a special place," she said.

She opened the box, took out a picture, and handed it to me.

I saw two women smiling, a mother and daughter reunited, sitting on the same couch I was. "This is really nice," I said. I was about to give the picture back, when my hand froze. That's when I saw it.

A simple date printed in the bottom-right-hand corner of the picture. The same date Conrad Birch had been stabbed more than fifty times. Hackers' Night.

I asked Evelyn if the date was right. Perhaps the camera had been programmed wrong, the internal calendar never set correctly.

"No," she said, looking at the picture again. "That's when Haley was here. It was the night before Halloween. I remember because the next day, before she left, she went to the market and bought me some candy to give out to the kids."

The next day? "You mean, Haley spent the night here with you?"

"Yes."

"The *whole* night, you're saying, right?"

"Yes. Why?"

My head was dizzy. If Haley was down in Georgia, she couldn't have been up in Manhattan. Then again, who said she was? She could've called me the night of the murder from anywhere. Now it was all making sense: Haley Morgan wasn't working alone.

"Ms. Stark, I have to ask you a favor," I said, trying to remain calm. "I need to borrow this picture for a day."

"Where are you going with it?" she asked.

"Home to Manhattan. I promise I'll overnight it back to you on Monday."

She hardly looked convinced. "It's not that I don't trust you—"

"I understand," I said. "But what I haven't told you is why I need the picture. I'm going to be showing it to the police."

"Why?"

"Because I think it proves your daughter didn't kill anyone."

The change in her face said it all. I represented a shot at redemption for Haley. "You say you promise to send it back?"

"Yes. You have my word."

I apologized again for having to be the bearer of such bad news. Then I hustled out of there, picture in hand.

I headed toward the airport. There was a plane to catch, but more important, there was a phone call to make. To Terry. I'd tell her what happened, and she'd tell the police. They needed to know there was a killer at large. Samantha Kent might still be a target.

I grabbed my cell phone and glanced at my watch—six twenty-five. I dialed Terry at her apartment. The good news about the hell I was about to catch for making this trip behind her back was that she was probably going to forget we had eight-o'clock dinner reservations. Three rings . . . four rings. *C'mon, Terry, be there.*

She wasn't. I left a message on her machine to call me as soon as possible and tried next to reach her on her cell phone. Not picking up at home, not picking up on her cell phone. *Where is she?*

I next tried Victor. I called his home and then his cell phone, both with no luck.

I drove another mile, thinking of what to do. The knee-jerk move was to call the police, maybe even try to get ahold of Detectives Trentino and Lopez. They'd never believed me before. Now they had to. In my mind, I went over what I'd tell them. That I'd gone to see Haley Morgan's birth mother and— I could see their faces. Hear their questions. Why was I visiting the mother? How did I find out who she was and where she lived? I'd have to give them answers while at the same time protecting Ethan. I'd have to lie.

Or better yet, I'd call Samantha Kent directly. She'd undoubtedly start to panic once she heard what I had to say. But I'd do my best to calm her down. Then I'd casually suggest she double-lock her door, slide a dresser against it, and immediately hide under the bed.

"What city, please?"

"Manhattan . . . the Drake Hotel."

I got the number and called, asking for her room. It rang eight times before switching to voice mail. I gave my cell number and told her to call as soon as she could. Then I called Delta to reserve a seat on the next New York flight.

"There's one leaving at nine-forty tonight," said the agent.

"Nothing earlier?"

"There's a seven-thirty, but that's in less than an hour."

I looked at my watch again—six thirty-five. She was right; there was no way I'd make it. "The nine-forty it is, then."

As soon as I hung up, my cell phone rang. "Hello?"

"Dr. Remler?" It was Samantha Kent. Thinking she might have called in for her messages, I immediately asked where she was.

"I'm here at the Drake. I was on the other line," she said. "Is there some sort of problem?"

"Not yet," I said. "But something's happened. It's a long story, but the bottom line is that Haley Morgan didn't kill your husband."

It took her a second. *"What?"*

"The night Conrad was murdered, Haley was in Griffin, Georgia. That's where Evelyn Stark lives—she's Haley's birth mother. Haley was staying with her that very same night."

"How do you know?"

"Because I just came from Georgia."

"If Haley Morgan didn't kill Conrad, who did?"

"She must have been working with someone."

"Oh, God, David. That woman from the trial: Gabrielle Dennis."

The other mistress. Maybe. Somehow working with Haley, she came forward *posing* as the mistress to try to derail my defense.

"What do you mean? Did you talk to her?" I asked.

"She called me yesterday," said Samantha. "She said she wanted to tell me in person how sorry she was."

"You didn't—"

"No. I told her that couldn't happen. I obviously want nothing to do with her. Except she was so persistent. Now I'm afraid."

"Does she know where you're staying?"

"Yes," she said, her voice quavering. "I had all the calls to my apartment automatically forwarded here to the hotel." She was sounding more and more terrified. "What should I do?"

I was about to tell her to call the police, when I heard a beep on the line. It was my call-waiting. I figured it was Terry. Thank God. "Hold on a second, okay?"

I switched over and was right. "We're still on for dinner, aren't we?" came Terry's voice, chipper.

"Not exactly," I said. "Where are you right now?"

"Walking out of the gym. Why? What's wrong?"

I told her as fast as I could. I also told her I had Samantha Kent on the other line. "She's scared to death," I said. "I was going to have her call the police."

Terry interrupted. "I have an idea. I don't want you to call the police until you're back here with that picture. In the meantime, she should go to my place. Give her my address, and tell her I'll be there myself in fifteen minutes."

"Good, thanks," I said. "I'll come straight there after I land."

I got back to Samantha and filled her in on the plan. Right as I finished, my cell cut off. My battery was toast. I floored it to try to make that seven-thirty Delta flight.

After spending the next twenty minutes violating every speed limit there was, doing a near tuck-and-roll from my rental car, and storming the ticket counter, I caught a break at security. It was sparse with passengers, and I was able to zip through and sprint for the gate.

Two and a half hours later, I arrived at Terry's brownstone in the West Village. I buzzed and heard the return buzz of the front entrance unlocking. Hers was the top floor of the three-story walk-up. I took the steps two at a time.

I walked into the apartment and saw Terry sitting on the couch in her living room. I started to smile. Then everything went black.

"YOU couldn't leave well enough alone, could you?"

Those were the first words I heard when I opened my eyes. They were being spoken by Samantha Kent.

"No, you had to go ahead and play junior detective." She was sitting at a small table in Terry's kitchen, legs crossed, lit cigarette in hand. "And look where it got you."

On the floor, to be exact. Facedown, arms and legs tied together with duct tape. Next to me was Terry in the same position. A gash on her forehead was caked with dried blood. No telling how long I'd been knocked out.

"So what do you have to say for yourself, David?"

It was a rhetorical question. The strip of duct tape over my mouth made sure of it. Terry's mouth was covered as well.

I was still groggy, but the big dots were easy to connect. Haley Morgan had been working with someone, all right. Though, as partnerships went, "confounding" didn't begin to describe it. A man's mistress and the wife he was cheating on. Score one for the ladies.

I tried to lift my head to get a better look at Samantha. I cringed in pain. If the piece of cookware sitting atop the table next to her was any indication, I'd taken a blow to the head from a saucepan.

"Mmmmph," I said.

Samantha looked at me with a pensive smile. "Got something to say, David? Of course you do. So many questions." She leaned forward. "You're not going to do anything stupid, like yell, are you?"

I shook my head.

She got up from her chair. Before walking toward me, however, she picked up the saucepan. Just in case.

In one motion, she grabbed the tape and ripped it off my mouth. For a moment, she stood there, hovering with the saucepan.

"Are you okay?" I immediately asked Terry.

She nodded.

Samantha sat back down. "Now, what would you like to ask?"

I summed it up in one word. "Why?"

She glanced at Terry before fixing her gaze back on me. "That is the question, isn't it—why? Why did I want Conrad dead? Why would I seemingly team up with the woman he was cheating with? And why were you the fall guy?" She looked at her watch. "As much as I'd like to fill you in, I'm afraid I'm a little short on time."

I glanced at my bound hands. "I was thinking the same thing."

"A morbid sense of humor. I like that. Conrad had one as well."

"Before you killed him."

"*Yes,* before I killed him."

"All because he cheated on you."

She drew off her cigarette. "Were this only about hurt feelings."

"What else could it be about?"

"Try money."

I didn't follow. She was an heiress. "An insurance policy?"

"You could call it that," she said. "The problem is, it expired early last year. Right on our tenth wedding anniversary."

I now followed. She was talking about a prenuptial agreement. Clearly, as successful as Conrad was, his money was no match for the Kent family fortune. "There was no infidelity rider?" I asked.

"Ah, you mean a bad-boy clause? Yes, it was in there, but in the legal give-and-take, it didn't carry on. I wanted it extended past the ten years, but that was the give for getting the ten years in the first place. His lawyer had been pushing for seven."

"How much did he stand to make off you?"

"About seventy million," she said coolly.

"So instead of paying Conrad, you preferred to kill him?"

"First off, we're talking about *seventy million dollars.* Second, there are more sympathetic figures than Conrad hanging on the wall in the post office. And were she still alive, Haley Morgan would've backed me up on that."

Now we were really getting into it. And the longer we talked, the better chance I had to think of something. An angle. A way out.

"You and Haley—a strange partnership, don't you think?"

"Actually, that was the beauty of it. There's something more dangerous than a woman scorned. *Two* women scorned."

"In Haley's case, because Conrad broke off the affair, right?"

"Haley was angry, all right, and when she showed up on my doorstep, her intent was to turn my world upside down. But all I could do was stare at her black eye. Conrad hit her right after she confronted him."

"About what?"

"The drug he secretly slipped her for a few days after she told him she was pregnant. The bastard. I know you're not *that* kind of doctor, but I suspect you've heard of mifepristone."

I had. It was now more commonly known as RU-486.

Samantha continued. "The doctor found traces of it in her blood after she lost the baby. Needless to say, she was ripe for revenge."

Okay. "But murder?"

"It wasn't her first impulse. That's why I supplied her with an additional five hundred thousand reasons to go through with it. Half up front, half on the back end, and all payable in cash. It was a lot of money for someone who didn't have any, especially with her sugar daddy having left."

"So what went wrong?" I asked. "Haley wanted to kill you."

"No. The only thing she wanted that morning in my apartment was the balance of her money. I, naturally, had other plans."

"Killing her, you mean."

"She *was* having an affair with my husband, after all. Besides, she got made. Her picture was everywhere." Samantha took a final pull off her cigarette and stubbed it out on the table. "I must say, though, it was like she had eyes in the back of her head."

I could envision Samantha going after Haley. Using a knife—Conrad's murder weapon—so it would appear to be the other way around. But Haley had sensed the ambush. She turned just in time. A struggle ensued. Then I came rushing in.

Samantha clapped her hands slowly. "You saved the day, David."

I could see Haley's face now. I could see her eyes. They were staring into mine at the moment she picked up the knife from the living-room carpet. I was sure she was going to lunge at me. Now I knew otherwise. What I was really looking at in that split second was a woman trapped.

In the promise of a lie.

And when the bullet had ripped through her body another split second later, Samantha made sure it would stay that way.

"Given what you've said about Haley's being pregnant, I'm beginning to think Conrad never used me as a foil with her."

"You're right. She never knew Conrad had seen a psychologist. But I did."

"How?"

"I happened to stumble across the check Conrad had written you for his first session. Problem was, I never saw another."

"Because there never was another session."

"Exactly. Only I couldn't know that for sure. So months later, when the prenup expired and I learned about Haley, you became a serious loose end. Had Conrad been seeing you on a regular basis, there was no telling the things you knew. Were Conrad suddenly to die, I could ill afford to have you coming forward and implicating me. As it was, he ended up saying plenty in just your one session."

"He intended to break off the affair."

"No, but he intended to establish that *impression*. If I was to find out about the affair while the prenup was still in force, his lawyers would drag you into court to show his conflicted state of mind. Maybe instead of seventy million, he'd end up with thirty-five."

"So I was being used by everybody."

"Nothing personal on my part. I didn't even know you."

"Which unto itself was instrumental to your plan."

"Yes, but that paled in comparison to your book." She laughed. "What a premise—good people doing bad things for seemingly no apparent reason. Hell, David, it was like you were asking for it."

"So you had no problem framing me? It was that easy for you?"

She shook her head. "You're trying to turn this into a session. Get the facts, and then get inside my head. Maybe talk your way out of this. Nice of me to play along, don't you think?"

"Let me just ask you another question."

Samantha looked at her watch again. "I'm afraid I've indulged you long enough." She rubbed her chin, her eyes darting back and forth between Terry and me. "What am I going to do with you two?"

If only I thought she was actually mulling it over.

She stood up and walked over to me, the strip of duct tape in her hand. She slapped it back on my mouth.

She turned a knob on the stove. From the corner of my eye, I could see a blue flame. She blew it out. The pungent smell of gas began to fill the kitchen.

Samantha proceeded over to one of the cabinets and opened it. She knelt and reached in. Out came a square metal baking pan.

"I suppose there's a chance the police will ask why you called me earlier, David."

She stepped over Terry and me to the sink and turned the faucet on. She hummed while filling the pan up with some water.

"I'll tell them, of course, you were inviting me over for dinner with your new steady."

The gas, the metal baking pan, the water—there was only one place Samantha was heading next: the microwave.

"Shame, I had other plans."

She slid the pan in, slammed the door shut, and punched a few buttons. The microwave lit up with a soft glow.

"Otherwise they'd have to get *three* sets of dental records."

There'd be no more lingering. No more Q&A. After all that, Samantha simply looked at us with a sick grin. "*Bon appétit,* guys."

Out the door she walked. She was gone. And in about five or six minutes, Terry and I would be as well. We were smack in the middle of a time bomb. That metal pan was destined to spark and catch fire, turning the microwave into a pressure cooker. Aided by the boiling water, the latch would eventually give, blowing the thing open right into the gas-filled room. *Boom.*

I looked at Terry. We couldn't talk, but we needed to communicate. More than that, we needed to think fast. Somehow we had to get free and out of that kitchen. That's when I saw her eyes go wide. She thought of something and, with a jerk of her head, tried to tell me. She motioned toward the cabinet next to the stove. There was something in there, she was trying to tell me.

With a rocking motion, I began to inch closer to the cabinet. Hands behind my back, I stretched and leaned, my fingertips just catching the front of the cabinet. Except the handle was too high. I dug my nails into the edge of the door until I could get a grip. I pulled it open. Inside were dish towels, oven cleaner, and tinfoil.

I turned back to Terry. *What am I looking for?*

She rolled her eyes around in circles.

Huh?

The tinfoil. The *roll* of tinfoil. Specifically, the serrated metal edge on the box. The next best thing to a knife.

I'd started to reach for it, when I heard a loud popping and looked up to see the first spark. Time was running out.

I fixed on the box again. It was propped on a shelf, midway up the cabinet.

I got it and pulled, clinging to it while I rocked back to Terry. *Pop!* Another spark lit up the microwave with an orange glow.

She tried to meet me halfway. We were back-to-back. She pushed her hands out, exposing as much of the tape around her wrists as possible. I angled the box, serrated edge down, until I had it aligned. Then I sawed. Above us, the microwave groaned, its walls beginning to feel the inexorable push. It was a matter of seconds.

Frantically I kept sawing as Terry tried to force the cuts in the tape with all her might. It wasn't working fast enough. I dropped the box and grabbed her wrists, feeling for the tape. If I could turn the cuts into tears, we had a shot. If not, we were surely dead.

I gave it all I had and all I had to live for. Until, with a sticky rip, the tape gave. Terry's hands were free. She immediately pushed herself up, rising to her bound feet and lunging for a drawer. She pulled out a pair of scissors and cut between her ankles, dropping back on the floor to do the same for me. As she hurried to release my arms, I looked at the microwave. Smoke was billowing out from the edges, thick and black. The pan was completely on fire.

With one last yank, the rest of the tape gave, and I sprang to my feet. We sprinted out of the kitchen and headed into the hallway. The floor, the walls, the ceiling—they all shook. The noise was deafening. The sheer force of the explosion slammed into our backs, practically lifting us off the ground. Were it not for Terry's last-minute pull on my arm, we would've been engulfed in flames.

The pull led to a dive and a crash landing in the bathroom. Amid the toppled walls and shattered glass, it was probably the thick porcelain tub we fell next to that saved us. We were bruised, and we were bloody. But we were alive.

I held Terry tight in my arms. Our bodies intertwined and our eyes locked.

"Mmmmph," she said. The duct tape was still on our mouths. We both ripped the strips off, easing the sting with a long kiss.

"So," I said when we took a breath, "do you still want to look at that picture of Haley and her mom before we call the police?"

"WE'RE going to have to change the ending from there."

"Why?"

"Every studio will balk. It would never test well," he said. "It's not *satisfying* enough."

"It sure was to me," I said.

Kevin Daniels smiled and ran a hand through his unruly brown hair. He was back for the first time since he'd left for Hollywood. The belly of the beast. In the interim, the *culturally retarded wayward whores destined to make feel-good-movie johns out of all of us* had finally bought one of his scripts. He was officially a screenwriter. Now, only a week after Samantha was arrested and charged with both first- and second-degree murder, he'd flown three thousand miles to meet with me. He wanted to adapt my story.

"All I'm suggesting is a slight change," he said. "Instead of you and Terry calling the police after the explosion, you go after Samantha yourselves. You need to be there when she's busted."

Truth was, I wish I had. It would've been great to see. The look on her face. The shock. The disbelief. It couldn't have been much different from *my* face when I first saw her for who she really was.

Sam Kent. Samantha Kent. Mrs. Samantha Kent.

There was only one other person who knew Haley Morgan didn't kill Conrad Birch, and that was her mother. And there was only one other person who knew she knew: Samantha. I'd conveniently supplied the name, the town, the state—everything she needed to track the mother down. So after bidding Terry and me a fond farewell, Samantha was no doubt off to Griffin, Georgia, to pay a visit to Evelyn Stark. She was going to make sure the secret died with her.

She never made it onto the airplane. With one phone call from Terry to the police, patrol cars were dispatched to Kennedy and La Guardia. They nabbed her at La Guardia.

After being caught, Samantha had the right to remain silent, but she chose to talk. Her lawyers weren't about to stop her. Their angle was criminal insanity, and despite the premeditation, they felt it was their best shot. I couldn't help marveling at what this meant: She immediately had to be evaluated by a shrink.

Don't ask me how I got my hands on the report. All I'll say is that it was filed electronically and logged in to a "lame" 128-bit encrypted computer network. Sorry, but after all that had happened, I couldn't resist looking at it.

In the course of two sessions, Samantha managed to be very forthcoming. She explained how she had slipped out of the Ritz-Carlton in Boston and made the drive down to Manhattan and back undetected. It was a round-trip that fell neatly between the time she placed her wake-up call request and when she received it.

There was also her getting Conrad's signature on the letter planted in my apartment. She simply caught him as he was rushing out to work and thrust in his face a stack of things for him to sign. "He doesn't bother to read anything," she claimed. "He just scribbles his name and barks out, 'Next!' "

Meanwhile, there was Haley. On the night of the murder, she had one job—calling me. What she obviously didn't tell Samantha was that she'd decided to do it from Griffin, Georgia. Maybe it was happenstance. Or maybe it was the shrewd move of someone who didn't trust her partner. Visiting her real mother for the first time doubled as an alibi for Haley. If it ever came to that. It never did.

Having Haley call me after my trial got suspended was Samantha's idea. The sprayer device they used belonged to Conrad. He apparently was paranoid about people taping his business dealings over the phone.

Threatening to kill the "bitch of a wife" Conrad ran back to would further insulate Samantha from suspicion. At least that's how she explained it to Haley. In reality, the call was about her getting away with murder for a second time. Were there to be any doubt, Samantha knew I'd gladly come forward and, seeking my own vindication, tell of the phone call I'd received.

Of course, how fast I came forward was of considerable surprise to her. She obviously had no idea I'd be staking out her apartment.

Still, she turned that miscalculation to her advantage. What's more, my showing up that morning most likely saved her life. Who knows what would've happened if I hadn't come bursting in.

And I had no clue what was really going on.

SPEAKING of which . . .

A few days after meeting with Kevin Daniels, I was walking from my office to the corner deli when a limousine pulled up. The rear-seat passenger called my name. It was Arnold Kesper.

His tinted window was half down, and he was peering out at me. I walked over to the curb.

"It's nice to see you again, Dr. Remler."

"You as well, Mr. Kesper."

"Can I give you a lift to wherever it is you're going?"

"It would be a short ride," I said. "I'm just going to the corner."

"In that case, can I delay your arrival there for a few minutes?"

He opened the door and began to slide over. I got in.

The first thing I noticed was that this wasn't the limo that took my date and me to the prom. This was a feast of burled walnut and soft leather. To either side were plasma screens and LCD monitors, all brandishing the latest news and market figures. Across from us sat the same petite and humorless-looking minion who'd ushered Kesper around the night of his cocktail party. She nodded slightly before going back to some paperwork in her lap.

Kesper watched as I took it all in. "On the subject of rides, you've had quite a wild one in the past year or so. First the rabbi trial and then your own."

"You heard about that, huh?"

"It was hard not to," he said. "I was quite intrigued."

"What did you think?"

"Do you mean whether I first thought you were guilty?" He flicked a piece of lint from his trousers. "To be perfectly honest, at first I was indifferent to your plight. Guilty or innocent, you seemed to face a predicament that was similar to the rabbi's. Two men asking to be taken at their word. Except you didn't believe the rabbi, did you? So perhaps it would've made sense if I didn't believe you."

"Mr. Kesper, I'm not offended if you had your doubts."

"You were right. I was wrong. You saw the situation for what it was, while I saw it for what I hoped it wasn't. Your vision proved to be far more enlightened than mine." He nodded at his minion, who reached to her side and picked up an envelope, handing it to me.

"What's this?" I asked.

"Something I no longer need."

I opened the envelope. Inside were pages of contact sheets, plus their negatives. In every picture was the same person: me.

Me walking into my office. Me hailing a cab outside my apartment building. Me exiting a Starbucks.

"One of the trappings of preposterous wealth, David, is the ability to do almost anything you want. Including finding out almost anything you want to know about anybody. There are people who, for one reason or another, fascinate me. You were such a person because of your role in the rabbi trial and the book you'd written. It made me curious about the kind of man you really are."

I sat there groping for a proper reaction. I wanted to be angry, wanted to lay into Kesper for his arrogance and disrespect. But most of all, I wanted to thank him. Because I knew what he'd done. Behind the last contact sheet was an enlargement of one of the shots. It had been taken the night of the Kesper Society cocktail party—my Mystery Patient and me standing outside the Metropolitan Museum of Art.

I stared at the picture, flashing back to that night, as well as to when I saw it for the first time in the chambers of Judge Lomax.

Said Kesper, "After I heard about the rabbi's confession note, my indifference to your situation changed. That's when I took a second look at the pictures I'd arranged to be taken. Miracle of miracles, there you were with the woman who fit your description."

"How did you know Judge Lomax would do what he did?"

"I didn't. But I figured sending him the photo would be a good first move. As it turned out, it was the only one needed."

"It certainly turned things around," I said. "For that, I can't thank you enough." I slid the pictures back into the envelope. I started to hand them to Kesper.

"No. Those are yours to keep. Or dispose of, whichever you prefer. I no longer have a need for them. I know what kind of man you really are." Arnold Kesper extended his hand. We shook. "Good luck, David."

"Thank you," I said. "Thank you for everything."

I reached for the door handle.

"Oh, I almost forgot," he said. "I have something else for you."

He nodded at his minion, who opened a file on the seat. She took out another envelope and handed it to me. I began to open it.

"Actually, why don't you do that outside," he said.

"Oh, okay, sure." I stepped out of the limo, which promptly took off. I watched it disappear into the traffic. I opened the envelope. Inside was a check made out to Crescent House. It looked like a check for a million dollars. Except it had an extra zero attached.

THREE years later.

It's got all the trappings of an official happy ending, but forgive my reluctance to call it that. Life, for all its wonders, has a nasty habit of reminding you that you're never *really* in control.

I'm still a practicing psychologist. I've got a full load of patients again. Mila remains my Mamka.

Samantha Kent got life without the possibility of parole. Not a single juror in her trial bought into the insanity plea. Interestingly enough, as pointed out by Victor, they were all college graduates.

Much to the consternation of Debra Walker Coyne, my agent, I never wrote a firsthand account of what happened to me. Instead, I let Kevin Daniels take his crack at the story. I must admit, he wrote a pretty good script, which a studio finally bought. But after floundering in development for a time, the project is now in turnaround.

"Them's the breaks," said my new bride.

Normally, Terry's falling for a guy she'd represented in a murder trial would've been an extremely bad career move. Except she always knew her career was changing. As of a year ago, she said good-bye to the world of criminal law to oversee the expansion of Crescent House to other cities. Owing to Arnold Kesper's ten-million-dollar donation, there's already been a few ribbon-cutting ceremonies. With more to come.

However, Terry won't be able to make the next one, which takes place in Chicago in a few weeks. You can't fly when you're beyond seven months pregnant.

We don't know if it's a boy or a girl. As for what we do know, Parker and Stacy will be the godparents. Also, we have the name picked out. In an effort to come up with a kid-friendly unisex name while still giving a nod to Terry's favorite book, we've decided on Harper Lee Remler. The nursery is ready.

Which brings me to one final thing. A while back, Terry found a safe-deposit-box key. She asked what it was for, and I told her.

I shared with her the story of the list my first wife had made when she was pregnant and how I'd found it after she died. Terry asked what was on the list, and I told her. I still had it memorized.

She listened and nodded. A lesser person would've left it at that. My past would've remained my past, and that list would've remained in that safe-deposit box. But not Terry. She's never worried about living in anyone's shadow. Which is why she'll never have to.

When she asked me if I'd get the list from the bank, I didn't know why she wanted it. Two days after I gave it to her, I found out. That's when I walked into the nursery and saw the list framed and hanging on the wall. "It's what *every* child should be taught," she said.

> *To love.*
> *To laugh.*
> *To laugh some more.*
> *To listen and learn.*
> *To say please and thank you.*
> *To have opinions.*
> *To respect those of others.*
> *To be honest.*
> *To be a friend.*
> *To be yourself.*

*N*ew York, New York—it's a wonderful town, or at least it was for Howard Roughan. After almost ten years of living among the city's many "cultures, restaurants, theaters, and maniac taxi drivers," Roughan and his wife moved to Connecticut to start a family. "People often feel compelled to wax poetic about their years living in Manhattan," says Roughan. "Truth was, we didn't want to raise a child who would be more clever and hip than his parents by the age of five."

Roughan, a former creative director in the advertising industry, admits that certain aspects of his personality tend to crop up in his writing—"especially the humor," he says. But what inspired him to make the main character of his second novel a psychologist? "I had a conversation with a woman who was seeing a psychologist," he recalls. "She spoke of how important trust was in her therapy. It got me thinking . . . and plotting. What if the doctor could be trusted, but not the patient? Before I knew it, I was outlining *The Promise of a Lie."*

Although he enjoyed the collaborative aspects of advertising, Roughan says that after a while, he wanted to do something creative that was all his own, and thus his full-time writing career was born. Says the author hopefully, "We'll see if I made the right decision."

"We didn't want to raise a child who would be more clever and hip than his parents."

My name is

Christopher John Francis Boone.

I know all the countries of the world

and their capital cities and

every prime number up to 7,507. . . .

I am writing a murder mystery novel.

the curious incident

of

the dog

in

the night-time

a novel

by

mark haddon

2.   IT WAS 7 minutes after midnight. The dog was lying on the grass in the middle of the lawn in front of Mrs. Shears's house. Its eyes were closed. It looked as if it was running on its side, the way dogs run when they think they are chasing a cat in a dream. But the dog was not running or asleep. The dog was dead. There was a garden fork sticking out of the dog. I decided that the dog was probably killed with the fork, because I could not see any other wounds in the dog and I do not think you would stick a garden fork into a dog after it had died for some other reason, like cancer, for example, or a road accident. But I could not be certain about this.

I went through Mrs. Shears's gate, closing it behind me. I walked onto her lawn and knelt beside the dog. I put my hand on the muzzle of the dog. It was still warm.

The dog was called Wellington. It belonged to Mrs. Shears, who was our friend. She lived on the opposite side of the road, two houses to the left.

Wellington was a poodle. Not one of the small poodles that have hairstyles, but a big poodle with curly black fur.

I stroked Wellington and wondered who had killed him and why.

My name is Christopher John Francis Boone. I know all the countries of the world and their capital cities and every prime number up to 7,507. Eight years ago, when I first met Siobhan, she showed me this picture

and I knew that it meant *sad,* which is what I felt when I found the dead dog.

Then she showed me this picture

and I knew that it meant *happy,* like when I'm reading about the Apollo space missions, or when I am still awake at 3:00 a.m. or 4:00 a.m. and I can walk up and down the street and pretend that I am the only person in the whole world. Then she drew some other pictures

but I was unable to say what these meant.

I got Siobhan to draw lots of these faces and then write down next to them exactly what they meant. I kept the piece of paper in my pocket and took it out when I didn't understand what someone was saying. But it was very difficult to decide which of the diagrams was most like the face they were making, because people's faces move very quickly.

When I told Siobhan that I was doing this, she got out a pencil and another piece of paper and said it probably made people feel very and then she laughed. So I tore the original piece of paper up and threw it away. And Siobhan apologized. And now if I don't know what someone is saying, I ask them what they mean or I walk away.

I PULLED the fork out of the dog and lifted him into my arms and hugged him. He was leaking blood from the fork holes.

I like dogs. You always know what a dog is thinking. It has four moods: happy, sad, cross, and concentrating. Also, dogs are faithful, and they do not tell lies, because they cannot talk.

I had been hugging the dog for 4 minutes when I heard screaming. I looked up and saw Mrs. Shears running toward me from the patio. She was wearing pajamas and a housecoat, and she had no shoes on. She was shouting, "What have you done to my dog?"

I do not like people shouting at me. It makes me scared that they are going to hit me or touch me and I do not know what is going to happen.

"Let go of the dog!" she shouted.

I put the dog down on the lawn and moved back 2 meters.

She bent down. I thought she was going to pick the dog up herself, but she didn't. Perhaps she noticed how much blood there was and didn't want to get dirty. Instead she started screaming again.

I put my hands over my ears and closed my eyes and rolled forward till I was hunched up with my forehead pressed onto the grass. The grass was wet and cold. It was nice.

3.   THIS is a murder mystery novel.

Siobhan said that I should write something I would want to read myself. Mostly I read books about science and maths. I do not like proper novels. In proper novels people say things like "I am veined with iron, with silver, and with streaks of common mud. I cannot contract into the firm fist which those clench who do not depend on stimulus." (I found this book in the library when Mother took me into town once.) What does this mean? I do not know. Nor does Father. Nor do Siobhan or Mr. Jeavons. I have asked them.

Siobhan has long blond hair and wears glasses made of green plastic. And Mr. Jeavons smells of soap and wears brown shoes that have approximately 60 tiny circular holes in each of them.

But I do like murder mystery novels. So I am writing a murder mystery novel.

In a murder mystery novel someone has to work out who the murderer is and then catch them. It is a puzzle. If it is a good puzzle, you can sometimes work out the answer before the end of the book.

Siobhan said that the book should begin with something to grab people's attention. That is why I started with the dog. I also started with the dog because it happened to me and I find it hard to imagine things that did not happen to me.

Siobhan read the first page and said that it was different. She put this word into inverted commas by making the wiggly quotation sign with her first and second fingers. She said that it was usually people who were killed in murder mystery novels. I said that 2 dogs were killed in *The Hound of the Baskervilles*—the hound itself and James Mortimer's spaniel—but Siobhan said they weren't the victims of the murder; Sir Charles Baskerville was. She said that this was because readers cared more about people than dogs, so if a person was killed in a book, readers would want to carry on reading.

I said that I wanted to write about something real and I did not know any people who had been killed except Edward's father from school, and that was a gliding accident, not murder, and I didn't really know him. I also said that I cared about dogs because they were faithful and honest, and some dogs were cleverer and more interesting than some people. Steve, for example, who comes to the school on Thursdays, needs help to eat his food and could not even fetch a stick. Siobhan asked me not to say this to Steve's mother.

THEN the police arrived. I like the police. They have uniforms and numbers, and you know what they are meant to be doing. There was a policewoman and a policeman. The policewoman had a hole in her tights on her left ankle and a red scratch in the middle of the hole. The policeman had a big leaf stuck to the bottom of his shoe.

The policewoman put her arms round Mrs. Shears and led her back toward the house.

I lifted my head off the grass. The policeman squatted down beside me and said, "Would you like to tell me what's going on here, young man?"

I sat up and said, "The dog is dead."

"I'd got that far," he said.

I said, "I think someone killed the dog."

"How old are you?" he asked.

I replied, "I am fifteen years and three months and two days."

"And what, precisely, were you doing in the garden?" he asked.

"I was holding the dog," I replied.

"And why were you holding the dog?" he asked.

This was a difficult question. It was something I wanted to do. I like dogs. It made me sad to see that the dog was dead. I wanted to answer the question properly, but the policeman did not give me enough time to work out the correct answer.

"Why were you holding the dog?" he asked again.

"I like dogs," I said.

"Did you kill the dog?" he asked.

I said, "I did not kill the dog."

"Is this your fork?" he asked.

I said, "No."

"You seem very upset about this," he said.

He was asking too many questions and he was asking them too quickly. They were stacking up in my head like loaves in the factory where Uncle Terry works. The factory is a bakery and he operates the slicing machines. And sometimes the slicer is not working fast enough, but the bread keeps coming and there is a blockage. I sometimes think of my mind as a machine, but not always as a bread-slicing machine. It makes it easier to explain to other people what is going on inside it.

The policeman said, "I am going to ask you once again . . ."

I rolled back onto the lawn and pressed my forehead to the ground again and made the noise that Father calls *groaning*. I make this noise when there is too much information coming into my head from the outside world. It is like when you are upset and you hold the radio against your ear and you tune it halfway between two stations, so all you get is white noise, and then you turn the volume right up, so this is all you can hear, and then you know you are safe because you cannot hear anything else.

The policeman took hold of my arm and lifted me onto my feet.

I didn't like him touching me like this. And this is when I hit him.

The policeman looked at me for a while without speaking. Then he said, "I am arresting you for assaulting a police officer."

This made me feel a lot calmer because it is what policemen say on television and in films.

Then he said, "I strongly advise you to get into the back of the police car, because if you try any of that monkey business again, I will seriously lose my rag. Is that understood?"

I walked over to the police car, which was parked just outside the gate. He opened the back door and I got inside. He climbed into the driver's seat and made a call on his radio to the policewoman who was still inside the house. He said, "The little bugger just had a pop at me, Kate. Can you hang on with Mrs. S. while I drop him off at the station? I'll get Tony to swing by and pick you up."

And she said, "Sure. I'll catch you later."

We drove off. The police car smelled of hot plastic and aftershave and take-away chips.

I watched the sky as we drove toward the town center. It was a clear night and you could see the Milky Way.

Some people think the Milky Way is a long line of stars, but it isn't. Our galaxy is a huge disk of stars millions of light-years across, and the solar system is somewhere near the outside edge of the disk.

And I thought about how, for a long time, scientists were puzzled by the fact that the sky is dark at night, even though there are billions of stars in the universe and there must be stars in every direction you look, so the sky should be full of starlight, because there is very little in the way to stop the light from reaching earth.

Then they worked out that the universe was expanding, that the stars were all rushing away from one another after the Big Bang, and the farther the stars were away from us, the faster they were moving, some of them nearly as fast as the speed of light, which was why their light never reached us.

I like this fact. It is something you can work out in your own mind just by looking at the sky above your head at night and thinking without having to ask anyone.

5. CHAPTERS in books are usually given the cardinal numbers 1, 2, 3, 4, 5, and so on. But I have decided to give my chapters prime numbers 2, 3, 5, 7, 11, and so on because I like prime numbers.

This is how you work out what prime numbers are. First you write down all the positive whole numbers in the world.

1	2	3	4	5	6	7	8	9	10
11	12	13	14	15	16	17	18	19	20
21	22	23	24	25	26	27	28	29	30
31	32	33	34	35	36	37	38	39	40
41	42	43	44	45	46	47	48	49	etc.

Then you take away all the numbers that are multiples of 2. Then you take away all the numbers that are multiples of 3. Then you take away all the numbers that are multiples of 4 and 5 and 6 and 7 and so on. The numbers that are left are the prime numbers.

	2	3		5		7			
11		13				17		19	
		23						29	
31						37			
41		43				47			etc.

The rule for working out prime numbers is really simple, but no one has ever worked out a simple formula for telling you whether a very big number is a prime number or what the next one will be. If a number is really, really big, it can take a computer years to work out whether it is a prime number.

Prime numbers are useful for writing codes and in America they are classed as Military Material, and if you find one over 100 digits long, you have to tell the CIA and they buy it off you for $10,000. But it would not be a very good way of making a living.

Prime numbers are what is left when you have taken all the patterns away. I think prime numbers are like life. They are very logical, but you could never work out the rules, even if you spent all your time thinking about them.

WHEN I got to the police station, they made me take the laces out of my shoes and empty my pockets at the front desk in case I had anything in them that I could use to kill myself or escape or attack a policeman with.

The sergeant behind the desk had very hairy hands. This is what I had in my pockets

1. A Swiss army knife with 13 attachments, including a wire stripper and a saw and a toothpick and tweezers

2. A piece of string

3. A piece of a wooden puzzle that looked like this

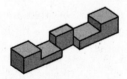

4. 3 pellets of rat food for Toby, my rat

5. £1.47 (This was made up of a £1 coin, a 20-pence coin, two 10-pence coins, a 5-pence coin, and a 2-pence coin.)

6. A red paper clip

7. A key for the front door

I was also wearing my watch and they wanted me to leave this at the desk as well, but I said that I needed to keep my watch on because I needed to know exactly what time it was. And when they tried to take it off me, I screamed, so they let me keep it on.

They asked me if I had any family. I said I did. They asked me who my family was. I said it was Father, but Mother was dead. And I said it was also Uncle Terry, but he was in Sunderland and he was Father's brother, and it was my grandparents, too, but three of them were dead and Grandma Burton was in a home because she had senile dementia and thought that I was someone on television.

Then they asked me for Father's phone number.

I told them that he had two numbers, one for at home and one that was a mobile phone, and I said both of them.

It was nice in the police cell. It was almost a perfect cube—2 meters long by 2 meters wide by 2 meters high. It contained approximately 8 cubic meters of air. It had a small window with bars and, on the opposite side, a metal door with a long, thin hatch near the floor for sliding trays of food into the cell and a sliding hatch higher up so that policemen could look in and check that prisoners hadn't escaped or committed suicide. There was also a padded bench.

I wondered how I would escape if I was in a story. It would be difficult, because the only things I had were my clothes and my shoes, which had no laces in them.

I decided that my best plan would be to wait for a really sunny day and then use my glasses to focus the sunlight on a piece of my clothing and start a fire. I would then make my escape when they saw the smoke and took me out of the cell.

I wondered whether Mrs. Shears had told the police that I had killed Wellington and whether, when the police found out that she had lied, she would go to prison. Because telling lies about people is called *slander*.

I FIND people confusing. This is for two main reasons.

The first main reason is that people do a lot of talking without using any words. Siobhan says if you raise one eyebrow, it can mean lots of different things. It can mean *I want to do sex with you,* and it can also mean *I think that what you just said was stupid.*

Siobhan also says that if you close your mouth and breathe out loudly through your nose, it can mean that you are relaxed or that you are bored or that you are angry, and it all depends on how much air comes out of your nose and how fast and what shape your mouth is when you do it and how you are sitting and what you said just before and hundreds of other things that are too complicated to work out in a few seconds.

The second main reason is that people often talk using metaphors. These are examples of metaphors

> **I laughed my socks off.**
> **He was the apple of her eye.**
> **They had a skeleton in the cupboard.**
> **We had a real pig of a day.**
> **The dog was stone dead.**

The word *metaphor* means *carrying something from one place to another,* and it comes from the Greek words μετα (which means *from one place to another*) and φερειν (which means *to carry*), and it is when you describe something by using a word for something that it isn't. This means that the word *metaphor* is a metaphor.

I think it should be called a lie because a pig is not like a day and people do not have skeletons in their cupboards. And when I try to make a picture of the phrase in my head, it just confuses me, because imagining an apple in someone's eye doesn't have anything to do with liking someone a lot and it makes you forget what the person was talking about.

My name is a metaphor. It means *carrying Christ,* and it comes from the Greek words χριστος (which means *Jesus Christ*) and φερειν, and it was the name given to St. Christopher because he carried Jesus Christ across a river. Mother used to say that it meant Christopher was a nice name because it was a story about being kind and helpful, but I do not want my name to mean a story about being kind and helpful. I want my name to mean me.

IT WAS 1:12 A.M. WHEN FATHER arrived at the police station. I did not see him until 1:28 a.m., but I knew he was there because I could hear him.

He was shouting, "I want to see my son," and "Why the hell is he locked up?" and "Of course I'm bloody angry."

Then I heard a policeman telling him to calm down. Then I heard nothing for a long while.

At 1:28 a.m. a policeman opened the door of the cell and told me that there was someone to see me.

I stepped outside. Father was standing in the corridor. He held up his right hand and spread his fingers out in a fan. I held up my left hand and spread my fingers out in a fan, and we made our fingers and thumbs touch each other. We do this because sometimes Father wants to give me a hug, but I do not like hugging people, so we do this instead, and it means that he loves me.

Then the policeman told us to follow him down the corridor to another room. In the room was a table and three chairs. He told us to sit down on the far side of the table and he sat down on the other side. There was a tape recorder on the table, and I asked whether I was going to be interviewed and he was going to record the interview.

He said, "I don't think there will be any need for that."

He was an inspector. I could tell because he wasn't wearing a uniform. He also had a very hairy nose. It looked as if there were two very small mice hiding in his nostrils.

He said, "I have spoken to your father and he says that you didn't mean to hit the policeman."

I didn't say anything, because this wasn't a question.

He said, "Did you mean to hit the policeman?"

I said, "Yes."

He squeezed his face and said, "But you didn't mean to hurt the policeman?"

I thought about this and said, "No, I didn't mean to hurt the policeman. I just wanted him to stop touching me."

He said, "You know it is wrong to hit a policeman, don't you?"

I said, "I do."

He was quiet for a few seconds, then he asked, "Did you kill the dog, Christopher?"

I said, "I didn't kill the dog."

He said, "Do you know that it is wrong to lie to a policeman and that you can get into a very great deal of trouble if you do?"

I said, "Yes."

He said, "So do you know who killed the dog?"

I said, "No."

He said, "Are you telling the truth?"

I said, "Yes, I always tell the truth."

And he said, "Right. I am going to give you a caution."

I asked, "Is that going to be on a piece of paper like a certificate I can keep?"

He replied, "No. A caution means that we are going to keep a record of what you did—that you hit a policeman, but that it was an accident and that you didn't mean to hurt the policeman."

I said, "But it wasn't an accident."

And Father said, "Christopher, please."

The policeman closed his mouth and breathed out through his nose and said, "If you get into any more trouble, we will take out this record and see that you have been given a caution, and we will take things much more seriously. Do you understand what I'm saying?"

I said that I understood.

Then he said that we could go, and he stood up and opened the door, and we walked out into the corridor and back to the front desk, where I picked up my Swiss army knife and my piece of string and the 3 pellets of rat food for Toby and my £1.47 and the piece of the wooden puzzle and the paper clip and my front-door key, which were all in a little plastic bag, and we went out to Father's car, which was parked outside, and we drove home.

7. I DO not tell lies. Mother used to say that this was because I was a good person. But it is not because I am a good person. It is because I can't tell lies.

Mother was a small person who smelled nice. And she sometimes wore a fleece with a zip down the front that was pink, and it had a tiny label that said BERGHAUS on the left bosom.

A lie is when you say something happened that didn't happen. But there is only ever one thing that happened at a particular time and a particular place. And there are an infinite number of things that didn't happen at that time and that place. And if I think about something that didn't happen, I start thinking about all the other things that didn't happen.

For example, this morning for breakfast I had Ready Brek and some hot raspberry milk shake. But if I say that I actually had Shreddies and a mug of tea, I start thinking about Coco Pops and lemonade and how I wasn't eating my breakfast in Egypt and there wasn't a rhinoceros in the room and Father wasn't wearing a diving suit and so on, and even writing this makes me feel shaky and scared, like I do when I'm standing on the top of a very tall building and there are houses and cars and people below me, and my head is so full of these things that I'm afraid that I'm going to forget to stand up straight and hang on to the rail and I'm going to fall over and be killed.

This is another reason why I don't like proper novels, because they are lies about things that didn't happen and they make me feel shaky and scared.

And this is why everything I have written here is true.

THERE were clouds in the sky on the way home, so I couldn't see the Milky Way.

I said, "I'm sorry," because Father had had to come to the police station, which was a bad thing.

He said, "It's OK."

I said, "I didn't kill the dog."

And he said, "I know." Then he said, "Christopher, you have to stay out of trouble, OK?"

I said, "I didn't know I was going to get into trouble. I like Wellington and I went to say hello to him, but I didn't know that someone had killed him."

Father said, "Just try and keep your nose out of other people's business."

I thought for a little, and I said, "I am going to find out who killed Wellington."

And Father said, "Were you listening to what I was saying, Christopher?"

I said, "Yes, I was listening to what you were saying, but when someone gets murdered, you have to find out who did it so that they can be punished."

And he said, "It's a bloody dog, Christopher, a bloody dog."

I replied, "I think dogs are important too."

He said, "Leave it."

And I said, "I wonder if the police will find out who killed him and punish the person."

Then Father banged the steering wheel with his fist, and the car weaved a little bit across the dotted line in the middle of the road, and he shouted, "I said leave it, for God's sake."

I could tell he was angry because he was shouting. I didn't want to make him angry, so I didn't say anything else until we got home.

When we came in through the front door, I went into the kitchen and got a carrot for Toby, my rat, and I went upstairs and I shut the door of my room and I let Toby out and gave him the carrot. Then I turned my computer on and played 76 games of **Minesweeper** and did the Expert Version in 102 seconds, which was only 3 seconds off my best time, which was 99 seconds.

At 2:07 a.m. I decided that I wanted a drink of orange squash before I brushed my teeth and got into bed, so I went downstairs to the kitchen. Father was sitting on the sofa watching snooker on the television and drinking Scotch. There were tears coming out of his eyes.

I asked, "Are you sad about Wellington?"

He looked at me for a long time and sucked air in through his nose. Then he said, "Yes, Christopher, you could say that. You could very well say that."

I decided to leave him alone because when I am sad, I want to be left alone. So I didn't say anything else. I just went into the kitchen and made my orange squash and took it back upstairs to my room.

MOTHER died 2 years ago.

I came home from school one day and no one answered the door, so I went and found the secret key that we keep under a flowerpot behind the kitchen door. I let myself into the house and carried on making the Airfix Sherman tank model I was building.

An hour and a half later Father came home from work. He runs a business and he does heating maintenance and boiler repair with a man called Rhodri, who is his employee. He knocked on the door of my room and opened it and asked whether I had seen Mother.

I said that I hadn't seen her and he went downstairs and started making some phone calls. I did not hear what he said.

Then he came up to my room and said he had to go out for a while and he wasn't sure how long he would be. He said that if I needed anything, I should call him on his mobile phone.

He was away for 2½ hours. When he came back, I went downstairs. He was sitting in the kitchen staring out the back window, down the garden to the pond.

Father said, "I'm afraid you won't be seeing your mother for a while." He didn't look at me when he said this. He kept on looking through the window.

Usually people look at you when they're talking to you. I know that they're working out what I'm thinking, but I can't tell what they're thinking. It is like being in a room with a one-way mirror in a spy film. But this was nice, having Father speak to me but not look at me.

I said, "Why not?"

He waited for a very long time, then he said, "Your mother has had to go into hospital."

"Can we visit her?" I asked, because I like hospitals. I like the uniforms and the machines.

Father said, "No."

I said, "Why can't we?"

And he said, "She needs rest. She needs to be on her own. She has a problem . . . a problem with her heart."

I said, "We will need to take food to her," because I knew that food in hospital was not very good. David from school, he went into hospital to have an operation so that he could walk better, and he hated the food, so his mother used to take meals in every day.

Father waited a long time and said, "I'll take some in to her while you're at school and I'll give it to the doctors and they can give it to your mum, OK?"

I said, "But you can't cook."

Father put his hands over his face and said, "Christopher, look, I'll buy some ready-made stuff from Marks and Spencer's and take those in. She likes those."

I said I would make her a get-well card because that is what you do for people when they are in hospital.

Father said he would take it in the next day.

11. IN THE bus on the way to school next morning we passed 4 red cars in a row, which meant that it was a **Good Day,** so I decided not to be sad about Wellington.

Mr. Jeavons, the psychologist at the school, once asked me why 4 red cars in a row made it a **Good Day,** and 3 red cars in a row made it a **Quite Good Day,** and 5 red cars in a row made it a **Super Good Day,** and why 4 yellow cars in a row made it a **Black Day,** which is a day when I don't speak to anyone and don't eat my lunch and

Take No Risks. He said that I was a very logical person, so he was surprised that I should think like this, because it wasn't very logical.

I said that I liked things to be in a nice order. And one way of things being in a nice order was to be logical. Especially if those things were numbers or an argument. But there were other ways of putting things in a nice order. And that was why I had **Good Days** and **Black Days.** And I said that some people who worked in an office came out of their house in the morning and saw that the sun was shining and it made them feel happy, or they saw that it was raining and it made them feel sad, but the only difference was the weather, and if they worked in an office, the weather didn't have anything to do with whether they had a good day or a bad day.

I said that when Father got up in the morning, he always put his trousers on before he put his socks on and it wasn't logical, but he always did it that way because he liked things in a nice order too. Mr. Jeavons said that I was a very clever boy.

I said that I wasn't clever. I was just noticing how things were, and that wasn't clever. That was just being observant. Being clever was when you looked at how things were and used the evidence to work out something new. Like the universe expanding or who committed a murder.

Mr. Jeavons asked me whether this made me feel safe, having things always in a nice order, and I said it did.

Then he asked if I didn't like things changing. And I said I wouldn't mind things changing if I became an astronaut, for example, which is one of the biggest changes you can imagine, apart from becoming a girl or dying.

He asked whether I wanted to become an astronaut and I said I did. He said that it was very difficult to become an astronaut. I said that I knew. You had to become an officer in the air force, and you had to take lots of orders and be prepared to kill other humans, and I couldn't take orders. Also I didn't have 20/20 vision. But I said that you could still want something that is very unlikely to happen.

Terry, who is the older brother of Francis, who is at the school, said I would only ever get a job collecting supermarket trolleys or cleaning up after donkeys at an animal sanctuary and they didn't let spazzers drive rockets that cost billions of pounds. When I told this to Father, he said that Terry was jealous of my being cleverer than him. Which was a stupid thing to think, because we weren't in a competition. But Terry is stupid, so *quod erat demonstrandum,* which is Latin for *which is the thing that was going to be proved,* which means *thus it is proved.*

I'm not a spazzer, which means *spastic,* and even though I probably won't become an astronaut, I am going to go to university and study mathematics because I like mathematics and physics and I'm very good at them. But Terry won't go to university. Father says Terry is most likely to end up in prison. Terry has a tattoo on his arm of a heart shape with a knife through the middle of it.

But this is what is called a digression, and now I am going to go back to the fact that it was a Good Day.

Because it was a Good Day, I decided that I would try to find out who killed Wellington because a Good Day is a day for projects and planning things.

When I said this to Siobhan, she said, "Well, we're meant to be writing stories today, so why don't you write about finding Wellington and going to the police station."

And that is when I started writing this.

MOTHER died 2 weeks after she went into hospital.

I had not been into hospital to see her, but Father had taken in lots of food from Marks and Spencer's. He said that she had been looking OK and seemed to be getting better. She had sent me lots of love and had my get-well card on the table beside her bed. Father said that she liked it very much.

The card had pictures of cars on the front. I did it with Mrs. Peters at school who does art, and it was a linocut, which is when you draw a picture on a piece of lino and Mrs. Peters cuts round the picture with a Stanley knife, and then you put ink on the lino and press it onto the paper, which is why all the cars looked the same, because I did one car and pressed it onto the paper 9 times.

And I colored all the cars in with red paint to make it a **Super Super Good Day** for Mother.

Father said that she died of a heart attack and it wasn't expected.

I said, "What kind of heart attack?" because I was surprised.

Mother was only 38 years old and heart attacks usually happen to older people, and Mother was very active and rode a bicycle and ate food that was healthy and high in fiber and low in saturated fat, like chicken and vegetables and muesli.

Father said that he didn't know what kind of heart attack she had had and now wasn't the moment to be asking questions like that.

Then he said, "I'm sorry, Christopher. I'm really sorry."

But it wasn't his fault.

Then Mrs. Shears came over and cooked supper for us. And she was wearing sandals and jeans and a T-shirt that had the words WINDSURF and CORFU and a picture of a windsurfer on it.

And Father was sitting down, and she stood next to him and held his head against her bosoms and said, "Come on, Ed. We're going to get you through this."

And then she made us spaghetti and tomato sauce. After dinner we played Scrabble and I beat her 247 points to 134.

13. I DECIDED that I was going to find out who killed Wellington even though Father had told me to stay out of other people's business.

This is because I do not always do what I am told.

And this is because when people tell you what to do, it is usually confusing and does not make sense.

For example, people often say "Be quiet," but they don't tell you how long to be quiet for. Or you see a sign that says KEEP OFF THE GRASS, but it should say KEEP OFF THE GRASS AROUND THIS SIGN, because there is lots of grass you are allowed to walk on.

Also people break rules all the time. For example, Father often drives at over 30 mph in a 30-mph zone and sometimes he drives when he has been drinking and often he doesn't wear his seat belt. And in the Bible it says, *Thou shalt not kill,* but there were the Crusades and two World Wars and the Gulf war and there were Christians killing people in all of them.

Also, I don't know what Father means when he says, "Stay out of other people's business," because I do lots of things with other people, at school and in the shop and on the bus, and his job is going into other people's houses and fixing their boilers and their heating. And all of these things are other people's business.

Siobhan understands. When she tells me not to do something, she tells me exactly what it is that I am not allowed to do. And I like this. But when other people tell you what you can't do, they don't do it clearly, so I decide for myself what I am going to do and what I am not going to do.

That evening I went round to Mrs. Shears's house and knocked on the door and waited for her to answer it.

When she opened the door, she was holding a mug of tea and she was wearing sheepskin slippers, and she had been watching a quiz program on the television, because there was a television on and I could hear someone saying, "The capital city of Venezuela is . . . a) Maracas, b) Caracas, c) Bogotá, or d) Georgetown." And I knew that it was Caracas.

She said, "Christopher, I really don't think I want to see you right now. What are you doing here?"

I said, "I wanted to come and tell you that I didn't kill Wellington. And also, I want to find out who killed him."

Some of her tea spilled onto the carpet.

I said, "Do you know who killed Wellington?"

She didn't answer my question. She just said, "Good-bye, Christopher," and closed the door.

Then I decided to do some detective work.

I could see that she was watching me and waiting for me to leave because I could see her standing on the other side of the frosted glass in her front door. So I walked down the path and out of the garden. Then I turned round and saw that she wasn't standing in her hall any longer. I made sure that there was no one watching and climbed over the wall and walked down the side of the house into her back garden to the shed where she kept her gardening tools.

The shed was locked with a padlock and I couldn't go inside, so I walked round to the window in the side. Then I had some good luck. When I looked through the window, I could see a fork that looked exactly the same as the fork that had been sticking out of Wellington. It had been cleaned, because there was no blood on the spikes. I could see some other tools: a spade and a rake and one of those long clippers people use for cutting branches that are too high to reach. And they all had the same green plastic handles like the fork. This meant that the fork belonged to Mrs. Shears. Either that or it was a *Red Herring,* which is a clue that makes you come to a wrong conclusion, or something that looks like a clue but isn't.

I wondered if Mrs. Shears had killed Wellington herself. But if she had killed Wellington, why did she come out of the house shouting, "What have you done to my dog?"

I thought that Mrs. Shears probably didn't kill Wellington. But whoever had killed him had probably killed him with Mrs. Shears's fork. And the shed was locked. This meant that it was someone who had the key to Mrs. Shears's shed, or that she had left it unlocked, or that she had left her fork lying around in the garden.

I heard a noise and turned round and saw Mrs. Shears standing on the lawn looking at me.

I said, "I came to see if the fork was in the shed."

And she said, "If you don't go now, I will call the police again." So I went home.

When I got home, I said hello to Father and went upstairs and fed Toby, my rat, and felt happy, because I was being a detective and finding things out.

MRS. Forbes at school said that when Mother died, she had gone to heaven. That was because Mrs. Forbes is very old and she believes in heaven.

But when Mother died, she didn't go to heaven, because heaven doesn't exist.

Mrs. Peters's husband is a vicar called the Reverend Peters, and he comes to our school sometimes to talk to us, and I asked him where heaven was, and he said, "It's not in our universe. It's another kind of place altogether."

I said that there wasn't anything outside the universe and there wasn't another kind of place altogether. Except that there might be if you went through a black hole, but a black hole is what is called a *singularity,* which means it is impossible to find out what is on the other side, because the gravity of a black hole is so big that even electromagnetic waves like light can't get out of it, and electromagnetic waves are how we get information about things that are far away. And if heaven was on the other side of a black hole, dead people would have to be fired into space on rockets to get there, and they aren't or people would notice.

I think people believe in heaven because they don't like the idea of dying, because they want to carry on living and they don't like the idea that other people will move into their house and put their things into the rubbish.

The Reverend Peters said, "Well, when I say that heaven is outside the universe, it's really just a manner of speaking. I suppose what it really means is that they are with God."

And I replied, "But where is God?"

And the Reverend Peters said that we should talk about this on another day, when he had more time.

What actually happens when you die is that your brain stops working and your body rots, like Rabbit did when he died and we buried him in the earth at the bottom of the garden. And all his molecules were broken down into other molecules and they went into the earth and were eaten by worms and went into the plants, and if we go and dig in the same place in 10 years, there will be nothing except his skeleton left. And in 1,000 years, even his skeleton will be gone. But that is all right because he is a part of the flowers and the apple tree and the hawthorn bush now.

When people die, they are sometimes put into coffins, which means that they don't mix with the earth for a very long time until the wood of the coffin rots.

But Mother was cremated. This means that she was put into a coffin and burned and ground up and turned into ash and smoke. I do not know what happens to the ash, and I couldn't ask at the crematorium, because I didn't go to the funeral. But the smoke goes out of the chimney and into the air, and sometimes I look up into the sky and I think that there are molecules of Mother up there, or in clouds over Africa or the Antarctic, or coming down as rain in the rain forests in Brazil, or in snow somewhere.

17. THE next day was Saturday and there is not much to do on a Saturday unless Father takes me on an outing to the boating lake or to the garden center, but on this Saturday, England was playing Romania at football, which meant that we weren't going to go on an outing, because Father wanted to watch the match on the television.

So I decided to do some more detection on my own. I decided that I would go and ask some of the other people who lived in our street, which is called Randolph Street, if they had seen anyone killing Wellington or whether they had seen anything strange happening in the street on Thursday night.

Usually I do not like talking to strangers. This is because I do not like people I have never met before. They are hard to understand. It is like being in France, which is where we went on holiday sometimes when Mother was alive, to camp. And I hated it, because if you went into a shop or a restaurant, you couldn't understand what anyone was saying, which was frightening.

It takes me a long time to get used to people I do not know. For example, when there is a new member of staff at school, I do not talk to them for weeks. I just watch them until I know that they are safe. Then I ask them questions about themselves, like whether they have pets and what is their favorite color and what do they know about the Apollo space missions, and I get them to draw a plan of their house, so I get to know them. Then I don't mind if I am in the same room as them and don't have to watch them all the time.

So talking to the other people in our street was brave. But if you are going to do detective work, you have to be brave, so I had no choice.

First of all, I went out and I knocked on the door of Number 40, which is opposite Mrs. Shears's house, which means that they were most likely to have seen something. The people who live at Number 40 are called Thompson.

Mr. Thompson answered the door. He said, "Can I help you?"

I said, "Do you know who killed Wellington?"

I did not look at his face. I do not like looking at people's faces, especially if they are strangers. He did not say anything for a few seconds. Then he said, "Who are you?"

I said, "I'm Christopher Boone from Number Thirty-six and I know you. You're Mr. Thompson."

He said, "I'm Mr. Thompson's brother."

And I said, "Do you know who killed Wellington?"

He said, "Who is Wellington?"

I said, "Mrs. Shears's dog. Mrs. Shears is from Number Forty-one."

He said, "Someone killed her dog?"

I said, "With a garden fork. Do you know who killed him?"

He said, "I haven't a clue."

I said, "Did you see anything suspicious on Thursday evening?"

He said, "Look, son, do you really think you should be going around asking questions like this?"

And I said, "Yes, because I want to find out who killed Wellington and I am writing a book about it."

And he said, "Well, I was in Colchester on Thursday, so you're asking the wrong bloke."

I said, "Thank you," and I walked away.

There was no answer at Number 42.

I had seen the people who lived at Number 44, but I did not

know what their names were. They were black people and they were a man and a lady with 2 children, a boy and a girl. The lady answered the door. There were 5 bracelets made out of a silver-colored metal on her wrist and they made a jangling noise. She said, "It's Christopher, isn't it?."

I said that it was, and I asked her if she knew who killed Wellington. She knew who Wellington was, so I didn't have to explain, and she had heard about him being killed.

I asked if she had seen anything suspicious on Thursday evening that might be a clue, but she said she hadn't.

And then I decided to do what is called *Trying a Different Tack,* and I asked her whether she knew of anyone who might want to make Mrs. Shears sad.

And she said, "Perhaps you should talk to your father about this."

And I explained that I couldn't ask my father, because the investigation was a secret, because he had told me to stay out of other people's business.

She said, "Well, maybe he has a point, Christopher."

And I said, "So you don't know anything that might be a clue?"

And she said, "No," and then she said, "And you be careful, young man."

I said that I would be careful and then I said thank you to her for helping me with my questions and I went to Number 43, which is the house next to Mrs. Shears's house.

The people who live at Number 43 are Mr. Wise and Mr. Wise's mother, who is in a wheelchair, which is why he lives with her, so he can take her to the shops and drive her around.

It was Mr. Wise who answered the door. He smelled of body odor and old biscuits and off popcorn, which is what you smell of if you haven't washed for a very long time, like Jason at school smells because his family is poor.

I asked Mr. Wise if he knew who had killed Wellington on Thursday night.

He said, "Policemen really are getting younger, aren't they?" Then he laughed.

I do not like people laughing at me, so I turned and walked away.

I did not knock at the door of Number 38, which is the house next to our house, because the people there take drugs and Father says that I should never talk to them, so I don't. They play loud music at night and they make me scared when I see them in the street.

Then I noticed that the old lady who lives at Number 39, which is on the other side of Mrs. Shears's house, was in her front garden, cutting her hedge with an electric hedge trimmer. Her name is Mrs. Alexander. She has a dachshund, so she is probably a good person because she likes dogs. But the dog wasn't in the garden with her. It was inside the house.

Mrs. Alexander was wearing jeans and training shoes, which old people don't normally wear. There was mud on the jeans. And the trainers were New Balance trainers. I went up to Mrs. Alexander and said, "Do you know anything about Wellington being killed?"

She turned the electric hedge trimmer off and said, "I'm afraid you're going to have to say that again. I'm a little deaf."

So I said, "Do you know anything about Wellington being killed?"

And she said, "I heard about it yesterday. Dreadful. Dreadful."

I said, "Do you know who killed him?"

And she said, "No, I don't."

And I said, "Thank you for helping me with my investigation."

And she said, "You're Christopher, aren't you?"

I said, "Yes. I live at Number Thirty-six."

And she said, "We haven't talked before, have we?"

I said, "No. I don't like talking to strangers. But I'm doing detective work."

And she said, "I see you every day going to school. It's very nice of you to come and say hello."

I didn't reply to this, because Mrs. Alexander was doing what is called chatting, where people say things to each other that aren't questions and answers and aren't connected.

Then she said, "Even if it's only because you're doing detective work."

And I said, "Thank you," again.

And I was about to turn and walk away, when she said, "I have a grandson your age."

I tried to do chatting by saying, "My age is fifteen years and three months and three days."

And she said, "Well, almost your age."

Then we said nothing for a little while until she said, "You don't have a dog, do you?"

And I said, "No, but I have a rat. He's called Toby."

And she said, "Oh."

And I said, "Most people don't like rats, because they think they carry diseases like bubonic plague. But that's only because they lived in sewers and stowed away on ships coming from countries where there were strange diseases. But rats are very clean. Toby is always washing himself. And you don't have to take him out for walks. I just let him run around my room so he gets some exercise."

Mrs. Alexander said, "Do you want to come in for tea?"

And I said, "I don't go into other people's houses."

And she said, "Well, maybe I could bring some out here. Do you like lemon squash?"

I replied, "I only like orange squash."

And she said, "Luckily, I have some of that. And what about Battenberg?"

I said, "I don't know, because I don't know what Battenberg is."

She said, "It's a kind of cake. It has four pink and yellow squares in the middle, and it has marzipan icing round the edge."

And I said, "Is it a long cake with a square cross section that is divided into equally sized, alternately colored squares?"

And she said, "Yes. I think you could describe it like that."

I said, "I think I'd like the pink squares, but not the yellow squares, because I don't like yellow. And I don't know what marzipan is, so I don't know whether I'd like that."

And she said, "I'm afraid marzipan is yellow too. Perhaps I should bring out some biscuits instead. Do you like biscuits?"

And I said, "Yes. Some sorts of biscuits."

And she said, "I'll get a selection."

Then she turned and went into the house. She moved very slowly because she was an old lady, and she was inside the house for more than 6 minutes and I began to get nervous, because I didn't know what she was doing. I didn't know her well enough to know whether she was telling the truth about getting orange squash and Battenberg cake. And I thought she might be ringing the police and then I'd get into much more serious trouble because of the caution. So I walked away. And as I was crossing the street, I had a stroke of inspiration about who might have killed Wellington. I was imagining a Chain of Reasoning inside my head, which was like this

> **1.** Why would you kill a dog?
> **a)** Because you hated the dog.
> **b)** Because you were mad.
> **c)** Because you wanted to make Mrs. Shears upset.
> **2.** I didn't know anyone who hated Wellington, so if it was **(a)**, it was probably a stranger.
> **3.** I didn't know any mad people, so if it was **(b)**, it was also probably a stranger.
> **4.** Most murders are committed by someone who is known to the victim. In fact, you are most likely to be murdered by a member of your own family. This is a fact. Wellington was therefore most likely to have been killed by someone known to him.
> **5.** If it was **(c)**, I only knew one person who didn't like Mrs. Shears, and that was Mr. Shears, who knew Wellington very well indeed.

This meant that Mr. Shears was my **Prime Suspect.**

Mr. Shears used to be married to Mrs. Shears and they lived together until two years ago. Then Mr. Shears left and didn't come back. This was why Mrs. Shears came over and did lots of cooking for us after Mother died, because she didn't have to cook for Mr. Shears anymore and she didn't have to stay at home and be his wife. And also Father said that she needed company and didn't want to be on her own.

And sometimes Mrs. Shears stayed overnight at our house, and I liked it when she did because she made things tidy and she arranged the jars in order of their height on the shelves in the kitchen and she put the knives, forks, and spoons in the correct compartments in the cutlery drawer. But she smoked cigarettes and she said lots of things I didn't understand, e.g., "I'm going to hit the hay," and, "It's brass monkeys out there." And I didn't like it when she said things like that, because I didn't know what she meant.

And I don't know why Mr. Shears left Mrs. Shears, but if Mr. Shears didn't want to live in the same house as Mrs. Shears anymore, he probably hated her and he might have come back and killed her dog to make her sad.

I decided to try to find out more about Mr. Shears.

ALL the other children at my school are stupid. Except I'm not meant to call them stupid, even though they are. I'm meant to say that they have learning difficulties or that they have special needs. But this is stupid because everyone has learning difficulties, because learning to speak French or understanding relativity is difficult, and also everyone has special needs, like Father who has to carry a little packet of artificial sweetening tablets around with him to put in his coffee to stop him from getting fat, or Siobhan who has glasses so thick that they give you a headache if you borrow them, and none of these people are Special Needs, even if they have special needs.

I am going to prove that I'm not stupid. Next month I'm going to take my A level in maths and I'm going to get an A grade. No one has ever taken an A level at our school before and the headmistress, Mrs. Gascoyne, didn't want me to take it at first. She said they didn't have the facilities to let us sit A levels. She said they didn't want to treat me differently from everyone else, because it would set a precedent. And I could always do my A levels later, at 18.

I was sitting in Mrs. Gascoyne's office with Father when she said these things. And Father got really cross. He said, "Christopher is getting a crap enough deal already, don't you think? This is the one thing he is really good at."

Then Mrs. Gascoyne said that she and Father should talk about this at some later point on their own. But Father asked her whether she wanted to say things she was embarrassed to say in front of me, and she said no, so he said, "Say them now, then."

And she said that if I sat an A level, I would have to have a member of staff looking after me in my own separate room. And Father said he would pay someone £50 to do it after school and he wasn't going to take no for an answer. And she said she'd go away and think about it. And the next week she rang Father at home and told him that I could take the A level and the Reverend Peters would be what is called the invigilator.

And after I've taken A-level maths, I am going to take A-level further maths and physics and then I can go to university. There is not a university in our town, which is Swindon, so we will have to move to another town where there is a university, because I don't want to live on my own or in a house with other students.

Then, when I've got a degree in maths, or physics, or maths and physics, I will be able to get a job and earn lots of money, and I will be able to pay someone who can look after me and cook my meals and wash my clothes, or I will get a lady to marry me and be my wife and she can look after me, so I can have company and not be on my own.

I USED to think that Mother and Father might get divorced. That was because they had lots of arguments, and sometimes they hated each other. This was because of the stress of looking after someone who has Behavioral Problems like I have. I used to have lots of Behavioral Problems, but I don't have so many now, because I'm more grown up and I can make decisions for myself and do things on my own, like buying things at the shop at the end of the road.

These are some of my Behavioral Problems

A. Not talking to people for a long time
B. Not eating or drinking anything for a long time
C. Not liking being touched

D. Screaming when I am angry or confused

E. Not liking being in really small places with other people

F. Smashing things when I am angry or confused

G. Groaning

H. Not liking yellow things or brown things and refusing to touch yellow or brown things

I. Not eating food if different sorts of food are touching

J. Not noticing that people are angry with me

K. Not smiling

L. Saying things that other people think are rude. (You are not allowed to tell old people that they are old and you are not allowed to tell people if they smell funny. And you are not allowed to say "I do not like you" unless that person has been horrible to you.)

M. Doing stupid things like emptying a jar of peanut butter onto the table in the kitchen and making it level with a knife so that it covers all the table right to the edge or burning things on the gas stove to see what happened to them, like my shoes

N. Hitting other people

O. Hating France

P. Getting cross when someone has moved the furniture

Sometimes these things would make Mother and Father really angry, and they would shout at me or they would shout at each other. Sometimes Father would say, "Christopher, if you do not behave, I swear I shall knock the living daylights out of you," or Mother would say, "Christopher, I am seriously considering putting you in a home," or "You are going to drive me into an early grave."

19. WHEN I got home, Father was sitting at the table in the kitchen and he had made my supper. He was wearing a lumberjack shirt. The supper was baked beans and broccoli and two slices of ham, and they were laid out on the plate so they were not touching.

Father said, "Where have you been?"

And I said, "I have been out." This is called a white lie. A white lie is not a lie at all. It is where you tell the truth, but you do not tell all of the truth. And I said a white lie because I knew that Father didn't want me to be a detective.

Father said, "I have just had a phone call from Mrs. Shears."

I started eating my baked beans and broccoli and two slices of ham.

Then Father asked, "What the hell were you doing poking round her garden?"

I said, "I was doing detective work, trying to find out who killed Wellington."

Father replied, "How many times do I have to tell you, Christopher? I told you to keep your nose out of other people's business."

I said, "I think Mr. Shears probably killed Wellington. He is my Prime Suspect. Because I think someone might have killed Wellington to make Mrs. Shears sad. And a murder is usually committed by someone known—"

Father banged the table with his fist so that the plates and his knife and fork jumped around and my ham jumped, so it touched the broccoli, so I couldn't eat the ham or the broccoli anymore. Then he shouted, "I will not have that man's name mentioned in my house."

I asked, "Why not?"

And he said, "That man is evil."

And I said, "Does that mean he might have killed Wellington?"

Father put his head in his hands and said, "Jesus wept."

I could see that Father was angry with me, so I said, "I know you told me not to get involved in other people's business, but Mrs. Shears is a friend of ours."

And Father said, "Well, she's not a friend anymore."

And I asked, "Why not?"

And Father said, "OK, Christopher. I am going to say this for the last and final time. I will not tell you again. Look at me when I'm talking to you. Look at me. You are not to go asking Mrs. Shears about who killed that bloody dog. You are not to go asking anyone about who killed that bloody dog. You are not to go trespassing in other people's gardens. You are to stop this ridiculous bloody detective game right now."

I didn't say anything.

Father said, "I am going to make you promise, Christopher. And you know what it means when I make you promise."

I did know what it meant when you say you promise something. You have to say that you will never do something again, and then you must never do it, because that would make the promise a lie. I said, "I know."

Father said, "Promise me that you will stop doing these things. Promise me that you will give up this ridiculous game."

I said, "I promise."

I THINK I would make a very good astronaut.

To be a good astronaut you have to be intelligent and I'm intelligent. You also have to understand how machines work and I'm good at understanding how machines work. You also have to be someone who would like being on their own in a tiny spacecraft thousands and thousands of miles away from the surface of the earth and not panic or get claustrophobia or be homesick or insane. And I like really little spaces, so long as there is no one else in them with me. Sometimes when I want to be on my own, I get into the airing cupboard in the bathroom and pull the door closed behind me and sit there and think for hours, and it makes me feel very calm.

So I would have to be an astronaut on my own or have my own part of the spacecraft that no one else could come into. And also, there would be no yellow or brown things in a spacecraft, so that would be OK too. I wouldn't be homesick, because I'd be surrounded by the things I like, which are machines and computers and outer space. And I would be able to look out a little window in the spacecraft and know that there was no one else near me for thousands of miles, which is what I sometimes pretend at night in the summer when I go and lie on the lawn and look up at the sky and put my hands round the sides of my face so that I can't see the chimney and the washing line and I can pretend I'm in space. And all I could see would be stars. And stars are the places where the molecules that life is made of were constructed billions of years ago.

And I would like it if I could take Toby with me into space, and that might be allowed because they sometimes do take animals into space for experiments, so if I could think of a good experiment you could do with a rat that didn't hurt the rat, I could make them let me take Toby.

But if they didn't let me, I would still go because it would be a Dream Come True.

THE next day at school I told Siobhan that Father had told me I couldn't do any more detecting, which meant that the book was finished. I showed her the pages I had written so far, and she said that it didn't matter. She said the book was really good as it was and that I should be very proud of having written a book at all, even if it was quite short. But I said that it wasn't a proper book, because it didn't have a proper ending, because I never found out who killed Wellington, so the murderer was still At Large.

And she said that was like life, and not all murders were solved and not all murderers were caught. Like Jack the Ripper.

I said I didn't like the idea that the person who killed Wellington was still At Large and could be living somewhere nearby and I might meet him when I went out for a walk at night.

Then I said, "Father said I was never to mention Mr. Shears's name in our house again and that he was an evil man and maybe that meant he was the person who killed Wellington."

And she said, "Perhaps your father just doesn't like Mr. Shears."

And I asked, "Why?"

And she said, "I don't know, Christopher. I don't know, because I don't know anything about Mr. Shears."

I said, "Mr. Shears used to be married to Mrs. Shears and he left her, like in a divorce. But I don't know if they were actually divorced."

And Siobhan said, "Well, Mrs. Shears is a friend of yours, isn't she? Perhaps your father doesn't like Mr. Shears, because he left Mrs. Shears. Because he did something bad to someone who is a friend."

And I said, "But Father says Mrs. Shears isn't a friend anymore."

And Siobhan said, "I'm sorry, Christopher. I wish I could answer all these questions, but I simply don't know."

Then the bell went for the end of school.

The next day I saw 4 yellow cars in a row on the way to school, which made it a **Black Day,** so I didn't eat anything at lunch, and I sat in the corner of the room all day and read my A-level maths course book. And the next day, too, I saw 4 yellow cars in a row on the way to school, which made it another **Black Day,** so I didn't speak to anyone, and for the whole afternoon I sat in the corner of the library, groaning, with my head pressed into the join between two walls, and this made me feel safe. But on the third day I kept my eyes closed all the way to school until we got off the bus because after I have had 2 **Black Days** in a row, I'm allowed to do that.

It wasn't the end of the book, because 5 days later I saw 5 red cars in a row, which made it a **Super Good Day,** and I knew that something special was going to happen. Nothing special happened at school, so I knew something special was going to happen after school. And when I got home, I went down to the shop at the end of our road to buy some licorice laces and a Milky Bar with my pocket money. And when I had bought them, I turned round and saw Mrs. Alexander, the old lady from Number 39, who was in the shop as well. She wasn't wearing jeans now. She was wearing a dress, like a normal old lady. And she smelled of cooking.

She said, "What happened to you the other day? I came out again and you'd gone. I had to eat all the biscuits myself."

I said, "I went away."

And she said, "I gathered that."

I said, "I thought you might ring the police."

And she said, "Why on earth would I do that?"

And I said, "Because I was poking my nose into other people's business, and Father said I shouldn't investigate who killed Wellington. And a policeman gave me a caution, and if I get into trouble again, it will be a lot worse because of the caution."

Then the Indian lady behind the counter said to Mrs. Alexander, "Can I help you?" and Mrs. Alexander said she'd like a pint of milk and a packet of Jaffa cakes, so I went out of the shop.

When I was outside, I saw that Mrs. Alexander's dachshund was sitting on the pavement. It was wearing a little coat made out of tartan material, which is Scottish and check. She had tied its lead to the drainpipe next to the door. I like dogs, so I bent down and I said hello to her dog and it licked my hand. Its tongue was rough and wet, and it liked the smell on my trousers and started sniffing them.

Then Mrs. Alexander came outside and said, "His name is Ivor."

I didn't say anything.

Mrs. Alexander said, "You're very shy, aren't you, Christopher?"

And I said, "I'm not allowed to talk to you."

And she said, "Don't worry. I'm not going to tell the police and I'm not going to tell your father, because there's nothing wrong with having a chat. Having a chat is just being friendly, isn't it?"

I said, "I can't do chatting."

Then she said, "Do you like computers?"

And I said, "Yes, I like computers. I have a computer at home in my bedroom."

And she said, "I know. I can see you sitting at your computer in your bedroom sometimes when I look across the street."

Then she untied Ivor's lead from the drainpipe.

I wasn't going to say anything, because I didn't want to get into trouble. But then I thought that this was a **Super Good Day** and something special hadn't happened yet, so it was possible that talking to Mrs. Alexander was the special thing. She might tell me something about Wellington or about Mr. Shears without me asking her, and that wouldn't be breaking my promise.

So I said, "And I like maths and looking after Toby."

And she said, "I bet you're very good at maths, aren't you?"

And I said, "I am. I'm going to do my A-level maths next month. And I'm going to get an A grade."

And Mrs. Alexander said, "Really? A-level maths?"

I replied, "Yes. I don't tell lies. I'm the first person to do an A level from my school because it's a special school."

And she said, "I am very impressed. I hope you do get an A."

And I said, "I will."

And then I did some reasoning. I reasoned that Father had only made me do a promise about five things, which were

1. Not to mention Mr. Shears's name in our house
2. Not to go asking Mrs. Shears about who killed that bloody dog
3. Not to go asking anyone about who killed that bloody dog
4. Not to go trespassing in other people's gardens
5. To stop this ridiculous bloody detective game

And asking about Mr. Shears wasn't any of these things. And if you are a detective, you have to *Take Risks,* and this was a **Super Good Day,** which meant it was a good day for *Taking Risks,* so I said, "Do you know Mr. Shears?" which was like chatting.

And Mrs. Alexander said, "Not really, no. I mean, I knew him well enough to say hello and talk to a little in the street, but I didn't know much about him. I think he worked in a bank."

And I said, "Father says that he is an evil man. Do you know why he said that? Is Mr. Shears an evil man?"

And Mrs. Alexander said, "Why are you asking me about Mr. Shears, Christopher? Is this about Wellington?"

And I nodded because that didn't count as being a detective.

Mrs. Alexander sucked in a big breath and said, "Perhaps it would be best not to talk about these things, Christopher."

And I asked, "Why not?"

And she said, "Because." Then she stopped and decided to start saying a different sentence. "Because maybe your father is right and you shouldn't go around asking questions about this."

And I asked, "Why?"

And she said, "Because he is going to find it quite upsetting."

And I said, "Why is he going to find it upsetting?"

Then she sucked in another breath and said, "Because . . . because I think you know why your father doesn't like Mr. Shears much."

Then I asked, "Did Mr. Shears kill Mother?"

And Mrs. Alexander said, "Kill her? No. Of course he didn't."

And I said, "Did he hurt her, so that she had to go into hospital?"

And Mrs. Alexander said, "Did she have to go into hospital?"

And I said, "Yes. And it wasn't very serious at first, but she had a heart attack when she was in hospital. And she died."

And Mrs. Alexander said, "Oh, my goodness," and then she said, "Oh, Christopher, I am so, so sorry. I never realized."

Then I asked her, "Why did you say, 'I think you know why your father doesn't like Mr. Shears very much'?"

Mrs. Alexander put her hand over her mouth and said, "Oh dear, dear, dear." But she didn't answer my question. Instead she asked me a question. She said, "So you don't know?"

And I said, "Don't know what?"

She replied, "Christopher, I probably shouldn't be telling you this." Then she said, "Perhaps we should take a walk in the park together. This is not the place to be talking about this kind of thing."

I was nervous. I did not know Mrs. Alexander. I knew that she was an old lady and that she liked dogs. But she was a stranger. And I never go into the park on my own, because it is dangerous and people inject drugs behind the public toilet in the corner.

But I was excited too. Because I thought she might tell me a secret. And the secret might be about who killed Wellington. Or about Mr. Shears. And if she did that, I might have more evidence against him or be able to *Exclude Him from My Investigations.*

So because it was a **Super Good Day,** I decided to walk into the park with Mrs. Alexander, even though it scared me.

When we were inside the park, Mrs. Alexander stopped walking and said, "I am going to say something to you, and you must promise not to tell your father that I told you this."

I asked, "Why?"

And she said, "I shouldn't have said what I said. And if I don't explain, you'll carry on wondering what I meant. And you might ask your father. And I don't want you to do that, because I don't want you to upset him. So I'm going to explain why I said what I said. But you have to promise not to tell anyone I said this to you."

And I said, "I promise." Because if Mrs. Alexander told me who killed Wellington, or she told me that Mr. Shears had really killed Mother, I could still go to the police and tell them because you are allowed to break a promise if someone has committed a crime.

And Mrs. Alexander said, "Your mother, before she died, was very good friends with Mr. Shears."

And I said, "I know."

And she said, "No, Christopher, I'm not sure that you do. I mean that they were very good friends. Very, very good friends."

I thought about this for a while and said, "Do you mean that they were doing sex?"

And Mrs. Alexander said, "Yes, Christopher. That is what I mean." Then she said, "I'm sorry, Christopher. I really didn't mean to say anything that was going to upset you. But I thought you knew. That's why your father thinks that Mr. Shears is an evil man. And that will be why he doesn't want you going around talking to people about Mr. Shears. Because it will bring back bad memories."

And I said, "Was that why Mr. Shears left Mrs. Shears, because he was doing sex with someone else when he was married to Mrs. Shears?"

And Mrs. Alexander said, "Yes, I expect so." Then she said, "I'm sorry, Christopher. I really am."

And I said, "I think I should go now."

And she said, "Are you OK, Christopher?"

And I said, "I'm scared of being in the park with you because you're a stranger."

And she said, "I'm not a stranger, Christopher. I'm a friend. And if you want to talk about this, you can come and see me any time you want. You only have to knock on my door."

And I said, "OK."

And she said, "Christopher, you won't tell your father about this conversation, will you?"

And I said, "No. I promised."

Then I went home.

23. WHEN I got home, Rhodri was there. Rhodri works for Father, helping him do heating maintenance and boiler repair. And he sometimes comes round to the house in the evening to drink beer with Father and watch the television and have a conversation.

Rhodri was wearing white dungarees, which had dirty marks all over them, and he smelled of something I do not know the name of, which Father often smells of when he comes home from work.

I put my licorice laces and my Milky Bar in my special food box on the shelf that Father is not allowed to touch, because it is mine.

Then Father said, "And what have you been up to, young man?"

And I said, "I went to the shop to get some licorice laces and a Milky Bar."

And he said, "You were a long time."

And I said, "I talked to Mrs. Alexander's dog outside the shop. And I stroked him and he sniffed my trousers." Which was another white lie.

Then Rhodri said to me, "So how are you doing, Captain?"

And I said, "I'm doing very well, thank you," which is what you're meant to say.

And he said, "What's 251 times 864?"

And I thought about this, and I said, "216,864." Because it was a really easy sum, because you just multiply **864 x 1,000,** which is **864,000.** Then you divide it by **4,** which is **216,000,** and that's **250 x 864.** Then you just add another **864** on to it to get **251 x 864.** And that's **216,864.**

And I said, "Is that right?"

And Rhodri said, "I haven't got a clue," and he laughed.

I don't like it when Rhodri laughs at me. Rhodri laughs at me a lot. Father says it is being friendly.

Then Father said, "I'll stick one of those Gobi Aloo Sag things in the oven for you, OK?"

This is because I like Indian food, because it has a strong taste. But Gobi Aloo Sag is yellow, so I put red food coloring into it before I eat it. And I keep a little plastic bottle of this in my special food box.

And I said, "OK."

Then I went into the garden.

Siobhan said that when you are writing a book, you have to include some descriptions of things, and she said it was best to describe things that were interesting or different. I said that I could take photographs and put them in the book. But she said the idea of a book was to describe things using words so that people could read them and make a picture in their own head.

She also said that I should describe people in the story by mentioning one or two details about them. Which is why I wrote about Mr. Jeavons's shoes with all the holes in them and the policeman who looked as if he had two mice in his nose and the thing Rhodri smelled of but I didn't know the name for.

So I decided to do a description of the garden. But the garden wasn't very interesting or different. It was just a garden, with grass and a shed and a clothesline. But the sky was interesting and different because usually skies look boring, because they are all blue or all gray or all covered in one pattern of clouds and they don't look like they are hundreds of miles above your head. They look like someone might have painted them on a big roof. But this sky had lots of different types of clouds in it at different heights, so you could see how big it was, and this made it look enormous.

Farthest away in the sky were lots of little white clouds that looked liked fish scales or sand dunes that had a very regular pattern. Then, next farthest away and to the west were some big clouds that were colored slightly orange because it was nearly evening and the sun was going down. Then closest to the ground was a huge cloud that was colored gray because it was a rain cloud. And it was a big pointy shape and it looked like this

And when I looked at it for a long time, I could see it moving very slowly, and it was like an alien spaceship hundreds of kilometers long, like in *Blake's 7* or *Close Encounters of the Third Kind,* except that it wasn't made of solid material; it was made of droplets of condensed water vapor, which is what clouds are made of.

It could have been an alien spaceship. People think that alien spaceships would be made of metal and have lights all over them and move slowly through the sky because that is how we would build a spaceship if we were able to build one that big. But aliens, if they exist, would probably be different from us. They might look like big slugs or be flat like reflections. Or they might be bigger than planets. Or they might not have bodies at all. They might just be information, like in a computer. And their spaceships might look like clouds or be made up of unconnected objects like dust or leaves.

Then I listened to the sounds of the garden and I could hear a bird singing and I could hear traffic noises and I could hear someone playing music somewhere and children shouting.

Then I sniffed the air to see if I could see what the air in the garden smelled like. But I couldn't smell anything. And this was interesting too.

Then I went inside and fed Toby.

THE *Hound of the Baskervilles* is my favorite book.

I like *The Hound of the Baskervilles* because it is a detective story, which means that there are clues and Red Herrings.

I also like *The Hound of the Baskervilles* because I like Sherlock Holmes, and I think that if I were a proper detective, he is the kind of detective I would be. He is very intelligent, and he solves the mystery, and he says

The world is full of obvious things that nobody by any chance ever observes.

But he notices them, like I do. Also, it says in the book

Sherlock Holmes had, in a very remarkable degree, the power of detaching his mind at will.

And this is like me, too, because if I get really interested in something, like practicing maths or reading a book about the Apollo missions or great white sharks, I don't notice anything else and Father can be calling me and I won't hear him. And this is why I am very good at playing chess, because I detach my mind at will and concentrate on the board, and after a while the person I am playing will stop concentrating and start scratching their nose or staring out of the window and then they will make a mistake and I will win.

Also, Dr. Watson says about Sherlock Holmes

His mind . . . was busy in endeavoring to frame some scheme into which all these strange and apparently disconnected episodes could be fitted.

And that is what I am trying to do by writing this book.

I am going to finish this chapter by including two interesting facts about Sherlock Holmes

1. In the original Sherlock Holmes stories Sherlock Holmes is never described as wearing a deerstalker hat, which is what he is always wearing in pictures. The deerstalker hat was invented by a man called Sidney Paget, who did the illustrations for the original books.

2. In the original Sherlock Holmes stories Holmes never says, "Elementary, my dear Watson." He only ever says this in films.

29. THAT night I wrote some more of my book, and the next day I took it into school so that Siobhan could read it and tell me if I had made mistakes with the spelling and the grammar.

Siobhan read the book during morning break, when she has a cup of coffee and sits at the edge of the playground with the other teachers. After morning break she came and sat down next to me and said she had read the bit about my conversation with Mrs. Alexander, and she said, "Have you told your father about this?"

And I replied, "No."

And she said, "Are you going to tell your father about this?"

And I replied, "No."

And she said, "Good. I think that's a good idea, Christopher." And then she said, "Did it make you sad to find out that your mother and Mr. Shears had an affair?"

And I said, "No."

And she said, "Are you telling the truth, Christopher?"

And then I said, "I always tell the truth."

And she said, "I know you do, Christopher. But sometimes we get sad about things and we don't like to tell other people that we are sad about them. We like to keep it a secret. Or sometimes we are sad, but we don't really know we are sad. So we say we aren't sad. But really we are."

And I said, "I'm not sad."

And she said, "If you do start to feel sad about this, I want you to know that you can come and talk to me about it. Because I think talking to me will help you feel less sad. And if you don't feel sad, but you just want to talk to me about it, that would be OK too. Do you understand?"

And I said, "I understand."

And she said, "Good."

And I replied, "But I don't feel sad about it. Because Mother is dead. And because Mr. Shears isn't around anymore. So I would be feeling sad about something that isn't real and doesn't exist. And that would be stupid."

And then I practiced maths for the rest of the morning, and at lunch I didn't have the quiche, because it was yellow, but I did have the carrots and the peas and tomato ketchup. And for afters I had blackberry-and-apple crumble, but not the crumble bit, because that was yellow, too, and I got Mrs. Davis to take the crumble bit off before she put it onto my plate because it doesn't matter if different sorts of food are touching before they are actually on your plate.

Then, after lunch, I spent the afternoon doing art with Mrs. Peters and I painted some pictures of aliens.

MY MEMORY is like a film. That is why I am good at remembering things, like the conversations I have written down in this book, and what people were wearing, and what they smelled like, because my memory has a smell track, which is like a sound track.

And when people ask me to remember something, I can simply press **Rewind** and **Fast Forward** and **Pause,** like on a video recorder, but more like a DVD player, because I don't have to Rewind through everything in between to get to a memory of something a long time ago.

If someone says to me, "Christopher, tell me what your mother was like," I can Rewind to lots of different scenes and say what she was like in those scenes.

For example, I could Rewind to July 4, 1992, when I was 9 years old, which was a Saturday, and we were on holiday in Cornwall, and in the afternoon we were on the beach in a place called Polperro. And Mother was wearing a pair of shorts made out of denim and a light-blue bikini top, and she was smoking cigarettes called Consulate, which were mint flavor. And she wasn't swimming. Mother was sunbathing on a towel that had red and purple stripes, and she was reading a book by Georgette Heyer called *The Masqueraders.* And then she finished sunbathing and went into the water to swim, and she said, "Bloody Nora, it's cold." And she said I should come and swim, too, but I don't like swimming, because I don't like taking my clothes off. And she said I should just roll up my trousers and walk into the water a little way, so I did. And Mother said, "Look. It's lovely." And she jumped backward and disappeared under the water, and I thought a shark had eaten her and I screamed, and she stood up out of the water again and came over to where I was standing and held up her right hand and spread her fingers out in a fan and said, "Come on, Christopher, touch my hand. Come on now. Stop screaming. Listen to me, Christopher. You can do it." And after a while I stopped screaming and I held up my left hand and spread my fingers out in a fan and we made our fingers and thumbs touch. And Mother said, "It's OK, Christopher. There aren't any sharks in Cornwall," and then I felt better.

Except I can't remember anything before I was about 4, because I wasn't looking at things in the right way before then, so they didn't get recorded properly.

And this is how I recognize someone if I don't know who they are. I see what they are wearing, or if they have funny hair or a certain type of glasses, and I do a **Search** through my memories to see if I have met them before.

And this is also how I know how to act in difficult situations when I don't know what to do. For example, if people say things that don't make sense, like, "See you later, alligator," or "You'll catch your death in that," I do a Search and see if I have ever heard someone say this before.

Other people have pictures in their heads too. But they are different because the pictures in my head are all pictures of things that really happened. But other people have pictures in their heads of things that aren't real and didn't happen. For example, sometimes Mother used to say, "If I hadn't married your father, I think I'd be living in a little farmhouse in the south of France with someone called Jean. And he'd be, ooh, a local handyman. And we'd have a veranda with figs growing over it, and there would be a field of sunflowers at the bottom of the garden and a little town on the hill in the distance, and we'd sit outside in the evening and drink red wine and watch the sun go down."

And sometimes when someone has died, like Mother died, people say, "What would you want to say to your mother if she was here now?" or, "What would your mother think about that?" which is stupid because Mother is dead and you can't say anything to people who are dead and dead people can't think.

And Grandmother has pictures in her head, too, but her pictures are all confused, like someone has muddled the film up, and she can't tell what happened in what order, so she thinks that dead people are still alive and she doesn't know whether something happened in real life or whether it happened on television.

31. WHEN I got home from school, Father was still out at work, so I unlocked the front door and went inside and took my coat off. I went into the kitchen and put my things on the table. And one of the things was this book. I made myself a raspberry milk shake and then went through to the living room to watch one of my *Blue Planet* videos about life in the deepest parts of the ocean, about sulfur chimneys, which are underwater volcanoes where gases are ejected from the earth's crust into the water. Scientists never expected there to be any living organisms there, because it was so hot and so poisonous, but there are whole ecosystems there.

I like this bit because it shows you that there is always something new that science can discover, and all the facts that you take for granted can be completely wrong. And also, I like the fact that they are filming in a place that is harder to get to than the top of Mount Everest but is only a few miles away from sea level. And it is one of the quietest and darkest and most secret places on the surface of the earth. And I like imagining that I am there sometimes, in a spherical metal submersible, with windows that are 30 cm thick to stop them from imploding under the pressure. And I imagine that I am the only person in it and that I can control the motors and move anywhere I want to on the seabed and I can never be found.

Father came home at 5:48 p.m. I heard him come through the front door and into the living room. He was wearing a lime-green-and-sky-blue-checked shirt.

He said, "Howdy, pardner," which is a joke he does.

And I said, "Hello."

I carried on watching the video and Father went into the kitchen.

I had forgotten that I had left my book on the kitchen table, because I was too interested in the *Blue Planet* video. This is what is called *Relaxing Your Guard,* and it is what you must never do if you are a detective.

It was 5:54 p.m. when Father came back into the living room. He said, "What is this?" But he said it very quietly, and I didn't realize that he was angry, because he wasn't shouting. He was holding the book in his right hand.

I said, "It's a book I'm writing."

And he said, "Is this true? Did you talk to Mrs. Alexander?" He said this very quietly as well.

And I said, "Yes."

Then he said, "God, Christopher. How stupid are you?"

This is what Siobhan says is called a rhetorical question. It has a question mark at the end, but you are not meant to answer it, because the person who is asking it already knows the answer. It is difficult to spot a rhetorical question.

Then Father said, "What did I tell you, Christopher?" This was much louder.

And I replied, "Not to mention Mr. Shears's name in our house. And not to go asking Mrs. Shears, or anyone, about who killed that bloody dog. And not to go trespassing in other people's gardens. And to stop this ridiculous bloody detective game. Except I haven't done any of those things. I just asked Mrs. Alexander about Mr. Shears because—"

But Father interrupted me and said, "Don't give me that. You knew exactly what you were bloody doing. I've read the book, remember?" And when he said this, he held up the book and shook it. "What else did I say, Christopher?"

I thought that this might be another rhetorical question, but I wasn't sure. I found it hard to work out what to say, because I was starting to get scared and confused. I said, "I don't know."

And he said, "Come on. You're the memory man."

But I couldn't think.

And Father said, "Not to go around sticking your nose into other people's business. And what do you do? You go sticking your nose in other people's business. You go raking up the past and sharing it with every Tom, Dick, and Harry you bump into. What am I going to do with you, Christopher? What am I going to do with you?"

I said, "I was just doing chatting with Mrs. Alexander. I wasn't doing investigating. I didn't want to talk to Mrs. Alexander. It was Mrs. Alexander who—"

But Father interrupted me and grabbed hold of my arm really hard.

Father had never grabbed hold of me like that before. Mother had hit me sometimes because she was a very hot-tempered person, which means that she got angry more quickly than other people and she shouted more often. But Father is levelheaded, which means he doesn't get angry as quickly and he doesn't shout often. So I was very surprised when he grabbed me.

I don't like it when people grab me. And I don't like being surprised either. So I hit him, like I hit the policeman when he took hold of my arms and lifted me onto my feet. But Father didn't let go and he was shouting. And I hit him again. And then I didn't know what I was doing anymore.

I had no memories for a short while. I know it was a short while because I checked my watch afterward. It was like someone had switched me off and then switched me on again. And when they switched me on again, I was sitting on the carpet with my back against the wall and there was blood on my right hand and the side of my head was hurting. And Father was standing on the carpet, looking down at me, and he was still holding my book in his right hand, but it was bent in half and all the corners were messed up, and there was a scratch on his neck and a big rip in the sleeve of his green-and-blue-checked shirt and he was breathing really deeply.

After about a minute he turned and he walked through to the kitchen. Then he unlocked the back door into the garden and went outside. I heard him lift the lid of the dustbin and drop something into it. Then he came into the kitchen again, but he wasn't carrying the book anymore. Then he locked the back door and put the key into the little china jug that is shaped like a fat nun, and he stood in the middle of the kitchen and closed his eyes. Then he opened his eyes and said, "I need a drink." And he got himself a can of beer.

THE next day Father said he was sorry that he had hit me and he didn't mean to. He made me wash the cut on my cheek with Dettol to make sure that it wasn't infected, then he got me to put a plaster on it so it didn't bleed.

Then, because it was a Saturday, he said he was going to take me on an expedition to show me that he was properly sorry, and we were going to Twycross Zoo. So he made me some sandwiches with white bread and tomatoes and lettuce and ham and strawberry jam for me to eat because I don't like eating food from places I don't know. And he said it would be OK because there wouldn't be too many people because it was forecast to rain, and I was glad about that because I don't like crowds of people and I like it when it is raining. So I went and got my waterproof, which is orange.

Then we drove to Twycross Zoo.

I had never been to Twycross Zoo before, so I didn't have a picture of it in my mind before we got there, so we bought a guidebook from the information center and then we walked round the whole zoo and I decided which were my favorite animals.

My favorite animals were

1. **RANDYMAN,** which is the name of the oldest **Red-faced Black Spider Monkey** ever kept in captivity. Randyman is 44 years old, which is the same age as Father.
2. The **PATAGONIAN SEA LIONS** called **Miracle** and **Star.**
3. **MALIKU,** which is an **Orangutan.** I liked it especially

because it was lying in a kind of hammock made out of a pair of stripy green pajama bottoms, and on the blue plastic notice next to the cage it said it made the hammock itself.

Then we went to the café and Father had plaice and chips and apple pie and ice cream and a pot of Earl Grey tea, and I had my sandwiches and I read the guidebook to the zoo.

And Father said, "I love you very much, Christopher. Don't ever forget that. And I know I lose my rag occasionally. I know I shout. And I know I shouldn't. But I only do it because I worry about you, because I don't want to see you getting into trouble and I don't want you to get hurt. Do you understand?"

I didn't know whether I understood. So I said, "I don't know."

And Father said, "Christopher, do you understand that I love you?"

And I said, "Yes," because loving someone is helping them when they get into trouble, and looking after them, and telling them the truth, and Father looks after me when I get into trouble, like coming to the police station, and he looks after me by cooking meals for me, and he always tells me the truth, which means that he loves me.

And then he held up his right hand and spread his fingers out in a fan, and I held up my left hand and spread my fingers out in a fan, and we made our fingers and thumbs touch each other.

Then we went and looked at the giraffes. And the smell of their poo was like the smell in the gerbil cage at school, and when they ran, their legs were so long, it looked like they were running in slow motion.

Then Father said we had to get home before the roads got busy.

37. WHEN I got home from school on Monday, Father was still at work, so I went into the kitchen and took the key out of the little china jug shaped like a nun and opened the back door and

went outside and looked inside the dustbin to find my book.

I wanted to get my book back because I liked writing it. Also, I still didn't know who had killed Wellington, and my book was where I had kept all the clues that I had discovered and I did not want them to be thrown away. But my book wasn't in the dustbin.

I put the lid back on the dustbin and walked down the garden to have a look in the bin where Father keeps the garden waste, but my book wasn't in there either.

One other possibility was that Father had hidden my book somewhere in the house. So I decided to do some detecting and see if I could find it. Except I had to keep listening really hard all the time so I would hear his van when he pulled up outside the house so he wouldn't catch me being a detective.

I started by looking in the kitchen. My book was approximately **25 cm x 35 cm x 1 cm,** so it couldn't be hidden in a very small place, which meant that I didn't have to look in any really small places. I looked on top of the cupboards and down the back of drawers and under the oven, and I used my special Mag-Lite torch and a piece of mirror from the utility room to help me see into the dark spaces at the back of the cupboards where the mice used to get in from the garden and have their babies.

Then I detected in the utility room.

Then I detected in the dining room.

Then I detected in the living room, where I found the missing wheel from my Airfix Messerschmitt Bf 109 G-6 model under the sofa.

Then I went upstairs, but I didn't do any detecting in my own room, because I reasoned that Father wouldn't hide something from me in my own room unless he was being very clever and doing what is called a *Double Bluff,* like in a real murder mystery novel, so I decided to look there only if I couldn't find the book anywhere else.

I detected in the bathroom, but the only place to look was in the airing cupboard and there was nothing in there.

Which meant that the only room left to detect in was Father's bedroom. I didn't know whether I should look in there, because he had told me before not to mess with anything in his room. But if he was going to hide something from me, the best place to hide it would be in his room. So I told myself I would not mess with things in his room. I would move them and then I would move them back. And he would never know I had done it, so he wouldn't be angry.

I started by looking under the bed. There were 7 shoes and a comb and a piece of copper pipe and a chocolate biscuit and a dead bee and a Homer Simpson–patterned tie, but not my book.

Then I looked in the drawers on either side of the dressing table, but these only contained aspirin and nail clippers and dental floss.

Then I looked in his clothes cupboard. This was full of his clothes on hangers. In the bottom of the cupboard was a large plastic toolbox that was full of tools for doing Do-It-Yourself, like a drill and some screws and a hammer, but I could see these without opening the box because it was made of transparent gray plastic.

Then I saw that there was another box underneath the toolbox, so I lifted the toolbox out of the cupboard. The other box was an old cardboard box that is called a shirt box because people used to buy shirts in them. And when I opened the shirt box, I saw my book.

Then I didn't know what to do.

I was happy because Father hadn't thrown my book away. But if I took the book, he would know I had been messing with things in his room and he would be very angry and I had promised not to mess with things in his room.

Then I heard his van pulling up outside the house and I knew that I had to think fast. So I decided that I would leave the book where it was because I reasoned that Father wasn't going to throw it away if he had put it into the box, and I could carry on writing in another book that I would keep really secret and then, maybe later, he might change his mind and let me have the first book back again and I could copy the new book into it. And if he never gave it back to me, I would be able to remember most of what I had written, so I would put it all into the second secret book, and if there were bits I wanted to check to make sure that I had remembered them correctly, I could come into his room when he was out and check.

Then I heard Father shutting the door of the van.

And that was when I saw the envelope.

It was addressed to me and it was lying under my book in the shirt box with some other envelopes. I picked it up. It had never been opened. It said

> Christopher Boone
> 36 Randolph Street
> Swindon
> Wiltshire

Then I noticed that there were lots of other envelopes and they were all addressed to me. And this was interesting and confusing.

And then I noticed how the words Christopher and Swindon were written. They were like this

Christopher

Swindon

I only know 3 people who do little circles instead of dots over the letter *i*. And one of them is Siobhan; one of them was Mr. Loxely, who used to teach at the school; and one of them was Mother.

And then I heard Father opening the front door, so I took one envelope from under the book and I put the lid back on the shirt box and I put the toolbox back on top of it and I closed the cupboard door really carefully.

Then Father called out, "Christopher?"

I said nothing, because he might be able to hear where I was calling from. I stood up and walked round the bed to the door, holding the envelope, trying to make as little noise as possible.

Father was standing at the bottom of the stairs and I thought he might see me, but he was flicking through the post that had come that morning, so his head was pointing downward. Then he walked away from the foot of the stairs toward the kitchen, and I closed the door of his room very quietly and went into my own room, where I hid the envelope underneath my mattress. Then I walked downstairs and said hello to Father.

And he said, "So what have you been up to today, young man?"

And I said, "Today we did *Life Skills* with Mrs. Gray. Which was *Using Money* and *Public Transport*. And I had tomato soup for lunch and 3 apples. And I practiced some maths in the afternoon and we went for a walk in the park with Mrs. Peters and collected leaves for making collages."

And Father said, "Excellent. What do you fancy for chow tonight?"

Chow is food. I said I wanted baked beans and broccoli.

And Father said, "I think that can be very easily arranged."

Then I sat on the sofa and I read some more of the book I was reading called *Chaos* by James Gleick.

Then I went into the kitchen and had my baked beans and broccoli while Father had sausages and eggs and fried bread and a mug of tea.

Then Father said, "I'm going to put those shelves up in the living room, if that's all right with you. I'll make a bit of a racket, I'm afraid, so if you want to watch television, we're going to have to shift it upstairs."

And I said, "I'll go and be on my own in my room."

And he said, "Good man."

And I said, "Thank you for the supper," because that is being polite.

And he said, "No problem, kiddo."

And I went up to my room. I shut the door and I took out the envelope from underneath my mattress. I held the letter up to the light to see if I could detect what was inside the envelope, but the paper of the envelope was too thick. I wondered whether I should open the envelope, because it was something I had taken from Father's room. But then I reasoned that because the envelope was addressed to me, it belonged to me, so it was OK to open it.

So I opened the envelope. Inside, there was a letter. And this is what was written in the letter

Dear Christopher,

I'm sorry it's been such a very long time since I wrote my last letter to you. I've been very busy. I've got a new job working as a secretery for a factory that makes things out of steel. You'd like it a lot. The factory is full of huge machines that make the steel and cut it and bend it into watever shapes they need. This week they're making a roof for a cafe in a shopping centre in Birmingham.

Also we've moved into the new flat, as you can see from the address. It's not as nice as the old one and I don't like Willesden very much, but it's easier for Roger to get to work and he's bought it (he only rented the other one), so we can get our own furnature and paint the walls the colour we want to. And that's why it's such a long time since I wrote my last letter to you because it's been hard work packing up all our things and then unpacking them and getting used to this new job. I'm very tired now and I must go to sleep and I want to put this into the letterbox tomorrow morning, so I'll sign off now and write you another letter soon.

You haven't written to me yet, so I know that you are probably still angry with me. I'm sorry Christopher. But I still love you. I hope you don't stay angry with me forever. And I'd love it if you were able to write me a letter.

I think about you all the time.

Lots of Love,
Your Mum x x x x x

Then I was really confused because Mother had never worked as a secretary for a firm that made things out of steel. Mother had worked as a secretary for a big garage in the center of town. And Mother had never lived in London. Mother had always lived with us. And Mother had never written a letter to me before.

There was no date on the letter, so I couldn't work out when

Mother had written the letter, and I wondered whether someone else had written the letter and pretended to be Mother.

And then I looked at the front of the envelope, and I saw that there was a postmark with a date on it, and it said

Which meant that the letter was posted on October 16, 1997, which was 18 months after Mother had died.

And then the door of my bedroom opened, and Father said, "What are you doing?"

I said, "I'm reading a letter."

And he said, "I've finished the drilling. That David Attenborough nature program's on telly if you're interested."

I said, "OK."

Then he went downstairs again.

I looked at the letter and thought really hard. It was a mystery and I couldn't work it out. Perhaps the letter was in the wrong envelope and it had been written before Mother had died. But why was she writing from London? The longest she had been away was a week, when she went to visit her cousin Ruth who had cancer, and Ruth lived in Manchester.

And then I thought that perhaps it was a letter to another person called Christopher, from that Christopher's mother.

I was excited. When I started writing my book, there was only one mystery I had to solve. Now there were two.

I decided that I would not think about it anymore that night, because I didn't have enough information and could easily *Leap to the Wrong Conclusions,* which is a dangerous thing to do because you should make sure you have all the available clues before you start deducing things. That way you are less likely to make a mistake.

I decided that I would wait until Father was out of the house. Then I would go into the cupboard in his bedroom and look at the other letters and see who they were from and what they said.

I folded the letter and hid it under my mattress. Then I went downstairs and watched the television.

41.
IT WAS 6 days before I could go back into Father's room to look in the shirt box in the cupboard.

On the first, second, third, and fourth days, which were Wednesday, Thursday, Friday, and Saturday, nothing interesting happened.

On the fifth day, which was a Sunday, it rained hard. I like it when it rains hard. It sounds like white noise everywhere, which is like silence but not empty.

I went upstairs and sat in my room and watched the water falling in the street. It was falling so hard that it looked like white sparks. And there was no one around, because everyone was staying indoors. And it made me think how all the water in the world was connected, and this water had evaporated from the oceans somewhere in the middle of the Gulf of Mexico or Baffin Bay, and now it was falling in front of the house and it would drain away into the gutters and flow to a sewage station, where it would be cleaned, and then it would go into a river and go back into the ocean again.

And in the evening on Monday, Father got a phone call from a lady whose cellar had flooded and he had to go out and fix it in an emergency.

Father told me to behave and to ring him on his mobile phone if there was a problem, and then he went out in the van.

So I went into his bedroom and opened up the cupboard and lifted the toolbox off the top of the shirt box and opened the shirt box. I counted the letters. There were 43 of them. They were all addressed to me in the same handwriting.

I took one out and opened it. Inside was this letter

3rd May

451c Chapter Road
London NW2 5NG
0208 887 8907

Dear Christopher,

We have a new fridge and cooker at last! Roger and I drove to the tip at the weekend to throw the old ones away. It's where people throw everything away. There are huge bins for three different colors of bottles and cardboard and engine oil and garden waste and larger items (that's where we put the old fridge and the cooker).

Then we went to a secondhand shop and bought a new cooker and a new fridge. Now the house feels a little bit more like home.

I was looking through some old photos last night, which made me sad. Then I found a photo of you playing with the train set we bought for you. And that made me happy because it was one of the really good times we had together. Do you remember how you played with it all day and you refused to go to bed at night because you were still playing with it? And do you remember how we told you about train timetabels and you made a train timetabel and you had a clock and you made the trains run on time. And there was a little wooddden station, too, and we showed you how people who wanted to go on the train went to the station and bought a ticket and then got on the train? And then we got out a map and we showed you the little lines which were the trains lines connecting all the stations. You played with it for weeks and weeks and we bought you more trains and you knew where they were all going. I liked remembering that a lot.

I have to go now. It's half past three in the afternoon. I know you always like to know exactly what time it is. And I have to go to the Co-op and buy some ham to make Roger's tea with. I'll put this letter in the post box on the way to the shop.

Love,
Your Mum x x x x x

Then I opened another envelope. This was the letter that was inside

Dear Christopher,

I said that I wanted to explain to you why I went away when I had the time to do it properly. Now I have lots of time. So I'm sitting on the sofa with this letter and the radio on and I'm going to try to explain.

I was not a very good mother, Christopher. Maybe if things had been differant, maybe if you'd been differant, I might have been better at it. But that's just the way things turned out.

I'm not like your father. Your father is much more pacient. He just gets on with things and if things upset him he doesn't let it show. But that's not the way I am and there's nothing I can do to change that.

Do you remember once when we were shopping in town together? And we went into Bentalls and it was really crowded and we had to get a Christmas present for Grandma? You were frightened because of all the people in the shop. And I was talking to Mr. Land who works on the kichen floor and went to school with me. And you crouched down on the floor and put your hands over your ears and you were in the way of everyone. So I got cross, because I don't like shopping at Christmas, either, and I told you to behave and I tried to pick you up and move you. But you shouted and you knocked those mixers off the shelf and there was a big crash. And everyone turned round to see what was going on. And Mr. Land was realy nice about it but there were boxes and bits of broken bowl on the floor and everyone was staring and I saw that you had wet yourself and I was so cross and I wanted to take you out of the shop but you wouldn't let me touch you and you just lay on the floor and screamed. The maniger came and asked what the problem was and I was at the end of my tether and I had to pay for two broken mixers and we just had to wait until you stoped screaming. I had to walk you all the way home which took hours because I knew you wouldn't go on the bus again.

I remember that night I just cried and cried and your father was really nice about it at first and he made you supper and he put you to bed and he said these things happen and it would be OK. But I said

I couldn't take it any more and eventually he got really cross and he told me I was being stupid and should pull myself together.

We had a lot of argumants like that. Because I often thought I couldn't take any more. And your father is really pacient but I'm not, I get cross, even though I don't mean too. And by the end we stopped talking to each other very much because we knew it would always end up in an argumant and it would go nowere. And I felt realy lonley.

That was when I started spending lots of time with Roger. I mean obviously we had always spent lots of time with Roger and Eileen. But I started seeing Roger on his own because I could talk to him. And when I was with him I didn't feel lonley anymore.

And I know you might not understand any of this, but I wanted to explain, so that you knew. And even if you don't understand now, you can keep this letter and read it later and maybe you might understand then.

Roger told me that he and Eileen weren't in love with one another anymore, which meant that he was feeling lonely too. So we had a lot in common. And then we realized that we were in love with one another. He suggested that we should move into a house together. But I said that I couldn't leave you, and he was sad about that but he understood that you were realy important to me.

And then you and me had that argumant. Do you remember? It was about your supper one evening. I'd cooked you something and you wouldn't eat it. You hadn't eaten for days and you were looking so thin. You started to shout and I got cross and I threw the food across the room. Which I know I shouldn't have done. And you grabbed the chopping board and you threw it and it hit my foot and broke my toes. Then, of course, we had to go to the hospital and I had that plaster put on my foot. And afterward, at home, your father blamed me for getting cross with you. And he said I should just give you what you wanted, even if it was just a strawberry milk shake. And I said I was just trying to get you to eat something healthy. And he said that you couldn't help it. And I said well I couldn't help it either. And he said that if he could keep his temper then I should bloody well keep my temper. And it went on and on like this.

And I couldn't walk properly for a month, do you remember, and your father had to look after you. And I remember looking at the two of you and seeing you together and thinking how you were really differant with him. Much calmer. And you didn't shout at one another. And it made me so sad because it was like you didn't really need me at all. It was like I was invisible.

And I think that was when I realized you and your father were probably better off if I wasn't living in the house. Then he would only have one person to look after instead of two.

Then Roger said that he had asked the bank for a transfer to London and he was leaving. He asked me if I wanted to come with him. I thought about it for a long time, Christopher. Honestly, I did. And it broke my heart, but eventualy I decided it would be better for all of us if I went. So I said yes.

I meant to say goodbye. I was going to come back and pick up some clothes when you were back from school. And that was when I was going to explain and say that I would come back and see you as often as I could and you could come down to London to stay with us. But when I rang your father he said I couldn't come back. He was really angry. He said I couldn't talk to you. I didn't know what to do. He said that I was being selfish and that I was never to set foot inside the house again. So I haven't. But I have written you these letters instead.

I wonder if you can understand any of this. I know it will be very difficult for you. But I hope you can understand a little. Christopher, I never meant to hurt you. I thought that what I was doing was the best for all of us. I hope it is. I want you to know this is not your fault.

I used to have dreams that everything would get better. Do you remember you used to say that you wanted to be an astranaut? Well, I used to have dreams you were an astranaut and you were on the television and I thought that's my son. I wonder what it is that you want to be now. Has it changed? Are you still doing maths? I hope you are.

Please, Christopher, write to me sometime, or ring me on the telephone. The numbers at the top of the letter.

Love and Kisses,
Your Mother x x x x x

Then I opened a third envelope. This was the letter that was inside

18th September

> *Flat 1, 312 Lausanne Road*
> *London N8 5BV*
> *0208 756 4321*

Dear Christopher,

Well, I said I'd write you every week, and I have. In fact, this is the second letter this week, so I'm doing even better than I said.

I have got a job! I'm working in Camden, at Perkin and Rashid, which is a Chartered Survayors. It's a nice office. I don't know how long I'll stay here, though. I have to do a lot of adding up of numbers for when we send bills out to clients and I'm not very good at doing this (you'd be better at it than I am!). The pay is not very good either. So I shall be looking for something better as soon as I get the chance.

I went up to Alexandra Palace the other day. It's a big park just round the corner from our flat, and the park is a huge hill with a big conference center on the top and it made me think of you because if you came here we could go there and fly kites or watch the planes coming into Heathrow airport and I know you'd like that.

I have to go now, Christopher. I'm writing this in my lunch hour. Please write to me sometime and tell me about how you are and what your doing at school.

> *Loads and loads of love,*
> *Your Mother x x x x*

And there was a fourth letter, but I stopped reading because I felt sick. Mother had not had a heart attack. Mother had not died. Mother had been alive all the time. And Father had lied about this.

I tried really hard to think if there was any other explanation, but I couldn't think of one. And then I couldn't think of anything at all, because my brain wasn't working properly.

I rolled onto the bed and curled up in a ball. My stomach hurt.

I don't know what happened then, because there is a gap in my memory, like a bit of the tape had been erased. But I know that a lot of time must have passed because later on, when I opened my eyes again, I could see that it was dark outside the window. And I had been sick, because there was sick all over the bed.

I heard Father coming into the house and calling out my name, which is another reason why I know a lot of time had passed.

And then I heard him come up the stairs and walk into the room. He said, "Christopher, what the hell are you doing?" and his voice sounded tiny and far away, like people's voices sometimes do when I am groaning and I don't want them to be near me.

And he said, "That's my cupboard, Christopher. Those are . . . Oh, damn . . . Damn, damn, damn."

He said nothing for a while. Then he put his hand on my shoulder and moved me onto my side, and he said, "Oh, God." But it didn't hurt when he touched me, like it normally does. I could see him touching me, like I was watching a film of what was happening in the room, but I could hardly feel his hand at all.

And he was silent again for a while. Then he said, "I'm sorry, Christopher. I'm so, so sorry. You read the letters."

Then I could hear that he was crying because his breath sounded all bubbly and wet. He said, "I did it for your good, Christopher. Honestly I did. I never meant to lie. I just thought it was better if you didn't know . . . that . . . that . . . I didn't mean to . . . I was going to show them to you when you were older."

Then he was silent again. Then he said, "I didn't know what to say. . . . I was in such a mess. . . . She left a note and . . . Then she rang and . . . I said she was in hospital because . . . because I didn't know how to explain. It was so complicated. So difficult. And I . . . I said she was in hospital. And I know it wasn't true. But once I'd said that, I couldn't . . . I couldn't change it. Do you understand, Christopher? It just . . . It got out of control and I wish . . ."

Then he was silent again for a really long time.

Then he touched me on the shoulder again and said, "Christopher, we have to get you cleaned up, OK?"

He shook my shoulder a little bit, but I didn't move.

And he said, "Christopher, I'm going to go to the bathroom and

I'm going to run you a hot bath. Then I'm going to come back and take you to the bathroom, OK? Then I can put the sheets into the washing machine."

I heard him get up and go to the bathroom and turn the taps on. I listened to the water running into the bath. Then he came back and touched my shoulder again and said, "Let's do this really gently, Christopher. Let's sit you up and get your clothes off and get you into the bath, OK? I'm going to have to touch you, but it's going to be all right."

Then he lifted me up and made me sit on the side of the bed. He took my jumper and my shirt off and put them on the bed. Then he made me stand up and walk through to the bathroom. And I didn't scream. And I didn't fight. And I didn't hit him.

43. AFTER Father had given me a bath and dried me off with a towel, he took me to my room and put some clean clothes on me.

Then he said, "Have you had anything to eat yet this evening?"

But I didn't say anything.

Then he said, "Can I get you something to eat, Christopher?"

But I still didn't say anything.

So he said, "OK. Look, I'm going to put your clothes and the bedsheets into the washing machine and then I'll come back, OK?"

I sat on the bed and looked at my knees.

So Father went out of the room and picked up my clothes and put them on the landing. Then he got the sheets from his bed and brought them onto the landing, together with my shirt and jumper. Then he picked them all up and took them downstairs. I heard him start the washing machine and I heard the boiler starting up and the water in the water pipes going into the washing machine.

I doubled 2's in my head because it made me feel calmer. I got to **33,554,432**, which is 2^{25}, which was not very much, because I've got to 2^{45} before, but my brain wasn't working very well.

Then Father came back into the room again and said, "How are you feeling? Can I get you anything?"

I didn't say anything. I carried on looking at my knees.

And Father didn't say anything either. He just sat down on the bed next to me and put his elbows on his knees and looked down at the carpet between his legs.

Then I heard Toby waking up, because he is nocturnal, and I heard him rustling in his cage.

And Father was silent for a really long time. Then he said, "Look, maybe I shouldn't say this, but . . . I want you to know that you can trust me. And OK, maybe I don't tell the truth all the time. I try, Christopher, but . . . life is difficult, you know. It's hard telling the truth all the time. Sometimes it's impossible. And I want you to know that I'm trying, I really am. And perhaps this is not a very good time to say this, and I know you're not going to like it, but . . . You have to know that I am going to tell you the truth from now on. About everything. Because if you don't tell the truth now, then later on . . . later on it hurts even more. So . . . ."

Father rubbed his face with his hands and pulled his chin down with his fingers and stared at the wall. I could see him out of the corner of my eye. And he said, "I killed Wellington, Christopher."

I wondered if this was a joke, because I don't understand jokes, and when people tell jokes, they don't mean what they say.

But then Father said, "Please, Christopher, just let me explain." Then he sucked in some air and said, "When your mum left, Eileen . . . Mrs. Shears . . . was very good to us. Very good to me. She helped me through a very difficult time. And I'm not sure I would have made it without her. You know how she was round here most days. Helping out with the cooking and cleaning. Popping over to see if we needed anything. . . . I thought . . . Well, I thought she might . . . eventually . . . want to move in here. Or that we might move into her house. We got on really, really well. I thought we were friends. And I guess I thought wrong. . . . In the end, it comes down to . . . We argued, Christopher, and she said some things I'm not going to say to you, because they're not nice, but they hurt. . . .

I think she cared more for that bloody dog than for me, for us. And maybe that's not so stupid, looking back. Maybe we are a bloody handful. Anyway, we had quite a few rows. After this particularly nasty little blowout, she chucked me out of the house. And you know what that bloody dog was like after the operation. . . . Nice as pie one moment, roll over, tickle its stomach. Sink its teeth into your leg the next. Anyway, we're yelling at each other and it's in the garden relieving itself. So when she slams the door behind me, the bugger's waiting for me. And . . . I know, I know. Maybe if I'd just given it a kick, it would probably have backed off. But all I could think was that she cared more about this bloody dog than she did about you or me. And it was like everything I'd been bottling up for two years just . . ."

Then Father was silent for a bit. Then he said, "I'm sorry, Christopher. I promise you, I never meant for it to turn out like this."

And then I knew that it wasn't a joke and I was really frightened.

Then he held up his right hand and spread his fingers out in a fan. But I screamed and pushed him backward so that he fell off the bed and onto the floor.

He sat up and said, "Look, Christopher, I'm sorry. Let's leave it for tonight, OK? I'm going to go downstairs and you get some sleep and we'll talk in the morning. It's going to be all right. Honestly. Trust me." Then he stood up and took a deep breath and went out of the room.

I sat on the bed for a long time. Then I heard Toby scratching in his cage. I looked up and saw him staring through the bars at me.

I had to get out of the house. Father had murdered Wellington. That meant he could murder me, because I couldn't trust him, even though he had said, "Trust me," because he had told a lie about a big thing. But I couldn't get out of the house straightaway, because he would see me, so I would have to wait until he was asleep.

The time was 11:16 p.m. I tried doubling 2's again, but I couldn't get past 2^{15}, which was **32,768.** So I groaned to make the time pass quicker and not think.

Then it was 1:20 a.m., but I hadn't heard Father come upstairs to bed. I wondered if he was asleep downstairs or whether he was waiting to come in and kill me. So I got out my Swiss army knife and opened the saw blade so that I could defend myself. Then I went out of my bedroom and listened. I couldn't hear anything, so I started going downstairs really quietly. And when I got downstairs, I could see Father's foot through the door of the living room. I waited for 4 minutes to see if it moved, but it didn't. So I carried on walking till I got to the hallway. Then I looked round the door of the living room.

Father was lying on the sofa with his eyes closed. I looked at him for a long time. Then he snored and I jumped and I could hear the blood in my ears and my heart going really fast.

Father's eyes were still closed. He was asleep.

That meant I could get out of the house if I was really quiet, so I didn't wake him. I took both my coats and my scarf from the hooks next to the front door and I put them all on because it would be cold outside at night. Then I went upstairs again really quietly, but it was difficult, because my legs were shaking. I went into my room and I picked up Toby's cage. He was making scratching noises, so I took off one of the coats and put it over the cage to make the noise quieter. Then I carried him downstairs again.

I went into the kitchen and I picked up my special food box. I unlocked the back door and stepped outside. Then I held the handle of the door down as I shut it again, so that the click wasn't too loud. Then I walked down to the bottom of the garden.

At the bottom of the garden is a shed. It has the lawn mower and the hedge cutter in it, and lots of gardening equipment. It would be a bit warmer in the shed, but I knew that Father might look for me there, so I went round the back of the shed and squeezed into the gap between the wall of the shed and the fence, behind the big, black, plastic tub for collecting rainwater. Then I sat down. I decided to leave my other coat over Toby's cage because I didn't want him to get cold and die.

I opened up my special food box. Inside was the Milky Bar and two licorice laces and three clementines and a pink wafer biscuit and my red food coloring. I didn't feel hungry, but I knew that I should eat something, because if you don't eat something, you can get cold, so I ate two clementines and the Milky Bar. Then I wondered what I would do next.

BETWEEN the roof of the shed and the big plant that hangs over the fence from the house next door, I could see the constellation **Orion.**

People say that **Orion** is called Orion because Orion was a hunter and the constellation looks like a hunter with a club and a bow and arrow, like this

But this is really silly because it is just stars, and you could join up the dots in any way you wanted and you could make it look like a lady with an umbrella who is waving, or the coffeemaker that Mrs. Shears has, which is from Italy, with a handle and steam coming out, or like a dinosaur

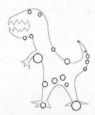

And there aren't any lines in space, so you could join bits of **Orion** to bits of **Lepus** or **Taurus** or **Gemini** and say that they were a constellation called **The Bunch of Grapes** or **The Bicycle** (except that they didn't have bicycles in Roman and Greek times, which was when they called **Orion** Orion).

And anyway, **Orion** is not a hunter or a coffeemaker or a dinosaur.

It is just Betelgeuse and Bellatrix and Alnilam and Rigel and 17 other stars I don't know the names of. And they are nuclear explosions billions of miles away.

And that is the truth.

47. I STAYED awake until 3:47. That was the last time I looked at my watch before I fell asleep. It has a luminous face and lights up if you press a button, so I could read it in the dark.

I looked at the sky a lot. I like looking up at the sky in the garden at night. In summer I sometimes come outside at night with my torch and my planisphere, which is two circles of plastic with a pin through the middle. On the bottom is a map of the sky and on top is an aperture that is shaped in a parabola and you turn it round to see a map of the sky that you can see on that day of the year from the latitude 51.5° north, which is the latitude that Swindon is on.

And when you look at the sky, you know you are looking at stars that are hundreds and thousands of light-years away from you. And some of the stars don't even exist anymore, because their light has taken so long to get to us that they are already dead or they have exploded and collapsed into red dwarfs. And that makes you seem very small, and if you have difficult things in your life, it is nice to think that they are what is called *negligible,* which means that they are so small, you don't have to take them into account when you are calculating something.

I didn't sleep very well because of the cold and because the ground was very bumpy underneath me and because Toby was scratching in his cage a lot. But when I woke up properly, it was dawn and the sky was all orange and blue and purple. And I stayed where I was for another 2 hours and 32 minutes, and then I heard Father come into the garden and call out, "Christopher?"

So I turned round and I found an old plastic sack that used to have fertilizer in it and I squeezed myself and Toby's cage and my special food box into the corner between the wall of the shed and the fence and the rainwater tub and I covered us with the fertilizer sack. And then I heard Father coming down the garden, and I took my Swiss army knife out of my pocket and got out the saw blade and held it in case he found us. And I heard him open the door of the shed and look inside. And then I heard his footsteps in the bushes round the side of the shed and my heart was beating really fast and I think he might have looked round the back of the shed, but I couldn't see, because I was hiding, but he didn't see me, because I heard him walking back up the garden again.

Then I looked at my watch and I stayed still for 27 minutes. And then I heard Father start the engine of his van. And when I heard him drive away from the house, I knew it would be safe to come out.

And then I had to decide what to do. I did this by thinking of all the things I could do and deciding whether they were the right decision or not.

I decided that I couldn't go home again.

And I decided that I couldn't go and live with Siobhan, because she couldn't look after me when school was closed, because she was a teacher and not a friend or a member of my family.

And I decided that I couldn't go and live with Uncle Terry, because he lived in Sunderland and I didn't know how to get to Sunderland and I didn't like Uncle Terry, because he smoked cigarettes and stroked my hair.

And I decided I couldn't go and live with Mrs. Alexander, because she wasn't a friend or a member of my family, even if she had a dog.

And then I thought that I could go and live with Mother because I knew where she lived, because I could remember the address from the letters, which was 451c Chapter Road, London, NW2 5NG. Except that she lived in London and I'd never been to London before. I'd only been to France, and to Sunderland to visit Uncle Terry, and to Manchester to visit Aunt Ruth. I had never been anywhere apart from the shop at the end of the road on my own. And the thought of going somewhere on my own was frightening.

But then I thought about going home again or hiding in the garden every night and Father finding me, and that made me feel even more frightened. And I felt like I was going to be sick again.

And then I realized that there was nothing I could do that felt safe. And I made a picture of all the possibilities in my head and imagined crossing out all the possibilities which were impossible, which is like in a maths exam, when you look at all the questions and decide which ones you are going to do, and you cross out all the ones that you are not going to do, because then your decision is final and you can't change your mind. And the picture in my mind was like this

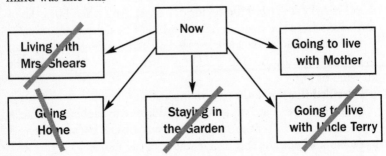

Which meant that I had to go London to live with Mother. And I could do it by going on a train because I knew all about trains from the train set, how you looked at the timetable and went to the station and bought a ticket and looked at the departure board to see if your train was on time and then you went to the right platform and got on board. And I would go from Swindon station, where Sherlock Holmes and Dr. Watson stop for lunch when they are on their way to Ross from Paddington in *The Boscombe Valley Mystery*.

And then I thought that I had to be like Sherlock Holmes and I had to detach my mind at will to a remarkable degree so that I did not notice how much it was hurting inside my head.

And then I thought I would need money if I was going to go to London. And I would need food to eat because it was a long journey. And then I thought I would need someone to look after

Toby when I went to London because I couldn't take him with me.

And then I *Formulated a Plan*. And that made me feel better.

I took the licorice laces and the pink wafer biscuit and the last clementine out of my special food box and put them in my pocket and hid the special food box under the fertilizer bag. Then I picked up Toby's cage and my extra coat and I climbed out from behind the shed. I walked up the garden and down the side of the house to the front. I made sure there was no one in the street. Then I went to Mrs. Alexander's house and I knocked on the door.

Then Mrs. Alexander opened the door, and she said, "Christopher, what on earth has happened to you?"

And I said, "Can you look after Toby for me?"

And she said, "Who's Toby?"

And I said, "Toby's my pet rat."

Then Mrs. Alexander said, "Oh . . . Oh, yes. I remember. You told me."

Then I held Toby's cage up and said, "This is him."

Mrs. Alexander took a step backward into her hallway.

And I said, "He eats special pellets and you can buy them from a pet shop. But he can also eat biscuits and carrots and bread and chicken bones. But you mustn't give him chocolate, because it's got caffeine and theobromine in it, which are methylxanthines, and it's poisonous for rats in large quantities. And he needs new water in his bottle every day too. And he likes to come out of his cage, but it doesn't matter if you don't take him out."

Then Mrs. Alexander said, "Why do you need someone to look after Toby, Christopher?"

And I said, "I'm going to London."

And she said, "How long are you going for?"

And I said, "Until I go to university."

And Mrs. Alexander said, "Are you and your father moving?"

And I said, "No."

And she said, "So why are you going to London?"

And I said, "I'm going to live with Mother."

And she said, "I thought you told me your mother was dead."

And I said, "I thought she was dead, but she was still alive. And Father lied to me. And also, he said he killed Wellington."

And Mrs. Alexander said, "Oh, my goodness."

And I said, "I'm going to live with my mother because Father killed Wellington and he lied and I'm frightened of being in the house with him."

And Mrs. Alexander said, "Is your mother here?"

And I said, "No. Mother is in London."

And she said, "So you're going to London on your own?"

And I said, "Yes."

And she said, "Christopher, why don't you come inside and we can talk about this and work out what is the best thing to do."

And I said, "No, I can't come inside. Will you look after Toby for me?"

And she said, "I really don't think that would be a good idea, Christopher. Where's your father at the moment?"

And I said, "I don't know."

And she said, "Well, perhaps we should try and give him a ring. I'm sure he's worried about you. And I'm sure that there's been some dreadful misunderstanding."

So I turned round and I ran across the road back to our house. And I didn't look before I crossed the road, and a yellow Mini had to stop and the tires squealed on the road. And I ran down the side of the house and back through the garden gate.

I tried to open the kitchen door, but it was locked. So I picked up a brick that was lying on the ground and I smashed it through the window and the glass shattered everywhere. Then I put my arm through the broken glass and I opened the door from the inside.

I went into the house and I put Toby down on the kitchen table. Then I ran upstairs and I grabbed my schoolbag and I put some food for Toby in it and some of my maths books and some clean pants and a vest and a clean shirt. Then I came downstairs and I opened the fridge and I put a carton of orange juice into my bag and a bottle of milk that hadn't been opened. And I took two more clementines and two tins of baked beans and a packet of custard creams from the cupboard, and I put them in my bag as well, because I could open them with the can opener on my Swiss army knife.

Then I looked on the surface next to the sink and I saw Father's mobile phone and his wallet. He must have left them when he left the house. And I took his bank card out of his wallet because that was how I could get money, because the card has a PIN number, which is the secret code that you put into the machine at the bank to get money out, and Father hadn't written it down in a safe place, which is what you're meant to do, but he had told me because he said I'd never forget it. And it was 3558. I put the card into my pocket.

Then I took Toby out of his cage and put him into the pocket of one of my coats because the cage was very heavy to carry all the way to London. And then I went out the kitchen door into the garden again. I went out through the garden gate and I started walking toward the school because that was a direction I knew, and when I got to school, I could ask Siobhan where the train station was.

It takes 19 minutes for the bus to get to school from our house, but it took me 47 minutes to walk the same distance, so I was very tired when I got there, and I hoped that I could stay at school for a little while and have some biscuits and some orange juice before I went to the train station. But I couldn't, because when I got to the school, I saw that Father's van was parked outside in the car park. And I knew it was his van because it said **Ed Boone Heating Maintenance & Boiler Repair** on the side with a crossed-spanners sign.

And when I saw the van, I wanted to curl up on the ground and do groaning. But I knew that if I curled up on the ground and did groaning, then Father would come out of the school and he would see me and he would catch me and take me home. So I took lots of deep breaths, like Siobhan says I have to do if someone hits me at school, and I counted 50 breaths and I concentrated very hard on the numbers and did their cubes as I said them.

And then I made a decision that I would have to find out how to get to the train station, and I would do this by asking someone, and it would be a lady because when they talked to us about Stranger Danger at school, they say that if a man comes up to you and talks to you and you feel frightened, you should call out and find a lady to run to because ladies are safer.

So I got out my Swiss army knife and I flicked out the saw blade, and I held it tightly in the pocket that Toby wasn't in so that I could stab someone if they grabbed hold of me, and then I saw a lady on the other side of the street with a baby in a pushchair and a little boy with a toy elephant, so I decided to ask her. And this time I looked left and right so that I wouldn't be run over by a car, and I crossed the road.

And I said to the lady, "Where can I buy a map?" And I could feel the hand that was holding the knife shaking even though I wasn't shaking it.

And she said, "Patrick, put that down, it's dirty. A map of where?"

And I said, "A map of here."

And she said, "I don't know. Where do you want to get to?"

And I said, "I'm going to the train station."

And she said, "You don't need a map to get to the train station."

And I said, "I do, because I don't know where the train station is."

And she said, "You can see it from here."

And I said, "No, I can't."

And she pointed and said, "That building. Says *Signal Point* on the top. There's a British Rail sign on the other end. The station's at the bottom of that. Patrick, I've told you a thousand times. Don't pick things off the pavement and stick them in your mouth."

And I looked and I could see a building with writing at the top, but it was a long way away, so it was hard to read, and I said, "Do you mean the stripy building with the horizontal windows?"

And she said, "That's the one."

And I said, "How do I get to that building?"

And she said, "Follow that bus," and she pointed to a bus that was going past.

So I started to run. But buses go really fast and I had to make sure that Toby didn't fall out of my pocket. But I managed to keep running after the bus for a long way, and I crossed 6 side roads before it turned down another street and I couldn't see it anymore.

And then I stopped running because I was breathing really hard and my legs hurt. And I was in a street with lots of shops. And there were lots of people doing their shopping, but I didn't want them to touch me, so I walked right at the edge of the road. And I didn't like all the people being near me and all the noise, because it was too much information in my head and it made it hard to think, like there was shouting in my head. So I put my hands over my ears and I groaned very quietly.

And then I noticed that I could still see the ⇌ sign that the lady had pointed at, so I kept on walking toward it.

And then I couldn't see the ⇌ sign anymore. And I had forgotten to remember where it was, and this was frightening because I was lost and because I do not forget things. Normally I would make a map in my head and I would follow the map, but there was too much interference in my head and this had made me confused. So I stood outside the green-and-white canvas roof outside a green-grocer's shop and made a plan.

I knew that the train station was near. And if something is nearby, you can find it by moving in a spiral, walking clockwise, and taking every right turn until you come back to a road you've already walked on, then taking the next left, then taking every right turn and so on.

And that was how I found the train station. I concentrated really hard on making a map of the center of town in my head as I walked, and that way it was easier to ignore all the people and all the noise around me.

And then I went inside the train station.

I SEE everything. That is why I don't like new places. If I am in a place I know, like home, or school, or the bus, or the shop, or the street, I have seen almost everything in it beforehand and all I have to do is to look at the things that have changed or moved.

Most people are lazy. They never look at everything. They do what is called *glancing*, which is the same word for bumping off something and carrying on in almost the same direction. And the information in their head is really simple. For example, if they are in the countryside, it might be

1. I am standing in a field that is full of grass.
2. There are some cows in the fields.
3. It is sunny with a few clouds.
4. There is a village in the distance.

And then they would stop noticing anything, because they would be thinking something else, like, "Oh, it is very beautiful here," or, "I'm worried that I might have left the gas cooker on." (This is really true because I asked Siobhan what people thought about when they looked at things, and this is what she said.)

But if I am standing in a field in the countryside, I notice everything. For example, I remember standing in a field on Thursday, June 15, 1994, because Father and Mother and I were driving to Dover to get a ferry to France and we did what Father called *Taking the Scenic Route,* which means going by little roads and stopping for lunch in a pub garden, and I had to stop to go for a wee, and I went into a field with cows in it and I stopped and looked and I noticed these things

1. There are 19 cows in the field, 15 of which are black and white and 4 of which are brown and white.

2. There is a village in the distance that has 31 visible houses and a church with a square tower and not a spire.

3. There are ridges in the field, which means that in medieval times it was what is called a *ridge-and-furrow* field and people who lived in the village would have a ridge each to do farming on.

4. There is an old plastic bag from Asda in the hedge and a squashed Coca-Cola can with a snail on it.

5. I can see 3 different types of grass and 2 colors of flowers in the grass.

6. The cows are mostly facing uphill.

And there were 31 more things in this list of things I noticed, but Siobhan said I didn't need to write them all down. And it means that it is very tiring if I am in a new place because I see all these things, and if someone asked me afterward what the cows looked like, I could ask which one, and I could do a drawing of them at home and say that a particular cow had patterns on it like this

When I am in a new place, because I see everything, it is like when a computer is doing too many things at the same time and the central processor unit is blocked up and there isn't any space left to think about other things. And when I am in a new place and there are lots of people there, it is even harder, because people are not like cows and flowers and grass and they can talk to you and do things that you don't expect, so you have to notice everything that is in the place, and also, you have to notice things that might happen as well. And sometimes when I am in a new place and there are lots of people there, it is like a computer crashing and I have to close my eyes and put my hands over my ears and groan, which is like pressing **CTRL + ALT + DEL** and shutting down programs and turning the computer off and rebooting so that I can remember what I am doing and where I am meant to be going.

53. MY TRAIN set had a little building that was two rooms with a corridor between them, and one was the ticket office, where you bought tickets, and one was a waiting room, where you waited for the train. But the train station in Swindon wasn't like that. It was a tunnel and some stairs and a shop and café and a waiting room.

And it was like standing on a cliff in a really strong wind because it made me feel giddy and sick, because there were lots of people and it was really echoey, and there was only one way to go and that was down the tunnel, and it smelled of toilets and cigarettes. So I stood against the wall to make sure that I didn't fall over. And I wanted to go home, but I was frightened of going home and I tried to make a plan of what I should do in my head, but there were too many things to look at and too many things to hear.

So I put my hands over my ears to block out the noise and think. And I thought that I had to stay in the station to get on a train and I had to sit down somewhere, and there was nowhere to sit down near the door of the station, so I had to walk down the tunnel. So I said to myself, in my head, "I will walk down the tunnel and there might be somewhere I can sit down and then I can shut my eyes and I can think," and I walked down the tunnel, trying to concentrate on the sign at the end that said **WARNING CCTV in operation.** And it was like stepping off the cliff onto a tightrope.

And eventually I got to the end of the tunnel and there were some stairs, and I went up the stairs and there were still lots of people and I groaned. And there were signs saying **Great Western** and **cold beers and lagers** and **CAUTION WET FLOOR** and **Your 50p will keep a premature baby alive for 1.8 seconds** and **transforming travel** and **Refreshingly Different** and **No Smoking,** and there were some little tables with chairs next to them and no one was sitting at one of the tables, and it was in a corner and I sat down on one of the chairs next to it and I closed my eyes. And I put my hands in my pockets and Toby climbed into my hand and I gave him two pellets of rat food from my bag and I gripped the Swiss army knife in the other hand, and I groaned to cover up the noise, but not so loud that other people would hear me groaning and come and talk to me.

And then I tried to think about what I had to do, but I couldn't think, because there were too many other things in my head, so I did a maths problem to make my head clearer.

And when I looked up, I saw that there was a policeman standing in front of me, and he was saying, "Anyone at home?" but I didn't know what that meant.

And then he said, "Are you all right, young man?"

I looked at him, and I thought for a bit so that I would answer the question correctly, and I said, "No."

And he said, "You're looking a bit worse for wear. The lady at the café says you've been here for 2½ hours, and when she tried talking to you, you were in a complete trance. What's your name?"

And I said, "Christopher Boone."

And he said, "Where do you live?"

And I said, "Thirty-six Randolph Street," and I started feeling better because I like policemen and it was an easy question, and I wondered whether I should tell him that Father killed Wellington and whether he would arrest Father.

And he said, "What are you doing here?"

And I said, "I needed to sit down and be quiet and think."

And he said, "OK, let's keep it simple. What are you doing at the railway station?"

And I said, "I'm going to see Mother. She lives in London."

And he said, "So you don't live with your mother?"

And I said, "No. But I'm going to."

And then he sat down next to me and said, "So where in London does your mother live?"

And I said, "Four Fifty-one c Chapter Road, London NW2 5NG."

And he said, "Bloody Nora, what is that?"

And I looked down, and I said, "That's my pet rat, Toby," because he was looking out of my pocket at the policeman.

And the policeman said, "A pet rat?"

And I said, "Yes, a pet rat. He's very clean and he hasn't got bubonic plague."

And the policeman said, "Well, that's reassuring. Have you got a ticket?"

And I said, "No."

And he said, "Have you got any money to get a ticket?"

And I said, "No."

And he said, "How precisely were you going to get to London?"

Then I didn't know what to say, because I had Father's cashpoint card in my pocket and it was illegal to steal things, but he was a policeman, so I had to tell the truth, so I said, "I have a cashpoint card," and I took it out and showed it to him. And this was a white lie.

But the policeman said, "Is this your card?"

And then I thought he might arrest me, and I said, "No. It's Father's."

And he said, "OK," but he said it really slowly.

And I said, "He told me the number," which was another white lie.

And he said, "Why don't you and I take a stroll to the cashpoint machine, eh?"

And I said, "You mustn't touch me."

And he said, "Why would I want to touch you?"

And I said, "I don't know. But I got a caution for hitting a policeman. I didn't mean to hurt him, and if I do it again, I'll get into even bigger trouble."

Then he looked at me, and he said, "You're serious, aren't you?"

And I said, "Yes."

And he said, "You lead the way."

And I said, "Where?"

And he said, "Back by the ticket office," and he pointed with his thumb.

And then we walked back through the tunnel, but it wasn't so frightening this time, because there was a policeman with me.

And I put the cashpoint card into the machine, like Father had let me do sometimes, and it said **ENTER YOUR PERSONAL NUMBER** and I typed in **3558** and pressed the **ENTER** button and the machine said **PLEASE ENTER AMOUNT** and there was a choice.

And I asked the policeman, "How much does it cost to get a ticket for a train to London?"

And he said, "About thirty quid."

And I said, "Is that pounds?"

And he laughed. But I didn't laugh, because I don't like people laughing at me, even if they are policemen. And he stopped laughing and said, "Yep. It's thirty pounds."

So I pressed **£50** and five £10 notes came out of the machine, and I put the notes and the receipt and the card into my pocket.

And the policeman said, "Well, I guess I shouldn't keep you chatting any longer."

And I said, "Where do I get a ticket for the train from?" because if you are lost and you need directions, you can ask a policeman.

And he said, "You are a prize specimen, aren't you?"

And I said, "Where do I get a ticket for the train from?" because he hadn't answered my question.

And he said, "In there," and he pointed to a big room with a glass window on the other side of the train-station door, and then he said, "Now, are you sure you know what you're doing?"

And I said, "Yes. I'm going to London to live with my mother."

And he said, "Has your mother got a telephone number?"

And I said, "Yes. It's 0208 887 8907."

And he said, "And you'll ring her if you get into any trouble?"

And I said, "Yes," because I knew you could ring people from phone boxes if you had money, and I had money now.

And he said, "Good."

And I walked into the ticket office and I turned round and I could see that the policeman was still watching me, so I felt safe. And there was a long desk at the other side of the big room and a window on the desk, and there was a man standing in front of the window and a man behind the window, and I said to the man behind the window, "I want to go to London."

And the man in front of the window said, "If you don't mind," and he turned round so that his back was toward me and the man behind the window gave him a bit of paper to sign and he signed it and pushed it back under the window and the man behind the window gave him his ticket. Then the man in front of the window looked at me and said, "What are you looking at?" before walking away. I kept my hand on my Swiss army knife in case he touched me.

And then there was no one else in front of the window, and I said to the man behind the window, "I want to go to London." I turned round and saw that the policeman had gone and I was scared again, so I tried to pretend I was playing a game on my computer and it was called **Train to London,** and you had to solve lots of different problems to get to the next level, and I could turn it off at any time.

And the man said, "Single or return?"

And I said, "What does *single or return* mean?"

And he said, "Do you want to go one way, or do you want to go and come back?"

And I said, "I want to stay there when I get there."

And he said, "For how long?"

And I said, "Until I go to university."

And he said, "Single, then. That'll be thirty-two pounds."

And I gave him the £50, and he gave me £10 back and a little yellow-and-orange ticket and £8 in coins, and I put it all in my pocket with my knife. And I didn't like the ticket being half yellow, but I had to keep it because it was my train ticket.

And then he said, "If you could move away from the counter."

And I said, "When is the train to London?"

And he looked at his watch and said, "Platform One, five minutes."

And I said, "Where is Platform One?"

And he pointed and said, "Through the underpass and up the stairs. You'll see the signs."

And *underpass* meant *tunnel* because I could see where he was pointing, so I went out of the ticket office, but it wasn't like a computer game, because I was in the middle of it and it was like all the signs were shouting in my head and someone bumped into me as they walked past and I made a noise like a dog barking to scare them off. And I pictured in my head a big red line across the floor that started at my feet and went through the tunnel, and I started walking along the red line, saying, "Left, right, left, right, left, right," because sometimes when I am frightened or angry, it helps if I do something that has a rhythm to it, like music or drumming, which is something Siobhan taught me to do.

And I went up the stairs and I saw a sign saying ➜ **Platform 1** and the ➜ was pointing at a glass door, so I went through it and someone bumped into me again with a suitcase and I made another noise like a dog barking, and they said, "Watch where you're going," but I pretended that they were just one of the Guarding Demons in **Train to London** and there was a train. And I saw a man with a newspaper and a bag of golf clubs go up to one of the doors of the train and press a big button next to it and the doors were electronic and they slid open and I liked that. And then the doors closed behind him. And I looked at my watch and 3 minutes had gone past since I was at the ticket office, which meant that the train would be going in 2 minutes.

And I went up to the door and I pressed the big button and the doors slid open and I stepped through the doors.

And I was on the train to London.

59. THERE were lots of people on the train, and I didn't like that, because there were lots of people I didn't know and I hate it when I am in stuck in a room with lots of people I don't know, and a train is like a room and you can't get out of it without moving.

So I stood very still in the train carriage and didn't move.

And then I heard someone say, "Christopher."

It was the policeman again. And he said, "Caught you just in time," and he was breathing really loudly and holding his knees. And he said, "We've got your father at the police station."

And I thought he was going to say that they had arrested Father for killing Wellington, but he didn't. He said, "He's looking for you."

And I said, "I know."

And he said, "So why are you going to London?"

And I said, "Because I'm going to live with Mother."

And he said, "Well, I think your father might have something to say about that."

And then I thought that he was going to take me back to Father and that was frightening because he was a policeman and policemen are meant to be good, so I started to run away, but he grabbed me and I screamed. And then he let go.

And he said, "OK, let's not get overexcited here. I'm going to take you back to the police station and you and me and your dad can sit down and have a little chat about who's going where."

And I said, "I'm going to live with Mother, in London."

And he said, "Not just yet, you're not."

And I said, "Have you arrested Father? He killed a dog. With a garden fork."

And the policeman said, "Did he now?"

And I said, "Yes, he did."

And he said, "Well, we can talk about that as well." And then he said, "Right, young man, I think you've done enough adventuring for one day."

And then he reached out to touch me again and I started to scream again, and he said, "Now listen, you little monkey. You can either do what I say or I am going to have to make—"

And then the train jiggled and it began to move.

And then the policeman said, "Dammit." And he put his hands together in front of his mouth like people do when they are praying to God and he breathed loudly into his hands and made a whistling noise. Then he stopped because the train jiggled again and he had to grab hold of one of the straps hanging from the ceiling.

And then he said, "Don't move." And then he took out his walkie-talkie and pressed a button and said, "Rob? . . . Yeah, it's Nigel. I'm stuck on the bloody train. . . . Yeah. Don't even . . . It stops at Didcot Parkway. So if you can get someone to meet me with a car . . . Cheers. Tell his old man we've got him, but it's going to take a while, OK? . . . Great."

And then he clicked his walkie-talkie off, and he said, "Let's get ourselves a seat," and he pointed to two seats nearby that faced each other, and he said, "Park yourself. And no monkey business."

And we sat down facing one another. And he said, "You are a handful, you are."

And I wondered whether the policeman would help me find 451c Chapter Road, London NW2 5NG.

And I looked out the window and we were going past factories and scrap yards and there were 4 caravans in a muddy field with 2 dogs and some clothes hanging up to dry. And there were so many things it made my head hurt, so I closed my eyes, but then I opened them again because it was like flying, but nearer to the ground, and I think flying is good. And when I opened my eyes, the policeman was reading a newspaper called *The Sun*.

And then I wanted to go for a wee, but I was on a train. And I didn't know how long it would take us to get to London and I felt a panic starting, and I started to tap a rhythm on the glass with my knuckles to help me wait and not think about wanting to go for a wee, and I looked at my watch and waited for 17 minutes, but when I want to go for a wee, I have to go really quickly, which is why I leaked a bit and wet my trousers.

And the policeman looked across at me and put his newspaper down and said, "Oh, for heaven's sake, go to the toilet, will you?"

And I said, "But I'm on a train."

And he said, "They do have toilets on trains, you know."

And I said, "Where is the toilet on the train?"

And he pointed and said, "Through those doors there. But I'll be keeping an eye on you."

I got up out of my seat and I closed my eyes so that my eyelids were just little slits so I couldn't see the other people on the train and I walked to the door, and when I got through the door, there was another door on the right and it was half open and it said **Toilet** on it, so I went inside.

And it was horrible because it smelled of poo, and I didn't want to use it, but I had to because I really wanted to wee. So I closed my eyes and went for a wee and I flushed the toilet and then I tried to use the sink, but the tap didn't work, so I put spit on my hands and wiped them with a paper tissue and put it into the toilet.

Then I went out and I saw that opposite the toilet, there were two shelves with cases and a rucksack on them and it made me think of the airing cupboard at home and how I climb in there sometimes and it makes me feel safe. So I climbed onto the middle shelf and I pulled one of the cases across like a door, so that I was shut in, and it was dark and there was no one in there with me and I couldn't hear people talking, so I felt much calmer and it was nice.

And I did some quadratic equations like

$$0 = 437x^2 + 103x + 11$$
and
$$0 = 79x^2 + 43x + 2089$$

and I made some of the coefficients large so that they were hard to solve. And the train started to slow down and someone came and stood near the shelf and knocked on the door of the toilet, and it was the policeman, and he said, "Christopher?" He opened the door of the toilet and cursed and he was so close that I could see his walkie-talkie and his truncheon on his belt, but he didn't see me.

And then he went away again, running.

And then the train stopped and I wondered if it was London, but I didn't move, because I didn't want the policeman to find me.

And then a lady with a jumper that had bees and flowers made of wool on it came and took the rucksack off the shelf over my head, and she said, "You scared the living daylights out of me."

But I didn't say anything.

And then she said, "I think someone's out there on the platform looking for you."

But I carried on not saying anything.

And she said, "Well, it's your lookout," and she went away.

And then 3 other people walked past and one of them put a big parcel on the shelf above my head, but he didn't see me. And then the train started going again.

I WONDERED whether I should have got off the train because it had just stopped at London, and I was scared, because if the train went anywhere else, it would be somewhere where I didn't know anybody.

And then I closed my eyes and did some more maths puzzles so I didn't think about where I was going.

And then the train stopped again, and I thought about getting off the shelf and going to get my bag and get off the train. But I didn't want to be found by the policeman and be taken to Father, so I stayed on the shelf and didn't move, and no one saw me.

And then I remembered that there was a map of England and Scotland and Wales on the wall of one of the classrooms at school, and it showed you where all the towns were and I pictured it in my head with Swindon and London on it, and it was like this

And I had been looking at my watch since the train had started at **12:59 p.m.** And the first stop had been at **1:16 p.m.**, which was 17 minutes later. And it was now **1:39 p.m.**, which was 23 minutes after the stop, which meant that we would be at the sea if the train didn't go in a big curve. But I didn't know if it went in a big curve.

And then there were another 4 stops, and 4 people came and took bags away from the shelves and 2 people put bags on the shelves, but no one moved the big suitcase that was in front of me.

And then the train stopped and a lady with a yellow waterproof coat came and took the big suitcase away.

And then the train was really quiet and it didn't move again and I couldn't hear anyone. So I decided to get off the shelf and go and get my bag and see if the policeman was still sitting in his seat.

So I got off the shelf and I looked through the door, but the policeman wasn't there. And my bag had gone as well.

And then I heard the sound of feet and I turned round and it was another policeman, not the one who was on the train before, and I could see him through the door, in the next carriage, and he was looking under the seats. And I decided that I didn't like policemen so much anymore, so I got off the train.

And when I saw how big the room was that the train was in and I heard how noisy and echoey it was, I had to kneel down on the ground for a bit because I thought I was going to fall over. And then I worked out which way to walk, and I decided to walk in the direction the train was going when it came into the station because if this was the last stop, that was the direction London was in.

So I stood up and I imagined that there was a big red line on the ground that ran parallel to the train to the gate at the far end, and I walked along it, and I said, "Left, right, left, right . . ."

And I carried on walking. And I covered my ears with my hands and I went and stood against the wall of a little shop that said **Hotel and Theatre Reservations Tel: 0207 402 5164** in the middle of the big room, and then I took my hands away from my ears and I groaned to block out the noise and I looked round the big room at all the signs to see if this was London. And the signs said

Sweet Pastries **Heathrow Airport Check-In Here** *Bagel Factory* **Stationlink** Buses W H Smith MEZZANINE **Heathrow Express** First Class Lounge easyCar.com *The Mad Bishop and Bear Public House* **Fuller's** London Pride **Dixons** *Our Price* **Paddington Bear at Paddington Station** Tickets Taxis Toilets First Aid **Way Out** Praed Street **The Lawn** Q Here Please *Upper Crust* Sainsbury's **Local** ⓘ**Information** GREAT WESTERN FIRST Ⓟ Position Closed Position Closed

There were too many signs and my brain wasn't working properly, and this frightened me, so I closed my eyes again and counted slowly to 50 but without doing the cubes. And I stood there and I opened my Swiss army knife in my pocket and held on to it tight.

And then I made my hand into a little tube with my fingers and I opened my eyes and I looked through the tube so that I was only looking at one sign at a time, and after a long time I saw a sign that said ⓘ**Information** and it was above a window on a little shop.

I went into the shop and I could feel my heart beating very hard and I could hear a noise like the sea in my ears. And when I got to the window, I said, "Is this London?"

And the lady behind the window was black, and she had long fingernails that were painted pink, and she said, "Indeed it is."

And I said, "How do I get to Four Fifty-one c Chapter Road, London NW2 5NG?"

And she said, "Where is that?"

And I said, "It's Four Fifty-one c Chapter Road, London NW2 5NG. And sometimes you can write it *Four Fifty-one c Chapter Road, Willesden, London NW2 5NG.*"

And the lady said to me, "Take the tube to Willesden Junction, honey. Or Willesden Green. Got to be near there somewhere."

And I said, "What sort of tube?"

And she said, "Are you for real?"

And I didn't say anything.

And she said, "See that big staircase with the escalators? See the sign? Says *Underground.* Take the Bakerloo Line to Willesden Junction or the Jubilee to Willesden Green. You OK, honey?"

And I looked where she was pointing and there was a big staircase going down into the ground and there was a big sign over the top of it like this

And I thought, "I can do this," because I was doing really well and I was in London and I would find my mother. And I had to think to myself, "The people are like cows in a field," and I just had to look in front of me all the time and make a red line along the floor in the picture of the big room in my head and follow it.

And I walked across the big room to the escalators. And *the escalators* was a staircase, but it was moving and people stepped onto it and it carried them down and up and it made me laugh because I hadn't been on one before and it was like something in a science fiction film about the future. But I didn't want to use it, so I went down the stairs instead.

And then I was in a smaller room underground and there were lots of people and there were pillars that had blue lights in the ground around the bottom of them and I liked these, but I didn't like the people, so I saw a photo booth like one I went into on March 25, 1994, to have my passport photo done, and I went into the photo booth because it was like a cupboard and it felt safer and I could look out through the curtain. And I did detecting by watching and I saw that people were putting tickets into gray gates and walking through. And some of the people were buying tickets at big black machines on the wall.

And I watched 47 people do this, and I memorized what to do. Then I imagined a red line on the floor and I walked over to the wall where there was a poster, which was a list of places to go, and it was alphabetical and I saw **Willesden Green** and it said **£2.20** and then I went to one of the machines and there was a little screen that said PRESS TICKET TYPE and I pressed the button that most people had pressed, which was ADULT SINGLE and **£2.20** and the screen said INSERT **£2.20** and I put 3 £1 coins into the slot and there was a clinking noise and the screen said TAKE TICKET AND CHANGE and there was a ticket in a little hole at the bottom of the machine and a 50p coin and a 20p coin and a 10p coin and I put the coins in my pocket and I went up to one of the gray gates and I put my ticket into the slot and it sucked it in and it came out on the other side of the gate. And someone said, "Get a move on," and I made a noise like a dog barking and I walked forward and the gate opened and I took my ticket like other people did and I liked the gray gate because that was like something in a science fiction film too.

And then I had to work out which way to go, so I stood against a wall so people didn't touch me, and there was a sign for **Bakerloo Line** and **District and Circle Line,** but not one for **Jubilee Line** like the lady had said, so I made a plan and it was *to go to Willesden Junction on the Bakerloo Line.*

And there was another sign for the **Bakerloo Line** and a list of place names. And I read all the words and I found **Willesden Junction,** so I followed the arrow beside it and I went through the left-hand tunnel and there was a fence down the middle of the tunnel and the people were walking straight ahead on the left and coming the other way on the right like on a road, so I walked along the left and the tunnel curved left and then there were more gates and a sign said **Bakerloo Line** and it pointed down an escalator, so I had to go down the escalator and people were standing close to me and I wanted to hit them to make them go away, but I didn't hit them, because of the caution.

And then I was at the bottom of the escalator and there were two ways to go and one said **Northbound** and I went that way because **Willesden** was on the top half of the map and the top is always north on maps.

And then I was in another train station, but it was tiny and it was in a tunnel and there was only one track and the walls were curved and they were covered in big adverts and they said **WAY OUT** and **London's Transport Museum** and **Take time out to regret your career choice** and **For Stations beyond Queen's Park take the first train and change at Queen's Park if necessary** and **Hammersmith and City Line.** And there were lots of people standing in the little station, and it was underground so there weren't any windows, and I didn't like that, so I found a bench and I sat at the end of the bench.

And then there was a sound like people fighting with swords and I could feel a strong wind and a roaring started and I closed my eyes and the roaring got louder and I groaned loudly and I thought the little station was going to collapse or there was a big fire somewhere and I was going to die. And the roaring turned into a clattering and a squealing and it got slowly quieter and then it stopped and I kept my eyes closed because I felt safer not seeing what was happening. And then I could hear people moving and I opened my eyes and I saw that they were getting onto a train that wasn't there before and it was the train that was roaring. And there was sweat running down my face from under my hair and I was moaning, not groaning, but different, like a dog when it has hurt its paw and I heard the sound, but I didn't realize that it was me at first.

And then the train doors closed and the train started moving and it roared again, but not as loud this time and it went into the tunnel at the end of the little station and it was quiet again and the people were all walking into the tunnels that went out of the little station.

And I was shaking and I wanted to be back at home, and then I realized I couldn't be at home, because Father was there and he told a lie and he killed Wellington, which meant that it wasn't my home anymore. My home was 451c Chapter Road, London NW2 5NG and it scared me, having a wrong thought like I wish I was back at home again, because it meant my mind wasn't working properly.

And then more people came into the little station and then the roaring began again and I closed my eyes and felt sick and I found it hard to breathe. And then the people went away on the train and the little station was empty again. And then it filled up with people and another train came with the same roaring. And I wanted to go to sleep so that I wouldn't have to think, because the only thing I could think was how much it hurt because there wasn't room for anything else in my head, but I couldn't just go to sleep and I just had to sit there and there was nothing to do but wait and hurt.

AND this is another description because Siobhan said I should do descriptions and it is a description of the advert that was on the wall of the little train station opposite me, but I can't remember all of it.

The advert said

Dream holiday,
think Kuoni
in Malaysia

and behind the writing, there was a big photograph of 2 orangutans swinging on branches and there were trees behind them, but the leaves were blurred because the camera was focusing on the orangutans and not the leaves, and the orangutans were moving.

And *orangutan* comes from the Malaysian word **ōranghūtan**, which means *man of the woods*.

And adverts are pictures or television programs to make you buy things like cars or Snickers or use an Internet service provider. But this was an advert to make you go to Malaysia on a holiday. And Malaysia is in Southeast Asia and it is made up of peninsular Malaysia and Sabah and Sarawak and Labuan and the capital is Kuala Lumpur and the highest mountain is Mount Kinabalu, which is 4,101 meters high, but that wasn't on the advert.

And Siobhan says people go on holidays to see new things and relax, but it wouldn't make me relaxed and you can see new things by looking at earth under a microscope or drawing the shape of the solid made when 3 circular rods of equal thickness intersect at right angles. And I think that there are so many things just in one house that it would take years to think about all of them properly. And, also, a thing is interesting because of thinking about it and not because of it being new.

61. AND I kept my eyes closed and I didn't look at my watch at all. And the trains coming in and out of the station were in a rhythm, like music or drumming. And it was like counting and saying, "Left, right, left, right, left, right . . ." which Siobhan taught me to do to make myself calm. And I was saying in my head, "Train coming. Train stopped. Train going. Silence. Train coming. Train stopped. Train going . . ." as if the trains were only in my mind.

And I didn't open my eyes and I didn't look at my watch. And it was like being in a dark room with the curtains closed, so I couldn't see anything, like when you wake up at night and the only sounds you hear are the sounds inside your head. And that made it better because it was like I was in bed and I was safe.

And then the silences between the trains coming and going got longer and longer. And I could hear that there were fewer people in the little station, so I opened my eyes and I looked at my watch and it said 8:07 p.m. and I had been sitting on the bench for approximately 5 hours, but it hadn't seemed like approximately 5 hours except that my bottom hurt and I was hungry and thirsty.

And then I realized that Toby was missing, because he was not in my pocket. I didn't want him to be missing, because we weren't in Father's house or Mother's house and there wasn't anyone to feed him in the little station and he might get run over by a train.

And then I looked up at the ceiling and I saw that there was a long black box that was a sign and it said

1 Harrow & Wealdstone	2 min
3 Queen's Park	7 min

And then the bottom line scrolled up and disappeared and a different line scrolled up into its place and the sign said

1 Harrow & Wealdstone	1 min
2 Willesden Junction	4 min

And then it changed again and it said

1 Harrow & Wealdstone
STAND BACK TRAIN APPROACHING

And then I heard the roaring of a train coming into the station and I worked out that there was a computer somewhere and it knew where all the trains were and it sent messages to the black boxes in the little stations to say when the trains were coming, and that made me feel better because everything had an order and a plan.

And the train came into the little station and it stopped and 5 people got onto the train and 7 people got off and then the doors closed automatically and the train went away. And when the next train came, I wasn't so scared anymore, because the sign said TRAIN APPROACHING , so I knew it was going to happen.

And then I decided that I would look for Toby. So I stood up and I looked up and down the little station and in the doorways that went into tunnels, but I couldn't see him anywhere. And then I looked down into the black lower-down bit where the rails were, and then I saw two mice and they were black because they were covered in dirt. And I liked that because I like mice and rats. But they weren't Toby, so I carried on looking.

And then I saw Toby. I knew he was Toby because he was white and he had a brown egg shape on his back. So I climbed down off the concrete. And he was eating a bit of rubbish that was an old sweet paper. And someone shouted, "What are you doing?"

And I bent down to catch Toby, but he ran off. And I walked after him and I bent down again, and I said, "Toby . . . Toby," and I held out my hand so that he could smell that it was me.

And someone said, "Get out of there, for God's sake," and I looked up and it was a man wearing a raincoat and he had black shoes and his socks were showing and they were gray with diamond patterns on them. And he tried to grab my shoulder, so I screamed. And then I heard the sound like sword fighting and Toby started running again, and I grabbed at him and I caught him by the tail.

And then I heard the roaring and I lifted Toby up and grabbed him with both hands and he bit me on my thumb and there was blood coming out and I shouted and Toby tried to jump out of my hands. And then the roaring got louder and I turned round and I saw the train coming and I was going to be run over and killed, so I tried to climb up onto the concrete, but it was high and I was holding Toby in both my hands.

And then the man with the diamond patterns on his socks grabbed hold of me and pulled me and I screamed, but he kept pulling me up onto the concrete and we fell over and I carried on screaming. And the train came into the station and I stood up and I put Toby into the pocket inside my jacket.

And the man with the diamond patterns on his socks was standing next to me, and he said, "What do you think you were playing at?"

But I didn't say anything.

And he said, "What were you doing?"

And the doors of the train opened and people got off and there was a lady standing behind the man with the diamond patterns on his socks and she was carrying a guitar case like Siobhan has.

And I said, "I was finding Toby. He's my pet rat."

And the man with the diamond patterns on his socks said, "Bloody Nora."

And the lady with the guitar case said, "Is he OK?"

And the man said, "Him? Thanks a bundle. And all for a pet rat. Oh dammit, my train." And he ran to the train and banged on the door, which was closed, and the train started to go away and he cursed again.

And the lady said, "Are you OK?" and she touched my arm, so I screamed again. And she said, "OK. OK. OK."

And I was sitting on the ground and the woman knelt down on one knee, and she said, "Is there anything I can do to help you?"

And if she was a teacher at school, I could have said, "Where is Four Fifty-one c Chapter Road, Willesden, London NW2 5NG?" But she was a stranger, so I said, "Stand farther away," because I didn't like her being so close. And I said, "I've got a Swiss army knife and it has a saw blade and it could cut someone's fingers off."

And she said, "OK, buddy. I'm going to take that as a no," and she stood up and walked away.

And the man with the diamond patterns on his socks said, "Mad as a damn hatter," and he was pressing a handkerchief against his face and there was blood on the handkerchief.

And then another train came and the man with the diamond patterns on his socks and the lady with the guitar case got on and it went away again.

And then 8 more trains came and I decided that I would get onto a train and then I would work out what to do.

So I got on the next train.

And there were 11 people in the carriage and I didn't like being in a room with 11 people, so I concentrated on things in the carriage. And there were signs saying **There are 53,963 holiday cottages in Scandinavia and Germany** and **Penalty £10 if you fail to show a valid ticket for your entire journey** and **Discover Gold, Then Bronze** and **TVIC** and **EPBIC** and **Obstructing the doors can be dangerous.**

Then the train wobbled a lot and I had to hang on to a rail and we went into a tunnel and it was noisy and I closed my eyes and I could feel the blood pumping in the sides of my neck.

And then we came out of the tunnel and went into another little station and it was called **Warwick Avenue** and it said it in big letters on the wall and I liked that because you knew where you were.

And I timed the distance between stations all the way to Willesden Junction and all the times between stations were multiples of 15 seconds like this

Paddington	0:00
Warwick Avenue	1:30
Maida Vale	3:15
Kilburn Park	5:00
Queen's Park	7:00
Kensal Green	10:30
Willesden Junction	11:45

And when the train stopped at **Willesden Junction** and the doors opened automatically, I walked out of the train. And then the doors closed and the train went away. And everyone who got off the train walked up a staircase and over a bridge except me, and then there were only 2 people that I could see and one was an Indian man in a shop that was a little window in a wall.

And I didn't want to talk to him, because I had already talked to lots of strangers, which is dangerous, and the more you do something dangerous, the more likely it is that something bad happens. But I didn't know how to get to 451c Chapter Road, London NW2 5NG, so I had to ask somebody.

So I went up to the man in the little shop, and I said, "Where is Four Fifty-one c Chapter Road, London NW2 5NG?"

And he picked up a little book and handed it to me and said, "Two ninety-five."

And the book was called *LONDON AZ Street Atlas and Index,* and I opened it up and it was lots of maps.

And the man in the little shop said, "Are you going to buy it or not?"

And I said, "I don't know."

And he said, "Well, you can get your dirty fingers off it if you don't mind," and he took it back from me.

And I said, "Where is Four Fifty-one c Chapter Road, London NW2 5NG?"

And he said, "You can either buy the A-to-Z or you can hop it. I'm not a walking encyclopedia."

And I said, "Is that the A-to-Z?" and I pointed at the book.

And he said, "No. It's a sodding crocodile."

And I said, "Is that the A-to-Z?" because it wasn't a crocodile and I thought I had heard wrongly because of his accent.

And he said, "Yes, it's the A-to-Z."

And I said, "Can I buy it?"

And he said, "Two pounds ninety-five, but you're giving me the money first. I'm not having you scarpering," and then I realized that he meant £2.95 when he said *Two ninety-five.*

And I paid him with my money and I went and sat down on the floor against the wall and I opened up the book.

And inside the front cover there was a big map of London with places on it like **Abbey Wood** and **Poplar** and **Acton** and **Stanmore.** And it said KEY TO MAP PAGES. And the map was covered with a grid and each square of the grid had two numbers on it. And **Willesden** was in the square that said **42** and **43.** And I worked out that the numbers were the numbers of the pages where you could see a bigger scale map of that square of London. And the whole book was a big map of London, but it had been chopped up so it could be made into a book, and I liked that.

But Willesden Junction wasn't on pages 42 and 43. I found it on page 58, which was directly under page 42 on the KEY TO MAP PAGES and which joined up with page 42.

And it took me a long time to find Chapter Road because it wasn't on page 58. It was back on page 42 and it was in square 5C.

And this was the shape of the roads between Willesden Junction and Chapter Road and this was my route

So I went up the staircase and over the bridge and I put my ticket in the little gray gate and went into the street and I looked around and it was dark and there were lots of bright lights and I hadn't been outside for a long time and it made me feel sick. And I kept my eyelids very close together and I just looked at the shape of the roads and then I knew which roads were **Station Approach** and **Oak Lane,** the roads I had to go along, so I started walking.

I got to 451c Chapter Road, London NW2 5NG, and it took me 27 minutes and there was no one in when I pressed the button that said **Flat C.**

So I decided to wait and I hoped that Mother was not on holiday, because that would mean she could be away for more than a whole week, but I tried not to think about this, because I couldn't go back to Swindon. So I sat down on the ground behind the dustbins in the little garden that was in front of 451c Chapter Road, London NW2 5NG. And then it started to rain and I got wet and I started shivering because I was cold.

And then it was 11:32 p.m. and I heard voices of people walking along the street.

And a voice said, "I don't care whether you thought it was funny or not," and it was a lady's voice.

And another voice said, "Judy, look. I'm sorry, OK," and it was a man's voice.

And the other voice, which was the lady's voice, said, "Well, perhaps you should have thought about that before you made me look like a complete idiot."

And the lady's voice was Mother's voice.

And Mother came into the garden and Mr. Shears was with her, and the other voice was his.

So I stood up, and I said, "You weren't in, so I waited for you."

And Mother said, "Christopher."

And Mr. Shears said, "What?"

And Mother put her arms round me and said, "Christopher, Christopher, Christopher."

And I pushed her away because she was grabbing me and I didn't like it, and I pushed really hard and I fell over.

And Mr. Shears said, "What the hell is going on?"

And Mother said, "I'm so sorry, Christopher. I forgot."

And I was lying on the ground and Mother held up her right hand and spread her fingers out in a fan so that I could touch her fingers, but then I saw that Toby had escaped out of my pocket, so I had to catch him.

And Mr. Shears said, "I suppose this mean Ed's here."

And there was a wall round the garden, so Toby couldn't get out and I grabbed him and put him back in my pocket, and I said, "He's hungry. Have you got any food I can give him, and some water?"

And Mother said, "Where's your father, Christopher?"

And I said, "I think he's in Swindon."

And Mr. Shears said, "Thank heavens for that."

And Mother said, "But how did you get here?"

And my teeth were clicking against each other because of the cold and I couldn't stop them, and I said, "I came on the train. And it was really frightening. And I took Father's cashpoint card so I could get money out and a policeman helped me. But then he wanted to take me back to Father. And he was on the train with me. But then he wasn't."

And Mother said, "Christopher, you're soaking. Roger, don't just stand there." And then she said, "Christopher. I didn't . . . I didn't think I'd ever . . . Why are you here on your own?"

And I said, "I'm going to live with you because Father killed Wellington with a garden fork and I'm frightened of him."

And Mr. Shears said, "What the hell . . ."

And Mother said, "Roger, please. Come on, Christopher, let's go inside and get you dried off."

So I stood up and I went into the house, and Mother said, "You follow Roger," and I followed Mr. Shears up the stairs and there was a landing and a door that said **Flat C** and I was scared of going inside because I didn't know what was inside.

And Mother said, "Go on, or you'll catch your death," but I didn't know what *you'll catch your death* meant, and I went inside.

And then she said, "I'll run you a bath," and I walked round the flat to make a map of it in my head, so I felt safer.

And then Mother made me take my clothes off and get into the bath and she said I could use her towel, which was purple with green flowers on the end. And she gave Toby a saucer of water and some bran flakes and I let him run round the bathroom.

Then Mother came into the bathroom and she sat on the toilet, and she said, "Are you OK, Christopher?"

And I said, "I'm very tired."

And she said, "I know, love." And then she said, "You're very brave."

And I said, "Yes."

And she said, "Why didn't you write to me? I wrote you all those letters. I kept thinking something dreadful had happened, or you'd moved away and I'd never find out where you were."

And I said, "Father said you were dead."

And she said, "What?"

And I said, "He said you went into hospital because you had something wrong with your heart. And then you had a heart attack and died and he kept all the letters in a shirt box in the cupboard in his bedroom and I found them because I was looking for a book I was writing about Wellington being killed and he'd taken it away from me and hidden it in the shirt box."

And then Mother said, "Oh, my God."

And then she didn't say anything for a long while. And then she made a loud wailing noise like an animal.

And I didn't like her doing this, because it was a loud noise, and I said, "Why are you doing that?"

And she didn't say anything for a while, and then she said, "Oh, Christopher, I'm so sorry."

And I said, "It's not your fault."

And then she said, "Bastard. The bastard."

And then, after a while, she said, "Christopher, let me hold your hand. Just for once. Just for me. Will you? I won't hold it hard," and she held out her hand.

And I said, "I don't like people holding my hand."

And she took her hand back, and she said, "No. OK. That's OK." And then she said, "Let's get you out of the bath and dried off."

And I got out of the bath and dried myself with the purple towel. But I didn't have any pajamas, so I put on a white T-shirt and a pair of yellow shorts, which were Mother's, but I didn't mind, because I was so tired. And while I was doing this, Mother went into the kitchen and heated up some tomato soup because it was red.

And then I heard someone opening the door of the flat and there was a strange man's voice outside, so I locked the bathroom door. And there was an argument outside, and a man said, "I need to speak to him," and Mother said, "He's been through enough today already," and the man said, "I know. But I still need to speak to him."

And Mother knocked on the door and said a policeman wanted to talk to me and I had to open the door. And she said she wouldn't let him take me away and she promised. So I picked Toby up and opened the door.

And there was a policeman outside the door, and he said, "Are you Christopher Boone?"

And I said I was.

And he said, "Your father says you've run away. Is that right?"

And I said, "Yes."

And he said, "Is this your mother?" and he pointed at Mother.

And I said, "Yes."

And he said, "Why did you run away?"

And I said, "Because Father killed Wellington, who is a dog, and I was frightened of him."

And he said, "So I've been told." And then he said, "Do you want to go back to Swindon to your father, or do you want to stay here?"

And I said, "I want to stay here."

And he said, "And how do you feel about that?"

And I said, "I want to stay here."

And the policeman said, "Hang on. I'm asking your mother."

And Mother said, "He told Christopher I was dead."

And the policeman said, "OK. Let's . . . let's not get into an argument about who said what here. I just want to know whether—"

And Mother said, "Of course he can stay."

And then the policeman said, "Well, I think that probably settles it as far as I'm concerned."

And I said, "Are you going to take me back to Swindon?"

And he said, "No."

And then I was happy because I could live with Mother.

And the policeman said, "If your husband turns up and causes any trouble, just give us a ring. Otherwise, you're going to have to sort this out between yourselves."

And then the policeman went away and I had my tomato soup

and Mr. Shears stacked up some boxes in the spare room so he could put a blowup mattress on the floor for me to sleep on.

And I went to sleep and then I woke up because there were people shouting in the flat and it was 2:31 a.m. And one of the people was Father and I was frightened. He was shouting, "I'm talking to her. And I am not going to be told what to do by you of all people."

And Mother shouted, "Roger, don't. Just—"

And Mr. Shears shouted, "I'm not being spoken to like that in my own home."

And Father shouted, "I'll talk to you how I damn well like."

And Mother shouted, "You have no right to be here."

And Father shouted, "No right? No right? He's my son, in case you've forgotten."

And Mother shouted, "What did you think you were playing at, saying those things to him?"

And Father shouted, "What was I playing at? You were the one that bloody left."

And Mother shouted, "So you decided to just wipe me out of his life altogether?"

And Mr. Shears shouted, "Let's all just calm down here, shall we?"

And Father shouted, "Well, isn't that what you wanted?"

And Mother shouted, "I wrote to him every week. Every week."

And Father shouted, "Wrote to him? What use is writing to him? I cooked his meals. I cleaned his clothes. I looked after him every weekend. I looked after him when he was ill. I worried myself sick every time he wandered off somewhere at night. I went to school every time he got into a fight. And you? What? You wrote him some letters."

And Mother shouted, "So you thought it was OK to tell him his mother was dead?"

And Mr. Shears shouted, "Whoa, whoa, whoa."

And Father said, "I'm going to see him. If you try to stop me—"

And then Father came into my room. But I was holding my Swiss army knife with the saw blade out in case he grabbed me. And

Mother came into the room as well, and she said, "It's OK, Christopher. I won't let him do anything. You're all right."

And Father bent down on his knees near the bed, and he said, "Christopher? I'm really, really sorry. About Wellington. About the letters. About making you run away. I never meant . . . I promise I will never do anything like that again. Hey. Come on, kiddo."

And then he held up his right hand and spread his fingers in a fan so that I could touch his fingers, but I didn't, because I was frightened.

And Father said, "God, Christopher, please."

And there were tears dripping off his face.

And no one said anything for a while.

And then Mother said, "I think you should go now," but she was talking to Father, not me.

And then the policeman came back because Mr. Shears had rung the police station and he told Father to calm down and he took him out of the flat.

And Mother said, "You go back to sleep now. Everything is going to be all right. I promise."

And then I went back to sleep.

67. AND when I was asleep, I had one of my favorite dreams. Sometimes I have it during the day, but then it's a daydream. But I often have it at night as well.

And in the dream nearly everyone on earth is dead, because they have caught a virus. But it's not like a normal virus. It's like a computer virus. And people catch it because of the meaning of something an infected person says and the meaning of what they do with their faces when they say it, which means that people can also get it from watching an infected person on television, which means that it spreads around the world really quickly.

And when people get the virus, they just sit on the sofa and do nothing and they don't eat or drink and so they die. And eventually there is no one left in the world except people who don't look at other people's faces and who don't know what these pictures mean

and these people are all special people like me. And they like being on their own, and I hardly ever see them, because they are like okapi in the jungle in the Congo, which are a kind of antelope and very shy and rare.

And I can go anywhere in the world and I know that no one is going to talk to me or touch me or ask me a question. But if I don't want to go anywhere, I don't have to, and I can stay at home and eat broccoli and oranges and licorice laces all the time, or I can play computer games for a whole week, or I can just sit in the corner of the room and rub a £1 coin back and forward over the surface of the radiator. And I wouldn't have to go to France.

And I go out of Father's house and I walk down the street, and it is very quiet even though it is the middle of the day and I can't hear any noise except birds singing and wind and sometimes buildings falling down in the distance, and if I stand very close to traffic lights, I can hear a little click as the colors change.

And I go into other people's houses and play at being a detective and I can break the windows to get in because the people are dead and it doesn't matter. And I go into shops and take things I want, like pink biscuits or computer games or books or videos.

And I take a ladder from Father's van and I climb onto the roof, and when I get to the edge of the roof, I put the ladder across the gap and I climb to the next roof, because in a dream you are allowed to do anything.

And then I find someone's car keys and I get into their car and I drive, and it doesn't matter if I bump into things and I drive to the sea and I park the car and I get out and there is rain pouring down.

And I take an ice cream from a shop and eat it. And then I walk down to the beach. And the beach is covered in sand and big rocks and there is a lighthouse on a point, but the light is not on, because the lighthouse keeper is dead.

And I stand in the surf and it comes up and over my shoes. And I don't go swimming in case there are sharks. And I stand and look at the horizon and I take out my long metal ruler and I hold it up against the line between the sea and the sky and I demonstrate that the line is a curve and the earth is round. And the way the surf comes up and over my shoes and then goes down again is in a rhythm, like music or drumming.

And then I get some dry clothes from the house of a family who are dead. And I go home to Father's house except it's not Father's house anymore, it's mine. And I make myself some Gobi Aloo Sag with red food coloring in it and some strawberry milk shake for a drink, and then I watch a video about the solar system and I play some computer games and I go to bed.

And then the dream is finished and I am happy.

THE next morning I had fried tomatoes for breakfast and a tin of green beans, which Mother heated up in a saucepan.

In the middle of breakfast Mr. Shears said, "OK, he can stay for a few days."

And Mother said, "He can stay as long as he needs to stay."

And Mr. Shears said, "What's he going to do? There's no school for him to go to. We've both got jobs. It's bloody ridiculous."

And Mother said, "Roger, that's enough."

After Mr. Shears had gone to work, she made a telephone call to the office and took what is called *Compassionate Leave,* which is when someone in your family dies or is ill.

Then she said we had to go buy some clothes and some pajamas and a toothbrush and a flannel for me. So we went out of the flat and we walked to the main road, which was Hill Lane, and it was really crowded and we caught a number 266 bus to Brent Cross Shopping Centre. Except there were too many people in John

Lewis and I was frightened and I lay down on the floor next to the watches and I screamed and Mother had to take me home in a taxi.

Then she had to go back to the shopping center to buy me some clothes and pajamas and a toothbrush and a flannel, so I stayed in the spare room while she was gone because I didn't want to be in the same room as Mr. Shears, because I was frightened of him.

And when Mother got home, she brought me a glass of strawberry milk shake and showed me my new pajamas, and the pattern on them was 5-pointed blue stars on a purple background.

And I said, "I have to go back to Swindon."

And Mother said, "Christopher, you've only just got here."

And I said, "I have to go because I have to sit my maths A level."

And Mother said, "You're doing maths A level?"

And I said, "Yes. I'm taking it on Wednesday and Thursday and Friday next week. The Reverend Peters is going to be the invigilator."

And Mother said, "I mean, that's really good."

And I said, "I'm going to get an A grade. And that's why I have to go back to Swindon. Except I don't want to see Father. So I have to go to Swindon with you."

Then Mother put her hands over her face and breathed out hard, and she said, "I don't know whether that's going to be possible."

And I said, "But I have to go."

And Mother said, "Let's talk about this some other time, OK?"

And I said, "OK. But I have to go to Swindon."

And she said, "Christopher, please."

And I drank some of my milk shake.

And, later on, at 10:31 p.m., I went out onto the balcony to find out whether I could see any stars, but there weren't any, because of what is called *light pollution,* which is light from streetlights and lights in buildings reflecting off tiny particles in the atmosphere and getting in the way of light from the stars. So I went back inside.

But I couldn't sleep. And I got out of bed at 2:07 a.m. and I felt scared of Mr. Shears, so I went downstairs and out the front door onto Chapter Road. And there was no one on the street and it was quieter than it was during the day, so it made me feel calmer.

Then I heard two people coming along the road, so I crouched down between the end of a skip and a Ford Transit van, but they didn't see me. And I liked it between the skip and the Ford Transit van, so I stayed there for a long time. And the only colors you could see were orange and black and mixtures of orange and black. And you couldn't tell what colors the cars would be during the day.

And then I heard Mother's voice, and she was shouting, "Christopher? Christopher?" and she was running down the road, so I came out between the skip and the Ford Transit van and she ran up to me and pointed her finger at my face and said, "If you ever do that again, I swear, Christopher, I love you, but . . . I don't know what I'll do."

So she made me promise never to leave the flat on my own, because it was dangerous and because you couldn't trust people in London, because they were strangers. And the next day she had to go to the shops again and she made me promise not to answer the door if anyone rang the bell. And when she came back, she brought some food pellets for Toby and three *Star Trek* videos and I watched them in the living room until Mr. Shears came home and then I went into the spare room again.

And the day after that the office where Mother worked rang and told her she couldn't come back to work, because they had got someone else to do her job for her, and she was really angry and she said that it was illegal and she was going to complain, but Mr. Shears said, "Don't be a bloody fool. It was a temporary job."

And when Mother came into the spare room before I went to sleep, I said, "I have to go to Swindon to take my A level."

And she said, "Christopher, not now. I'm getting phone calls from your father threatening to take me to court. I'm getting it in the neck from Roger. It's not a good time."

And I said, "But I have to go because it's been arranged and the Reverend Peters is going to invigilate."

And she said, "Look. It's only an exam. I can ring the school. We can get it postponed. You can take it some other time."

And I said, "I can't take it another time. It's been arranged. And Mrs. Gascoyne said we could use a room at school."

And Mother said, "Christopher, I am just about holding this together. But I am this close to losing it, all right? So just give me some . . ." Then she stopped talking and she put her hand over her mouth and she stood up and went out of the room. And I started feeling a pain in my chest because I thought I wasn't going to be able to go back to Swindon and take my A level.

And the next morning I looked out the window in the dining room to count the cars in the street to see whether it was going to be a **Quite Good Day** or a **Good Day** or a **Super Good Day** or a **Black Day,** and I looked out the window for 3 hours and I saw 5 red cars in a row and 4 yellow cars in a row, which meant it was both a **Good Day** and a **Black Day,** so the system didn't work anymore. But if I concentrated on counting the cars, it stopped me thinking about my A level and the pain in my chest.

And in the afternoon Mother took me to Hampstead Heath in a taxi and we sat on the top of a hill and looked at the planes coming in to Heathrow Airport in the distance. And I had a red ice lolly from an ice-cream van. And Mother said she had rung Mrs. Gascoyne and told her that I was going to take my maths A level next year, so I threw my red ice lolly away and I screamed for a long time and the pain in my chest hurt so much that it was hard to breathe and a man came up and asked if I was OK, and Mother said, "Well, what does it look like to you?" and he went away.

And then I was tired from screaming and Mother took me back to the flat in another taxi and the next morning was Saturday and she told Mr. Shears to go out and get me some books about science and maths from the library, and they were called *100 Number Puzzles* and *The Origins of the Universe* and *Nuclear Power,* but they were for children and not very good, so I didn't read them, and Mr. Shears said, "Well, it's nice to know my contribution is appreciated."

And when Mother and Mr. Shears argued, I took the little radio from the kitchen and I went and sat in the spare room and I tuned it halfway between two stations, so all I could hear was white noise, and I turned the volume up really loud and I held it against my ear and the sound filled my head and it hurt, so I couldn't feel any other sort of hurt, like the hurt in my chest, and I couldn't hear Mother and Mr. Shears arguing and I couldn't think about not doing my A level or the fact that I couldn't see the stars at 451c Chapter Road.

And then it was Monday. And it was very late at night and Mr. Shears came into my room and woke me up and he had been drinking beer because he smelled like Father did when he had been drinking beer with Rhodri. And he said, "You think you're clever, don't you? Don't you ever, ever think about other people for one second? Well, I'll bet you're really pleased with yourself, aren't you?"

And then Mother came in and pulled him out of the room and said, "Christopher, I'm sorry. I'm really, really sorry."

The next morning, after Mr. Shears had gone to work, Mother packed lots of her clothes into two suitcases and told me to come downstairs and bring Toby and get into the car. And she put the suitcases into the boot and we drove off. But it was Mr. Shears's car, and I said, "Are you stealing the car?"

And she said, "I'm just borrowing it."

And I said, "Where are we going?"

And she said, "We're going home."

And I said, "Do you mean home in Swindon?"

And she said, "Yes."

And I said, "Is Father going to be there?"

And she said, "Christopher, don't give me any hassle now, OK?"

And I said, "I don't want to be with Father."

And she said, "Just . . . Just . . . It's going to be all right, Christopher, OK? It's going to be all right."

And I said, "Are we going back to Swindon so I can do my maths A level?"

And Mother said, "What?"

And I said, "I'm meant to be doing my maths A level tomorrow."

And Mother spoke very slowly, and she said, "We are going back to Swindon because if we stayed in London any longer . . . someone was going to get hurt. And I don't necessarily mean you."

And I said, "What do you mean?"

And she said, "Now I need you to be quiet for a while."

And I said, "How long do you want me to be quiet for?"

And she said, "Half an hour, Christopher. I need you to be quiet for half an hour."

And we drove all the way to Swindon and it took 3 hours 12 minutes and we had to stop for petrol and Mother bought me a Milky Bar, but I didn't eat it. And we got caught in a long traffic jam and I fell asleep.

And when we got to Swindon, Mother had keys to the house and we went in, and she said, "Hello?" but there was no one there, because it was 1:23 p.m. And I was frightened, but Mother said I would be safe, so I went up to my room and closed the door. I took Toby out of my pocket and I let him run around and I played **Minesweeper** and I did the Expert Version in 174 seconds, which was 75 seconds longer than my best time.

And then it was 6:35 p.m. and I heard Father come home in his van and I moved the bed against the door so he couldn't get in and he came into the house and he and Mother shouted at each other.

Father shouted, "How the hell did you get in here?"

And Mother shouted, "This is my house too."

And Father shouted, "Is your fancy man here, as well?"

And then I picked up the bongo drums that Uncle Terry had bought me and I knelt down in the corner of the room and I pressed my head into the join between the two walls and I banged the drums and I groaned and I carried on doing this for an hour, and then Mother came into the room and said Father had gone to stay with Rhodri for a while and we would get a place to live of our own in the next few weeks.

Then I went into the garden and I found Toby's cage behind the shed and I brought it inside and I cleaned it and put Toby back in it.

And I asked Mother if I could do my maths A level the next day.

And she said, "You're not listening to me, are you, Christopher? I told you. I rang your headmistress. I told her you were in London. I told her you'd do it next year."

And I said, "But I'm here now and I can take it."

And Mother said, "I'm sorry, Christopher. I was trying to do things properly. I didn't know we'd be coming back."

And my chest began hurting again and I folded my arms and I rocked backward and forward and groaned.

And Mother said, "Come on. This isn't going to solve anything."

Then she asked if I wanted to watch one of my *Blue Planet* videos about life under the Arctic ice or the migration of humpback whales, but I didn't say anything, because I knew I wasn't going to be able to do my maths A level and it was like pressing your thumbnail against a radiator when it's really hot and the pain starts and it makes you want to cry.

Then Mother made me some carrots and broccoli and ketchup, but I didn't eat them. And I didn't sleep that night either.

The next day Mother drove me to school in Mr. Shears's car because we missed the bus. And when we were getting into the car, Mrs. Shears came across the road and said to Mother, "You've got nerve."

And Mother said, "Get into the car, Christopher."

But I couldn't get into the car, because the door was locked.

And Mrs. Shears said, "So has he finally dumped you too?"

Then Mother opened her door and got into the car and unlocked my door and I got in and we drove away.

And when we got to school, Siobhan said, "So you're Christopher's mother." And Siobhan said that she was glad to see me again and she asked if I was OK and I said I was tired. And Mother explained that I was upset because I couldn't do my maths A level, so I hadn't been eating properly or sleeping properly.

And then Mother went away and I drew a picture of a bus using perspective so that I didn't think about the pain in my chest.

And after lunch Siobhan said that she had spoken to Mrs. Gascoyne and she still had my A-level papers in 3 sealed envelopes in her desk.

So I asked if I could still do my A level.

And Siobhan said, "I think so. We're going to ring the Reverend Peters this afternoon to make sure he can still be your invigilator.

And Mrs. Gascoyne is going to write a letter to the examination board to say that you're going to take the exam after all. And hopefully they'll say that that's OK. But we can't know that for sure." Then she said, "Is this what you want to do, Christopher?"

And I thought about the question, and I wasn't sure what the answer was, because I wanted to do my maths A level, but I was tired, and when I tried to think about maths, my brain didn't work properly, and when I tried to remember certain facts, like the logarithmic formula for the approximate number of prime numbers not greater than x, I couldn't remember them and this made me frightened.

And Siobhan said, "You don't have to do it, Christopher. If you say you don't want to do it, no one is going to be angry with you."

And I said, "I want to do it," because I don't like it when I put things in my timetable and I have to take them out again.

And Siobhan said, "OK."

And she rang the Reverend Peters and he came into school at 3:27 p.m., and he said, "So, young man, are we ready to roll?"

And I did **Paper 1** of my maths A level sitting in the Art Room. And the Reverend Peters was the invigilator and he sat at a desk while I did the exam and he read a book called *The Cost of Discipleship* by Dietrich Bonhoeffer and ate a sandwich. And in the middle of the exam he went and smoked a cigarette outside the window, but he watched me through the window in case I cheated.

And when I opened the paper and read through it, I couldn't think how to answer any of the questions and also I couldn't breathe properly. And I wanted to hit somebody or stab them with my Swiss army knife, but there wasn't anyone to hit or stab with my Swiss army knife except the Reverend Peters and he was very tall, and if I hit him or stabbed him with my Swiss army knife, he wouldn't be my invigilator for the rest of the exam. So I took deep breaths, like Siobhan said I should do when I want to hit someone in school, and I counted 50 breaths and did cubes of the cardinal numbers as I counted like this: **1, 8, 27, 64, 125, 216, 343, 512, 729, 1,000, 1,331, 1,728, 2,197, 2,744, 3,375, 4,096, 4,913 . . . etc.**

And that made me feel a little calmer. But the exam was 2 hours long and 20 minutes had already gone, so I had to work really fast and I didn't have time to check my answers properly.

And that night, just after I got home, Father came back to the house and I screamed, but Mother said she wouldn't let anything bad happen to me and I went into the garden and lay down and looked at the stars in the sky and made myself negligible. And when Father came out of the house, he looked at me for a long time and then he punched the fence and made a hole in it and went away.

And I slept a little bit that night because I was doing my maths A level. And I had some spinach soup for supper.

And the next day I did **Paper 2** and the Reverend Peters read *The Cost of Discipleship,* but this time he didn't smoke a cigarette and Siobhan made me go into the toilets before the exam and sit on my own and do breathing and counting.

And I was playing **The 11th Hour** on my computer that evening when a taxi stopped outside the house. Mr. Shears was in the taxi and he got out and threw a big cardboard box of things belonging to Mother onto the lawn. And they were a hair dryer and some knickers and a box of muesli and a photograph of me in a silver frame. And the glass in the frame broke when it fell onto the grass.

Then he got some keys out of his pocket and got into his car and drove away, and Mother ran out of the house and into the street and shouted, "Don't bother coming back either!" And she threw the box of muesli and it hit the boot of his car as he drove away and Mrs. Shears was looking out her window when Mother did this.

The next day I did **Paper 3** and the Reverend Peters read the *Daily Mail* and smoked 3 cigarettes. And this was my favorite question

> Prove the following result: "A triangle with sides that can be written in the form $n^2 + 1$, $n^2 - 1$ and $2n$ (where $n > 1$) is right-angled." Show, by means of a counterexample, that the converse is false.

And I was going to write out how I answered the question, but Siobhan said it wasn't very interesting. And then my chest didn't hurt so much and it was easier to breathe. But I still felt sick because

I didn't know if I'd done well in the exam and because I didn't know if the examination board would allow my paper to be considered after Mrs. Gascoyne had told them I wasn't going to take it.

It's best if you know a good thing is going to happen, like an eclipse or getting a microscope for Christmas. And it's bad if you know a bad thing is going to happen, like having a filling or going to France. But I think it is worst if you don't know whether it is a good thing or a bad thing that is going to happen.

And Father came round to the house that night and I was sitting on the sofa watching *University Challenge* and just answering the science questions. And he stood in the doorway of the living room, and he said, "Don't scream, Christopher. I'm not going to hurt you."

And Mother was standing behind him, so I didn't scream.

Then he came a bit closer to me and he crouched down like you do with dogs to show that you are not an Aggressor, and he said, "I wanted to ask you how the exam went."

But I didn't say anything.

And Mother said, "Tell him, Christopher."

But I still didn't say anything.

And Mother said, "Please, Christopher."

So I said, "I don't know if I got all the questions right, because I was really tired and I hadn't eaten any food, so I couldn't think properly."

And then Father nodded and he didn't say anything for a short while. Then he said, "Thank you."

And I said, "What for?"

And he said, "Just . . . thank you." Then he said, "I'm very proud of you, Christopher. Very proud. I'm sure you did really well."

And then he went away and I watched the rest of *University Challenge.*

And the next week Father told Mother she had to move out of the house, but she couldn't, because she didn't have any money to pay rent for a flat. And I asked if Father would be arrested and go to prison for killing Wellington, because we could live in the house if he was in prison. But Mother said the police would only arrest

Father if Mrs. Shears did what is called *pressing charges,* because the police don't arrest people for little crimes unless you ask them and Mother said that killing a dog was only a little crime.

But then everything was OK because Mother got a job on the till in a garden center and the doctor gave her pills to take every morning to stop her feeling sad except that sometimes they made her dizzy and she fell over if she stood up too fast. So we moved into a room in a big house that was made of red bricks. And the bed was in the same room as the kitchen, and I didn't like it, because it was small and the corridor was painted brown and there was a toilet and a bathroom that other people used. And Mother had to clean it before I used it or I wouldn't use it. And the corridor outside the room smelled like gravy and the bleach they use to clean the toilets at school. And inside the room it smelled like socks and pine air freshener.

And I didn't like waiting to find out about my maths A level. And whenever I thought about the future, I couldn't see anything clearly in my head and that made a panic start. So Siobhan said I shouldn't think about the future. She said, "Just think about today. Think about things that have happened. Especially about good things that have happened."

And one of the good things was that I helped Mother paint her room **White with a Hint of Wheat** except I got paint in my hair and she wanted to wash it out by rubbing shampoo on my head when I was in the bath, but I wouldn't let her, so there was paint in my hair for 5 days and then I cut it out with a pair of scissors.

But there were more bad things than good things.

And one of them was that Mother didn't get back from work till 5:30 p.m., so I had to go to Father's house between 3:49 p.m. and 5:30 p.m. because I wasn't allowed to be on my own and Mother said I didn't have a choice, so I pushed the bed against the door in case Father tried to come in. And sometimes he tried to talk to me through the door, but I didn't answer him. And sometimes I heard him sitting on the floor outside the door quietly for a long time.

And another bad thing was that Toby died because he was 2

years and 7 months old, which is very old for a rat, and I said I wanted to bury him, but Mother didn't have a garden, so I buried him in a big plastic pot of earth like a pot you put a plant in. And I said I wanted another rat, but Mother said I couldn't have one, because the room was too small.

And Mother picked me up from Father's house one day after she had finished work, and Father said, "Christopher, can I have a talk with you?"

And I said, "No."

And Mother said, "It's OK. I'll be here."

And I said, "I don't want to talk to Father."

And Father said, "I'll do you a deal." And he was holding the kitchen timer, which is a big plastic tomato sliced through the middle and he twisted it and it started ticking. And he said, "Five minutes, OK? That's all. Then you can go."

So I sat on the sofa and he sat on the armchair and Mother was in the hallway, and Father said, "Christopher, look . . . Things can't go on like this. I don't know about you, but this . . . this just hurts too much. You being in the house but refusing to talk to me . . . You have to learn to trust me. . . . And I don't care how long it takes. If it's a minute one day and two minutes the next and it takes years, I don't care. Because this is important. This is more important than anything else. Let's call it . . . let's call it a project we have to do together. You have to spend more time with me. And I . . . I have to show you that you can trust me. And it will be difficult at first, because . . . because it's a difficult project. But it will get better. I promise."

Then he rubbed the sides of his forehead with his fingertips, and he said, "You don't have to say anything, not right now. You just have to think about it. And, um, I've got you a present. To show you that I really mean what I say. And to say sorry. And because . . . Well, you'll see what I mean."

Then he got out of the armchair and he walked over to the kitchen door and opened it and there was a big cardboard box on the floor and there was a blanket in it and he bent down and put his hands inside the box and he took out a little sandy-colored dog.

Then he came back through and gave me the dog, and he said, "He's two months old. And he's a golden retriever."

And the dog sat in my lap and I stroked it.

And no one said anything for a while.

Then Father said, "Christopher, I would never, ever do anything to hurt you."

Then no one said anything.

And Mother came into the room and said, "You won't be able to take him away with you, I'm afraid. The bed-sit's too small. But your father's going to look after him here. And you can come and take him out for walks whenever you want."

And I said, "Does he have a name?"

And Father said, "No. You can decide what to call him."

And the dog chewed my finger.

And then it was 5 minutes and the tomato alarm went. So Mother and I drove back to her room.

And the next week there was a lightning storm and the lightning hit a big tree in the park near Father's house and knocked it down and men came and cut the branches up with chain saws and carried the logs away on a lorry, and all that was left was a big black pointed stump made of carbonized wood.

And I got the results of my maths A level and I got an A grade, which is the best result, and it made me feel like this

And I called the dog Sandy. And Father bought him a collar and a lead and I was allowed to take him for walks to the shop and back. And I played with him with a rubber bone.

And Mother got the flu and I had to spend three days with Father and stay in his house. But it was OK because Sandy slept on my bed, so he would bark if anyone came into the room during the night. And Father made a vegetable patch in the garden and I helped him.

And we planted carrots and peas and spinach and I'm going to pick them and eat them when they're ready.

And I went to a bookshop with Mother and I bought a book called *Further Maths for A Level* and Father told Mrs. Gascoyne that I was going to take A-level further maths next year and she said, "OK."

And I am going to pass it and get an A grade. And in two years' time I am going to take A-level physics and get an A grade.

And then, when I've done that, I am going to go to university in another town. And it doesn't have to be in London, because I don't like London, and there are universities in lots of places and not all of them are in big cities. And I can live in a flat with a garden and a proper toilet. And I can take Sandy and my books and my computer.

And then I will get a First Class Honors degree and I will become a scientist.

And I know I can do this because I went to London on my own, and because I solved the mystery of **Who Killed Wellington?** and I found my mother and I was brave and I wrote a book and that means I can do anything.

A Conversation with
MARK HADDON

by Dave Weich

"**W**hen I was writing," Mark Haddon says, "I really thought to myself, Who on earth is going to want to read about a fifteen-year-old kid with a disability living in Swindon with his father? And I thought, I better make the plot good." The plot is significantly better than good, but it's the irresistible voice of Mark Haddon's young narrator, Christopher Boone, that elevates this literary debut to fantastic heights.

It was 7 minutes after midnight. The dog was lying on the grass in the middle of the lawn in front of Mrs. Shears's house. Its eyes were closed. It looked as if it was running on its side, the way dogs run when they think they are chasing a cat in a dream. But the dog was not run-

Vital Stats

Born: Northampton, England
Residence: Oxford, England
Profession: Writer/Illustrator
Previous Works:
    The Sea of Tranquility (Writer)
    The Agent Z series (Illustrator)
Spouse: Sos Eltis
Children: Two boys, Alfie & Zac
Recently Read: Bill Bryson's *A Short History of Nearly Everything*

ning or asleep. The dog was dead. There was a garden fork sticking out of the dog.

"This is a murder mystery novel," explains the boy with Behavioral Problems a few pages further on. As you've seen, Christopher, a fan of Sherlock Holmes stories, decides to investigate the dog's death and turn the story into a book of his own. Here, Mark Haddon discusses how he brought Christopher's story to life.

DAVE WEICH: Where did you find the original impulse to write this novel? I know that it wasn't a matter of you thinking you'd write a book about an autistic boy, as some might presume.

MARK HADDON: No, very deliberately not. And I think if I had done that, I'd have run the risk of producing a very stolid, earnest, and over-worthy book.

It came from the image of the dead dog with the fork through it. I just wanted a good image on that first page. To me, that was gripping and vivid, and it stuck in your head. Only when I was writing it did I realize, at least to my mind, that it was also quite funny. But it was only funny if you described it in the voice that I used in the book.

So the dog came along first, then the voice. Only after a few pages did I really start to ask, Who does the voice belong to? So Christopher came along,

Is Christopher Autistic?

While he never uses the term to describe himself, Christopher suffers from Asperger Syndrome, a developmental disorder falling within the spectrum of autism but with generally milder symptoms. As with all forms of autism, it appears much more often in boys than in girls, which some researchers suspect could be due to interactions between male hormones and fetal brain development. More information is available from the Asperger Syndrome Coalition of the United States, which can be reached on the Internet at www.Asperger.org.

in fact, after the book had already got under way.

WEICH: Did that seem a daunting prospect at first? How long did it take to develop Christopher into the character he became?

HADDON: I think once I heard the voice, I knew that Christopher would be quite easy. I started writing in that voice, and I found it so engaging myself that I knew I could write in the voice for a long time.

The more difficult thing was constructing the shape of the story. I knew there was a story; once you find a dog with a fork through it, you know there's a story there. The more difficult puzzle was this: I wanted the whole book to be in Christopher's voice, but the paradox is that if Christopher were real, he would find it very hard, if not impossible, to write a book. The one thing he cannot

Hounds, Dogs & Detectives

It's downright elementary why the hyper-logical fictional detective Sherlock Holmes holds such allure for Christopher. In Christopher's favorite book, *The Hound of the Baskervilles,* Holmes confronts the forces of superstition and exposes the all-too-human source of a supposedly supernatural family curse. Oddly enough, *Hound* was first published almost exactly one century before *Dog*, in 1902. To bring things full circle, a story about *The Curious Incident* was recently featured on the website of The Sherlock Holmes Society of London, where Baker Street loyalists meet to ponder all things Sherlock.

do is put himself in someone else's shoes, and the one thing you have to do if you write a book is put yourself in someone else's shoes—the reader's shoes. You've got to entertain them, and there's no way he could have done that.

It took me a while to figure out that puzzle. The answer I came up with is having him be a fan of the Sherlock Holmes

Real Rain Men
Mystifying Islands of Brilliance

Christopher's math talents are impressive for his age, but a few autistics' skills are so far off the charts they fall into the rare and mystifying category of savants. According to Dr. Darold Treffert, author of *Extraordinary People: Understanding Savant Syndrome,* this is "a rare condition in which persons with developmental disorders have astonishing islands of ability, brilliance, or talent that stand in stark contrast to overall limitations. The skills are always combined with prodigious memory of a special type—extraordinarily deep but very narrow."

Frequently these skills involve mathematics. Raymond Babbitt, for instance, the character portrayed by Dustin Hoffman in the film *Rain Man* (1988), was a mathematical savant whose talent his brother (played by Tom Cruise) tried to exploit at the Las Vegas blackjack tables. Hoffman closely studied several real savants to build his characterization, and his accuracy was highly praised by experts.

Among the most mystifying expressions of mathematical savant syndrome is the phenomenon of calendar calculating. Dr. Treffert notes that calendar calculating includes such feats as "being able to name all the years in the next 100 in which Easter will fall on March 23rd, for example."

One historical instance involved Thomas Fuller, an unlettered African American slave who lived in the 1700s. When asked how many seconds a man had lived who was 70 years, 17 days, and 12 hours old, Fuller's correct answer came in less than two minutes: 2,210,500,800 seconds. The figure included adjustments for all 17 leap years!

Savant syndrome appears in only about 10 percent of autistics but accompanies some other developmental disabilities as well. "Thus," says Dr. Treffert, "not all savants are autistic, and not all autistics are savants."

But all are unquestionably fascinating.

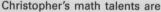

stories. That way, he doesn't have to put himself in the mind of a reader. He just has to say, "I enjoy Sherlock Holmes stories, and I'll try to do something similar." That was the biggest puzzle for the book. When I solved that, I began to see how I could shape the story.

WEICH: The book is being marketed as both a literary novel and a story for young adults. Did you have a readership in mind as you were putting it together?

HADDON: It was definitely for adults. Consequently, I was quite surprised when I gave it to my agent and she said, "Let's try it with both adult and children's publishers and see what happens." I was really quite surprised and, truth to tell, perhaps a bit disappointed, because I'd spent a lot of effort trying to move away from writing for children.

WEICH: You still have to sit at the kids' table.

HADDON: But what happened in the U.K. was that we got a very good adult publisher and a good children's publisher that wanted to publish a

parallel edition, so who can complain about that? It's the same book in a slightly different cover.

WEICH: Yet what makes the book so successful is that it would seem to transcend those kinds of targeted marketing efforts. Christopher, in a way, is ageless. You don't necessarily think of him as a child when you're reading, because many of his faculties are advanced well beyond an adult's.

HADDON: One of the things I like about the book, if I'm allowed to say that about my own book, is something I realized quite early on: It has a very simple surface, but there are layers of irony and paradox all the way through it. Here is a fiction about a character who says he can only tell the truth—he can't tell lies—but he gets everything wrong. Here is a narrator who seems to be hugely ill-equipped for writing a book—he can't understand metaphor, he can't understand other people's emotions, he misses the bigger picture—and yet it makes him incredibly well suited to narrating a book. He never explains too much. He never tries to persuade the reader to feel about things this way or that way; he just kind of paints this picture and says, "Make of it what you will." Which is a kind of writing that many writers are searching for all the time.

Also—and this has become something very important to me—it's not just a book about disability. Obviously, on some level it is, but on another level, and this is a level that I think only perhaps adults will get, it's a book about books, about what you can do with words and what it means to communicate with someone in a book. Here's a character whom if you met him in real life, you'd never, ever get inside his head. Yet something magical happens when you write a novel about him. You slip inside his head, and it seems like the most natural thing in the world.

WEICH: The father and the mother—I imagine their world, and I see two people who didn't plan for this situation. They weren't prepared to take this on. Now they don't know how to cope.

HADDON: One of the strange things about his parents is that different readers feel very, very different things about them. Particularly his father. Some people say he's a good man struggling in difficult conditions; other people say, "The guy's a psychopath." And I think that's one of the functions of Christopher's voice. He paints a very sparse picture of the world around him. You only see little bits of his father and little bits of his mother. Readers bring to those characters what they want. Some people paint one picture, and some people paint another.

People have said to me that it's a desperately sad book and they wept most of the way through it. Other people say it's charming and they kept laughing all the time. People say it has a sad ending; people say it has a happy ending. Because Christopher doesn't force the reader to think one thing and another, I get many different reactions.

One Book, Two Covers, Three Cheers!

Like the book itself, everything about *The Curious Incident*'s original publishing plan in England defied convention. Issued in two editions (identical except for the covers), one by a leading adult publisher and another by an unrelated children's publisher, the many prizes it has won reflects its curious history:

- The Whitbread Book of the Year Award
- The Whitbread Novel Award
- The Booktrust Teenage Prize
- The South Bank Show Literature Award
- The *Guardian* Children's Fiction Prize

WEICH: You worked with children with disabilities, but that's a while back in your past.

HADDON: It is. In fact, it's so far in my past—it's eighteen or twenty years ago now—that autism wasn't a term that was even used much at the time, and only in retrospect do I realize that some of the people I worked with had autism, although they had it much more seriously than Christopher does.

WEICH: The math is also something that you bring to the book from your own background.

HADDON: I'm most like Christopher in respect of his math. Most of that came straight out of my own head. Obviously, the puzzles ultimately come from somewhere else, but most of those puzzles are things that I've enjoyed doing at one time in my life. And if you enjoy math and you write novels, it's very rare that you'll get a chance to put your math into a novel. I leapt at the chance.

WEICH: In another interview, you mentioned that it's not so much the idea of writing about a disability as much as the different worldview a disability might impose on the narrator, some unconventional perspective, that's of interest to you in creating characters.

HADDON: Disability crops up here and there in my work. Since I finished the novel, one of the things I've done was I wrote a radio play for BBC Radio 4 in the U.K. about two brothers, one of whom has Down's syndrome.

For me, disability is a way of getting some extremity, some kind of very difficult situation, that throws an interesting light on people. But it's also something that's terribly, terribly ordinary. There are these extreme situations, but they're happening somewhere in your street at this very moment. And that's important to me— to find the extraordinary inside the ordinary.

Dave Weich works for Powell's Books in Portland, Oregon. This interview first appeared on www.Powells.com and is used by permission.

Further Reading...

Let Me Hear Your Voice: A Family's Triumph Over Autism
by Catherine Maurice
A mother writes of the struggle to understand her daughter's autism.

Flowers for Algernon
by Daniel Keyes
A science-fiction classic that explores the human dimensions of genius and disability.

Songs of the Gorilla Nation: My Journey Through Autism
by Dawn Prince-Hughes, Ph.D.
A woman with Asperger Syndrome overcomes isolation through pioneering work with primates.